Sue Russell is an internationally syndicated reporter and author. A past associate editor of *Woman* magazine and U.S. correspondent for the *Sunday Express Magazine*, she is a regular contributor to the major British magazines and newspapers. Born and educated in London, she is now based in Los Angeles, from where she covers a diverse range of stories. She has written several nonfiction books, and this is her first in the true-crime genre.

BOOK YOUR PLACE ON OUR WEBSITE AND MAKE THE READING CONNECTION!

We've created a customized website just for our very special readers, where you can get the inside scoop on everything that's going on with Zebra, Pinnacle and Kensington books.

When you come online, you'll have the exciting opportunity to:

- View covers of upcoming books
- Read sample chapters
- Learn about our future publishing schedule (listed by publication month *and author*)
- Find out when your favorite authors will be visiting a city near you
- Search for and order backlist books from our online catalog
- Check out author bios and background information
- Send e-mail to your favorite authors
- Meet the Kensington staff online
- Join us in weekly chats with authors, readers and other guests
- Get writing guidelines
- AND MUCH MORE!

**Visit our website at
http://www.kensingtonbooks.com**

LETHAL INTENT

SUE RUSSELL

PINNACLE BOOKS
Kensington Publishing Corp.
http://www.kensingtonbooks.com

Some names have been changed to protect the privacy of individuals connected to this story.

PINNACLE BOOKS are published by

Kensington Publishing Corp.
850 Third Avenue
New York, NY 10022

All Kensington Titles, Imprints, and Distributed Lines are available at special quantity discounts for bulk purchases for sales promotions, premiums, fund-raising, and educational or institutional use. Special book excerpts or customized printings can also be created to fit specific needs. For details, write or phone the office of the Kensington special sales manager: Kensington Publishing Corp., 850 Third Avenue, New York, NY 10022, attn: Special Sales Department, phone: 1-800-221-2647.

Pinnacle and the P logo Reg. U.S. Pat. & TM Off.

First Printing: November 2002
10 9 8 7 6 5 4 3

Printed in the United States of America

In the prime of my life,
must I go through the gates of death
and be robbed of the rest of my years?

AILEEN CAROL WUORNOS,
a born-again Christian since
April 1991, paraphrasing
Isaiah 38 while awaiting trial
in Volusia County Jail, Florida

AUTHOR'S NOTE

I'd like to acknowledge Jackelyn Giroux, a woman of great passion, tenacity and true grit, and to give special thanks to Katherine Grace, my longtime research assistant, who survived another book. Thanks, too, to my friends Randi Kaplan and Jane Lovelle Drache for their support and insight.

This book involved hundreds of hours of interviews, and special gratitude is due to the victims' families who shared their memories, however painful it was to do so.

Thanks to Karen Combs, paralegal with Florida's Marion County State Attorney's Office, for her much appreciated cooperation. Gratitude, too, to the many law enforcement officers, attorneys and good people of Florida, Michigan, and Kansas (both named and unnamed in the book), who generously gave of their time. In addition to those interviewees who specifically requested anonymity, I've elected to substitute pseudonyms for a handful of other parties unrelated to the crimes. All of their characters are real, however.

I'm especially grateful to agent Linda Konner, who worked so hard and had faith. To my publisher, Michaela Hamilton and to my editors, Karen Haas and Richard Ember, for their support and enthusiasm. And to Ken Benjamin, whose loving support helped me find the fortitude to see this long project finally come to fruition.

For their invaluable help: Chris Lavin, Denise Stubbs, Nick Von Klock, Marilyn Greene, Harry Shannon, Roger St. John Webster, Joan Bellefontaine, Tanya Everett, Randy Doh, John Fort, Eddie Sanderson, Jean-Paul Chaillet, Alva and John Lusky. They each know why.

Last but not least, I'd like to thank my beloved father, Norman Markham Chapman, whose influence propelled me toward writing—and questioning.

ILLUSTRATIONS

Aileen Carol Wuornos (*Photo courtesy of Lori Grody*)
Keith Wuornos (*Photo courtesy of Lori Grody*)
The young Diane Wuornos, Aileen and Keith's natural mother (*Photo courtesy of Lori Grody*)
Leo Pittman, Aileen's natural father
Barry, Keith, Aileen and Lori Wuornos (*Photo courtesy of Lori Grody*)
Keith Wuornos with his father/grandfather, Lauri Wuornos (*Photo courtesy of Lori Grody*)
Aileen and Keith with their grandmother Britta Wuornos (*Photo courtesy of Lori Grody*)
Britta Wuornos (*Photo courtesy of Lori Grody*)
Aileen in 1969 during a summer vacation (*Photo courtesy of Lori Grody*)
Aileen and Keith's childhood friend Mike Fearn (*Photo by Jackye Giroux*)
The Wuornos home (*Photo courtesy of John Majestic*)
The Wuornos home in Troy, Michigan (*Photo by Jackye Giroux*)
Aileen riding her bike in her Troy neighborhood (*Photo courtesy of Lori Grody*)
Tyria Jolene Moore, the big love of Aileen's life (*Photo courtesy of Cammie Greene*)
Shirley and Dick Humphreys (*Photo courtesy of Shirley Humphreys*)
Troy 'Buddy' Burress with his sister Letha Prater (*Photo courtesy of Letha Prater*)
David and Dee Spears (*Photo courtesy of Dee Spears*)
The central Florida woods where Lee took her victims (*Photo by Jackye Giroux*)
One of the trailer homes that Lee and Ty lived in at Homossassa Springs (*Photo by Jackye Giroux*)
Wet Willie's bar in Daytona, Florida (*Photo by Jackye Giroux*)
Aileen Carol Wuornos shortly after her arrest in 1991
The shrine erected to Lee Wuornos at the Last Resort Bar where she was arrested in 1991 (*Photo by Jackye Giroux*)

1

Snarling with rage, she rammed the barrel of her .22 revolver into Dick Humphreys' ribs with such violent, malevolent force that it broke the skin right through his shirt, roughly scraping away the top layer of flesh.

Out of his car, he stumbled backwards in his shocked effort to evade her. Tripping and falling, struggling to regain his balance, back on his feet, then down again. And thinking about dying here and now, out in the middle of nowhere, and Shirley, and the kids . . . was it all going to end like this?

Breathing hard, moving in for the kill, she'd shot fast, aiming straight for his torso, wanting to see the flying bullet hit home. One was never enough. He was a big guy, too, this one. Must have been over six feet, around 200 pounds. She pumped a second. Then a third. Later, she'd forget in a haze of violence about the fourth, the fifth, the sixth, and the seventh. Three of the bullets were fired ruthlessly into the back of a helpless man, twisting, turning, trying to run.

Blood flew, spattering onto his spectacles and his gold wedding band.

It was the day after his 35th wedding anniversary, and he didn't die easily. An ex-police chief, an expert in hostage negotiations, the unlikeliest of victims, none of it mattered now as he groaned, gasping for air. He was slumped down on the ground, right by the concrete culvert he'd stumbled over. And still he was fighting for life. When she heard him making gurgling noises she felt kinda sorry for him and re-aimed her pistol, unloading the shot to the back of his head. Better put him out of his misery.

Couldn't let him live. If he lived, he'd rat on her. Her ass would be up on attempted murder. Her face would be plastered all over

9

the place. She could kiss hooking goodbye if that happened. And then what? The only way she could make money was to hustle.

No, she was definitely going to let him die. Then die.

Each time it was easier. The fear, the body coursing with adrenalin, and oh God, it felt good. She had her prey. She had the power. She had the control.

The bastards deserved to die, anyway, she thought bitterly. They probably would have raped her, skipped off without paying her, tried to screw her in the ass, beaten the shit out of her, strangled her, maybe even killed her. Maybe they had a gun, too? Who knows what they might have done? That's how she had to look at it.

Well, it wasn't going to happen. Now she was the one calling the shots.

You bet, she took their cash and their stuff. That was out of pure hatred. The final revenge. You bastards. Dirty sons-of-bitches. You would have hurt me. Damned right, she'd take their things. Get her money's worth.

After they were dead, there were no regrets. It didn't bother her, what she'd done. They were old. Their fathers and mothers were probably dead. Why worry about it?

She knew in her heart she was a good girl.

Shirley Humphreys' first clue that Dick was home from work was customarily the sound of his Firenza's tyres scrunching along the curving, pine-needle-scattered driveway of their spacious, tree-surrounded home in Crystal River, Florida. On the evening of Tuesday 11 September 1990, that sound didn't come at 6.10 as usual and Shirley noted its absence within minutes. Dick ran his life like clockwork and after three and a half decades she knew his orderly patterns as well as her own.

At 6.30 p.m. she began speculating that he'd had car trouble. At 7 p.m., that he'd stopped for a beer with the fellas. Fifty-six-year-old Dick, an investigator who worked child custody cases for Health and Rehabilitative Services, always made a point of calling, even if he was going to be just a little late, but it was his last day in the Sumter County office; perhaps they'd decided to celebrate? By 7.30 p.m., when the telephone sat silent in its cradle, Shirley began to worry.

Just the previous night they'd shared a doubly sweet celebration. Dick had taken her for a beautiful prime rib and chicken dinner at the Sheraton Hotel near their home, and they'd toasted 35 years of happy marriage. They'd also toasted life.

When cancer strikes a family, it has a way of excising extraneous, niggling worries and cutting straight to the heart of everything. So it was for Shirley, also 56, who had been battling the big 'C' since 1984 and had learned to savour and cherish the small moments and victories.

First the cancer struck her mouth, then, in 1987, she'd needed two breast cancer surgeries. On their anniversary night, she was optimistically in remission and she and Dick were counting their blessings anew. Charles Richard Humphreys, known as Dick, was also celebrating a long-anticipated transfer to the Ocala office. He'd been very unhappy with his female supervisor in Sumter County and was content to be making a demotional move to intake community control worker. He'd be behind his new desk on Wednesday. He'd already have been on his way had his old supervisor not asked him to stay just one or two days longer than planned to help them out of a spot.

The Humphreyses enjoyed full, busy lives, swimming together in their pool, going ballroom dancing, and taking a lively interest in their three grown children. Thirty-two-year-old Elizabeth (nicknamed Libby) and 25-year-old Terry Ann were married and living in Pennsylvania and Georgia respectively. Charles Michael, Mike to his friends, was 22, and lived close by Mom and Dad. Dick was also an active member of the Loyal Order of the Moose in Crystal River, and was a member and past commander of the VFW (Veterans of Foreign Wars).

With a serviceman's stately bearing, Dick Humphreys was an imposing man, but a warm, friendly character with an abiding love for children, particularly those who had been dealt a rough hand in life. He didn't generally take case work home with him, but often, on a Friday evening, he'd visit Tony, a little fellow he'd placed in a foster home and couldn't quite get out of his mind.

He'd tell Shirley: 'I just had to stop and see Tony tonight, and you should have seen him. He hugged my leg and I bounced him up in the air! He looked great!'

The son of a tool and dye worker, his father was born in Birmingham, in England's industrial Midlands. Dick grew up in Detroit, then signed on with the Navy, doing four years of service, spending a year in Vietnam and serving on a ship in Korea. When he came out, he started working for his bachelor's degree in police administration at Michigan State. Dick and Shirley met at a party on New Year's Eve, 1954, fell hard, and married nine months later. Dick graduated in March 1960 and informed his wife: 'I've learned policing at this level, now I need to bring it down to street level.'

They moved to Ann Arbor where Dick pounded the pavements as a patrolman for three years until a recruiter talked him into signing up for the Air Force, where he specialised in security and law enforcement.

Starting in 1969, the Humphreyses and their three young children spent almost four years in Europe, with Dick based in Germany. Encouraged by Shirley, and looking towards securing their family's future, while there, Dick began taking external courses towards a master's degree in business administration at Ball State University in Muncie, Indiana. With that credential under his belt, he went on to do graduate work in criminal justice at Georgia State, but dropped out short of his doctorate.

He stayed in the Air Force almost twenty years, eventually holding the rank of Major and working as an adjunct professor at Park College, Missouri.

Retiring in November of 1981, Dick segued into the post of Police Chief in Sylacauga, Alabama, which he held for two years. The Humphreyses also spent time in Miami where Dick worked in nuclear security for the Wackenhut Corporation.

On his last day in the Sumter HRS office, Dick cleared his desk, switched off his beeper, and headed out to clear up a couple of final loose ends. There was a medical examiner's report to be checked on at the Wildwood Police Department, which he did some time after 2.30 p.m., speaking to Assistant Police Chief, David Jesse.

He also stopped at the Journey's End Motel (since renamed the Budget Motor Lodge). A then-dingy, brown, two-storey, L-shaped building fringing a pool and set amidst a sandy parking lot, it later bore a sign advertising singles for $23.95 a night and freshly painted turquoise doors. Juxtaposed as it is to the busy Speedway truck stop, with its steady procession of truckers looping around to use the certified scales, re-fuel, and buy Cokes and hot dogs, it is hellishly noisy. At around 3.45, Dick checked in by phone with the office secretary at Sumter to see if anyone needed him. All was quiet.

If the average citizen asked the police for help because their spouse was less than two hours late home from work, they'd get short shrift, but with his history, Dick enjoyed a good rapport with local law enforcement.

At 8 p.m., Shirley called the Highway Patrol—she needed a phone number for Ken Jones (Dick was his supervisor), who surely would know what was keeping Dick. Highway Patrol referred Shirley back to the Sheriff's Department, which she had no luck reaching. Next, she called the Wildwood Police Department, with whom Dick worked closely, and asked them please to help her locate Ken Jones. She assumed, correctly, that protocol would prevent them from giving her Ken's home number. Ken finally responded at around 9.30 p.m.

'Dick hasn't shown up. Something's wrong. I know there's something wrong!' Shirley told him, her anxiety evident in her voice.

That anxiety mounted considerably when Ken couldn't readily explain Dick's absence. He suggested that she check the Moose Lodge and the VFW. Shirley was certain that if her methodical, disciplined husband had gone to either place he'd have called her to meet him. She checked anyway. Ken notified the Wildwood Police Department, who in turn alerted the Sheriff's Department, who in turn went to work immediately checking the ditches along Dick's route home, hoping to spot his blue 1985 Oldsmobile Firenza.

In a matter of hours, Dick Humphreys, husband, father, and friend, was officially listed in the state's computer as missing/endangered.

Shirley Humphreys sat alone with her thoughts through that long night, cold fear gripping at her. An unexplained absence was completely out of character, as was the notion that Dick would take off unexpectedly. That he wouldn't call her was literally inconceivable.

She thought about how Dick would have liked to carry a gun, but that to do so would have been against the laws of Florida in his current job. Her husband was a big, highly trained man, but basically defenceless. It seemed as if the night would never end. She prayed he was all right.

By 6.30 p.m., Wednesday 12 September, the sun was slipping low in a vibrantly clear, panoramic Florida sky as teenagers Paul Babb and Michael Smith pedalled their bicycles aimlessly, casually exploring a largely undeveloped wasteland intercut with a patchwork maze of dirt trails and paved roads, each ending abruptly in a cul-de-sac just short of the bushes. Less than half a mile off CR 484, just west of I-75 and Marion Oaks (a luxurious, gated housing community with a waterfall at its entrance), they weren't far from home, yet this was new territory to them. It was a somewhat desolate expanse of low-lying brushland behind a power station, unpopulated save for a sparse scattering of houses.

Three-quarters of an inch of rain had fallen that day, barely cooling what had been a balmy 91 degrees. It was the prettiest, somehow laziest, time of day.

Pulling down one paved strip of cul-de-sac abutting some farmland, Paul and Mike (seventeen and fifteen years old, respectively) idly observed what looked at first sight like a lumpy heap of clothing piled close to the edge of the grass, to the left of a concrete culvert. Drawing closer, Michael was in the lead when, wide-eyed with horror, he focused in on the clothes.

'Come here quick!' he yelled to Paul.

'What? It's just a pile of clothes,' Paul retorted uninterestedly.

Slowed by the sandy road, he had dismounted from his bicycle and casually wheeled it towards his friend. He was within a foot of the clothing before he saw just what it was that seemed to have rendered Mike speechless. What had appeared from afar a shapeless form came into focus as something horribly different.

First Paul saw a man's face, framed with grey hair, curled among the fabric. His bloody spectacles were raised up on his forehead. The man was wearing brown trousers and shoes and argyle socks, and was hunched forward in almost a sitting position, his torso curved over towards his knees. His white, short-sleeved shirt was heavily stained with blood both at the front and on the left shoulder. Protruding from his pocket was a Cross pen-and-pencil set. His left front trouser pocket had been turned inside out as if ransacked. He was still wearing his watch and his wedding ring. And he was obviously dead.

The boys' shock was followed rapidly by plain fear. Might whoever was responsible still be lurking nearby? Their systems pumping into high gear, they clambered aboard their bicycles and furiously rode the two and a half miles back to Paul's house without exchanging a word. Their progress was slowed when a piece on Paul's bicycle chain came adrift forcing him to push his bike, running to keep up with Mike.

The exhausted boys could barely catch their breath but words spilling over, managed to tell their anxious mothers, Janet Babb and Carol Smith, why they were in such a state. Janet, a nurse at a Florida Correctional Institution, immediately notified the police, arranging to meet them out on the main road. Within minutes, an emergency vehicle bearing four rescue personnel pulled up, and the boys led the way to their gory discovery.

As law enforcement officers converged on the scene and confirmed that they were dealing with a homicide brought about by multiple gunshot wounds, the sun finally sank out of sight.

Separating Paul and Mike so that they could not confer or compare stories, the officers spoke into their radios, reporting the discovery of an unidentified male victim, then launched into a barrage of questions. Each boy was asked how he got to the site. Why he'd come. Whether he knew the victim. Whether he'd touched the body. Whether he'd rifled through the man's pockets looking for valuables. Whether he'd taken anything. Thoroughly scared, they answered as best they could, as a growing assembly of police officers, detectives and technicians congregated for the slow and laborious task of processing the crime scene. The officers would work through the night hours, securing evidence and scouring the area for clues.

When their questioning was over, Paul and Mike were told they were free to go home. But their ordeal wasn't over; Paul, for one, didn't sleep for three days. The nightmares lasted longer.

Shirley Humphreys' husband had been missing more than twelve hours when, at 7.15 that Wednesday morning, she called Ken Jones again to tell him there was no news.

Hanging up the phone, she then sucked in a deep breath. There was no avoiding it any longer. She'd better call her son. 'I'll be right out!' cried Mike, who was devoted to his dad and immediately sounded desperately worried. Mother and son sat together in the horribly empty house through the long hours of that day. Hours punctuated by seemingly non-stop phone calls from concerned friends to whom word had quickly spread.

Thankfully, there were practical matters to occupy Shirley. Dick had never been fond of using their credit cards, most of which were usually left on his desk, but with the advice and help of friends, Shirley immediately cancelled them all, including her own, since those were jointly held. She had cashed a cheque for Dick on Monday for $110 but they had paid for their anniversary dinner from that. Shirley imagined he probably had about $45 left on him when he disappeared.

Night fell and, eventually, knowing there was nothing more to be done but wait, Shirley and Mike went to their beds, finally overtaken by sheer exhaustion. Shirley must have drifted off because suddenly, she awoke with a start. Disoriented, she thought it was around 2.30 a.m. when she left the refuge of sleep to face again the terrible realisation that she was living, not dreaming, a nightmare.

She slipped on her robe and walked slowly out into the living room, worn out and thoroughly drained but restless. Sitting on the couch with her feet up, she flicked a flame to a cigarette. Suddenly, the doorbell rang, rudely loud and jarring in the still of the night. Walking past the front door, Shirley reached for the light switch to throw on the porch light. As she did so, through the glass she could see the looming silhouettes of four large men. She had been a policeman's wife long enough to know what it meant.

'Oh no! Mike!' she cried.

And her scream shattered the silence.

David Taylor of the Marion County SO had arrived at the undeveloped subdivision just before 10 p.m. in response to patrol officers requesting the presence of a major crimes investigator at a homicide scene. By 10.30, Sergeant Kerry Crawford had instigated a search of possible missing persons, which almost immediately turned up the report on Mr Humphreys. Phone calls flew between the various divisions working in concert, and CID Captain Steve Binegar announced that he was on his way. Painstakingly, photographs were taken, recording the details of the body and the crime scene.

Meanwhile, just before midnight, Ken Jones was called out to the scene and given the grim task of identifying his colleague's body. And it was he who, with Captain Jim Fussell and Chief Deputy Greg Matthews, stood on Mrs Humphreys' doorstep, in fact sometime before 1 a.m.

An autopsy the next day by Dr Janet Pillow, a forensic pathologist in the medical examiner's office in Leesburg, would note the doughnut-shaped abrasion and bruising on the victim's side, consistent with a gun barrel, and the other mysterious small bruises inside his upper right arm. Of the seven bullet wounds, her expert opinion was that the only shot to have completely incapacitated the victim was the one to the back of his head. Shattering as it entered, lead bullet fragments flew through his brain with enough force to bruise his left eyelid.

Six hollow-point bullets were recovered, all told. The one that struck Dick Humphreys' wrist was not. A toxicology examination of his blood came back negative as to alcohol and drugs and marijuana.

Shirley Humphreys had buried her mother the past January, and her father-in-law, to whom she was very close, in March. Now, she was burying her beloved husband.

Thirty-five years and one day after they wed, Shirley was a widow.

'How much more can I take?'

She asked that question of God, more than once.

Mike took the loss of his father very, very hard, losing the greatest friend he ever had; they had been very, very close. It was no easier for Dick's daughters. As Terry firmly informed the assistant state attorneys: 'My daddy was twenty-seven feet tall.'

It was after her daughters had had to return to their own lives that the gaping emptiness of the house hit hardest. The Moose ladies rallied and did their best to busy her, but company alone was not enough. The months between Dick's death and the arrest of a suspect were also very scary for Shirley Humphreys.

Somebody, somewhere out there, had the keys to her house and her car. She had the locks on both changed, of course, but still, every little noise 'created a big trauma'. Each night when she took out her hearing aids to go to bed, she felt even more defenceless. Mike, who was also frightened, had moved back into the house to keep her company and urged her to get a dog.

'For twenty-eight years I've raised a dog along with my kids—I don't need another dog! Dogs are too hairy,' Shirley retorted.

Trying to find reason in madness, every possible scenario floated through Shirley's mind regarding the identity of Dick's murderer. Given his professional history, the most likely seemed to be someone from one of his cases. 'I went through beaucoup paperwork on some case he was involved with in Alabama involving drugs, and handed that to the Sheriff's Department,' Shirley recalls. And Ken Jones scoured the case files at the Sumter County HRS office, groping for any kind of clue or connection.

On 19 September, Dick's car was finally located in Live Oak, 125 miles north of the spot where his body was found. It was parked in a space behind an abandoned service station.

Shirley Humphreys eventually received her late husband's Cross pen, dented where a bullet had hit it. And when the sheriff handed over Dick's gold wedding band and his spectacles, both mercilessly still bore her husband's blood. Cruel mementoes. Chilling reminders of the brutality of her loss.

Who could have done such a thing?

2

The Wuornos home, an unprepossessing one-storey ranch, its wood siding a sad, faded yellow, sat amidst a cluster of trees away from the roadside in suburban Troy, Michigan, just 16 miles north of Detroit. Benign-looking and otherwise unnoteworthy, it was nevertheless a house of secrets.

Near neighbours who over the years were never once invited to set foot inside for even casual pleasantries, recall the curtains always being drawn tightly across its small windows, excluding the outside world.

Behind those windows frequent clashes of will took place between young Aileen and her father, Lauri Wuornos. The omnipresent third party: a wide, brown leather belt with western-style tooling that Lauri kept hanging on a peg on his bedroom door, and which was cleaned almost ritualistically by Aileen at his bidding with saddle soap and conditioner kept in the dresser drawer.

When she was made to pull down her shorts and bend over the wooden table in the middle of the kitchen, when the doubled-over belt flew down onto her bare buttocks, little Aileen railed against her father, petrified and crying noisily. Sometimes she lay face down, spread-eagled naked on the bed, for her whippings.

Behind those windows she listened, a captive and impressionable audience, as her father repeatedly told her that she was evil. Wicked. Worthless. Should never have been born. She wasn't worthy of the air she breathed. She already knew she was different. Born on 29 February 1956, she only celebrated a birthday every four years. When she was twelve, the other kids taunted her, saying she was three.

Her blond brother Keith, sharing the same broad facial structure and wide-set eyes, was often taken for her twin but was eleven months older. Like Aileen, Keith clashed with Lauri's discipline head on.

There were others in this family, sharing the Wuornos name but with little else in common. Diane, an older daughter, had already left home. Nobody talked about her. But Barry Wuornos, twelve years older than Aileen, was Lauri's blue-eyed boy, his golf buddy and his pal, and rarely put a foot wrong. When Barry joined the Air Force in 1967, Lauri was definitely sorry to see him go.

Even Lori, who was just two and a half years older than Aileen and grew up alongside Aileen and Keith, was spared the abuse they suffered. True, her dad was strict, authoritarian, stubborn, and always right. 'An ornery s.o.b.', as one neighbour called him. Sure he drank; two, three, sometimes more bottles of wine a day. But only wine. Sure, he was intimidating if you crossed him. Lori never did. She didn't dare. But she didn't see him as the tyrant Aileen and Keith made him out to be. Aileen and Keith, they just couldn't seem to stop themselves going up against him. It was as if they had the devil in them.

By the time she was eleven, Aileen was already incorrigible, with a fearsome and socially unacceptable temper. Her volcanic explosions were unpredictable and seemingly unprovoked, and inevitably they drove a wedge between her and her peers. It was as if even those who wanted to like her somehow just couldn't. Lori echoed that ambivalence herself. Jekyll and Hyde, everyone called Aileen.

She had another life outside, and regularly made her escape through the window of the bedroom she shared with Lori, rebelling against being confined to the house as a punishment for one offence or another. An escape to her other world; a world in which she felt omnipotent.

Across the street from Clark gas station, which sat part-way between the townships of Troy and Rochester, there was in those days a heavily wooded, ravine-like dip close to the side of Emerald Lakes. Houses have since sprung up changing the face of the landscape, but in 1967 the shallow ravine and the wooded pathway linking the two small towns was a well-trodden short cut for local youngsters, and a hangout. The terrain provided ample natural cover for their antics: from eight-year-olds burying a forbidden copy of *Playboy* under twigs and leaves, to teenagers playing hooky and drinking and making out.

In a depression in this ravine, tucked at the foot of a huge spreading tree, sat one of a number of makeshift, fort-like constructions, patched together from logs, tree stumps, pieces of plasterboard, plywood and scraps. To prepubescent Aileen, this was no playhouse, however. It was a place of business; a hideaway where she calculatingly removed her clothes and performed sexual acts on boys for which they rewarded her with cigarettes or loose change. This little girl had learned at a frighteningly early age to disassociate herself from her body; to blank off her emotions.

Small, fair-haired and slender, this child-woman was courted by the youth from Troy and Rochester, in so far as they enjoyed her unusual services. But more significantly she was constantly derided and denigrated by them, pummelling the shaky self-esteem that lay beneath her bravado. Sought after one moment, rejected the next. Used and cast aside.

One not so unusual night, when Aileen was twelve, on the brink of thirteen, she slipped out from her room to keep a midnight rendezvous at the fort with a boy called Johnny, barely older than she. While they were coupled on the ground, a noise from above disturbed Aileen. Looking up, she caught sight of a trio of boys hiding in the branches of the tree spying on them, and doing a rather inferior job of keeping quiet. Realising that they had been spotted, they snickered out loud. The laughter's volume built; infectious schoolboy stuff. But as it increased, so did Aileen's fury. Close to tears, feeling humiliated and badly betrayed, she started pulling on her clothes and backing away from the fort, but, not yet content, the descending boys harassed her further. They even had the gall to shout at her, noisily demanding a refund on Johnny's behalf as if he were a dissatisfied customer at Kmart. As she ran off into the woods, she could hear the sound of their laughter pealing out behind her.

Playing hooky from school later, and still enraged by the incident, Aileen returned and scavenged bits and pieces with which to create her own fort.

There seemed some kind of superficial acceptance of her outcast role. At her tender age she had already come to expect such treatment. But that didn't mean she liked it.

There was no shortage of testosterone-driven clientele for Aileen, who worked not just in the forts but in the backs of cars, or simply lay down in the dirt, stripping off her clothes without inhibition or emotion, sometimes taking on three boys at a time. Those boys are now men who today admit that she took no pleasure in it and there was little if any conversation. Certainly no kissing. Just business. Aileen's earnings went on cigarettes, beer, and, before long, on the drugs with which she became increasingly involved—mescaline, acid, and downers like pot and pills, were her preference.

The money also went on trying to buy something that she wanted desperately but that continued to elude her: popularity and acceptance. With money, she felt empowered. It gave her status, and a means by which she could have people in her life.

Frank Tremonti lost his virginity to Aileen when he was twelve or thirteen, which is reason enough for the sunny afternoon she followed him home to be indelibly etched in his mind, even if the date is not. Aileen, at eleven or twelve a slim, pretty, young creature in shorts, watched intently from across the street while he took out a gasoline-powered rotary lawn mower and began methodically mowing his parents' lawn, one of his designated chores. Slowly, calculatedly, Aileen rode her bicycle back and forth along the path in front of his house so that Frank would have had to have been myopic not to notice. Watchfully assessing the situation, he soon found himself waiting keenly for each return pass. Eventually, Aileen made her move towards him, slipping him a folded-up note, then riding off. Frank, hormones raging, couldn't believe his eyes: 'Meet me at Clark station. For a pack of cigs I will suck and fuck.'

Trembling with anticipation, he hurriedly returned the lawn mower to its place in the garage and rushed inside the house to scrabble for some change before racing down the street; a young man with an urgent purpose. Out of breath, he reached the gas station to find Aileen waiting, calmly sitting astride her bicycle, exuding a confidence beyond her years. Following her instructions, Frank went inside Clark's and purchased her the requisite packet of Marlboros, then rode the bicycle, with Aileen perched on the handlebars, heading off the road and down among the trees to her fort.

Some 23 years later, after Aileen Carol Wuornos's arrest for the murders of six men and her confession to the murders of seven, Frank broke down and cried. The thought that tormented him?

If he hadn't had sex with her, would she have turned out the way she did?

He was hardly alone, of course. When Aileen had barely reached puberty herself she claimed the virginities of a number of Troy and Rochester's neighbourhood boys. Virginities they were anxious to dispose of. She allowed them to initiate themselves into the tantalising world of sex at an age where it seemed to them that so-called free love was only available elsewhere. Jerry Moss, Keith's close friend, was among Aileen's first lovers. At the time, he categorically believed he was *the* first.

'I know damn well it was *my* first time. She *said* it was hers,' he recalls with a hint of indignation. Later, the duplicate stories of other males cast serious doubt on her claim. Somehow, Aileen had managed to convince a not inconsiderable number of gullible boys that they were being given the gift of her virginity. As the years went by, however, local lore accorded Dean that honour.

Jerry Moss and his clan lived on Cambria, separated only by Dean's house from the Wuornoses' home on Cadmus. When sex wasn't involved, he and the other boys wanted little or nothing to do with Aileen. When Jerry and Keith went out walking, they'd often notice her sneaking around the bushes that edged the field, following them to see where they went. They lobbed rocks at her to try to scare her off, yelling: 'Get your ass home!'

'I'm telling Dad!' Aileen retorted.

'Tell whoever the hell you want,' Keith shouted back, angrily. 'Just get the hell outta here.'

During ceasefires, a common topic was getting out of the

neighbourhood, and ruminating on what their lives would be like when they did. Jerry, the son of a Marine, fancied going into the Navy; Keith was going to be an Army officer; Lori wanted to finish high school. Aileen? Aileen wanted to be a movie star. Everyone knew that.

Jerry was fourteen and Aileen twelve in the summer of '68 when they first began exploring each other's bodies one day in Jerry's parents' upstairs bedroom. They were interrupted when the clunking sound of the garage door opening signalled his folks' unexpected return, and as Aileen scurried to slip out of the house unnoticed, they paused long enough to make plans to finish what they'd started.

Later that same day they sneaked up into the attic above Jerry's garage, this time armed with a blanket and pillow. Their handful of sexual encounters began in an 'I'll show you mine, if you show me yours' vein, and were tender enough with some gentle kissing. Aileen, who hadn't yet developed breasts or body hair, evidently knew more than Jerry. The true source of her own sexual initiation by eleven was a mystery, but it was she who initiated taking things a step further.

They were both a little tipsy from sipping some unpleasantly vinegary old apple cider that had turned potent enough to grease the wheels of inhibition. Aileen customarily conducted her sexual activities in her neighbourhood in secret, and suggested to Jerry that they keep what had happened between them to themselves. Jerry readily agreed, knowing discretion was in his best interests.

Far from aching to rush off and brag about his lost virginity, he had already decided he wasn't going to tell anyone, even his close friends. And that included Keith. He certainly had no intention of telling Keith that he'd lost his virginity to Aileen. And to have announced he'd 'lost it' at all would have meant revealing with whom. The prevailing sexual climate in their age group and the unavailability of sex would alone have been enough to point the finger at Aileen. So he kept quiet. Not until he was seventeen did he belatedly announce that he'd just lost his virginity—with his 14-year-old wife. He never told a soul the truth.

'I wouldn't want nobody in that neighbourhood knowing that

I screwed the hell out of Aileen in my dad's garage,' he says emphatically. Then and now, Jerry never felt anything but ashamed of the liaison.

At a shockingly young age, Aileen had become an object of ridicule, and no neighbourhood boy would have willingly admitted to being involved with her.

'Everybody called her bitch, slut, whore, an ugly bitch, before she even was,' Jerry recalls. 'If I'd a went out and said, "Hey, I screwed the hell out of Aileen Wuornos," everybody in the neighbourhood woulda went crazy and said, "What the fuck? That ugly bitch!" She was ridiculed or whatever . . . abused . . . I'm sure somebody slapped her around. I never hit the girl. I might have pushed her in an argument or something. Broke up a fight between her and her brother or Lori, something like that, but I never slapped that girl or did anything like that.'

Since Jerry was such a close friend, Aileen didn't ask for payment for her sexual favours, which was unusual in itself. He might have given her a couple of tabs of acid or PCP, or shared a couple of joints with her, but no money changed hands.

Their secret encounters in the attic halted abruptly just a few weeks later. Aileen's agenda had changed, or perhaps merely revealed itself. Unusually vulnerable, she had begun talking dreamily about how nice it would be to have a boyfriend and she had been trying to press Jerry into the role. 'Not me!' retorted Jerry, who didn't even plan on being seen in public with her. He didn't want to hurt her feelings but his bottom line was 'No way!'

Aileen didn't shed a tear at this rejection. Instead she became angry, shouting, 'Fuck off, Jerry!'

Well, if Aileen chose to ignore him for the rest of the summer, so be it. Jerry's mind was made up.

After this rift, when Jerry knocked on the Wuornoses' door looking for Keith, if he was unlucky enough to have Aileen answer, she greeted him with, 'Fuck you! Keith isn't here!' even when Jerry could see his friend standing right there behind her.

Gary Kopietz was also fourteen when he first had sex with Aileen. It was the summer of '69 and she was then thirteen. Without Aileen, Gary surmised that he would probably have had to wait until he was sixteen to be relieved of his burdensome virginity. As it was, he'd heard about her services and Aileen, dressed tomboyishly in the hippie style of the sixties in jeans, a simple blouse and a beginner's bra, looked quite appealing. Gary's hormones were calling loudly and he wanted some action too.

He soon got his chance the day a friend rode by on his bicycle, calling out, 'Come on! We got Cigarette Pig! We're gonna go down and fuck her! Get thirty-five cents.'

Aileen first smoked when she was ten years old, sitting under the slide in the backyard with an older girlfriend, puffing away, and practising her new-found vocabulary of profanities.

Cigarettes, and Aileen's addiction to them, were her downfall, decided Gary, not that the thought deterred him. Since he didn't have a bicycle, he ran to keep up with Frank who pedalled the mile or so to a spot Aileen had nominated behind the Wuornos house.

Revisiting the spot in the fall, when the leaves had tumbled from the trees, although it was tucked at the foot of a three-foot slope, he was astonished to see how exposed it was, and how close to the cars on nearby South Boulevard. But shielded by summer's greenery it had sufficed that day.

The boys were gentle with Aileen and didn't manhandle her. At her invitation, they peeled all her clothes off, then had an energetic discussion about who should be first in line. 'I really put up a squawk,' Gary recalls, 'saying, "This is my first time, let me go first!" Finally the others agreed and went and sat maybe fifteen or twenty feet away and turned their backs.'

Intercourse took place with the minimum of pleasantries. 'There wasn't like a big discussion. This was not boyfriend–girlfriend. She definitely wasn't the type you'd want for a girlfriend at that point. She put it in, and I'm sitting there going for ten, fifteen minutes. And these guys are heckling me in the background after five minutes, saying, "Hurry up! Come on! We want our turn!" And nothing was happening. I'd never come before, and it didn't happen. I finally just said, "Well, that's it."'

He promptly ran home and leapt in the bathtub. In his eyes, she was a whore, basically, and although he was pleased no longer to be a virgin, he also felt the urgent need to make contact with water.

From that day on, Aileen initiated ten or so encounters with Gary. She offered 'a fuck, a blow job, or whatever you want' for a fee. 'There was never a time when anybody said no. Not when you're fourteen,' Gary emphasises.

'Cigarette Pig' and the marginally less degrading and more romantic-sounding 'Cigarette Bandit' were the nicknames she earned for her trouble. Cruel words that with repeated use gnawed away at her.

Clark gas station, which boasted two islands with two pumps apiece, was also the scene of many sexual encounters. When one of the local youngsters was working a shift running the place, sex took place behind the cooler, in the bathrooms, and in the small storage room out back. One of the Clark employees, who was around eighteen at the time, was also approached by Aileen and offered oral sex in the back room. When she needed cigarettes, it was a deal she often struck. She was a quick learner in the art of negotiation.

Unaware of the Cigarette Pig reputation, the young man triumphantly announced that he'd kissed Aileen and made love to her in the back room. Gary and the others couldn't resist spoiling his moment of glory by telling him that Aileen had given them all blow jobs earlier that afternoon. Besides, they felt they were doing him a service. Imagine if he'd blindly become her boyfriend? 'Basically, all we did was tell him that she was a dog,' Gary recalled.

Keith's best friend, Mark Fearn, who was a year younger than Aileen and had known her since they were toddlers, also lost his virginity to Aileen when he was ten or eleven. Before that, he once stumbled across Aileen and Dean copulating in the field over by the willow trees (Dean being the boy neighbourhood kids generally credited with having started Aileen off on sex).

'I didn't even know what I was doing,' Mark says of his own first encounter. 'I don't even remember it being fun or anything. You did it, I guess, so you could brag, "I did it!"'

On one occasion, Jerry Moss kept a lookout while Mark Fearn and Aileen had sex in a bedroom in his parents' home. Aileen also told Mark that she'd had sex with her father, Lauri. (Everyone pronounced it 'Larry'.) At the time, he didn't believe her.

With his dark good looks, Mark became a natural target for Aileen's hunger for love. As with Jerry, she tried desperately through the device of sex to win Mark's true affection—and failed. Mark didn't want Aileen, of all people, for a girlfriend. He tried to let her down as gently as he could. But it was another rejection.

Young Aileen's sexual activities were not confined to friends and strangers. There was incest between Aileen and Keith, although with just eleven months between them in age and with Keith the virgin, it was by mutual consent.

Aileen told Gary Kopietz yet another variation on the story of her deflowering, saying that the first time she had had sex was when she was eleven with her own brother. He was shocked, which is why it stuck in his mind. It was probably more common than he thought. It certainly didn't seem like a big deal to her. But he knew it wasn't right.

All of Keith's friends knew that shy Keith was deeply embarrassed by his sister's reputation as the local 'loose goose', 'the first one off with her shorts'. But many knew that Keith also took advantage of her promiscuity. Since she knew about sex, he urged her, please would she teach him so that girls wouldn't laugh at him? Aileen agreed and there were a number of voluntary encounters between them, some of which took place in the presence of Mark Fearn.

On one memorable occasion, Aileen and Keith were almost caught in the act. They were playing around in the little loft above the garage when Lauri suddenly came in and started up the makeshift ladder. Mark, Keith and Aileen lay frozen, scared to move a muscle, while Lauri, seemingly oblivious, reached up perilously close to them to retrieve his stash of cheap wine. Which is how Aileen and Keith first learned he had a hiding place up there. 'Scared the hell out of us,' Mark recalls.

While outsiders noted such encounters and the bond between the siblings, their sister Lori would always find it hard to believe that Aileen and Keith had sex. Such intimacy didn't gel with her memories of two adversaries who fought vigorously and constantly. They even sat at the breakfast table hiding their faces behind cereal boxes so that they wouldn't have to look at one another.

But this sexual aspect of Keith and Aileen's relationship was no less mercurial than any other. Mark remembers Keith once, for a lark, a bit of boyish silliness, urinating on Aileen as she lay on the ground in the garage. He also remembers Aileen's fury.

3

Aileen's rampant promiscuity flew in the face of the firm discipline at home. The Wuornos household was nothing if not structured. Lori and Barry, whose opinions were generally in accord, would later recall their family life thus: if it wasn't quite of the fairy-tale, white picket-fence variety, it was certainly normal, uneventful, and just like everyone else's. They describe Lauri Wuornos as strict, firm, a disciplinarian, but in no way tyrannical or abusive. In Barry's eyes his father was 'someone you could look up to'.

With his dark skin, high cheekbones, and Scandinavian facial structure, Lauri looked almost Native American. Despite a superficial resemblance to comedian Jackie Gleason, his stern demeanour and imposingly bushy eyebrows always scared and intimidated Lori's friends, and Lori had to reassure them that he wasn't as mean as he looked.

Lauri Wuornos would be remembered in Troy as a man who put on a suit to go to work and comported himself with a superior attitude, as if designating himself as a cut above the rest. Bullishly opinionated, he was also a vehement anti-Republican. Just seeing a car with its headlights on early in the evening would prompt a snide remark about wastefulness. 'That's a Republican,' he'd say.

He behaved as if he bore a grudge against the world. John Majestic, whose family moved into the house next door in 1956, quickly measured Lauri as an arrogant, pompous know-it-all, best taken in small doses. John, Barry's peer, wore a path through the grass to Barry's bedroom window where almost daily he'd crawl in for a chat. In summer, when they were in their teens and Aileen was a toddler, Barry joined John to camp out in the tent pitched in Barry's backyard, or to spend the night in the back of an old Dodge station wagon that Lauri kept.

Lauri always insisted that Barry do his chores, like tending their huge lawn. If John was around, he'd be corralled into them too. 'You guys get out there and chop that wood!' said Lauri, pointing them to the heap of kindling that had to be neatly split each week to fire up the sauna. Not one for idle pleasantries, he'd sometimes snap at John, 'Go home!' And John did. Instinctively, kids knew to give him a wide berth. 'He was boisterous,' John recalls. 'He was like a walrus, a bull.'

If neighbourhood kids stepped in his yard when it didn't suit him, Lauri chewed them out without a second thought. Jerry Moss, for some reason he himself never understood, seemed especially to antagonise old man Wuornos. Lauri singled him out if he tried to take a short-cut through the Wuornos yard like the other kids, skipping along to catch the school bus.

'Hey, you fuckin' bum. Hey, what are you doing? You ain't coming in my yard,' Lauri growled.

'Asshole,' Jerry retorted, not exactly diplomatically. 'Fuck you! I'm going through there, I'm gonna be late. My bus is out there right now!'

Many more houses have since sprung up to plug in the neighbourhood's vacant lots, but in those days Aileen's home had a cyclone fence around the front and a huge backyard of close to two acres, planted with a weeping willow and an imposing maple tree. Out back lived the children's menagerie—a changing cast of dogs, cats, pigeons, ducks, turtles, fish and birds. Aileen wasn't as besotted with animals as Lori, but held a particularly soft spot in her heart for a mutt called Coco.

The subdivision was cliquish but—with the exception of the almost reclusive Wuornoses—most of the inhabitants got along reasonably well, and even socialised. At Christmas, things turned positively festive. The Moss home was strung with coloured lights and Mrs Moss made eggnog and baked fruit cakes for her neighbour friends, who all stopped by, again with the exception of the Wuornoses. Lauri let the kids go

Christmas carolling, but that was the extent of their participation.

None the less, Lori remembered merry family Christmases when the house was decorated and the family sang carols and played Christmas music. Lauri didn't go to church, but Britta (whose full name was Aileen Britta) took the children to services regularly throughout the year.

Since Aileen's 29 February birthday fell only on leap years, another day was generally designated to celebrate it, with cake, candles, gifts and singing. Sometimes during the summer when there was a tent pitched in the backyard, friends like Lori's pal, Janet Craig, were invited to spend the night out there with Aileen and Lori, just as Barry's friends had done with him in the past.

The childish pleasure of sleepovers, however, was interrupted by Aileen's late-night forays out into the dark world of prostitution. She'd return after a couple of hours, clutching a fistful of dollars, plus alcohol or drugs.

Incongruously, the days began in the Wuornos household with Britta rousing them by singing 'Wake up little sleepyhead . . .' If that sounds borderline Brady Bunch, a happy, normal, if strict, family is exactly what Lori believes she grew up in.

Supper was always a family affair, but a subdued one. Talking was minimal because Keith and Aileen inevitably argued, which in turn meant Lauri got angry. It was easier just to keep quiet.

The 5 p.m. meal was followed by chores and homework. Aileen showed considerable artistic promise, but her home environment was not conducive to maximising that potential or to putting her into any situations where she could shine, rather than being perennially the bad girl. Her negative behaviour drew attention, not her positive.

Strict rules were enforced, with each child being delegated duties like dusting and vacuuming. Edicts were issued rather than requests made: 'Aileen, clean your room spotless now!' 'Keith, mow the lawn now!' Bedtime was 8 p.m. during the week, 9 p.m. at weekends. There was no question of being ten or twenty minutes late or straggling. They all knew that the consequences of rebelling or being mouthy were to be grounded, spanked, or both.

Once, catching them skipping school, Lauri grounded them for a month. They were allowed to play in the front yard but were forbidden to see friends or to receive phone calls. Even Lori felt that that was a little excessive. For most of her friends, it would have been two weeks, tops.

Rashomon-like, Lori and Barry report quite different punishments from Aileen.

'We got spankings and groundings but we never got beat,' Lori insists. 'We *did* get yelled at.'

Aileen describes being hit with a leather belt on bare skin, sometimes on consecutive days with the skin still painfully raw from the previous session. Sometimes with the belt folded in half and grasped in the middle, so the loose ends and buckle struck the skin. That by far exceeds the commonly accepted idea of spankings. Aileen has not proved herself to be a consistent source of information, but her account is definitely long-standing. Both Aileen and Keith complained at the time to friends of the 'bare-ass spankings'. Other kids knew they were harshly punished.

Some neighbours heard Lauri's screaming and yelling echoing around the neighbourhood so loudly it could be heard from half a block away. 'That was just how he talked,' Cheryl Stacy would recall. 'He didn't treat them like human beings. He treated them worse than anybody would treat an animal.'

For being ten minutes late, Lauri hollered, 'Get in your rooms and pull your pants down!' and went to fetch his belt. Britta just stood back compliantly and did nothing to stop him. 'Maybe that will teach you to come home when I tell you to,' Lauri announced when they cried.

'It wasn't so bad that we had bruises . . . but it hurts when you're little,' Lori reluctantly admits, obviously pained by giving or hearing any criticism of her father. 'I got smart enough eventually to start crying right away because then the spanking was shorter. We were spanked until we cried.'

Being yelled at was far more upsetting to Lori than being spanked. A spanking was soon over. Being yelled at hurt your feelings, making you feel unloved or even hated; an emotional pain that could last for days.

In the sixties, before corporal punishment was the politically incorrect hot potato it is today, it wasn't uncommon to see a neighbourhood kid dancing around in the yard trying to elude an angry parent wielding a strap. In what is more than mere semantics, however, the wicked, sadistic beatings that Aileen claimed terrorised her were categorically minimised and dismissed as just spankings by Lori and by Barry. Barry even claims that while the boys got spankings, the girls did not. (Barry's experiences should be put in context: he was out of the house and off in the Air Force by 1967 when Aileen was eleven and coming into her era of greatest conflict with Lauri.)

Whom to believe? Major discrepancies in memories within the same family are common. (Barry, for instance, described Aileen as a 'well-liked' child. A unique claim.) But it's also true that adults in denial of childhood abuse sometimes belittle the punishment they suffered.

In a fashion common in alcoholic families, much remained hidden. Lori maintains she knew nothing of Aileen's teenage prostitution, or of Britta's alcoholism until after her mother's death. She can't remember her ever drinking. She only remembers that her mom seemed worn down from trying to exert herself in the face of Lauri's domineering personality and temper.

Lauri was a habitual, blatantly overt drinker. He didn't care who knew it. He sat in his armchair each night, imbibing cheap wine (often two or three bottles of muscatel) and brandishing a cigar in his stubby fingers until he all but passed out. At the last moment he'd come to and would shuffle off to bed. At weekends, he drank more.

Occasionally he was rowdily drunk. He had a fierce aversion to motorcycles and once when he and Lori visited Veterans Hospital, he stopped the car outside and deliberately let his foot off the brake, sliding into a motorcycle and bumping its rider off into the road. Lori was petrified. Lauri laughed.

The alcohol generally made him quiet rather than violent, but he nevertheless had a fearsome temper and a dogmatic manner. What he said was law, Lori concedes: 'I'd say, "It's raining out," and he'd say, "No, it's not," and he'd be right. He had to be right—and it didn't matter if you could prove him wrong.'

As a couple, Lauri and Britta seemed distant. There was little warmth between them. Their interaction focused primarily on mundane chores like bill-paying. Even in Lori's accepting eyes, they were like a couple married so long that they had nothing left to say to one another. They rarely went out together even for a meal unless they were on vacation. They shared a bed but, around the family at least, there was no physical affection between them or really towards their children. Certainly not as much as Lori would have liked. Lauri wasn't the type to sit a child on his lap and offer a kind word or affection, yet the children were made to ritualistically kiss each parent goodnight, something Keith loathed. Finally, Lauri relented, allowing him to shake his hand.

Like Barry, Keith also detested the short, neat 'butch' haircuts that Lauri insisted on, but Lauri was skilled with the scissors. When the mood took him, he'd bellow for the boys to come in and get their hair cut.

Keith so hated following any of Lauri's orders that by the age of ten, even carrying a little garbage out back was enough to reduce him to tears of frustration. He always argued with Lauri, but Lauri never backed down. Yet he wasn't a merciless tyrant and on weekends chauffeured groups of children to see a film like The Beatles' *A Hard Day's Night,* or to go tobogganing or ice-skating. And he saw to it that Aileen was included . . . whether the other kids wanted her along or not.

Each summer the family shared a two-week vacation up north, camping and staying in motels. Evenings at home were spent, with the television tuned to Lawrence Welk or Jackie Gleason, or to old World War II movies, which Lauri loved. Having served in the Army, Lauri proudly regaled his family with war stories including a tale of how he claimed he earned a Purple Heart. When his parents were out, Barry sometimes sneaked John into their dark room for a look at Lauri's war medals and photographs. Barry was proud his dad had fought in the trenches and got shrapnel in his back. (Lauri said he was injured by fallout from a hand grenade.) A stout and stocky figure of 5 feet 9 inches, he had the tips of two fingertips missing from a bout of frostbite during a logging expedition. Lauri Wuornos didn't keep guns in the house or have any interest in hunting. Aileen didn't learn about firearms at home.

Like Aileen, Keith made it plain to his closest friends that he hated his parents, reporting that they were often locked in their rooms for long periods. Both sometimes bore bruises, but they never told their friends how they got them.

The 'cat incident' made a lasting impact not just on them but a number of neighbourhood children. A family of wild kittens had been living in the attic, and all but one had been taken to the pound when the remaining kitten scratched at Aileen's face. The next day it was playing nicely with her when Lauri demanded, 'Is that the damned cat who scratched you?' Hearing her 'yes', he grabbed the flailing animal and made her follow him into the sauna and watch while he held the kitten under water until it was dead.

Like every other childhood, theirs wasn't free of misadventure and near disaster. It was Keith's bright idea to mix gasoline and oil in a little trail and then set light to it. Aileen, who was nine, and Lori decided to copy him, but they carelessly splashed too heavy a trail and the flames licked up instantly, burning Lori's leg and catching Aileen's face and hair. Hearing Aileen's screams, Lauri came running but couldn't extinguish the fire before Aileen was burned badly enough to leave scars on her face and to warrant a few days in the hospital. She was traumatised.

'That's when everybody started to tease me. I was like a misfit,' she now says. To her mind, Lori then refused to have anything to do with her and treated her like a freak. An accusation everyone scoffs at. Aileen describes blisters the size of fifty-cent pieces all over her face and her hair being charred. Certainly there was swelling initially, but the scars weren't disfiguring. With a fringe, they weren't even visible. Yet to Aileen it all assumed monumental importance.

Keith was definitely mischievous, his antics ranging from rock fights to BB gun fights, and at least five times, at Keith's suggestion, he and Mark set fire to a nearby field. 'Keith'd say, "We're just gonna light a little one",' Mark recalls, 'and we'd end up with the whole damn field on fire.' Aileen also lit fires in a nearby field, and, in junior high, she set some toilet paper alight in the school bathroom. Lori would never forget the ruckus that caused.

As an adult, Aileen often claimed to be part of a singing group, and indeed always fancied herself as a singer. As a child, with her short hair swept back like a boy's, she pretended she had a microphone and pranced around the living room as if she was out onstage.

It was the prospect of the attention she relished, of being admired and idolised—that and being rich. She was always preoccupied with money or, rather, with what having it could do for her.

She began shoplifting in her early teens, at first on a minor scale, stealing record albums from a store in nearby Rochester and smuggling them out under her coat. Inevitably, she was caught. Store officials telephoned Lauri, who, fuming, had to collect her. Presumably it was no accident that Aileen also targeted for shoplifting the very Kmart store where Britta worked part-time. Completely humiliated, Britta decided she couldn't live with the embarrassment and quit her job.

She was no less mortified the time a gaggle of neighbours gathered to watch open-mouthed as a couple of policemen chased Aileen down the street. Aileen was clutching a take-away tub of spaghetti she obviously didn't want to lose, but finally dumped it so she could run faster. Gathering speed, she then took off across the field with the cops in pursuit.

'Aileen and Keith both could rip you off pretty quick,' Mark admits. Yet brother and sister had markedly different temperaments. Keith held things inside and let them fester, but if something bothered Aileen, she'd just blurt it out without editing. It took a lot to get Keith to say what was on his mind.

The Wuornos kids had it worse than any others in the subdivision, that was the consensus. It seemed nobody ever cared about Aileen. She was on her own and no one appeared to give a damn.

While other families rose in the morning and lifted their blinds, letting sunlight stream over their breakfast tables, the Wuornoses lived in gloom. 'It was like a dungeon most of the time,' one friend observed. 'The Wuornoses were lucky if they got a bowl of breakfast cereal, let alone lunch money for school. Sometimes a teacher gave them a loan or other kids shared a sandwich with them. Generally, they took bag lunches because they couldn't afford hot lunches.'

As Aileen and Keith entered their teens they were already alienated at home. It was unthinkable that Aileen might have confided how she felt about the other kids in school not liking her. Her parents would never have understood. The friction was so bad that it seemed Aileen and Keith's very existence infuriated Lauri. He couldn't tolerate them being sassy. When they became rebellious and uncontrollable things only got worse.

'Do the dishes now,' Lauri commanded them.

'I don't want to right now,' Aileen whined.

'Now!' Laurie retorted, his voice rising.

'I'm sick of you ordering us around,' Aileen shot back, growing wilder by the moment.

'Go to your room,' Lauri ordered.

When the moment came, Aileen took her spanking but kept screaming, 'I hate you, old man!'

Aileen and Keith often accused Lori of being the favourite. 'No way,' Lori argued back. 'I get grounded and spanked just as much as you, and I don't get any extra toys or extra clothes or extra love.'

Aileen did not have a single good, healthy, supportive or nurturing relationship with a man during her formative years.

Aileen and Keith heard the distressing news of their adoption when Aileen was eleven and just beginning her sexual acting out. Aileen and Keith were being passed off as Lori and Barry's siblings but were in fact their nephew and niece. Dad and Mom weren't their parents after all. And it wasn't Lauri Wuornos who dropped the genealogical bombshell. In an era when divorce was still a disgrace in school, this had a major shaming effect on

Aileen and Keith. Their real mother, Diane (Lauri and Britta's eldest), had just upped and abandoned them when they were babies. Lauri and Mom had officially adopted them. But Lauri refused to reveal the identity of their real father.

The revelations made relations deteriorate still further. And when Lauri went from being their dad to being their mean old grandfather, the discipline problems escalated, too. Aileen and Keith taunted Lauri with their new weapon: 'You're not my real father!' Lauri shot back at them with equal force. Lori merely watched, distressed, or ran crying to her room.

The truth was out, but the subject of Diane (let alone Leo Pittman, their real father) was tantamount to taboo. The only time her name was mentioned was at Christmas. Diane sent gifts which Lauri promptly confiscated. It seemed to Aileen, Keith and Lori that Diane had disowned her mother and father and that they in turn had disowned her. Dimly, the children were made aware that Diane had remarried and had two more children, Rusty and Kathy, but their paths never crossed and details remained very sketchy.

Frequent runaways, Aileen and Keith took to going off, separately and together, hitchhiking until they were stopped and picked up by the police who telephoned for the Wuornoses to come and collect them. They'd then be grounded for two weeks, but the cycle was soon repeated.

Once Aileen and Keith informed Lauri in advance that they were running away together.

'Good!' he shouted. 'And don't you ever try to come back to this house again, do you hear me?'

'Fine! We don't ever want to come back because we hate your guts!' they retorted in unison.

When Lauri received the customary call—Aileen and Keith had been picked up by the police—he was true to his word and refused to collect them. Aileen was taken for the first of her visits to juvenile hall. She ran away.

Even Lori ran away from home briefly, but when Lauri collected her and gave her a choice between going home or to juvy, Lori unhesitatingly chose home. She didn't run off because she hated her parents, either. She did it just to do it. Aileen and

Keith's hatred for Father (as they continued to refer to Lauri) was monumental. Sufficiently powerful, Lori often thought, to prompt Aileen to get even. She could imagine her thinking in some perverse way, 'I'll show you! Even after you're dead, I'll ruin you!'

She's sure that the idea of bringing her father low would have given Aileen and Keith great pleasure.

4

Lured by its promise of beer, cigarettes and a laissez-faire atmosphere, Aileen, like many of the other local kids, often gravitated to the home of the Podlacks. The ramshackle, cluttered dwelling of Alfonse Podlack, commonly known as Chief, and Dixie, his common-law wife, provided a haven. It was different from their own homes, somewhere to hang out and drink and swear without censorship. Birds and rabbits inhabited the yard and the enclosed front porch was piled high with junk and boxes. Sometimes, kids stayed on the bunk in the old camper that sat out back on cement blocks among the chicken coops, or used it for making out, which no one seemed to mind.

Chief ('Chief of the Polacks') was an eccentric character, a one-time polio victim with a withered leg and a severe limp, who wore a bandanna around his head. After work at night, he made his rounds, rifling in the garbage cans behind the local grocery stores for food for his chickens. Tuesdays and Thursdays, they threw out baked goods and Chief would be there with his fireplace tongs, retrieving them from the Dumpsters.

While described as 'a grouchy old sonofabitch who reminded you of Aileen's dad' by some, others would recall Mr Podlack fondly, remembering how he'd always help fix a broken bike, or be ready to play chess, or to teach them to use a bow and arrow or to care for a gun. (He was a hunter.) He enjoyed regaling the kids with tales of the adventures of his youth, hopping trains and travelling the world.

Dixie, a retired burlesque dancer, was definitely the wild one. A vivacious, if blowsy, fun-loving drunk, she was a sociable soul who often chattered about her own childhood days

42

in Alabama in the 1920s and the back-breaking work picking cotton on the farm.

She liked having the youngsters around, particularly when Chief wasn't there, because they all chipped in for beer, which, because of the legal age limit, she would be dispatched to go and buy. She and Chief brewed their own elderberry and dandelion wine in the basement, but Chief was always chastising Dixie for her excessive drinking. Hanging out with the kids was a way of getting access to more liquor. Some of the visiting kids smoked dope with the Podlacks, buying weed and rolling joints.

Dixie, then in her fifties, was nothing if not memorable, often dressed in flimsy clothes. Her tales of burlesque seemed to enthral young Aileen, for whom Dixie became kind of a role model; a representative of worlds more exotic than Troy. Others would describe her rather ruthlessly as looking more like an old farm lady from a remote part of Italy than an ex-dancer, but Aileen didn't see her that way.

Teenage Mark found Dixie not seductive but 'A scary looking thing with red hair, the typical drunk. You could see whatever she had if you wanted to look, but who wanted to look? To me at that time she was like looking at an eighty-year-old woman. She wasn't that old, but she looked it, from all the drinking. She had a filthy mouth. I don't think she really talked about sex but she cussed a lot which was something you didn't see much of then in an older woman.'

While other adults thought they were a lonely old couple making up for not having children, there was more afoot. Even back in the early sixties, when Aileen was little, the Podlacks' was the scene of a lot of crazy times and major partying. Had Aileen spent much time there, it would not have been a good influence, admits one ex-regular. He remembers Mrs P., though, as a 'beer-buying, loving old granny' who showed off her aged newspaper clippings and reminisced about her days as an actress. For the previous wave of youngsters, as for Aileen and her peers, much of the attraction of the Podlacks' was having an adult who took little persuasion to go and purchase beer for minors.

By the time Aileen was on the scene, Dixie was generally believed to be having sex with Jimmy, a hippie who wore flowers in his hair, flounced around in big capes, and who people also thought was bisexual. When there was a party in the backwoods, Jimmy would often appear with Mrs Podlack, also done up in hippie attire, draped all over him.

Dixie did have a penchant for young boys and at least one teenager who made a pass at her had sex with her. (Which others thought very strange because of the age difference.) Dixie also had a longtime salesman boyfriend who came round when Mr Podlack was out of the way. By all accounts, together they'd get 'drunker than hell'.

Dixie enjoyed teasing the youngsters with titillating tales, and sometimes accompanying gestures, describing, for instance, what she liked to do to men with whipped cream and cherries—and what she liked to have them do to her in return. The whipped cream story became a minor legend. But Dixie didn't name names, so the kids could only speculate whether the incident involved Chief, Jimmy, or her boyfriend. She also talked brazenly and shockingly about oral and anal sex.

Aileen's sexual liaison with Mr Podlack, who sometimes visited the forts, too, became common knowledge in the neighbourhood. She frequently rode in his pick-up truck purportedly to go and get beer, or just to have a ride. If anyone questioned her directly about it she generally said, 'No way! You don't know what you're talking about.'

Yet one day, Aileen announced to the entire school bus that she'd had sex with Mr Podlack.

And Dixie, while she spoke to Aileen and even went fishing with her, often ranted and raved publicly about Chief having sex with 'the blonde bitch'.

'Aileen could walk down to the end of the block and come back with twenty or forty bucks, and never reach Rochester Road,' reports Jerry, who thought that was a neat trick.

Another of Mr Podlack's eccentricities was that he didn't believe in banks and kept his money in the house. And despite (or perhaps because of) his extreme frugality, he seemed to have plenty of it. So did Aileen, after seeing Podlack. And when she had money, she made no attempt to hide it. The point was to share it.

'Look what I've got,' she'd boast with a smile.

'Well, where did you get it?' the boys asked.

'Somebody owed it to me.'

'Well, what are you gonna buy?'

'Oh, I was thinking about we'll buy some beer and go have a party,' she'd reply, perennially in pursuit of popularity.

Mr Podlack drank too, but he made plain his disgust with Dixie. Pulling into his driveway in his old Ford pick-up truck after a day on the job at General Motors, the insults would often start flying. 'Fucking drunk again!' Chief would shout. 'I hope you didn't drink mine!'

The couple had some terrible fights. Dixie often bore the marks of what could have been a beating, but would say she had fallen down the stairs or slipped or something. Sometimes, however, she came right out and said Chief had beaten her, but at least one regular visitor disputes that claim. At first he believed her stories: 'But one time I saw her slip and fall on her butt and hurt her knee . . . the next day it was like, "Oh, he beat me up! Look what he did to me!" I said, "Well, I seen you fall! Remember that?"'

One night, long after Barry's friend, John Majestic, had outgrown the scene at Podlacks', he tooled down their street in his 1958 Chevy with its powerful spotlight, and as the blaze of light hit Podlack's front porch it looked to him as if all hell broke loose. 'Kids were like rats jumping off the porch. Beer bottles flew all over the place.'

He knew immediately that nothing had changed.

Although it was possible to live in Aileen's subdivision and avoid the drug scene, at times it seemed that drugs and alcohol were all-pervasive. The infestation of illegal substances really took hold there after servicemen first began returning from Vietnam. It began with pot-smoking, spreading to LSD and downers. Heroin was still inner-city fare, and cocaine was off on the horizon.

By the time Aileen and Keith came of age, however, the scene was more hard-core. Neighbourhood crimes centred on car-theft rings, burgling houses, stealing stereos and TVs (a speciality of Keith and his friend Don), gun-running, and, of course, drug dealing. The latter involved cocaine, heroin, LSD, mescaline and large shipments of pot. Aileen, with money in her pocket and an appetite to buy, was spoiled for choice.

Just as the boys with drugs traditionally got the girls, so Aileen with drugs usually landed herself some fair-weather friends.

Keith, who both used and dealt drugs, was into the heavy heroin scenario, using needles, junkie works and spoons. Others, like Aileen, stuck with peyote from out West, mushrooms, Seconals, Tuinals, mescaline capsules and tablets (sometimes consumed in a local spot nicknamed Mescaline Mountain), and an eclectic menu of other so-called party pills.

Drugs were the pivot around which this social clique's life revolved. The uppermost thoughts in their minds were not about their futures, but when could they next get high? A normal weekend night would likely be spent lying round a campfire, stoned out of their minds, 'totally ripped'.

On one occasion, Aileen, Jerry, Keith, and a couple of other boys took hallucinogens together and just spent the whole night walking through the woods. They must have wandered 25 miles, ending up in Dodge Park near Utica, their minds spilling over with psychedelic imagery. Drifting by the big Ford plant, cutting across the grass, the merry band of revellers wove in and out of the floodlights just as the sprinkler system spurted into action, soaking them through. Oblivious to their wet clothes, they rambled on, laughing, finally finding their way home the next morning.

Whenever someone's parents left town, it was immediately the signal for a party, the rowdier the better. With no adult supervision, these affairs inevitably got out of hand, as did one at Jerry Moss's house. A boy called Danny, rejected by the girl he was wild about—and also high and drunk—pulled one of Jerry's mom's butcher knives on the object of his desire, threatening to cut her. Jerry intervened, chasing him out of the house, only to have Danny return and put his fist through the window.

'He came crying to me, dripping blood all over my mom's house, so I said, "Come on, idiot!"—I probably wasn't that nice—and threw him in my car and took him to the hospital and kicked him out at the emergency room.'

This same Danny was a participant in a dangerous game of cowboys and Indians in the woods with real live guns and once came back with a .30-30 bullet in his shoulder. Kids grew up feeling they had to be tough and macho to survive. That was the system, even in school. Certain hallways, they instinctively knew better than to walk down unless they wanted to be knocked, pushed, and shoved. 'We did violent things, but we didn't hurt anybody,' Jerry claims.

Aileen hung out with this crowd, until she angered someone and was told to get the hell out. Then she'd wander off on her own. She was regularly thrown out of parties because she was vulgar, belligerent, and would try to start a fight.

'I think Aileen liked to cause trouble,' says Jerry Moss. 'I don't think she liked to get right down dirty into the fighting part. She liked to argue and start something. She wasn't afraid to call somebody a name or say, "Get the hell away from me."'

It fell to Keith or Lori to try to calm her down, and Keith stuck up for his sister a lot. 'Lori would be out there trying to help and Keith would send her away,' Jerry recalls. 'There was a bond between them, most definitely. You couldn't miss it.'

'She'll be all right. I'll take care of her,' Keith would say, putting his arm around Aileen as she wrapped hers tightly around him. 'We've got to stick together,' he'd whisper to his misfit sister.

In the subdivision, ethics between best friends were shaky, and nobody was to be trusted except immediate family. 'Everybody shit on everybody,' Jerry observed. 'Relatives, friends, girlfriends. They were all two-timing. The whole neighbourhood was back-stabbers and two-timers.'

Some of the girls were almost as rowdy as the boys, getting into fights and turning the air blue with their language. At the time, Jerry was involved with a tougher greaser chick from Detroit, who wore a black leather jacket and a 'Fuck you, I'll kick your ass!' attitude. He once saw her slap a couple of guys in the face and say, 'Come on. You want to fight with me? I'll fight with you.'

He found that exciting, even though he knew she had at least one other boyfriend. What he didn't know was that Keith was one of them.

'She was a little whore. She was whoring around with my best friend! I caught them that day. I almost ran Keith over. I was really very, very pissed. They had to jump out of the way of the car. I hit Keith with the door and we immediately started fighting in the ditch. And we were best friends. After that I still married her.'

Jerry (who was soon divorced) quickly forgave Keith. They patched things up while sitting in someone's yard, 'probably doing some acid'.

For formal socialising, Troy had a couple of teen clubs; one at a local church and one at the school. There were teen dances, but they were tame. Youngsters would go for a while, but only as a prelude to something wilder.

The biggest neighbourhood hot spot, in fact the only place in town, was 'the pits': huge, sprawling gravel pits filled with water so they looked like lakes, rimmed with abandoned cars and junk. They were frequented by motorcycle gangs, and by school kids skipping class. On Senior Skip Day, Aileen's entire school congregated there for a big party and beer bash, and sometimes everyone slept out there. It was private property, but the rules were rarely enforced unless things got out of hand, in which case the police arrived and chased everyone off.

The gravel pits were also the scene of some nasty fights among motorcyle gangs like the Renegades and others from Detroit, in which youths were cut up and beaten with motorcycle chains. The kids from the subdivision stayed clear of those, watching the action from a safe vantage point.

Kids from other neighbourhoods knew better than to straggle into their turf and respected the boundaries—they'd be chased out if they didn't. And so it was with the pits. They claimed the territory for their own and turned it into a mini-society. Where outsiders didn't care and littered the place, the local kids picked up trash and cleaned up the forts, even sweeping the floors.

The forts, which were scattered in the wooded area around the pits, were the scene of much of the social interaction: drinking, smoking (some of it pot), and lots of making out. There was little philosophising or discussion of putting the world to rights. The male inhabitants' desires were simple. 'Smokin' dope and trying to get one of the best-looking girls to make out with you.'

With acid rock, then known as psychedelic rock—Led Zeppelin, Steppenwolf, Moody Blues, J. Geils, Savoy Brown—wailing in the background on someone's hot stereo, the kids played kissing games, seeing who could make out the longest. Keith, who had become a handsome young man with fine, longish, Beatles-style, blond hair, and Jerry would sit either side of Sally. Each would take a turn at kissing her to see who could beat the record. Lori and the other girls all joined in the kissing contests with other guys.

Aileen sat across the fire. Watching. The only one there with nobody to kiss. The Cigarette Pig. Sometimes she just stayed and watched. Sometimes she got up and left. While many of these same boys had sex with her, when they were with their friends everything changed. Nobody wanted to make out with her, ever.

'I guess it would be a double standard,' Jerry Moss admits, with a shrug. 'But nobody cared about feelings then.'

One summer, Jerry worked at Clark gas station on the midnight shift. At fifteen, he was left in charge of the place all night, but the pumps were self-service and all that Jerry, or the other guys on the roster, had to do was collect money in the register and drop anything over twenty dollars in a drop slot.

A gang of kids would often convene around the station and filter across to the house next door (which would later be occupied by local musicians, Bob Seger and the Seger System). With its assortment of young male inhabitants in their late teens and early twenties, it became a frequent party house. In those days, drugs were an integral part of the attraction there as everywhere else.

Aileen was a regular at the party house and often took guys across the street into a field. She never came out and admitted to being paid for sex, not among those in her own subdivision, but everyone knew where she got her money.

Kids from other neighbourhoods were always around picking

up the Cigarette Bandit for a blow job. And subtlety and finesse were soon foreign to Aileen who solicited openly, approaching a man at a party and offering, 'I'll suck your dick right off.'

Wild affairs, with each bedroom soon occupied by couples making out, the parties often turned rowdy, with drunken and stoned kids tearing up the place, tipping furniture over, fighting, breaking windows and destroying property.

Clearly the pits were the safest places for such mayhem since there was less to damage. In theory. One huge party took place in a two-storey fort a dozen youngsters had built from wood they'd stolen from a construction site. By the end of that wild night, the fort was wrecked, torn down to the ground by the traffic and the fights. No matter. When the police found one of these products of stolen property, they tore them down anyway. The kids merely moved on and started building somewhere else.

Kids were left on lookout to tip everyone off when cruising cops were nearby. Parents' stores of liquor, sometimes half-gallons of something sickening like cooking sherry, were purloined and brought along. 'We're gonna have a big blast tonight!' the message went out. And the word spread to other subdivisions.

One pit party was so huge that hundreds came: car headlights and tail-lights and people sitting up on car hoods and standing shoulder to shoulder, as far as the eye could see. Silhouettes lit by the flames of two or three big bonfires. Whooping and hollering you could hear for miles around.

That night there were so many bodies that when cops rode in from Troy, Rochester, Clauson, Oakland County and the State Police, and surrounded the place, nobody realised until the uniforms were in their midst. Those who'd come by car were trapped, but people scattered in all directions, scurrying to escape the strong arms of the law. Jerry and Keith swam across the lake and got away. Lori and Aileen also made it to safety; one advantage of being pedestrians.

Occasionally, a parent would straggle down to the notorious pits, hoping to retrieve a wayward child. One neighbourhood father, Mr Small, was always complaining about the older kids smoking in front of his younger sons and often tried to break up parties. Unintimidated, the young men shouted, 'You'd better get the hell out of here before we carry you out!'

That didn't stop Small wrecking one underground fort that Aileen stayed in for a while. He stamped on top of it, trying to cave it in, and Jerry and Rob got out just in time. A couple of days later they sought sweet revenge. It was a balmy summer night close to 4 July, and they took some zig-zag firecrackers, jimmied their way into Small's front door, set them on the couch and lit them. Just as they were beating a hasty retreat, Small saw them. He jumped in his car and followed them to Clark station.

'Come here, Jerry, I want to talk to you,' he said, calm and cool as a cucumber.

'I don't want to talk to you,' Jerry retorted.

'I want to talk to you,' Small said, without a trace of anger. As Jerry gave in and walked up to him, he pulled a .22 pistol and held it to Jerry's head, right there at Clark station.

'Do you think you're smart? Do you think you're funny?' he snarled. 'I'm gonna blow your head off.'

Meanwhile Rob had called the police who came speeding up and pulled guns on Mr Small. The tables were turned, and the indignant adult was suddenly in the hot seat. He was far from the only adult to be pushed to the limit.

Once, when her father was away, Lori got a taste of what her parents had gone through with Aileen, who showed up at the house after running away from a juvenile hall. Aileen's drug use had escalated considerably, although she didn't like marijuana and she didn't do uppers because they made her feel 'nuts'. 'She had to have something to calm her down,' Lori recalls. 'Aileen's thing was downers.' For a while that meant 'reds' (barbiturates), Quaaludes, or whatever kinds of downers she could get her hands on to get wasted at weekends. She also took some prescribed but nameless 'nerve pills' and drank vast quantities of alcohol, at who knew what long-term cost to her body.

Lori wasn't a paragon of virtue; she was doing drugs too. But she found that with these drug cocktails inside her, Aileen's temper became downright impossible to deal with. In desperation, she once sent Aileen off to get a pizza from a few blocks away, then quickly called the police and asked them to pick her up. She was afraid of what Aileen might do if she found out who was behind the tip-off, but she felt she had no choice.

'She just made me so mad I just couldn't take it, and I thought she needed help again,' Lori recalls. 'I don't know if she was on mescaline or what, but she was scratching at the windows saying, "Lori, don't let them take me!" She was crying and screaming and just flipping out. And oh God, it hurt . . . but I knew she needed to go back.'

Aileen's considerable, if raw, artistic talent was largely overlooked at school as it was at home, bringing her little reinforcement. But her 'anti-social behaviour', low grades and very poor relationships with classmates and teachers, did not go unnoticed at Smith Junior High. At fourteen, she was prescribed a mild tranquilliser that failed to improve her behaviour. She'd also run away from home. Indeed, a report by diagnostician Carolyn Marcy, completed in April 1970, ended on an emphatic warning note.

Aileen heartily disliked school and had always had problems there. Her poor hearing and slight vision impairment were noted by staff early on. She was prescribed glasses, which out of vanity she refused to wear. Her hearing difficulties had been noted as far back as kindergarten, but with the rider that they would not handicap her comprehension in the classroom. By the age of eight, the right ear was identified as having greater hearing loss, and it was suggested that she be properly tested, and also be seated near the front of the classroom with her left ear towards the rest of the class. She was still considered unhandicapped in classroom.

Curiously, while her family doctor's later report noted an ear infection and earache at age ten, it failed to register her as 'hard of hearing'. An oversight? Or had Britta Wuornos, who believed Aileen's sole problem was that she was temperamental and disliked taking direction, deliberately omitted to tell the doctor about the school diagnosis? It seems the most likely explanation since that same year a further school report concluded: 'There are many indications that Aileen has a hearing problem. However, her mother is very defensive about this and says Aileen simply does not pay attention. She refuses to permit a professional evaluation.'

The same report observed that Aileen 'loses interest quickly and can easily become a leader in discipline problems.'

Other tests found her to have a low verbal IQ (80) and an average performance IQ (106): 'Everyday judgement based upon experience tested average. Motivation for assimilation of facts, numerical concepts, word knowledge and social awareness were far below average.'

Tests also yielded the nebulous if prophetic conclusion that Aileen was not 'comfortable' in the female role.

The report also commented: 'A well developed super ego results in guilt feelings, as behaviour is seen affecting the emotional well-being of those close to her. The outstanding feature was a remarkable concern for strong family ties.' And noted that 'Culturally nonconforming behaviour is of great concern to Aileen. Moral values, concern for her family's hurt, contribute to her guilt feelings.'

While Barry Wuornos had already made a layman's observation of Aileen as being 'hard-headed' and 'without conscience', here was a test result from a counsellor seeing something altogether different. Guilt, concern for others and for the rules of society.

Would that she had been right.

Marcy's report ended with the prophetically urgent words: 'It is vital for this girl's welfare that she receive counselling immediately.'

The warning was not heeded. Aileen never did receive any counselling, either as an in-patient or out-patient. With each year that passed, the broad, open smile of an innocent little girl gradually slipped from her face.

5

Both Aileen Britta Moilanen's and Lauri Jacob Wuornos's parents were born in Finland. As first generation immigrants, like many of their countryfolk they settled in Michigan's upper peninsula. Britta was one of thirteen children raised by a mother who went blind in middle age. Britta's sister Alma, the youngest, married Ben Kuopus, himself the oldest of fourteen. It was one of many unions between sprawling clans, and Aileen had no shortage of kinfolk.

Lauri and Britta moved to the Rochester area in 1936. When Aileen and Keith were small, Lauri was transferred from Chrysler in Michigan to the Firestone Tire factory in Akron, Ohio. Lauri rented out his house on Cadmus to Alma and Ben, but a year later he was laid off and he and his family returned to Troy. Alma, Ben, and their children, Elaine, Kathy, and Larry, then moved across the street, where they stayed for the next twelve years.

Bill, the eldest Wuornos brother, was found dead by the tracks one day, thought to have been hit by a train. Brother Eno was next oldest, then Lauri, then their sister Gertrude. Eno and his wife, Pat Ullman, lived a couple of blocks away, and there were family poker games at Cadmus. Lauri had one rule for his own debts but another for others', and when he wouldn't let Eno owe him, Eno reached right across the table and punched him in the nose. The short, stocky ex-Marine was the only person to stand up to Lauri.

Later, there was a serious rift between Aileen's grandparents and Eno and Pat. Eno died in the late sixties and Pat later lived with another man, but that estranged branch of the family remained shrouded in mystery for the younger generation. Lauri told the kids to stay away from Pat but never explained why. They thought she must be nutty and suppressed their urge to knock on the door and find out.

Eventually, Lauri's drinking put a strain on his relationship with his sister-in-law, Alma. Lauri was never parted from a bottle of wine, keeping one at home, one in his car, and one in a drawer at work, and when Barry left home, Alma believed Lauri's alcoholism contributed. 'Lauri was dominant, and Barry was a nice kid, didn't want to fight.'

Britta, by contrast, was quiet and introverted, with a sweet disposition. 'Almost a saint,' in Barry's eyes. Sturdily built, she wore her hair in a bun and dressed in pretty, long skirts, giving her a look of the old country. She was a familiar if distant figure to neighbours, kneeling outside, tending her flowerbeds. Aileen idolised and idealised her, viewing her as adorable, with a perfect figure. Britta painted, wrote poetry, played the accordion, and babysat part-time, and took Aileen and Keith on field trips in the backyard to see how insects live at night.

Despite her solid appearance, Britta was frail, if not sickly— and a terribly nervous driver. When the car skidded, it was Lori who had to calm her mother.

Britta and John Majestic's mother, Opal, were pals. Sociable Opal, perhaps Britta's only confidante, was famous for her home-baked cookies and doughnuts; but she also liked to drink. They used to chat while hanging their washing out on the line. The only time Lori saw her mother shed tears was when Opal died.

Home saunas were commonplace items among the Finnish community. Lauri's, housed in the garage on Cadmus, was in the ethnic tradition, created from a metal barrel with the top cut out, and with a wood-burning, chimneyless stove in the bottom. Rocks were placed over the stove. Water was then poured in to create the steam. The barrel sat against one wall, opposite two benches, one high and one low. Naked or wrapped in a towel, they sat there, inhaling the hot steam and waiting for the purifying and cleansing sweat to break out, glistening on their skins. The ritual was a part of Wuornos family life. Yet when Lori's high school screened its educational film on the facts of life to the latest body of students to reach adolescence, and parents were required to sign a letter of consent, to Lori's excruciating embarrassment, Lauri refused. She was forced to sit alone out in the hallway, her view into the classroom blocked by black paper that was put up specially to mask the windows for the Wuornos child.

There seemed a grotesque kind of paradoxical inconsistency in the behaviour of a man who forbade his daughter to watch sex education films, yet thought nothing of locking three naked adolescents together in the sauna. Sexual repression contrasted with a blatant disregard for the presence of adolescent urges.

'Don't spread your legs until you are married,' Lauri often chided Lori, but he was otherwise vehemently opposed to any mention of sex and didn't allow her to date. Lori dutifully remained a virgin until she was eighteen. She assumed her parents didn't want her to screw up her life like Diane.

Lauri explained the Finnish rituals, bragging that as a child, after a session in the sauna, he'd run to the end of the docks, chop a hole in the ice and jump in. Commanded by Lauri, John and Barry would 'stoke that baby up till it got red hot', then whip themselves with the traditional whisks of birch twigs. In winter, they sometimes put a big pile of snow in the garage and would scurry from the sauna and fling themselves into it, naked as the day they were born. Sometimes Lauri joined in, pouring a bucket of ice water over each of them and, warmed by the glow of alcohol into something approaching bonhomie, passed round his bottle of wine.

As he had done with Diane and Barry before them, Lauri sometimes closeted Aileen, Lori and Keith in the sauna as a punishment.

'Keith, don't you go in the sauna without clothes?' Jerry Moss asked him, riddled with curiosity about this mysterious foreign ritual.

'Yeah. We didn't even have a towel.'

'What'd you do in there?'

'We didn't do nothin'. Waited for my dad to let us out.'

Still, everybody thought it a strange scenario. Imagine—locking up three stark-naked kids together? And Lauri Wuornos talked up such a good story about sexual purity.

Titillated by the idea, and convinced they'd see more than just nudity, Jerry and a friend sneaked around a couple of times in an abortive effort to peak inside for a glimpse of Aileen and Keith. They'd heard there was a peephole from the attic above, but when they tried to creep up there, Lauri came out and they had to make a run for it.

Lori Grody believes her father could not have sexually abused Aileen in the house without her knowing. Viewing it from the street, to the left lay two bedrooms: the front one Aileen and Lori's, the rear one occupied by Keith and, when he was still living there, Barry. Lauri had added a spacious room on to the centre back of the house, where he and Britta slept on a foldout couch.

There was an attic space above Lori and Aileen's bedroom, but the floorboards creaked. By Lori's account it was small, one step up from a crawl space, yet Aileen detailed the room as having contained a bed, a desk and bookshelves, and Diane remembered staying up there.

If Aileen was sexually abused in the house, it would certainly have been possible for Lori not to have known, or, if she was aware of it, for her to have blocked out her memories. It would definitely be consistent with the minimal communication in the family for Aileen to have kept it to herself.

Specifically, Aileen told only one story of highly inappropriate behaviour by her grandfather when she was in her early teens. In front of Britta, Lauri grabbed Aileen and kissed her on the mouth, forcing his tongue down towards her throat. Retelling this, Aileen laughed: she found the whole thing not so much abhorrent as very funny.

It might have been the tip of the iceberg; the sole, readily accessible memory of full-blown abuse. Or it might have been a bizarre incident born of a drunken binge. There would be other clues.

57

6

Aileen Wuornos never came face-to-face with her biological father, Leo Arthur Pittman, to whom she owed a large part of her genetic heritage. Leo's marriage to Diane was over before Aileen took her first breath in this world. He didn't even know she was pregnant when he left.

Yet the lives of these genetically linked strangers ran uncannily similar paths. Just like Aileen, Leo before her was abandoned by his natural parents, Lorraine Pittman Briggs and her husband Arthur. When he was five months old, they left him and his two sisters alone in an apartment overnight. Also like Aileen, Leo was rescued and raised by his grandparents. Ida and Leo Herbert Pittman adopted him along with Nancy, the younger of his sisters. His other sister, Patsy, was adopted by another family.

Leo's grandparents, who ran the local garbage dump and owned a pleasant house across the street from it, doted on him. His grandfather died of throat cancer when Leo was in his early teens, but Leo remained devoted to his grandmother, Ida. Almost worshipful of her. She spoiled him terribly, baking him his favourite cookies and constantly indulging his whims. She also overlooked his chronic truancy and pathetic academic performance in school, not to mention his repeated discipline problems.

As a kind of sinister mark of his affection, Leo (a bed wetter until he was thirteen) also hit her and abused her. Significantly, she turned a blind eye to his behaviour, as she and her late husband had always done, still over-compensating for his rough start in life. In that household, young Leo definitely called the shots.

The red-haired, freckle-faced boy managed to check his rotten temper most of the time at Troy High, but it manifested itself at home. If he didn't get his way with Grandma, he'd react violently, punching the refrigerator or kicking down a door:

'His grandma was the sweetest person in the world and Leo was "it" for her, but he treated her like a dog,' recalls Larry Larson, who met him at fifteen. 'I know he struck her when he'd get mad. Still, that was her Leo.'

Leo never talked about his real parents and Larry rapidly learned it was a touchy subject, best avoided. Leo, Larry, and another friend, Fritz Sturms, whiled away their spare time fishing or swimming in the same gravel pits that a generation later would so attract Aileen. Leo at 5 foot 8 inches was stocky, solidly built, athletic and a good, strong swimmer. He and Larry walked in the woods that then fringed the water, shooting rabbits or rats with a .22 rifle (Leo was 'a hell of a shot', one friend recalls) and generally looking for mischief. Their idea of a laugh was to tie a couple of cats' tails together and throw the animals over a clothes line to see feline war break out.

'We weren't angels,' Larry reflects. 'It's not that Leo was a bad guy and I was a good guy. I was just as rotten.'

Before he knew Leo, Larry was already a close friend and neighbour of Diane's and of Marge Moss (Jerry's older sister). The trio were in the same grade and rode the school bus together.

Diane was quiet, sweet and friendly. But Larry, a jokester by nature and certainly not given to deep reflection at that age, nevertheless picked up the strong impression that there was something strange about her family. The neighbourhood kids perceived Lauri Wuornos as some kind of a big-shot executive because he wore a suit to his job at Beaver Tool and Dye and because he had a sauna attached to the house. Larry's own dad was a mechanic and Marge's a carpenter, so Lauri was seen as something a step up. Furthering that impression, the aloof Wuornoses didn't frequent Connie's Bar like the rest of the locals. Everyone respected Lauri Wuornos. No one ever questioned him.

Yet there was something odd about the Wuornoses. Larry and Marge's families welcomed other kids, but not Diane's. On Sundays, Lauri allowed Diane to ride the bus to the cinema in Rochester with Marge, but Diane wasn't allowed to go to a basketball game, even with a group. Lauri kept her on a tight rein, but it was more than that. A cloud of secrecy hung over Diane's family and she, too, was secretive and somehow troubled.

Once, before Leo came into her life, Diane asked Larry to hide her from her folks and he stowed her away in his family's attic for a couple of days, sneaking her down into the kitchen for food when his parents went out to work.

'Why did you leave?' Larry asked. Diane just shook her head. Larry found his unofficial house guest attractive and tried making advances, but Diane turned him down.

Years later, Larry's second wife, JoAnn, heard about Diane's secret stay—from his parents. They'd known all along but decided not to intervene, despite realising that Diane's parents might be worried about her whereabouts. Intuitively, they knew that if Diane was hiding out, she had a good reason.

Larry Larson liked Leo Pittman and hung out with him a good deal, but was mystified as to why Diane, petite, dark-eyed and pretty like her mother, took up with him. Yet Diane's attraction to the moody, explosive Leo was in many ways so predictable. She'd been hoping for a white knight, and he cut an appealing, wildly rebellious figure on his motorcycle, representing a freedom she could only have dreamed of. They soon became inseparable and were often seen holding hands, heading for the privacy of the woods. Just as Aileen would do later on her secret missions, Diane sneaked out of her bedroom window to meet Leo. Larry didn't doubt that Leo loved Diane: 'He'd probably go to the end of the earth for her—as long as she did what he said.'

When Lauri was safely out of the way, Diane and Leo, Larry and Marge (who were by then dating), used the sauna, too. The girls were discreetly wrapped in towels and it was far from an orgy atmosphere, yet the environment was conducive to the gratification of strong teenage impulses that wouldn't be quieted. In those days, no one bothered with condoms or thought too much of the consequences.

By Lauri's rulebook, Diane was forbidden to date. Something that so angered Leo that he once put sugar in Lauri's gas tank. Diane, who was regularly grounded, would cry on the phone to Marge, saying that she had to get out. When Fritz, a classmate, innocuously asked to come around to study with her, Lauri wouldn't even allow that. He didn't want Diane hanging around with boys and watched her like a hawk.

Predictably, Lauri vehemently disapproved of Diane's liaison with the reckless and unsavoury Leo Pittman. No father would have been thrilled with the match. Leo was generally regarded as a bit of a hood. He even kept guns in the back of the car. (Another foreshadowing of Aileen's behaviour.) Yet Larry Larson had a curious encounter with Lauri as a result.

Larry had really never even seen Lauri up close before but out of the blue, Diane's dad extended him an extraordinary offer, saying he would pay his way through trade school. The fee, around $300, was a lot of money back in the late fifties, and Larry was mystified. Only with hindsight would he notice what eluded him then: Lauri had accompanied the offer with a barrage of questions about Leo, and Leo's relationship with Diane. Lauri was trying to buy inside information about his daughter and her beau.

With all the precautions Lauri took, he was beside himself when Diane defied him and eloped with Leo, marrying him on 3 June 1954. Permission for the underage couple was given by Leo's grandmother. Diane was fourteen and Leo seventeen, but they lied about their ages, both claiming to be eighteen. The Wuornoses were furious, feeling Diane had brought disgrace to the family.

Diane and Leo's first child, Keith Edward Pittman, was born on 14 March 1955, ten months after their marriage. Keith was a fretful, unhappy baby who cried all the time, as Aileen would be too.

Leo's true personality was soon unleashed with the security of a marriage certificate. Uncontrollably jealous, as if gripped by sickness, he made a prisoner of Diane. If she was at home alone with the baby, Leo made her keep the shades drawn and the doors locked, even in 90-degree heat. She couldn't go out. She couldn't look out. She was not allowed to wear makeup in case anyone noticed how pretty she was. She had to hang her washing indoors because if she went outside another man might spot her. She was a love prisoner—only it wasn't love. It was a stultifying possessiveness.

Diane wasn't allowed to receive phone calls. If she answered the door to the mailman, she'd be beaten. If he found out she had disobeyed him, Leo beat her. If she hadn't disobeyed him, he beat her anyway. Behind closed doors, she met a far worse fate than Leo's grandmother.

Even Larry wasn't trusted by Leo, his supposed best friend. Larry also saw first-hand how little prompting Leo needed to lash out at Diane when Leo once 'beat the shit out of her pretty bad' in his presence. Visiting their apartment one afternoon, not knowing Leo wasn't home, Larry was astonished when Diane refused to let him in.

'I can't open the door. I can't talk to you. He'll beat me!' she cried.

She'd been willing to incur the considerable wrath of her father by eloping with Leo, but that obviously wasn't enough to prove her love to him. Good-natured and easy-going, Diane didn't give Leo any reason to question or doubt her fidelity, but she didn't seem able to stand up to this 'extremely violent' man any more than she had to Lauri.

She craved freedom but to her horror, she'd gone from the proverbial frying pan into an open, roaring fire. During their year or so together, 'He beat me up probably about every other day.'

Leo had lost his virginity at ten to an older woman. Hypersexual Leo's libido demanded gratification five or six times a day, and Diane complained to her friends about his enormous appetite, asking if it was normal. But marriage did nothing to halt his quest to see how many women he could have on the side. Until he had his own car—bought for him by his grandmother—Leo enlisted Larry to chauffeur him around.

Diane trusted Leo but her belief in his fidelity was grossly misplaced. Larry's car served as a place for Leo to 'see' the other girls he was 'dating' and one skinny, young slip of a girl in particular.

'Leo was always banging her in the back seat,' Larry recalls. 'A couple of times he'd leave her with me. He'd say, "Don't you dare touch her—I'll kill you if you touch her!" I wouldn't touch her with a ten-foot pole, but I didn't say that. But he'd say, "I'll kill you." It didn't scare me or nothing like that, it was just the way he talked.'

Leo wasn't exactly Mr Popularity. Like both Lauri and Aileen, his attitude didn't win him any points for charm or social graces, and he rapidly alienated potential friends. Since Larry refused to be intimidated by him, they got along just fine. Larry could whip Leo's ass and vice-versa. The mix worked.

Leo and Fritz once dated a pair of twins, with Leo carefully selecting the more promiscuous one for himself. Fritz, who was always rather taken by Diane, couldn't understand why Leo didn't just go home to his wife.

Leo liked to drink, but (again like Aileen) the demon liquor had a very detrimental effect, making his moods uglier and meaner than ever. On a typical night, their marital status notwithstanding, Leo and Larry cruised around, threw back a few beers, then pulled in at Tony's Drive-in restaurant, whistling at waitresses and munching burgers and fries. Larry even worked there for a while, slopping cheeseburgers and slinging hash, and put in tiring ten-hour days in a greasy factory. But Leo didn't do much of anything, although he liked to talk about his various jobs—gardening, driving a truck, working at a gas station, and being a grinder/polisher—and the big money he made. Lauri Wuornos once landed Leo a job in a vain attempt to make him face up to his responsibilities, but Leo refused to take it.

Leo had one job making chrome bumpers where he was supposed to wear a mask to protect him. He deliberately left it off, inhaling the fumes, so that he wouldn't pass the employees' lead-level tests and could stay at home and still get paid.

Diane spent a lot of time alone with Keith, and Lauri often drove over to take them to Cadmus for a visit—being helpful or interfering, depending upon your point of view; Leo took the latter. Diane loved Leo, but fate took a hand and the break came in the summer of 1955, when Keith was just a few months old and she was newly pregnant with Aileen, but didn't know it. Leo was, like a number of his contemporaries, a blossoming petty criminal who had progressed from stealing hubcaps to cars. (He was also arrested for furnishing liquor to minors.) In the fashion of the times, he took the option of going into the service rather than doing jail time and stayed in the Army until October 1957, thereby helping sixteen-year-old Diane liberate herself from their miserable life together.

Their divorce decree, issued on 14 November 1955, cited Leo as guilty of 'several acts of extreme and repeated cruelty'. The divorce court ordered him to pay $15 a week child support and hospital costs for her second labour.

Diane was afraid of Leo and doubted he'd stay away.

With the help of an Army allowance she received, she'd been able to rent the top floor of a duplex, and Larry and Marge moved in too, sharing the expenses. Their troubled marriage ended shortly after. Drawn together during these painful times, Diane and Marge continued to be roommates. Bright, and a hard worker, Diane was over the moon when she landed a desirable operator's job with Michigan Bell. She made good money and seemed to be picking up the pieces in her young life. While she worked, Marge babysat, then Diane babysat so Marge could go out. The system worked well enough for a while.

Diane had a brief affair with Fritz. When she divorced Leo, Fritz had gone with her to Pastor Cook, speaking up on her behalf to confirm Leo's adulteries. Yet Diane never told Fritz about Leo's temper or the physical abuse that, heaven knows, provided her with equally strong justification for ending her marriage. Then again, she rarely confided in anyone.

Diane reported a trouble-free pregnancy with Aileen during which she smoked less than a pack of cigarettes a day and says she didn't drink. Working backwards, Diane eventually realised that she must have been a week or two pregnant and not known it when Leo subjected her to a particularly savage beating.

Aileen was born on 29 February 1956, via breech birth. Diane listed her parents' address on Aileen's birth certificate. After parting company with Leo, she did indeed make a couple of short-lived stabs at moving in with her folks, but it never worked out.

Aileen was, like Keith, a colicky, fractious baby, and Diane wondered about the effect on them both of all the stress she was under as she emerged from being a battered wife, only to end up arguing with her parents.

She tried to make a go of things as a single mother for about a year. For that brief time, she was a devoted mother. Larry Larson imagined that 'she would die for those goddamn kids'.

The only less-than-exemplary incident came when Diane was dating Fritz. Working shifts in a bakery, he arrived at Diane's home one lunchtime to hear loud wailing baby noises as he climbed the stairs. Entering by the back door, he saw Diane sprawled on the couch, sound asleep. She had been in the same room as the cots yet oblivious to her babies' cries.

When Fritz shook her awake, she jumped up immediately, telling him she'd been drunk and hadn't heard anything.

Later, Fritz ran into Diane in the street. She told him she'd had a fight with her downstairs neighbour who'd complained Diane had let her children cry all morning.

'I don't let my kids cry!' Diane said indignantly.

'That woman was right,' Fritz countered. 'I heard them right downstairs when I started walking up. I woke you up. They were hungry. They was probably crying all morning.'

That incident aside, Diane nevertheless completely confounded all who knew her by one day going out for dinner and not returning.

No explanation. No phone call. Nothing.

Aileen was somewhere between six and nine months old. Marge couldn't figure out what had prompted her to run off or, indeed, where she had gone. In fact, she never heard from Diane again. As best friends, their intimacy was obviously severely limited.

That Diane abandoned Aileen and Keith is not in question. That it was perhaps the first in a long line of dominoes that tipped over, adversely affecting both their lives, is also clear. But Aileen's woeful tale that she and Keith were found in the attic at her grandparents' home, covered with flies, is inaccurate.

Marge, who was babysitting that night, hung on to them for almost a week, fully expecting Diane to return and not wanting to get her into trouble with her family.

Marge couldn't imagine ever leaving her own kids under any

circumstances, but she felt shocked, upset and mystified rather than angry. Perhaps her own marital troubles made her especially empathetic.

'People that walk off and leave their kids usually have a tendency to not give a damn what they do; not care if they're washed or fed,' she points out. 'Diane did all that. She went to work every day and she fed them, kept them clean.'

Diane's desertion came at a painful time for Marge, a young mother. Her own brief marriage disintegrated after Larry's infidelity, and Diane had been supporting her, paying the rent. Suddenly, Marge was forced to move back in with her folks and to get a job in a local restaurant. When, in desperation, Marge finally informed Lauri and Britta that Diane had taken off, they were understandably shocked. 'Mr Wuornos was upset. Who wouldn't be? He had a fit about it.' But he took in his grandchildren all the same.

Diane, it turned out, had gone to Texas. (Even Aunt Alma never learned why, and Diane, at this point in history, chooses not to clarify this era.) Some of her friends believed she'd run off with a girlfriend, or a young serviceman from one of the nearby Army bases. Marge doubted that, believing Diane would have told her about something like that. Yet it seems the most likely explanation.

After their separation, Leo Pittman had no contact whatsoever with Diane or his children. Besides his own lack of interest and concern, 'Ain't no way he would come around Mr Wuornos,' Fritz Sturms says categorically. 'He would have killed him. Mr Wuornos would have shot him dead.'

Diane wrote to her parents from Texas and in due course, signed the papers necessary for them to adopt Aileen and Keith officially. At eighteen she was facing a second failed marriage and returned to Troy briefly at her father's request, even going back to school. (Marge, by then starting a new life away from Troy, knew nothing of this second chapter.) But Diane's attempt to reintegrate herself into the family didn't work. Her presence seemed to make Britta jealous, as if she felt threatened by Diane showing Aileen and Keith any love. Diane had always suspected that Britta lied to Lauri about her and undermined her. Suddenly, she heard it first-hand. Lauri and Britta were shut in their bedroom arguing when, unbeknownst to them, Diane overheard her mother say, 'She's just come back and she wants these children to love her more than they love me! And do you know what she does when you're gone to work? She beats these children, Lauri.'

Diane wouldn't have dared lay a hand on them even if it seemed warranted. They were no longer officially hers. But Diane's niggling suspicions that Britta had been trying to drive a wedge between her and her father were confirmed in that one incident. Diane also cites an episode that may well have contributed to making living at home seem so unpalatable. A friend stayed over one night after a party in the house and she and Diane slept in the same bed that night. The next morning her friend recounted an incident that bothered Diane greatly:

'She said that in the middle of the night she woke up and he was there and he . . . you know, that he wanted to ah . . . with her. And she said, "Lauri, for God's sake, get out of here. Diane is right there. Get out of here and go back to your bedroom."'

Learning that her father had sexually propositioned her friend made Diane wonder, 'What was he doing in my bedroom in the middle of the night . . . and how often did he go in there before?'

Lauri had told Diane that Britta didn't much care for him physically. And Britta had told Diane that sex was an unpleasant chore that a woman had to do for her husband. Even before she left with Leo, Diane had had problems with Britta.

'Daddy treated me and Barry equally, but my mother especially zeroed in on me. Just hateful, that's all I can tell you,' she'd later recall. Britta turned on her when Diane hit puberty at eleven or twelve. Whereas her dad seemed proud of her good school work, her mom seemed jealous. Perhaps, too, her dad was treating her differently as she blossomed into womanhood, and Britta knew something that Diane did not. Looking back, she'd wonder: 'Was she seeing something in Daddy that I was too young to even understand? Was she seeing that his affection for me was possibly more than normal father-daughter affection?'

Yet Diane denies that any full-blown sexual abuse took place.

Being interviewed by investigator Marvin Padgett in 1991, she admitted her father 'would just maybe accidentally touch me like he shouldn't, and then I can remember one disgusting awful time when I was about fourteen and my mother was standing right there and he . . . I had never been kissed by anyone, and he said he wanted to kiss me. Like, you know, "Give your daddy a big kiss." And he kissed me, now I realise, like a man would kiss a woman and it was just awful. But if Mother saw that, why wouldn't she be angry, you know? She's a human being too.'

Diane, who knew nothing of Aileen's similar experience, can see that Britta had no choice but to stay with Lauri back in the late fifties. How could she have supported a family alone?

Ultimately, Diane realised she didn't have the maturity to pull off living alone as a single mother, and when Aileen was two and Keith three, she headed back to Texas. That time, Alma and Ben's 15-year-old daughter, Elaine (now Carol Connell), was left holding the babies.

After Diane had left for the evening, a man stopped by at her apartment. Elaine's memory is blurred and she cannot be sure, but she wonders if it was perhaps Diane's ex-husband, Leo Pittman. (Pittman did reappear at some point in Troy, wearing a paratrooper's uniform.) Clearly, it was a man she knew because she was unafraid to let him in, but he soon left.

As the hour grew late, and Diane didn't return at the appointed time, she remembers waiting, waiting, waiting, and growing more and more anxious. Finally, the telephone rang. It was Diane. She wasn't coming back. Elaine sat on the couch in a state of shock and disbelief, then called Alma. She in turn alerted Lauri and Britta, who drove over with Barry to pick up the children and their baby clothes.

'I was hysterical,' Elaine admits, saying, '"How could a mother do that?" It was really traumatic for me . . . especially because I always liked Diane. A lot of people always said how we looked so much alike.'

Diane had always struck her as the perfect, caring mother, making considerate preparations for her each time she babysat, leaving, for instance, a little bowl of peaches and a chair right next to the crib.

The way that old upstairs apartment looked, with its back staircase, is also etched in Elaine's memory. There, doubtless, lies the root of Aileen's story about being abandoned, covered with flies. There was no screen on the door and when it was open, flies came in.

Did Diane return to a man in Texas? Or did Leo Pittman blow through town on furlough and rekindle the old flame? Either way, Diane had gone again and this time for good. It was thirteen years before she returned to Troy after Britta died.

In 1958, Leo Pittman was given three years' probation for breaking and entering. He was becoming a blight on society and his criminal record was building steadily. In 1959, he was sentenced to Federal prison at Chillicothe, Ohio, for car theft and for transporting stolen cars across state lines, serving three of six years before being paroled.

In the early sixties, Diane got a rudely blatant hint about the kind of path her ex had taken when detectives turned up at her door in Texas. They wanted to question her about Leo's whereabouts way back on 24 March 1955, apparently hoping to tie him into an unsolved rape and child murder. Prompted by them to cast her mind back, she could recall the date with startling clarity, primarily because of its proximity to Keith's birth just ten days earlier. She described to the detectives a scenario in which Leo had come into the apartment acting as if he were hiding from someone. He kept peeking out from behind the drapes and refusing to answer knocks on the door. As usual, he beat her, too.

Surveying her second marriage, which she also described as a trip from frying pan to fire, Diane later asked Aunt Alma: 'Why does this have to happen to me? I get rid of one, and get another one just like him.'

Thankfully, not quite like him. Leo Pittman's descent into depravity was just beginning.

7

The year was 1962, the month September, and the man, having violated his Federal parole, was on the run. He took his pregnant wife and small daughter and went into hiding 926 miles away in Wichita, Kansas. He couldn't stay out of trouble for long, however, and the next time it was of a far darker nature.

On Friday 23 November his eye was caught by a group of young children romping in a school play-ground, and his fascination was far from innocent. A black temptation stirred within him. It was an impulse that he knew he should fight, and at first he did struggle to quash it, driving on by and pulling to the side of the road to think it over.

'And then I got this urge, and I started west again.'

He wheeled his way back to the school and parked his car alongside the playground. Casually, he sidled over to join in the kids' play, ingratiating himself with the group. Then he moved in on the target, chatting to the pretty seven-year-old who had drawn him there, easing her gently into a private conversation.

'Would you like to go for a ride and see my pony?'

'Well, yes. But I have to take my little sister home first.'

'OK, but don't tell your friends or anyone else about it.'

Dutifully, the little girl escorted her small sister back to Grandma's across the street, then returned to the man who waited, heart pounding, preparing to spring his trap.

He drove the little girl a few miles out into the country and as she lay along the front seat, trustingly, her head resting against his lap, the tone of the outing changed. Before stopping the car, he warned his by then terrified captive that if she tried to resist him, he would kill her. Once in a suitably deserted spot away from the road, he brutally raped and sodomised her. Afterwards, with perverse consideration, he drove her right back to her neighbourhood, dropping her off near the school. Letting her go, he warned her again that if she told on him, he'd kill her mother and grandmother.

Once free, the child ran straight back into the warmth and safety of her grandmother's arms. Immediately, she blurted out, 'Some man picked me up and took me out in the country and done something real dirty to me.'

Her grandmother rushed her to the emergency room at the nearby hospital. The child was so traumatized, so distraught, that the doctor's examination had to be cut short, but not before it had categorically confirmed the sexual assault.

According to her grandmother, 'For a long time afterwards, she would wake up in her sleep and scream and carry on.'

Gently questioned by the deputy sheriff, the little girl managed to proffer a surprisingly sharp description of her attacker. The sheriff also coaxed her into drawing the design of the car upholstery that she'd described. She carefully reproduced a diamond pattern, interspersed with bars.

The observant child's physical description of the pony man was good enough for a gas station attendant, questioned by police during a mass canvass of the area, to recognise him.

The station worker led detectives straight to the door of Leo Arthur Pittman, father of Aileen Carol Wuornos. They arrested this inept, but none the less sinister and dangerous sex offender the very day after the assault, finding him easily at his cabin in a hotel right round the corner from the school. He'd been helping pay his bill by doing odd jobs around the motel yard.

On his person when he was taken into custody was a private detective badge that he'd bought in California. He had recently left that state, he told officers, with his pregnant wife and daughter. In a line-up, the little girl readily picked out Leo, as did two young male witnesses who'd been at the playground.

A detective described Leo, just after his arrest, as being dirty and long-haired, bearing the 'wild look of a man caught'.

Leo confessed to the assault of the little girl and the next day was examined by a court-appointed psychologist, but he refused to take a lie detector test. His introduction to sex at the age of ten with an older female neighbour emerged, as did his pattern of promiscuity. He no longer drank, he said, because it made him aggressive, giving him an uncontrollable urge to pick fights.

He was held without bail on charges of First Degree Kidnapping, and was shaken to learn that he'd committed a capital offence and could earn the death penalty. He was also charged with forcible rape and 'the abominable and detestable' crime against nature of sodomy.

His preliminary hearing (at which he contradicted his previous story and claimed to be single and unemployed) was set for 10 December.

What followed was what the then prosecutor, Keith Sanborn, would always remember as 'The most amazing identification I was ever witness to.' When Leo was led into the courtroom, the girl reacted so strongly to his very presence that she broke out in hives before his eyes—and the eyes of everyone else in the courtroom.

Sanborn recalls it as vividly as if it were yesterday. 'That was pretty hair-raising to me as a young prosecutor,' he explains, '. . . and then he got away.'

Leo Pittman was arraigned without bond. He confided in three cellmates (young men who were AWOL from the Navy) of his plan to convince everyone he was insane so that he'd be sent to a mental hospital instead of prison, and could then escape. The cellmates spilled the beans and testified to what Leo had told them, and Sanborn argued an effective case for Leo's manipulative behaviour.

In June of 1962, Leo had been considered a suspect in a case in Michigan of indecent liberties taken with two ten-year-old girls. On 12 March 1963, the Detroit Police Department had also begun investigating him in connection with a child murder charge, yet in April he was ruled by Judge Clement F. Clark to be schizophrenic and unable to comprehend his situation. To Sanborn's dismay, he was ferried off to Larned State Hospital for psychiatric observation and evaluation, edging his escape plan one step closer to fruition.

Sure enough, just thirteen days later, Leo seized his opportunity. Along with two other prisoners, he sawed through the steel bars of a hospital window, then made a run for it.

'We were pretty hot at Larned State Hospital for not letting us know immediately he escaped,' recalls Keith Sanborn. He wasn't notified until noon the next day and detectives told him that Pittman had threatened to return to Wichita and kill Sanborn's entire family, just so that everyone would know for sure he was crazy.

FBI agents picked Leo up in Cassanova, Michigan, in August as a parole violator, at which point he was charged with the earlier sex offence, which he denied. He was found innocent by reason of insanity. He was then sent to Ionia State Mental Institution in Michigan where he was held until February 1965. Word filtered out that he was due to be released as cured. Getting wind of this, with just a matter of days to go, County Attorney Sanborn and Wichita law enforcement pulled out all the stops, determined to avert his release. They used an unlawful flight warrant to hold him and return him to Wichita.

Finally, three whole years after the crime, he was brought to trial for his assault on the little girl. In January 1966 such was the social climate that only seven of the 151 prospective jurors were excused because they could not, under any circumstances, impose the death penalty.

In the courtroom, the child was flanked for support by her mother and aunt. Everyone was a little nervous about the solidity of the victim. Years had passed. How good would her young memory prove to be? But as Leo was escorted in, she turned to her mother and without wavering for an instant said: 'There he is, Mommy!'

A member of the defence team approached the grandfather, planting the idea that Sanborn was just pushing the trial for publicity, and that testifying would do irreparable harm to the child. Sanborn saw that as 'an attempt at psychological warfare to scare the grandfather to try to get him to come and see me and ask me to drop the case'.

Sanborn knew his motives were pure, but was relieved all the same to learn from a psychiatrist that testifying would actually be cathartic for the child.

With the jury finally seated, Leo denied committing the self-same crimes to which he'd earlier confessed. He also accused the detective of threatening to take his children (one, and another on the way) from him and his wife if he didn't take sodium pentothal.

'I could not tell Detective Williamson anything about the crime because I did not commit the crime,' he complained.

His defence attorney, not surprisingly, set out to prove an insanity defence. One psychiatrist testified that Leo was insane on the day of the assault and had been for 'at least ten years'. Another also testified for Pittman, saying, 'I found this man was suffering from schizophrenic reaction, paranoid type, which involves a thought disorder, disassociation between emotion and thought control, and general feelings of hostility towards society, and also some degree of depression. And I felt that if this man knew what he had been doing . . . that he was not emotionally or intellectually able to appreciate that he was doing wrong like other people, as I understand it.'

County Attorney Sanborn argued that being diagnosed a paranoid schizophrenic did not prove Pittman's insanity. There were plenty of such individuals, he was at pains to point out, who functioned well in society without doing anything wrong. Sanborn then took a sledgehammer to Pittman's already dubious credibility, bringing on a clinical psychologist who testified that in his professional opinion, the defendant had fudged the answers on his sanity tests, hoping to con his way to a lighter sentence. Dr Roy B. Henderson said Pittman 'overplayed the role of being unable to comprehend'.

One test had required Leo to reproduce geometric designs and Dr Henderson found fault with the manner in which he did so. He said Pittman reproduced them 'In a real distorted fashion . . . not as you would expect a psychotic to do. When you try to fake something, there is a tendency to over-fake, and this, I think, is what happened here.'

Also testifying for the state was psychologist Dr Paul G. Murphy. Dr Murphy said that while Pittman had a 'schizoid personality', he was not psychotic when he examined him in 1962. Dr Murphy pointed up Pittman's sexual obsession—citing the fact that in the ink-blot test he took, in almost every case he identified the blots with female genitals.

In another of Dr Henderson's tests, Pittman was unable to add two single-digit numbers correctly. Yet when he believed he wasn't being observed, the doctor watched Leo play a good game of Ping-Pong, keeping score perfectly well as he went.

The *Wichita Eagle* newspaper reported that Leo's con-man abilities had been put to yet another test by Dr Henderson. After making certain that Pittman was within earshot and listening, Dr Henderson rather loudly declared to a colleague that if Pittman was suffering from the disorder he indeed thought he was suffering from, he would make an 'x' in a particular place on a piece of paper. Falling headlong into the trap, Leo did just that.

The mental health professionals who testified for the defence began by claiming Leo didn't know right from wrong. Yet eventually, under the careful and persistent questioning of prosecutor Sanborn, they were pushed to concede that he did.

More damning still for Leo was the child's testimony, and her accurate drawing of the slipcover on the front seat of his car—a drawing that was done before Leo's car was even found.

Just before closing arguments, word was sent to Keith Sanborn: Leo's faithful grandmother was threatening his life.

'She had said that if Leo was convicted, I was going to be shot. So I told some press in the courtroom, "Don't sit between me and her!" Of course, nothing like that happened, but I do remember it, naturally. I'd already made the only decision that a person can make, and that's that you don't worry about stuff like that. A detective once told me, "Don't worry about the ones that tell you they're going to do it."'

At 8.45 p.m. on Saturday 15 January 1966, the jury retreated to deliberate, returning just after midnight. Leo's beloved grandmother was present in the courtroom for the reading of the three guilty verdicts and looked on impotently as he was sentenced to life imprisonment at hard labour. On 28 January an extra 31 years were added to his life sentence after the judge denied a defence motion for a new trial.

Leo was incarcerated at the Kansas State Penitentiary in Lansing to serve out his sentence and was put to work in the cannery.

Keith Sanborn, now a judge, was finally satisfied. 'I was a prosecutor for twenty-four years, and I never got to the point where anything wasn't personal. And it wasn't a matter of me against him. It was a matter of what he did. It was really a terrible thing.'

Prison officers found Leo in his cell, hanging from a rope that he'd fashioned from his bedsheet and strung over his cell bars. It was January of 1969, and he was 33 years old.

He was rushed first to the prison hospital then to Kansas Medical Center, in a coma. A few days later he was returned to the Kansas State Penitentiary. He died there on 30 January from complications arising from the suicide attempt, without ever regaining consciousness.

The autopsy noted that Leo's body was adorned with eight tattoos including, on his chest, one of a woman's head.

Later that year, Aileen Carol Wuornos, the daughter Leo had never met, gave birth to her only child, a baby boy, propelling the Pittman genes one generation further.

Leo's legacy of love to Aileen was non-existent. Instead, his potent contribution to the recipe for a ticking time bomb that was his daughter, was an inherited predisposition towards criminal behaviour.

Being raised by adoptive parents with a criminal record increases the probability that a child will follow suit. But studies have shown that the biological legacy of criminality is even more powerful than the environmental in determining the outcome of the child. Even if that child is removed from the parent soon after birth (or, in Aileen's case, before it) and raised in a different environment, the odds are that they will be a chip off the old block.

8

Aileen's pregnancy when she was fourteen was a better kept secret than her incest with Keith. Set against the backdrop of her inappropriate and premature sexual activity, it could hardly be called a surprise, yet it had a catastrophic effect on her already tenuous family relationships.

An inhabitant of this household of denial, where everything even mildly unpleasant was brushed under the carpet, Aileen not surprisingly concocted a story that seemed at least partially fantasy. She said a brutal rape by an Elvis Presley look-alike led to her pregnancy and that she had been molested at gun- and knife-point for six hours.

'He was almost going to kill me but I begged for my life, and he let me go,' she says.

It was a story that, in various guises, she returned to over the years, but just one among many. Sometimes she said that the man was a friend of Lauri's. Like the boy who cried wolf, Aileen said so many things, gave so many different versions, that any truths were lost in the shuffle. She has claimed to have been raped nine times in her life, and was doubtless raped at some stage, probably more than once. Perhaps the nameless stranger was an easier culprit to latch on to to have brought about such dire consequences? Tellingly, however, despite Aileen's tender age, Britta and Lauri didn't believe her. Regardless of whether Britta and Lauri knew of Aileen's prostitution, evidently they considered her a liar, promiscuous, or both.

During her pregnancy, Aileen continued to name other men as the baby's father. Keith. Lauri. Dean—a neighbourhood boy she earlier claimed had raped her. And Mr Podlack. She confronted some with the paternity issue. Dean laughed in her face, and

Keith scoffed that there was no way she could know who the father was.

Condoms later became part of her prostitute's paraphernalia, but her teenage partners didn't wear them, relying instead on coitus interruptus.

It was a lonely, frightening time for Aileen, who was more isolated than ever with her secret. She first confided her fears in her neighbour and friend, Cheryl Stacy, a student assistant in cooking class and (more relevantly) in family planning. What were the first signs of pregnancy? Aileen asked. How could she tell? Cheryl explained that her breasts would swell and she'd have morning sickness, and demanded to know who was the father. She was floored when Aileen told her that it was old Mr Podlack: 'But she always said that he was very nice to her and he'd give her money and they'd go places together.'

The idea of Aileen and Mr Podlack was so sublimely ridiculous to Cheryl that it almost had to be true. It certainly wasn't news to her that her friend had learned to make money through sex, but she was amazed at how well Aileen hid her condition. She put it down to the fact that they weren't a very close family. Her own mom would have known immediately.

By the time Aileen broke down and told Lori, her pants were so stretched to capacity that they left angry red marks ingrained in her flesh. In the privacy of their bedroom, she pulled up her sweater and revealed her protruding belly. Tearfully, she explained that she hadn't had her period in months, but was petrified about telling Mom and Dad, afraid they would throw her out. Lori begged her to see that she had no choice. Besides, Mom would notice she hadn't been using sanitary pads. (But Mom *hadn't* noticed or had looked the other way.) Lori felt sorry for Aileen, but she didn't believe her rape story for a second. When Aileen finally plucked up the courage to tell, Lauri yelled and Britta cried. Lauri wanted Aileen—and the disgrace she'd visited on the family—gone as quickly as possible. Britta was embarrassed, shamed, and bitterly disappointed in her. They were convinced their unhappy history with Diane was destined to repeat itself.

Britta sought advice at Troy High in January of 1971 and was sent to the Michigan Children's Aid Society for help. Aileen was fourteen when she became pregnant, not thirteen as she claims, and had just passed her fifteenth birthday by the baby's birth. Mrs Verduin, her case worker, was struck by her immaturity. Aileen didn't seem to look beyond the moment. She seemed to find the subject of her future a completely alien concept.

Despite Barry's claim that he was never out of work while Aileen lived at home, Lauri had been unemployed since the previous October, so DSS paid for the baby's delivery. On 19 January, Aileen was whisked off to the sombre institution-like Florence Crittenton Unwed Mothers' Home in Detroit. Cheryl didn't even get a chance to say goodbye to her. It was only Aileen's second visit to the big Motown. She viewed with distaste its dirt, noise and pollution, deciding it wasn't at all a place she'd ever choose to live, although she had one fond memory of a family outing to a ball game there. She could still remember the hot dogs, peanuts and popcorn tasting so good to her young tastebuds. 'Too bad Dad couldn't always be affectionate and full of bubbliness like that.'

'The wretched man', as she more often thought of him, drove her to the unwed home. 'With that damn drinking of his, the car stunk like leftover puke.' She couldn't help feeling he took pleasure in abandoning her in a strange place. And because of the way they parted, she didn't even know if she had a home to go back to. She cherished Britta's letters, but no visits were forthcoming. Lauri wouldn't allow it; nor would he drive her. Britta told Aileen she could only make one call a week.

Given her tender age, there was really no decision to be made about whether or not she would keep the baby, but she did want to see it just once before it was taken away and put up for adoption. Lauri, however, wouldn't hear of it. Aileen's short life thus far had been one long series of rejections and losses. It was just one more.

Aileen claims she did get one peek of her son through a window. He was born, she remembered, on 24 March, weighing 7 pounds 11 ounces. The new mom was 4 feet 11 inches and weighed 145 pounds.

'I'd see a baby that had two little front teeth,' she muses in

79

what seems story-like fashion. 'Very, very tiny, like just about to protrude out of the gums. And also, long fingernails on his fingers making his face have itty-bitty scratches here and there. And his hair was full and dark brown on his head, which made me think he'd probably turn blond later on. He was cute. A real cute little boy.' Again, her language sounds indicative of fantasising: 'I'd look at him and say, "Sorry, young 'un, but if you knew my living situation, you'd understand why I have to give you up. You'll be ten times better off."'

She reminisces about being sorry to say goodbye to the friends she'd made. But while she was certainly bonded to the unwed home's other young inhabitants by their mutual plight and common fear of the pain of labour, she did not get along well with them. Again, she fantasised about bonds that did not exist.

With Aileen safely removed from the house, her pregnancy was never discussed, becoming another family secret so shameful that Britta didn't even confide in her own sister. Aunt Alma didn't learn that Aileen had a child until many years later. Timid Lori didn't dare ask questions, but took her parents' fury and the fact that they didn't call the police as evidence enough that they didn't believe Aileen's rape story. The whole episode was so successfully hushed up that no one in school besides Cheryl even had a clue where Aileen was. They just assumed she was off in juvy hall.

Aileen named the baby Keith Wuornos in honour of her brother. Entering the father's name on sealed official forms, she sometimes claims to have written Lauri Wuornos, at others, 'rapist'. Lauri relented and allowed her to return home, but fear froze on her face when he showed up to pick her up.

'I was praying inside that he was not by himself. I was just so scared. Even if Keith or Lori was with him, I'd feel better. To be with him alone terrified me. Then he blurted out, "Mom's in the car. She's been sick lately. She's sleeping in the back seat."' What ailed her would be debated later.

Relations between Aileen and Lauri reached their nadir. It was almost as if she finally abandoned any pretence that she loved him, or he her. Certainly, she felt abandoned by Britta. Old way beyond her years, a woman now, not a child, Aileen no longer pretended to tolerate being told what to do, or when to come home, or when she could leave.

Frank and Gary went looking for her one day, both a little afraid that she might have named them as the baby's father. They tracked her down at a friend's house in as mean a mood as they'd ever seen. She told them the baby was 'an old man's'. Then again, they heard on the grapevine that she'd fingered Keith. By then, Aileen's paying customers began noticing that her young body was marred by stretchmarks.

Aileen re-enrolled in Troy High School that spring but dropped out after a few months. Simultaneously, the Oakland Juvenile Court requested her records from Smith Junior High for a pending court hearing, and her next stop was the Adrian girl's home. Lori visited her there as she'd done in the previous juvy, listening to her litany of complaints all about the dykes she was shut in with, and her terror of their cat-calls and sexual propositions. On a more upbeat note, she had become quite proficient at shooting pool—a skill that stood her in good stead later, hustling in pool halls.

Lori couldn't help worrying that instead of getting psychiatric help to straighten her out, her sister's eyes were only being opened to even more avenues of potential trouble.

By the time she was finally allowed to return home several months later, Aileen was incurably restless, soon running away again. That time, when Lauri told her never to come back, he meant it.

Sleeping rough in the woods and in abandoned cars, hitch-hiking on the highway, hanging out with men of all ages, whose treatment of her ran both ends of the spectrum, she wasted countless days on drugs and drinking binges. It was only a matter of time until she would be lost for ever.

9

Britta Wuornos's alcohol problem ran a different course from Lauri's. While neighbours believed that she was drinking behind closed doors, she either sustained a long period of abstinence or of extreme secrecy—because Lori didn't see her touch a drop.

Aileen and Keith had been banished from the house in disgrace (Aileen was living in the woods and Keith with friends), when Lauri took Britta away for a few days vacation to help her frayed nerves recover.

The night of their homecoming, Lori spotted something strange: three bottles of beer nestled on the top shelf of the refrigerator.

'Whose is this?' she asked her dad, knowing he never drank anything but wine.

'Oh, it's your mother's,' Lauri replied.

'Mom's?' Lori thought.

Certainly, Britta was acting strangely. What was odder still was that Lori suspected she'd been drinking. If so, Lori felt sure she'd done it because of her heartbreak over Aileen and Keith. The pregnancy, the truancy, the shoplifting, all of it. She could only resort to speculation because her mother never told her what was going on. There were never any intimate mother-daughter talks. (Lori started her periods without a clue what they were.) From that night on, Britta became so ill that Lori seriously doubted she could have lifted a beer bottle. She even missed Lori's high school graduation on 7 June. She was so groggy that, visiting her in the back bedroom, Lori wondered if she might be suffering from the d.t.'s.

Repeatedly, Britta instructed Lori to open the front door

and to yell out to the motorcyclists she could hear roaring past the house to quit riding up and down the road. Lori knew there was nobody there but it seemed easiest to humour her mother, so, embarrassed, she opened the door and shouted, 'Stop! Stop!', then quickly closed it. But Britta wasn't satisfied. 'They didn't hear you! They're driving me nuts.' Lori opened the door and yelled again and again until her mother fell back asleep.

One afternoon soon after, Lori was on the couch watching TV when Britta suddenly pointed to the telephone directories, asking, 'Lori, will you call AA?'

'I looked in the phone book,' Lori recalls, 'and I didn't know what AA was, so I said, "Well, there's AAA here? I don't know what you mean." And she said, "Do you think I need AA?" I said, "What's AA?" Then she dropped the subject. And now, of course, I know that AA is Alcoholics Anonymous.'

Britta's condition continued to deteriorate and she started having convulsions. Once, as Lori was helping her to the bathroom, Britta's eyes began to bulge and Lori was afraid she was going to swallow her tongue. She screamed for her father who rushed in and held Britta's tongue down hard with a pencil until the spasms passed. Frightened, Lori pleaded with him, not for the first time, to call an ambulance. He told her they didn't have insurance and couldn't afford it. He merely helped Britta back to the bedroom and closed the door. Lori sat outside listening. All she could hear was the low drone of the television. She couldn't turn to Aunt Alma and Uncle Ben for help because they were away on vacation. On 7 July 1971, Lauri emerged from the bedroom and told Lori to go in and check on her mother.

'Feel her pulse. Feel if she's alive.'

Immediately scared, Lori retorted, 'No! I don't want to.'

But when had she ever disobeyed her father? Despite herself, she edged gingerly towards Britta's lifeless form. To her horror, her mother felt chillingly cold to the touch. Looking back, Lori knows she had been manipulated: 'I knew he knew she was dead, but he wanted *me* to know it as part of an experience, or something. Like teaching me to change a tyre or balance the cheque-book. *I* didn't think that was a good experience—but *he* thought it was.'

(Aileen, who was off in the woods, later claimed this experience for her own, telling Diane how Lauri had made her and Lori sit with Mom's body from 5 a.m. until they notified police at noon, just so that they could experience death.)

Finally, but all too late, Lauri telephoned for an ambulance. Numb with shock and immobile, Lori watched as it pulled into the driveway and the drivers came into the house, put a sheet over her mother and removed her body.

Lori knew she had to find Aileen immediately, and tracked her down at the pits where she had been sleeping in an abandoned car. Then she located Keith.

Britta had believed in reincarnation and it had been her wish to be cremated. An Edgar Cayce fan, 'She wanted to come back as a bird because birds are so free,' Aileen recalls. 'I told her, "Yeah, well what if an eagle comes and gets you?" "Well, that's what I want to be—an eagle!" She was cool, she was neat, she was hip. A very humble lady.'

Finally, Lori, Aileen and Keith learned what their father, Diane and Barry had known all along: Britta was an alcoholic. Her liver had been in such poor condition that she'd been warned by doctors that if she drank again, it would kill her.

'The autopsy said she died from cirrhosis of the liver from drinking, but how could she die from three bottles of beer?' Lori ruminates. 'I think she wanted to die. After what she went through with Diane, now it was starting all over again with Keith and Aileen, and I don't think she could handle it.'

Aileen always spoke reverentially and adoringly of her grandmother, but this was the same woman who stood by and didn't intervene when Aileen was abused by Lauri. Inappropriately dressed in blue jeans, Aileen showed up at the funeral home, viewed Britta's casket, then frivolously switched the nameplates on the men's and ladies' restrooms. She then had to be thrown out for lighting up a cigarette and defiantly puffing smoke in Britta's face, saying, 'If I want to blow smoke in the old slob's face, I will!'

Behind her rampant idealising lay Aileen's anger at Britta for deserting her and not saving her from Lauri.

Lauri notified Diane of her mother's death—but not until after the cremation.

'He said, "The funeral is over and she's been cremated . . . but I just wanted you to know you killed your mother." That's the kind of abuse that we put up with,' Diane recalled.

His own role aside, Lauri certainly laid considerable blame for what happened to Britta at the feet of Aileen and Keith. There was no doubt she was devastated by Aileen's pregnancy and by having police show up on the doorstep. And talking to Diane that day, Lauri threatened that he would kill the children if she didn't come and get them.

Responding to his manipulation, she immediately drove to Michigan, but not until she'd called Uncle Ben, who strongly warned her against going to the house alone.

'Go get Barry,' he advised, 'and then you go with Barry . . . because your daddy is really gone off the wall.'

Following Ben's advice, Diane informed her father that she had checked into a local motel, saying she didn't want to be in his way and also preferred to be by herself.

'What's the matter?' sniped Lauri. 'If you stay, you think I'm going to kill you too?'

Diane couldn't help but notice the revealing 'too'. It seemed to have slipped out by accident.

He also continued his litany of complaints about Aileen and Keith: 'Those kids are no good . . . they're rotten through and through. They're no good, just like you.'

'Daddy, I've listened to that being no good all my life, and I thought I was no good until I left home, went far away, and realised that I was a good person. And don't you ever say that to me again, that I'm not any good.'

To Diane's astonishment, her retort silenced him. But she felt a painful pang of realisation. Her children had probably been even more abused than she had, just by virtue of the fact that they were hers.

While Diane was reassured that there was no sign of foul play, her mother was dead at 54 of a fatty liver and chronic thyroiditis, and she wasn't satisfied. Puzzled, she rang the coroner to request a copy of the autopsy report, thereby learning that Britta had died with bruises all over her body. She also smelled as if she had been drinking.

That was no surprise to Diane, 'because that was the problem . . . it was alcohol . . . that was the problem . . . in the house.'

The coroner asked if Britta had often fallen down drunk. Diane was adamant. Definitely not. She staggered, maybe, but never fell. And she could think of no legitimate explanation for the bruises. Something else struck Diane as odd. Although no one ever accused Lauri of taking Britta's life, until his own death five years later he repeatedly told people that he didn't kill her. Meanwhile, in Troy, Diane was getting her first glimpse of the juvenile delinquents Aileen and Keith had become. Seeing them over a period of a few days, she was shocked by how hard they were; how unlike her other two children. She told Aileen that she wanted to take her back to Houston with her, saying, 'You haven't gotten love here and I made a mistake.'

How hard Diane worked to try to take them, only she knows for sure. She later said she explored the possibility but that Texas authorities wouldn't permit it, predicting that without a husband she would be unable to cope with two more children who were already in trouble with the law and wards of the court.

'It sounds so cold . . . not being able to take your own children . . . but there's only so much a person can do,' she said.

Aileen and Keith were ambivalent about the move anyway since Diane made it plain she intended to lay down some firm rules. It wasn't going to be party time and she wouldn't allow them to smoke marijuana. All in all, a rather unattractive agenda.

Lori later reflected on her father's refusal to call an ambulance. At the time, she hadn't known that an emergency call would have summoned immediate help, money or no. Slowly, she came to a painful realisation. Her father must have thought she was so dumb that she wouldn't figure out what happened. And as an adult, she tearfully faced the disquieting truth. Her father had let her mother die.

Sometimes, she felt she hated him. Most of the time, she willed herself to block it out. She kept repeating to herself, 'It's over with. Thinking about it won't do any good.'

Lonely and isolated for the bulk of her young years, Aileen finally met one kindred spirit in 10th grade. Dawn Nieman first became aware of Aileen as the kid all the others teased and whispered about behind her back. They said she carried around her mother's ashes.

Dawn, who was eight days younger, wasn't as wild as Aileen but was a fellow troublemaker and was expelled from school for fighting just around the time Aileen dropped out. She was frankly intrigued by her friend's renegade reputation and the fact she'd already had a child and was a prostitute. Aileen never talked about the baby. She acted as if it was nothing. And she never said she'd been raped. The more the other kids urged Dawn to give Aileen a wide berth, the more she was drawn to her. A friendship, albeit a mercurial one, developed between them.

Britta's death had marked a crucial turning point for Aileen. All semblance of family ties had disintegrated and by her fifteenth summer, while most of her peers were preoccupied with junior proms and the like, she was out of the nest completely, living in a kind of no-man's-land, answering the call of the wild.

Dawn, for some long-forgotten reason, also ran away from home for a while, and together they took to living rough and sleeping in the abandoned cars they found in fields, in backyards and even in neighbours' yards and driveways. Aileen briefly moved into an old Oldsmobile up on blocks in one family's yard, and the Kretsches briefly allowed her to sleep in their old VW. After her benefactors left home for work, she went inside to shower. For a time, Aileen and Keith also stayed with the Richey family. Then when Dawn returned home, Aileen spent odd nights with her folks, too.

Dawn thought of Aileen as a Jekyll and Hyde. She could be a

bitch at times, but she also had an endearing side. When they hung out in bars (passing themselves off as eighteen wherever people weren't too fussy about i.d.), or went to the mall or to eat at a burger joint, it was always Aileen's treat. She enjoyed being generous, buying jeans for Dawn, who didn't have any money of her own. And her apparently fearless friend carried a knife, so Dawn knew she'd look out for her even when they went panhandling.

Dawn knew exactly how Aileen got her pocketfuls of cash, they just never talked about it outright. Whereas Cheryl Stacy and Janet Craig tried to challenge Aileen about messing around with men, Dawn didn't get on her case about the prostitution, even though Aileen sent her away a couple of times a day while she took care of business. Dawn didn't judge her. Her silence was a mark of her respect for Aileen, who she thought was doing what was necessary to be able to give money and drugs to Keith and Lori. Although Aileen was the youngest, she seemed admirably protective of Lori, who was still into Barbie dolls and seemed much younger. Aileen even tried to shield Lori from sex by aggressively warning off Lori's boyfriends. Dawn found something noble in the way Aileen took care of her family, albeit by questionable means.

Unlike Aileen's previous attempts at friendship, her alliance with Dawn endured, weathering its storms.

Lori continued to live with Lauri and while he was off on a few days' vacation, broke his cardinal rule, inviting Aileen and Keith to stay over. When he returned unexpectedly at seven o'clock one morning, he caught Keith sleeping in Lori's bedroom. Enraged by the sight of him, he yelled so loudly that Keith didn't even think of leaving by the door—he frantically crawled out through the bedroom window.

Shortly thereafter, Lauri sold the house, but he didn't leave until he was forced to. And when he couldn't get his piano out through the doorway, he chopped it up and threw it away. He was too mean-spirited to leave it for the next inhabitants. Lori cried over the fate of the piano. To her, he was closing the whole chapter of their lives involving Mom with that single, destructive gesture. 'After what he did to my mother, I'm sure his head wasn't in the right place.'

With Britta gone, Lori also sensed that Lauri had lost some of his steam. He barely reacted when he found out she smoked. There was no outburst. He simply told her not to smoke in front of him.

'I don't know what was in his head. He was an angry sort of person, period,' she muses. 'It wasn't as bad as it sounds, but he was always temperamental. He always had to be right. It seemed to me he got a little bit more quiet and sad and lonely after my mom died. Maybe he dreaded what he did.'

Lori moved with him for a while to Utica nine miles away, into a little house next to Barry. Aileen and Keith were who knows where. But at eighteen, Lori felt trapped by Lauri's demands that she stay home with him night after night to keep him company. And he got upset when she refused. So when he moved up to rugged northern Michigan where he had family, envisaging a remote cabin in the woods, she declined to go with him. She still loved her father, but it was time to forge her own life. When her friends, the Richeys, left Troy for the Mancelona ski resort area, Lori, who was anxious to break away from drugs and partying, went with them.

Lauri was lonely. Like Aileen, he wasn't gifted at making or keeping friends and his bad temper seemed to isolate him. Having trouble making ends meet, he eventually moved back down into Barry's home. If Lauri was disappointed in Diane, he'd also been let down by Barry who dropped out of college after three semesters. Lauri, who'd staved off unemployment with a number of unskilled jobs over the years, working as a janitor, cab driver and bus driver, wanted something better for Barry. Barry had joined the Air Force but as soon as he came out, Lori and her friend fixed him up and Barry married Judy in September 1970. He was 25, she 19. Lauri was not pleased. He was also angry because they didn't visit more often with their baby, Becky.

As a boy, Barry had shone at golf. He and a friend, John Majestic, lifted weights together and often rose at 4 or 5 a.m. to caddy at the Rochester Golf Course, where they were rewarded with free golf. Practising in the back yard, he hit balls into the field out back, then took the family dog to help retrieve them. His golfing talent became family legend, but he didn't pursue it as a career. John Majestic thought the way Lauri rammed it down his throat didn't help. Instead, Barry moved into clerical work in a factory.

10

It was so long ago that Lori couldn't pinpoint when it first struck her that Aileen was just plain different from all the other kids. It was just something she felt she'd always known. Aileen did try to fit in, she really tried, but she simply couldn't. It seemed beyond her capabilities. By the time she was eight, she was constantly falling out with other kids, despite Lori's frequent counselling to be nice and not lose her temper. If Lori invited Aileen to join in with her friends, she soon regretted it. Inevitably, Aileen whined that this or that was unfair. Then she'd blow up, making everyone else angry and embarrassing Lori. She seemed unable to sustain her 'good self' for extended periods of time, and sometimes, to Lori's chagrin, her friends didn't mince words: 'We don't want to go if Aileen's going too.'

Aileen could be nice, but Lori always had the curious sense that the niceness was fake, a veneer. It registered even then that her sister's mannerisms and smiles lacked authenticity; her mood and sociability seemed phony and forced. It was as if she knew that she didn't fit and tried hard to tailor her personality to something she thought people would like and accept. But then, in a split second, her temper erupted and it was all over. No one wanted to be around her. Lori felt sorry for her, but she couldn't sacrifice her own life and friendships.

Lori believed Aileen was troubled not by the way she was treated at home, but by something inside her. Something in her personality. And with her chemical abuse, the temper worsened. Aileen's rages were a sight to behold. Her fury would sweep over her, turning her red in the face and unleashing a torrent of ugly verbiage. She didn't seem able to control herself.

Lori was eighteen at the time of one particularly frightening altercation, when Aileen, heavily under the influence of alcohol and downers, popped in to see her at the Kretsches' where she was babysitting. Infuriated by her embarrassing intrusion, Lori yelled, 'You're crazy!' A grave tactical error since 'crazy' and 'nuts' were adjectives that struck a sore personal chord with Aileen. Hearing them was guaranteed to send her into an absolute rage, and she ran into the Kretsches' kitchen, grabbed a skewer, and rushed back into the living room, wielding it like a weapon. Brandishing it a quarter-inch from Lori's throat, she launched into a tirade saying she hated her and should kill her. Lori was scared and mad and shouted at her to leave her alone. 'I started bawling and crying, then she backed off and I ran out of the back door.'

From that day forth, Lori never quite trusted Aileen again and if they ever had occasion to sleep under the same roof and Aileen went to bed angry, Lori barely slept a wink. She couldn't help wondering what she might do for revenge.

As a kid, Aileen had sorely tried Lori's patience. As an adult, nothing changed. Periodically, Aileen called or visited Lori and her husband Ervin Grody, and lived with them briefly three times, once when they were living in Colorado before their wedding. They never made it past two or three weeks without getting into a major blow-out argument. It was usually Aileen's loud music, or her unwillingness to help with chores or contribute to the rent, that set it off. Lori felt she and Erv were being used.

Lori often ached to help Aileen, particularly when she called from a hospital in another state and announced that she'd tried to kill herself, but nothing worked. A woman affiliated with a church telephoned Lori soon after, saying that they were buying Aileen a plane ticket so she could fly to be with Lori and Erv. 'We couldn't be civil to one another for too long, no matter when or where it was.' On one occasion, Lori seriously thought of having Aileen committed and discussed it with Barry. What stopped her was her fear—if Aileen had ever found out she was behind it, she'd be 'dead meat'.

Eventually, the dramatic calls merged and blurred in Lori's mind. Was that the time Aileen overdosed on pills and had to have her stomach pumped? Or the time she shot herself in the abdomen? Aileen seemed hell-bent on sabotaging Lori and Erv's efforts to help by making herself downright impossible to live with. She paid lip service to a dream of having a regular job and a regular life, but in reality destroyed anything good. If she had a job she'd lose her temper with someone, then quit or get fired. She even stole from friends or the very people who'd taken her in (including Barry and his wife), then took off. She hardly helped herself.

There were clues everywhere to Aileen's deep anger. Once she went after Keith with a knife. It was imperative to Keith to hold his own with Aileen. He couldn't let her get the upper hand. He wasn't violent by nature, but neither was he afraid to fight. And things often turned physical with Aileen. It was he who gave Aileen a black eye when she drunkenly totalled his car after careering through the Richeys' front yard, knocking down the mailbox, hurtling into a ditch and finally coming to a standstill amidst the trees. She was only about sixteen at the time.

Aileen once threatened Barry's wife, Judy, saying, 'If you don't shut up, I'll kill you!'

'Oh yeah, right!' Judy retorted.

'Well, I've already killed somebody and chopped them up in little pieces and put them out in the field,' Aileen shot back.

Dawn had her turn with a threat with a cue ball, but when they went head-to-head and actually fought, Dawn came out on top, flipping Aileen over a car. Afterwards, they shook hands. Dawn's brother once bore the marks of Aileen's fingernails as the result of some name-calling offence.

Lori was overwhelmingly thought of as being sweet with a sunny disposition, Aileen was thought of as mean. 'A number one bitch, she was too hard to cry. She was always pissed off at everyone,' recalls one neighbour. 'Maybe one time out of ten she'd be in a good mood.'

Her neighbour, Jean Kear, saw Aileen as 'rather unsavoury, that's putting it mildly', but also as very troubled. 'She was unloved, unwanted, and always in the way, and I think it gave her one hell of a chip on her shoulder. If you walked down the street and didn't look at her, she'd give you a mouthful. And if you *did* look, she'd say, "What the f*** are you looking at!"'

Cheryl Stacy saw something else. 'If you look into her eyes, you see she's been crying for someone to love her. Someone to care about her.'

Aileen was rarely viewed with such sensitivity. She struck one local boy as being hard, with a 'motherfuck this, motherfuck that, fuck you' attitude. 'She'd fly off the handle and get upset over trivial bullshit.'

He described her as ugly. While Aileen didn't wear makeup or pretty herself up like the other girls, it was clear that it was her aura rather than her physical features he meant. In the face of even dire provocation, she never showed her vulnerable side. Never cried.

'A lot of her peers treated her like shit,' said Dawn Nieman, remembering the time Aileen was in an unusually super mood having decided to throw a party in the old family home which sat briefly empty after Lauri moved up north and before the new tenants moved in. Aileen was elated at the prospect of playing hostess.

'They'd have to stop calling her a sleazebag whore and everything,' was how Dawn interpreted her thinking.

But Aileen seemed to attract such abuse like a magnet.

As usual, she tried to buy the companionship and relationships she craved, using her wages of sin to gather people together, then to include herself. Indignant at the unfairness of it all, Dawn recalls the common outcome.

'She'd go get money for liquor for a party or whatever, then the others would end up kicking her out of her own party because they knew what she did [sexually]. She'd give blow jobs or whatever to buy the stuff, and they hated it and treated her like shit. Like dirt.'

Watching while Aileen was thrown out of one of her parties, Dawn looked on helplessly, afraid to go out on a limb for her friend.

'It's terrible she was used in that way,' agrees Lori, who also felt powerless to stop the maltreatment. She herself once called the police when a party got out of hand. Someone had stuffed a beer can down the toilet which was overflowing.

'One time Aileen was coming out of the store and these guys

hit her with their car,' Dawn recalls. 'Not enough to hurt her, but they just knocked her. Aileen was emotional, but she never sat there and cried to have people feel sorry for her. She'd get pissed off. That way, they didn't feel sorry for her. They hated her even more for getting mad.'

Another time, another party. As Aileen arrived in the field bringing in beer supplies, someone accidentally knocked her down with a car door, but no one even bothered to check and see if she was OK.

Blissfully free of school, Dawn and Aileen hitchhiked all over, living the low life and the high life, running into a bad part of town to buy drugs, or swanning off to the racetrack. It was while on one of their famous hitchhiking jaunts that in 1973 Dawn met her husband, Dave Botkins, whom she married a year later. It was another abandonment for Aileen.

11

Keith found a lump on his neck roughly a month after successfully passing his physical and enrolling in the Army in 1974. It was diagnosed as cancerous. After surgery, the doctors reassured him that they had removed all the insidious cells.

That they were wrong became glaringly apparent when at a party one day he took a drunken fall down a short flight of steps. His leg broke because his bones were so brittle. Back at the hospital, he learned that the cancer he thought he'd beaten had begun a slow but unstoppable spread and was ravaging his body. There was a period of remission, but the disease continued to gain on him and he spent eighteen months in Veterans Hospital, south of Detroit, being treated with chemotherapy.

This turn of events did nothing to improve things between him and Lauri, the old adversaries who once came to blows, with Keith almost knocking Lauri to the ground. Lauri did visit Keith in Veterans Hospital, but it wasn't long before they got into an argument, and Lori admits: 'I don't know if my father loved him, or if he went to see him knowing he was in bed, for the spite of it.'

Keith was dying at the tender age of twenty. But first he was determined to fulfil his own prophecy and outlive Lauri.

Lauri, meanwhile, was living in the basement of Barry's home in Rochester where he spent most of his time watching TV, glued to war movies in particular. He had his own room, complete with couch and chair, but took his meals upstairs with the family. He no longer worked and was plagued by poor health, brought about by diabetes and his alcoholism.

Seemingly in the grip of a depression that never quite lifted after Britta's death, there were days when Lauri, once so proud of his well-groomed appearance, didn't even bathe.

His death when it came was, like Britta's, disturbing. Lauri's father had committed suicide, hanging himself in an aircraft hangar, and Lauri had once tried to kill himself by going into a basement that was flooded with water after torrential rain and standing up to his ankles in water, then turning on an electric switch. It didn't work.

On 12 March 1976, he was successful. Barry had gone to work and Judy had gone back to bed when Lauri went out to the garage, turned on his car ignition, and omitted to open the garage door. He passed out from the toxic engine fumes and his son found him hours later, after pulling his car in alongside, lying across the front seat. At first the family thought he'd had a stroke because the car had run out of gas and stalled. But the death certificate said carbon monoxide poisoning and intoxication. Generally, the family accepted it as suicide.

Maybe there wasn't much to live for any longer. Perhaps he wanted to be with his wife. Just because he deliberately failed to save Britta's life, so ran Lori's rationalisation, didn't mean he hated her, or didn't care about her, or didn't love her.

Aileen did not attend her hated grandfather's funeral. Nor did Keith, who was then clinging to his own life by a fragile thread. Keith had waged his battle against cancer for two years but by then the cancer had spread throughout his throat, brain, lungs and bones. His drug-dealer friend, Ducky (since deceased), took Keith's cheque and brought drugs into his hospital room, feeding them right into his intravenous drip when no one was looking.

This was also the year Aileen married Lewis Gratz Fell. A curious match, to describe it in the most moderate of terms. Fell, with his reputable Philadelphia bloodline, was 69 years old, she twenty. They met when he spotted her hitching and offered her a ride. Interestingly, they married in Kingsley, Georgia, less than two months after the death of her grandfather. At 65, Lauri had been younger than Aileen's beau. And what would Lauri have made of it?

Most who knew Aileen viewed this union cynically, finding it impossible to judge it as anything other than a purely mercenary move. Obviously, the unwitting Lewis Fell had no idea what he was letting himself in for. Erv Grody saw it this way: Fell wanted a young blonde on his arm, and Aileen was after his money.

'He wanted the prize—and they both got the prize, all right. *Sur*-prise.'

Early in July, she and Lewis rolled into Michigan in a spiffy, new, cream-coloured Cadillac and checked into a motel. Aileen had sent Lori and Barry newspaper clippings of their wedding announcement from the society pages of the Daytona press, complete with a photograph of a man who looked old enough to be her grandfather, describing Fell as the president of a yacht club. Mailing it to Barry, to whom she'd never been close, she was merely milking her big chance to show off. She told Lori she was blissfully happy.

Arriving back in her hometown, apparently unembarrassed by the vast age difference between her and her spouse, the girl who had always wanted to be a movie star proudly displayed her silver-haired husband and her valuable diamond engagement ring, not necessarily in that order. He had more money than anyone she'd ever known and a plush beachside condominium. And just as she had always wanted, she was the talk of the town.

But Aileen was quickly torn. Her desire to get drunk and hang out in bars bubbled so close to the surface that it rapidly broke through the token marriage. To Lewis's fury, his young wife went out at night, bar-hopping, exactly as she'd done when single.

Calculating or otherwise, whatever Aileen's hopes and intentions were, she didn't seem able to stick to them and her fleeting marriage was immediately in dire straits. After just one month of this less-than-love match, Lewis took to the hills before Lori and Erv had even got to meet him. Back in Florida, he filed a restraining order against his estranged wife, claiming she had beaten him with his walking cane.

The divorce decree stated: 'Respondent has a violent and ungovernable temper and has threatened to do bodily harm to the Petitioner and from her past actions will injure Petitioner and his property . . . unless the court enjoins and restrains said respondent from assaulting . . . or interfering with Petitioner or his property.'

Not for the first time, Aileen simply inverted the facts, flipping over this story and accusing Fell of doing what she herself had done. Repeatedly, she claimed that he beat her, but at odd moments, the truth broke through. She admitted it to Lori, who was appalled (particularly by her addendum that she'd made Lewis fall by taking away his cane, then fallen about laughing). She also told the truth to Diane, during one of their rare meetings. It was an anecdote that only exacerbated Diane's fear of her daughter, which had been building steadily with every horror story she heard about Aileen's anger.

'Why would you do that?' she asked in astonishment. 'This man's a multi-multi-millionaire and he can take care of you, and he must evidently care about you!'

Aileen's explanation was that her clothes-buying sprees had finally gotten too much for Fell, who meted out money thirty dollars at a time, and when he reprimanded her, she grabbed his cane and beat him.

No stranger to drunken arguments in bars, on 13 July she made a lasting impression on Bernie's Club (later Club 131) in Mancelona. The evening began peaceably enough with Earl Junior Castle (more commonly known as Bud), a slightly built 27-year-old construction worker, dropping in after work as was his custom to relax over a couple of drinks.

His eye was caught by an attractive young blonde in blue jeans and a cream sweater who was busy hustling pool for money and drinks. He'd never seen her before and decided he'd like to get to know her. When she challenged him to join her at the table, he rose to the bait, playing three or four games, which she won. Bud kept watching her and noticed that as the evening wore on she grew rowdier, shouting obscenities, uttering threats to other patrons, and generally being objectionable.

Sometime after midnight, the bartender and manager, Danny Moore, had finally had enough. He also smelled trouble brewing. Young, tough and confident, he ran the establishment in a 'kick ass' fashion (meaning he wasn't afraid to 'kick ass' when need be), yet something prompted him to handle this differently. He casually walked over to the pool table, sweeping the balls together and announcing that the table was closing down. Just as he was doing so, he heard someone shout, 'Duck!' He turned just in time to see Aileen aim a cue ball at his head. It flew past, missing him only by inches, but she had hurled it with such incredible force that it literally lodged itself in the wall. If she had been on target, she might have killed him.

Once again guided by the wisdom of experience, something told Danny not to try to deal with this incendiary situation himself. He called the police.

When Deputy Jimmie Pattrick of the Antrim County Sheriff's Department arrived, being single, he noted how attractive Aileen was and was baffled as to why someone so good-looking should be involved in a barroom scuffle. Yet Aileen was duly arrested for Assault and Battery and hauled off to jail. She was also charged on fugitive warrants from the Troy Police Department requesting that she be picked up within a hundred-mile radius for charges of consuming alcohol in a car, unlawful use of a driver's licence, and for not having a Michigan driver's licence.

Small town that it was, Jimmie Pattrick knew Erv and telephoned to tell him what had happened to his sister-in-law. Erv and Lori quickly jumped in their grey pick-up truck and headed for the bar to try to persuade them to drop the charges, but Danny wouldn't budge. 'If I drop the charges now, then every time I call a cop, they won't come out,' he argued.

Filling in the jail forms, Aileen noted that she was under a doctor's care and on nerve medication. She was living back at the Grodys' home, but had a motel key in her purse along with $20.78. She then slept off the liquor in the drunk tank, but not before she threatened the officers present, saying, 'I'm an undercover narcotics agent in Colorado and you guys will be really sorry!'

Despite the different charges against her, Aileen was quickly released on bail after an unidentified friend arrived with her purse containing $1,450. It certainly wasn't Erv Grody: 'She could have stayed there and rotted for all I really cared.'

Erv and Lori had grown more accustomed to Aileen's exploits than they cared to. When Aileen was playing pool, she loved to flirt and flaunt her body. Reading her blatant availability signals, a couple of womanising married men set their sights on getting her into the backwoods.

Paul, once a friend of Erv's, took her for a ride in his car out into a desolate area and parked, thinking he'd got lucky. But the encounter then went awry. Reporting back to Erv, he said, 'Man, that sister-in-law of yours is a wild person.' They'd been making out for a while and both had their clothes off, but just as Paul was about to climb on top of her, Aileen snapped at him: 'What do you think you're going to do with that?'

'You know what I'm going to do.'

'No, you aren't!' Aileen shouted, as she began pounding on him with her fists, kicking furiously and screaming her head off.

'I kicked her ass out of the car and told her she was walking home,' Paul said, showing Erv the scratches he bore to back up his story.

Aileen reprimanded Barry for hardly visiting Keith in the hospital—blithely ignoring the fact that it was Barry who took him in and cared for him when the hospital could do no more. She had hitchhiked halfway across the country to see him. Yet, for all this lip-service Aileen paid to the importance she put on Keith, no one remembers her visiting her dying brother. Dawn, however, stopped by weekly with candy and books. (She didn't tell her husband, who might have misinterpreted it.) Lori went too, meeting Keith's curious craving for chocolate-covered cherries which he explained he hoped would help him put on weight. He couldn't chew anything solid, or even brush his teeth. His gums and teeth were too fragile. Keith also requested *Playboy* magazines which Lori duly took him.

When his body could stand no more and doctors knew it was near the end, they allowed Keith his dying wish to live out his last days at home. Jerry Moss drove him to Barry's house in Keith's new Corvette: he'd bought it with cash from the Army cheques he'd saved, but never had a chance to drive it himself.

It was just three days after Aileen's cue ball incident arrest, on 17 July, that Keith finally lost his fight against the cancer. He was just 21. On 19 July, Aileen's marriage officially ended with a divorce issued at the Volusia County courthouse in Florida. She pawned the ring. Two days after that, Keith was cremated at the same funeral home as Britta and Lauri. Aileen arrived late.

Having rejected him in life, but acknowledging him in death, Diane arrived from Texas for the funeral. Other mourners were surprised to see her apparently too distraught to sit through the service for her abandoned son. She attended the viewing of Keith's body, carefully avoiding being left alone in a room with Aileen, who also put in a surprise appearance. Aileen, seeming uncharacteristically vulnerable, followed her around like a little puppy looking for attention. Diane left just as the mourners reached the steps.

Aunt Alma, Uncle Ben, and Jerry Moss didn't know it then, but it was the last time they'd see Aileen. And they'd remember the way she gently slipped a rose into her brother's hand.

Lori didn't fare well that day, breaking down in floods of tears. She also got into an argument with Dawn because she thought the drugs Dawn's brother Ducky had taken Keith in the hospital, supposedly to relieve the pain, might have hastened his death. Janet Craig had to usher Lori into the bathroom and help settle her down.

Had Keith lived, Lori would later reflect, he'd probably have ended up in trouble for dealing and using drugs. But she couldn't imagine in her worst nightmares that he'd ever be capable of committing any violent crime. He had a temper, but never like Aileen's.

Fondly, Lori recalled how in an effort to get her to be less timid and more outgoing, he had once bought her a provocatively sheer, sexy, black blouse. She was too shy to wear it.

On 4 August, Aileen pleaded guilty to the Assault and Battery charge for the cue ball outburst, paying a fine and costs of $105. She'd left town again by Lori and Erv's wedding. But not before issuing one of her unfriendly warnings to Erv: 'If you ever hurt Lori, I'll kill you and bury your body where no one will ever find it. Don't think I can't do it.'

A few months after Keith died, each of his siblings inherited $10,000, courtesy of payments on his Army life insurance. Aileen claimed to have camped out on the doorstep of the insurance company until they issued her a cheque. With money in hand, she promptly put a down payment on a shiny black Pontiac (which was soon repossessed) and tooled over to Lori and Erv's, flashing her wad of money.

She also bought a mixed bag of antiques and a massive stereo system (she had no home but apparently saw no incongruity), and blew the lot in three months, pronouncing, 'This is death money—I don't want it!' Referring back to their inheritances, Aileen said: 'Barry's money-hungry too, by the way. I'm not the only black sheep of the family. I'm not materialistic because I got into the Lord.'

When, inevitably, she moved out of Lori and Erv's, her purchases went into storage. She called a while later—by which time the storage rental fees were delinquent—asking Lori and Erv to retrieve her stuff. They did so and kept it in their home until her next visit.

The stereo system was hooked up to two powerful speakers set outside the house. Lori and Erv returned one day to find Aileen, the self-professed 'music freak', totally oblivious to any need to show consideration for other residents, blasting it out across the whole neighbourhood. She was inside the house, clutching the plug-in mike and crooning along.

Her visits always ended in animosity. Acting as if it were her home, not Lori and Erv's, she would come in and change the TV channel at whim overriding Lori and Erv and never consulting anyone else in the room. She might be on her best behaviour for a couple of days, then she'd settle into her usual routine. She contributed nothing to the household expenses, didn't cook a single meal, didn't clean, and generally lounged around the house all day without even a semblance of pulling her weight.

She sometimes took three showers a day. And each night she'd say, 'I need a beer to help calm my nerves,' as though she'd been working hard all day and was under pressure. Unlike them, she had no responsibilities. At least she didn't break the place up, Lori thought, saying a silent 'thank you'. Erv often imagined the sisters coming to blows, yet, miraculously, they didn't. There was no doubt, however, that Aileen's prolonged presence would put a lethal strain on their marriage. Ultimately, it was them or her, and she had to go.

She bragged openly about her dubious survival methods, such as finding the minister in a new town and conning him and his family into taking her in. 'That was her way of getting back on her feet several times,' Erv Grody recalls. 'Then she'd end up robbing them blind.' When she hitched, she boasted, there were always plenty of truckers who stopped, ready for sex.

On one of her visits, Erv drove her to a storage unit she'd rented. In it, she kept an old trunk of clothing, a crossbow, and an antique .22 calibre rifle. That time, when Lori and Erv asked her to leave after a couple of tense weeks, she pleaded poverty. To help her out, Erv found someone willing to buy her stereo with its huge home-made speakers for $450. For his trouble, Erv received another of the by then familiar warnings about treating Lori right. As always, he knew instinctively that she meant what she said.

Instead of using the money to fly to Florida as she'd promised, Aileen asked Lori to drive her to the highway.

They bid farewell that time on a rainy morning. Lori felt bad about leaving her sister out there, but what could she do? 'It killed me, but I couldn't have her living with us.' Off went Aileen, her thumb extended.

Not long after Keith's death, Aileen turned up unannounced at Diane's home in Texas for a two-week stay; an unwelcome guest in what Diane would call 'a very horrible experience'. By then, Diane's fear of her estranged daughter was sky high. What she had witnessed during her stay in Michigan for Keith's funeral had primed her for trouble. 'I could see the violence in her, and she frightened me to death,' she said. Barry had tried to soothe her fears, but Diane wouldn't be placated, saying, 'There's something that's in her that frightens me, that's all I can tell you.'

It hadn't helped when the family had got together and discussed Aileen's threatening of Lori with the skewer. Nor did the infamous cue ball incident—which in Diane's mind translated into attempted murder—alleviate her deep anxiety.

Its root cause, of course, harked back to her firm belief that Aileen had been raised to hate her by Lauri and Britta. If Aileen had such vast quantities of anger seething inside her, how much of it might be aimed at Diane?

When she arrived on her doorstep, Aileen got off on the right foot, informing Diane that she planned to find a job. But it rapidly became apparent that this was just a token gesture designed to keep Diane off her back. When Diane returned from work each day, Aileen would be either drunk or high. Diane didn't know what she'd been taking because—she's not sure why—she didn't ask her.

('She kept trying to get me drunk on whisky,' Aileen would allege, referring to Diane as a 'wet-brain'.)

Diane would claim not to be averse to giving Aileen a home, it was just that Aileen wouldn't stop the violent talk, the drink, the drugs. The violent talk, the drink and the drugs, of course, *were* Aileen. So, hard though it may have been to admit, Diane didn't actually want this troublesome daughter at all.

And who could blame her? She'd heard what the Texas authorities said about children's personalities being locked in by the age of ten, and the prognosis for sudden miraculous change did not look good. However much her heart ached to be able to, it just seemed too late to start over.

Lori believed it wasn't so much that Diane hated Aileen as that she felt guilty for having left her and Keith, particularly for having left them with her parents. And, of course, she had made another life for herself. A life upon which she didn't want a disruptive influence like Aileen to intrude.

The upshot was that each night Diane went to bed in fear that Aileen would kill her in her sleep. She slept restlessly with her keys tucked inside her pillowcase the entire time, thinking that at the very least, her daughter might try to steal her car. That was no way to live.

After a couple of weeks, Aileen grew tired of Diane's rules and regulations. She complained that she didn't like it there and wanted to leave. But faster than Diane could heave a sigh of relief and offer her the money for a bus ticket, Aileen changed her mind again. She'd stay.

Diane's frayed nerves, however, could take little more. She told Aileen that it would be best if she went and handed her the bus money. Diane told the family that when she drove her to the bus terminal, she had watched from her car as Aileen walked in the front door of the terminal, went right through and straight out the back, obviously intent on hitching.

Aileen's version? 'I hated her guts, and I told her to take me to the freeway, and then let me out of here. She took me to I-10 in Texas. I wasn't going to put up with her shit.'

12

Aileen's teenage runaway jags and well-honed hitchhiking skills had segued into a permanent lifestyle of rootless wanderings. Her natural habitat was, by the late seventies, the vast expanse of flat woodlands fringing the central Florida highways. The sun-belt, with its casual way of life, was a seductive magnet that had long exerted its powerful pull on the shiftless and uncon-nected. But Aileen also harboured a special fondness for the starkly contrasting mountainous peaks of Colorado. She often spoke of them longingly, saying, 'It was the prettiest place that I really liked to be in and that felt right.'

Hanging out there with a rough biker crowd, she was in her element. She'd always been drawn to the outlaw life, ever since as a little girl at the pits she'd watched the biker gangs from afar. Now, she was among them, riding motorcycles in the Rockies and living dangerously. She claims she was once run off the road by a rival bunch of bikers who managed to send her sailing over the handlebars, right into a ditch. Drink flowed, and on one oc-casion when she'd been out riding with the guys, she'd imbibed such vast quantities of alcohol that she passed out cold. She felt safe because of one guy in particular whom she liked. She had the feeling he would look out for her. Wrong. She awoke the next morning to find herself tied hand and foot to a bed and had to scream blue murder until the biker boys relented and cut her loose.

Also legend according to Wuornos is that, while living the wild life in Colorado, she had a job to do for the guys she ran with. She had to get all decked out in her leather jacket, leather pants and thigh-high boots, then position herself outside a restaurant or truck-stop, acting as bait to lure a rival bike gang into a fight. Or worse.

On an earlier visit to Colorado, in May of 1974, she was arrested as 'Sandra B. Kretsch' for disorderly conduct (with the stolen licence of the woman in whose abandoned VW she had briefly slept). She spent ten days in jail. But when she moved there in 1977, her crimes became more serious. She had two DUI (driving under the influence) arrests and two arrests for weapons offences.

That August, Aileen was spotted driving a brown Grand Prix (highly erratically), and blithely waving around and firing a handgun out of the car window—much to the horror of passing motorists. The car weaved from lane to lane without signalling, its driver apparently unaware of the other vehicles that were being forced to swerve to avoid it. It hurtled through red lights, then slowed to 30 m.p.h., or screeched to a halt only suddenly to speed up again to close to 60 m.p.h., tyres squealing. Finally intercepted, Aileen stepped from the car, her breath preceding her. She fairly reeked of alcohol (a blood test would reveal a level of .129 per cent), her eyes were blood-red, her speech slurred and her gait staggering.

A .25 calibre automatic pistol containing three hollow-point bullets was found in the car's console. Aileen told the officers that her boyfriend owned the car and the gun.

On 23 December 1977, she was arrested again for the same charges: prohibited use of a firearm, no operator's licence, and DUI.

Along with her money hunger, Aileen's craving for love unarguably remained a major driving force in her life. Her poor track record for relationships notwithstanding, Aileen was repeatedly propelled into situations by that urgent hunger she had to bond closely with another human being.

She was 25 when her path crossed that of Jay Watts, a 52-year-old automobile worker, in the spring of 1981. She approached him at the Talk of the Town, a lounge in the Daytona Beach area. (Daytona, home of the International Speedway, with its 23 miles of 500-foot wide, hard-packed, pale, sandy beaches, would repeatedly draw her.) The Talk of the Town boasted a pool room at the back, but Aileen didn't attempt to hustle Jay, they just had a drink together. An innocuous and rather pleasurable encounter that they repeated six or seven times. Jay 'didn't spot her as being on the make or anything'. Aileen always offered to buy him a drink but gentleman that he is, he insisted on paying.

Jay could always tell immediately when Aileen was in the bar because he'd spot her decrepit, white, ten-speed bicycle, which couldn't have been worth more than five bucks, chained to the lamp-post outside. The chain—hefty enough to hold a tractor—always struck him as funny.

One night the pattern changed when Aileen tapped Jay for a $15 loan with a hard-luck story about being short on her rent at the old Troy hotel. A couple of weeks later she reappeared, planted a kiss on his cheek and, without any prompting, paid him back in full.

Another month went by before he next heard her customary greeting—'Hey, Jay'—drift down the darkened bar. She had nowhere to stay; could she crash with him for a couple of nights? He said yes, without knowing whether she would sleep with him. One step at a time, he thought. They stopped to buy a fifth of whisky then drove on to his mobile home.

'I've got to go to the bathroom,' Aileen said when they arrived.

'Go. If you're going to stay here, you might as well make yourself at home.' Sex or no was OK with him. One thing about Daytona Beach, men didn't have to worry about their sex lives.

'I fixed us a couple of real nice drinks,' he remembers, 'turned on the stereo, turned on the TV. She was gone for the longest kind of time, then I saw the lights go off in the bedroom and she said, "Hey, Jay! Aren't you going to come back here?" I walked back and she was in bed. She said, "Let's go." And I said, "Why not?"'

It was a curious alliance. And, informal arrangement that it was, it was experienced—and remembered—very differently by the parties involved. To Jay, since the affair lasted just a couple of months before 'the incident', it was very much a casual involvement.

To Aileen, it assumed monumental importance, being the closest thing to stability she'd experienced in years. Jay worked in used cars and acquired an old 1971 Ford station wagon for her to tool around in so she could go to the beach and (at his prodding) job-hunting. She treated the gift as if it were a Mercedes, cleaning it until she could see her face in it and seeming happily content with their semblance of domestic bliss. When Jay said he needed a vacuum cleaner, Aileen leapt up, saying, 'I can take care of that.' She returned an hour later with one so antiquated it looked as if it had come over on the *Mayflower*.

'Where did you get that?'

'I borrowed it from the hotel. I just went in and got it and put it in the station wagon.'

'You're going to take it back, though, aren't you?'

'Oh sure,' she said.

She liked sex. But she also loved being affectionate. She loved nothing better than to cuddle up when they lay back and relaxed in the evenings, just watching TV. She'd craved a boyfriend ever since Mark Fearn and Jerry Moss turned her down. With Jay, she had one.

She shared some of her past: her one-month marriage to a man of 69 who beat her with his cane. She spoke, too, of another Mark whom she described to Jay as the first man she'd ever wanted to marry. She said his mother was responsible for splitting them up because she disapproved of Aileen's drinking, and she threatened to shoot Aileen rather than let Mark marry such a no-good. If what Aileen told Jay was true, it marked another major rejection. A crushing blow.

Jay got the feeling that Aileen liked the idea of being able to put a man on a pedestal and to lean on him. He didn't know it, but that was very much Aileen's way of relating to other human beings. Either putting them on pedestals or hating them.

Aileen also confessed that back in 1978 she'd drunkenly shot herself in the stomach; that she had been an unhappy girl. Jay didn't think she sounded suicidal when she was with him, but wouldn't remember anyway. As a policy, he never paid any attention when women talked that way.

By contrast, he would have good reason to recall the night of 19 May 1981.

'We were watching one of those slam-bang, cops-and-robbers things they had on TV, something like *Miami Vice*. After it was over, she said, "You know," and she got that faraway look in her eyes—and I never will forget this, it's the first thing I remembered when I heard about her being in trouble—she said, "You know, I think it would really be neat to be . . ." Then I'm not sure if she said Ma Barker or a gun moll, but where she'd be famous and *be* somebody. I said, "Well, yeah, if you want to spend the rest of your days in the slammer or worse." Dumb question followed by a dumb answer.'

Later that evening they had a few angry words but they were sufficiently inconsequential for Jay not to remember for the life of him what about. Perhaps it was about sex, which Jay believed she really liked. 'OK, shweetheart,' she'd say in a Bogey imitation, 'this will be the time of your life!' The sex was OK, but not especially memorable. Personally, he'd just as soon play golf with her. When she had a pitcher of Manhattans and got on the golf course, she was great fun. She had a natural talent for golf. Jay took her to the clubhouse once but suddenly worried that everyone might think she was his daughter. Just to tease him, she started calling him Daddy. They had a good laugh about that.

They went to bed together that night of the argument, but Aileen couldn't settle down. She got up, went outside and lay on a chaise-longue in her favourite spot above the carport for about four hours before finally going back to bed. She was moody, but Jay never saw any glimpse of violence. Never saw her do drugs either, except that she liked Qualuudes and sometimes took some of the prescription Libriums that he himself used to wind down after a tense day selling cars.

'The next day, the police were calling me at work. "Do you know Aileen Wuornos?" I said, "Yup!" They said, "Well, Jay, she's really bought it this time. We got her down at the truck stop. In her bikini bathing suit. We got the gun, we got everything. She hit a Majik Market."'

At approximately 1.25 p.m. on 20 May, like something out

of a bad movie, Aileen held up Elizabeth Smith, the cashier of the Majik Market on Ridgewood Avenue in Edgewater, Florida, brandishing a .22 calibre pistol.

'Would you believe this is an armed robbery? Give me all your money and make it fast,' she said.

She was formally charged with Robbery with a Deadly Weapon, a first-degree felony. And all for $35 and two packs of cigarettes. She had $90 on her when she was arrested. Neither Jay nor attorney Russell Armstrong knew where she got the money to buy the gun. And she refused to tell them.

Before her sentencing, she wrote a letter to Judge Hammond, pleading for lenience. Her naïve language, her child-like handwriting and her poor spelling indicated a far more youthful author. Simplistically, she explained how in 1976 she was madly in love with a fellow and wanted to marry him but that his mother had broken them up. She became depressed to a degree she could not explain, and began drinking herself to craziness. Because she loved Mark so much, losing him made her want to die and so, in 1978, she shot herself in the stomach and spent two weeks in the hospital recovering.

She began to realise that it was stupid to try to take her own life over a guy, when she'd probably meet another one just like him some day. But first loves die hard and she couldn't get Mark off her mind.

Her degree of obsession doubtless explains why Jay was under the impression that she and Mark had split up just a month or two before they met—not three or four years earlier.

'When I fall in love, I know I fall too deep,' Aileen observed in a poignant postscript to the judge who held her fate in his hands.

Aileen's recollection of her argument with Jay the previous night predictably differed from his. She'd had a lot on her mind and wanted to be alone to think, so when Jay came out of the shower and into the bedroom, she'd asked if he wanted to be in there? She needed some privacy, so maybe she'd better go outside to think? Jay took it all the wrong way, as if she was trying to tell him what to do in his own home.

'You can leave my room and the rest of the house for that matter!'

'Good, I'll sleep in the car!' Aileen retorted.

She didn't, but she cried herself to sleep. The next morning, still feeling angry and hurt, she convinced herself that she had lost him. Leaving the mobile home at around 7 a.m., she stopped at the fridge to grab a six-pack, then drove to the beach and drank it. She bought more beer, picked up a .22 pistol at a pawn shop, thinking she would kill herself. She stopped at Kmart and bought the bullets, but still didn't feel quite high enough to do the deed, so added whisky and Librium to the day's cocktail.

Driving around, she noticed a light flickering on the dashboard, signalling that the car was overheating. A gas station attendant helped her locate a big hole in the radiator, but told her she should make it home.

Pulling away, she spotted the Majik Market across the street and parked in front and just sat there, staring at the pay phones. Should she call Jay to find out if they were really breaking up or not? She was pretty darn drunk (the cashier claimed differently) when she entered the Majik Market, an unlikely bikini bandit. When she pulled out her newly acquired gun, thoroughly terrifying the cashier, Aileen says she wasn't thinking ahead to the repercussions. (A theme in her life.) She was too busy wondering what Jay would do if she was caught robbing a store. If he loved her, he'd stand by her and rescue her. Bail her out and take her home. Then she'd know for sure. It would be a true test of his love.

Leaving the Majik, Aileen climbed back into her complaining car and headed towards Jay's place. (She was no longer sure whether it was her place or not.) When the car sputtered to a halt, two Good Samaritans in a pick-up truck helped her push it to the nearest gas station. And there she waited.

When the arresting officers arrived, Aileen went quietly. With her plea of guilty to Robbery with a Weapon, her history as a runaway surfaced, as did the fact that Aileen Carol Wuornos was wanted by the Pueblo, Colorado, Sheriff's Department for Grand Larceny, a crime allegedly committed in 1979.

The complainant was a woman who'd befriended Aileen, given her a place to stay and even handed over $25 for a bus ticket. Aileen had repaid her kindness by stealing a diamond ring worth $1,200, a cassette tape recorder, and a set of luggage. The state of Colorado wanted to extradite her to answer these charges.

Meanwhile, on 4 June 1981, a bewildered Jay Watts enlisted attorney Russell Armstrong to represent his wayward and emotionally precarious young girlfriend. It was a move prompted by friendship and compassion for a fellow human being, rather than an act of love or an investment in a joint future. Russell Armstrong, however, had a profound effect on Jay's course of action. He persuaded Jay that his continuing presence in Aileen's life was essential for her well-being. He was the only thing she had to cling to.

'It's kind of humorous,' Jay recalls. 'Russell said I had such an intense effect on her and she was so deeply involved with me, that he thought it would be traumatic if I just cut the girl off after she got convicted.'

'I told Jay, "If you just cut it cold, I worry about her emotional status,"' Armstrong confirms. So Jay, who never had any intention of getting involved but had a good heart and often came to the aid of lame ducks, stayed in her life. His conscience was clear. He'd never led her on into thinking he had deep feelings for her. But he felt compassion for her, all the same.

Aileen was observed in a psychiatric evaluation for the Department of Corrections to be an unstable individual who, besides claiming to have been repeatedly sexually abused, had suffered a lot of emotional upheavals in her life.

Dr Barnard wrote in his report: 'Clinically, she is judged to be of average intelligence. She has a mild deficit in recent and remote memory. There is no indication of a thought disorder and specifically no loosening of associations or delusions.

Russell Armstrong, however, said it was hard for him to communicate with her: 'I thought her train of thought wasn't following what we were doing. She would fantasise. I wondered if she was in touch with reality.'

Her plea for probation denied, Aileen was sentenced to three years' imprisonment in the Correctional Institute in Lowell, Florida. Dutifully, Jay kept her bicycle and Keith's Bible, and visited weekly. In between times, aching for contact, Aileen wrote him an average of three to five letters a week. Repetitive in content, they addressed her loathing of being shut in with all the lesbian inmates, her embracing of the Bible, and her overwhelming longing to get out and be back with Jay. Whenever he visited her, she lavished him with affection and declarations of love.

'The first time I went, she just started crying a little bit. I said, "Honey, cheer up. I'll be back out here again." Sometimes, Aileen was downright sexually aggressive. 'I'd think I'd need a crowbar to get her off of me. She didn't have any lesbian tendencies then!'

He kept up the visits for a year, but when, one Saturday, he couldn't get there, she just went to pieces. During visits, they were allowed to sit out in the courtyard to get some sun and while guards looked the other way, inmates and their visitors did just about anything short of intercourse. On Jay's last visit before she was moved to Hollywood Community Correctional Center in Pembroke Pines, down near Fort Lauderdale, they were allowed to go back into the laundry area. Before Jay knew it, Aileen was hungrily peeling off his clothes, but he stopped her short. He didn't care how *she* felt about it, but he had no intention of having sex in some prison laundry room.

Languishing in Pembroke Pines, with Jay's letters and visits increasingly scarce, Aileen put an ad in the personals of a biker magazine. In her last letter to Jay, she wrote that she was afraid he was falling out of love with her. She'd had a hundred replies to her ad, which she'd narrowed down to the ten best, and a man from Maryland had been sending her money. She thought Jay should know. He was ecstatic, thinking, 'Wunderbar! The annuity stops!' Finally, she would be out of his hair, and he could stop sending her the fifty bucks or so he mailed off each month.

By the time Aileen was released a few months later, after serving eighteen months, she had lined up a new life for herself. It was to this total stranger that she went, not to loyal, faithful Jay—the proclaimed great love of her life—whose actions had gone so far beyond the call of duty.

13

The 47-year-old Maryland engineer Aileen had corresponded with had answered ads and joined a lonely-hearts-type club looking for romance. Ed was divorced and his brood of grown children had left home. He was the caretaking kind of man who loved having a woman to be good to, but found it increasingly difficult to find one willing to admit she needed help. Aileen, who wrote back to him three times, seemed like she might be the answer to his prayers. She was a country and western singer who was temporarily having problems with her voice. He knew she was incarcerated but was intrigued, and sent her a letter, too. He had no idea of the seriousness of her crime since she dismissed it as a mix-up in a fast-food store. Someone thought she'd been stealing when she hadn't.

Upon her release in August 1983, Aileen hitched her way right to Washington, DC, to meet this new target of her affections. Without warning, she telephoned Ed. She was out, and wanted directions to his place. Excitedly, Ed drove into DC to pick her up, but when his eyes first lit upon his pen pal, she was hardly the personification of his fantasies. She looked older than 27. Slender, though. But very puffy around the eyes. What is more, she was blind, roaring drunk. Somehow, through the haze of alcohol, she slurred out an even less appealing message. She was gay, and he was to keep his hands off her. 'There was to be no touching. She stressed that very strongly,' he recalls.

This news bulletin, coupled with her unattractive inebriation, shifted his mind right away from any tingle of anticipation he'd been feeling. What in heaven had he gotten himself into?

117

There was one point in her favour. She seemed determined to go straight.

'I'll *never* go back to prison,' she hissed fiercely. 'I'll kill myself first! I'll die before I ever go back!'

A tumultuous relationship ensued, and it wasn't even a romance. Aileen was in Ed's life for approximately three rollercoaster months during which she hitched down to Florida twice, only to return like the proverbial bad penny. If he added it up, he doubted she spent more than a total of four weeks under his roof, but it felt like longer. Much longer.

He paid her to do some yard work and housework, and to clean the basement. It gave her some pin money, and she did a decent job. A veritable motor-mouth, she talked incessantly, but nevertheless had a knack with a story and a good sense of humour. She told Ed about her fantasies, or visions, or whatever you'd like to call them. Once, on her way to Florida, she'd seen a spaceship or chariot-like vision in the sky. She talked about religion, too.

One subject she returned to repeatedly was her grandmother Britta, for whom she obviously cared deeply. She didn't talk much about her grandfather, except to say that he beat her and favoured his own children over her and Keith. She wasn't close to Barry, but one day she telephoned Lori for a chat. She spoke of Keith as if her life had been progressing fine until he died of cancer. She'd sat there and watched him die, she said.

She was positively vitriolic when she spoke of her ex-husband, because he mistreated her. She said he was probably lucky to have got out of the marriage alive. Ed got the clear impression that very few men in her life had treated her decently. Just Jay Watts and himself, really. Aileen told Ed he reminded her of her grandmother. A thoughtful man with a kind heart, he took that as a compliment.

He didn't know she was a hooker. But he realised she was getting extra money from somewhere.

Ed was painfully aware of her alcoholism from the very first day they met and they talked often about her drinking. She wanted so much to kick all her bad habits. One day, driving up in the mountains, she made Ed stop the car while, ceremoniously, she tipped all her cigarettes out onto the ground and stomped them into oblivion. She then took her omnipresent bottle of booze, poured it out and smashed it. She climbed back into the car with a smirk of satisfaction spreading across her face.

'I'm never gonna do that again!' she announced.

Yet before they made it back to the house, she made Ed pull in somewhere so she could buy herself a can of beer.

As the days went by, despite his desire to think the best of her, Ed reluctantly concluded that she wasn't merely an alcoholic—she was pretty crazy, too. It seemed like she was either at one end of the spectrum or the other, espousing religion or violence. Nothing in between.

Out of the clear blue sky, a Ford Torino, two-door, hardtop in vivid fire-engine red, pulled into the car place where Jay was working. He noticed the details because he was into cars. Behind the wheel sat Aileen, wearing a neat little hat. That shocked Jay, who had never seen her in anything but a bikini, Levis or buck naked. She looked pretty good to him: trim figure, good-looking, nicely dressed. And she wheeled on over and wrapped him in a big hug and a kiss as if they'd never been apart.

'Hey, Jay! I need a place to stay for a couple of days.'

'This is where we came in, isn't it? What are you saying?'

'Well, I want to stay down here, get some rays.'

Same thing, second course, Jay found himself thinking. But more cautious this time, he added: 'For how long?'

'Maybe a week.'

She moved into his bachelor apartment, bringing in her suitcases, unpacking them neatly and precisely. The car, she said, belonged to the man in Maryland.

'Well, you've hit the big time! That's nice.'

'Come on, let's go for a ride in it.'

When they arrived back in the apartment, nothing sexual transpired between them and Jay decided that staying platonic might be for the best. They went their separate ways that evening. However, by the time Aileen returned in the small hours of the morning, Jay was feeling amorous. He told her to go take a shower and get into bed so they could have sex. But when he joined her under the sheets, she turned him down. At first, he accepted that graciously, but the more he thought about it, the madder he became.

He got up out of the queen-sized bed, walked around the other side, grabbed hold of the covers beneath her and tugged hard, flipping her out of the bed and onto the floor. She just lay there, puzzled and indignant.

'What did you do that for?' she demanded.

'What do you think? And I'm not through yet!'

'You're not going to beat me, are you?'

'No, I don't beat nobody. Have I ever beat you?'

'No, you never have.'

'I'm not going to. You can get back up in bed, or you can stay down there. I don't care what you do. But I have to be at work at 8.30, and I want you out of here by noon. That will give you plenty of time.'

'I need gas for the car. I can't go back there without.'

'It's worth fifty dollars to me to get your ass out of here. OK. I got to write you a cheque, but go through a drive-thru and they'll cash it for you.'

Leaving home in the morning, he found her sleeping on the couch. Tapping her on the rear end, he reminded her of the noon deadline. And sure enough, about thirty minutes ahead of time she pulled into the car lot in the little red car.

'I just want to tell you, bye!' she called, waving to him.

'Good luck, goodbye,' said Jay. 'Go back to your man. Happy life to you!'

And that was the last he saw or heard of her. Almost.

Later, he discovered that she'd stolen the $80 in change he'd saved in a jar, and that she'd cashed the $50 cheque and used it to forge another cheque for $100. The coins made him madder. It was the principle of the thing. He dialled the Maryland number and with flawless timing, reached Aileen, who had just pulled up from her trip.

'I don't know what you think you're doing, but your ass has gone too far with me!' Jay shouted. 'As good as I've been to you, and as much as I've done for you, you rip me off! You can tell

Daddy Warbucks up there that if he wants to keep your ass from going back in again, just send me back the money!'

To his immense surprise, a cheque arrived within a week.

While living with Ed, Aileen kept a baseball bat propped behind the door, but no gun that he knew of. There was no mistaking her fascination with Bonnie and Clyde-type stories or with leather-clad bikers. She had a whole cache of biker yarns and spoke, too, of a woman she'd lived with in Colorado. But she couldn't go back there, she told Ed. She was wanted out there. (That much was true.) Her taste for hanging out in biker bars remained, and one night she took Ed along with her.

'I embarrassed her because I don't shoot pool . . . and one of my shots went over on the floor. She grabbed me by the arm and marched me out of there real quick!'

A couple of times a man she'd met in a biker bar collected her from Ed's place in his pick-up truck. She once returned home from one of these outings, shaken and very scared, muttering something about a rape and saying that she was going to get into trouble. Ed never could get the story straight.

One of her Colorado tales that made a particularly lasting impression featured a hefty, 6 foot 2 inch biker she'd dated who had tried to rape her. Somehow, she'd managed to turn the tables and kick him in the groin; then she got him on the ground and started stomping on his head, Aileen told him, acting out the role as she went.

'Apparently, she really got a bit high out of beating his face into a pulp,' Ed recalls.

And yet, in her own way, Aileen always struck him as very feminine. She owned no clothes beyond those she stood up in when she arrived in Maryland and had since commandeered some of Ed's, wearing a T-shirt to sleep in. She had some quirks. She didn't like toes in socks, so cut them out of the pairs he loaned her. Nor did she like clothes that came up high around her neck. She took the scissors to a couple of Ed's good sweaters and chopped the necklines down.

Ed took her shopping at the local mall and bought her a few gifts and was struck anew by the fascination for leather that had

121

emerged in her biker stories when she saw a leather jacket. She just *had* to have it. She talked a lot about boots, too. But he didn't let her con him into buying her any boots.

One lazy Sunday afternoon after lunch, Aileen took Ed completely by surprise. He'd had no reason to doubt her claim that she was gay and had put sex with her out of his mind altogether. So he was shocked when she suddenly declared: 'I'm horny as hell and I'm bored. Let's go have sex!'

'I thought you told me you were gay? You told me not to ever touch you.'

'I was just joking! Let's go find out how gay I am.'

Taking the initiative, she led him into her bedroom, where Ed entered her from behind. It wasn't what he'd describe as a kinky encounter by any stretch of the imagination. In fact, it was very pleasant.

Afterward, he lay on the bed in her room, relaxed and satisfied, his ego nicely rubbed by her statement that it was the best sex she'd ever had. Ed had two marriages behind him but wasn't the most experienced man in the world and rather felt the same.

Then, five minutes later, Aileen stunned him for the second time that day. Faster than he could fathom what had hit him, her mood had done a 180-degree turn. She came into the room brandishing a kitchen utensil and snarling, 'I'm gonna kill you!'

'Aileen! I don't understand! What's wrong?' Ed cried, flying to his feet and talking to her in as soothing a voice as he could muster. He had seen her flare up before and seen her change in an instant, and while it was nothing like this, he knew that he could only wait for whatever had happened in her mind to pass.

He uttered a silent prayer of thanks that he didn't keep guns in the house. He was also grateful that some time earlier, put on guard by her erratic behaviour, he'd had the foresight to gather all his butcher knives and hide them on top of the downstairs heat duct where she would never find them.

Deep down, Ed had the feeling that her threat to kill him was a perverse way of trying to get his attention. He knew he lived a bit in his own world, oblivious to others. He could easily get wrapped up in reading a newspaper or watching TV and wasn't the most attentive fellow. But the timing of her outburst, the proximity to the sex, was curious, to say the least.

During the next couple of weeks, her last under Ed's roof, Aileen sat up all night, glued to the TV. She lay in the Lazy Boy wearing his big, heavy robe and encased in a couple of blankets. She was always cold. You'd think it was December in Alaska instead of August in Maryland, the way she bundled up, cuddling with Lady, the little dog she'd found. She treated Lady like a baby, she loved her so much.

Aileen couldn't get enough of those TV preachers whose rhetoric seemed to enthral her, hour after hour. (Ed did not share her viewing tastes.) She even wrote a fan letter to Jim Bakker, telling him that she'd been watching him on TV. Jim and Tammy's ministries sent her a large, expensive-looking, fake-leather-bound Bible in the mail, which she kept. She didn't pay for it, of course. And when she'd had her fill of TV evangelism, she'd snuggle under the bedcovers and sleep all day long.

One night Aileen persuaded Ed to drive her to a local medical centre for some pills. What she wanted were mild tranquillisers, but Ed couldn't see the doctors handing them over to her.

'I'll drive you, but they're not gonna give you what you want,' he warned her. 'They're only going to give you Valium.'

Outside the waiting-room, her previously jovial mood snapped as she suddenly flew into a screaming fit, hurling abuse at him. But inside, she behaved herself. Questioned about how she would pay for her treatment, she straight-facedly announced that she was a movie star and filled in the application form accordingly. Of course, she had no money. Ed was taken to one side for a little chat by a female counsellor, and when he confided the threats she'd made against him, he was warned to take them very seriously. The counsellor advised him to get her out of his life as quickly as possible, and preferably to get her out of the state. (He put the emphasis on the state down to the fact that the hospital didn't want her being a financial burden on Maryland.) He had a feeling the counsellor was right, but that didn't help him get rid of Aileen.

Back outside, her mood shifted just as quickly again as she

gloated about coercing the quack psychologist into giving her exactly what she wanted.

The situation at home was becoming urgent and Ed's agenda all too clear—he had to get her out of the house before she made good her threat to kill him. Things came to a head the day the Maryland State Police knocked on the door while Ed was at work, issuing her a summons for passing a school bus while it was stationary. Burning with righteous indignation, she telephoned Ed to inform him of this development.

He was not pleased. This reckless creature was driving his car, and heaven knows what havoc she'd wreak with his insurance. That was all he needed.

By the time Ed got home, Aileen had methodically drunk herself into a stupor. It was a worse than usual episode triggered, he didn't doubt, by her fear that she'd end up in jail again. And while he was convinced that alcohol was the major contributor to her condition, something about her behaviour made him suspect that she'd taken drugs, too, that day. When he walked in, she staggered out into the hall and collapsed; passed out cold. It just confirmed for him the wisdom of his plan to have her admitted for psychiatric testing at Finan Center in Cumberland. The stumbling block had been that he hadn't figured out quite how he was going to get her down there. In a way, this episode was heaven-sent.

'A gift from the gods!' thought Ed, who was nevertheless scared she might die in his house. He quickly picked up the telephone and summoned the rescue squad, who took Aileen to the hospital overnight. From there, she would be taken to Finan the next morning.

Later, while cleaning out her room, Ed stumbled across an old news clipping of Aileen's that informed him that his recently departed house-guest had, in fact, been convicted of armed robbery.

Later, Aileen gave her account of what transpired with Ed: they'd had a fight, she'd got drunk on Mad Dog wine, and she'd then let loose a vacuum cleaner bag full of dirt and dust all over Ed's white furniture. He'd been so mad at her that he had her committed to a mental institution.

Ed thought that story showed flair and imagination. He didn't even own a white sofa.

Neither one of them held any grudge despite Ed's insistence that it was time she moved on. In fact, Ed visited her a couple of times during her short spell in the hospital and listened to her plans to join Jim and Tammy Faye Bakker's religious community, Heritage USA, in North Carolina. As a member of Jim and Tammy's flock, she would go out and save the world. True to her word, she did hitch there (sending Ed a postcard) and stayed a couple of weeks before heading back to her old stamping ground of Florida.

About six months later, Ed took a call from Lori, who was trying to track Aileen down. Apparently, the cops had been looking for her.

When everything went quiet for a year in Maryland, Ed thought he'd heard the last of Aileen. Then, out of the blue, he received a letter. She was living with a female lover, running a carpet-cleaning business, and things weren't going so well. Could she come back? No way, he thought.

14

Aileen dropped the bombshell during a phone call to Lori, who was then, in 1984, living in Arizona. 'I'm gay, and I know you're not going to like that,' she cheerfully announced, explaining that she was very much in love with a woman named Toni. Toni was the first homosexual lover Aileen acknowledged having, although it wasn't the first time she'd described herself as gay. Since she had chosen to instigate sexual encounters with men when there was no pressure to do so, and seemed to enjoy sex with men, she might have described herself as bisexual, but 'gay' was her word of choice. She and Toni were going to start a pressure-cleaning business together, she told Lori. If they saved enough money, they planned to buy a house with a yard and a fence. All very domestic and cosy. (During this period, Aileen was arrested in Key West on two counts of forgery after passing a couple of cheques totalling $5,595. She skipped off to Daytona and failed to show up for her sentencing hearing, saying later that they were trumped-up charges.)

Lori, who had noticed how her sister often talked about wanting to own a car and material things, but never voiced the desire for a husband and children, wished she could shut out what she was hearing about Aileen being gay. She tried not to let Aileen sense how she felt—what good would that do?—but in truth, she was so shocked to learn that Aileen was a lesbian that she couldn't even bring herself to share this piece of unwanted news with her own husband. Erv didn't learn the truth for years. Just as her father had swept Aileen's pregnancy under the rug, Lori swept this. Another family skeleton in the closet.

'It was embarrassing enough to have a sister like that, much less pile on more stuff, you know?' she explains. 'It just galled me.'

When Aileen proudly mailed Lori a photograph of Toni—a short, chunky woman with cropped, dark hair—Lori was so appalled that she threw it out immediately. Later, when Aileen wanted the picture back, Lori had to lie and pretend to be looking for it. And she lived in fear that Aileen might actually carry out her promise that she and Toni would stop and visit when they hitchhiked across the country.

'I thought, "I'll die! I swear I'll die if she comes over with this girl. I'll be so embarrassed I have a lesbian sister."'

It was no surprise to Lori, of course, that Aileen hated men. She recalled only too well the way Aileen had treated her own boyfriends before she married Erv, threatening them: 'You keep your hands off her!' or 'Don't you ever touch her, or I'll get you!'

When she telephoned, Aileen always demanded to know how Erv was treating Lori. Was he hitting her? (Not that he ever had.) She threatened to 'come and take care of him' if he didn't treat Lori properly. Then, she'd always been protective. Back when they were teenagers and Lori expressed excitement at the prospect of trying drugs, Aileen had ordered, 'You're not touching them!' She always wanted to shield her from anything dangerous or ugly.

Whenever Aileen talked about men, it seemed associated with violence or with being used.

She once told Lori she belonged to a motorcycle gang and complained of being gang-banged. But then she also said that out in Colorado she was some kind of FBI agent or government worker. 'Yeah! Right! Sure!' thought Lori.

Aileen's various claims to having been raped also told Lori there was no love lost between Aileen and the males of the species. But Lori thought that would make you become a loner, not get romantically and sexually involved with women.

She came to dread Aileen's periodic calls. She never knew exactly where Aileen was calling from because Aileen always kept her whereabouts a secret, saying, 'You'll only get in trouble if I tell you.' Inevitably, Lori hung up worrying terribly about her anew, wondering if she was living on the streets and what kind of trouble she was in, but impotent to do anything. It seemed as if each time life was getting back to normal, Aileen would surface and shake her up all over again. Lori felt some relief when the calls all came from the state of Florida. She could comfort herself by imagining that perhaps Aileen had settled down.

The calls were often prolonged, disjointed, rambling monologues, and Lori held the receiver away from her ear in frustration and let Aileen drone on, particularly when her sister was preaching God and the Lord to her, hardly pausing for breath. The end of the world was nigh, Aileen announced, urging Lori to go to church, to read the Bible, and to believe in God for her sins so that she would go to heaven.

'She'd say, "Oh, I've changed. I'm a good person now. I'm serving the Lord and I'm reading the Bible and I'm on page such-and-such." She could quote from the Bible without even picking it up.'

Somehow, Lori couldn't help feeling instantly depressed when she heard Aileen's voice, and couldn't wait for the conversations—if you could call them that—to end. She always felt a strong sense of impending disaster. A feeling (something akin to that experienced by the family members of hardline drug addicts) that her sister's life was bound to end in tragedy and it was only a matter of time. She often envisaged her being hit by a car or killed by some crazy person.

'It sounds terrible to say it and well, she isn't . . . but I knew in my mind she would end up dead eventually. You can't hitchhike on the streets for ever and not have something happen. . . . I was just waiting for that day to come, and it would be over with, and I wouldn't have to worry about her any more.'

Prowling the highways, looking for rides, Aileen didn't passively wait for men to stop, but targeted specific vehicles, flagging down likely drivers. She invariably singled out older men, believing she'd be safer riding with them. There was less likelihood they'd be heavy druggies or flying high on crack, which in turn meant less likelihood of aggression or problems. A little pot or alcohol she could handle, but she didn't want men who were out of control.

She liked her customers. She liked having sex with them. Perhaps she was gay. Perhaps not.

She didn't sexually proposition every man who stopped for her. At least, not right off. Her opening gambit was often to pass herself off as a woman in trouble and therefore, of course, in need of money. She varied her tales of woe from 'My babies are sick at home' to 'My rent is due' or 'My car's broke down'.

Whether portraying herself as a pressure-cleaner operator or a professional call girl (as she liked to call it), she always laid claim to a host of regular, satisfied customers, many of whom, she said, were police officers, detectives, FBI men, attorneys. Making her point, she flashed her wallet full of business cards (not lingering long enough to allow careful scrutiny) to anyone interested enough to look.

In 1985, she stopped a man called Dennis just south of Ocala on I-75, telling him her name was Lori Grody. They quickly dispensed with the polite preliminaries and drove off to his business trailer for sex. When she took off her clothes, he noted a puncture wound in her stomach area. Looked like a gunshot or stab wound, but he didn't know which. After the sex, 'Lori' asked for a ride down to New Port Richey. Dennis obliged. Only after she'd got out, did he notice he'd been robbed for his trouble. She'd stolen the .38-calibre Welby revolver that he kept in his car.

Aileen's grandiose behaviour had begun to take full flight and, not entirely coincidentally, her criminal record kept building. In 1985 she was stopped in Florida's Pasco County in a stolen car without a valid licence. In January of 1986, she was at it again with one of her more ludicrous episodes. Finding herself confronting a driver's licence check point, she tried to evade it by hastily turning around the brown Chevy Blazer she was driving and speeding off in the opposite direction. She was spotted and stopped anyway, and asked to produce a licence. She'd left it in a store—could she go get it? No. And please get out of the car, she was told, politely but firmly. As the officers ran the Blazer's plates and learned that the woman who called herself Lori Grody was in a stolen vehicle, she repeatedly asked to be allowed to leave.

She seemed unduly anxious to get back to the car. Suspicions aroused, one officer strolled over to the Blazer and did a search, quickly uncovering a pistol and a box of .38 specials in the console.

Just as the second officer moved to arrest her, Aileen suddenly made a run for it, employing a desperate measure that might have been comical were it not for the poor innocent driver involved. Racing across the highway, she hurtled towards another car whose driver had innocently stopped at the check point. Reaching the astounded man's car she literally lunged through his open passenger window, screaming for him to get out. Before the motorist had any idea what had hit him, one of the officers in hot pursuit finally caught up with her, pulled her back out by her legs, and triumphantly slapped on the handcuffs.

For Aileen, it was typically short-sighted, impulsive behaviour. As a solution to a problem, it was doomed to failure.

She was arrested again in June. (A busy month in which she was also ticketed for driving at 72 m.p.h. while carrying the licence of one Susan Lynn Blahovec.) She was riding with a man called Wayne Manning, heavily engrossed in an argument over whether or not he'd stolen her money, when a park ranger stopped their 1982 Dodge pick-up truck near Bulow Creek State Park. The ranger was acting on what turned out to be an unfounded report of a robbery in progress. Routinely checking out the pick-up, however, he learned it had been listed by Manning's grandfather as stolen.

Searching the truck, the Volusia County deputies who arrived on the scene found a loaded .22 revolver in a brown paper bag, tucked under the passenger seat. Aileen (using the name Lori Grody) denied owning the gun. She claimed she didn't know it was there. 'My eyes popped out of my head, though, 'cause I couldn't believe it. This guy mighta killed me or something, you know!' Only problem: she trapped herself by denying that 'the .22' was hers: no one had said anything about a .22. She then launched into various alternative scenarios, veering from saying she and Manning were off on a shooting expedition, to saying she'd seen the gun only because Manning showed it to her. 'I said why should I be charged with a concealed weapon when it's not even my damned gun?'

When twelve rounds of .22-calibre ammo were subsequently found in her overnight bag, she still stuck to her colander-like story. Never quick to take responsibility, she then changed her stance: Manning had planted the ammunition on her. Manning's more plausible story was that they'd got into an argument after Aileen accused him of stealing $200 from her and that she'd then pulled the gun on him.

That day, as Lori Kristine Grody, Aileen was arrested on an outstanding warrant from Pasco County for carrying a concealed firearm. There was another concealed firearm warrant for her in Volusia. Manning was also arrested.

And the brown bulldog who'd sat patiently in the back of the pick-up throughout this fiasco was collected by the Humane Society.

15

'There's someone in bed with Tyria!' Cammie and Dinky Greene's two young sons blurted out, rushing into their parents' bedroom. It was an otherwise normal Saturday morning in June 1986. The boys, shocked, had beaten a hasty retreat after sticking their heads around the bedroom door as was their ritual to wake their buddy, Ty.

In the two years the Greenes had known her, Ty had never brought anyone home. Cammie and Dinky were taken aback, but pleased. Perhaps she'd finally met someone nice?

'It's a girl in there with her,' was the boys' postscript.

Cammie and Dinky exchanged glances. Cammie had realised pretty swiftly that her short, squat and stocky red-headed friend was attracted to women, not men. At first sight, from a distance, Cammie had even thought she was a guy. Ty, with a small heart tattooed on her left upper arm, and her uniform of shorts, T-shirt and one of those ball caps with a beer logo, didn't advertise her sexual preference at first, but had soon opened up to non-judgemental Cammie. If they saw some pretty girls on TV, Ty would say how cute one was, and they'd all laugh. She'd been gay as long as she could remember. But her parents didn't know, and she didn't want them to know, either. She'd been stabbed at the age of thirteen for messing with another girl's girlfriend and she'd even managed to keep that from them.

Tyria Jolene Moore's real mom died when she was just two. Tyria (pronounced Ty-ra) was raised in Ohio by her father, Jack Moore, and his next wife Mary Ann, to whom Ty was close. She had just one photograph by which to remember her real mother. She lost all her other mementoes after once putting her possessions in storage. When she couldn't pay the rental fee to retrieve

132

them, the owner confiscated everything, family albums and all, and they were lost for ever.

Tyria and Cammie's family first became neighbours on Halifax Drive in Holly Hill near Daytona Beach, early in 1984. Ty's front door faced Cammie's back door and inevitably the two women bumped into each other the very day the Greenes moved in. One of Cammie's small sons was stung by a bee and Ty rallied around, trying to soothe the sting with mud. They felt a connection: they were both born in August 1962. Ty was fun, easygoing, and had a sunny disposition. She was never in a bad mood. Ever. And for a long time she was Cammie Greene's only true friend.

After Ty was evicted from her apartment, the Greenes took her under their wing as an extended-family member and, depending upon her fluctuating circumstances, she lived with them from time to time. When they moved into a spacious house on Highridge in Holly Hill, Ty went too, while she waited for a room to become vacant at the motel where she was working. She'd made herself popular (and somewhat indispensable) to her employers because of her knack with maintenance jobs. Ty was quite the Ms Fix-It. The Greenes often stopped by to swim in the motel pool. When Ty had to give up her room there, she simply moved in with Cammie and Dinky. Their door was always open.

Ty had moved out to Florida from Ohio in 1983 (the year the Greenes' son Jason was born) using the money she received from a car accident settlement. She met a woman called Marcia and lived with her and her two children in a house that no longer exists, on a boat dock along the Halifax River. The two broke up after a fight amidst great animosity. Indeed, after Ty slipped back to Marcia's to collect her belongings, the police picked her up for breaking and entering. It was the only criminal blot on her otherwise pristine record.

When Cammie and Dinky met Ty, she was still raw from the recent split with her girlfriend, in fact they sometimes ran into Marcia and she'd often holler and cuss at Ty. Sometimes, they'd get into a full-scale fight.

When Cammie met her, Ty was a regular churchgoer, attending two or three services a week at the local Baptist church and socialising with other churchgoers. She repeatedly asked Cammie to go with her, but Cammie declined. Ty often took the boys though, and even babysat for the preacher's kids. After work, Ty often had her head stuck in a Bible. She found no conflict between her belief in the Good Book and her lesbianism. The only things she vehemently opposed were all references implying that women should obey men. No way.

Ty met Aileen Wuornos (who'd adopted the name Lee, a truncated version of Aileen) in the Zodiac bar, a gay hangout in Daytona that has since closed. For Lee, it was love at first sight when she saw Ty drinking at the bar. Aileen/Lee did not know it but Ty, with her strawberry-blonde hair and freckles, had colouring that was uncannily similar to Leo Pittman's.

All Cammie knew was that the two women stayed in Ty's room for three straight days and nights. Ty emerged only to fetch food.

'I met somebody last night!' she whispered to Cammie when they ran into each other in the kitchen. 'I'll introduce you to her over the weekend.'

The lovers went shopping for sex toys, including a long white rubber dildo that Cammie stumbled across one day and that Dinky would periodically produce when the women were gone to give his friends a good laugh, saying, 'See what these girls play with?'

Certainly, when Ty and Lee were in the Greenes' household, sex played a part in their relationship. Ty confided in Cammie and even had a joke about it. She hobbled around awkwardly, complaining that she hurt. Lee, who apparently took on the male role, was just too much for her, she said.

Lee kept a low profile through that entire first weekend until the Monday morning. She came out and showed her face after Dinky (whose real name is Monnin) had left for work. Even as a little girl, Ty had thought girls were cuter than guys. She liked men as friends, she just had no desire to be in a relationship with them. Lee, on the other hand, hated men. Or so she said. Cammie thought she was pretty, if a little chunky, and a somewhat unlikely companion for the homely and hefty Tyria. Cammie was torn. She was happy for Ty that she'd found a girlfriend, but she couldn't shake a bad feeling she had about Lee. She couldn't put her finger on it, but it just wouldn't go away.

Lee had said that she was in the pressure-cleaning business and she went off hitchhiking for days at a time, supposedly to Zephyrhills or Ocala or wherever. Sometimes Cammie dropped her off near I-95 which is where she'd start hitchhiking.

'Aren't you scared?' asked Cammie.

'No. Not as long as middle-aged guys pick me up,' Lee replied. She told Cammie she never rode with young guys or with 'coloureds'.

Often, she left on a Monday or Tuesday and was back before Friday, then she and Ty spent the weekend at the house. She always returned with hundreds of dollars in cash which she and Ty promptly blew in bars, only occasionally chipping in on a household bill.

Lee never washed dishes or did any chores around the house, but the pattern of her relationship with Ty was emerging. Cammie noticed she was pretty good at bossing Tyria around. Lee shaved her legs and insisted Ty also shave hers. It was something that Ty, whose legs were often as hairy as Dinky's, hated doing but she did as Lee said. Lee didn't like her woman working and soon Ty gave up her low-paid motel job and lay in bed all morning, sleeping.

Ty, who'd also given up churchgoing since she met Lee, wasn't afraid of work, but she enjoyed taking it easy while Lee brought home the bacon. Lee definitely liked having her woman there, waiting. When she was gone, affable Ty helped Cammie around the house, folding clothes, doing dishes. But Lee did not like it one little bit if Ty was off helping Cammie with something when she came home.

Neither Ty nor Lee ever made a pass at Cammie, a petite, slender, fair-haired woman with a strikingly pretty, heart-shaped face. Yet Cammie knew Lee was somehow threatened by her relationship with Ty, even though it was only friendship. Indeed, Ty confirmed her suspicion, telling her: 'Lee is really jealous over me and you!'

'She *is?*' Cammie replied.

'Cammie, I really respect you and I would never try anything with you.'

'What about Lee? Don't you respect her?'

'No.'

Ty had a good heart. She enjoyed doing things for people, particularly when Lee was away, and once brought home some orange paint from her job, knowing it was Cammie's favourite colour. For a surprise, she painted Cammie's bathrooms, kitchen cabinets and even her refrigerator. Cammie certainly was surprised. It was a veritable orange onslaught.

'She was so happy because she thought I'd be happy,' she recalls. 'I said, "Well, it's *nice*, Tyria! It's nice and bright!"'

Lee became a familiar sight, drifting around with a beer in her hand first thing in the morning. Tyria groaned and said she couldn't handle it that early in the day. But they could plough through a case of beer in a day with no problem. Sometimes more. They ate separately and Ty cooked for them, fixing noodles or burgers or other simple fare. Lee always avoided sitting at the table and eating with Dinky.

Sometimes Cammie knocked on Ty and Lee's bedroom door to see if Lee was going to work and wanted a ride. One morning, Lee called back that she wasn't, then opened the door. Cammie saw a big, shiny black eye staring back at her. She must have been beaten up.

'Shouldn't you call anybody?' asked Cammie, shocked.

'No, it's no big deal. I was raped,' Lee replied dismissively. Later, Ty explained to Cammie that Lee had spent the night in a motel where somebody had tried to snatch her money. When she wouldn't let them have it, they got in a fight and the guy then raped her. The story didn't quite ring true to Cammie. Somehow, she just couldn't imagine Lee being raped.

Already suspicious of her mystery house-guest, Cammie was waiting for an opportunity to look inside the vanity-sized, square, tan suitcase that Lee always took on the road with her. She might learn something about her if she could get a peek inside. When Lee was safely out of the house, Cammie grabbed her chance and went into their room and sifted through her belongings. The suitcase housed a sizable stock of condoms—not

136

generally part of a gay woman's paraphernalia—and a collection of men's business cards. Lee never wore jewellery but Cammie had noticed that she owned a couple of men's rings and watches. She said they came from customers who couldn't pay their cleaning bills. She told Cammie she had a storage place full of belongings, too. Would Cammie like to buy a ring for Dinky? Cammie declined. Dinky didn't care for rings.

'Don't tell him that I wanted to sell you any,' Lee instructed her. 'Don't tell him I have any rings or anything.'

'Ty,' Cammie said one day when they were alone, 'I don't think Lee has a pressure-cleaning business. I think she's prostituting.'

When Ty first met Lee, Lee had billed herself as a drugs dealer, but Ty had long since learned that her lover was a hooker. Put on the spot by Cammie, however, she played dumb. She told Cammie she shared her suspicions.

'Aren't you gonna say anything to her about it?' Cammie asked.

Ty said she didn't want to rock the boat.

'Isn't Lee scared of riding with strangers?'

'No. She knows who to ride with. Older guys.'

Looking back, Cammie was sure Ty knew about Lee's hooking all along, but Lee never did admit to it in Cammie's presence.

Lee owned a CO_2 cartridge BB gun. She said she needed it for protection in case anyone messed with her, and often she and Ty practised shooting at beer cans or the trees in the backyard. Cammie finished work at two in the afternoon, and she sometimes sat out there with them and practised too. Lee wasn't any great shakes at hitting a target. Cammie was definitely a better shot than either Lee or Tyria. Cammie never knew Lee to have a real gun, but a BB gun with a CO_2 cartridge was quite powerful. About as powerful as a .22.

Lee once showed Cammie a scar on her stomach, claiming she'd been shot while holding up a store. Cammie didn't believe her. She didn't even believe it was a bullet wound.

For some curious reason, Lee hated the idea of Dinky knowing anything about her. She didn't like him, true, but it was more than that. Perhaps she thought he could see through her. She told

Cammie, however, that she'd been abused as a child. She also spoke of an ex-husband who was the richest man in Georgia, and an ex-lover in Key Largo called Toni with whom she had lived in a big mansion.

'That woman took everything from me,' Lee complained. 'I wish I could kill her.' After they split up, Lee said, she knew she wouldn't get anything so she went back to the house to destroy everything.

Cammie thought Lee just liked to come off as tough, but she certainly had a temper. Once she commented on a big bruise on Ty's leg. Lee had hit her, Ty said, but she'd hit her back. Husky Ty could give as good as she got and by sheer weight alone could have doubtless overpowered Lee. Cammie wasn't too concerned about her that way. Besides, by August, the girls had moved out to be on their own and the Greenes rarely saw them.

They drifted from one motel to another until by fall, Tyria finally landed a job. She was hired as a maid at the Pierre Motel in Zephyrhills. She and Lee had just ridden up on her moped, one backpack between them, hoping to find work and needing a place to stay. They checked in for two nights, but when Kathy Beasman, the Pierre's owner, insisted the blonde fill out the guest register, she thought it odd the way her new guest seemed to be casting around, confused, for a name to use. Eventually, she signed in Cher-style. Lee was the only name Kathy ever knew for her.

Kathy needed help but could only afford to hire one person. Within a couple of days, she liked Ty enough to hire her, throwing in a free room as part of the pay deal. With her work history and gentler demeanour, Ty was the natural choice. The Pierre's clientele was primarily retired folk. Regulars. It was almost like a family community. They came each year and stayed for the season, which lasted anything from three to six months. Tyria's warm personality made her very popular with the guests. She was a good worker. Very pleasant, minded her own business. And Lee gave the guests a wide berth. The arrangement worked well.

It was clear to Kathy that Lee was the boss, yet she sensed a lost quality in her. Lee kept following her around, intently saying: 'I'm looking for a good Christian person. It's very important to me to find a good Christian person.'

Kathy, who believed she fitted the bill, listened understandingly to Lee's tales of being verbally abused and hit by both her mother and father. And, oh, she missed her brother, Keith, so much! Kathy's strong sense that Lee had not been loved was compounded by her revelation that she'd been on the streets prostituting to survive since she was eleven. She'd had a baby, too, but said, 'I don't ever want to meet him or have him find out who I am.' How sad, Kathy thought.

She told Kathy that she'd been partners in a pressure-cleaning business with her ex-lover, Toni, until they had a major falling out, but she still owned part of the business. Finally satisfied that Kathy wouldn't condemn her for it, she admitted she was a hooker. She hated it, and only did it out of necessity when they ran out of cash. She had to keep them fed and get them shelter. Ty hated her hooking, too. Kathy never knew Lee actually to go look for any regular employment, but at least she kept her prostitution well away from the motel. She never hitched nearby and never brought any guys back.

'When I was married to Lewis Fell, I sang in a nightclub,' Lee wistfully told Kathy, and hearing her sing, Kathy was surprisingly impressed. A gorgeous voice, she thought. But if she'd sung once, why didn't she do it again? Surely, it had to be better than prostitution?

'There'll be a book written about me one day,' Lee told her confidently. Kathy thought that unlikely, but why burst her bubble?

At night, Ty sometimes sat and wrote long, chatty letters to her stepmother, Mary Ann Moore, and to her family in Ohio. Seeing her girlfriend engrossed in that intimate ritual made feelings of jealousy and discomfort erupt in Lee. It bothered her greatly that Ty had someone else in the world besides her to whom she felt close. Someone that cared enough about her to want to know where she was at any given moment. It hurt her that Ty had a family she cared for and that she didn't. It would have suited Lee to see Ty cut off from her family altogether. She'd have felt more secure if they were both in the same lonely boat. She wished she was Ty's whole world, just as Ty was hers. She hated the way she felt inside if she ever thought about life without her. After Mom and Keith, she just couldn't stand to lose somebody else. She knew she couldn't ever let that happen.

Ty and Lee settled into a routine at the Pierre. Kathy gave them permission to shoot the BB gun out back and they duly practised every day. Kathy thought it rather funny, the way Lee pulled her gun out of her pocket like a parody of a western gunslinger. Pull, aim, fire. Pull, aim, fire. She seemed bent on perfecting her quickdraw technique.

Lee and Ty rarely ate anything nutritious, all they did was drink beer. Lots of it. Indeed, Lee bloated up so badly, she was convinced she had some kind of tumour. She took herself off for a rare trip to a doctor, but he assured her that it was nothing more sinister than beer bloat. She'd better cut down on her drinking.

When money ran out, Kathy sometimes helped them with a small loan, but they always honoured it, even paid her back double, handing over a ten here, a twenty there. So Kathy didn't even worry when at one point the loan rose to $200. She trusted them. Sure enough, they paid her back in full. But trouble was brewing. Kathy asked them to leave in the spring of '87. It wasn't just their excessive drinking. They had been flaunting their gay relationship—kissing and holding hands out by the pool. It had offended and upset some of her elderly guests. Kathy was sorry, there was nothing she could do.

By then, Ty had sold her moped, so they left what had been a semblance of security on foot. For a month or so, they motel-hopped, resuming their earlier nomadic existence. Sometimes, they took their backpack and slept out in the orange groves or camped in the woods, or by the railroad tracks. The weather was reasonably kind, but by April 1987, they'd had enough of roughing it.

Ty and Lee reappeared at Cammie and Dinky Greene's door. Could they stay? Ty told them how they'd been sleeping outdoors but had picked out a spot where they could see a bread truck make its 3 a.m. delivery drop at a supermarket. That way, Ty could run over and pick off a couple of loaves before the store opened.

To Cammie, that was stealing, plain and simple. It put her in mind of the time she and Dinky were looking for a camper top for their truck, and Ty and Lee took her to see one they'd spotted.

'Come on, Ty, help me pick this up and we'll put it on her truck,' Lee had said, bending down to lift a corner to assess how heavy it was.

'What are you doing?' Cammie had interrupted anxiously. 'Let me go up there and ask the guy what size it is and see what he wants for it.'

'Oh, we don't have to do that. We'll just throw it on the truck and take off!' Lee replied.

'No! We ain't gonna do that!' Cammie shot back.

'Hey! What are you all doing?' Suddenly a man was walking towards them.

'Is this your camper top?' Cammie called. 'Why don't you come down here, and let's talk about it?'

Ultimately the size was wrong, but there was no doubt in Cammie's mind that they'd have stolen it in a hot minute. Cammie thought, not for the first time, that Lee was definitely not a good influence on Ty. Now, here they were, back again. Cammie and Dinky didn't mind Ty moving back in, but they categorically did not want Lee. Not wanting to say that, they just acted hesitant. Lee was going to be gone a lot on the road and she just hated the idea of leaving Ty alone in a motel, she said, appealing to their soft hearts. She'd pay the Greenes if they would please look after Ty for her. Ty was always welcome. She could stay without paying, they said. To their utter dismay, when Ty moved back in, Lee simply wormed her way back in with her. This time round, Lee Wuornos and Dinky Greene clashed badly. Even with Cammie and Tyria playing peacemakers, they simply couldn't get along. The Greenes reluctantly went along with it for Ty's sake. They certainly didn't do it for the rent money. For all their talk, Lee and Ty only ever handed over small amounts, $20 here and $30 there.

'Every family needs a Tyria,' Cammie used to say. Ty was so

great with the kids. When Lee was gone, she fitted back in as one of the family, going to the boys' baseball games, popping to the grocery store, getting all fired up at a wrestling match with Cammie and Dinky, watching football games on TV, playing catch with the kids. She did everything they did.

Ty bought a motorcycle for $50 and she and Dinky played around with it every night until finally they got it running. Then they rode it hard in the woods until they drove it right into the ground.

Cammie once took Ty and Lee to the beach with the kids. She couldn't believe it. They all lay there on the sand, relaxing. Lee and Ty were both watching the girls walk by—then they got furious at one another for ogling.

At home, Lee kept to her man-hating line. When Dinky's friends came over she stormed through the house, loudly asking Ty: 'When are those guys leaving?' But Cammie could never quite get out of her mind the feeling that the man-hating business was an act she put on. Somehow it just didn't seem genuine.

Lee was never rude to Cammie, although Cammie instinctively knew that there were times it was better to give her a wide berth. Dinky, who thought she was an obnoxious know-all, wasn't so diplomatic and couldn't resist baiting her.

'You think you know everything!' he'd say.

'Oh yeah? I do know everything!' Lee screamed back.

Much as Dinky liked Ty, he wasn't keen on what they were doing under his roof and in front of his sons. They kissed just like boyfriend and girlfriend.

'We told them we didn't care what they did in the bedroom but not to be doing it in front of the kids,' Cammie recalls. 'And I think Lee just would do it because she knew it aggravated us.'

Dinky decided that they'd been on their best behaviour when they were angling to move in, but once they got their way about that, they just started doing as they pleased. Finally, he told them they would have to take their stuff and get out. Lee threw one of her fits. Dinky, unimpressed, just laughed. But they stayed put. Things came to an ugly head again the night Lee wanted to eat in the living room and Dinky told her she must eat at the dining table. She flew off the handle, leapt from her chair shouting, 'I'll kill him! I'll kill him!'

Dinky didn't take the threat seriously, but Cammie was stunned, and scared. Judging by Ty's reaction, Cammie had the distinct feeling that she also believed Lee could do it. Ty struggled to pick Lee up bodily and somehow managed to manoeuvre her into the bedroom where she eventually calmed her down. Once again, things settled down.

For Mother's Day in May 1987, a whole family entourage including Cammie, Dinky, the kids, Dinky's mother, brothers and sisters, set off on a truck ride up to North Carolina to visit Cammie's mom for a week's vacation. Sandra, Cammie's three-year-old niece, was living with her at the time and Ty suggested that since the truck was so full, they leave Sandra with her and Lee. Cammie, trusting Ty completely, agreed. She did not trust Lee, but she knew Tyria would never let any harm come to Sandra. In fact, little Sandra had a fine time being ferried around in taxicabs since Ty and Lee didn't have a car.

Up in the Carolinas, Cammie suddenly missed her driver's licence. She had a habit of sticking it in her back pocket, then forgetting it was there when she threw her jeans in the wash. By the time Cammie called about it, concerned, Lee had already spotted it where it had fallen by Cammie's dresser, and had pocketed it, deciding to keep it. They hadn't seen it, Ty and Lee told Cammie, who couldn't think what happened to it . . . then.

Months later, Cammie had a notice from the local library. A couple of books she'd checked out were overdue. Cammie had never heard of either title, yet the slip bore the number of her missing driver's licence. Then she noticed they were survival books. How odd. Suddenly, she had the eeriest feeling Lee was behind it. But why?

Cammie held many lingering memories of Ty and Lee, but over the years found one especially hard to shake. She could still picture them coming home one day, bubbling over with excitement about a mysterious plan. It was going to make them *all* rich, Lee bragged.

'How would you like to have enough money where **you**'d

never have to work again? Where your kids would never have to work?' she asked breathlessly.

'I'd like my kids to know the value of a dollar,' Cammie drily retorted.

'But how would you like it if you had so much money you didn't have to work?'

'Sounds like a pretty good deal,' Cammie conceded warily.

'I'm gonna do something no woman has ever done before and everybody will respect me,' Lee boasted.

What could she possibly do, Cammie wondered with mild disgust, that would make people respect her?

Lee didn't offer Cammie any concrete explanation for quite how this triumph was supposed to take place, and something stopped her from probing further.

What Lee *did* say was that she and Tyria were going to be like Bonnie and Clyde.

That they'd be sitting back, raking in all the money.

That they'd be doing society a favour.

That everyone would look up to her.

And that one of these days they'd be writing a movie or a story about her.

Was Cammie *sure* she didn't want to be a part of it?

'Only if it's legal,' Cammie said suspiciously, immediately sure that it couldn't be.

She knew Bonnie and Clyde were bandits who robbed banks and killed people. She didn't know they wound up dead.

The subject was then dropped as suddenly as it had arisen. Then, a couple of months later, Lee and Ty asked Cammie strange questions. If she and Dinky saw them in court later on down the line, would they try to help them out? Would they testify for them? Would they show up in court?

Cammie couldn't imagine what on earth Lee was talking about but, once again, something stopped her from pressing for specifics. Not that it crossed Cammie's mind that they were talking about anything really bad. She envisaged something dumb and innocuous. Trespassing somewhere exciting, perhaps. Even so, she was non-committal.

'I don't know. It depends what it's about,' she hedged.

Frankly, most of what Lee said went in one ear and out the other, like so much hot air. Dinky was right, Lee was a big talker. She'd even spun some story once about being a special agent in another state! She was always boasting she was going to buy Tyria this and that. Saying Tyria would never have to work again. She was going to take care of her. Cammie took it all with a grain of salt. Years later, she'd wish she'd paid more attention and asked a truckload more questions.

To Dinky's great relief, Ty and Lee left again that summer, but their shifty eventual departure was like a daylight version of a moonlight flit.

A couple of days before, Lee informed Cammie that she was due to be getting some money and would be giving her something towards the rent. Nothing had been forthcoming. Surprise, surprise. Dinky *had* told them to leave by then. Besides not contributing to the rent, they ate their food. Dinky and Cammie had their work cut out supporting their family, without supporting them too. They didn't mind so much with Ty, but given the wad of money Lee always had, why on earth should they subsidise her?

Ultimately, however, the Greenes had no idea the two women were actually planning to leave.

At the time, Cammie worked in the school cafeteria across the street, and coincidentally, Dinky, a roofer, was working on the school roof that very morning. The task gave him a bird's eye view of activities outside their home. Clambering down the ladder, he hurried inside the cafeteria to warn Cammie that it looked as if Ty and Lee were moving out. She'd better get over there, Dinky said. Make sure they weren't taking anything they shouldn't.

Cammie hurried in the door and just couldn't believe her eyes. Her home looked as if it had been blitzed by a tornado. There were Ty and Lee, literally throwing stuff around, as they hastily loaded up some white car they'd pulled in the driveway. Something along the lines of an Oldsmobile Cutlass or a Monte Carlo, it was a car Cammie and Dinky had never seen before. In fact, there'd never been any kind of car in all the time they'd known the two women.

'What are you doing?' Cammie demanded nervously.

'Movin' out,' Ty replied, sounding unusually hostile.

'Tyria, we don't have time to talk,' Lee interjected. 'Let's get our stuff and get out.'

'Whose car is that?' Cammie wanted to know.

'A friend of mine's,' said Lee. 'Don't worry about it.'

That, too, struck Cammie as strange. To the best of her knowledge, Lee didn't have any friends.

Being packed was the stereo that Ty had fought over so bitterly with Marcia. Then Cammie also spotted some of her blankets and a sleeping bag, stacked up ready to be moved.

'You're not going to take the sleeping bag, are you?' Cammie asked, her hand shaking with anger as she drew hard on her cigarette.

'Well, Cammie, you gave that to me,' Ty replied. Cammie was shocked. 'No! I said you can use it while you are here. That doesn't mean when you leave you take it with you!'

Watching them leave, Cammie was even *more* shocked by Tyria's attitude. What had happened to her buddy? She seemed so cold. So angry and unpleasant. Nothing at all like the Ty she knew. Or thought she knew.

16

In the steaming haze of the summer of 1987, Lee and Ty's nomadic existence found them drifting aimlessly around the highly
transient Daytona Beach area. With its boardwalk, lackadaisical
lifestyle and proliferation of bars, arcades and cheap motels, it
was the perfect hangout spot. A week here. A week there. Lazy
days rolling by. Nights dulled by alcohol.

Together, Lee and Ty raised a little hell. That was how people
would remember them: together. An inseparable and sometimes
rowdy duo. The short, heavy one. And the tall, blonde one. In
fact, Lee hovers below 5 feet 6 inches, but her broad-shouldered
frame and strong manner are deceiving. People repeatedly took
her for 5 feet 7 or 5 feet 8, even 5 feet 10. So much for eyewitness accuracy. Ty, on the other hand, with her close-cropped hair
tucked under a cap, and her cumbersome, lumbering gait, was
often mistaken for a chunky guy.

Ty's recorded offences were chicken-feed compared to her
companion's. Ty was arrested in July of 1986 for failing to
obey a traffic sign, and was cited for driving without headlights in March of 1987. After whooping it up on 4 July 1987,
Ty was treated at the Halifax Medical Center for scalp lacer-
ations. She'd had an altercation in the Barn Door Lounge and
a man knocked her to the ground. Tame stuff, by Lee's standards.

One of their many pit stops in Daytona was the Carnival
Motel, although there was little festive about it. They had no
phone in their spartan room, so Lee would use the pay phone
outside a nearby convenience store, then pop in to pick up cigarettes and other life-sustaining essentials. Sometimes, she hung
around outside.

The heavens opened the day that Paul, acting as assistant manager of the store to help a friend, stuck his head around the door. 'Why don't you step inside to take shelter?' he asked, assuring her she didn't have to buy anything. They'd exchanged a few words before. He remembered her saying she worked for a cleaning business or maid service or something. And since she had no wheels of her own, she had to wait in the street for someone to pick her up.

Single at the time, he found himself a little turned on by her. She wasn't bad looking at all. Making conversation, though, Paul felt she was a bit of a cold fish. Maybe a little hostile. Yet as soon as he mentioned that he was a part-time writer, her demeanour changed dramatically. It was as if a light bulb had switched on somewhere. She'd been looking for a ghost writer to help her with her autobiography, she enthused. And she was willing to pay a lot of money. Several thousand dollars. Could they meet later at her motel room, to discuss it in more detail?

Paul headed over to the Carnival that night, armed with a healthy degree of scepticism born of experience and past disappointment. He wasn't seduced by her talk of big bucks. Thinking logically, his first concern was whether this woman had any kind of original story to tell. Was it even worth his while to get involved? He'd worry about the specifics later.

When he arrived, Lee welcomed him. She then gave her pudgy, homely, and decidedly masculine-looking companion a highly memorable introduction, saying: 'This is my wife, Ty.' It was Paul's first intimation of Lee's lesbianism.

Staying professional, he opened the meeting by delivering his usual speech, just laying out the basics. The uninitiated always needed to be set straight on the way things worked. Paul pointed out grimly that in order to write anything commercial, you must have an audience. That you must identify a group of people out there who will be sufficiently fascinated to buy your product. Lots of famous people have biographies and autobiographies gathering dust on bookstore shelves because no one cared to spend money on them, he said.

What did Lee feel was so special about her life? She was a little ticked off by this confrontational tactic, but he'd seen that reaction before. People never liked marketplace realities interfering with their dreams and aspirations.

Lee thought he was questioning her worth and, challenged, she rose to the bait. What did she have that was special? Well, she'd tell him what. She knew of some unsolved murders, that's what. And she could name names.

That got Paul's attention.

Two facts emerged. One: Lee *desperately* wanted to become a public figure, and was hell-bent on trying to gain some kind of notoriety for herself; two: Lee and Ty had been drinking before he arrived, which put him off since he himself was on the wagon and in the AA programme. Yet she'd aroused his curiosity enough to make him delve deeper.

Lee's sinister stories began to tumble out, the flow lubricated by her beer consumption. What they lacked in detail, they made up for in mood. He had a creeping but certain feeling that she was capable of anything. She tried to cajole him into drinking with them. She didn't like it when he told her he'd been sober for a few years. Kept pushing beers at him regardless.

While Lee talked, Ty listened, pacing the room, feeling left out. She was more passive, yet every so often she chimed in, each interjection some feeble attempt to outdo Lee and her heavy-duty stories. Paul quickly deduced that Ty wasn't that bright, and found her competitive efforts rather comical.

Undeterred and still intent on her potential autobiography, Lee pulled out an old newspaper clipping detailing her 1976 marriage to Lewis Fell. It hadn't lasted long, but he had megabucks. She'd lost out badly there. Been dealt out of the fortune and didn't get a thing. Pissed her off so bad, she picked up with a biker gang. She had a wild streak, and that crazy biker lifestyle had always appealed to her.

Gradually, Paul got a taste of her stories. While she was living in Fell's penthouse, she told him, and sunbathing nude on the terrace, she'd deliberately flashed her body, luring a telephone or TV-cable worker. She'd driven him so crazy with desire that he came over to try and get friendly. Then she took her revenge. Hit him, then screamed. She liked to know she had the power to draw a man to her—then to reject him. Pretty sick stuff, Paul decided, liking the sound of her and her life less and less by the minute. Not something he wanted to get involved in. It was glaringly obvious she was full of anger at men, but he didn't know why. In all her stories, she made no mention of being beaten as a child, or of being sexually abused.

She claimed that when running with the bikers, she'd been used as bait, flaunting her body to entice men into a trap, but hating them all along and getting pleasure out of making them suffer.

She hinted around the subject of killing, tantalising rather than revealing. Never came right out and admitted to killing anyone herself, or even to witnessing any murders. Just sat there with a kind of smug smile, repeating her claim that she knew about some murders no one else knew about. She also bragged how tough she was and said she knew her way around weapons. When she ran with the biker gang, she was into a lot of violence.

The beer supply was drying up and Lee was anxious to replenish it. There were people who owed her money, so she didn't have any cash right now: could Paul loan her some?

'You know I work in the store and it doesn't pay,' he hedged, not liking this turn of events. 'I don't have but a few dollars on me.'

'Give me what you've got,' she said aggressively.

'No, ma'am. I have to live till pay day.'

'Don't give me that bullshit you don't have any money. What are you afraid of?'

With his refusal to comply, the so-called interview took a vicious turn. Lee grew belligerent, calling him ugly names and using foul language.

Paul tried to steer the conversation back onto the presumably safer ground of her book. Privately, he'd already decided he wanted no part of it. He didn't want to deal with her, let alone write about her.

Making his excuses, he edged towards the door with Lee still pushing for money. By the time he pulled away from the Carnival, she had somehow talked him out of ten bucks. That left him just five for himself.

'I'll bring it into the store in a couple of days,' she promised.

'Fine.'

'What are you going to do about the writing?'

'I'll be in touch,' Paul lied, more than happy to write off the ten bucks to experience. He decided this must be her pattern. Hitting people up for cash. He counted himself lucky to get off so lightly. But he still felt rattled. It had been an upsetting, disturbing encounter and he wanted to forget it as quickly as possible.

Predictably, he didn't see his money again, but he did see Lee a few months later, bumping into her back in the store. He was then dating one of the staff (who later became his wife) and had just stopped by when Lee appeared in the company of a homely-looking, much older man. The fellow was perhaps in his late sixties and behaved as if he thought he'd struck pay dirt with her.

Lee ran up and down the aisles, gathering beer and stacking it on the counter, giggling merrily. Then she went over to her companion and held out her hand, and he pulled out a wad of bills. Paul was alarmed. She then scampered over to another aisle and returned with a pack of condoms which she waved, teasingly, under the man's nose. He looked happier than a clam. He paid for everything, then they took off in his beaten old van.

Paul agonised over what he'd seen. During their evening together, she had not mentioned prostitution. But she had mentioned violence. What was going to happen to that old fellow? Was she going to rob him blind? He thought hard about calling the cops and debated it with his girlfriend.

'I know what they'll tell me,' he fretted. 'They'll say, "Nobody has committed any crime. Forget it!"' He had talked himself out of doing anything.

But Lee's ambition to have an autobiography burned on, undimmed. She talked to another writer and clipped and carefully saved those questionable advertisements that run in the backs of magazines, enticing amateur hopefuls with messages like, 'Looking For a Publisher?' or 'Be An Author'. One day there'd be a book about her.

Meanwhile, Lee railed against the world with a sense of righteous indignation that sometimes drove her to put pen to paper herself.

In January of 1988, she wrote to the clerk of the circuit court contesting a traffic offence—she'd been caught walking on the interstate on 18 December 1987—for which she felt she'd been wrongfully ticketed. She ended her letter with the postscript. 'I wrote this in all honesty. Now Please, get it squared away. Because I'll be *#D if I am falsely charged or accussed *[sic]*.'

Early in February, having had no reply, she once again committed her sense of outrage to paper. She had only walked on the interstate when she stepped out of a car to retrieve a piece of paper that had flown out of the window! She wrote: 'FHP decided to [lie] and accuse us of improperly pulling over for no emergency reasons . . .'

She complained that another ticket had been written out later, outside her presence, for something she felt was irrelevant. What did it matter that the licence she carried (Susan Lynn Blahovec's) was suspended? She didn't drive on it anyway, she grandly asserted, she had someone to drive for her.

Equally grandly, she wrote: 'If this is not erased from my record and I get arrested from this improper accussation *[sic]* Well then be prepared for one hell of a lawsuit against the department the county, the jail system, the officers and what else my lawyer can dig up from law books. I will not tolarate *[sic]* a made up conjecture of lies.' (Actual punctuation.)

It would not be the last time she would bandy around threats of a lawsuit. Then, after accusing the authorities of having 'the gall' to do all this, she herself had the gall to blithely sign off as Susan Blahovec.

One of the troublesome tickets bore a telling little notation by the citing officer: 'Att. poor. Thinks she is above the law.'

Since August '87, Ty and Lee had been ensconced in a rear apartment on Oleander Avenue in the Daytona area. Ty worked variously at the El Caribe Motel, where she'd been employed when she first met Lee, and at a laundry from which she was eventually fired (unjustly they'd claim) after some money disappeared. It had been a relatively stable period, but on 25 July a police officer was dispatched to their apartment in response to a vandalism complaint lodged by Brian Donley, the landlord. Donley could hear banging and crashing and was afraid the place was being wrecked. His upstairs tenant had also complained that the women had made too much noise the night before.

At first, Lee and Ty refused to let the officer in. Eventually, he gained access, along with Donley who, taking a look around, noted that a fifty-dollar carpet had been removed without his permission and that the walls had been re-painted brown, also without his permission. Lee and Ty maintained that they'd had his OK. And the noise? They'd just been having a party. Donley evicted them anyway, giving them notice to be out by 1 August.

Homeless again, they briefly camped out in the woods, living very primitively, but soon hitched back over to Zephyrhills and knocked on Kathy Beasman's door at the Pierre Motel. Kathy, who needed someone, agreed to give them a second chance. This time, they seemed anxious to fit in and made an effort to play by the rules. Kathy was pleased.

But every so often, Lee had an outburst. She just seemed to lose control, and it invariably happened when she got into a debate with one of the male guests. It was as if she couldn't bear to be wrong and a man to be right; she had to have the last word. She never yelled at Kathy, only at the men.

In their room, Lee and Ty kept a cat called Zephyr, which Lee babied completely, bathing it and sitting it out in the sunshine to dry. The cat became pregnant, and when the kittens were born, Kathy said they could keep them just until they were old enough to farm out to good homes. At which point, Kathy's father stopped by to tell them it was time to get rid of them.

Hearing that, Lee spat out a torrent of abuse so vicious that it quite upset him. He'd never seen a woman so angry. It was positively frightening. If only Kathy could have seen it for herself.

Lee was always so sweet to her. He felt sure that Lee had something seriously wrong with her to change like that.

Lee got into another altercation in the Publix store in the shopping centre next to the motel. She'd bought some lottery tickets and when the assistant manager, Robert McManus, made a mistake on the numbers she wanted, she turned abusive. Finally, she stormed out, but, soon after, McManus began getting nasty, harassing phone calls at the store. An anonymous woman threatened him with bodily injury. She'd put him in the hospital! She had a contract out on him! McManus had a pretty good idea who she was. Even so, he was sufficiently scared to wear a bulletproof vest to work, and to call the police.

With the help of the Pierre Motel's phone records, they were able to track those calls to their source. Room 5. The residence of Lee and Ty. When confronted, Lee admitted to having had a run-in with McManus and to calling Publix's main office to have him fired. But she flatly denied making the calls to the store. McManus had taken the precaution of having a couple of fellow employees listen in on the line as witnesses, and the time and date they cited coincided exactly with a call on the Pierre's records. Proof enough. Lee was trapped. She was given a stern warning to back off.

The staff of Votran, the East Volusia Transit System, became all too familiar with Lee Wuornos (known to them as Cammie Greene) in the spring of 1988. She was a regular rider, normally boarding on Spruce Creek Road and riding to the end of the route, close to the Amoco on I-95, her hitching beat. During these rides, she'd had some hassles with late-night trolley driver, Gary Thomson. When the police were called to a Union '76 station to check out a report of assault and battery on a bus passenger, the complainant was 'Cammie Greene'.

According to Thomson, she had pulled him out of his seat and struggled with him, before crashing through the glass doors. But 'Cammie' accused Thomson of standing up and making vulgar comments at girls while driving, of taking the wrong route, and as she exited, of knocking her down the steps, making her fall. When she tried to climb back aboard, she said, he kicked her in the stomach, then drove off. Ty Moore was a witness for 'Cammie', who actually sued Votran and was given a small settlement. When the police arrived, 'Cammie' said she wanted to press charges against the driver but a few days later, changed her mind. Thomson was subsequently fired by Votran on an unrelated matter.

George Soloway, the director of transportation, didn't meet 'Cammie' that time, but wasn't deprived of the pleasure. She had yet another verbal run-in with a driver and threatened to sue again. Soloway was alerted immediately. In a diplomatic gesture, he went to pick her up at the bus stop where the altercation took place, then drove her to her destination himself in the company van, calming her down.

(In December of 1990, another Votran supervisor, David Hope, received one more angry, vulgar phone call complaining that a driver had failed to stop for 'Cammie'. She'd sued Votran once, and she could certainly sue them again!)

By January of 1989, Lee and Ty had left the Pierre, and since Ty was unemployed were slowly meandering their way over to Homosassa Springs on Florida's east coast, north of Tampa. First they stayed in a motel, then shuttled around a few trailer parks, the proliferation of which leads to the observation that much of Florida is on wheels. Landing at the RV park Billy Copeland managed, they settled into a trailer for a bargain $95 a month. During those lazy days, Lee and Ty made no attempt to hide their firearms as they hung around outside, taking aim at beer cans. Hardly unobtrusive neighbours, they fought loudly and often. Billy and Cindy Copeland say they saw Lee 'beat the hell' out of hefty Tyria. Intrigued by their traffic of male visitors, Billy and Cindy nevertheless presumed the women to be lesbians.

'She met ugly old Ty and Ty was a good lover to her,' Billy observed, 'and she had her own little wife right there. Lee saw something she could grab onto and have somebody to come home to. Somebody she could have and love . . . good love.'

Ty and Lee were sometimes given vegetables and groceries by the Copelands, and Cindy frequently gave Lee a ride to the highway. Neither of them fell for the 'pressure-cleaning business in New Port Richey' line. Lee just disappeared for four hours, then reappeared. 'There's no way you could even get to New Port Richey in four hours, much less pressure clean!' Billy noted disbelievingly.

One day, Lee strolled over to Billy, complaining bitterly about a male visitor Billy had seen arrive, clutching a TV. He also saw him leave again in his van. Didn't notice the colour, just that it was a van.

'Billy, you're going to have to do something if this sonofabitch comes back,' Lee said. 'I don't want him coming back after his TV. He gave it to us, and now he wants it back.'

'Listen, Lee, let me tell you something,' Billy snapped. 'I don't want any trouble. But if that sonofabitch wants some of my ass, you just tell him to come in my back door and I'll give it to him.'

The next time the man appeared, he joined them all in a barbecue. He seemed the argumentative sort, though, and Billy didn't take to him. Before long, Lee was fighting with him again and storming over to Billy, saying, 'The sonofabitch thinks we're gonna do a threesome with him! The hell with him!'

The man then left in a hurry. Billy's snap assessment was that, like the rest of their male visitors, he merely wanted a piece of ass and showed no human kindness towards her. He was glad she kept the TV. Not that he had any particular love for Lee. And he was sure she could take care of herself. Underneath those sunglasses she always wore, he couldn't help thinking a bizarre thought. Death-row eyes, that's what Lee had. He and Cindy wouldn't forget them.

Later, they'd recall (and question) the man with the TV, and the day Lee and Ty walked up the campsite driveway calling, 'Look, Billy! Look! Me and Ty won the Lotto!' and flashing around six one-hundred-dollar bills.

James Dalla Rosa picked Lee up in Port Orange. She'd been standing at the side of the road and he was out running some errands. Where did she want to go? Cutting straight to the chase, she told him that she was a professional prostitute and wanted to get to Orlando.

She showed him a picture of her two kids—a boy and a girl—and told him about a home she owned. He had a feeling all was not 'as advertised'. She slipped the photos back in the purse she had on the floor between her feet, then produced a wallet full of business cards. Judges, state attorneys, police officers, were all her clients, she said. Keeping one eye on the road, he thought he spotted the outline of a sheriff's star on one.

She listed her fees as $75 in the woods, $100 in a motel room. Straight sex. With condoms. Not exactly a direct proposition, but the offer was there.

Not wanting to offend her, he muttered something about taking a rain check.

'It's now or never!' she retorted.

Then she changed dramatically. Went quiet on him. He could tell she was angry by the jerky way she was moving, and when he pulled to the side of the road to let her out, she slammed the door and stalked off without so much as a thank you.

17

Like Cammie Greene before her, Sandy Russell gravitated to Tyria Moore. The two women wrangled linens alongside one another in the Casa Del Mar's sweat-inducing laundry room. Ty landed her job with the housekeeping department of the seven-storey, 150-room, upscale, ocean-front hotel in Ormond Beach in the autumn of 1989. Initially, this did not thrill Sandy, a delicately pretty, all-American blonde from West Virginia whose wide blue eyes, fair luscious lashes and translucent pale skin all contributed to her looking considerably younger than her 29 years. Ty's arrival elbowed Sandy temporarily into the lobby area where, under the gaze of the paying public, she had to mop and sweep every inch of the huge floor. A tedious job she hated.

Yet despite this state of affairs, she and Ty clicked immediately. She admired Ty's feisty personality and the two shared a wildly wacky, offbeat sense of humour and a love of sports. In so many other ways they were the veritable odd couple. Sandy so overtly feminine; almost girlishly so, with her wispy hair and equally wispy voice, and Ty so butch in dress, manner, and posture. Sandy liked men, and strongly suspected Ty didn't share her taste. Not that that bothered her in the slightest.

If she liked Ty a lot, she was decidedly less sure about Lee whom she met at Thanksgiving and presumed to be Ty's lover. The holiday fell on Thursday 23 November. Being far from their respective families, they all planned to have dinner together. Since Sandy and Ty were on duty at the Casa Del Mar, it fell to Lee to prepare their festive repast. No gourmet chef, Lee cooked an oven-ready, TV-style turkey dinner that was all pre-compartmentalised with vegetables, utilising the limited facilities of the Ocean Shores motel room in Ormond Beach, their home for the past month.

It seemed so peculiar to Sandy that even on a traditionally social occasion like Thanksgiving, Lee was obviously downright uncomfortable about dining with a stranger. In fact, she didn't. She *claimed* to have already eaten, but Sandy didn't believe her. It was downright unnerving, the way Lee sat there peering intently at her and Ty while they hungrily tucked into their food. She didn't seem able to quite join in. She wondered if it was her presence somehow making her off-balance.

Other factors contributed to Sandy's conclusion that Lee was odd. Sandy didn't relish seeing Lee waving a gun around in a temper. Sandy was no stranger to firearms: her ex-husband owned a long-barrelled .357 that looked similar to Lee's. She wasn't afraid. She didn't even know for sure the weapon was loaded, but that was hardly the point. Sandy knew enough about firearms to have a healthy respect for them. She didn't want anyone waving a gun around in front of her, loaded or not.

Lee, who hoisted her shirt up over her beer-inflated stomach to show Sandy her bullet scar, was friendly enough and, in a slightly odd way, could be likeable. She was even affectionate. Hugging Sandy, she'd cry, 'Oh Sandy, I love you like a sister!' Yet Sandy couldn't shake her deep misgivings about Ty's mate. At first, it was more of a gut feeling than anything she could put a name to.

When Richard Charles Mallory of Clearwater, Florida, disappeared a week after Thanksgiving, near and dear ones didn't exactly rise up in force. Fifty-one-year-old Mallory, who had his own VCR and TV repair shop in a strip shopping mall in Palm Harbor, was last seen on the night of Thursday 30 November 1989, and in a sad echo of his life, he seemed alone then, too.

Grey-haired, moustachioed Mallory was 5 feet 11 inches, with hazel eyes behind wire-rimmed glasses. He cut a trim figure, tipping the scales at just under 170 pounds. A long-time divorcé, he was a loner, a man who loved to party in the carnal sense, a frequenter of the kinds of establishments dedicated to catering to pleasures of the flesh. He was a sufficiently regular customer at the topless bars in the Tampa and Clearwater area on Florida's west coast that the strippers, go-go dancers and hookers mostly knew him by sight, if not by name.

He paid some of those women quite generously for sex, either with cash or with his other viable currency, TVs and VCRs, and was known for being an extremely generous tipper. His special favourite on the sexual repertoire was watching two women together.

In his other life, he was depressed over a recent break-up with Jackie Davis, a warm, chestnut-haired, rather demure-looking woman who wore spectacles and floral dresses and with whom he'd been involved for about eighteen months. Jackie had got fed up with Richard's lifestyle.

Richard had also been seeing a woman called Nancy he'd met through a dating group called MCI, but Nancy gave up on Richard when she learned that Jackie was still in the picture.

Richard Mallory's solitary status and relationship difficulties were unlikely to be helped by his considerable appetite for encounters with women of the night.

He liked to drink and smoked a little pot. Jackie Davis found him kind and gentle but prone to mood swings. Sometimes he was sweet and easygoing, at others, he shrank back into his shell. He could be a little paranoid. Sometimes, he confided in Jackie, he felt as if he was being followed. In the three years he'd lived in his apartment at The Oaks, he'd had his lock changed at least eight times.

Jackie last spoke to Richard on 26 November. They'd talked about getting away for a long weekend in Daytona Beach. Jeff Davis, Jackie's son, who worked part-time for Richard at Mallory Electronics, last saw him around 6.10 p.m. on the 30th, after closing up the shop. As always, he was clutching his black attaché case. He said he was off to do a service call.

Mallory was in dire financial straits: another predicament his rampant night life did nothing to ameliorate. Nor did his irresponsible behaviour. He'd been known to take off unannounced and even to fail to show up with the keys to open the shop, leaving his employees standing out on the street. He was almost $4,000 in arrears on his rent, and was due to be audited by the IRS.

He owned two vans, one white and the other maroon. But the night he disappeared, heading for Daytona (minus Jackie) for a weekend of what was euphemistically called socialising, he was driving his light beige, two-door, 1977 Cadillac Coupe de Ville, with its brown interior and racily tinted windows. A vehicle better suited to the pursuit.

By early evening, a handful of north-bound rides from Fort Myers had deposited her outside Tampa on I-4, right at the point where it passes under I-75. She was lingering there when Richard Mallory stopped to pick her up. They had a common destination in Daytona so he invited her to hop in. They whiled away a pleasant drive across the state, chatting companionably and drinking. Richard smoked a little pot, but she wouldn't join him. Not a drug she'd ever cared for, herself. It made her heart race and her hands and feet swell up, she complained. He stirred her a vodka and orange. Somewhere along the highway they made a pit-stop and he bought her a six-pack. A die-hard beer drinker, she was more at home with that.

She was tired. She'd spent a profitable day turning tricks in the Fort Myers area and was on her way home, but as they hit the fringes of Daytona close to midnight, Richard asked: 'Do you mind if we stop somewhere to talk some more?' She suggested a spot near Bunnell where they parked again, talking and drinking, while Richard poured out a few of his troubles. He complimented her; she was a good listener. She thought he was nice, too. At first, she maintained the pressure-cleaning charade, then she admitted to being a professional call girl.

'Do you want to help me make some money, 'cause I need some money for rent and everything?' she asked. He was ready, willing and able, so they talked prices and moved to a still more deserted spot in the woods.

It was around 5 a.m. when Richard finally initiated sex. She

161

peeled off her clothes before he did. It was her custom to make her clients more comfortable. She made self-deprecating references to her stretch marks and beer belly but he reassured her. 'You'll do,' he'd said, switching on the dome light for a better look. They hugged and kissed a little.

'Why don't you take off your clothes? It will hurt if you don't,' she said finally, referring to his blue jeans' metal studs and zipper. But Richard didn't want to undress. His old demon paranoia was surfacing. Naked, he would have felt horribly vulnerable. What if she ran off or robbed him? No, he'd just unzip his pants, thank you very much.

Colliding with his mental machinations was a woman with plenty of her own. In her mind, she was in jeopardy. What if this guy took back the money he'd given her, or rolled her? What if he was going to rape her?

Two individuals beleaguered by their separate mind games. A potentially lethal combination.

Yet, given the pleasant hours preceding this exchange, there was no way that Richard could possibly have imagined the sudden and horrific turn of events. This usually unduly cautious man had made a fatal error in judgement.

He was still sitting in a non-threatening position behind his steering wheel when she made her move. She had been standing just outside the open passenger door when suddenly she reached in, making a grab for her small blue bag containing her spare clothes which lay on the car floor.

How could he have known that she always kept its zipper partially undone for easy access?

How could he have known she was carrying a loaded, nine-shot, .22-calibre revolver?

Yet, instinctively, he smelled danger and lunged across to try to stop her getting the bag. The struggle was brief. She already had a firm grasp on it and quickly wrenched it out of his reach. Moving at lightning speed, utilising all her hours of practice, she yanked out her gun and aimed it towards her companion.

'You sonofabitch! I knew you were going to rape me!'

'No, I wasn't! No, I wasn't!' he protested.

Without more ado, she leaned into the car and fired quickly, pumping a bullet that first hit his right arm, then travelled lethally onward, striking him in the right side.

His blood flowed onto the car upholstery behind him.

Fighting for his very survival in the midst of darkness with this apparently crazy woman, he had no time to think. He had but one potential escape route and he took it, crawling out of the driver's door, slamming it behind him, trying desperately to put something between him and his attacker.

She had not finished. She ran around the front of the car to where he stood, disabled. 'If you don't stop, man, right now, I'll keep shooting!' she growled. She liked the .22's hairpin trigger and now she put it to the test, mercilessly firing a second bullet, which hit him in the torso, knocking him back up and making him fall to the ground.

Then a third.

Then a fourth.

He did not die immediately. But the bullet that struck the right side of his chest had gone on to penetrate his left lung, travelling through it and out the other side, coming to rest in the chest cavity. It caused a massive and fatal haemorrhage.

Lying there, with the life blood seeping from him, death was inevitable. But he gasped for air, desperately trying to suck in the oxygen he needed, desperately trying to cling on. He struggled for ten, maybe even twenty, long minutes.

And she watched him die.

When he was gone, she did not attempt to drag her victim's lifeless body away, but just moved him enough to get at his pockets, taking his identification and money. (She'd later say she only found about forty dollars, but Mallory customarily carried several hundred dollars; possibly more on a trip.)

The luminous moon shone brightly. Casting glances all around her, she spied some cardboard and a discarded piece of red carpeting and she dragged those over to where he lay. First she put the cardboard over his body, then she stretched out the carpeting on top to hide as much of him as it would. (Later she'd say that she didn't want the birds picking at his body.) Only the tips of his hands were exposed.

Still naked, she found the ignition keys and moved the Cadillac to Quail Run, another isolated spot nearby, where she hastily dressed. She drank her last beer while pondering her next move.

She considered putting the car through a car wash before going home to shower, then thought better of it. She didn't have time. But she was forced to stop to get gas. She threw some of the dead man's clothing into the woods, far from his body. Later, she would throw the rest into trash Dumpsters.

Finally, she drove back to the Ocean Shores motel. Back to her woman.

The sun was still inching towards its first peek through the early morning haze as Ty's peaceful sleep was shattered by a knock on the door, signalling that Lee wanted to be let in. Ty, who didn't need to be at the Casa Del Mar until 9 a.m., had been counting on the alarm to wake her. She didn't know it as that first day of December dawned, but by nightfall she would be sleeping in a new home.

She and Lee had already looked into renting a converted garage apartment over on Burleigh Avenue in nearby Holly Hill. Some of their belongings were already in boxes because they planned to move soon—but not that day. Suddenly, as Ty was stretching and yawning herself awake, Lee was urging her on, telling her to get ready, she'd got the money they needed. They were going to move right that minute, before she went to work.

'I made a lot of money, and some guy loaned me this car,' Lee told her, 'and we can get our stuff moved over to the other apartment.'

Ty could smell the alcohol wafting on her drunken partner's breath, but Lee was perfectly coherent. Just her usual self. Nothing out of the ordinary. She set to and helped Ty pack, handing Ty a man's grey, Members Only jacket with a zip-in, fur-type lining, and a scarf. Boxing their belongings, Ty noted a few other items she hadn't seen before. A suitcase, a blanket, a box of papers. She made no comment.

Loading their worldly possessions into Richard Mallory's beige Cadillac, they were off. Ty, not having seen the car be-

164

fore, registered the University of Florida Gators tag on the front and the tinted windows. Within minutes, they were dropping their stuff at the new place. Without stopping to unpack, Lee then quickly ferried Ty the 9.3 miles back to the Ocean Shores motel. Just in time for Ty to pick up her moped and make it to work.

'I gotta go and bring this car back, so I'll see you later, honey,' Lee said brightly, heading off.

Executing the next part of her plan, she stashed her ten-speed bicycle in the boot, and drove twelve or so miles to a deserted dirt trail near the beach. She took everything out of the car, scooped a hole in the sandy soil and buried it, then she methodically wiped away all her fingerprints with a red towel. Next she retrieved her bicycle and rode away from the dead man's car, tossing his keys into the bushes of someone's yard on the way. It was over.

By the time Ty came home from work, the 'borrowed' car had vanished and she never saw it again.

Alarm bells were sounded that very same day after Richard Mallory's car was spotted, apparently abandoned, by Deputy Bonnevier of the Volusia County Sheriff's Office who was out on routine patrol.

The Cadillac had been backed roughly thirty feet into a narrow, wooded dirt road that ran east–west off John Anderson Drive in Ormond Beach. John Anderson Drive was frequented only by those folk who used it to reach their homes. The fire trail itself was one of several that had been carved through the undergrowth ready to give access for more building developments that were already in the works.

Bonnevier ran the Cadillac's VIN number and tags which promptly threw up the owner's name of Richard Mallory. Finding the car out there in the bushes near the sand dunes with no sign of its owner, Bonnevier immediately suspected that something was amiss. It was Bonnevier's guess that the Cadillac had been driven within a couple of hours of him finding it.

Hastily buried in a small depression about thirty feet behind the car was a blue nylon wallet containing two long-expired credit cards and car ownership papers, a red car caddy, Richard Mallory's business cards and some miscellaneous papers. A piece of white cloth lay like a curious camouflage between the items and their thin, sandy covering. A sinister discovery.

Volusia investigators contacted Detective Bonnie Richway at the Pinellas County Sheriff's Office, located near Richard Mallory's home on the west coast, and requested that she try to locate Mallory at his apartment or business address. She was unsuccessful, but came back with a good physical description of the man.

There would be further reason to suspect that Mallory had met with foul play. What appeared to be a blood stain loomed ominously on the backrest of the driver's seat.

Judging by the way the driver's seat had been pulled forward as far as it would go, the last person behind the wheel had been considerably shorter than Mallory himself. The ignition key was missing and the car had been stripped of identification and wiped clean of fingerprints. Someone seemed to know just what they were doing. Richard Mallory's spectacles were the only item left in the car.

Also found half-buried were two clear plastic tumblers and a brown bag containing a half-empty Smirnoff vodka bottle. Apparently, Mr Mallory had had a companion.

'I killed a guy today.'

Shocking words uttered with alarming dispassion. Lee's disclosure sounded almost nonchalant. A memorable punctuation to their first evening in the Burleigh apartment which was being spent in an otherwise normal fashion, sitting around on the floor, knocking back a few beers, staying glued to the TV.

Equally shocking was Tyria's ostrich-like reaction. Whatever Lee was saying, she didn't want to hear about it. Didn't want to believe her ears. *Didn't* believe them at first. Thought it was a lie or some kind of joke. Lee lied all the time.

If the strange 'borrowed' car they'd used, or the man's jacket she'd been given, or the unfamiliar possessions—the suitcase, the clothing, the blanket, the comforter, the tool box, the Polaroid camera—she had seen Lee clean out of the car that morning or bring into the apartment later, were setting off any alarm bells, she didn't let on. She didn't even ask Lee what on earth she was talking about. Rather, she merely let the enormity of her girlfriend's statement sit there like a twenty-ton white elephant.

They then simply went back to watching TV.

Later, more details trickled out, whether Ty wanted to hear them or not. Lee told her that she'd shot the man, then put his body in the woods. Covered it with carpet, then taken his car and dumped it up in Ormond Beach. As Ty worked desperately to avert her eyes, Lee tried to flash in front of her a photograph of the man she'd killed, plus a piece of paper. Don't tell me! Don't show me! Determined not to look, Ty successfully avoided the photograph. But before she could push away the paper Lee was waving, she saw the name 'Richard'.

Hearing about the hooking was bad enough, why would she want to hear about something like that?

She was afraid. Truly afraid. While she had been able to block it out, it had been OK. But knowing for sure that Lee had killed meant she should do something about it—like go to the authorities.

Why did Lee kill him? She didn't ask, maybe afraid of what she'd hear. Lee certainly never said that Richard Mallory had hurt or raped or abused her. She bore no bruises. No physical signs she'd been attacked. It was no secret that Lee hated men, although Ty had never quite understood the logic of being a hustler if she hated them so much.

Now Ty felt stuck in quicksand. 'I wanted to get out of the relationship then . . . but I just . . . I was scared,' she recalled. Lee had always told her she would never hurt her, but Ty didn't trust Lee's words any more.

If there was any lingering doubt as to where fiction ended and fact began in her lover's murderous confession, it didn't last for long. It was rudely replaced by cold, hard facts a couple of weeks later when Ty saw a TV news bulletin reporting Richard Mallory's murder and showing his car. Ty definitely recognised it. It was the car they'd borrowed.

167

So, the woman who said she'd die for Ty was really a killer.

Reluctantly banging up against reality, Tyria Jolene Moore was faced with a number of choices, none of them easy and some more unpalatable than others. She could have blown the whistle by calling the police. She could have hot-footed it out of Florida as fast and as far as a Greyhound bus would carry her. She could have left Lee immediately, but maintained her silence.

Instead, she stayed put.

On 6 December, using her Cammie Greene i.d., Lee pawned Richard Mallory's camera and radar detector for $30 at the OK Pawn Shop in Daytona.

Dutifully, she pressed her thumb into the inkpad, transferring a nice, clear print into the shop's receipt book where it would remain for posterity.

Richard Mallory's body was found across the river from his car on Wednesday 13 December, five miles away as the crow flies. Thirteen days after his disappearance, he bore little resemblance to the man he was in life. With nature working its inevitable course, the empty shell was already in an advanced stage of decomposition. A couple of young men out sifting trash and debris, scavenging for scrap metal, stumbled across it when they noticed birds circling and a hand sticking out. They rushed to a pay phone and alerted police.

It seemed Richard Mallory had come to an ignominious rest in a small clearing amidst the palmettos. It was an area littered with debris and garbage because of its proximity to an illegal dump site in a deeply wooded area to the west of US 1, about three-quarters of a mile north of I-95. An insultingly ugly environment.

Summoned to the murder scene that afternoon, lead investigator Larry Horzepa noted that this dump site, accessed by a trail worn down by a traffic of trucks and cars, was in fact visible from US 1.

Horzepa, a tall, lean, serious-looking man with dark hair, spectacles and a dry sense of humour, came to the Mallory case after six years with the Volusia County Sheriff's Office and ten with the Brevard County Sheriff's Department. He'd first heard Mallory's name on 4 December when paperwork on his abandoned car filtered through his office.

As Horzepa approached, stepping over the crime scene tape with which deputies had cordoned off the area, he saw at once that it was no accident that the body had lain almost entirely hidden from view. Someone had had the foresight to cover it with a rubber-backed, red carpet runner. Working with video and still cameras and floodlights, technicians recorded the scene.

With the video still running and camera clicking, as darkness fell the rug was finally lifted away, revealing to Horzepa and the other officers the remnants of a man lying face down, his legs crossed at the ankles. He was fully clothed in a short-sleeved white shirt, blue jeans, two pairs of socks and brown loafers. As he was turned over, a full set of dentures fell away from the decaying body. His jeans were fastened and fully zipped and his brown belt was buckled, though the buckle was twisted four inches or so off-centre.

His front pants pockets were pulled slightly inside-out as if they had been emptied.

Horzepa didn't know for sure the man's identity, but he had a pretty good hunch. He thought back to that car that had been found about twelve miles away and the description Bonnie Richway had provided. He thought he had his man.

Later, at the autopsy, law enforcement would learn that four gunshot wounds to the chest had sucked the life out of him. The bullets used would turn out to be of the copper-coated, hollow-nosed variety and fired from a .22 handgun.

At least one had penetrated his body while he was still sitting in his car, accounting for the blood stain on the backrest.

But surveying his body that day, just on the surface, the progression of the decomposition struck Larry Horzepa as strange. The body was totally skeletonised from the collarbone to the top of the head.

'It led me to believe there was a possibility if there had been a wound, it might have been a knife wound where his throat might have been slashed,' he recalls. The autopsy could be no more conclusive.

Given Florida's temperate climate, the corpse was actually in relatively good condition, preserved at least a little by some recent cold snaps. Horzepa had no idea whether the carpet would have hindered disintegration of the body, or accelerated it. The body was also sufficiently decayed that it was impossible to see any bullet holes. Even the experts wouldn't be able to say whether the victim's body had also been bruised, battered, or beaten.

A blood alcohol test later revealed a level of .05 per cent, so if Richard Mallory was under the influence of alcohol at the time of his death, he was very much at the lower limits of the scale. There was not yet any sign in the blood sample of the bacteria that eventually grows after death, changing the blood alcohol level and clouding the picture as far as determining the true source is concerned.

The victim's hands were removed and taken separately to the FDLE (Florida Department of Law Enforcement) crime lab where a set of latent prints were taken. Thanks to a match with a set of fingerprints on file from Richard Mallory's single DUI arrest, the corpse was positively identified.

Mr Mallory was a man who wore jewellery, particularly when he was going out on the town, but none was found. It must have been stolen on his drive of death.

Painstakingly piecing together what had befallen him, the Volusia County investigators worked against the disadvantages inherent in dealing with a private man, a loner, a man who didn't confide his every move to anyone. There was no doting wife or girlfriend waving him off to work each day. They didn't have the luxury of knowing about Richard Mallory and what he had with him in gloriously detailed description.

Horzepa worked with what he'd got. Both Mallory's Clearwater apartment and his shop were searched, but there was no sign of foul play in either place—although lots of complaining letters and work receipts showed that the victim was clearly way behind in his repairs. A Christmas card was found from a sister in Texas and she was duly notified of her brother's death.

Richard also had two brothers who lived in Virginia and Maryland who had to be told.

Detectives combed the victim's home, work and social environments, interviewing everyone they could find who knew him. Most importantly, they talked to Jackie Davis. From her, they learned that when Richard disappeared he probably had with him a 35mm Minolta camera, a Polaroid 600 (helpfully distinctive because of its highly unusual maroon colour), a gold Seiko watch, and a Radio Shack radar detector. Jackie Davis handed over pictures of her son Jeff at his birthday party that actually showed the Polaroid camera in the background.

Maryann Beatty, the worried president of the MCI dating service Mallory had belonged to, was instructed to notify the females among her thousand-plus members that the sheriff's office would be contacting them. Detectives busily canvassed the motels and bars in the Daytona area. Perhaps the victim checked in somewhere before he died. No luck.

Horzepa had no reason to suspect that Mallory had deviated from his customary ritual of religiously carrying with him his black attaché case with its Mallory Electronics stationery, personal papers and cash supply inside. His assortment of luggage would have held items like his weekend clothing, his hairbrush and hair dryer. He had had a tool box, too, judging by the deep impression mark in the lining of the boot, alongside the spare tyre. There was no sign of a single one of them.

Later, viewing photographs taken after the FDLE evidence technicians had coated the Cadillac from one end to the other with fingerprint powder, Horzepa could clearly observe the white arcing curves revealing where it had been wiped down. It was so clean that it looked as if it had come fresh from a car wash.

By the end of January 1990, Larry Horzepa had established that prior to leaving town his last night alive, Richard Mallory had already engaged in a paid sexual encounter with two dancers named Chastity and Danielle, whom he'd met previously at Tampa's 2001 Odyssey club. Chastity left the club in the early hours of 1 December and didn't return until mid-December.

Both women's phone numbers were found on Mallory's kitchen counter, scribbled on slips of paper.

Working with the Tampa homicide department, Volusia investigators Horzepa and Bob Kelley first tracked down 26-year-old Danielle. She confirmed that in November Mallory had tried to date her, but that she'd told him she was gay. He gave her a 19-inch TV, a Fisher VCR and $50 in exchange for bumping and grinding 'lap dances' and sex.

Within a week, Larry Horzepa had found Chastity, a thin, large-breasted, heavily tattooed, 27-year-old blonde (like Lee, an adoptee with a wild streak, a string of aliases and a history of violent behaviour) and her bouncer boyfriend, Doug. Chastity, who had danced at local clubs like Circus, Candy-Bar and Boobie Trap, told Horzepa that she and Danielle had fulfilled one of Mallory's favourite fantasies, having sex with him and with each other, back at his repair shop where he'd driven them in his van.

Chastity was somewhat foggy on dates, but piecing together eyewitness accounts, Horzepa pinpointed her as one of the last people to see Richard Mallory alive in the Clearwater area.

Ronnie Poulter, a female night manager at the 2001, said she'd spent Christmas with Chastity who had made a couple of tantalisingly suspicious comments. She said, 'I'm hot as a firecracker, I've got to get out of town', 'I've seen and done everything now', and 'I'm in big trouble'.

By 30 March, when Horzepa and Kelley went back across the state to Tampa hoping to polygraph the two women, Chastity had left for South Carolina. She and Doug had split up because of her violence. While being re-interviewed, Doug broke down and cried. Chastity had told him things concerning the Mallory homicide. The investigators' ears pricked up.

First, Chastity told Doug that she had gone to Daytona for a few days with Richard Mallory to party. She also told Doug, not once but several times, that she had killed Richard Mallory. She repeatedly threatened to call Volusia investigators and admit to killing him.

On the face of it, Chastity seemed a likely, close to perfect, suspect, particularly in light of her confession. She had a criminal history and had in the past been seen with a .22 calibre handgun. She was adopted when she was nine but after two years her adoptive parents gave her up, unable to handle her violence and stealing. She was familiar with some of the Daytona area bars and streets, whereas Mallory was not. He had, it seemed, no friends, relatives or business in Daytona. So it was not hard to envisage her being his tour guide to Daytona's notoriously decadent underbelly.

A warrant was issued on 5 April for Chastity's arrest for first degree murder and a search began for her in the South Carolina area (where she worked for an escort service), in San Francisco and in Texas. On 25 May, Horzepa learned she had been arrested in New Orleans on local prostitution charges and was also wanted in Orange County, Florida, for a drug-related parole violation. Flying to New Orleans to interview her, Horzepa and Kelley found Chastity by then denying any involvement in Richard Mallory's murder. She was extradited to Florida but Horzepa worried that something just didn't smell right.

It had all seemed to fit so neatly. Too neatly, apparently.

'I don't know,' he says, recalling that day with a half-smile and shaking his head. 'After sixteen years of doing this job and interviewing people, when she was talking to me, it was just a sort of a gut feeling I had that it wasn't her, even though everything pointed to her.'

Horzepa concluded that Chastity's confession to Doug had more to do with their fights, 'and something in the air about him wanting her to move out', than with reality. 'I think she just might have said that to get his attention,' Horzepa surmised. 'And she just happened to say the wrong thing.'

Back in Volusia, he and Kelley consulted with assistant state attorney David Damore, and shared their misgivings. Meanwhile, Chastity's friend Danielle, although at one time implicated by Chastity, had passed a polygraph test. All law enforcement parties were in accord that there simply wasn't physical evidence tying Chastity to Mallory's murder. The charges were dropped.

Chastity or no, Horzepa didn't waver from his original position. Mallory's homicide bore the female imprint. Women generally kill people they know, but there was good reason to think that a woman had murdered Mr Mallory, given his personality. He never confided in anyone. He was wary. Wary of men, especially. The women in his life were adamant that he would never, ever, have stopped to pick up a male, not under any circumstances. If he gave someone a ride, all logic demanded it had to have been a woman.

'It would be very easy for him to stop and pick up a lone, female hitchhiker. He would not have felt threatened by that,' Horzepa reasoned.

Despite Mallory's encounter with two women on the very night he was murdered, Larry Horzepa was also convinced he'd had a single companion on his journey.

His educated deduction, based on long acquaintance with the quirks of human behaviour, was that Mr Mallory's enjoyment of two women would not supersede his underlying paranoia. A man like Mallory simply would not undertake that kind of drive with two women because one would have had to sit behind him. This was a man who always needed to feel in control, to have the upper hand. The kind of wary man who, in a restaurant, probably chose a table where he could have his back against the wall. It seemed highly unlikely he'd put himself in a vulnerable situation with women he didn't know well. It just wasn't his style. No, the encounter was one-on-one, Horzepa felt sure of it. And two, not three, glasses were found behind the car, bearing out his theory.

But if Chastity was no longer in the picture, who was?

18

Lee hated to share Ty. She loathed not having every scrap of her woman's undivided attention. She 'loved her to the max'. Why did Ty feel the need to have anyone else around? Especially guys. Lee couldn't understand Ty wanting to hang out with them. When Ty brought Dion, a drinking buddy of hers and colleague from the Casa Del Mar, home for a beer, Lee'd gotten so mad she'd thrown a yelling and screaming fit, scaring him off in short order. Other women were an unwelcome intrusion, but she *really* couldn't stand having men around the place. In their three years together, they'd developed remarkably few outside friendships as they moved around Florida, a tightly-wound, self-contained, isolated little unit, deflecting just about everyone from getting close. It was the way Lee liked it.

Cammie Greene was firmly ensconced in Ty's life before Lee came along. There was little Lee could do about that, although waves of jealousy surged over her about Ty's attachment to the pretty young woman. Lee was resentfully fearful of the fact they seemed to enjoy each other so much. Then again, Cammie was married. Safely preoccupied with Dinky and the boys. At the end of the day, Lee could warm herself with the knowledge that Ty chose to stay with her, not with Cammie. Crucially, when Lee told Ty that they were moving on, she went along with the plan.

Sandy Russell presented Lee with a different kind of threat, as did the Casa Del Mar itself, with its extra-curricular team spirit.

As always in her life, Lee was excluded from the team.

Ty had made friends with some of the staff. Unhampered by her size, she joined the hotel volleyball team, adding an after-hours activity to her life in which Lee had no part.

175

The separations while Lee went on her highway sorties seemed a necessary evil. They badly needed the money, but they made Lee nervous all the same and she kept them to a minimum. She was infinitely happier out there if she knew that Ty was lying around at home alone, just waiting for her to return.

'I make a hundred and fifty dollars a day and you only make a hundred and fifty dollars a week. I'll support you!' Lee grandly proclaimed when they first met, persuading Ty to be a stay-at-home wife. Her greater earning power and the knowledge that she had the means to take care of her lover were crucial to Lee's tenuous hold on any sense of security. The calculation was quite simple: while she was Ty's mainstay of support, she felt less afraid of being abandoned.

On the other hand, Ty's pay was regular and Ty liked her job. The Casa Del Mar became an important part of Ty's life, whether Lee liked it or not.

So did Sandy. Ty made no secret of how much she loved her company at work and after hours. To Lee, Ty's pretty, unattached friend represented a threatening combination. Sandy was supposedly straight, but who knew? She kept coming around to the Burleigh apartment for a few beers, or they'd go out and visit a bar or two. Lee liked her though, in spite of herself.

Sandy wasn't so fond of Lee, however nice and sweet and friendly she tried to be. For one thing, Sandy grew tired of Lee's hunger to be the centre of attention the whole time. When they were trying to pay attention to a video, it was wearing the way Lee kept turning to Ty and demanding, 'Hold me! Hold me!' Downright annoying. Just like a big kid, Sandy thought. 'Shut up!' Ty admonished Lee, without taking her eyes off the screen. Duly reprimanded, Lee would briefly fall silent, but the attention-getting behaviour soon started up all over again. She seemed driven to make everyone focus on her and she'd do whatever it took.

Sandy's deepening friendship with Ty, however, amply compensated for her growing dislike of Lee and the discomfort she felt around her. Sandy was no stranger to difficult partners who had to be catered to, and didn't sit in judgement.

Despite her and Ty's core difference in sexual orientation,

they'd become like soul sisters, sharing secrets and exchanging confidences, spending long hours chewing over the minutiae of their personal lives.

Of course, Ty's chewing over had severe limitations. Ty had trouble admitting to herself what Lee had done to Richard Mallory; hell might have to freeze over before she'd voluntarily admit it to someone else. Talking about it would have made it seem more real. No, it was best buried.

Sandy, who was blissfully unaware of her friend's shocking, black secret, had already decided that for Ty's sake she would endure Lee and her foibles. Since Ty and Lee were all but joined at the hip, it was the price Sandy had to pay.

Ty, with her irresistible, simpatico sense of humour, provided a veritable ray of sunshine in Sandy's otherwise rather grey and mundane life. They had even more fun during football season when Ty carted a small, portable television set into the laundry room and the two avid sports fans raucously cheered on their teams. Ty favoured the Georgia Bulldogs, Sandy the Cleveland Browns. Good-naturedly lobbing repartee—and hotel towels—back and forth, made the work go easier.

Their colleagues, who weren't privy to the intimate conversational shorthand that developed between them, affectionately decided they were both nuts. Both Sandy and Ty were popular. Witnessing the two women's special rapport and affection for one another, some also questioned the exact nature of Ty and Sandy's relationship. Inevitably, rumours flew. They were lovers. They were sleeping together. They were having a mad affair. Sandy and Ty had a good chuckle about it, then promptly ignored it. Nothing they couldn't handle.

In truth, Ty's preference for women came as a relief to Sandy, who had few women friends. With Ty, there was none of that competitive stuff that had soured so many of her other relationships with women. Sandy was definitely of the shy rather than flirtatious or sexually aggressive type, yet somehow that only enhanced her considerable appeal to men. As a result, she found women often took a dislike to her without even knowing her. She'd grown used to them making superficial, unfavourable judgements about her based on her looks, then leaping to their

177

erroneous assumptions that she was out to poach their husbands or boyfriends.

Sandy certainly didn't have to worry about Ty thinking she was coming on to Lee! And whatever Ty's underlying feelings might have been for Sandy (particularly when the going got rough with Lee), she treated her with too much respect ever to complicate their friendship by making any moves toward her. It was all nice and simple.

You didn't need to be Einstein to see how head over heels in love with Ty Lee was, and Sandy put Lee's possessiveness down to that love. It accounted for the way Lee tried to keep Ty on a taut rein. Ty and Lee's relationship was fiery, though. Sometimes their fights turned physical and they'd slap one another or wrestle around on the floor. Lee prided herself on being tough, but Ty was no featherweight pushover, mentally or physically. Built like the mascot of her favourite Georgia Bulldogs, it was hard for anyone to put one over on her, and that included Lee. They were pretty evenly matched.

Gary Kopietz had decided way back when Lee was a teenage prostitute that cigarettes were her downfall, but alcohol would have been a more appropriate culprit to earmark. No one knew better than Ty, who had learned it to her detriment, that Lee was transformed into a totally different person when she drank. Over the years, Ty had seen her go on some real cataclysmic binges. Ty liked to put away the beers, too, but she couldn't hold a candle to Lee. The woman was a bottomless pit. With every drink that passed her lips, she grew louder and more boisterous. When she tipped over the line from obnoxious to aggressive, though, she'd never once hurt Ty. If anything, she was downright protective of her, just as she used to be with Lori.

Lee repeatedly told Ty how much she loved her.

She would do anything for her.

She even said she would die for her.

When Ty and Lee finally dropped the party line about Lee having a pressure-cleaning business and keeping her equipment in a white van down in Orlando, Sandy was hardly shocked. But on hearing that Lee was 'a call girl', she couldn't help wondering about Lee's ability to draw customers. With her beer belly and butch outfits (sleeveless white T-shirts some-times worn without a bra, and cut-off jeans), she hardly struck Sandy as any kind of seductress. Prostitution was an odd ca-reer choice for someone who so loathed men. But Sandy often gave Lee a ride to the interstate and watched her walk off into the distance, carrying her little blue bag, looking for rides. And now she learned that Lee's modus operandi as a hitch-hiking prostitute was to work exit to exit, getting into any-where from eight to fifteen strangers' cars a day, and generally having sex with three, six, sometimes as many as eight of them. If one guy turned down her offer, she'd simply get out at the next exit and start all over again.

'Aren't you afraid of being out there hitchhiking and getting in a car with anybody?' Sandy asked, rather in awe of this brav-ery—or foolhardiness.

'I carry my gun. I'm not afraid,' Lee replied with a shrug.

'Aren't you afraid of getting AIDS?' Sandy persisted.

'I use condoms, even for head,' Lee retorted, very matter-of-factly.

Ty didn't like Lee turning tricks, but Ty did like partying and was perfectly willing to help Lee spend her money. Her usual haul could be anywhere from $20 to a hundred, maybe more. Later, Lee complained of Ty's extravagance. Ty was a spendthrift who frittered away her hard-earned cash, whereas she, Lee, was so frugal, so dedicated to saving up to buy a house, that she was reduced to wearing a bra held together with Band-Aids. Lee scathingly accused Ty of only being interested in going to the mall on spending sprees. Ty repeatedly put pressure on her to get out there and spread her legs, Lee alleged. 'She was constantly telling me I wasn't making enough money.'

Whether Ty's goal was in fact to send her girlfriend out onto the streets with renewed vigour, or to push her into getting a proper job, depended upon who was telling the story.

Sandy was only grateful for Lee's absences which she con-sidered a blessing. Sometimes, she was only gone for a few hours, but occasionally she disappeared overnight. Ty didn't seem to mind either. Ty and Sandy hung out together and watched TV without interruption.

As the summer rolled around, Ty began focusing her attention on the impending visit of her 18-year-old half-sister, Tracey Moore. Tracey planned to come down to Florida from Ohio during her college summer break so she could spend some time with Ty and combine a vacation with some kind of job. Excited at the prospect, Ty began fantasising about all the things they could do together. Tracey needed to make money for school and Ty was confident that she could get her in at the Casa Del Mar. On the strength of those assurances, Ty's parents, Jack and Mary Ann, sprang for Tracey's air ticket.

Tracey, who did not know Ty was gay, was woefully unprepared for the rude awakening awaiting her in Florida. She had not been warned that Ty and her friend Lee were lovers, let alone about Lee's anti-social behaviour.

Ty worked out the sleeping arrangements so that Tracey slept in the upstairs portion of the small, split level apartment, while she and Lee stayed together down below.

Watching her sister and Lee interact, Tracey soon suspected that it wasn't just a regular friendship. Only later, piecing together fragments of comments made by her parents, did she find out for sure.

Her more immediate problem was dealing with Lee. She didn't know what to make of her. No sooner had she unpacked her bags than Lee was asking if she ever did dope? No, Tracey said flatly. It was just that sometimes she got paid for her pressure-cleaning work with something other than money, or people gave her bonuses, Lee explained.

Lee also pointedly told Tracey that things were very tight financially. Someone had stiffed her in her business, then some substance she'd been exposed to on her job had made her sick, so Ty had been struggling to pay all the rent and they'd fallen a few months behind.

Tracey, who was ready to knuckle down to work, had no intention of lazing around and living off the fat of the land. She would pull her weight. And Ty was as good as her word. Tracey flew in on a Thursday in mid-May and the very next day, was hired by the Casa Del Mar. The sisters were thrilled. Working alongside one another in housekeeping, which carried a staff of close to thirty, they'd see lots of each other.

Revelling in their reunion, they were oblivious to the effect they were having on Lee. She didn't like the rival for Ty's attention or affections one little bit. Lee's perception of things was warped, misguided, and often blatantly wrong, but it was irrefutably how she saw the world. And at this moment Lee's world was inhabited by looming forces who threatened her very being.

Tracey couldn't possibly have known that just her presence activated some of Lee's deepest, most persistent fears of being abandoned by Ty. As the person in the relationship more afraid of being left, Lee was intensely vulnerable. And Tracey represented a dark threat to her shaky sense of well-being. She was not only a potent competitor for Ty's attention but was also, Lee decided, a spoiled little brat. Miss Goody Two-Shoes. Didn't drink. Didn't smoke. What did she do? How could she possibly fit in with them if she didn't drink?

Tracey, viewing her sister's relationship from the outside, heard Lee constantly talk about leaving to go to work, but it seemed there was far more talk than action. Lee's promises were just so much hot air. Tracey had no clue how hard it was for Lee to leave. Lee's worst fear was that Tracey might somehow talk Ty into leaving her, or might persuade her to go back to Ohio with her.

Tracey was no fonder of Lee than Lee was of her, not that she knew much about her. She didn't even know her last name, although she thought it was Polish and began with a 'B'. Lee gradually unfurled a potted (and heavily edited) life history, saying she'd been married and divorced when she was very young, and that her ex-husband, whom she called 'fuck face', was very wealthy.

To Tracey, Lee just seemed downright odd. When Tracey registered her surprise that people didn't always lock their doors, the next thing she knew, Lee, quite unsolicited, wandered up to her bedroom and handed her a black nightstick with an engraved knob at one end and a leather grasp strap. The weapon was just to keep with her in case she ever needed it. Lee said she had a gun in her room, too, should Tracey ever need that.

Tracey also found Lee completely unpredictable. Nice one minute, screaming her head off the next. Not someone she could imagine ever wanting to get close to. Heaven knows what her sister saw in her. Tracey never saw Lee being physically aggressive, but she certainly talked enough about violence. That, and hating cops. Something held Tracey back from asking just why she loathed them so much. Just as something held her back from asking about blood she saw on some clothes and shoes one day when she was doing laundry.

It was when Lee was drunk—which was often—that Tracey truly dreaded being around her. 'That is when she really got violent. Not violent but . . . kind of out of control . . . loud, boisterous,' she observed.

When it came to beer, Lee drank anything, whatever was on the table, but heaven help them if someone offered her a shot of spirit and she got into whisky or vodka. That really sent her over the top.

Lee showed no concern about fitting in with the rest of the world and blasted out her music so loudly that no one else could hear themselves think. Anyone telling her to turn it down sent her off the deep end.

Just living in her presence, waiting for the next explosion, made Tracey horribly tense and uncomfortable. She was shocked, too, that when Ty and Lee got into one of their petty arguments, her sister backed down. That was totally uncharacteristic. Unheard of. She'd never known Ty back down to anyone. And Ty, in so many ways, had the stronger personality of the two.

Summing up her feelings about Lee, Tracey admitted, 'I was just plain scared to death of her.'

19

As ex-husbands go, 47-year-old David Spears rated somewhere around dream come true. He was predictable, honest, hard-working, responsible, a man you could count on. Their divorce notwithstanding, David still cared enough for Dee, his wife of twenty years and companion of twenty-six, regularly to hand her a good chunk of his pay cheque from Universal Concrete. A shy, soft-spoken giant of a man, 6 feet 4 inches, bearded, greying and weather-lined from his outdoor lifestyle, David was everyone's idea of a nice guy. Quiet, and something of a loner. David and Dee, childhood sweethearts, met and fell in love in their native Kentucky when she was fifteen, he twenty-one. They married a year later. They'd divorced in '84, if you followed those pieces of paper, yet as man and woman they were unwilling and unable to stay apart. They were living under the same roof the day their divorce was finalised. Not only did the divorce not take, their remarrying was on the cards once their daughter, Deanna, had graduated. David bought Dee an engagement ring in April.

A creature of habit, David's weekend ritual was to go to stay with Dee. The mother of his three children lived just short of a hundred miles away in Winter Garden, near Orlando. On Saturdays, after signing out at his job as a loading supervisor, he hopped into his cream pick-up and headed on over. His usual route, certainly the most direct, was to go north from Sarasota on I-75, then flip east on I-4. He spent weeknights in a rented trailer, so he customarily arrived clutching an accumulation of dirty laundry.

Just before lunchtime on Friday 18 May 1990 David called Dee and told her to expect him somewhere between 2 and 2.30

the next day. Definitely no later than 3, he promised. He'd be bringing her a special gift, a sleek, black, ceramic panther that stood about ten inches high. He loved indulging her and her passion for big cats and pretty clothes. He'd also have the cash so they could run out and shop for Deanna's birthday on the 23rd, and her upcoming graduation. God, he was so proud of Deanna. Hard to believe his little baby girl was all grown up.

When Saturday rolled round, David waved goodbye to his colleagues at Universal Concrete at 2.10 p.m. after sharing a quick beer with them outside in the parking lot. He had a busy afternoon ahead. His son Jeff, who worked alongside him, tried to get him to go to a bar. 'No, I'm going home to your mama,' David replied.

But David simply did not materialise in Winter Garden. No phone call, no message, nothing.

He made his fateful decision and opened the door of his pickup to her somewhere near route 27. 27 intersects with I-4 just 36 miles from his Winter Garden destination. He'd have been at Dee's within thirty minutes. He might have stopped for gas. Most likely, she flagged him down on some pretext.

When it was all over, she, the only living witness, who could say whatever she liked about these men unchallenged—and did—claimed that even though it took him clear out of his way, David Spears willingly agreed to drive her to Homosassa Springs. Even though it would inevitably make him late (and how late, he could never imagine), he simply took off in the opposite direction.

David wasn't perfect, he wasn't an angel, but he was Dee's and she loved him. And it just wasn't like him to forget about his wife—for he never thought of her as anything else—knowing she'd be worrying herself silly. If he'd had devious intentions and planned, say, an illicit detour into the woods for sex, common sense and his own well-developed sense of responsibility would dictate that he'd first stop to make a phone call. It would have been so simple to call Winter Garden and make some excuse for being late. That would have been the end of it. Easy. He made no such call. And there were 'titty factories', as Jeff called them, right by the works. Why wouldn't he go there?

Homosassa was her old stomping ground, and, lying, she told him she lived there. Matter of fact, she had a plan. She always had a plan. She figured that once she and the pick-up fella parted company, she'd trick in Homosassa for a while. She knew some guys there who could put money in her pocket. They ended up on US 19 outside Homosassa, pulling off the road, then driving so deep into the woods that she was afraid his truck might get stuck. She said it was late, maybe even one or two in the morning, when it happened. More than nine hours had passed during which David Spears didn't make that phone call. Maybe, maybe not.

Her beer consumption goes without saying. Wherever she was, beer flowed. David liked it, too, and could handle it. It would have taken an awful lot of beer for that to become any kind of reason for not calling home. She never did account for those long, unexplained hours or the curious geography. But they were naked. They'd been 'screwing around', getting drunk, she said, when he wanted her to climb in the back of the pick-up where she saw a lead pipe. She says the gentle giant turned vicious. The gentle giant whose three kids knew Daddy would never hurt a fly. The gentle giant who happened to have hundreds of dollars in his pocket for his daughter's big day, got rough. Suddenly. Well.

Adrenalin coursing again, she leapt down from the back and made for the passenger door. He jumped out, too, but in a single, almost-fluid move she reached in, retrieved her bag and gun, then with lightning speed, fired. She plugged that first bullet in him right where he stood, by the tailgate.

He was wounded, but still mobile. Stunned, acting on pure survival instinct, her prey rushed around to the driver's door and hurried to clamber in. The move brought him closer to his attacker, but the truck seemed his sole refuge when there was no real place to hide. If he escaped her, he could drive away.

A vain hope. Watching him, she said: 'What the hell you think you're doin', dude . . . I'm gonna kill you, 'cause you were trying to do whatever you could with me!'

Blasting off another shot, she aimed right at him across the car seat. Close enough for the gunfire to tilt him back. Oh, she had the drop on him now. He was a big guy, but what could *he* do, naked and bleeding?

She was naked also, and barefoot. D'you think she had any intention of tearing up her feet by running through the woods and the briars? No way. What else would you have liked her to do? Hold the gun on him while she got dressed, then walk on out of there? Oh no. What if he—what if any of them—had come after her and run her down? What if they'd had guns, too? They might have had guns. Did you think of that?

With two bullets racking his body, as David Spears backed away from the truck, staggering, retreating, she shuffled her butt across the seat to the driver's side, then fired another shot that knocked him clean off his feet, tipping him backwards.

That was it. At least, that's how she remembered it.

Maybe there was a fourth bullet? Just to make sure he'd die. Hard to remember everything.

Indeed, there was a fourth. And a fifth. Even a sixth. One lodged itself in the back of his collarbone. A few were mercilessly pumped into a dying man's retreating back.

Her mind was brimming with other things. Like making sure he was dead. That she could remember. Couldn't let him live to tell the tale. Satisfied on that score, she drove off in his pickup. But first, she cleaned out his cash. His wages, Deanna's graduation money, plus the fallback, secret cash-stash he kept tucked in his truck for emergencies. He was a strictly cash kind of guy. No bank account, no credit cards.

All told, she probably stole between $500 and $700 from the dead man. For she was a robber, too, most assuredly. The money motivated her. And she needed it. Just as she'd always needed it. She was in control. Just let anyone try and mess with her.

She drove away aimlessly at first, then decided to head over to Burleigh Avenue, unloading those of his tools that she thought she could turn around for a few bucks.

Ty, who'd worked the 11 a.m. to 7 p.m. shift at the Casa Del Mar on the day David Spears died, spotted his truck through the window. She thought it was yellow, but she was always a bit off with colours. She didn't ride in it. Didn't even step outside to see it. Lee said she'd borrowed it and Ty didn't question her further. It was gone by the next day.

Lee drove it a good, long way before dumping it. She went west to I-75, then north to Orange Lake. Finally, she climbed out and ripped off the licence plate with her bare hands. Needing a suitably unobtrusive spot in which to dump it, she laid it in a ditch near the truck, and camouflaged it with grass. She then yanked the radio out of the truck—it was hanging by a wire, all she had to do was pull—and took it with her.

Drunkenly walking away, she spotted a homeless-type fellow sitting right there in the woods.

'Hey, man, you need a place to crash?' she called out. 'Go crash in that truck.' Suddenly Lady Bountiful.

Later, what would be endlessly puzzling to Dee was quite how Lee had enticed David away on the day he had Deanna's graduation on his mind. He can't have gone willingly.

She must have enjoyed the killing. If you fired one bullet into somebody, surely seeing the blood would be such a shock that you would throw the gun and start running? You wouldn't keep going, bullet after bullet.

Dee was so sure of David that she knew he was dead the very first day he didn't come home. Later, the lies made it harder for her to move on, to put the loss behind her.

When David Spears died, the mysteries went with him to his grave.

20

Forty-year-old Charles Carskaddon, a sometime road digger and rodeo rider, left his mother's Missouri home at around 4 p.m. on 31 May. Chuck was a good, considerate son who often paid Mom's gas or phone bill or set to and mowed her lawn. That Thursday, he was bound for Tampa, Florida, to pick up Peggy, his fiancée. A lover of the ultra-quiet Missouri farmland (he lived in Boonesville), Florida was not his cup of tea. He'd once considered living there if it meant finding work, but luckily didn't have to. He'd just landed a job as a press operator in Missouri and was bringing Peggy back to join him. He set off alone, persuaded by Mom to leave Muffin, his Sheltie dog, with her rather than cooping him up in the car for the long round-trip. (Ironic. Things might have gone differently if she'd seen a cute dog in the car with him.)

He cruised 24 south through Paducah, Kentucky, to I-75, caressing the wheel of the 1975 Cadillac he lovingly restored in his spare time. Chuck was handy with tools. No question, he'd stop and help someone with car trouble. A woman in distress? In a second. But no one knew what interrupted his journey.

Neither Peggy nor anyone else ever saw or heard from him again.

Darkness had engulfed the pancake-flat countryside by the time Chuck Carskaddon showed up, tooling along in what, missing the beauty he saw in it, she dismissed as 'a brown, whipped-looking, ugly thing'. Their destinies collided somewhere outside Tampa. He was barely short of his destination and his excited fiancée. So near, and yet so far.

He'd never be able to dispute her claim that he'd said he was a drug dealer. It wouldn't have been a sensible announcement, not for anyone with half a brain. Nor a likely one. Maybe a joke, if it was said at all. Whatever. It was, she said, a precursor to them striking a deal for sex and to him wheeling his Cadillac into a suitably deserted spot off Highway 52.

Chuck Carskaddon faced death in the back seat of his own car. She shot him there more than once. As always, once she began, she kept going. Pulling the trigger again and again and again, until all life had ebbed away.

When she was through, she searched his car. She found his .45 sitting on the hood. No one disputes he had one. (He had a stun gun, too, and planned to sell the .45 on his trip.)

Maybe he was planning to blow her brains out? That's what she thought—after she'd filled him with bullets. Hey! She had almost been hurt! That really pissed her off. Think what might have happened. It pissed her off so bad that she reloaded the .22 and fired a couple more bullets into his body for good measure.

She was fed up about something else, too. He only had twenty bucks in his wallet. That's what she said, as if it were a sin on his part that deserved retribution. Assuming it to be true. Even after filling up the car's huge gas tank, he'd have had close to three hundred dollars in cash. Unless he'd been robbed before he met her. And how much ill can befall a man in one day? Possible, as they put it in courtrooms, but not probable. Chuck's wallet was never seen again.

Another unlikely victim, he was younger, stronger, fitter, and faster on his feet, as befitted a rodeo rider. His physical fortitude didn't help him. Ultimately, by the time she had reloaded her seven-shot revolver, she'd fired nine bullets into his shaking, quivering body. Nine bullets. Nine. What else could you call it but sheer, cold-hearted overkill? Impulsive rage, outweighing rationale.

When he was safely dead and she'd scooped up all she wanted, she drove the car she found so ugly back to her apartment. She backed it, as she always did her temporary trophies, into her and Ty's spot, tucked conveniently away beside the house. Later, Ty (who was off work from 31 May until 3 June) took a perfunctory look at it through the window, but it was soon gone again. It seemed to Ty that it was there just a couple of days after the pick-up. In actuality, it was closer to ten days.

Even Ty's well-developed, ostrich-like tendencies couldn't completely block out the brief appearances of these mysteriously acquired vehicles that supposedly came back with Lee from her so-called trips to her pressure-cleaning business in Orlando. The trips, as Ty knew, were a con line anyway. So what did that make the cars? They turned up out of nowhere. Loaned by faceless friends to a woman Ty, of all people, knew to be friendless. Only to vanish in a manner disturbingly reminiscent of Richard Mallory's Cadillac. In the light of what had gone before, how could Ty not wonder, question and worry about the fates of their owners? Whatever thoughts sputtered through her denial system, though, she shut down. She did nothing. Told no one. Silently complicit.

By contrast, Ty's memory would log quite clearly Lee coming home with the .45 automatic. She remembered its pearly-white handle grips and the black, holster-style case that snapped on the side. She'd remember it with good reason. She used it, too.

Sometimes, after the bullets and the bloodletting, Lee felt guilty about what she'd done. It didn't last, though. No. Most of the time, she felt good. Like a hero or something. As if she'd done something really useful to benefit society.

Oh, she guessed she'd done a few crooked things in her life. But she'd only been protecting herself, that was all. That's why she knew she'd go to heaven.

Inside her, right inside, she knew she was a good person.

21

There is no rule decreeing that someone who finds a body is any kind of hero. Sometimes they become a prime suspect. So it was for the young man named Matthew who on 1 June 1990 spotted a dead body lying in the woods in a clearing amidst the pine trees and palmettos. He'd wandered far off the beaten track, passing an illegal dumping site on Fling Lane and walking down a rutted trail into a deserted wooded area.

Fling Lane is a dirt road south of Chassahowitzka and runs adjacent to US 19, and just north of the Citrus County/Hernando County line. Had anyone been able to do the impossible and plough through the woods in a straight line from US 19, they'd have found the body not much more than four hundred feet from the main road.

Alerted by Matthew and called to the scene late that afternoon, Sergeant William Burns and Investigator Wallace Griggs of the Citrus County Sheriff's Office were confronted with a badly decomposed body, nude except for a camouflage-design ball cap. Nature was far enough along in its course that at first glance they couldn't determine the sex or age or likely cause of death. It was, however, lying on its back, legs apart, arms outstretched, palms facing skywards. Securing the immediate area, they spotted some beer cans, papers, and assorted items close by, and a number of tyre tracks.

Sergeant David Strickland and Investigator Fred Johnson also showed up, as did Investigator Jerry Thompson of Citrus County's CID, a twenty-year law enforcement veteran who'd been summoned by a phone call to his home.

This Matthew behaved oddly, even for one who had recently had the shocking misfortune to stumble across a corpse. Interviewing him, Sgt Burns thought him evasive, nervous and inconsistent. Not unnaturally, this aroused his suspicions. Did people who committed such crimes ever report them, too? Matthew wanted to know. That didn't help either. He could know far more than he was letting on. With a word to the wise, Burns turned him over to Griggs who took him back to Citrus's Operations Center where he and Jerry Thompson would take a crack at questioning him.

Meanwhile, the dark thunderclouds that had been loitering ominously above the strength-sapping, ninety-degree humidity began to do their worst. Nothing hampers crime scene investigation quite so handily as a heavy downpour. After covering the body with plastic and cordoning off and securing the scene, most of the officers had no choice but to retreat and wait out the rain. Teletypes were circulated, though, feeding into the crowded system their limited description of a John Doe.

Under Jerry Thompson's questioning, Matthew stayed close to his original theme about being a surveyor looking for a section line for a friend—but changed other elements of his story a couple of times. Worse, he couldn't remember the friend's name. His shifty, downright suspicious behaviour propelled law enforcement down an investigative path that looked as fertile as any other, for the moment. He admitted to owning a .30-30 rifle, which he'd traded a week or so earlier for a .357 pistol. Finally, Thompson's prodding elicited an embarrassed confession: Matthew had really been looking for a place to masturbate. If true, it went some way towards explaining his curious behaviour. But why venture so deep into the woods? Under full investigation by then, he agreed to give blood, head hair and pubic hair samples.

The next morning, under kinder meteorological conditions, Fred Johnson took detailed photographs and videotape of the naked body and the damaged trees around it. The trees looked as if a vehicle might have ploughed through them, and might yield further clues. He also photographed a tyre track found on a plywood board (it could mean something, or absolutely nothing) and assorted items lying around the body—cigarette butts,

Busch and Budweiser beer cans, an open Trojan condom pack, a used condom and tissue papers.

Dr Janet Pillow carried out the autopsy on Monday 4 June with Dr Maples, a forensic anthropologist connected with the University of Florida Gainesville, in attendance. The man who weighed 195 pounds in life was reduced to around 40 in death. That's all that was left of him. Dr Pillow began with an X-ray that revealed six bullets in the torso. All six were recovered that day (although one later went missing somewhere down the evidence chain). At least one or two bullets were fired into Mr Spears from behind, one hitting him in the collarbone, the rest in the torso.

There might have been more bullets, but the state of the body precluded ever knowing for sure.

The victim was described as a 6 foot 2 male, over 45, with brown hair, moustache and perhaps a beard. A toxicology report was also impossible; decomposition was too far along for them to retrieve the necessary blood sample. So there was no way of knowing if the victim had ingested alcohol or drugs.

On 6 June Jerry Thompson called Dottie Young, a detective with the Sarasota Police Department, who had left a message for him in response to Citrus's BOLO teletype on the victim. Be on the lookout, it meant. Young was. She had a missing person, 6 feet 4 inches tall, 47 years old. David Andrew Spears. Might he be a match?

Detective Tom Muck, a seventeen-year veteran with Pasco County Sheriff's Office, also got a call on Wednesday 6 June. Another nude, white, male body had been found in some woods in his jurisdiction. When Muck arrived at the crime scene at around 4.30 p.m., what he saw was a decomposing, naked body covered with a green electric blanket and weeds. At first glance, he could tell it had probably lain there for a few days.

The medical examiner, Dr Joan Wood, had performed over five thousand autopsies, and was able to pin down the time of death more precisely. Approximately five days before discovery of the body. The cause? No less than nine .22-calibre gunshot wounds, maybe more. One bullet had hit the deceased's upper left arm, the remaining eight had struck his chest and abdomen. During the autopsy, Joan Wood retrieved eight of those bullets from the torso and labelled them accordingly. She then carefully extricated the bullet fragments from the arm.

The close grouping of the projectiles led her to deduce that the victim had probably moved very little while his life was being extinguished, and that he and his attacker were facing one another head on.

Because of the decomposition, it was impossible to determine the mystery man's height, weight or eye colour. A probable likeness was re-created graphically to help with identification, and what was left of his fingerprints were rolled. For the time being there was no other fate for him: he was another sad John Doe.

On 7 June, investigators Jerry Thompson and Marvin Padgett collected David Spears' dental X-rays from his dentist in the town of Ocoee as, simultaneously, Sergeant Strickland and Investigator Johnson picked up his skull. Both were taken to Dr Thomas G. Ford who successfully used them to make a positive identification. David Spears had been found dead, as Dee had supposed all along. And oh, it hurt so bad when she found out later that he'd been taken to pieces like that.

Thompson and Padgett then got a message from Pasco County's Tom Muck regarding his white, nude male victim who had also been found in a remote area near a major highway. Muck's man had been shot nine times with a .22 and he was wondering if their homicide might be related. They all agreed it was well worth exploring.

Padgett and Thompson informed Sarasota's Dottie Young of the positive i.d. on Spears, and she had news for them, too. Spears' 1983 Dodge pick-up had already turned up on a highway ramp in Marion County.

In a thousand-to-one long shot, it had been spotted back on 28 May by Robert 'Red' Kerr, none other than Spears' work supervisor. He and his wife Beverly had been driving back from a vacation in Nashville along I-75. As the Kerrs came out of Gainesville and passed ramp 318, Red spotted a truck sitting by the side of the highway, disabled by a flat. He turned to his wife and said, 'That looks like Dave's!' He wasn't sure until he reversed up the highway for a proper look, but it was not surprising he should recognise it, even with its tag missing. He'd sold it to Dave. Peering in the back, the pick-up's past owner recognised an axle that he knew for sure belonged to Dave. He also noted an inflated spare along with a couple of jacks. Dave would have changed the flat in a second. But there was no sign of the tools Dave usually carried. The passenger window was ajar, and the truck was unlocked. The Kerrs pulled off at the next exit and called 911.

Scrutinising the vehicle down in Sarasota, Jerry Thompson couldn't spot any overt signs of a struggle or of shooting inside the truck, but he did notice some dried blood on the driver's side, just on the inner running board. The evidence technicians collected that along with their other scrapings and vacuumings. An empty condom packet was also found in the truck. Spears' laundry was nowhere to be seen. Nor was the black panther he was taking to Dee.

With the murder investigation under way, the killer's sex inevitably became an issue. Their extensive interviewing had given detectives no reason to suspect that Spears had ever engaged in any homosexual activities. Anyway, Jerry Thompson and the others knew it would be unusual for two males having sex to leave a condom behind. The prophylactics near the body weren't proven to be Spears', but did seem to indicate the presence of at least one woman somewhere along the line. Perhaps he was killed by a man and woman team? Or a woman acting solo? Or two women acting in concert?

Inevitably, the question arose: was there another woman in Dave's life? Red felt it was possible. Dave and Dee's relationship was very volatile and he indicated to officers that there'd been problems. There'd been a blow-up at the works once when Dee had accused Dave of fathering her son's girlfriend's child. She didn't *really* think that. No way. But she was mad enough at him that day to hurl the accusation. Words, just words. It didn't sound good, though, when Dave disappeared. He'd taken out life insurance that year. Only $12,000, not a fortune. He wasn't a rich man. But Dee, the policy's beneficiary, felt the timing made her look bad. And struggling to survive without him, she learned the hard facts of life for common-law wives. She didn't qualify for any widow's benefit because they weren't legally married when he died.

Scared to death alone in her apartment, not knowing who had killed Dave, it seemed to her that the cops viewed her as a suspect. They thought he'd run off with a woman and that she'd got mad and shot him. They'd always fought. She never denied it. And if anyone was likely to lash out, it was Dee, not Dave. She provoked him sometimes, but he just stood there and took it.

Detectives learned that on Tuesdays, Dave patronised Ramano's bar. Most other weekday afternoons, he and some colleagues usually fished off the dock of a closed-up marina in Sarasota, had a few beers and relaxed. Dave was generally home before dark. There was no evidence of any other woman in his life.

22

Peter Siems, a 65-year-old retired merchant marine living near Jupiter, Florida, loaded into his Sunbird his ever-present stack of Bibles. Mr Siems, a balding, bespectacled, part-time missionary, took spreading the Word seriously, both in his everyday life and as a member of the Christ Is The Answer Crusade. In his neighbourhood, he lent a hand transporting folk and landscaping the grounds around the church.

Ursula, Peter's wife of over 25 years and a fellow missionary, was away in Europe working, as was their son, Leonard. Peter planned to drive I-95 all the way north to New Jersey to visit his mother, then, in July, to move on to Arkansas to spend a week with his 23-year-old son, Stefan, a mechanical engineer.

Setting off on 7 June, besides the Bibles, Peter packed a suitcase and a small holdall from the family's communal luggage pool—both navy blue, with a tan trim. He took the radio/tape-player Stefan had given him on their last visit, plus a few other distinctive items like his light windbreaker jacket and a yellow and black flashlight. He'd filled his toiletry bag with the usual basics and the favourite scissors he'd used to cut Stefan's hair when he was a kid. Memories. How time flew.

His neighbours watched him pack up and leave at around 9 p.m. Helen Slattery would be keeping an eye on things while he was gone. Then he simply disappeared without trace.

Peter Siems headed north out of Jupiter. She'd recall him picking her up on I-95 near its intersection with 100, not far from Bunnell. Another time, she said they met in a coffee shop. She was drunk. Very drunk. That's why she just couldn't remember precisely where they drove. She thought they crossed the state line into Georgia. Or was it Carolina? She vaguely recalled stopping somewhere past Fort Stewart military reservation (just ouside Savannah), but retreating back to the car after being descended upon by hundreds of swarming flies. Finally, they found a spot about ten miles off I-95 in the woods, a spot she couldn't pinpoint on a map.

Peter Siems, the missionary with the carful of Bibles, met his death after doing unspeakably sick things to her. So she said. When he carried a sleeping bag to lay out on the grass, she carried her murder bag.

They'd stripped off their clothes when the thought came. I'm *not* going to give you a chance to rape me. I don't wanna shoot you. I know you were gonna rape me. The illogic of this preemptive thinking escaped her.

When the time came to do her deed, they struggled over her gun, a couple of accidental shots escaping, ringing out, melting unheard into the air above them. Finally ripping the gun back from him, she deftly flipped it from her left hand to her right and fired. She aimed straight for his torso, wanting no doubt that the bullet hit home.

After the first shot, she justifed the rest. Told herself, I don't really want to do this to you, guy, but I'm gonna have to. If I did let you live, you'd tell who I am, and all this other jazz. And I'd probably get caught.

Why on earth did she drive so far with him? If he'd just turned out to be a trick, it would have spelled economic disaster. A major time investment for little return. Maybe she got him to tell her how much money he had on him. Maybe she'd decided it was going to be worth it.

When it was over, she rifled through his belongings like a hungry vulture picking over the bones, sifting out what might be saleable. She tossed the red sleeping bag in one direction, and threw his clothing in another.

She spotted the Bibles under the seat. Lots of them. What was this guy? A minister, or something? Curiosity aroused, she flipped open a cover, peering inside, expecting to see a reverend's name. It was blank. Moving on, she opened his suitcase, finding not just the small vestiges of a man's life but around four hundred dollars. One of her best hauls.

Odd, if he *was* a missionary. When she was a litle girl, you see, she'd always wanted to be a nun. Then, when she grew up, she thought of being a missionary herself. A missionary, or a cop. Matter of fact, she'd looked into being a cop. But you had to have all these grades she hadn't got, not to mention a ton of money for the tuition. Thousands of dollars. She'd had to forget that idea real quick.

Depriving Peter Siems's family of the finality of a funeral, her memory would falter irrevocably on where she left his supposedly naked body to rot in obscurity. On the other hand, she'd remember that Ty was in bed asleep when she pulled up in the Sunbird. She crept in silently. When Ty awoke, Lee was under the covers beside her.

The same day that Peter Siems disappeared, Marion County police found Chuck Carskaddon's brown, 1975 Cadillac just off I-75, just south of CR 484, pointing in a southerly direction. The licence plate had been taken off but the VIN number revealed the Missouri man's name. By the time the car was actually impounded one week later (the day that a distraught Mrs Florence Carskaddon reported her only son as missing), its back seat had been ripped out by vandals and its headlights smashed. There was one satisfactory fingerprint and one only. Unfortunately, it was Carskaddon's own.

It had turned into the bloodiest of summers, her pace accelerating into a veritable killing frenzy. Three lives snuffed out in less than three weeks. Three good men gone for ever. Three families devastated, just like that.

She was propelled by uncontrollable rages, by dark impulses she couldn't resist. She was driven on by a desperate need to somehow short-circuit the monumental fear and anxiety that welled up in her like poison. The pain and anger that tormented her were old and familiar. Pain and anger at knowing that Ty, Tracey, Sandy and their friend, Tammy, had piled merrily into Sandy's car for a day of frivolity and fun at Universal Studios down in Orlando. Frivolity and fun that excluded her. It resurrected all the old aloneness, the hollow emptiness, the frightening isolation, carrying her back to her childhood and to being left out. Everyone was afraid of being left. To Lee, with her warped thinking, it was more than that. It became a matter of survival.

Lee was put out if Ty did anything at all with other people, and that summer, the summer of Tracey, she burned with jealousy.

It seemed to Lee that Ty's bonds with the rest of the world were gathering strength and that she was slipping from Lee's grasp, inch by inch.

Then again, purely pragmatically, her need to lay her hands on some big money also nudged her forward. Ever since she'd been a little girl, having money had soothed her. The trouble was, pulling tricks was no longer easy for her with her body swollen from beer and inertia. The generous bloom of youth had long since been overtaken by her unhealthy pallor, her neglected teeth, her wrinkling skin. Unpleasant reflections of her decaying life.

In her warped perception of the world and its inhabitants, it seemed that everyone was out to get her. So why the hell shouldn't she get them first?

Upset by seeing Ty with Tracey—Ty entertaining Tracey, loving Tracey, caring about Tracey—an urgent lust had built up inside her. She needed power, needed control, and she was going to seize it with both hands.

While Ty and Tracey wedged some simple, almost childlike summer fun around their mundane work days in the laundry. Lee was off in an alien world. Spinning out of control. Living out a kind of madness. Although she kept one foot planted in their home life and maintained some semblance of normality, the veneer was increasingly fragile, and her other foot was precariously perched in an outlaw no-man's-land. Crossing back and forth during her killing spree, those worlds were rudely punctuated, one by the other. The lawful and lawless. Evil was winning and soon there would be no way back.

23

The small, silver-grey Sunbird outside their apartment window was cause for alarm. Backed hard into their parking spot, jammed as close to the wall as Lee could get it, its ongoing presence was definitely suspicious. Lee brushed it off by saying she'd borrowed it from a friend in Orlando. Tracey might have bought that story, even Sandy might not have questioned it. But Ty knew that Lee didn't have a cadre of rich, devoted friends with spare cars at their disposal. She also knew that last December when Lee had brought back a strange car, she had murdered its owner. A strange car, any car, would make her worry. Particularly when that car, unlike its predecessors, stayed and stayed. Particularly when Lee's story kept changing. First she said she'd borrowed it, then she turned right around and maintained the only reason it was stuck outside the house was that there was something wrong with it. At other times still, she claimed she'd rented it.

Rented it! That was really a red flag. It would be tough for Ty to rationalise that away. How could Lee rent a car with her non-existent credit rating? Lee didn't have any credit cards. Ty wasn't sophisticated or worldly, but she wasn't totally gullible either. But whatever annoying little doubts or questions flitted around in her head, they didn't stop her riding around in Lee's Sunbird.

As the days and weeks slipped by, Lee treated it as her own, which was the least likely of all possible scenarios. They were scratching to stay afloat financially. At the best of times, Lee would have been hard pressed to find a down payment. She certainly could never have conjured up a lump sum to buy a car outright; an '88 at that. Still, she carried on as though it were hers, sitting easily back behind the wheel, even giving another of the laundry room women a ride in it.

She even bought a Florida Challenger space-shuttle licence plate (bearing an Eagle and an American flag design) from a novelty shop down near Titusville.

Then she spun yet another yarn, saying she couldn't return the Sunbird to its owner because it was out of gas, and tapping Sandy for a loan so she could fill it up. That didn't ring true either. And it wasn't. The next time Sandy stopped by, there it sat, plain as day. Ty paid Sandy back her money.

Cars were not the only spoils of Lee's business forays. It wasn't unusual for Ty to see her come in armed with a motley assortment of goods—cameras, fishing rods, tools, you name it. Lee said they were bonuses from customers, or had been given to her in lieu of cash. There was an unfamiliar Bible on top of the refrigerator; another new acquisition. 'He must have been a religious man,' Lee muttered, flicking through its pages.

Since their cash-flow problem was no great secret, the sight of Lee flashing wads of bills made definite impressions on Tracey and Sandy. If only they'd made a note of the dates: but who could have guessed the significance?

Sandy vividly remembered Lee prancing in all smiles, bragging about having $600, then waving a fistful of bills in front of her and Ty's faces. It was May or June, that much she knew. And Tracey wasn't there. Tracey retained her own Technicolor memory. She and Ty were kicking back one night, relaxing in front of the TV, when Lee burst in. She seemed in almost deliriously good spirits about her windfall, crowing that some people who owed her money had finally paid her back. Unlike Sandy, Tracey could later pinpoint that occasion: it was precisely the night Lee first rolled up in the Sunbird.

After making her grand entrance with the cash, Lee ran upstairs and fetched her stereo, blasting out the thumping beat louder than ever. Magnanimously, Lee told Ty she could now take Tracey to Sea World and have some fun. Clearly lapping up the role of benefactor, she then decided to treat them all to hamburgers. As she swept out of the apartment, she also promised Ty that she'd take care of the rent problem.

Fridays and Saturdays were Ty's and Tracey's hard-earned days of rest and they savoured every minute of freedom from the laundry room. Ty, who was determined to show her little sister a great time in Florida, had lined up movies, trips to the beach, and various outings. A day trip to Sea World had long been high on the agenda. Better yet, as a perk of working at Casa Del Mar, Ty had acquired three discount tickets. One for her, one for Tracey, and one for Lee.

And how convenient: the Sunbird and the cash materialised right before the Saturday they were scheduled to go.

Worn down by Lee, Tracey finally went off to bed that night, but sleep did not come. The music blared out relentlessly, accompanied by the wavering strains of Lee singing along.

Lee knew that Tracey was unhappy and was thinking of packing up and returning to Ohio ahead of time. The little trouble-maker was going to go crying home, which Lee knew would upset Ty, whose family meant the world to her.

One day, armed with a few drinks inside her, Lee confronted Tracey, blaming her for things not working out between them. She didn't exactly threaten her, not in so many words, but the message got across and Tracey was intimidated and left in no doubt about the sinister subtext. She thought Lee was going to kill her, and even voiced her fears at the Casa Del Mar. Tracey had never actually seen Lee's gun, but she didn't for one second doubt its existence, and she finally had no wish to find out the hard way. Relations between Lee, Ty and Tracey were on fragile ground. Despite Ty's best efforts as mediator, Tracey's stay was turning into a torturous ordeal for everyone.

When the Sea World outing rolled around, Lee joined them as planned, seeming quite keen at first to drive them there, but the good humour didn't last. The outing definitely wasn't turning into the festive occasion Ty had envisaged. Drinking hard, Lee slipped into one of her sour, obnoxious moods. Suddenly she was behaving as if she was doing them a huge favour by acting as chauffeur and really didn't want to be there at all. Then she flatly refused to go into the park. Ty firmly refused to let Lee ruin their day. Lee could do what she wanted but she and Tracey were going to stay! Finally, in a truce of sorts, they agreed to meet outside later and Lee left. Inside, the sisters managed to have fun, but the black cloud of Lee's behaviour cast an unavoidable shadow.

Emerging several hours later, they looked around for their churlish companion and saw no sign of her. They sat down and waited. And waited. Finally, Ty spotted Lee off on the far side of the parking lot. She said she had been there the whole time. She was mad. Later, she made sarcastic cracks about not being included in any of the day's photographs, carefully ignoring the fact that it was she who had elected to leave.

Ty was mad, too. She'd wasted the price of a ticket and Lee had succeeded in spoiling everything.

Tracey couldn't bear the tension level that resonated around Lee or the stress of coping with these wildly fluctuating moods. She was by then 'a nervous wreck'. She'd simply had enough.

When they got home Tracey took Ty to one side and told her that she wanted to go home right away. She was upset about it, but she just couldn't be around Lee any more. She was just too unpredictable. Ty was upset and embarrassed. But she also understood. She knew how Lee felt about Tracey. Tracey didn't need to be a mind-reader to pick up on it. Perhaps it would be better all around if Tracey left, but Ty was livid that it had come to that. Now their parents would have to hear all about it. Together, they put a call in to Ohio and Tracey broke the news.

Later, Tracey reflected on that awful night and remembered how upset Lee became: 'Because I think she thought my sister was leaving too . . . and she wasn't . . . Ty didn't, you know, say that . . . but I think that's why she was upset with me . . . because she thought that my sister was leaving.'

24

While most citizens venture into the woods to spot wildlife, gather wildflowers, or to picnic, Lee and Ty went because Lee was anxious for Ty to hear the difference in sound between the shots fired from two weapons. There was the .45 she'd stolen from one victim, and the .22 with which she'd murdered others, although she didn't spell that out at the time. So it was that late one June afternoon they meandered their way into a quiet spot in the woods near Ormond Beach. Treating the loaded weapons in cavalier fashion and flagrantly flouting the law, Lee didn't lock them discreetly in the boot, but laid them on the floor by the back seat.

As they had done so many times before with the BB gun, they took turns in firing, peering intently along the barrels. Point, then fire. Since they weren't aiming for anything in particular, Ty couldn't evaluate Lee's marksmanship with these decidedly lethal weapons. But they both listened intently as the shots cracked in the stillness around them, like a couple of musicians with their ears tuned to pitch. Before the ammunition ran dry and without reloading, they stored the firearms back in the car and pulled away.

A curious outing, to say the least. If the dark spectre of Richard Mallory was hovering—if the very thought of his murder haunted and so terrified Ty that she couldn't bear to think or talk about it—why participate in such an event? Not for the first time, nor for the last, her behaviour begged the question: what on earth was she thinking?

On 19 June, Ursula Siems, still in Europe, waited in vain for her husband's promised call. When it didn't come as arranged, she repeatedly called their home, but no one ever answered. Worried, she called relatives and learned that no one had heard a word from Peter.

Three days later, Kathleen Siems, Peter's niece and a reporter, walked into the Jupiter Police Department and reported him missing. Because of his elastic and solitary touring schedule, because his wife was away in Europe, it had taken a couple of weeks for his disappearance to be noted, she explained. Now, they knew he'd neither arrived at his New Jersey destination after leaving Jupiter, nor called his mother, nor changed his plan and gone direct to Stefan's in Arkansas. The alarm was finally being sounded.

There was always the chance he was travelling with the Christ Is The Answer Crusade, the tent revival crusade headquartered in El Paso, Texas. Confusing the issue for Detective John Wisnieski, who began investigating, was the fact that the mobile Florida chapter had gone off and set up camp somewhere in Alabama. He did ascertain that Peter Siems had met with Bill Lowery from the Texas branch not long before. Beyond that, no one had any answers.

Stefan managed to procure his father's American Express account number and with it Wisnieski attempted to find out if there'd been any activity on the card since 7 June. He hit a brick wall. In an age of rampant computer information and virtually non-existent privacy, security-conscious American Express held that information sacred without a subpoena.

Wisnieski did the one other thing he could do. He sent out teletypes to law enforcement in Fort Payne, Alabama, asking that they try to locate Peter Siems or his car. Word filtered back: fellow Crusade members, many of whom knew and liked him, were concerned because no one had seen him.

On 20 June, Marvin Padgett and Jerry Thompson met up with Tom Muck to thrash out the possible similarities between their two cases. And on 28 June, Muck informed Thompson that the FDLE's monthly Florida Criminal Activity Bulletin detailed some homicides in Georgia that might also conceivably be linked. Muck had learned of a nude, white, male victim up there in Brooks County who had also been shot with a .22. Things seemed to be moving in an ominous direction.

So it was that on 9 July, a brainstorming session on the three I-75 cases was held in Tallahassee. Thompson, Padgett and David Strickland attended from Citrus County, Tom Muck from Pasco, two Georgia investigators, Wayne Porter of the FDLE, the FDLE's violent crime profiler, Dayle Hinman, and FDLE crime analyst, Teresa Gatlin. Pooling what they knew, the investigators felt a link was likely, and a spirit of co-operation was in the air.

For Ty 4 July 1990 began in a singularly unfestive fashion with the 9 a.m. to 4 p.m. shift at the Casa Del Mar. When she got off work, she and Lee got into the holiday spirit and decided to go find some firework displays. Attired in their usual T-shirts and beer caps, Ty wearing shorts and Lee blue jeans, they went for a drive at the tail end of the afternoon. They were killing time until it got dark. In the back of the Sunbird they'd stashed a few fire crackers and bottle rockets of their own, leftovers from the previous year, to set off later.

They stopped at a store on the coast road in Flagler Beach. While Ty went in to buy beer, Lee filled the car up—after conning her way into free gas by telling the store clerks that she was in the service and was waiting on her government cheque. They drove and drank some more, moseying along, enjoying the day. When they finished their beer, they pulled in at a Jiffy store to replenish the supply.

'I'm too drunk: do you want to drive?' Lee asked. 'OK,' Ty agreed.

It was Ty who spotted a sign for an Indian reservation. Never having seen a camp of Florida's American Indian Seminoles, she was curious and suggested they check it out. Lee agreed, so Ty turned back, navigating the winding road. When the camp didn't quickly reveal itself, they turned back, deciding to forget it. It was clear and dry at that point, but the hours of drinking had taken their toll and on the way out, Ty swung round a curve too fast and didn't quite make it. Losing control, she smashed the car through a steel gate and a barbed-wire fence. It listed as if to roll over, then righted itself, coming to a wounded halt in a field, the passenger side smacking into a tree.

'Man! We gotta get outta here! Get in the bushes,' Lee shouted, heaving herself out of the badly damaged car. She could hear the drone of other cars nearby. Responding on instinct, Ty ran out into the dirt road, but two thoughts soon flashed through her mind simultaneously. Was Lee afraid the gas tank was going to explode—or was the car stolen? But she did as she was told, stepping out of sight, swallowing her burning questions, but only momentarily. 'Why? What the fuck is the deal here?' she blurted seconds later.

'I'm going to tell you something,' Lee would later say she replied. 'We can't let the cops know anything right now. This is a cop car. I killed somebody! This is the car of a murdered guy.'

'What?' Lee claims Ty looked at her in horror.

'I said, I killed somebody.'

'You idiot! What are you? Crazy? Why did you do that?'

Lee says their incendiary exchange was nipped in the bud by the approach of local residents, Rhonda and Jim Bailey. They and Rhonda's cousin Brad had been out on the Baileys' porch when they heard the screech of tyres followed by a loud bang. They were all too familiar with the treacherously sharp curve by their house. Another accident, the Baileys groaned.

Their view partially obstructed by a profusion of greenery, they heard female voices screaming and saw a few beer cans flying through the air. Whoever it was had presumably been drinking and was dispensing with the evidence. The Baileys ran over to see if anyone needed assistance. They knew immediately that of the two women walking away from the car, the livid blonde had obviously been the passenger. Filling the air with profanities, she shouted to the other woman that she had warned her not to go so fast. Seeing the Baileys approach, the women returned to the car to talk to them and Lee's demeanour softened dramatically.

'Don't call the cops, please don't call the cops!' she implored them. 'My dad just lives up the road here a little bit. I'll go get him and we'll pull it out.'

'Do you want to come in here and use the phone or something?' Rhonda asked.

'No!' No!' the blonde assured them, leading her friend away, apparently anxious to leave.

The Baileys headed back to their home thinking, they'll never get that car out of there. It looked impossible because of the way the passenger side was rammed against the tree. But glancing back a minute or two later, they saw the women had obviously had a change of plan about fetching the father. They were running back down the road towards the car.

Lee used brute force to rip the licence plate from the Sunbird's rear with her bare hands, tossing it into a field. She then climbed in behind the wheel and tried to start the engine. Ty clambered into the back seat behind her as the tenacious little Sunbird sprang to noisy life. It sounded as if the fan belt was catching, but to the Baileys' amazement, it pulled away.

Both Lee and Ty felt considerably the worse for wear. Ty had banged her leg on both the steering wheel and the gear shift, but it was Lee who bore the brunt of it. Her shoulder and right arm were bleeding profusely where she'd been cut on broken window glass. In foul moods, they gingerly headed back down the dirt road and out on the highway. Within minutes, a front tyre completely collapsed. There was nothing for it but to leave it. Pulling over to the side, Lee once again instructed Ty to run but first she paused to rip off the front licence plate, tossing it as hard as she could into a field. Meanwhile, Ty grabbed the ice chest out of the back seat of the car. They didn't want to leave that: it still had beer in it. But they left the coasters (one Florida Gators, one Bass Fishing) they used to hold their cans.

Harmon Jeters saw the two women walking towards the fire station and SR 40. Thinking they were locals, he pulled over, planning to offer them a ride. As he drew close, however, the young man saw all the blood and quickly changed his mind. It seemed to him that they had blood on their faces, arms and hands, even around their fingernails. Lee told him they'd been in a bad accident and no one would give them a ride. They asked him for a lift to the main road but he refused and Lee became irate.

'Gee whizz! Thanks a lot! We're out here, just had an accident, and you won't take us nowhere!'

'Well, I got to go,' Harmon said, quickly pulling away.

Running into the woods, Lee cleaned some of the blood from her arm, then they headed down the road looking as nonchalant as possible. As they walked, Lee threw Peter Siems's car keys and registration into the foliage.

Immediately after he left them (at around 8.30 p.m.), Harmon stopped at his brother-in-law's and called Brenda and Hubert Hewett, his aunt and uncle. Hubert was Orange Springs' Volunteer Fire Department Chief and Brenda worked alongside him. On hearing Harmon's story, they promptly climbed into their fire vehicles and took to the road, looking for the accident victims. They must have passed by when Lee and Ty stepped into the woods, because they didn't see any sign of them.

After they turned around, however, and began heading back to home base, suddenly there were the women, carrying the distinctive red and white cooler Harmon had mentioned. But where was all the blood? Were they the people in the wreck, the Hewetts asked? No, they were not, Lee said emphatically, while her friend shook her head in agreement.

'Where did you get that idea? I don't know why people tell lies like that, but we haven't been in no accident,' Lee spat, cussing and carrying on.

They'd been out hitchhiking, she said, and two guys had picked them up, then dropped them off. They were on their way to Daytona to find some fireworks but they'd been given wrong directions. Lee did all the talking while Ty stood back and stayed silent. They were obviously keen to be on their way, and, puzzled, the Hewetts let them go.

They then hitched a couple of short rides, approaching a man whose house they came to, and a woman with a couple of children. Then they had a stroke of luck and met a man who was willing to take them almost to their door in Holly Hill.

Ty was shaken to the core and once they were safely away from the accident scene, her fear turned to fury. She was seething. At that moment, she hated Lee's guts. She could think of nothing she wanted more than to get as far away from her as possible.

Had she hurt this car's owner, too? Lee was always shooting her mouth off. Saying stuff that wasn't true. Getting drunk, playing with her mind. Hopefully, that's all it was. Ty's worst suspicions were all too horribly true. As the news reports would later confirm, Lee had indeed killed again.

Ever since Richard Mallory, Ty knew she should get out while the going was good. She knew she should turn Lee in, but she couldn't do that. She was confused and scared. Yet, somehow she couldn't tear herself away. Lee loved her. She was bonded to Lee. They needed each other. She didn't want to be alone. She was hurting and suffering, but she didn't know what else to do.

It was 9.44 p.m. when trooper Rickey responded to the accident scene in Orange Springs—or at least to the Sunbird's final resting place. Not until almost two months later would detectives learn where exactly the Sunbird had crashed or hear the Baileys' account. For now at least, they were dealing with part two of the incident. Marion County's Deputy Lawing was dispatched to investigate the abandoned, smashed-up vehicle. Looking it over, seeing the grass on its upper body regions, he surmised it had rolled over.

He also saw blood on the seat and on the exterior. Marvin Wood, who lived some five hundred yards away, had seen the blood, too. Wood told Lawing he'd watched Lee and Ty leave the Sunbird with the red and white cooler. He'd also seen what looked like blood on them. He'd thought it funny the way they kept disappearing into the bushes each time a car went by.

He described them as follows. A tall blonde of about forty, accompanied by an overweight white male of 280 to 300 pounds. He'd watched the blonde (who looked drunk) rip off the front licence tag and throw it in the grass nearby. After they walked off, he retrieved the tag, carefully picking it up with a piece of paper.

Checking the grey 1988 Sunbird's VIN number, Lawing found it to be registered to Peter Siems, a man who was listed as missing and endangered, so he immediately reported to his supervisor. Deputy Baskin arrived at the scene to relieve Lawing and

211

spoke briefly to Hubert and Brenda Hewett before escorting the car as it was towed into the impound yard for processing.

In response to their notification, Marion County soon received a teletype from Jupiter PD asking that the car be held and treated as a possible homicide crime scene.

Calling the Hewetts later to continue their conversation, Baskin learned about Harmon Jeters's call regarding the two women and how the Hewetts then searched for them. The Hewetts described the women as being dirty and wet, but with no sign of the blood Harmon Jeters had seen. Perhaps they'd cleaned up with the water hose outside the nearby Tappan Realty building? As it had been uncoiled and the tap turned on, this seemed likely, but it was also raining lightly. (The hose nozzle was taken in as evidence.)

The Hewetts' descriptions of the women were markedly different again. They told Baskin one was 5 feet 10 inches, maybe 5 feet 11, and 130 pounds, the other between 5 feet 4 and 5 feet 6, mannish in appearance, the more silent of the two, and weighing up to 200 pounds. Through the wet T-shirt of the short heavy one they'd seen a bra. It was definitely a woman.

Small witnesses customarily overestimate size just as tall ones often underestimate, and Harmon Jeters, who is short, described the blonde as around six feet, big-boned and heavy. The second, shorter girl had short, dark-red hair.

When Investigator Leo Smith, who works multitudes of stolen car cases, saw the Sunbird the next day, the decorative American Eagle tag Lee had bought was on the front seat where Mr Wood and the trooper had put it. Busch and Budweiser cans lay on the car floor along with bottle rocket fireworks and a multicoloured dishwashing cloth.

The car was in bad shape. Both side front windows were shattered and knocked out, and the windscreen had also shattered. There was blood, too, on the boot, on the left rear passenger door, on the column between the doors, on the driver's seat, on the passenger seat, on the steering wheel and on the driver's door handle.

On 7 July, forensic artist Beth Gee met with the Hewetts in Orange Springs and prepared sketches of the two females. Jeters showed up and added his input. The end product was ferried off to the FDLE and to various law enforcement agencies.

On 11 July, Sergeant Jacobsen and Detective Sprauer visited Siems's home and met up with his wife Ursula, who had just returned from Europe. Assuring the officers of the good state of her marriage and that she and Peter were devout Christians, she handed over a photograph of her missing husband.

25

Eugene 'Troy' Burress turned 50 in January of 1990, kicking, screaming and complaining all the way. Time to turn around and go backwards, he said, that was all there was to it. Slightly built, with blue eyes and blond hair, Troy was only around 5 feet 6 inches and weighed in at 155 pounds, but he exuded charm. Down-to-earth, popular and fun-loving, he was blessed with a natural gift of the gab. He could excite Eskimos about ice-creams, so what better place for him than working in sales?

Prior to moving to Ocala (a resort town in central Florida) a year earlier, he had his own company, Troy's Pools, in Boca Raton. Having gladly dropped the headaches that are the lot in life of a small business owner, he'd begun driving a delivery truck for the Gilchrist Sausage Company. Not that his new job was without problems. Those trucks—always breaking down at the worst possible moment. No air conditioning in the cabs, either—that was rough during the summer. Still, he liked Ocala. He didn't miss his old neighbourhood's seedier influences. Prostitution had been creeping too close for comfort. He could definitely do without that. And he didn't miss sniffing all those harsh pool chemicals. Workaholic that he was, he still did a little pool-cleaning work on the side for Glenn Miller Realty. You couldn't keep too busy, that was Troy's way of thinking. A proud grandaddy, he had two grown daughters, Wanda and Vicky, 29 and 32 respectively, from his first marriage, and three grown stepdaughters via his current wife of sixteen years, Rose 'Sharon' Burress.

The youngest of three children himself, Troy grew up in west Tennessee and had always been especially close to his sister, Letha Prater, two and a half years his senior. His childhood nickname, Buddy, bequeathed him by his father when he was sickly from anaemia, had stuck, especially with Letha, who never stopped taking care of her little Buddy. He'd been verbally slow as a child for some mysterious reason, jumbling certain words, but Letha understood his language and translated for the teachers in their small country school. Besides loving Buddy, Letha liked him a lot, and as adults, gravitating along separate lines to new lives in Florida, they never stayed far apart for long.

At weekends, they whiled away many happy hours together rummaging in flea markets, watching all the colourful characters. They were mutual confidants. Buddy poured out his heart to Letha as to no one else, and she to him. She knew she could always count on him for an unsparingly honest opinion. For all the years Sharon had been married to Troy, even she sometimes asked Letha what was on her husband's mind. Letha and Buddy had always fought between themselves, but their fierce family loyalty meant no one had better mess with Buddy or they'd have Letha's wrath to contend with, and vice-versa.

When their Momma, then 79 and a recent survivor of triple-bypass surgery, had paid a visit from Tennessee that spring, Buddy refused to let her ride back on the bus, and drove her all the way in his pick-up. He fought his natural bent to do everything in a hurry, and Momma said he'd been real good and had even made a detour to put flowers on Grandma's grave in Alabama.

Letha had been concerned about her brother of late. He'd been a bit down and worried about money. He'd expected to take a drop in his new line of work, but it was still disheartening and a struggle. And he was heartbroken over the loss of JC, one of his two black Chows, which had vanished into thin air. Every day he could, Troy stopped by the pound, just praying he'd be greeted by JC's face and wagging tail. If Troy had had his way, he would have had two of every kind of animal that walked the planet.

No one else could tell it. No one else was there. And she'd say it happened this way. The guy in the sausage truck was going to

215

kill her. Physically attacked her. She'd stripped her clothes off, trusting as ever, and the thanks she got was him pulling out a ten-dollar bill. This is all you fucking deserve, you fucking whore. Just threw the money down. Didn't know she had a gun. Started the ugly name-calling. I'm gonna get a piece of ass off you, baby. You whore. Said he was gonna rape her.

Kicking and fighting in the woods, they were struggling, tumbling, falling down into the weeds. She pushed him away—or he was backing away—now, which was it? Anyway, she pulled out her gun. You bastard. You're gonna rape me and shit. And she shot him right in the stomach. So she thought.

In fact, the first bullet coursing into the body of her bewildered victim hit the main artery to his heart, then ricocheted into his left lung, doing such massive damage there that it alone would prove fatal. He was only a little guy, but under threat like that, fear and fury pumping, he'd have fought for his life with every ounce of strength God delivered. If he'd had the chance. That first bullet shut down his options.

He didn't say a word. No way to talk his way out of this. Just turned, ready to run. Get away from her. They were out in the middle of nowhere. No lifelines to cling to. No telephones to call for help. No kindness of strangers to save him. No transport for miles and miles. What could he possibly have done to harm her? She was the one with the gun. He'd turned and was going to run from her, though. For her, at that moment, that was enough.

So she shot him again. In the back.

The bullet pierced its way through his diaphragm, coming to a stop in front of his fifth lumbar vertebra. Wherever she was standing when she pulled the trigger, she certainly wasn't looking into the eyes of the man whose life she was taking. Not possible, given the angle the bullet travelled. She shot him in the back.

Once she'd done it, he didn't get very far. Two bullets. That was all it took to snuff out his vibrant, love-filled life. That was all it took to rob Sharon of a husband. Letha of her Buddy. His mother of her youngest son. Wanda and Vicky of their Daddy, 'so precious' to them, Troy's grandchildren of their darling Grandaddy. Sharon's daughters of their stepfather.

Just two bullets.

Not thinking of that, though, she did what she had to do. They were old, remember? Probably didn't have anyone, anyway. Covering him up a little, making him blend in with the background, she draped some palm fronds across his body, camouflaging his blue Levis and the beige knit shirt that poignantly bore his name. Troy.

She'd say she wasn't expecting him to have all that money in the thingamajiggy in his truck. Herman Evans, though, a man she'd lived with back in the early eighties, also drove a sausage truck way back then. He'd remember distinctly telling her about the cash box all delivery drivers carried. (Herman knew Troy Burress, too. Such a nice guy.) Expected or not, the money was there—$310; something like that? A lot, anyway.

She left Troy's wedding ring on his finger, and the golden chain dangling around his neck.

When life had slipped away and he was no longer the man his loved ones knew, she drove off in his sausage truck and left him there. She was thinking. Stopping to throw out everything that might tie her to him. His gas credit card, his clipboard. Used to it by now. Kind of a ritual. She grabbed a pile of receipts and business cards, stuffing them into a dip in the pine needles near the foot of a tree. Still half-naked, she stopped again to finish getting dressed. Didn't get a whole lot farther down the road before the damn truck just sputtered to a halt, out of gas. She didn't know about the second tank, the switch she could have flicked to access it. Climbing down from his truck, she left it by the side of the road and walked clean away.

When Letha and Bob Prater's telephone rang at around eleven the night of Monday 30 July, Bob answered it.

'Troy ain't home,' came Sharon's anxious voice.

'Where is he?'

'I don't know. I wish I did know.'

Bob handed Letha the receiver and she went on the line with

217

Sharon, soothing her, telling her not to worry. For all her assurances, when she hung up, Letha was very concerned. Sure, Buddy liked to go out and have a good time, but he simply wasn't the flaky type who would just disappear without calling, knowing that Sharon was expecting him for dinner. On a normal night Buddy would have been home by seven, seven-thirty. Letha couldn't quash a terrible feeling that something was very wrong.

Within a matter of minutes, she dialled Sharon back: 'We'll be there.'

'OK. Will you stop and get me some cigarettes? I am really worried and nervous, and I'm afraid to leave the house.'

Feeling sick inside, Letha set off for Ocala. Seeing a sheriff's car by the Starvin' Marvin service station, she pulled over. She'd get Sharon's cigarettes but, more important, find out if the officers knew anything about Buddy. They'd been given his description. That meant that the search was on.

Troy Burress had left his home at around 5.45 a.m. that morning, reporting to Gilchrist and heading off on his rounds by 6.20. Mid-week, his route took him farther afield into southern Florida and he regularly spent Tuesday and Wednesday nights in motels, driving back on Thursday. But on a Monday, he stayed closer to home.

On what they called the Daytona route, he serviced stores in the local Ocala area, then headed east to Ormond Beach. From there he'd go north-west to the Harris Grocery in Bunnell, then to the Seville Grocery, south-west of there. That Monday, he arrived in Seville between two and half-past. He didn't make a sale, but he stayed and chatted for ten minutes or so before heading off to his next stop in Salt Springs.

Generally he took 17 South to SR 40 West to 19 North to get there, arriving between 2.30 and 3 p.m. So when he hadn't turned up by five, he was missed. Jeff Mason of the Salt Springs Grocery even drove down to where 19 intersects with SR 40, but saw no sign of the 1983 Ford truck with its distinctive black cab, white refrigerator back and Gilchrist logo.

In the seven months he'd worked for Gilchrist, Troy had always been punctual and when he didn't return between 4.30 and 5.30 p.m. as anticipated, the proprietor, Mrs Jonnie Mae Thompson, waited. At 6.10, she called the Salt Springs grocery store and learned that Troy had never made it there.

At seven, she headed home, leaving a note on the gate for Troy to call her son Michael immediately he got in. She returned to the office after 10 p.m. to find the note still there. Mrs Thompson's eldest son put in a call to Sharon, who had heard nothing either. It was most unlike Troy not to call if there was a problem. Returning home, Mrs Thompson filled in her husband, who called the Marion County SO, the Volusia County SO and the Lakeland County SO. None had any record of an arrest or accident involving Troy. At 11.30, Mr Thompson and his eldest son began backtracking over Troy's route.

Letha and Bob, driving the 30 miles from their home in Micanopy to Troy and Sharon's home in Ocala, were worried sick. Letha's mind was working overtime. Troy had visited her house just that Sunday and hadn't been his usual cheerful self. He'd come by to pick up some pears from Letha's trees for Sharon to make preserves, but he was irritable and seemed under a lot of stress. He'd had his grandson with him, so they couldn't really have a heart to heart.

Letha knew he enjoyed living in Ocala, meeting the public on his rounds, and selling, but she also knew he had serious misgivings about the job. He'd complained to her about having to carry large sums of cash around. Some of the stores he serviced were frequented by some unsavoury characters. The whole thing made him nervous. He'd vowed to give the job a proper chance and stick it out for a year, but he was definitely down. He was worried about money, too, and depressed because some of those he'd helped in the past weren't there for him now that he himself needed a little help. All these factors ran around in Letha's head.

While the Thompsons were still out searching for Troy and the truck, Letha put in one of a number of calls she made that night to the Sheriff's Office, and she didn't like what she heard. Perhaps he'd just run off? Just upped and left and taken Gilchrist's money? A grown person has every right to take off without notifying their husband or wife if they choose. With the majority of missing persons reports filed, that's exactly what has happened. The police were treating it accordingly.

Driving a company vehicle, it was against the rules to stop and pick up a hitchhiker. For one thing, the insurance didn't allow it. But might Troy have stopped for someone in trouble?

By 1.30 a.m., the Thompsons' search had drawn a blank and they called Sharon again to tell her to file a missing person's report which she did around 2 a.m. BOLOS were issued, but Troy wasn't officially listed on the NCIC/FCIC computer as missing or endangered until eleven the next morning.

It was around 2 a.m. when Bob Prater and patrol Deputy Chesser of Marion County SO spotted Troy's truck independently but almost simultaneously. It was parked southbound on the northbound side of CR 19 at its intersection with SR40 East. The truck was on Troy's route, but pointed in the wrong direction. It was cold and covered with dew and there was condensation on the windows. It looked as if it had been there for some time.

At first sight, there was no visible sign of a struggle or of foul play. The ignition keys were missing, though, and the refrigerator cab was locked. For Troy Burress's loved ones, the tension was almost unbearable as they waited for a locksmith to arrive. Bob had called Letha and Sharon to bring them up to date, and Letha didn't wait long before calling the Sheriff's Office back again. Had they found out if anyone was inside? She was told they were still waiting for the locksmith. Unable to bear it, Letha called back again. Had they unlocked the truck yet? The officer took pity on her. 'I really can't give out any information,' she said, 'but I will tell you this: your brother was not in the truck.'

Their immediate fears were allayed. Thank God. Troy was not inside—bound, gagged or any other way. But where was he?

Later, detectives searched the truck for any signs of a scratched message on the boxes or papers in the back. They even looked for words etched in the metal. Had he been transported in the back as a prisoner, he might have attempted to communicate the name or names of his attackers. There was nothing. But that came later. First, curiously, the Gilchrist folk were allowed to drive away the truck. That didn't seem right to the family. Didn't they have to check it for fingerprints before a host of other people put their hands all over it? It was a procedural error and procedural errors happen.

Speculating as to what had happened, the next logical assumption was that Buddy had been robbed since he was carrying company money and everything was gone from his truck. Letha knew with absolute conviction that whatever was troubling her brother, there was no way on this earth he would have left without confiding in her, without telling her she need not worry about him. Something bad must have happened.

Bob went out into the forest to search around the truck for any sign of Troy. Meanwhile, Letha and Sharon stayed at home awaiting a call from the sheriffs. The Praters spent the night with Sharon. No one slept a wink and Letha and Sharon were frantic by the next morning. While Bob popped home to feed their animals, Letha went to the sheriff's office. The platitudes she heard—the investigators had Troy's description and were doing all they could—did little to assuage her fears.

Finally convinced that Troy was unlikely to have done a flit, the search, utilising horses (and with Major Dan Henry in charge), began with a vengeance. It covered a four-mile radius from the truck, and that evening a helicopter dispatched from Volusia County scoured the area from the air.

Sharon didn't want to let Letha out of her sight.

'When you start to leave,' she said, 'I just can't stand it, because I know that you're my last link with him.'

'I don't have to go,' Letha reassured her.

She spent three nights at Sharon's place. She could easily have been a basket case herself, but somehow she found the strength to keep herself together. She kept busy talking to the local TV station and furnishing the local paper with a photograph of Buddy, driving it over herself so it would make the next edition.

'How do you do it?' Sharon asked. 'I always thought I was a strong person, and I'm falling apart.'

'I do it because I have to do it. I have to do it for him, and I *will* do it,' Letha said, as if convincing herself as well as Sharon.

On the third night, Letha went to bed for the first time. She stayed there for just one hour.

The rest of that long week, Troy's family went door to door and store to store, asking questions and putting up flyers. Trying to distract themselves with activity.

Troy's daughter Vicky broke the news to her younger sister, Wanda, down in Boynton Beach. Wanda, the baby (although a mother herself), was the last one to find out about her dad and was desperately upset. She immediately telephoned Sharon who filled her in and suggested she sit tight in Boynton Beach, 274 miles away, and wait for news. Wanda had seen her dad regularly because his route brought him by each week and he stopped in for dinner with the family. Not long before that, Troy had taken Wanda's elder daughter, Jennifer, who was eleven, back to Ocala with him to ride his horses.

By Wednesday, Wanda could bear it no longer. She had to be there. She and Gary made arrangements to leave the children with his parents, then drove to Ocala and joined Bob and Letha in their searches. They still prayed that if they found Troy in the woods he might be alive. Perhaps he was lying injured somewhere.

Sharon was enduring a different kind of pain; that of a woman whose husband has disappeared and who is not entirely convinced that he hasn't just upped and left her. Their marriage had been under stress and rumours had it that Troy had a lady friend down south whom he'd see on his mid-week stopovers. Letha tried to reassure her sister-in-law. She knew it was nothing like that. Buddy would have said something. Sharon was still not convinced. Letha understood. She might have felt the same in her shoes.

26

As the fractures in Ty's relationship with Lee deepened, so, too, did Ty's bond with Sandy. Sandy had had her share of man problems, contending with mates who didn't treat her well. She'd survived a failed marriage, then weathered a tempestuous time with an erratic, moody boyfriend. And Ty had Lee . . . with everything that that deceptively simple phrase entailed. Ty and Sandy's respective problems in affairs of the heart created an important area of common ground, forging and cementing their friendship. Running near parallel paths in their discontent, they lent comfort and support to one another. Sympathetic ears in the love wars.

Ty was increasingly unhappy at home and made no secret of it. Their sex life had withered into non-existence. Over the past months, Lee seemed to have lost all desire. True, she was having sex all day with her clients, but that didn't console Ty.

Compounding Ty's dissatisfaction was her annoyance at Lee's stubborn unwillingness to entertain the idea of getting some kind of regular work. Instead of her periodic forays onto the highways, she could have got a decent job like Ty's and brought in the same pay cheque. It would have made things easier and given them some kind of security. Lee, by whose unusual standards Ty was deemed 'a workaholic', had once worked (briefly) as a motel maid, but repeatedly moaned about how much she hated it. The managers were all assholes, she opined. It seemed she couldn't get along with anybody. Or chose not to.

What Ty viewed as a choice on Lee's part was largely, however, symptomatic of her inability to control her impulses in a fashion that would allow her to enter the workforce. Whatever her intentions, she simply couldn't maintain her good behaviour long enough to hold down a nine-to-five type job. This failing was nothing new. It was part of a lifelong pattern. One reason that prostitution worked for her in practical terms was because it involved encounters of limited and usually brief duration. She could move on before things turned sour. Most of the time, at least.

To Ty, however, Lee's change of lifestyle was a case of promises, promises. Lee talked like a big shot about how she supported her, but her income was actually very erratic. The flip-side of Lee's bragging was that, increasingly, Ty's hard-earned dollars went into subsidising her. True, Ty could knock back beer like a champion. Nevertheless, she faithfully roused herself each morning to roll into the Casa Del Mar on time. Lee, who drank round the clock, would often sit up all night, partying solo, then sleep in so late, recovering, that she'd effectively waste the next day. 'God,' Lee later admitted, '. . . all we did was stick around home and get drunk.' Meanwhile, Ty bust her ass for four dollars and change per hour.

Their biggest expenditure, next to keeping a roof over their heads, was the daily beer bill. Ty was often short of money, so Sandy sometimes paid for her lunch or gave her a loan. Ty never took advantage, however, and when Sandy was short, returned the favour.

While it was abundantly clear that Lee not only depended on Ty but was wild about her, Ty, on the other hand, seemed just to be making the best of things, to be hanging on. As disenchant-ment set in, what kept her might simply have been that she didn't have anywhere else to go—or anyone else to go to.

Later she said, 'I didn't really have any feelings for her . . . I was afraid of her . . . and I just stayed around her . . . because of fear, I guess . . .'

She didn't specify whether she was afraid of a woman who was capable of killing, or was afraid of being alone.

Living with Lee's ugly moods was not easy for Ty. It wasn't even easy for those at a distance. James Legary and his longtime lady friend, Beth, who owned the house next door to Lee and Ty's apartment, found having them for neighbours 'grossly unpleasant'. Mr Legary's first sight of Lee was of her glaring him down with an ugly 'I'll kick your ass' expression as he innocently pulled his car into his driveway. He laughed wryly to himself. It looked as if fate had bestowed upon him yet another in a seemingly long procession of less than perfect neighbours. Later, Legary heard Lee's perception of that first chilly (albeit distant) encounter from Lee's landlady. Lee had assumed he was laughing at her and took offence.

Over the months, Lee, who mangled anyone's minimum expectations of neighbourly peaceful co-existence, levelled three separate complaints against Legary's 15-year-old son, Lenny. He'd stolen her cat. He'd doused her garbage can with paint. And he'd stolen the hubcaps from her little car.

For good measure, each allegation was lodged to Legary Sr accompanied by a threat to kick his ass. That, or an equally antagonistic assurance that she had a gun and would shoot him. Once, she feigned taking a lunge at him. For a moment, it had looked for all the world as if she was about to come around the fence and tackle him physically.

Lenny eventually spoke directly to Lee about the cat incident and returned placated, bearing news of a truce. She wasn't really that bad a person, he informed his father. Legary was not impressed. His patience had by then been stretched to the limit by her perpetually blasting stereo. Worse, she once tossed firecrackers out of her window, cackling all the while like the Wicked Witch of the West.

One day, while Sandy was visiting Ty and Lee, a delivery man arrived to collect their rented stereo system to take it away to be fixed. Merely the messenger, he demonstrated no interest in anything beyond getting in and out as quietly and unobtrusively as possible. Lee wouldn't let it go at that. She laid into him, cussing him out as if he'd maliciously broken the thing himself. Livid about something that Sandy couldn't fathom, she paced back and forth in the hallway like a mad thing, cursing furiously.

Mild-mannered Sandy was appalled and absolutely mortified. She'd have loved the sofa to open and just swallow her up. Ty, on the other hand, seemed to take it all in her stride. She was accustomed to Lee's mood swings.

It is hard to reconcile the blandly compliant, unquestioning Ty with the picture painted by those who knew her as assertive and a generally dynamic individual. And it presented a dichotomy.

Take the Ty who accompanied Lee to throw out two big bags full of goodness knows what in a dump up near Holly Hill. Ty would have everyone believe that she didn't ask what was in the bags. Simple human curiosity makes that difficult to imagine. Either she lied, or she really did belong to the 'what you don't know won't hurt you' school of thought.

Ty was altogether too feisty a character to fit the classic parameters of the battered wife syndrome. They fought and wrestled around on the floor, but Ty gave as good as she got and the two women certainly didn't have the monopoly on such behaviour. Many couples functioned thus. More important, that alone did not provide evidence of any battering. And Ty always maintained that Lee never hurt her physically.

Secondly, there were too many contrary clues for the relationship to be labelled quite so easily. Scrutinised closely, it defied the pat, superficial assumption that Lee was dominant and Ty intimidated and subservient. Lee was unarguably aggressive, assertive and sometimes domineering. She was also clinging, babyish, and dependent. Often, her speaking voice adopted a sing-song, girlish tone belying her years, seeming to be an outward manifestation of the child within, reaching out and trying to get its needs met.

Cammie Greene was thoroughly disturbed when rudely presented with a glimpse of a thoroughly different Ty that ugly day when they suddenly flew the coop. Ty was equally culpable, if not more so, for the way, like a couple of mean-spirited ingrates, they left the friend who had been so supportive, generous and non-judgemental.

Lee's allegations later sowed the seeds for a different interpretation of her lover. Perhaps Ty was not a malleable, unquestioning, forgetful woman living in denial. Perhaps she was someone who enjoyed the fruits of Lee's labours, knew from whence they came, and was quite happy to submerge any qualms she had, so long as she wasn't directly or adversely affected.

Reinforcing the shadow of doubt cast over Ty as an abused wife, came an observation by Sandy made while trying to fathom the balance of power between them. She was perhaps closer to them than anyone, and believed their relationship broke the usual rules. It seemed to her that even in a union between two females, one partner generally adopted the stereotypically male role, and the other the female. Ty and Lee struck her as odd that way. 'Ty *always* acted like the man,' she observed. 'Lee acted like the woman sometimes, and the man sometimes. It was weird.'

As that sweltering summer rolled on, somehow Lee and Ty's alliance appeared to have weathered two more major hurdles: Tracey's departure, and the upsetting car crash. For all that was implicit in Lee's alleged revelation that it was the car of a man she'd murdered, Ty was still there at her side. By August, they were once again on the move. Ty approached Alzada Sherman, a co-worker of hers in the laundry room. Lee was leaving to go and live in Las Vegas so Ty needed a place to live. Alzada had an apartment nearby on Butler Boulevard and Ty asked whether she could move in as her roommate? Alzada, who liked Ty and could use help with the rent, agreed.

She was far from thrilled when Ty suddenly sprang another request for a favour. Could Lee stay, too, just for a couple of days, until she headed west? Alzada agreed, but only very reluctantly. She wasn't keen on having lesbians under her roof. (She had no idea Lee was a hooker and later found it hard to believe. She couldn't imagine anyone wanting her. She didn't even look clean most of the time.) Confirming Alzada's worst fears, this temporary stop-gap arrangement dragged on and on. Periodically, Lee disappeared for a day or so—but, to Alzada's dismay, she kept coming back.

During one such absence, Ty got to partying and was believed by her friends to have spent the night with a guy. If so, it was a sure sign of her disenchantment with Lee, who was wildly jealous of any men.

Another night at Alzada's, Lee, drunkenly shooting off her mouth, began veering into dangerous territory. She bragged pointedly about how she and Ty *used* to have a car until 'some bitch wrecked it'. Ranting on, she complained that she'd hurt her shoulder in the smash. Ignoring Ty's commands to 'Shut up!', Lee merely looked at her angry girlfriend, grinning wildly.

Right after Troy Burress's disappearance, the investigation took a detour following a male hitchhiker whom eyewitnesses had seen leaning against his Gilchrist truck. One witness who was shown Troy's picture identified him as being the barefoot hitchhiker in a flowered shirt and shorts that he'd picked up and given a ride. The hitchhiker said the truck on the roadside was his and that its fuel pump had broken. He asked for a ride to a camping area where he spent the night. He had next to no money and when asked why he wasn't wearing boots, he said that because it was hot he'd left them in the truck. Perhaps something had snapped in Troy Burress's mind?

Studying the area around Troy's truck later, Letha saw these male footprints and they looked huge, not even close to her brother's size seven and a half. So when officers told her that Troy had been spotted, she was adamant that it wasn't him. In fact, the mystery hitchhiker in the flowered shirt was soon identified as Curtis Blankenship, an apparently disturbed young man who had been involved in some minor scrapes with the law. Once, Blankenship had filed his own obituary with his hometown newspaper.

If he wasn't Troy Burress, perhaps he was a witness or was even Troy's murderer? Certainly, he was in the right place at the right time—or the wrong place at the wrong time.

Troy's daughter, Wanda, her husband Gary and Letha's husband Bob, were out searching the forest on the afternoon of 4 August. Running out of ideas, at around four they stopped to talk to a retired policeman who lived in the area. 'If anyone would know where to look, he would,' Bob told the others, approaching the house. Bob introduced Wanda and Gary and explained their plight. Unbeknownst to them, the ex-cop had been inside, monitoring his scanner.

'I want you to wait right here a minute,' he told them, going back into the house. He emerged a couple of minutes later and he looked at Wanda, then he turned to Bob and said gently, 'Take her home. Take her home and wait for a phone call.'

In that instant, Wanda knew it. She knew right then and there that her daddy had been found. Devastated, she asked Bob to drive her to where Troy's truck had turned up.

'No,' Bob said softly. 'We're going home.'

Back at the house, Letha, who had been cooking, was just getting ready to call her older brother and to go back out and join in the search.

'Don't call him yet,' Bob told her as they walked in. 'They found someone in the woods.'

They had been back just five minutes when a reporter from the Ocala *Star-Banner* called and informed Letha that a body had been found: they were pretty sure it was her brother. Then Investigator John Tilley telephoned and officially broke the news. There was little doubt it was Troy because of his clothes. Poignantly, his shirt still bore his name.

It had been around 2.30 p.m. when Margie and Ned Livingston, who were out sightseeing and looking for a pretty place to picnic, stumbled across the body of Troy Burress. Troy's body lay off a small dirt road in the National Forest approximately seven miles north of SR 40, just off CR 19, a spot just about three miles from where Bob, Wanda and Gary had been searching. When the police and emergency services personnel arrived, they saw a male lying face down. The two bullet wounds in his body would later be identified as having come from a .22 calibre weapon. Marion County's investigator John Tilley arrived on the scene at 4.22 p.m. and assumed control.

Partway down the dirt road, the victim's credit cards, Gilchrist cheques, receipts and clipboard were discovered among the bushes. The bank bag which would have held the day's cash receipts was nowhere in sight.

At 6 p.m. Tilley gently took the wedding ring from the body

and drove over to Sharon. She positively identified it as Troy's. Sharon gave Tilley the name of Troy's dentist so he could provide dental charts for positive identification. Wanda and her husband spent the night with Troy's widow, then drove back down south to fetch the children for the funeral.

Wanda, like the rest of the family, was reeling in shock. The abject horror hadn't sunk in. All she kept thinking was 'I'm too young to lose my father!' Her head swam with muddled thoughts. Her dad had wanted to retire in Ocala with his horses and chickens. That had been his dream. Now it was all gone. And Troy's mom; she'd never survive it. Wanda thought, too, of the trips her dad had taken her on as a kid to Sea World, to Monkey Jungle, Parrot Jungle and the Seaquarium down in Fort Lauderdale and Miami.

Over and over again, the same thoughts tumbled around. Why? Why would anyone do this? And *who* would do it? *Who* would want to kill him?

She felt sure, as did the rest of the family, that the only kind of person her dad would have stopped to help would be a woman having car trouble, something like that. 'He was a people person, he'd talk to everybody, very friendly.' She felt sure he'd never pick up a hitchhiker, though. They'd even talked about it. But he'd stop to help a woman because he'd want someone to do the same for the women in his family.

There was fear, too, mingled in with all the anger and sorrow and pain. Perhaps whoever did this might be after the rest of the family, too? For around 25 years her father had lived down near Wanda in Delray. Perhaps it was someone from down there?

After the discovery of Troy's body, the family posted a reward and pinned flyers up and down I-95, urging anyone who knew anything that could help find his murderer, to come forward. On 5 August, an autopsy was performed in Leesburg by Dr Shutze. Hearing how decomposed Troy's body was had been an added burden for the family.

On 7 August, Letha visited John Tilley for an interview at Marion County SO. She was distraught as she told him about Troy's money worries, about him not getting all he was owed on the sale of his pool business in West Palm Beach, and his problems at Gilchrist. Tears flowed as she talked.

The funeral, around a week later, was another ordeal that had to be endured. 'The hardest part for me,' Wanda recalls, 'was that my dad's casket was closed because he was in a body bag. The fact that I couldn't say goodbye to him, the fact I couldn't see him for one last time. He was just gone. Somebody took him, and it was unfair.'

Wanda's two children and Vicky's four kept asking their moms, 'Who would do this to my Grandpa?'

Wanda later arranged a memorial service down in Delray, inviting her father's legion of friends, who turned out in force to pay their respects. Vicky, who had remarried just a couple of months earlier, comforted herself remembering how happy her dad had looked at her wedding reception.

Fortunately, Troy's mother had Buddy's stepfather to console her up in Tennessee, but she kept a lot of her anguish locked inside. That was just her nature. She couldn't switch off her brain and all the thoughts that ran around inside it.

She just didn't understand, and never would, how someone could take her son out and shoot him in cold blood.

Curtis Blankenship, who was under investigation for the murder of Troy Burress, was arrested in Indiana on 8 August for vehicle theft in a truck that appeared to have been stolen back in Marion County. Its owner was Mr Biscardi, a man who had befriended Blankenship and let him stay with him. Blankenship clearly was in trouble and suicidally inclined. A local pastor, Pastor McWilliams, had visited him and prayed with him before he made off with the truck.

On 19 August, John Tilley and Sergeant Brian Jarvis flew to Indiana and came face to face with Blankenship at the State Police Headquarters in Connersville. He denied any knowledge of or involvement in the death of Troy Burress. He said he hadn't even walked up to Troy's truck, although he could remember saying he'd been in a truck that broke down. By 21 August, his story was that although he'd once tried to scare someone by claiming to own a gun, he'd made it up.

On 27 August, Troy's family were shocked at the news that tests had shown him to have 0.08 per cent blood alcohol level. Although he drank occasionally, they would all have sworn that he wouldn't have been drinking in the middle of the day. He was against drinking and driving, particularly while working. It seemed most out of character. Later, their minds would be put at rest. Although the point was not made in court, in fact the blood alcohol level had risen naturally after death as a result of decomposition.

Alzada Sherman had repeatedly urged Ty to move out and take Lee with her, and to her immense relief, she regained her apartment on 27 August. Her contention that she couldn't have that many people in the apartment without breaking the terms of her lease had finally been heeded. Lee and Ty checked into the optimistically named Happy Holidays, a cheap, clean motel right on Atlantic Avenue, making the trip in a white, compact, older-model car. Signing the motel register, Lee didn't log the registration, explaining to owner Vishnu Harripersaud that it wasn't her car. She'd just borrowed it from some friends who were helping her out with the move.

Lee told the Harripersauds that she had a job sandblasting houses in Orlando. That, they concluded, must be why she had so many tools.

Sandy also helped them move that day, agreeing to let them temporarily store some of their belongings in her garage. While shifting boxes, Sandy noted a couple of men's business briefcases among their stuff. It seemed inconsequential at the time, but it did flash through her mind: where did *those* come from?

27

Tyria's chequered work history was marred by lengthy (if often voluntary) periods of unemployment, but when she did hold down a job, she was generally regarded by employers as a reliable and diligent worker. When problems arose in her work arena, Lee invariably had a hand in them. The trouble at Casa Del Mar was no exception. The spark that ignited the flame came early in September when Lee telephoned to speak to Tyria and was told by the bellman of a new rule forbidding employees to receive personal calls. Lee did not handle this news well at all. Barely pausing for breath, she unleashed an ugly torrent of abuse in his ear. Annoyed, the clerk snapped back at her and promptly hung up. Furiously, Lee punched out the Casa Del Mar's number again and demanded to be put through to Ty. When the bellman refused, Lee, blithely ignoring the position she was putting Ty in, informed him that she was coming over to the hotel to beat him up. Even more annoyed, the bellman hung up a second time.

Not to be outdone, Lee dialled the Casa Del Mar back. Tired of the interruptions and sensing her calls would not stop, the bellman connected her with the laundry room. Finally getting Ty, Lee demanded to know who the asshole was she'd been talking to? At that juncture, Tyria also fell something short of a master diplomat. Without stopping to weigh her lover's complaints, she impetuously rushed out to the lobby. The bellman explained the new rule for which he was not responsible, but Ty launched into a tirade.

'Why are you talking to my woman like that? I'll kick your ass if you talk to her like that again! I don't give a shit about any new rule, this could have been an emergency! You put through *all* my phone calls!'

The bellman pointed out that he knew it was not an emergency because Lee had already identified herself. Ty resumed her screaming and threatening; soon the bellman had had enough. Furious, he reported her. (Or, as some staff members unsympathetically viewed it, 'went crying to our supervisor'.)

The next day was Tyria's day off, but she showed up as planned for the staff volleyball game. She was kicking back, chatting and puffing on a cigarette when Ahmad Bourbour, the Iranian supervisor, walked in. It struck him immediately that Ty was drunk.

Ahmad, attractive and dark-complexioned, had always got along well enough with Ty in the past. At one time, they'd been reasonably good buddies and Ahmad had occasionally bought her breakfast or lunch. Both being attracted to women, they'd tease one another when a pretty girl walked by. 'Tyria, put your tongue back in your mouth!' Ahmad would say, and she'd make some wisecrack back. But all that camaraderie was forgotten.

'Tyria, I'd like to talk to you. What was the problem with you and Dan?' he asked her.

'You're not my fucking boss! I don't have to fucking talk to you! Mind your own business!' Tyria retorted.

The bellman then put in an appearance and he and Ty renewed their bickering. Ahmad instructed Ty to go in his office, which she did. In her eyes, the issue had been settled the night before and there was no reason for Ahmad to get involved and to rehash it. But from Ahmad's perspective the whole affair looked rather different. Staff problems *were* his business. He and Ty went back and forth, voices rising, until they were screaming.

'You're not my boss!' yelled Tyria.

'For that you're fired!' the frustrated and angry Ahmad finally shot back.

Throwing her cigarette to the floor, Tyria defiantly challenged him: 'If you're going to fire me, you'd better have a good fucking reason!'

With that, she lunged at him across his desk. He was trapped behind it with no avenue of escape when she started pounding on him, pinning him up against the wall and hitting him in the head. At a slender 140 pounds, he was definitely outweighed. But he had the last word. Ty was terminated, and he meant it.

The rest of the housekeeping staff were shocked by Tyria's behaviour, although if anyone could take Ahmad on, it would have to have been tough-talking Ty, they agreed. Some, who were not too fond of Ahmad themselves, secretly admired her and wished they'd had her courage. From their safe vantage points, they savoured the whole affair.

For Ty, however, her outrageous outburst was a short-lived, bittersweet, and ultimately costly victory. 3 September found her unemployed, and genuinely upset about it. She went to Mr Romain to plead her case but did not like what she heard: Ahmad, who had worked at the Casa Del Mar for six years, had been right to fire her, Romain said, backing Ahmad one hundred per cent. Still not satisfied, Ty took her grievances a step further up the ladder, but Mr Bradley didn't see things her way, either. She'd hit a brick wall.

In Lee's mind, the firing of Ty would never be the logical result of flagrant insubordination at her place of work. In Lee's mind, the facts became mangled. First, it became an issue of sexual harassment because they were lesbians. Second, Lee believed the firing was a mean act of revenge by Ahmad because Ty wouldn't give him a piece of ass. Ahmad, married or no, may well have cast an eye over some of the female workers but if so, even his adversaries would doubt that Tyria was ever one of them.

Doubtless coached by Lee in the gentle art of crying lawsuit, Ty threatened to sue. Again revealing shades of Lee's influence, she snarled a number of 'I'll get you!' style threats at Ahmad. Ahmad took the threats seriously enough to file a police report in Ormond Beach.

Approximately ten days later, Ty appeared at the Casa Del Mar to return her uniform and to see Sandy. Crossing paths with Ahmad, she allegedly again hissed, 'I'll get you!'

After she left, Sandy and Alzada told Ahmad that Lee said she'd put a hit on him and was going to kill him. They also said

Lee was going to kill Paul, another worker, who had bought Ty's moped from her and angered Lee by paying for it with a cheque instead of cash. Fictional it all may have been, but, shaken, Ahmad returned to the police station and filed yet another report. It wasn't just himself he was worried about, but his family, his children. He didn't want them put in jeopardy. And if anything untoward should happen to him, he wanted everyone to know that Lee and Ty were behind it.

More than anything, he was shocked by the change he'd seen take place in Ty. It was as if she'd plunged downhill. True, she was drinking more heavily than when they'd first met, but all this recent behaviour just didn't seem like the same girl.

Worse, it seemed she'd started something with her talk of sexual harassment. Suddenly, other female employees were accusing him of this and that. He felt sure that they'd been egged on by Lee and Ty into trumping up charges against him. It was all ironic, he felt, since the door to housekeeping was always open and he was never alone in there with any of the women. Ultimately, he would move away from all the bad feeling at the Casa Del Mar into a job at another plush oceanside hotel nearby, and try to put it all behind him.

Unemployed again and unhappily so, Ty's long-voiced thoughts of moving back to Ohio and into the bosom of her family suddenly had more of a reality to them. Given her general discontent with Lee, maybe she should just pack up and leave? Perhaps now was as good a time as any to make the break?

While Lee was making forays out on the interstate, Ty drooped around the tiny motel room mulling it over. Besides her periodic walks to the store, she did nothing but think, wait for Lee to come back, and watch TV. Movies, *Wheel of Fortune,* and *Jeopardy.* What else was there to do? Pausing for a chat with Mary and Vishnu Harripersaud down at the desk, she told them she'd stopped working at the Casa Del Mar because a man had made a pass at her. She also confided that she was planning to move back to Ohio.

Lee had a lot on her mind. Nothing triggered her anxiety in quite the same way as the threat of losing Ty, and that fear was once again riding high. With her job gone, Ty's anchor to Florida had been perilously loosened. And Lee knew it. Ty was going to Ohio and she was going with her, Lee told the Harripersauds.

That wasn't what Ty had in mind at all.

28

Florida, by virtue of its high population of transients and drifters, is a tough state for crime detection. An almost invisible life is there for the asking. Those so inclined can move around virtually faceless and traceless, checking into cheap motels whose business is primarily cash and whose record-keeping is often perfunctory. Such establishments are accustomed to clients whose lives are elliptic. No phone listed in their name. Maybe no driver's licence. Credit cards? Bank accounts? Forget it. Nonexistent citizens, leaving the flimsiest of paper trails.

People like Lee and Ty are an investigator's nightmare.

Ensconced in the Happy Holidays, they were pedestrians in a state on wheels. Lee was a familiar sight, walking off, her wallet wedged, male-style, in her back jeans pocket, and clutching her plastic shopping bag. Because they were usually without transportation, the Harripersauds noted the night Lee showed up in a small, medium-blue car. A two-door, newish model that she said was her father's and that she'd be driving back to Orlando.

She kept it just a couple of days, but long enough for the Harripersauds to notice the back licence plate was missing. The car's arrival came right after Lee put down $100 on the room and promised to come back with more. She'd pulled up in it after dark, high as a kite and clutching $30. By checking their better-than-usual records later, they were sure that night fell between 12 and 18 September.

Ty had come home to find Lee perched on their bed, sifting through what looked like a collection of someone else's belongings—a couple of men's briefcases and boxes of paperwork. Lee was tossing things out as she went.

Ty listened as she explained away the 1985 Oldsmobile Firenza's presence, reassuring her nervous lover that she hadn't done anything to its owner, she'd only taken the car. But later, when Ty was digesting her usual hefty diet of TV, a news report popped up showing pictures of the little blue car and its owner. He'd been found murdered. Stark reality mingled in with the game shows. Dick Humphreys. He brought the horror total to three. Three murders that Ty definitely knew of. Three cars she had seen. It was on the news. She had no choice but to believe it.

Again, she stayed put. Again, she did nothing.

Lee could leave nothing to chance. Disposing of Dick Humphreys' car, she worked deliberately, calculatingly. She removed his old police chief badge from its wallet and tossed both pieces, separately, as hard and far as she could into the bushes lining the roadway.

She then drove the Firenza some seventy miles north up into southern Lake County. Pulling in off 27 to a desolate stretch known as Boggy Marsh Road, she methodically stripped the car of all her victim's other possessions. Those that she had not chosen to keep, that is. Things like his ice-scrapers. His maps. His personal and business papers, his warranties. She flung them all into the undergrowth. Dick Humphreys had always enjoyed drawing slowly on a good pipe and he kept it with his tobacco in a nicely sculpted wooden tray up on the dashboard. That went, too.

Anything that could link the car to the man.

She peeled a bright yellow Highway Patrol Association sticker from the back bumper, balling it up tightly before she tossed it away. She left the car behind the abandoned Banner service station in Live Oak at the intersection of I-10 and SR 40. But first she took out the Windex she kept in her bag and sprayed, carefully wiping down the car inside and out, meticulously ridding it of tell-tale fingerprints.

Marion County's John Tilley had contacted Citrus County's Jerry Thompson some weeks back and they'd compared notes on the Burress and Spears murders. Tilley had also hooked up with Tom

Muck in Pasco County after he read in the FDLE bulletin that Muck's victim was thought to perhaps be linked to Spears.

The Citrus and Pasco victims were found naked, which Troy Burress was not, but Tilley, Thompson and Muck thought the link of the small-calibre weapon was worth exploring. All the victims' bodies were left in remote areas, and in each case there'd been some attempt to cover them up with debris. Spears' and Burress's vehicles had been dumped away from their bodies. Muck's victim had not yet been identified, but again there was no car found close by the body.

When John Tilley finally met the Citrus investigators in the flesh on 6 September, as they brainstormed, he happened to grab the Peter Siems file and pull it out. It was one of those serendipitous moments. Late that night at home, sifting through the various files with the composite sketch of his Burress suspect, Curtis Blankenship, in hand, Tilley scrutinised the sketches of the two women seen leaving Siems's car. He was shocked. The sketch of Curtis Blankenship and the sketch of the short woman looked uncannily similar. They had to be the same person. The drawings were almost exactly alike.

On 11 September, the day Dick Humphreys died, Tilley went back to Orange Springs and re-interviewed the Hewetts about the two people they'd seen leaving Siems's car back on 4 July. He wanted to check whether they were absolutely sure that the short one was indeed a female. They were. It had been raining, her T-shirt was wet, and they'd been able to see her bra.

Tilley dug further. The area search around the Sunbird on 4 July had been somewhat limited. Anxious to check out Blankenship further to see if there was any correlation at all with the composites (perhaps it was a man/woman team?), Tilley expanded the search and back-tracked, finding the Baileys and the original crash site less than a mile away.

Ultimately, the explanation for the strikingly similar sketches wasn't all that mysterious. Forensic sketches do have a tendency to end up looking alike, and that's what had happened. But no matter. What was important was that Curtis Blankenship's composite had led Tilley to bring the Siems case into the loop. Every murder bears a signature that defines and ultimately reveals its author. Soon, detectives were playing around with the common denominators and contradictions, with the similarities and differences, and speculating that these homicides of men by the Florida highways were perhaps not isolated incidents. What if they were the work of a single killer?

Another really solid link between the homicides surfaced after the death of Dick Humphreys on 11 September, which alone bore enough resemblance to Troy Burress's murder in the same county to raise a red flag.

Both were white middle-aged men shot with .22 calibre weapons, both their bodies were found in remote spots far away from their vehicles. Dick Humphreys' pockets were found turned inside out. Troy Burress had been robbed. Unlike some of the others found in more wooded locations, Dick Humphreys' body had not been covered with debris, but then there was none handy in the sparse terrain, and the remote location in itself could classify as an attempt at concealment.

The bullets found in Dick Humphreys' body—.22 calibre, copper-coated, hollow-nosed, with rifling marks made by a 6-right twist firearm—led detectives to wonder if he might have been killed with the same weapon.

There was another death to fit into the equation. Douglas Giddens's body had been dumped off a dirt roadway and his car was found near an apartment complex in another part of Marion County. He had been shot in the head and killed by a single bullet from a .38 weapon while sitting in the passenger seat of his own car. A .38 broke the pattern of .22s, but since he owned a .38, there was always the possibility he'd been disarmed and shot with his own gun. Also fitting the pattern, some property had been stolen from his car, his wallet was left nearby, and his car was facing south, backed into a spot.

(All but two of the vehicles faced south, although no one knew why, or even if it mattered. A clue that could be meaningless—or crucial.)

Then there had been the mysterious disappearance of Peter Siems, whose wrecked car turned up on 4 July, after being abandoned by two women.

So it was that at 9.30 a.m. on Monday 17 September, there

241

was the biggest yet brainstorming session at Marion County SO. Clutching their morning coffees, investigators from all territories convened for a meeting of the minds. Besides the Marion County cases of Humphreys, Burress, Siems and Giddens, Pasco County's homicide of (the still unidentified) Charles Carskaddon and Citrus County's of David Spears, were also under discussion.

With remarkably little dissension, serious consideration was being given to the controversial theory being floated that the killer (or killers) might be female. Of course the Siems case really highlighted this female turn in the road of investigation. The fact that some of the victims were naked was not in itself that unusual. Nor did it especially suggest gay crimes, females, or even sex crimes. A more common explanation by far was that the killer(s) had merely removed the victims' clothing to try to avoid detection and to delay identification of the body. Gruesome though it may sound to the layman, the cops knew only too well that murderers frequently go to extreme lengths to achieve that end, sometimes removing a head, hands, or other body parts and scattering them in different locations.

The investigators also found it interesting that Dick Humphreys' belongings were scattered on both sides of the road. Had there been two women in his car, perhaps, tossing things to either side simultaneously? Then again, it might easily have been a woman working in tandem with a man.

It's a quantum deductive leap to go from suspecting a woman or women of a single homicide, to suggesting there might be a female serial killer (or killers) on the loose. No one took it lightly.

What nagged at many of the investigators was that these men did not seem easy marks. David Spears was 6 feet 4 inches and not easily overpowered. Investigator Munster couldn't imagine either Dick Humphreys or Troy Burress being conned by a male hitchhiker, or being kidnapped from a convenience store—a theory at one time tossed around regarding Troy Burress. Dick was very against hitchhiking and wouldn't pick up anyone with their thumb out. He was not a fearful man and would be difficult to intimidate, and an ex-cop of his experience would never go blindly where he smelled danger. But that didn't rule out the possibility that he'd fallen for a woman in distress. Both men would stop to help someone in trouble. And that someone could well be a woman.

More telling, to Munster's mind, was the preponderance of bullet wounds in the victims' torsos. There were head wounds, too, but those didn't strike him as being 'the purposeful wounds'. In the case of Dick Humphreys, the closest shot, the shot perhaps fired to make sure he was dead, had been aimed at his heart. In handling female suicides he'd learned a key difference between the sexes. Whereas men won't hesitate to execute someone by pumping a bullet into their head—hitmen traditionally aim a gun barrel point in someone's ear to blow their brains out—women are infinitely more delicate about such matters. On rare occasions a woman might end her life by putting a gun in her mouth, but generally women don't like to disfigure themselves. That theory would carry over into the way they killed others. Where a woman decides to kill a husband or lover, she generally aims for the heart or the torso. Also, .22 calibre revolvers are responsible for a high percentage of deaths nationwide because of their handy, readily concealable size, but are nevertheless generally considered a woman's choice. Increasingly, these homicides seemed to bear a female stamp.

The big question was: if investigators were seeking female serial killers, might these women be the first? The elusive answer depended upon your criteria. Certainly, a considerable number of women have killed multiple times, but what set such women apart from their male counterparts was that they functioned differently. They had not, as far as criminologists knew, infringed on that macabre, male-dominated turf of preying on strangers, picking them up and killing for the thrill of it. Predators stalking victims. That remained the dark province of men. The FBI's Behavioral Science Unit at Quantico, Virginia, defines a serial killer as someone who kills at least three times over a period of time in different locations with a cooling-off period in between. Very few, if any, multiple murderesses could be categorized in quite that way.

Despite the lack of precedent for women killing strangers, after weighing all the evidence, the investigators thought it made sense. And the FBI, when consulted, concurred.

With this new pooling of information, Marion County naturally evolved as the task force headquarters. Most of the bodies were found there, most of the cars dumped there.

Sergeant Brian Jarvis released the sketches of the two women seen leaving Siems's car to a local paper but no one was quite ready to show their hand and announce the women as possible murder suspects. The story came, was given low prominence, and went, drawing no concrete results.

(Later, Brian Jarvis claimed that he'd been reprimanded by his superior, Captain Binegar, then the CID commander responsible for overseeing major crime investigations, for releasing them at all. Jarvis discovered that Captain Binegar had decided to take over the job of funnelling information to the outside world himself.)

Meanwhile, investigators began scouring their female arrest reports and checking the criminal records, for instance, of women who'd been stopped hitchhiking or walking on the interstates. They were looking for two needles in a haystack.

Dick Humphreys' car was spotted by Deputy Cameron from the Suwannee County SO on 19 September—just one week after young Paul and Mike had found his bullet-riddled body, and just six days after the autopsy in Leesburg had officially classified the case a homicide.

Even to the naked eye, it was obvious the Firenza had been wiped down, inside and out. Someone was clearly hell-bent on not leaving any fingerprints. The deputy noted it had been stripped of its vehicle tag, manufacturer's and model identification, and bumper stickers.

Munster and Taylor went up to see the car where it had been towed, in the back yard of a private garage, and arranged for it to be moved down to Marion County's evidence bay on a flatbed trailer. Munster took photographs and he and Taylor interviewed people in the area and subpoenaed the records of a nearby pay phone. (It threw up some leads, but they didn't pan out.)

Closer inspection of the car about a month later revealed one good, old-fashioned clue that intrigued the detectives. On the car floor, beneath one of the pedals, lay a cash register receipt for the purchase of beer or wine. Using its Emro store number, 8237, investigators traced it to the Speedway truck stop and convenience store located in Wildwood, at SR 44 and I-75. The receipt was dated 11 September, the day of Dick's disappearance and murder, and marked with the register time of 4.19 p.m. It was a lead.

Investigators had already been busy asking questions, and had deduced that the last person who actually knew Dick Humphreys to have seen him alive was Gayle, a pretty, blonde, 28-year-old mother who was once part of his HRS caseload. Her HRS case file was closed, but after leaving the Wildwood Police Department on the last day of his life, Dick had made an unscheduled stop at her home in the Wildwood Commons housing complex sometime between 3.10 and 3.30 p.m.

Gayle had been outside and had watched him drive by. Thinking he was the insurance man, she waved. Seeing her, Dick stopped, backed up his car and got out. Only then did Gayle recognise him. He wasn't there for business, it was just a friendly stop. He seemed nervous, she thought, as he stepped inside with her. Gayle's live-in boyfriend, Michael, arrived shortly afterwards and the three chatted for a few minutes, then Mr Humphreys explained that he'd been looking for some people and must have had a wrong address. He went out to his car and abruptly left.

To Gayle, he seemed different that day; preoccupied and nervous. She thought back to the first time he'd called on her in the line of duty. She'd been defensive, like any mother whose suitability as a parent has been questioned and who finds herself under the magnifying glass. Despite her attitude, he was perceptive enough to win her over quickly. She admired that, just as she admired the fact he didn't take her neighbours' complaints at face value. He'd heard her out. She wasn't quite sure how to put it, but he seemed to have faith in her. That was something that Gayle, who had only recently escaped a husband who had sexually abused her young children, badly needed.

And whenever Mr Humphreys had dropped by and found her outside her apartment, sunning herself in her bikini, there was never any hint of sexual harassment or pressure. She was more used to being propositioned than treated with respect and she knew which she preferred. She liked the fact he told her about his happy marriage to Shirley.

The morning after his hasty departure, Gayle had an appointment with a counsellor in the next building and dropped in to see Dick Humphreys at his office, quite unaware of his disappearance. Ken Jones, Dick's co-worker, was tied up at the time, busily hitting the phones, calling sheriffs' offices, hospital emergency rooms and highway patrols, trying to find some trace of Dick. When Gayle was told Mr Humphreys wasn't in, she left, but fortunately, she'd told the secretary what she was doing and Ken, as soon as he heard, rushed after her. She filled him in on her last encounter with Dick.

Ken Jones duly passed this information on to the cops. So it was that Investigator David Taylor was in turn bringing Sergeant Brian Jarvis, the major crimes supervisor, and Investigator Bruce Munster up to speed at 3.36 a.m. on the morning of 13 September. Less than twenty minutes later, the witnesses were being ushered into CID Interview Room 2 and Taylor and Munster questioned first Gayle, then Michael. Their stories were the same. At around 5 a.m. Jarvis and Munster gave them a ride home and, with Gayle and Michael's permission, searched their apartment. They found nothing suspicious.

David Taylor, then the lead investigator on the Humphreys case, was at the Dunnellon Police Department the next evening, handing over a copy of the homicide bulletin on Humphreys, when he was paged by his office. He was to call a Ms Lori Stephens who might have some valuable information. Lori, an employee of the Journey's End Motel in Wildwood (close by the Speedway store where they'd later learn the beer or wine had been bought), had seen the news of Mr Humphreys' murder on TV. She thought she might have seen him on the day of his disappearance.

Talking to Journey's End employees, David Taylor took statements and began piecing the story together. One staff member remembered Mr Humphreys pacing up and down the halls that afternoon as if he were looking for someone. He also made a call from the pay phone. It might have been the call he made to his office.

Thanks to his own efforts, his presence at the motel had been memorable. At around 4 p.m., while a clutch of employees gathered around the desk in the lobby, chatting, he walked up, showed his i.d., then introduced himself as Dick Humphreys, HRS. Who owned the blue Buick Skylark in the parking lot with the child in it, he wanted to know? Motel employee, Tina Strickland, admitted that the boy was hers. Her son was sleeping peacefully where she could see him.

'Well you shouldn't leave him in the back seat. Go get that kid and bring him in here,' Humphreys told her.

He had a quiet air of authority which somehow automatically commanded respect, so she did as he said. Then she and the other employees, curiosity roused, watched as he headed down the street to a McDonald's. About ten minutes later, he was back at the motel. He didn't say anything, but again seemed to be looking for someone.

David Taylor checked the Journey's End records for 10 to 12 September for himself, but they only confirmed what the clerks had told him. Mr Humphreys had not booked a room. Introducing himself as Dick Humphreys, HRS, and bringing himself to the attention of a gaggle of employees, didn't sound much like a man who was up to no good.

With the task force in place, Jerry Thompson and Marvin Padgett found themselves spending a lot of time over in Marion County, and attended another meeting there on 21 September. Bruce Munster presented all the information on Burress, and Tom Muck did so on Pasco's still anonymous victim. For the first time, Volusia County's Richard Mallory was introduced into the mix. The investigators decided to send all the vacuumings, fibres and bullets found for laboratory comparison.

29

On Saturday 29 September, when Vishnu walked past Ty and Lee's open room door, he caught sight of them doling out some of their possessions to some women he'd seen before from the Casa Del Mar. It looked for all the world as if they were packing up and getting ready to leave. As they hadn't paid him since the 20th, he could be forgiven for suspecting they might be skipping out on their bill. Prompted thus, Vishnu confronted Lee.

'Are you guys leaving? I want my money,' he asked, good-naturedly enough.

'Oh no, no . . . we're not leaving or anything. We just want to give these people some of our stuff,' Lee reassured him, equally politely.

But sure enough, Vishnu later saw Lee and Ty about to take off. Hurrying past the open door of their bare room, he saw the room keys on the bed. She'd lied. They were doing a flit.

'You guys leaving?' he asked more sharply, running over to them. To his amazement, Lee snapped back at him.

'Don't mess with me, motherfucker! Don't mess with me!' She'd never cursed at him before. Suddenly, her expression and whole bearing had changed. She seemed like a totally different person.

'How can you guys be like that?' he cried.

Furious at her threat, he thought fast. He'd noticed they had a cab waiting for them out back and he was tempted to call the cops, then pull his car in front of the cab to block its exit. But he discarded the plan almost as soon as he came up with it. Cops always took too long. He couldn't stop them leaving.

Checking their vacant room later, Vishnu discovered a small

knife and a few odd tools and power sockets tucked in a drawer. The women had also left a TV which he plugged in and tried; it didn't work.

Mostly what they left behind was junk, their bill, and plenty of bad feeling.

When, later that same day, they checked into the Fairview Motel on Ridgewood Avenue in Port Orange, they arrived not by cab but wheeling their neatly boxed belongings on a dolly cart. The Fairview was a clean, respectable, family-owned establishment. Lee signed the register as Cammie Lee Greene and they paid $43.60 cash down, which was two days' rent in advance, for room No. 8. Rose McNeill, the owner, had a feeling they were lesbians.

As the days unwound, the usual pattern emerged. Ty, who was still not working, stayed pretty much behind their closed door. The only time Rose saw her, really, was when the two of them walked off together down the street. There was no reason to have much contact. Lee did all the talking. She seemed nice enough, and when she went off hitching for a couple of days' work, she was always concerned that Ty would be OK while she was gone, and would have enough money for food.

Just making casual conversation during one of her absences, Rose remarked to Ty that she thought it was terrible that Lee had to hitch all the way to Orlando to work. Ty soon shut her up.

'Her business is private. I don't talk about her business,' she said with a definite air of finality.

On 12 October 1990, one of Bruce Munster's numerous telephone calls brought good news from the Ocoee Police Department: Dick Humphreys' badge case and HRS i.d. had been found in a wooded field off 27 by a man who'd been out snake hunting. It could be the break they needed.

The next day, Munster and David Taylor rendezvoused with the snake-hunter and two Ocoee deputies at a hamburger joint, and they escorted them to the spot off Boggy Marsh Road in southern Lake County. They spread out and searched. Bingo. They found, scattered around, Dick's ice-scrapers, a wadded-up map, his pipe and tobacco, some personal and business papers, his car ownership and warranties. Near Dick's property they also found Miller Lite and Budweiser beer cans and one .22 calibre shell casing, lying in the sandy soil. There was also a ball of paper that turned out to be his yellow Highway Patrol Association bumper sticker.

Later, when technicians tested everything for fingerprints, they delicately separated the rolled-up bumper sticker, hoping to find a fingerprint or two. There was a single print and it lifted well—but it belonged to Dick Humphreys.

It was amazing. Whoever killed him hadn't even left a print in the sticky residue. Clever, or merely lucky? It was beginning to look like clever.

The drifting, delectable aromas of home-cooked Yugoslav fare drew Lee back to the Belgrade Restaurant, an old haunt from the early eighties. It was just past the RV lot a few doors down from the Fairview, and when she stopped by for a meal, she found it was still owned and operated by Vera Ivkovitch and her husband Velimir. Vel fixed cars in the garage out back and Vera ran the kitchen. She recognised Lee immediately, calling, 'Welcome home!' In the old days, Lee had come in regularly with clients to eat. Her hair was lighter now and she seemed a little more subdued, more bitter, somehow. Back then, she used to yatter like a typewriter, Vera remembered.

'I'm gonna be next door at the motel,' Lee explained, 'so I'm gonna stop in for breakfast and lunch.'

'OK,' Vera said, wiping her hands on her apron and smiling, pleased as always when a customer affirmed the appeal of her cooking.

True to her word, on Sunday 14 October, Lee took Ty, her 'friend', in for a meal. As they sat in the spartan restaurant, which does not serve alcohol, Lee asked Vera if she knew of any places to rent? They couldn't stay at the motel, it was too expensive. They'd lost their business and their car, in fact they'd lost everything they had. They had to find somewhere cheaper.

'We got room!' Vera cried in her heavily fractured English,

only too happy to oblige. 'Bathroom, TV, stereo. Fifty dollars a week.'

'We'll move in tonight!' Lee grinned without hesitating. She was excited by the saving. Fifty dollars a week! That was a real steal. She and Ty enlisted Sandy who, anxious to get rid of all their boxes from her garage, was only too glad to give them a hand to move.

Vera and Vel's guests kept themselves to themselves. No one ever stopped by to see them. No one drove by to pick them up. No one called. Once, a man called for Lee, but that was literally it.

They stayed holed up in their room at the back of the restaurant, the low drone of the TV emanating twenty-four hours a day. It had started out a loud drone, but Vel soon insisted they turn it down. Ty, especially, rarely ventured out and never alone. The Ivkovitchs thought it was odd, the way that when they went to the gas station next door to buy beer, they skirted round the back and through the bushes, rather than walk across the parking lot and out on the street. Odd, but not suspicious. Some nights, the women drank two cases of beer—48 cans. Vera couldn't believe her eyes when she saw all the empties spilling out of the trash. Sometimes, when Ty was holed up alone, Vera coaxed a cigarette from Vel for her. Of course, Vel thought Vera had taken up smoking again, but she didn't care. She felt rather sorry for Ty.

Vera, suspecting that Ty was Lee's lover, asked Lee outright if she'd become a lesbian. Lee was surprised more than angry, wanting to know how Vera could tell.

'I can tell on you,' Vera replied. 'But I respect. No problem.' The only thing that drowned their TV or music was the sound of Lee screaming at Ty. Screaming. Always screaming. 'She's my lover,' Lee explained to Vera, adding, in a manner eerily reminiscent of Leo Pittman, that she'd kill Tyria if she caught her with anyone else.

'How can she find another girl?' Vera retorted. 'She never leave the room!'

Lee and Ty's disputes never came to blows though, the Ivkovitches were pretty sure of that. Just screaming. 'I spank you, Lee! You're too bossy!' Vera chastised her. When the Yugoslav couple had another guest—a retired sheriff from New York City—they quietened down considerably.

As if intimidated by the presence of others, when they wanted to eat in the restaurant, they always checked first to make sure it was empty, then they'd venture out and sit at one of the chequered-tablecloth-covered tables. If anyone else came in to dine, they picked up their food and retreated to their room. Whatever the lighting and no matter the hour, Lee always wore a ball cap and sunglasses.

Just as their lesbianism was no problem, it was no problem, either, when the two women asked for credit. But with breakfast, lunch and appetisers, it soon mounted up, and they fell behind with their rent, too. The bill climbed to $230. More mornings than not, while Vera was up at dawn slaving over a hot stove, Lee languished in bed until lunchtime.

'Lee, honey, I'm sixty-five years old,' Vera finally said. 'I work seven days a week, sixteen hours a day. You're only thirty-three years old and work one day a week. No more credit!'

'I'll get you a cheque from my pressure-cleaning business if you give me a ride to I-95 and 44,' Lee promised.

'Where you going to go?'

'Pressure cleaning. But don't tell anybody about my business.' Vel drove her to the highway. The next day, she begged for another ride and, obligingly, he again dropped her off where she asked, near the same spot. How would she get where she was going from there, he asked? She'd walk, she reassured him.

'I don't think this girl's got business . . . maybe monkey business,' Vel reported to Vera. They speculated that she was either a prostitute or selling dope.

On 22 October Sergeant David Strickland of Citrus County SD's evidence identification department visited Marion County SO with Investigator Martin for a close-up look at Peter Siems's car. Searching for prints he could lift, Strickland noticed—as had other officers before him—what looked suspiciously like blood on the vinyl door handle, driver's side.

The part you slip your hand inside to open and close the door. He carefully removed the handle and carried it back to his office. A latent print was developed from it. And a palm print was also lifted from the right-hand side of the boot lid. They knew that was important. All they had to do was hope it didn't belong to Siems. Then all they would face was the minor task of locating its owner.

Having seen the condition of Mr Humphreys' car, Bruce Munster also decided to take a look at Peter Siems' car. The front ashtray was missing, presumably removed by technicians, but he noticed that the ashtray in the back was pulled out and brimming with cigarette butts that had apparently been overlooked. Prompted to take an even closer look, he removed the ashtray, then searched under the seats, finding under the passenger seat a bottle of Windex with an Eckerd's store price tag attached. A can of Busch also lay under the seat—a beer Dick did not drink. Munster had the items put into evidence and processed.

When the Windex led to a store in Atlanta, Georgia, where it was believed to have been sold back in February, that was even more intriguing. Jerry Thompson and Tom Muck were watching a couple of Georgia homicides that might be linked to the ones in Florida. In one, a white, male body was found outside Adel, Georgia, shot twice with a small-calibre weapon. But it bore tattoos, they learned. That ruled out Peter Siems.

On 23 October, Bruce Munster and David Taylor interviewed Anita Armstrong at the sheriff's office after being told she was the cashier on duty at Wildwood's Speedway store when the mystery Emro receipt found in Dick Humphreys' car was issued. Armstrong claimed to remember two women who resembled the composite drawings coming through the store.

Armstrong said she'd paid close attention because the two women fell into the precise category that put her antennae on full alert, since she was responsible for moving on any hookers who seemed to be dallying in the store, or even in the outside parking lot. The area was plagued with drug deals and prostitution, and anyone not buying fuel outside or produce inside was viewed with suspicion.

These two were just the kind of women she looked for. The blonde, at least, she felt sure was a hooker. She was around 5 feet 7, nicely built, well-proportioned and wearing a skirt with fringes hanging down. (Lee, of course, was something of an anomaly in the world of prostitution, ignoring the usual wardrobe and artifice, and working in T-shirts and shorts or jeans. She had never been known to wear a skirt.) The short one was a bit on the hefty side for hooking, but you never knew. She was around 5 feet 4 to 5 feet 6 inches.

Armstrong remembered them vividly because they were laughing and acting so silly and flamboyantly that everyone was looking. They walked straight through the store and out the back door: they didn't sit down or buy anything. Then they walked through a second time. By checking her work schedules, Armstrong was able to say they came through before 5 p.m. on 11 September. Just around the time Dick Humphreys, or someone who'd been in his car, had bought beer or wine there.

Her shift actually ran from 2 to 10.30 p.m. but she remembered it being late afternoon and probably before 5 p.m., because that's when the line backs up, particularly on Tuesdays, lottery night.

Anita did not remember Mr Humphreys from the photograph she was shown. But a respectable-looking man would hardly stand out in her mind.

Things were getting tense at the Belgrade. While Ty was easy-going enough, Lee was another story. She and Vel argued daily. She fought like a gypsy, that was how Vera saw her, with her volcanic personality and blazing eyes. At the heart of the trouble was money. Lee and Ty began chipping away at their debt, but far too slowly for the Ivkovitchs' liking.

Once, stopping by their room, Vera noted that they only seemed to have a couple of pairs of jeans and sneakers apiece. Everything else in there seemed to be tools. 'Why tools, Lee?' she asked.

'You know, my business people have no money, so they pay with tools,' she explained.

She tried offering Vera a gold chain in lieu of cash but Vera turned it down. She had gold jewellery of her own. It was money they wanted. Lee also presented Vera with a nice electric shaver for Vel. Vera took that just to try to keep the peace.

One night, Vera and Vel saw Lee standing inside the open doorway of her room. She was cleaning a gun. Did Vel have a gun, too? Yes, he replied. Of course. All over the place. One in every corner of every room. He didn't, but, instinctively, it had seemed the right thing to say.

Despite their financial bind, Lee and Ty offered to buy from the Ivkovitchs the three-dimensional picture of *The Last Supper* that hung above their bed. Vera wouldn't sell it. When Lee handed Vera a paltry $10 for Vel, she thought, 'Oh, no, Vel's going to get mad.' They'd never clear the debt, paying Vera $10 at a time. And indeed, he waved it at Vera angrily, saying, 'She thinks we're crazy.' Instead of catching up, they were falling further behind. Furious, he went and knocked on their door. Ty answered.

'I'm tired, who is it?' she called.

'You know who I am,' Vel called back. 'I want tomorrow my room empty!'

'Oh, no!' Ty cried.

'Oh, yes!' Vel shouted back.

Obviously, they took Vel seriously because, amazingly, they packed up and left the next day without waiting for any more warnings. They still owed the Ivkovitchs $34.

30

Ousted from the Belgrade, Lee and Ty showed their faces back at the Fairview on 17 November. It was undoubtedly their easiest option. It was near and it was familiar, they were almost out of cash, and Ty was leaving that day for Ohio to spend Thanksgiving with her folks. Please could they have a room, Lee begged Rose? She offered her a TV for collateral. They'd had to leave the Belgrade, Lee complained, because they'd had problems, none of which were their fault. Vel was always trying to put the make on her, or harassing her for owing money even when they had paid up in full, and now he'd told them to leave. Would Rose drive them over there so they could move their stuff back to the Fairview?

Obligingly, Rose pulled her car around by the Yugoslav restaurant and Ty and Lee loaded in their things. (With her muscular build, Lee had no problem lifting heavy-looking tool boxes in and out.) Meanwhile, Rose popped inside for a chat with Vera. Without being specific, Vera warned her, a fellow businesswoman after all, that the two women were trouble.

They hadn't given *her* any trouble in the past, Rose pointed out, thinking back. Nothing sprang to mind. She didn't always like Lee's attitude, but there'd never been any actual trouble. She'd never brought guys back or anything like that. If anyone gave her trouble, Rose called the police. There'd been nothing like that. True, they were sometimes a little late with her money, but that was about it.

Vera warned her again to be careful. Perhaps Vera sensed something Rose didn't, Rose fleetingly speculated. But she didn't pursue that line of thought. Her only complaint against the two women was, in fact, minor. More of a petty annoyance than

256

anything else. She'd told them more than once to please put their cans in separate bags and leave them outside their room for recycling. They always agreed, but never actually did it.

Just two days before their move, on Thursday, Lee Wuornos, shrouded by her Cammie Greene alias, had brushed perilously close to a branch of law enforcement. She was stopped by highway patrol officers for hitchhiking on I-95 up near St Augustine. It was always hitchhiking, never prostitution. She'd got it down to a fine art.

Those officers had no idea who had just slipped through their fingers. No idea that, tucked in her bag, she carried a smoking gun.

The day they moved back into the Fairview, Rose saw Ty and Lee leave on foot, dressed in their usual uniform of shorts, T-shirts and baseball caps, carrying a large, light brown suitcase. They were heading out to hitch a ride or catch a bus to Daytona airport for Ty to catch her flight to Ohio, then Lee would be going to Orlando for a day or two. She had a job down there sandblasting buildings, and when she came back, she'd have the money to pay Rose.

Since they were going to be away, Rose wondered if she could go in and clean their room and their screens? She'd been trying to get around to doing them. Lee said no, she'd rather she didn't. Rose wasn't in the least bit surprised—they'd never once taken advantage of the motel's maid service. They didn't want anyone poking around in their room.

Trying to be helpful, Rose suggested that while Lee was down in Orlando, she look up a motel owner friend of hers who might be interested in the sandblasting. It seemed curious, but Lee showed absolutely no interest in getting her name or number.

Ty was booked on flight 312 to Pittsburgh, Pennsylvania, and she couldn't wait. She was excited at the prospect of seeing her folks. Happy families. Fun and love and festivity. It would be a wonderful reunion.

It would be a wonderful reunion for her, at any rate. Lee would be spending the holiday at the motel, alone. She wasn't exactly swamped with Thanksgiving Dinner invitations.

The thought of Ty up in Ohio, the thought that Ty might never come back, bummed her out. Totally. Lonely. Drunk all the time. Not just drunk, but *really* drunk. Must have had a case of beer that day. Drunk as shit. Needed some money, so went hitchhiking. Picked somebody up, but couldn't remember where. Couldn't remember anything. Blackout time.

But this is the way it went. Older fella. Little short guy. On his way to Alabama. One thing about these men on their way to somewhere, they were usually heavy with cash.

So she asked the little guy if he'd help her make some money? Sure, he would.

They went far out in the woods down a dirt trail off Bar Pit Road. That crosses 19 about nine miles north of Cross City. Way, way out. Stripped off, both of them. Sat in the back seat of his Grand Prix. He took off his gold chain and put it on the seat. Dipped into his pants pocket, pulled out his wallet. Said he was a cop.

Oh, no. Not that line again. I'm a cop and I could arrest you, but if you have sex with me for free, I'll let you go. Told her what she had to suck or do to him, then he'd let her go. Another faker, after a free piece of ass. That was all she could think. Sick and tired of that old story. Cop? You're no cop. You can get badges like that through some detective magazine.

They were out of the car, arguing, when he ran around to her side. She whipped out her gun, and they struggled. He fell first, but he got back up on his feet and made a run for it. His life. He wanted to save his life.

Ice in her veins. No feeling for him. No feeling or caring for any of them. Their families would have to understand. These guys were trying to hurt her. She shot him right in the back as he went. He stopped and turned and looked at her. Disbelief on his face. Must have been. Who could believe this was happening?

He called her a name, she said. Cussed her out. Something. Whatever it was, she let him have it again. You bastard. One more in his back at close range.

That was it, wasn't it? Oh. Or did she shoot him in the back one more time? Near the head. Something like that. Did it just kind of randomly. Turned her head away and fired.

That bullet to the back of the head as he tried to get away hit him square on, just above his hairline. And yet a fourth bullet tore into the back of this man who was soon to be married and wanted so much to live. His life left him while he lay there on the ground, curled up in the fetal position.

Later, she'd ask if he survived. Even sounded kind of sorry to hear he hadn't. Could she really have thought she'd left him with a chance to cling to life? No. It wasn't her practice to let them live.

She was scared. Heart beating fast. She did it, but she was always afraid of being caught. Every time, she made sure that wouldn't happen. Made sure they wouldn't tell.

She threw some stuff out in the woods. Scavenging furiously through his car and glove box, she found his false teeth. Tossed them out, too. Not much good to her. You fucking bastard. Let me get something out of this. She pocketed his diamond and gold nugget ring. The one that had been lovingly chosen for him by his fiancée, Aleen. Took it off his finger when he was still alive, she'd thought. Would he have let her? And why? Well. She *thought* he was alive when she took it. So much beer.

She drove off in his car, naked. Pulled over, dressed. Threw out some more of his stuff. She was up off 27 by then, walking about, scattering things far and wide in all directions. Spectacles. A wallet with his Social Security card. His driver's licence. Credit card receipts. Underwear. Rubber boots. Box of denture cleaner. All kinds of junk. She tore off the licence plate and put it in the boot. Drove a bit further, then the damn car stopped. What the hell was wrong with it? Tried the ignition again, and it started back up.

You know, she'd had a hundred thousand guys. Meeting guys left and right, every moment of the day. Looking for clean and decent people. She'd say these guys were the only ones that gave her a problem. (She'd also say she'd been raped nine times, over the years.) It seemed like just in the past year men had started giving her hassles. Messing with her. She'd had to start taking retaliation. What else could she do?

She drove the dead man's car on back to the motel room that was her home of the moment, thoughts of Ty swimming around her head. Please let her come back soon. Parking the car outside the Fairview, she lifted a suitcase of his from the boot. Didn't remember much else.

Lee often popped her head into the Fairview's office about this or that. Would it be OK with Rose if she parked her boyfriend's car behind the motel? He was married, and they didn't want to leave it where his wife could see it. If it was spotted, she'd have to give it back and she hoped to be able to keep it until Ty flew back in so that she could pick her up from the airport. Ty would be arriving on a Sunday, when she wouldn't be able to get a bus and would have to pay for a cab. The car would really help.

Rose gave her the go ahead. Later, though, to keep her guest registration records straight, she stopped out back intending to take down the car's tag number. She saw it, pulled in almost behind the shed, a large, maroon two-door model with no licence plate.

The car was outside only briefly, a couple of days at the most, before disappearing as suddenly as it came. When she decided that the car was too hot to handle and that the pleasure of having wheels did not outweigh the risk, Lee drove south down I-95 past Edgewater. Getting off before Mims, in northern Brevard County, she'd turned towards the ocean and backed it into the abundant woods by US 1. Explaining its departure to Rose, she said that her boyfriend's wife had seen it and she'd had to give it back.

Seeing lamplight shining dimly through the window of Lee's room and hearing noises, a night when Rose had been led to believe she wouldn't be there, she knocked on the door to check it out. As Lee opened up and stood back for Rose to step inside, it was immediately apparent that Lee was as drunk as a skunk.

She held up a long, black wallet full of business cards, as if tantalising Rose with some highly classified information, and said that her business was private and personal, that she'd never give a recommendation from one place to another, that she completely protected her clients' privacy.

She was dressed just in a bra and panties, which struck Rose as odd, too, since they had complained before that the room was cold.

'I guess it got warm or something . . .' she commented. In response to which Lee whipped off her bra, threw it across the room and said, 'Oh, what the hell!'

'Well, no big deal, I have sisters,' Rose said, a little startled.

'Well, I do too,' said Lee.

Rose walked away, shaking her head, mystified after this curious interchange. The next day when she saw Lee, Lee acted as if nothing had happened. Who knew if she even remembered?

Lee was alone on Thanksgiving Day which fell on Thursday 22 November. The motel owner felt rather badly about that. She considered inviting her to join her and some friends who didn't have families in the area, but thought better of it. She really preferred to keep her distance. She didn't want to get involved.

Nor did the elderly gentleman who helped Rose out around the motel, although the two women in baseball caps would make an indelible impression on him. Lee stiffed him for quarters for the phone which she always promised to return and never did. Once, when he was retrieving his laundry from the line, Lee called out to him, 'Feel my panties! See if they're dry!' Things like that didn't happen every day.

Lee was a familiar face at the gas station near the Fairview, stopping in regularly to buy her twelve-packs of Busch, her Marlboro Lights and her coffee. She often chatted to Brenda McGarry, the clerk, and spoke lovingly of Britta, telling Brenda it was Lauri's fault that she died.

'She kept saying, "The pain, the pain . . . and the only thing that gets rid of the pain, slams it, is the hate."'

Once, Vel Ivkovitch bumped into her over there and asked her, 'Where's my money?'

'You're a sorry sonofabitch, you're lucky you're alive!' Lee snapped.

Of course, Vera and Vel thought she was joking. She was just mad because they'd kicked her out.

Lee once asked Brenda McGarry for a job application while simultaneously bragging that she made $2,000 to $3,000 a month in her current line of work.

Later, checking her records, Rose McNeill could tell that somewhere between 17 and 19 November, Lee paid another $90 for the room. The largest amount of cash she and Ty ever handed over during their stays. What Rose did know for sure was that on the 19th (which might, therefore, have been later that same day), Lee came in asking for a small loan. First she wanted a dollar, then two dollars. Rose handed it over, duly adding the small amounts to their card.

Rose struggled to pin down the date she received the $90, but was torn. On the one hand, she couldn't imagine herself letting them have a room without money down, which meant it must have been on the 17th. Then again it could have been the 19th, because she'd remembered it striking her as peculiar, Lee putting down a large sum one minute, then running out of money the next. Perhaps she took the TV on the 17th, and the cash on the 19th. The day after she killed him.

On 19 November, detectives in at least two counties were having busy days.

She'd assumed it would take them a while to find him. She hardly knew where the body was herself. But Walter Gino Antonio was found the very next day, pitifully naked, except for his tube socks. That was how he looked to Captain J. Small of the Tampa Police Department who came across him while out hunting near Cross City.

Jimmy Pinner of Dixie County Sheriff's Office was assigned to investigate.

Mr Antonio was identified by his fingerprints. Once his name was known, Pinner spoke to his fiancée, Aleen Berry, who racked her brain to draw up a list of the belongings she thought he had had with him when he left home.

There was the police badge from his days as a reserve deputy with the Brevard County Sheriff's Office, a police-style billy-club with a black, plaited handle, a black flashlight, and a pair of handcuffs. On a more mundane level there was his Timex watch, a few suitcases. Aleen also thought he had a red metal tool box full of mechanical tools and a green canvas military-style bag, also filled with tools. He might have had a baseball cap, possibly with NASA written on it. And there was the ring, of course.

The very same day, the white 1986 Olds Ciera belonging to Curtis 'Corky' Reid, a Titusville man who had been missing since 7 September, was at long last spotted by Orlando police, in a parking lot near Orlando's east–west expressway.

The mystery disappearance of the 50-year-old roofing engineer had been as perplexing as the Peter Siems case. Dan Carter, the Titusville detective investigating, had hit a brick wall. Corky, who worked for a company that serviced NASA, had gone missing on a Thursday; a pay day. He'd gone home, shaved, showered, left his security badge on the dresser. He left the air-conditioning on, obviously planning to return. On his way out again, he said 'Hi' to his neighbour, climbed into his car, and headed off, purportedly to keep a dinner date in Cocoa Beach with a buddy from work. Then he promptly disappeared off the face of the earth.

He, like the other missing men, didn't seem the type to do a disappearing act voluntarily. His house was on the market and he'd run up some substantial debts, but he was a devoted son who kept in almost daily contact with his mother who was dying of emphysema (and has since died). One of his sisters had cancer. His sister, Deanie, and her husband, Jim Stewart, were alerted to his disappearance on Tuesday morning by a phone call from his office wondering if they knew where he was. They were immediately alarmed. Corky's calls to his mom stopped stone cold. And there was no activity on his credit cards after the day he disappeared. A divorced man, he liked to visit bars and had recently had a female house-guest for a couple of weeks but she'd left by then. His 18-year-old son, John, had recently been living with him, too. They checked his home, found no sign of foul play, and immediately notified the Titusville Police Department.

Corky had been seen cashing a cheque the day he disappeared, and his family and Dan Carter suspected he was carrying anywhere from $600 up to $1,000. 'He couldn't hold on to money, bless his heart,' said Jim Stewart, noting that he'd recently paid out over $2,000 in back bills. If he'd planned to walk away from his life, why do that? Why not hang on to the money?

The discovery of Corky's car looked like the break Dan Carter needed. Carter had recently begun attending the task force meetings, but noted that Corky's Olds Ciera didn't quite fit the pattern. There were similarities. The driver's seat was pulled all the way forward, and the mirror was tilted down, so perhaps a woman had been driving it. There was also a blonde hair on the steering wheel. But the licence plates had not been removed, nor had the Masonic emblem on Corky's trunk. His passport and Masonic apron, which he usually kept in his glove box, were missing, though, as were his wallet, credit cards, jewellery. Both his car and house keys—breaking the pattern—were on the floor of the driver's side. Also, the car had not been wiped clean like the others. He was lost without his spectacles, and both pairs were in the car. It was a mystery.

The car was a break, but for Reid's family, the torment continued because there was still no sign whatsoever of Corky. It was the not knowing. The gaping hole of not knowing.

Walter Gino Antonio's maroon Pontiac Grand Prix was found on Saturday 24 November. Detectives came to learn he had a ritual; whenever he bought gas, he meticulously recorded his mileage on the receipts. From this methodical behaviour, they could deduce that in the week since his disappearance, his car had been put through its paces to the tune of over one thousand miles.

Ty was due to fly back into Daytona on Sunday 25 November, arriving on Eastern Airlines flight 301. No longer having the car, Lee headed out early to meet her, unsure of the

Sunday bus schedule and anticipating she might have to hitch a ride. As she walked down Spruce Creek Road, a small blue car that had already cruised past her once, pulled over and stopped. She recognised the man behind the wheel just as he'd recognised her.

She'd first officially met bearded Donald Willingham a year earlier in Geneva's bar down on Beach Street about a block from Wet Willie's, although they'd seen each other around for years. She was standing in the doorway that morning, combing the numbers on some Lotto tickets and 'waiting for my old man'. They went inside, played a little pool together, and she'd talked him into buying her some beers. Donald heard talk about her later, about how she'd turned loud and obnoxious. Since then, he'd spotted her numerous times out hitchhiking on the highway, and sometimes stopped and gave her rides in his red truck (later replaced by a blue car) and bought her a few beers. 'She needed me, and I needed her, it was a fair trade,' is how he summed up his acquaintance with the hitchhiking hooker. But he hadn't seen her in a good while before that November day.

'Where are you going?' he called out.

'I'm trying to get to the airport.'

'The airport? What are you going to the airport for?'

'My girlfriend is coming in.'

'Who?'

'Ty. Would you do me a favour and take me there?' Donald, who had no plans, told her to hop in.

'I need a beer,' Lee sighed.

Not averse to the idea himself, Donald stopped and bought some, then they just drove around, drinking, killing time and hanging out, until Ty's plane landed.

Ty was coming back, to all intents and purposes, of her own free will. Coming back one full year after Lee first confessed to her that she had killed someone. If indeed she feared for her life as she'd later claim, quite why she returned is a mystery. It wasn't as if she was bound to Florida by earthly possessions. They travelled light, weighed down for the most part by odd clutter. Stolen work tools can hardly have been the irresistible magnet pulling her back.

She was returning, but probably not for long. Lee knew that. Or at least strongly suspected it. Ty had warned her of that. Almost as soon as Ty emerged from the airport terminal, Lee hit on Donald for a ride for the next leg of their ongoing shuffle. Ty would be leaving, Lee said. They were splitting up, and she was going back up north. Then again, she'd threatened to leave before and Lee hoped to change her mind.

Meeting Ty took Donald by surprise. He'd never heard Lee was a lesbian and she'd never struck him that way. Ty was equally confused by his presence, wondering if he was one of Lee's tricks. Lee prevailed upon Donald to make another beer stop en route to the Fairview. Pulling up outside, Ty lugged her bags to their room while Lee heaved in the case of beer she'd bought to celebrate Ty's return.

Watching from her vantage point across the forecourt, Rose noted the beer, then quickly looked away. She tried to avoid seeing anything like that. Rose knew her mother would be furious if she knew they were buying cases of beer while they were behind with their bill.

In the privacy of their room, Lee presented Ty, her 'wife', with Gino Antonio's gold diamond ring. Ty slipped it on her finger.

Ty wasn't so afraid for her life that it stopped her from cheerfully showing Rose a happy family snap from Thanksgiving and waxing enthusiastic about her great vacation. Whatever Ty and Lee's plans were, they evidently weren't set in stone. Lee told Rose they'd seen an apartment they were hoping to get. But when Rose asked if it was nearby, Lee took umbrage. Ty, who was lounging on the bed, stayed silent as Lee angrily repeated her speech about her business being private. Once she left the motel, she informed Rose, in a tone that left no room for misinterpretation, she didn't want anyone knowing where she was or knowing anything about her.

'Fine,' retorted Rose, more than a little annoyed at being chastised. 'To tell you the truth, I couldn't care less what you're doing.'

Rose retreated back to the room next door where she and her mother had been cleaning. They both muttered darkly. One minute Lee was falling over herself with gratitude for being allowed to have the room back, then this! You just didn't know where you stood with the woman.

Shortly after, Lee came in and apologised for her behaviour. Ty had told her she'd been rude.

'Lee, I don't care what you do,' Rose replied, still irked about the whole episode. 'When people come here, I don't butt into their business.'

31

The discovery of Walter Gino Antonio's naked body and the knowledge that yet another victim had met his death at the end of a .22 calibre firearm, infused the investigators with a still greater sense of urgency. Official channels were buzzing. On 29 November 1990, just around the time Ty called her stepmother in Ohio and asked her to send her the bus fare home, a massive, inter-agency meeting was held at Marion County SO under the helm of Captain Steve Binegar. It drew in all involved law enforcement, not just from Marion County but also from Brevard, Sumter, Dixie, Citrus and Pasco Sheriff's Offices, from Titusville Police Department, and from the FDLE.

Investigators like Tom Muck and Jerry Thompson weren't the only ones to have been sharing information and collaborating on their homicides. Now it was time to knit together all the separate strands of detective work.

For Larry Horzepa of Volusia, who had just started attending the joint meetings, the task force's female theory certainly made perfect sense. It dove-tailed neatly with his own thoughts on Mallory, although he still held firm to the idea that Mallory had been murdered by a single female. Now, hearing about these other homicides in detail, Horzepa was even more convinced. He wasn't so much swayed by the preponderance of bullets to the torso as Munster had been, as by the way each murder victim appeared to have been accosted.

'We found that they were always alone, that they didn't have a wife or a girlfriend or family members in the car, that they were travelling extensively,' he recalls.

As the pace of the investigation accelerated, so, too, did the need to make a decision about whether or not to go public with the search for two female murder suspects. The local paper in Marion County, the *Ocala Star-Banner*, had run a piece suggesting a link between the murders, and had floated the possibility there was a highway serial killer on the loose. While the story had taken a back seat to the Gainesville student slayings, Captain Steve Binegar knew that would not continue indefinitely. It was a tough call. If they were tipped off about the search, there was a strong risk that the suspects might flee, disappearing without trace into the underbelly of the state. Or worse, leave Florida entirely.

Tom Muck of Pasco was especially vocal with his worry that the suspects might get nervous and dump the murder weapon. Those were the very real and major drawbacks. But the *Ocala Star-Banner*'s story would sooner or later have to be called false, or be confirmed and amplified. Weighing in on the other side of the scale was law enforcement's powerful duty to warn the public of the danger in helping or picking up women who appeared to be in distress on the road.

Above all, in broadcasting the search, the investigators were praying for help. Leads. Places to start. And with the strong likelihood that Siems's disappearance was part of the sinister chain of events, those composite drawings done by Marion County's in-house forensic artists in July, which had been given such a very limited release back in September, seemed the prime avenue to explore.

When the news release finally went out on 29 November, concerned citizens did not disappoint. The sketches of the two women seen fleeing the scene of missing missionary Peter Siems's crashed car were printed in newspapers and flashed on TV screens across the state and the response was immediate. Phone calls flooded the Marion County command post and poured into other law enforcement agencies across the state. Via the proliferation of leads generated, the uneasy alliance between media and public was showing its better face. In the words of Florida's own pre-eminent crime reporter, Edna Buchanan: Put it in the paper, it works. And work it did. The 'war room' that had been hastily set up with extra phones to man the calls, was soon under siege.

The team's best hope had been that repeated names and identities would be thrown up by the leads. Sergeant Brian Jarvis, a devout computer enthusiast, had devised a program to digest and sift the tips, picking up on common factors in names or geographic locations. Jarvis, who would have liked the sketches to have had broad distribution months earlier, watched intently as the process began to work.

The first three leads filtered in on the very night of the initial news break.

The next day, there were another twenty-six. Lead no. 5 came from Billy Copeland of Homosassa Springs, upon whom Lee's 'death-row eyes' had made such a lingering impression when she and Tyria Moore occupied a neighbouring trailer there a year earlier. He provided names, and the tip that when they left they had said they were going to head towards the East Coast. Copeland and his wife Cindy vividly remembered the women and the procession of men flowing to their trailer carrying TVs and other goods, and the way Lee went off hitchhiking with a gun for protection. They felt sure they were the two.

What is more, after seeing a photograph of Richard Mallory, the Copelands were so convinced that he was the man who'd visited Lee and Ty—the one who showed up in a van and gave them a TV, and that Lee later ran off the park—that they simply took to referring to him as Mallory. (Their account, unwittingly, would later pose an interesting question mark. Had Mallory been a regular of Lee's, not a stranger, Lee would not have met the FBI guidelines for a true serial killer. But Billy and Cindy's belief that they'd seen Mallory with her was never corroborated.)

Each day, criminal records were checked on any likely-sounding tips. Since the crime scenes had been so 'clean' and so devoid of physical evidence, that seemed to point to a pro. Someone knew what they were doing, and that someone probably had a record. The leads were priority-classified as As, Bs or Cs. And the sources of the leads seemed to cluster in the areas of the murders: another good sign they were on the right track.

There were the usual madcap calls, like the one saying the woman wanted was last seen in New York dressed as a nun.

But for all the red herrings, by 20 December, Tyria Moore's name had leapt to the fore. Ironically, the name Aileen Wuornos, diluted by Lee's long-time propensity for aliases, took longer to surface.

Tyria Moore watched the media blitz trumpeting the hunt for the two females with no less interest but with far less enthusiasm. She was badly shaken by this new development. The drawings were hardly perfect resemblances and wouldn't win any art prizes, yet uncannily they bore enough of a superficial likeness to scare Ty.

The input of the FBI's Behavioral Sciences Unit had suggested that the perpetrators of these homicides were likely to be transients, uninvolved in world politics, unexposed to newspapers. Yet Lee and Ty pored over the papers daily. And Ty was horrified to find herself centre stage in a drama she wanted no part of.

Suddenly, the prospect of capture and the slow realisation of how close she was to the fire, hit home. She was in over her head. She wanted to get out of there—fast.

Exactly when Ty finally decided to abandon ship was later hotly debated. After Thanksgiving, Lee had asked Donald Willingham to help them move out of the Fairview because Ty was going back up north. That was just before the sketches were released, but definitely before. Yet when on Sunday 2 December, the women announced to Rose McNeill that they were leaving and going their separate ways, it struck her as sudden and very peculiar. They'd seemed so close. She cast her mind back to all that talk of getting an apartment and Ty getting a job. To her, their splitting up came out of nowhere. And although Lee seemed 'a little bit bummed out by it', Rose would have expected them both to be a lot more upset.

Ty claims to have left for Ohio on the 3rd (although there'd be some questions asked about that), but first she took part in one last jaunt with Lee. Sandy Russell had flatly refused to store their stuff in her garage again. So when Donald Willingham picked them up to take Ty to the Greyhound station, they first made a stop at a storage unit Lee had found in Holly Hill. They'd been sealing up the last of their boxes when Donald arrived, and he stood and watched while they loaded them into the boot and the back of his car. Ty also had a couple of suitcases with her for her journey.

They headed over to Jack's Mini-Warehouses on Nova Road, where Lee rented a small unit under the name of Cammie Greene. She told the owners that she was a Marine on her way to Saudi Arabia and that's why she needed to store her stuff. While she stayed up front and filled out the necessary form and paid the deposit, Ty and Donald took the key and drove on back to the empty unit. Ty unlocked it and began throwing everything in. Lee appeared just in time to help her finish up.

(The next day, Lee returned to Jack's, complaining about the deposit they'd made her pay; she said she hadn't been told about it in advance.)

Donald hadn't the faintest idea that Lee, an almost-stranger, had rented the unit giving his address as her own. She must have stored it away in her mind from being at his house for a past sexual encounter.

What they put in the storage unit, Ty would recall, was a .45 handgun, a black tool box, a suitcase, a TV-radio, assorted clothing and knick-knacks, and a small briefcase. Ty knew of the bloody origins of at least some of those goods, but that didn't stop her helping Lee lock them away.

Ty hadn't left when Richard Mallory was murdered.

She hadn't left through that long year of killing.

She had even come back to Lee after going home to Ohio for Thanksgiving.

Now, finally, almost a year to the day Mallory met his death, she was baling out. Even to her mind, that was a hell of a long time in which to have done nothing.

Spending time in the warm bosom of her family had certainly given her a sharp reminder that another kind of life was open to her. But ultimately her timing was such that her departure seemed more spurred by the cold fear of capture. To Ty, there was a finality about her separation from her girlfriend, while Lee seemed to view it differently, as if it were part of a plan to split up and lie low for a while, then to reunite. If she believed that (or at least part of her did), it would explain why she took it in her stride, at least at first.

At the Greyhound station, there were no tears. No harsh words. No dramas. Donald stayed in the car while Lee walked Ty in to get her ticket. Five, maybe ten, minutes later, Lee emerged looking upset and climbed back in the car. 'Let's go,' she instructed her chauffeur.

There was still beer in the car and she grabbed one, tossing the familiar soothing liquid down her throat. Tears began to fall down her cheeks. She mumbled a little to herself. So, they'd split up, she muttered. So, she had to start a new life. Donald, sensing it best, didn't join in but just let her be. Then it seemed to pass, and she started chatting about anything and everything. She didn't mention Ty again.

As they drove towards Donald's house in Daytona, Ty, who had a two-hour wait alone for her bus, put in a call to Sandy. She wanted to tell her about the fight she'd had with Lee. She was leaving, she told her friend, because she needed to find out where she was at. She'd had it. And she'd told Lee that if she tried to find her, she'd call the cops.

Lee, meanwhile, soothed herself in bed with Donald. Feeling another body against hers. Hoping to feel less alone, at least for one night. She didn't charge him—after all, he'd been ferrying her around—but she asked him for money. He was broke, he told her, and even owed his landlord. (Funny, the way the landlord's dog, General Blackjack, had taken such a great dislike to Lee.) When they surfaced the next morning, she asked Donald to drop her off downtown, which he did, letting her out on Ridgewood and waving goodbye.

She ambled off, her face shielded by her ever-present sunglasses and a blue baseball hat perched on her head. It bore the friendly message: 'Go To Hell'.

Later, Donald realised that for his trouble she'd taken off with a green T-shirt and a pair of his sneakers. Later still, he missed a couple of pairs of blue jeans. He wouldn't mind betting she took those, too.

Taking another look at the 4 July Siems car crash, Bruce Munster was given some confusing input into the ever-fluctuating descriptions of the mystery women. On 3 December Rhonda Bailey, the woman who saw the actual smash take place before Lee and Ty dumped the car further down the road, described the blonde as being shorter than the brunette. The brunette was bigger in all directions. Rhonda hadn't come closer than within twenty feet of them and was sure she wouldn't be able to recognise their faces if she was shown a photo line-up. It had been too long and she simply couldn't remember.

Munster also learned from Rhonda that the car had not flipped over as speculated.

On 4 December, Munster drove over to Church Street in Orange Springs to interview Harmon Jeters. A further search of the area turned up Siems's licence plate, but there was still no sign of his body. On the 11th, Munster talked to Jim Bailey, Rhonda's husband. Jim's recollections varied yet again. He described the blonde as good-looking. Not fat, not thin, small-waisted, 5 feet 7 inches, 5 feet 8 inches. The brunette, he remembered as being on the heavy-set side, probably 5 feet 5 inches, 5 feet 6 inches, with a long, big face.

Rose McNeill, who had thought she'd seen the last of Lee, watched her sometime tenant reappear in the office on Wednesday 5 December, alone, upset, carrying a suitcase and asking for a room. She refused room 8 because she and Ty had stayed in it twice: it just held too many memories.

Rose allotted her room 7, just a thin wall and a few feet removed from all those memories. Her very first night back, Lee drew a complaint from the guest in the next room. Why had Rose given him such a noisy room? Rose asked him if he'd seen anyone coming or going. He said there was a tall man who must have left the next morning. Unfortunately, Rose didn't see him.

Lee finally checked out of the Fairview for the last time on Monday 10 December, owing $21.75 on her bill and leaving a gold-coloured ring for collateral. It wasn't valuable, but had sentimental value, she said, promising she'd be back to pick it up and to pay her debt. It was a pretty ring with a square red stone set amidst a cluster of white imitation diamonds. The effect was somewhat spoiled, however, by the rubber band Lee kept twisted around it.

On 11 December, Bruce Munster received a message to call Mrs Florence Carskaddon in response to her seeing something on TV about the search for two women. She told him about her son who'd been missing since June. His car had been found on I-75 in Marion County that same month and impounded, and there'd been no sign of him since. His body could be identified, she told Munster, by a wire in his jaw from an accident. Another light bulb went on.

Munster knew in an instant: it had to be Tom Muck's guy. Tom Muck had told him that the anonymous victim from Pasco County who they felt sure was tied to the case was a rodeo worker and that they'd found wire in his jaw. It was another big breakthrough.

Munster immediately informed Muck who in turn contacted Mrs Carskaddon and drove to the Ocala Highway Patrol post to pick up a copy of the impound report on Carskaddon's 1975 Cadillac. On 12 December, through a ridge detail taken from a fingertip on the decomposed body, a concrete i.d. was made. Finally, Mrs Carskaddon at least had the peace of mind of knowing what had happened to her son.

Lee checked into the Sea View Motel on US 1 down in Micco the night Mrs Carskaddon got the news. The next morning, through Tom Burton, a man she'd met in Bojos Bar in Melbourne, 'Lee Greene' met up with Tom's sister, Virginia Rocco. Lee had spun Tom a story about how her car had blown up in Miami and she'd had to leave it there, and how her husband had just died. She'd even had to pawn her gun to buy food, she told him. Playing on his sympathy, she went on to say she would have to sleep under a bridge because she had nowhere else to go. Caught up by this tale of woe that her brother relayed to her, Virginia, a good-hearted woman who happened to have a fishing cabin, had agreed to meet Lee and Tom in the bar.

Lee showed Virginia a heavy-link man's-style gold chain, and asked if she'd like to buy it for twenty bucks so that she could get something to drink? Virginia declined. She asked to see some i.d. and Lee produced a warehouse receipt for a place in Daytona where she was storing all her belongings.

After knowing her for just twenty minutes, Virginia agreed to let Lee stay at her cabin in Micco, just south of Cocoa Beach. In that short space of time Lee had also managed to cram in stories of her brother's death, a broken love affair, of being burnt in a fire as a kid, of having a baby at fourteen. She then regaled them with the story of the time she was in Colorado and had no place to stay so a man had loaned her a cabin. Her first night there, she told Virginia, a bear came smashing through a downstairs window and she shot it and killed it.

'Weren't you afraid?' Virginia asked.

'No. I'm a hell of a good shot,' Lee replied.

Virginia, who was rather tearful and preoccupied (she'd just come from visiting her father, who was terminally ill in hospital), didn't pay much attention to all this.

In return for Virginia's generosity with her cabin, Lee offered her a pawn ticket for a gun she said had belonged to her husband. She had no more use for it and she was getting rid of his stuff. Once again, Virginia refused her offer.

'Some day I'll pay you back,' Lee said gratefully.

'I don't want anything. All I want you to do is find a job and get yourself straightened out,' Virginia told her.

When Virginia next went to the cabin, on 19 December, Lee had already moved on. She'd left behind on the coffee table a handwritten note saying 'thankyou Virginia', a woman's purse and some men's clothing. That was the good news. The bad was that Lee had apparently taken a small gold charm of hers, a sterling silver ring and bracelet, and an ivory necklace. She had also taken her i.d., birth certificate and passport, but Virginia didn't miss those at the time. Indeed, she didn't find out about their disappearance for more than a year.

On 13 December, Kathy Beasman called in with lead no. 297, stating that Tyria Moore and Susan Blahovec used to work in her motel. The following day Sergeant Brian Jarvis took an anonymous call from a woman who claimed the two were violent, man-hating lesbians and were capable of hurting people. Before signing off, the nameless caller sealed her credibility: she supplied Jarvis with Ty Moore's mother's phone number in Ohio and said they'd bought an RV and moved to the Ocean Village RV park in Ormond Beach. Bruce Munster checked out the phone number and found it belonged to Jack Moore, Ty's father. He also checked out the RV park, where he was told of Blahovec's extremely violent past history and dislike of men. No one phoned the Moores at that stage. Ty was believed to be in Florida and they didn't want to tip anyone off.

On 14 December, Edward Michael McMann phoned in a tip. A woman he believed to be Lee had darted in front of his car. He'd have hit her if he hadn't slammed on his brakes. It was a Friday afternoon, between the third week in September and the third week in October, as he was driving home to Ocala, and he'd picked her up on Route 98 at 471, not far from Zephyrhills.

She asked to be dropped outside the populated part of town. She claimed not to know the area, but also claimed to have lived in Florida her whole life. Once he let her out, he watched her head off to find another ride. McMann remembered her carrying a purse and shopping bag and saying she was fussy about the men she chose and claiming she didn't fool with truck drivers. She tried to proposition him, saying she had no money and a couple of kids at home. She thought him decidedly odd when he turned her down, but he handed her a couple of bucks anyway. She wanted beer, but her luck was out. Edward didn't drink. He, too, saw the wallet with its array of business cards.

Over at the Casa Del Mar, Ty's ex-colleagues were poring over the sketches in the newspapers. Everyone chuckled when someone piped up, 'Look! There's Ty and Lee!' The sketches did seem to bear a strange resemblance to a couple they knew. No. Surely not. It couldn't be.

Paul Gribben, the aspiring writer Lee talked to back in 1987, was moved to call the police when he saw the sketches.

'I have a pretty good idea who they are,' he said. 'Their names are Lee and Ty, and I'd like to talk to somebody about it. I'd like to supply you with information.'

He was referred to a detective whom he was instructed to call during business hours, which proved impossible because of Paul's schedule as a tour bus driver. Still intent on passing on what he knew, he attempted to call other law enforcement agencies, including the FDLE, but to his immense frustration, he couldn't seem to get past the lower echelons and his calls went unreturned. Typical, he thought, annoyed. Screw them! Too much bureaucratic bullshit. Besides, it wasn't his job.

Unbeknownst to him, Larry Horzepa did try, unsuccessfully, to reach him.

That one aborted tip aside, ultimately a whopping 900-plus leads would pour in, many in response to a broadcast on the popular TV show, *America's Most Wanted*. The net was closing in.

The names of other pairs of women also cropped up more than once, but Ty and Lee were irrevocably being propelled to the fore as suspects.

On Thursday 20 December, Brian Jarvis handed Bruce Munster lead sheet no. 361. It bore the names Lee and Ty and had been marked 'Good Lead!', indicating it was the fourth time these names had cropped up. The tip came from a Port Orange detective who'd been told that the two women, supposedly lesbians and legally married, had been at Cathie's Toadl Pub in Port Orange and lived at the Fairview Motel.

That day there was a massive meeting embracing all the task force investigators including FDLE agents and the four hundred or so leads received thus far were sorted and prioritised. Arrangements were made to have driver's licence photographs and background checks flown in from the FDLE in Tallahassee on Susan Lynn Blahovec, Cammie Marsh Greene and Tyria Moore. (The name Wuornos was still notably absent.) Fingerprints were found on file in Tallahassee for both Blahovec and Tyria Moore.

The following day, 21 December, Munster telephoned Rose

McNeill of the Fairview Motel to quiz her about her guests. He listened intently as her account unravelled of their three stays there. It was the second time period that particularly grabbed him, especially when he learned from Mrs McNeill that somewhere between 17 and 19 November, Lee had put down what was for her an unusually large sum of cash. She could have put the cash down right after Walter Gino Antonio's murder, on the 18th.

Munster's attention, however, leapt to full alert when Rose said that while Tyria was away up north, Lee had pulled up with a maroon car with no tag and tucked it behind the motel. As the facts clicked together in his mind—she might have just put Walter Gino Antonio's car and one of the suspects at the Fairview together—he rose from the chair behind his desk. For a moment, he felt unable to speak. It was perfect. Just perfect.

Rose McNeill had just handed him a key.

With impeccable timing, Larry Horzepa and Bob Kelley from Volusia County happened to stop by just then to catch up on what they'd missed at the big Thursday meeting. Talking it over, they decided to run all the suspects' names—Tyria Moore, Susan Blahovec and Cammie Marsh Greene—through Volusia's computerised pawn shop records. Fortunately, an ordinance in Volusia meant anyone selling to pawn shops had to record their transaction by filling out a form and giving a thumbprint. It would turn out to be a useful little formality in this case as in a legion others.

Immediately, the system turned up a couple of hits on Cammie Marsh Greene. On 6 December 1989, just days after Richard Mallory's murder, she'd pawned a 35mm Minolta Freedom camera and a Micronta Road Patrol Radar Detector bought at Radio Shack (both of the type owned by Richard Mallory), at the OK Pawn Shop in Daytona Beach. Cammie got $30 for the trade, showed her driver's licence and duly left the obligatory thumbprint. Few people even own a Radio Shack radar detector, let alone coupled with a Minolta 35mm camera like the one that Jackie Davis, Mallory's ex-girlfriend, had said was also missing.

'That really piqued our interest,' remembered Larry Horzepa, a master of understatement. 'Putting those two together, we said, "OK, this has got to be the person we are looking for."'

With the all-important 'Cammie' thumbprint in hand, the FDLE was called in. Cammie had also pawned a box of tools in June of 1990 of the kind stolen from Spears. (Those, however, could not be traced.)

Looking back, the task force would designate 21 December a very good day indeed in the Wuornos investigation.

Early that evening, Jerry Thompson drove to Marion County SO and he and investigators from Pasco, Dixie and Marion then headed over towards Daytona Beach to be on the spot for a meeting Saturday morning at Volusia County SD.

At 10.10 a.m. on 22 December, the officers all met up with Bob Kelley there. By 10.30, Jenny Aherne from the FDLE lab in Orlando had good news. After she and a technician had sifted a thousand cards by hand, she'd made an i.d. on 'Cammie Greene's' pawn shop thumbprint to Lori Kristine Grody who'd been arrested in Volusia County for carrying a concealed firearm. It smelled right.

This wasn't the Lori Grody who sat with her family in Mancelona, Michigan, thinking pensively from time to time of her wayward sister. But the Lori Grody who had been arrested in Volusia County back in June of '86 for a driving licence charge while in a stolen vehicle and also while carrying a loaded .22 under the car seat along with twelve rounds of ammunition in a bag.

Checking Grody out, they learned that she had outstanding warrants for failure to appear in both Volusia and Pasco Counties. The FDLE folk were meanwhile burrowing deeper, and behind Lori Grody they found one Aileen Carol Wuornos and her prints from a past arrest.

In running her criminal history, up popped several more aliases, including Aileen Carol Wuornos, Aileen Carol Wuornot, Aileen Wuornot. Photo comparisons showed Lori Grody and Susan Blahovec to be one and the same person (Wuornos), whereas the photo on the Cammie Greene driver's licence was of someone else (the real Cammie Greene).

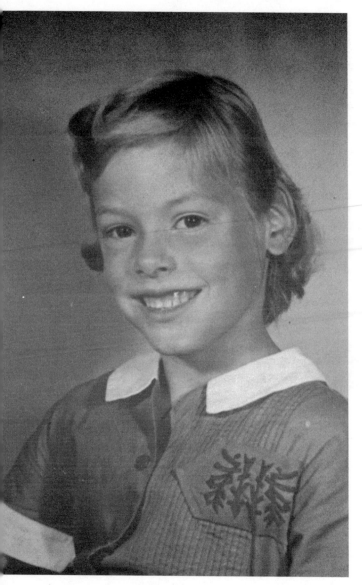

Aileen Wuornos, early school days in Troy, Michigan.

Keith Wuornos, early school days in Troy, Michigan.

The young Diane Wuornos, Aileen and Keith's natural
mother, before she married their father, Leo Pittman.

Leo Pittman, Aileen's natural father, eventually committed
suicide in prison. Sentenced to life behind bars
for raping a seven-year-old, his doomed existence
eerily foreshadowed Aileen's own.

The two-tier family in June 1962: clockwise from top, Barry, Keith, Aileen, and Lori Wuornos. Aileen and Keith were raised as siblings of their Aunt Lori and Uncle Barry.

Keith Wuornos with his father/grandfather,
Lauri Wuornos, on a family trip.

Aileen and Keith with Britta Wuornos, the grandmother
who raised them as if they were her own children,
on vacation two years before Britta's death.

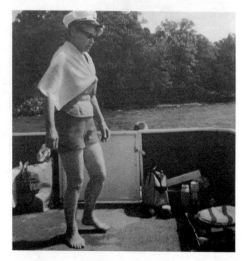

Britta Wuornos,
the same day.

Aileen in July 1969. A happy moment during one of her family's regular summer vacations.

Aileen and Keith's childhood friend Mark Fearn stands at the site where Aileen built the first of many forts in the woods close to her home.

The Wuornos home, above. Nearby neighbors heard Aileen's cries when her grandfather punished her.

What was once the Wuornos home in Troy, Michigan. Above the front door is one of the two windows from which Aileen regularly made her late-night escapes.

Aileen riding her bike in her Troy neighborhood shortly
before she became pregnant. She gave up the baby
for adoption immediately after his birth.

Redheaded like Leo Pittman, the father Aileen never met,
Tyria Jolene Moore became the big love of
Aileen Wuornos's life—and a fellow suspect in the
string of Florida murders.

Shirley Humphreys with her husband, Dick Humphreys. Aileen "Lee" Wuormos brutally murdered Dick the day after their 35th wedding anniversary.

Troy "Buddy" Burress, the sausage-delivery truck driver Lee murdered, seen here with his sister, Letha Prater.

Lee Wuornos stole the life of David Spears, seen here with Dee Spears, the mother of his three children. The Spearses divorced after twenty years, but were planning to remarry.

The flat, deserted roads amidst the dense central Florida woods where Lee took her prostitution clients...and, on her killing days, her robbery and murder victims.

One of the trailer homes that Lee and Ty lived in at Homossassa Springs, in 1989. Reminiscent of her childhood home, the trailer's windows were kept covered by Lee. Lee and Ty practiced shooting at trees and beer cans in the barren park.

Wet Willie's Tavern in a seedy stretch of the Daytona, Florida, area. One of Lee's many pool-playing and drinking hangouts.

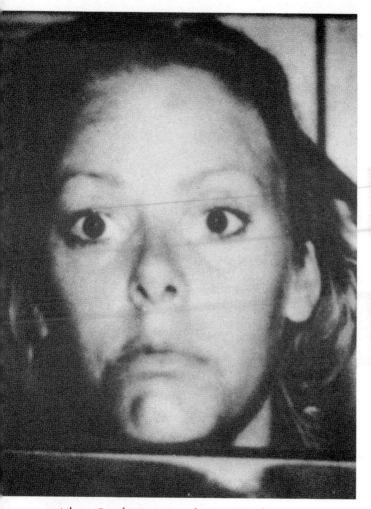

Aileen Carol Wuornos, aka Lori Grody,
aka Susan Blahovec, aka Cammie Marsh Greene,
shortly after her arrest in January 1991.

The shrine that has been erected to Lee Wuornos
outside the back of the Last Resort Bar
where she was finally arrested by investigator,
Larry Horzepa, on January 9, 1991.

From there, it was just a short leap to being able to 'make' the bloody palm print left behind on Peter Siems's abandoned Sunbird back on 4 July.

'We knew then that we definitely had the person we were looking for,' Larry Horzepa recalls.

Lee Wuotnos was in big trouble.

The real Cammie Marsh Greene was paid a cautious visit by law enforcement. They'd found an address for her and her husband in Bunnell and details of their two cars. She shared her story of Lee and Ty living in her home and of the not so coincidental disappearance of her driver's licence. There was one woman in the clear.

All the known fingerprints were sent off for comparison with all the latent fingerprints held in connection with the homicides. Then steps were taken to have all the technical evidence, which had been scattered among various crime labs, sent to Tallahassee so that all the evidence in all the homicides could be compared one to another.

That evening a team went down to Port Orange where Munster, Allen Blair, also of Marion County, and Jimmy Pinner of Dixie County SO all visited the Fairview to interview Rose McNeill in person. They trotted out photo-packs and Rose duly picked out Ty and Lee. Lee she knew as Cammie Greene. That was whose driver's licence Lee showed when registering. And Ty, she pointed out, looked considerably slimmer in the face in the photograph than in life. The officers took the cheap ring that Lee had left with Rose as collateral and, in fair exchange, left her a receipt.

Consulting with Ric Ridgway, the Marion County Assistant State Attorney, the investigators decided that they'd asked enough questions for the time being in Port Orange. Now it was time to lie low.

32

Lee Wuornos and Dick Mills collided like a pair of guided missiles the week before Christmas. Both were bar-hopping down Daytona's seediest, red-light strip, drowning their respective relationship sorrows in a hazy blur of alcohol. Lee was immediately drawn to Dick, a tattooed bulldog of a Vietnam veteran in his mid-forties who was just separated from his new wife. Something about him so resembled Ty that she couldn't get over it. Depressed and lonely, Dick missed Connie badly and was wallowing in his misery, propping up the bar at Wet Willie's, when Lee walked by him that afternoon.

She was in similar shape, grieving over Ty, but, working an angle as usual, Lee asked Dick if he had a car because she had some stuff at a Greyhound bus station she needed to pick up. He drove her there and took her on to Jack's Mini-Warehouses where Lee put down some more money on her storage unit and paused long enough to try to sell the owner, Melvin Colbert, some gold and silver. Colbert turned it down sight unseen: he didn't buy from clients, and he was broke.

Dick Mills, through his own fog of alcohol, was struck by the way Lee managed to be smart and trashy at the same time. That appealed to him. He also liked the way she could dart from talking about parapsychology to history. A couple of feisty, volatile and lively personalities, he saw them as two inhabitants of 'the pits of hell'. They filled the voids for one another and it worked out pretty well—for a while.

Even if he hadn't endured her constant stream of talk of Ty, Dick Mills had her pegged as a hard-core lesbian, but that didn't bother him. So she liked women? So did he. It was a taste they had in common. It didn't bother him, either, that she was a hooker. As was her wont, Lee treated him to a quick peek at her walletful of business cards and her speech about her regular, high-powered clientele. He looked and didn't really question it. When she said she got $100 per trick and once received $200 from an Orlando businessman for less than a minute of her time, he didn't question that either.

Over and over, she told him that she and Ty had done things together that no one else had ever done. He definitely didn't question that.

Lesbian or no, the only thing that came close to her insatiable appetite for beer was her voracious appetite for sex, and that appetite obviously wasn't restricted to women. She and Dick would be chatting and suddenly she'd exclaim: 'You wanna fuck?' or 'Let's fuck *now!*'

He'd remember her as 'a wild, savage, party animal'. But her obsession, there was no question, was with Ty. She wept over her lost lover more than once and when she tried calling Ty, she came back bawling. Wherever Lee and Dick's conversations rambled, they always returned to the same point: How could Ty do this to Lee? They'd done things together, pulled things off in this lifetime, that no other living being had ever done or would ever know.

One night, while out in Dick's car, they were pulled over by the police, and Lee made no attempt to disguise her loathing for the cops, uttering a mouthful that Dick was surprised didn't land her in jail.

Dick liked to walk on the wild side, but the novelty of this stop-gap relationship soon wore off, given Lee's dramatic mood swings and dreadful behaviour when she'd had too much beer. The last straw was when Dick took her over to his daughter, Reveshia's, for a family gathering that included his other daughter, Tammy Sibbernsen. He soon bitterly regretted it. Lee was a beast. She was rude, aggressive and very drunk, and would insist on regaling his daughters with stories of her fights in prison and her drug use.

Amidst her rambling diatribe, Lee also told the family she had been abused as a child. That didn't excuse her behaviour or make it any more bearable. As the night wore on, and Dick had placated her by buying her another half-case of beer, Reveshia could see that she was trying to bait her dad into a fight. She'd finally had enough. She pulled him to one side and told him, 'Just get her out of my home and don't bring her back.'

No matter. Dick didn't want Lee, anyway. Dick wanted Connie; he wanted to give it one more try. It was Christmas Eve, Connie filled his thoughts, and Lee had to go.

Kindly, Dick drove her to the Hawaii Motel on Ridgewood, handed her $50 and wished her luck. He didn't know it just then, but she'd made off with his LA Gear blue and white sneakers.

For Lee, with her limited tolerance for solitude, this parting of the ways was a dismal low point. Thanks to Dick's generosity, at least she had a bed to wake up in on Christmas Day, which was more than could be said for some nights, but holidays always heighten feelings of isolation for those without family. For Lee, being dumped by Dick like that, hot on the heels of the emotionally wrenching separation from Ty, was difficult to bear. The knowledge that she was a wanted woman didn't improve the mix. For Lee, the so-called season of goodwill was distinctly devoid of it.

She tried to alleviate her blues and isolation by spending money she could ill afford in bars and on motel rooms. She went through $600 (that magical figure again) in less than two weeks, she later told Ty, adding: 'Every time I was fucking in a room, I was so depressed and bored and crying. I was pissed when you left and shit, and I'd go to a bar and I'd just get myself floppy, fucking drunk. So money would just go.'

A few days after parting company with Dick, however, Lee demonstrated her resilience and optimism by calling in at Moore's Auto Lot, perusing the display of used cars, and enquiring about payments and terms. She was going to be coming into some money, she said, and she'd be back.

Despite its depressing name and greying array of underwear dangling from the ceiling, the infamous Last Resort biker bar was decidedly more upbeat than some of the watering holes

Lee frequented during her desperate hours. Animal dens, the locals call them. The worst of the worst. Rough, skid-row-type dives where hard-core drinkers and druggers spent long, wasted hours. The homeless and derelicts planted themselves along the sidewalks outside, propping up walls, the odour of human waste mingling heavily with that of dead beer and putrid smoke. Those confined by budgetary concerns to the sidewalk consumed liquids from bottles concealed in brown paper bags.

All of drug life was—and is—there, dope being the native currency. On the wrong side of Ridgewood Avenue, gangbangers boldly pushed nickel bags of rock in your face whether you liked it or not.

To entice a classier clientele, the nearby stripjoints and topless bars bore fresher paint. Lee once claimed to have been a dancer in such an establishment. With her potbelly and dishevelled appearance, if it was so, it was probably years ago. No one remembers her.

Commerce operated at all levels and some neighbourhood hookers, finding the pickings of solvent clients very slim, were reduced to giving blow jobs for two paltry bucks. That's right. Two bucks. If Lee ever worked that strip, where the sultry ladies of the night change their names more often than their eye makeup, no one remembers or cares.

Lee reappeared on Dick Mills's doorstep a week or so after he threw her out. Connie answered the door; Dick wasn't home. Lee stood there, clutching a can of Busch and a little suitcase. Seemed pleasant enough. Connie didn't invite her in, but neither did she say she couldn't wait. But Lee didn't show her face there again.

Word was out on the trucker grapevine. Some women were knocking off guys. Sam and Rowdy knew all about it. Truck drivers are rarely angelic and Sam and Rowdy never professed to be, rather proudly and cheerfully billing themselves 'two of the worst perverts on the road'. Both had been off on long hauls—Sam up north, Rowdy to Texas—when they cruised back into their Florida base and heard the warning: 'Don't pick up any hitchhikers or any hookers in Daytona. These girl killers are out there and they're whacko.'

Sam and Rowdy, who'd been running together for years, made a pact of sorts, a cursory nod in the direction of safety and survival. 'Well,' they decided, 'we just won't pick nothing up in the state of Florida.'

Good resolutions aside, they'd had a weird run-in with a girl hitchhiker in Gainesville. Pretty, too. The usual unwritten agreement when picking up a hitchhiker is the fair exchange theory: a ride in return for a sexual favour. But this woman started talking money right away, which rang an alarm bell. Then when she started sounding 'kooky', Rowdy didn't wait for the jury to come in, just kicked her right out of his truck to be on the safe side. Sam, who'd been having forty winks, felt sure his partner had lost it. 'That was a good-looking lady!' he complained. Rowdy didn't care. He wasn't taking any chances in Florida.

Not that he was afraid of much. He prided himself on that, too. In his private car, he carried more hardware than most law enforcement officers. Rowdy heard the warning again from the guys at Circus, a girlie bar in Daytona where they knew his appetite for sex on the road. His reputation preceded him, which he kind of liked. He was single, what the hell.

Truckers hear warnings all the time. Look out for this, watch out for that. The brotherhood keeping an eye out for its own. Not so long before, a driver lost his life over 38 cents. Stopped to phone and tell his wife he was an hour from home, and was shot for his trouble. The radio was a way of fighting back. Strength in numbers. Rowdy learned long ago that there's every kind of kook imaginable out there and maintained a lot of them were women. Word was already out on one who'd been dubbed The Strangler.

'If you pick her up and her bra comes off and she's got two eagles on her chest, you get rid of her,' Rowdy said flatly.

Very simple and to the point. Her *modus operandi* was to strip off her top then, while bending over to give a blow job, to wrap a piece of wire she'd got hidden in her hand around his jewels and castrate him, leaving him to bleed to death.

Why wait for the cops? The next time that broad bared her breasts in a truck she'd be history. Truckers, they looked out for their own.

33

It was time to move. On 26 December, Jerry Thompson and Marvin Padgett arrived at the Marion County SO bright and early to meet with the rest of the task force. The investigators now knew of Ty's job at the Casa Del Mar and of the motorcycle and moped she'd once had registered in her name. Slowly, the picture was being fleshed out.

A division of labour was worked out. Padgett and Investigator Jenny Combs would do a background check on the two suspects. Rickey Deen from the State Attorney's office would work on a subpoena for Ty's parents' phone in Ohio and for the pay phones in Port Orange. The FDLE folk would do further checks on pawnshops to see if the suspects had pawned anything else.

Jerry Thompson and Tom Muck were in for a little surprise. The two investigators who'd worked so hard on the case for so long had been all set to go to Ohio to execute the background check on Tyria, but at the last minute were told there'd been a change of plan. Marion County's Binegar and Henry would put down their pencils, emerge from behind their desks and do it themselves. (That move, particularly on the part of Major Henry, gave rise to questions later.) They'd leave the next day.

As the two senior officers made their way north, Jerry Thompson picked up from the old evidence storage the .22 revolver that Lori Grody had been carrying when she was arrested in June of '86. It was sent to the lab for comparison with the bullets in an old homicide case. Throughout the entire investigation, all the detectives were constantly combing old files for unsolved murders that might turn out to be linked to these suspects.

Meanwhile an updated outstanding warrant was issued for that 1986 arrest of Lori Grody, this one listing all her known aliases. When they found Lee Wuornos, they'd be ready for her.

On 28 December, Jerry Thompson was back at Marion County SO, and Bruce Munster filled him in on a call from a woman on Highridge in Holly Hill. She said she'd rented an apartment to Ty and Lee, that Lee hated men, that she and Ty hitchhiked everywhere, and that the two had first met in a lesbian bar in 1985 in Daytona.

Tom Muck reported in, too. He'd found out that Lori Grody was a suspect in the 1985 theft of a .38 gun in his county.

On 31 December, Bob Kelley checked in. Volusia's hand search of pawn records had turned up something else. Cammie Marsh Greene had pawned a man's gold nugget diamond ring on 7 December for $20. She'd used the same licence, date of birth and address as before.

Bruce Munster perused the three pawn slips he had; to the naked eye, all three signatures looked identical.

Bob Kelley called back. He'd collected the nugget diamond ring from the pawn shop and Jimmy Pinner of Dixie County had driven it over to the family of the late victim's fiancée. Sure enough, Aleen Berry and her daughters, Linda and Carol, verified that it was identical to the one stolen from Walter Gino Antonio on 18 November. They'd had it sized down to fit Gino, and Pinner checked with the jeweller who, while not able to identify his own work, confirmed the ring had been sized the same as Antonio's.

Bruce Munster added the information that Ty had flown Eastern Airlines to Pittsburgh on 17 November at 5.30 p.m., and had flown back into Daytona on 25 November at 2.30 p.m. She, at least, had the beginnings of a good alibi for the Walter Gino Antonio murder.

That same day, he received Lee's Colorado arrest history which included the prohibited use of a firearm. A clear picture was emerging of a career criminal. He and all the other key detectives headed over to Volusia County and, through interviews, learned of Lee and Ty's stay at the Belgrade restaurant.

Bruce Munster was the first to interview Vera Ivkovitch, who confirmed that they'd kept lots of tools in their room and she had once seen them cleaning a small handgun which Lee said she had because she was a lesbian. Vera made no mention of the black ceramic panther statue that victim David Spears was believed to have been carrying in his truck to give to his wife, Dee. (Later, she told Jerry Thompson she had seen it in their room, but it was never recovered.)

Susan Lynn Blahovec.

Cammie Marsh Greene.

Lori Kristine Grody.

Aileen Wuornos's stolen personae were steadily rising up, en masse, to haunt her.

Meanwhile, up in Ohio, Binegar and Henry had been working on the assumption that since Ty had spent Thanksgiving with her family, it was a fair bet that she might show up there again for the holidays. In the best possible scenario, they would locate her. Moving cautiously, the out-of-towners attempted to slip unnoticed into Cadiz's tight-knit community of less than five thousand people. Fat chance. Cadiz is no Ocala. According to Dan Henry, the Harrison County Sheriff, Richard Rensi, received phone calls tipping him off about their unmarked car within minutes of their arrival.

With the help of local law enforcement, however, they started in what is often a highly illuminating place: the school records. For a suspect who's never been in prison, it is often the *only* place to start trying to build a picture of them. They met with Harrison County School Superintendent, Don Hyde, and learned that Tyria's files had no notation of discipline problems or psychological problems or anything else untoward. She was a C-grade student and in 11th and 12th grades, transferred to Harrison Hills Vocational School, leaving in 1980. Getting a handle on Ty's personality was crucial.

Ty's father Jack, Binegar and Henry learned from Sheriff Rensi who knew him, was an industrious carpenter and bricklayer, well regarded in the community. Ty's mother, Janet, died when she was a toddler, and her father then married Mary Ann. One sister, Twyla, who was then living in Pennsylvania with her husband, an ex-deputy sheriff, had been through a wild stage. The Sheriff said she was one of the first streakers in the country. Besides her sisters, Ty also had three brothers registered with the school board: James, Jackie (known as Brent) and Michael. Sheriff Rensi cruised by the Moore residence, showing it to Binegar and Henry.

Later, they would be told that Ty had been there, but had they made a move on her too soon, before Lee was in custody, the big question had been, what would she do? There were no grounds for arrest right then. If investigators had approached her head on, asking questions about the murders, she might have told them to get out of her house, picked up the phone, and tipped off Lee. They had to tread softly.

Another vital item on the agenda was verifying Ty's travel arrangements for the Thanksgiving period, a task that fell to Special Agent Gerald Mroczkowski of the Ohio Bureau of Criminal Investigation. If, as Henry and Binegar believed, Ty had indeed been in Cadiz at that time, it would give her an ironclad alibi for when Walter Gino Antonio was murdered. It would also support the swelling belief that Ty was the weak link in the duo and as such, once they were apprehended, she would be the first one they would try to break. Binegar and Henry headed back to Florida.

An airline check soon confirmed that Ty had indeed travelled on dates that put her well out of the vicinity when Antonio was murdered. She was, however, far from out from under suspicion. She might conceivably have travelled to Ohio on the 17th, slipped back down to Florida, back up to Ohio, then still have flown back on the 25th. Plus, there was still the not insignificant matter of her being seen fleeing Peter Siems's car.

By 4 January 1991, the strategy for a two-pronged attack was in place. Up in Ohio, there'd be a renewed effort to find Tyria. Meanwhile the home team (with Captain Steve Binegar at the helm) concentrated on scouring the Daytona Beach area for Ty and for Aileen 'Lee' Wuornos, a.k.a. Cammie, a.k.a. Susan, a.k.a. Lori. The FDLE would supply mobile phones, pagers and expense money for the joint task force and surveillance would begin the next day.

While Wuornos *could* be picked up on the outstanding 1986 arrest warrant, it was agreed she should only be taken into custody as an absolute last resort.

First, it was thought to be premature to actually pick her up without first finding Tyria Moore. But there was also some legitimate worry about the wisdom of executing that warrant. Prosecutor Ric Ridgway, of the Marion County State Attorney's Office, explained it. At that moment in history, neither the Florida Supreme Court nor the United States Supreme Court had ruled on whether you could go into jail and question someone who is behind bars on one charge, about another unrelated case. Subsequently, the ruling came down that you could do just that, but back then it looked like a potential headache definitely best avoided.

Ridgway and his colleagues were concerned that when she made her first court appearance on the old charge, the moment she was assigned a court-appointed lawyer, they might find that they'd blown any chance of ever speaking to her about the homicides. Things were complicated enough, legally speaking. Had the Florida Supreme Court or the US Supreme Court ruled differently on two cases, any previous confession might have been lost anyway.

All things considered, the prudent course of action was to locate Wuornos, watch and wait.

In an ideal world, the suspects would lead law enforcement to their current residence, which could then be searched and might be a treasure trove of incriminating evidence linking them to the victims. By all accounts, the two women moved around with tool boxes. There could be much more. They just had to find it before the women realised they were being watched and got rid of it.

On 7 January, Major Henry flew to Ohio to spearhead the Ohio-Michigan effort. Stealthily, a web was slipped into place that would hopefully trap Tyria. A pen register was requested to allow law enforcement to tap the telephone at the Moore residence, and a mail cover was started to monitor the family's mail. The Moores' phone records were also subpoenaed. All part of the effort to find Tyria before she became aware that she was the object of a womanhunt. The legal formalities, however, would take around a week, and Major Henry had another chore to tackle meanwhile in the northern part of the state—checking out the real Susan Blahovec. The woman behind Lee's alias also happened to be an Ohio resident. As with Lee's other aliases, there'd been some hesitation about approaching their rightful owners. Because Wuornos seemed to use her a.k.a.'s with confidence, it was possible she was using them with permission. Were that the case, one false move could have tipped her off that they were on to her.

Local law enforcement in Berea, Ohio, already had the unwitting genuine Susan Blahovec under surveillance when Dan Henry arrived. The plan was to approach her on the old Florida traffic citations and see what she knew about them. They moved in, stopping her outside her home. Dan Henry posed as another Ohio man, blending in with the locals. Blahovec was immediately co-operative. She was only too aware that someone had been using her driver's licence and committing traffic offences in her name. In fact, she could document all her past efforts to prove that she had been in Ohio at the time of the offences and to try to get them off her record.

But how might someone have got a Florida licence in her name? It turned out that she'd lived at the Seahorse Campground down in the Keys area prior to 1985 with her common-law husband whom she'd later left when he got involved with drugs. She'd never met Lee Wuornos or Ty Moore, but clearly that was the link. When they'd stayed at the Seahorse later, her ex, out of animosity, blithely gave Lee Susan's birth certificate and duplicate Ohio driver's licence. From the Ohio licence, Lee had been able to get a Florida licence which was later suspended because of the unpaid tickets.

Susan had learned of the licence problem when she went to renew her Ohio licence and was told about the Florida tickets.

Dan Henry showed her the signature on the Florida traffic citations which she was able to show was not her own. Very rapidly, the real Susan Blahovec had neatly removed herself from under the cloud of suspicion.

34

Aileen Carol Wuornos, suspected serial killer, was finally spotted and placed under surveillance at 9.19 p.m. on Tuesday 8 January 1991. She was in the Port Orange Pub on Ridgewood Avenue in Harbor Oaks, about half a mile north of the Last Resort. On her tail were a couple of undercover officers who'd been handpicked for the task. Mike Joyner, a sergeant in the Citrus County SO Special Investigations Unit, worked undercover constantly, primarily narcotics operations. He'd ridden with biker gangs and was adept at infiltrating their environs.

Joyner already had a low-level awareness of the case that was shaping up. He'd first heard about the David Spears homicide when Mr Spears's body had turned up in Citrus County's jurisdiction, although at that stage Joyner's only personal involvement was taking part in a search through the woods.

On Saturday 5 January, Joyner, Jerry Thompson, and investigator Imperial of Citrus County had attended a joint meeting at the command post the task force had set up at the Pirate's Cove motel in Volusia, a move made because the Daytona area seemed to be the suspects' favoured terrain. That day, a game plan was put in place. They'd worked out a shift system for a moving surveillance operation that would get officers out covering the streets. The FDLE had supplied portable phones. There would be absolutely no radio communication so that the news media could not monitor the operation and ruin everything.

Investigators Imperial and Buscher had worked a Sunday shift together and had visited 'Our Place', a bar on Ridgewood in South Daytona. The bartender recognised a picture of Lee/Susan Blahovec and said she'd been in the previous day with another woman. They'd had a couple of beers, then left. They were getting close. Imperial stayed for a couple of hours in case they returned, but no such luck.

Joyner, it had been decided, would work with Martin, another undercover man. Having familiarised themselves with photographs of the two women, Joyner and Martin (a.k.a. Drums and Bucket), attired in their biker gear, would team up on the night shift, drifting into area bars, spending a few minutes in each—just long enough to see if the suspects were there—before moving on to the next.

On the Tuesday afternoon, Larry Horzepa and Special Agent Chouinard spent five hours checking the US 1 strip, but it wasn't their lucky day. Joyner and Martin were about to strike paydirt. Martin was driving their silver Chevy pick-up when, close to 9 p.m., they turned into the parking lot of the Port Orange Pub. Joyner, a lean fellow with long dark hair and a full beard, told his partner to stay put. He'd get out and take a walk around.

It wasn't hard to recognise Lee, not once he saw her face to face. As soon as he set foot inside, he knew he had her, standing alone and shooting pool.

Whenever she set down the pool cue, Joyner noted, she went right back to a tan suitcase that was clearly hers. Puffing steadily on Marlboros, she swigged her beer. Just as they were beginning to build a nice little rapport, Joyner (who'd of course introduced himself as 'Drums') watched in dismay as out of the blue a couple of uniformed officers came in and yanked her from the pub.

The very secretive nature of such an undercover operation almost guarantees that even with the best of efforts and intentions, wires sometimes cross, jeopardising a delicate operation. That, Joyner realised, was precisely what seemed to be happening before his very eyes.

Officer Proctor, it turned out, had been acting on an anonymous tip that one of the two suspected female serial killers was having a drink in the pub. The tipster said that they'd seen the same female about six weeks earlier with a girlfriend and overheard talk of guns, Colorado, and being able to 'take a man out'. Proctor had hurried over there and met up with Detective Belz who went in and confirmed that the female matching the description was indeed in the bar. Officers Proctor and Stiltner moved in, asking her to step outside.

Would she think they were on to her, Joyner worried? He had her in his sight as she stood across the parking lot with them, but could only guess. He certainly couldn't hear what was being said.

She co-operated with the cops to the extent that she produced a driver's licence in the name of Cammie Marsh Greene, but they had noticed she didn't match the photograph and seemed confused about her birthdate. She told them she was 'starting to get mad', and refused to show another piece of i.d. She wanted to go back into the bar. When asked for her address, she said she was between apartments. Joyner watched from afar, as she stood with her hands on her hips, her body language clearly showing her growing aggravation. Since she seemed to be getting so agitated, the officers let her go, then radioed in her licence information.

Little did they realise the frantic behind-the-scenes activity they had stirred up in an effort to stop their innocent efficiency from aborting the operation. Before going outside, Joyner quickly tipped off 'Bucket' to contact Jerry Thompson outside. He was running the show that day since Bruce Munster was back in Marion County doing more background work. Thompson swung into immediate action and was able to pluck the right phone number from memory and within seconds was patched through to Port Orange dispatch. Understood, the dispatcher said. Luckily, the officers were on the radio that very moment.

Only when they were told via radio to back off, did they learn that Lee was already under the eagle eye of the Volusia County Sheriff's Office. In fact, there were twenty, maybe even twenty-five, people on the surveillance at that point, many of them street soldiers from Marion and Citrus Counties and the FDLE, all in unmarked cars, except for the FDLE agents posted in a surveillance van across the street.

Lee later told the undercovers she was being hassled because she looked like a serial killer they were looking for and she had nowhere to stay, but there had been no mention of murders. The souls of discretion, the officers had merely thanked her politely and let her go. They left the scene with no visible harm done.

Free once more, an angry Lee had gone back into the bar cussing and shouting, then promptly threw her pool stick down on the table and ran into the bathroom, slamming the door behind her. She'd had a close call and she must have been shaken.

When she came out, her mood began to pick up again. She drank more beer, lots of it. Cans of Busch and Budweiser.

Sensing an available ear, Lee moaned to 'Drums' about her break-up with her girlfriend Ty. She was real depressed about losing her lover. At first, she thought the world had come to an end, but she was strong, she'd get over it. Joyner encouraged that line of thinking. He also went out to his truck and armed himself. His partner was already armed.

What were Drums and Bucket doing in town, Lee wanted to know? Non-committal and very cool, Joyner said they were just taking care of some business.

Everything she owned was in her little suitcase, she said. It was all she had left. She also showed him a small, silver, Eagle padlock key on a brass ring on her belt which she described as 'my life'. Then, just as suddenly, the chatting stopped and they would be back to playing pool or, with Lee pumping quarters steadily into the juke box, dancing together. She was definitely rowdy, but not overtly drunk. At times, she was downright affectionate, coming up and hugging him.

Then, quick as a flash, her mood could snap. At one point she accidentally bumped into Joyner and in an instant, she'd pulled back her pool stick as if ready to hit him with it. Jollying her out of it, he asked what she was doing. 'Gosh, damn, girl. I'm the one shooting pool!' he quipped. Then she was all right again.

Joyner, an old hand with almost a decade of undercover work under his belt, was adept at consuming the minimum of alcohol while giving the impression that he was knocking it back as fast as his companion. Ordering his beer in a can or brown bottle, he made restroom trips to tip out their contents and fill them up with water. That way he could keep up with her beer for beer. It was all nice and sociable, and she was none the wiser. Joyner was buying. He bought her a pack of Marlboros, too, plus maybe four or five beers over a three-hour period. And he saw her scars. The one on her arm from the car wreck, and the one in her stomach from being shot.

Martin made periodic calls from the cellular phone in their pick-up, reporting to command post. And Dixie County's Jimmy Pinner called Bruce Munster at home to say, 'We've got her under surveillance.' Munster immediately headed back over to Volusia.

When she was ready to leave the bar an hour later, she pushed Drums and Bucket for a ride. The edict had already come down that the undercovers weren't to get in a vehicle with her. To Joyner, that also meant not letting her get in his pick-up with him. Having made a firm mental note of how frighteningly quickly she could veer from affable to downright aggressive, he declined. They had a previous engagement, he said, but they'd probably catch up with her later.

Not only was this a suspected serial killer whose modus operandi was killing men she drove around with, but as a sergeant, he that day happened to have around $2,000 in investigation expense money stuffed in his pocket. He'd already accidentally pulled it out at one point, within her sight. He didn't particularly fancy feeling a gun rammed in his ribs that night. And he wasn't sure she didn't have one.

Staggering off, still tightly clutching her suitcase, she walked half a mile south down Ridgewood to the Last Resort Bar, her old haunt. Drums and Bucket pulled away in the opposite direction. Their shift was over and they handed over surveillance to another team.

Cannonball, the Last Resort's ultra-burly bartender, didn't pass judgement on Lee or any other street girls. Seemed to him, no one would wake up one morning and simply decide to be a hooker. Most of them were doing what they did because of what had been done to them by their fathers or uncles or someone. No, he wouldn't say anything bad about Lee. He remembered Ty, the lover who'd left, as looking like a little bulldog with a big, round face. She'd always liked playing the claw machines and fishing for soft toys and animals which it spat out as rewards. When she and Lee got into some heavy-duty drinking together, Ty seemed to be able to keep a lid on Lee. Sure, she got brassy and bold, but she never gave him any problems. But then, who'd want to tangle with him?

That night, since she had nowhere else to stay, Lee slept under the stars of what was indeed for her the last resort, curling up on an old, tan car seat on the porch. Silently the surveillance team watched over her while she snatched a few hours' shuteye. Had she but known it, she might have enjoyed the fact that she had more undivided attention focused on her than at any other time in her life.

When morning came, completely unaware of her minders, she sleepily stretched and staggered back into the bar. It was Wednesday 9 January. Scraping her stringy hair up into a ponytail, she freshened up and changed into blue shorts and a flowery blue shirt. By noon, she was back at the pool table, comforting herself with its familiarity.

Up north, Dan Henry was moving on from Ohio to Michigan to look in on the investigation that was under way there into the women behind the aliases Lori Grody and Sandra Kretsch.

Back in Florida, things were about to hot up. By early afternoon, the weather had turned chilly. Lee had changed into jeans and a beige windbreaker jacket; vital information that was duly circulated among her watchers. The jacket was the Members Only kind.

It was close to 3 p.m. when Drums and Bucket casually dropped back into the Last Resort, feigning surprise at finding Lee there, drinking. This time, Bucket was wired for sound with a body transmitter, and the surveillance team outside was able to listen in directly. She told the guys where she'd spent the night, even took Drums outside to show him the car seat. The tan suitcase, they noted, was still close by her side.

Outside, surveillance teams came and went, following departing Last Resort patrons to their next destinations and checking out their vehicles, tracing back owner names and addresses. They were covering all the bases.

Lee said she'd been on the road and had spent $600 in the last two weeks and was broke. She said her friend had stolen all her belongings and left her with nothing. She also regaled the undercovers with a tale of how she'd been in Mexico and when someone made her angry by touching her motorcycle, she'd pulled a .22 out of her boot and opened fire. She didn't know if she'd hit them or not.

Joyner, who gave her money for the juke box, noticed she seemed obsessed with playing one song—'Digging Up Bones' by Randy Travis—over and over again. It was an ode to lost love, but the irony of the title wasn't lost on the undercovers. Periodically, Lee moved over to the pay phone on the wall and went through the motions of making a call. Somehow, Joyner got the distinct feeling that it was all a charade and that she wasn't talking to anybody.

Drums and Bucket had also got chatting to Cannonball, the bartender. They listened with concern to his announcement that there was a big party planned for that night. A pig roast, the works. That meant crowds, and crowds meant trouble.

Joyner decided a pre-emptive strike was in order: he offered to give Lee the money for a room in the motel down the street. Hadn't she been saying she was tired and wanted a bath? He wanted her where they could keep an eye on her. Not unnaturally, Lee, who was unused to favours of any kind, greeted the offer with great suspicion. Was he putting her on? She was still sceptical when he came back and handed her a room key after saying he'd go and register her. (Meanwhile, he'd tipped off two FDLE agents outside about the party and the motel plan.)

Whereas the plan had been clear, suddenly all bets were off. As Larry Horzepa explains: 'As long as she didn't endanger anybody else, and she didn't attempt to pick anybody up, or to leave with anybody, we were just going to keep close surveillance on her.'

With a pig roast in progress? Forget it. As Larry Horzepa and the other locals knew all too well, if such a party ran true to Last Resort form, it would be a wild and crazy affair attracting literally hundreds of people. Those shindigs often spilled out into the back behind a privacy fence where there were old bus benches and abandoned cars and lots of opportunity for sex and drugs.

There was no doubt the bash could spell disaster for the operation. It was not as if they had a battalion of long-haired, biker undercovers who could suddenly slip into the Last Resort unnoticed. And should anything break inside the bar that meant they had to go in to get her, they could find themselves dealing with hundreds of bikers, too.

In all their gear, those biker chicks all looked alike. So all Lee would have to do would be to pop on a cycle helmet and leap on the back of a hog, and she'd be history, before the surveillance team had even figured out which one she was. Since she'd slept on the car seat the previous night, it also looked very much as if she had no home to lead them to.

Inevitably, it was a controversial decision either way. Assistant State Attorney Anthony Tatti was present. Everyone knew of the lawyers' concern and understood the wisdom of waiting. But what if they did nothing and lost her in the shuffle? The way Larry Horzepa saw it, it was ultimately Volusia County's decision to make since they were in their jurisdiction. In fact, on learning there would be a task force involved, Horzepa alerted his superior, Sergeant Jake Erhardt, that he might need to call on him to make some decisions. Of paramount importance while stalking Wuornos was the safety of the citizens of Volusia. There were also liability issues to consider.

'It's nice to be able to play out a scenario of "We'd like to follow her and see what she does",' Larry Horzepa points out. 'But at the same time, on the other edge of that double-edged sword, is that you also have to take responsibility if she picks somebody up and injures them.' Forget injure: what if she killed again before they caught up with her? That wouldn't have been pretty.

It would have been nice to see if she led them to Ty, but Sergeant Erhardt's decision was that she should be brought out of the Last Resort while they still had control of the situation and while she was clearly under surveillance. So it was that it fell to Joyner to figure out how to get her outside. First, he gave Lee the room key. Still suspicious, she went straight to the pay phone and called the motel to make sure he'd actually signed her in. While she was gone, Joyner quickly filled in Martin on the arrest plan.

Lee came back, finally convinced, and told Joyner she was going to go take a shower and clean up. Her parting shot was her last nice words to him. 'Come pick me up around seven, eight o'clock. Come by yourself and we'll party,' she promised.

The undercover officers then left, got in the silver pick-up, and pulled right alongside the front door of the bar. Stepping out of the truck, Joyner called through the doorway to Lee. 'I need directions! Come here a minute!'

Affably, she walked towards him. That was it. All of a sudden, there were cops everywhere. Larry Horzepa and Bernard Buscher, who were in the first car, confronted her, approaching her as Lori Grody. At just after 5 p.m., Larry Horzepa told 'Lori' that he'd been looking for her, and quietly handcuffed her and placed her under arrest.

'I don't know why you're bothering with me!' Lee retorted. 'I don't know what you're talking about!'

Horzepa and the other officers duly put on a bit of a show for the folk inside the bar, protecting the covers of Bucket and Drums. After Lee was set in the back seat of a police vehicle, they turned their attention to Drums, pushing him around a little bit, cuffing him, then throwing him in the back seat with her while they checked him out on the computer. Bucket, meanwhile, the very picture of concern, ran back and forth in the bar, saying, 'Hey, my pal's being arrested! Anyone know a good lawyer or bondsman?'

There was another motive to all this. Joyner was wired for sound and the back of the car was fitted with a hidden camera. They might get something useful. But when he asked her what was going on it was all too apparent that it was the end of a beautiful friendship. She unleashed a stream of expletives and snapped at him to keep his mouth shut.

Eventually, an officer came back, unlocked his cuffs, read him the riot act, then told him he could go. End of performance.

Lee's purse was retrieved from the bar, along with her tan suitcase, which she'd had chained up for safety. Looking alternately enraged and dazed, she was then driven to Volusia County Branch Jail and officially booked. While the paperwork was completed, Bruce Munster ambled in and offered to get her coffee and some cigarettes, getting his first glimpse of their dirty, dishevelled and sleep-deprived suspect. She seemed very unemotional.

It had been a long haul for Lee. Every mile of it, every year, was reflected in her hard, ravaged face. Just like Leo Pittman, who had relinquished his freedom long before her, she exuded the fearful menace of a caged wild animal. Beneath it all, she was tired, worn down and somehow beaten. She would be sleeping in a different kind of wild that night.

After Larry Horzepa had explained to her about the outstanding 1986 warrant for grand theft and carrying a concealed firearm in the name of Lori Grody, Lee knew that that part of her game, at least, was up. Lori Grody, she admitted, was her sister. She knew why she was being arrested.

Which was more than could be said for Marion County Assistant State Attorney Ric Ridgway, who was shocked by a call late that evening informing him that Wuornos had been taken into custody. Furious, he contacted Marion's State Attorney Brad King, who was of like mind.

'He hit the roof,' Ridgway recalls. 'We wound up driving over there—flying low over there—that night, and there was a bit of a confrontation over that decision between Brad and I, and Steve Binegar and Bruce Munster. There was a lot of emotion involved. Everybody was tired. We were hot, we were mad, and so we all kind of flared up.'

Lee became quite agitated when her property was inventoried at the jail. Her purse and tan suitcase had been taken from her, but what bothered her most of all seemed to be the safety of her Eagle key. Over and over, she asked that it be kept with her property, begging, 'Please don't lose that key, it's my life.'

Had no one been suspicious of her before, her blatant anxiety would have soon tipped them off. And while she was fingerprinted, it really got the better of her. Later, she complained to anyone who would listen that they'd taken more prints than was usual. In addition, they'd also taken a palm print. That really worried her.

Disappointingly, a search of her purse and suitcase drew a blank on stolen items, although she did have a couple of knives. The search yielded something, however: receipts from Jack's Mini-Warehouses on 1104 North Nova Road in Daytona Beach. Dated 3 and 19 December, they revealed that 'Cammie Greene' had possession of space C-1-G. Bernie Buscher passed the information straight over to Bruce Munster.

If those slips weren't enough to give her away, her rampant indiscretion would have sufficed.

In anticipation of Lee's arrival, Karen Collins, a Pasco County detective, had already gone undercover in the detention centre holding cell after being placed under fake arrest for aggravated battery. A seven-year veteran of undercover vice and narcotics work, she had the guts to spend the night in the holding cell with Lee and to get her chatting. Collins opened up the conversation by asking Lee what she was in for? Taking the bait, Lee said they'd had an old warrant for her for carrying a concealed firearm. Collins said she'd shot someone. Common ground. The communication door was open.

Lee talked about her guns and mentioned a friend accidentally shooting her with a .22 rifle. Later, she said she'd shot herself because she'd had a problem. Unable to see the wisdom of keeping her own counsel, Lee chatted on about getting a .45 calibre revolver through a man who'd known she was down and out and had given her $25 to go pawn it for $100. Lately, she'd been hitchhiking around town and 'doing men' for money. She tried to come off like a call girl who wouldn't touch anything for under $200, but later admitted she serviced people in biker bars for $20 or $25. She was worth more than $20, she said indignantly.

She spoke, too, of an incident that sounded like a variation on the 1986 arrest that led to the outstanding warrant. Only the story omitted to mention that she'd had twelve rounds of ammunition in her overnight bag. Instead it had grown to include an attempted rape on the part of her companion. She also said he'd stolen $150 from her.

Lee became very upset when she saw that Collins still had her shoelaces while hers had been taken from her.

More poignantly, she confided that she'd lost her lover and her home before Christmas. Since then, she'd been drinking heavily and living on the streets. She'd used the Cammie Greene i.d., which she'd found on the beach, to rent the storage unit in which she kept her life's possessions. Little did Lee know that a search warrant was already under way.

Obviously unfamiliar with the maxim that loose lips sink ships, she expressed her concern that police suspected her of killing all those men who'd been murdered near the interstates. Since they seemed to think she resembled the sketches, she'd been keeping up with the case. In fact, she leapt upon the daily newspaper with such fervour that she had to be told she must let the other girls enjoy it before she commandeered it. She spent much of her time scribbling personal letters, her head encased in radio earphones.

Most memorably, she talked about her boyfriend, Barry, with whom she'd broken up before Christmas. He didn't love her any more, she told Collins, saying nothing about being gay. But when she changed clothes, Collins thought, 'Oh God!'—Lee was wearing red men's briefs. Putting two and two together, Collins surmised the Barry she was talking about must be Ty. (Of all the names she could substitute, how strange she should pick her brother Barry's. Maybe she thought it would be easy to remember.)

Lee talked again about her storage unit. It had a stereo in it, an Eagle blanket, clothing, knick-knacks and some small figurines. Collins was getting the picture. Lee was obviously afraid something incriminating might be found there.

After breakfast the next morning, Collins was taken out to be debriefed by Tom Muck, then she went back in, was given proper prison clothes, and put in a pod. Unlike Lee, she knew she could get out, yet she still didn't relish her tiny taste of incarceration. Meanwhile, the trustee inmates had been getting suspicious because the holding cell was sealed off. It was time to pull Karen Collins out again.

The next day, 10 January, Investigator Buscher drove over to Jack's Mini-Warehouses where he met the owners, Alice and Melvin Colbert, and learned that Cammie Greene had paid up on her locker until February. Spotting an Eagle padlock on the bin, Buscher passed that little titbit on to Bruce Munster. By 4 p.m., Sergeant Mike Joyner had it and its mysterious contents under round-the-clock surveillance.

The wisdom of putting stolen goods into a rented bin was dubious to say the least, but then, she wasn't expecting to get caught. Lee's aliases, Larry Horzepa noted, had been highly successful for her for a very long time. She had hidden behind someone else's name and i.d. for every key act, from pawning stolen goods to renting the storage unit. And if anyone ever questioned her too closely on the fact that she didn't quite resemble her Cammie Greene photograph, she brought up her old burn scars as an excuse. She was manipulative enough to brazen it out, claiming the picture really *was* her, but her face had gone through a windshield in an accident. Hearing that, who would dare call her a liar?

Dick Humphreys' Sylacauga police chief badge was but one item on a very lengthy list of evidence the detectives hoped to find when they unsealed her stash of treasures. On 14 January, Judge Foxman signed Bruce Munster's 22-page affidavit for the search warrant and Bernard Buscher served it that same day. When they finally opened the storage unit, Larry Horzepa had the videotape camera running throughout.

The motley collection of goods inside was seized and taken into evidence by FDLE evidence technicians. It included everything from tools to a scrap of a Daytona newspaper and an open Handiwipe sachet with the wipe still inside. There were three football playing cards, six shower-curtain rings, an electrical cord, a vibrator, a bottle of aftershave, a guitar pick, a butter container, matchbooks, a shoehorn and numerous wire coat-hangers. Thankfully, some items were decidedly more intriguing, like the driver's licence receipts, birth and baptism certificates and

Social Security card for Susan Blahovec. Disappointingly, there was no sign whatsoever of David Spears's distinctive black ceramic panther.

Needless to say, it took some time to disseminate the hundreds of items, but Larry Horzepa was soon amply satisfied. There it was. A maroon Polaroid 600 camera of the type that Richard Mallory was carrying when he died.

35

Before Aileen's arrest, the Ohio-Michigan effort was still under way. Dan Henry had gone on to Michigan to do further checks on the aliases Lori Grody and Sandra Kretsch on 9 January, meeting up with Detective-Sergeant Leonard Goretski and Detective-Lieutenant Richard Duthler of the Michigan State Police. Together, Henry and Goretski had uncovered Aileen Wuornos's lengthy list of run-ins with police.

Sandra Kretsch was found to be an old neighbour of Aileen's from Troy and was cleared on the strength of mug shots on her 'record'. Dan Henry had had a little more background checking to do before visiting Lori Grody in Mancelona. Lori was by then known to be Aileen's aunt by bloodline and sister by adoption.

At the time Wuornos had been spotted in Daytona and was under surveillance, Dan Henry later wrote, there were mounting fears that 'Tyria may have been eliminated by Wuornos'. Some of the detectives thought that a bit far-fetched since the real nitty-gritty search for Ty had barely begun. In any event, after consulting with Steve Binegar back in Florida and hearing that Lee had been picked up, Dan Henry headed straight back to Cadiz, where the local law enforcement was finally instigating intensive surveillance on the Moore family, the next morning, Thursday 11 January. That same morning, the court-ordered phone tap would finally be on line. The local officers didn't plan to move in until 3 p.m., giving Dan Henry time to make it back from Michigan by car.

When he arrived, Henry found that Ty's father had been under the eagle eyes of deputies since 7.20 a.m. Her brother Jackie had also been located, as had her stepmother, Mary Ann, plus another female who did not fit Ty's description and who later turned out to be Ty's stepsister, Tracey Moore.

Sheriff Rensi picked up Jack Moore and brought him in for questioning. Jack Moore knew just where his daughter Ty was, but he was playing it cautious at first and was wary of handing her number over to Dan Henry. Eventually he did so, on the understanding that he and Mary Ann would get a chance to call her before he spoke to her. Henry agreed, but immediately Jack Moore had written down the number, Chief Neely slipped out of the room to trace it.

Obviously, at that juncture, they had no intention of letting Ty slip through their net. They didn't have enough evidence to charge her and they didn't want her skipping off or even calling an attorney if they could help it. Neely traced the number to Swoyersville, Pennsylvania, and rang it. No one was home.

Dan Henry spoke next to the Pennsylvania State Police who were asked to locate the residence, to secure it and endeavour to find Tyria. Very soon, the address was ascertained to be that of Ty's sister Twyla. Descending upon the house, they learned that Ty was at work. Within minutes, the state police had, with her permission, embraced her in protective custody: her only proviso being that she would only talk to Florida authorities.

Major Henry reported back to Captain Binegar, who was ensconced in the command post at the Pirate's Cove motel in Daytona, and they put their heads together to determine the next step. Binegar's immediate instinct was to send up what he considered the two most experienced homicide detectives he could lay his hands on to conduct the all-important Ty interview. Without hesitating, he picked Bruce Munster and Jerry Thompson. They both had excellent track records and had been 'part of the core work group since the beginning'. They'd fly to Pennsylvania, but Dan Henry would meanwhile hotfoot it over there and take up the slack until they arrived, meeting up with Ty in the hotel next to Scranton airport where the state police had lodged her. Captain Binegar felt comfortable with his decision.

'I felt that these two were the best people for the job. I mean, this was going to be kind of like the Super Bowl,' he explained in his deposition. 'You send what I consider to be the best people in.

'Well, I got a call back. There was some dissension as to who was going to go. The group wanted to have Tyria put on a bus . . . sent down, and then they would all interview her. Well, that's just not . . . I mean, that's just not practical. It's not good police practice.

'My job through most of this investigation . . . I spent ninety per cent of my energies keeping everybody from killing each other.'

Binegar understood all the keen minds who'd worked so hard wanting to stay involved in the high points of the case. He didn't take it personally. But neither was he swayed.

In a neatly dove-tailed manoeuvre, Ty's brother Jackie and Mary Ann Moore had been approached by agents at exactly the same time as Jack Moore was picked up. They were all interviewed separately and given no chance to communicate with one another beforehand, though Mary Ann was joined by Ty's half-sister, Tracey. Through these family members, officers learned of Tracey's stay in Florida the previous summer for a period that covered the time of Peter Siems's disappearance. Tracey confirmed that Lee had appeared with a vehicle like Mr Siems's. And Mary Ann readily handed over a package and letter addressed to Ty that had recently arrived from Lee. Mary Ann impressed upon the officers how terribly afraid Ty was of Lee.

Arriving at the Victoria Inn in Scranton, Dan Henry later wrote a report that summarised his first encounter with the suspect, Tyria Moore:

> I found Tyria to be tired, apprehensive, but otherwise in good shape. After reassuring her that she was not under arrest, could make phone calls, and leave if she so desired, she seemed to relax. She indicated she wanted to stay and she felt she could trust me. I told her it was late and she looked very tired and all I wanted her to do was get some sleep. I asked her if she would speak to my investigators when they arrived in the morning and help us 'clear up'

311

the problems in Florida. She said she would. I made sure she had whatever she needed and the Pennsylvania State Police were most accommodating. I felt that an interview at this time would not be in our best interest.

I checked into the room next to Tyria's, gave her my phone number and asked her to call me when she woke up and wanted to go to breakfast. Writer retired, having begun the day in Michigan, driving to Ohio, and flying to Eastern Pennsylvania.

Tyria phoned me around 8.45 a.m. the next morning, Friday, January 11th, and said, 'Major, this is Ty, do we still have a date? I'm hungry.' I told her we sure did and I'd be there in about 20 minutes.

Dan Henry then placed reassuring phone calls to Twyla and to Mary Ann Moore to let her worried family know Ty was not under arrest and could leave if she chose to do so. Dan Henry was biding his time, waiting for Bruce Munster and Jerry Thompson to do the interview, and in the meanwhile he was being extremely solicitous. Ty's family suggested sending a lawyer to the hotel room but thankfully Ty kept refusing. She thought it would only complicate things.

Bruce Munster and Jerry Thompson arrived just before noon, to conduct their interview in Ty's room. Facing her in the flesh for the first time, Munster and Thompson were convinced Lee was the trigger woman, but they still considered Tyria a murder suspect, still felt that two people had been involved. What they did not know just then was that she had left Florida with the belongings of murdered men in her possession.

Tyria was read her Miranda rights in which she was advised that she had the right to stay silent, that anything she said could be used against her in court, and that she had a right to talk to a lawyer for advice before questioning and to have a lawyer with her during the questioning. If she could not afford a lawyer, one would be appointed for her. And if she chose to proceed without a lawyer, she could change her mind and request one at any time. Ty waived her right to a lawyer, then launched straight into a lengthy interview during which she told what she knew about the murders. She told how Lee had sat before her on the floor that evening in December '89 and announced, with no spectacular show of emotion, that she had killed a man that day and had then covered his body with a piece of carpet. Tyria recounted how they'd used his two-door Cadillac, with its University of Florida Gator tag, to move from the Ocean Shores Motel in Ormond Beach to the converted garage apartment at 332½ Burleigh in Holly Hills.

Apparently co-operating fully, Ty told Bruce Munster of the maroon-coloured briefcase Lee had brought home, along with the combination numbers Lee had given her to open its lock. The six digits just so happened to coincide neatly with the first six digits of Dick Humphreys' Social Security number. Ty also identified a photograph of Mr Humphreys' blue car as being the kind Lee was driving in at the time of Dick's murder. One in a long, fast-changing line of vehicles Lee acquired. Listening to Ty, Munster and Jerry Thompson soon had more than an inkling that Lee Wuornos might have acted alone. The transcripts of those interviews give the impression that Tyria Moore was questioned more as an innocent bystander than as a full-blown suspect, but Bruce Munster was well-known for his soft-pedal approach designed to gain the target's confidence. He'd got a lot of confessions that way. The majority of interviewees try to minimise their involvement in the crime at hand and he had found that going along with them in that minimisation was an effective tool. That day, Munster and Thompson listened to what Ty claimed to be the truth, and although they had no way of verifying what she said right on the spot, they instinctively believed her.

After lunch, she agreed she'd go with them to Florida the next morning, so they then stopped by at Twyla's home to pick up clothes for the trip and the belongings of the murdered men that Ty had in her possession. While Munster talked to Twyla downstairs, Thompson went upstairs with Ty and gathered them up. There was the briefcase and notation of serial numbers, some clocks, a word processor, assorted clothing, a clipboard and a grass pipe; all of which had been given to her by Lee and could have belonged to the victims.

Dan Henry did not plan to fly back with them since his car

was still in Pittsburgh. Before he left, Ty said: 'Major, I just want you to know, after coming clean yesterday, I got the best night's sleep since this all began.'

Dan Henry had one last stop to make back in Cadiz. He went to the Moores' home to pick up a few other items Ty had told them about—a book of definitions called the *Legal Word Book*, GE '21 Memory' telephone and a pair of men's gloves, all of which had been given to her by Lee. Bruce Munster had also asked him to pick up Lee's recent letter, a Western Union moneygram receipt, two T-shirts and a set of airline ticket receipts.

36

By virtue of her inaction through Lee's killing rampage, Tyria had cast a black shadow over her own character. Turning a blind eye as she did, she would meet few people's criteria for an upstanding citizen or even an empathetic human being. Yet in terms of any actual culpability she might have for the homicides, once she began co-operating with authorities, every step she took solidified her role as the benign partner. Although Ty was not suspected of pulling the trigger in the Richard Mallory homicide, officially she did remain a suspect. She knew about at least three murders and had victims' property in her possession. As time went on she looked less and less like a *key* suspect. Suspicions to the contrary, she had not been granted immunity, and had there been any evidence of her being involved in the brutal crimes themselves, Bruce Munster insisted she would have been arrested.

Agreeing to help with no holds barred, Ty promptly flew back to Florida alongside Bruce Munster and Jerry Thompson. Both parties had clear agendas. Ty's was to exonerate herself of any involvement in the murders; law enforcement's was to give Lee the opportunity—within the confines of the law—to incriminate herself beyond a reasonable doubt.

Although forensic evidence linked Lee to Peter Siems's car, physical evidence was thin on the ground in some of the homicides, and they badly needed a confession.

On the flight down to Florida, Jerry Thompson allotted Ty a task that kept her busy: he wanted her to put together a list of all her and Lee's various addresses during 1989 and 1990. No small feat. She scratched her head and scribbled, memories popping up with each temporary home she recalled.

The original plan had been to send Ty into the jail upon arriving in Daytona so she could make direct contact with Lee, but red tape prohibited that approach. Instead, she would have to spin her web by telephone. Ty was willing to help and signed consent forms allowing the calls to be taped. Once Ty was ensconced in room 160 at the Quality Inn, she put together a natural-sounding letter that was rushed over by hand to Lee.

'Hi there,' Ty wrote. 'My mom told me you had called and said you were in trouble. I couldn't call you so I'm down here in Florida for a few days to see you. I wasn't able to get on your visitors' list so if you would like to call me, I'll try to help you out.'

So it went on. Ty had done her part. Now she and the changing shifts of female FDLE agents staying in the adjoining motel room, and the procession of investigators—primarily Munster and Thompson—who came in and out had simply to bide their time and wait for Lee's collect call. It was a call that had to come. Starved for contact, bitterly missing her lover and isolated behind bars, how could Lee resist? Ty's willingness to get on the telephone with Lee while surrounded by cops only strengthened the feeling about her that was already permeating the operation. Ty was certainly behaving as though she had little to hide or fear. She didn't balk at talking to Lee cold, with no opportunity to tip her off that they were being taped. No wonder, Bruce Munster recollects, 'We were becoming less convinced that Tyria was involved.'

It was not a new thought as far as he was concerned. From the outset in the Troy Burress case, a couple of pieces of the puzzle kept niggling at him. They were searching for two women, yet Burress's sausage truck was found with a hefty equipment box lodged on the front seat. It took up so much space that there was no way it left enough room for three people to have squeezed in there together—especially women of Tyria and Lee's size—unless one had sat on the other's lap. Possible, but not likely. Of course, if Burress had been abducted from a market or convenience store, he could have been transported in the refrigerated back. But Munster didn't think so. It seemed to him that Lee had acted alone.

Everything the investigators learned about the two women had seemed to substantiate Wuornos's role as the protagonist. Whether it was handling the witnesses when they crashed Siems's car, or having altercations with the Votrans drivers, Lee was always at the forefront. The other strong factor pointing the finger in Lee's direction was her longtime familiarity with firearms.

'When wasn't she arrested without a gun?' was Bruce Munster's point. 'She was arrested in Colorado with a .25 automatic, driving a car, shooting it. She was arrested in Orlando with a .38 revolver, driving a stolen car. She was arrested in Volusia County with a .22 revolver. She just had guns all the time. Tyria Moore, on the other hand, graduated high school, I believe. Had one arrest that we could find.'

Backing up her promise of co-operation, Tyria was coming through in other ways, too. She said she'd give the investigators a conducted tour of the homes in which she'd lived with Lee (in fact, they went alone to the addresses Ty gave them) and she showed them the very spot in Rose Bay where Lee had dumped her gun.

Bruce Munster came to believe Ty's claim that she had gone to Pennsylvania to hide out because of her fear of Lee. He also felt that eventually she would have come forward and told what she knew.

'Tyria realised that she was in a lot of trouble,' he notes. 'She didn't love Wuornos any more, she didn't want anything to do with Wuornos any more, because of what Wuornos had done. I think Tyria felt real bad that she didn't come forward because she could have saved a lot of lives.'

He came to view Ty's relationship with Lee as something akin to an abusive husband and dominated wife. Lee seemed to take charge and take care of paying the bills while Ty either worked or played Suzy Homemaker.

'Lee had quite a temper and was fairly physical when she had to be,' Larry Horzepa concurred, also noting her stout build at the time of arrest and that it took considerable brute strength to rip off licence plates with bare hands as she had done.

On Monday 14 January, at 3.32 in the afternoon, the officers tested their tape set-up to make sure it was working properly. The door between Ty's and the FDLE agents' rooms was open at all times, day and night. As if on cue, Lee's first collect call took place soon after.

'Hey, Ty?' Lee said, her voice small, anticipatory.

'Yeah,' Ty growled, in her huskier tones.

'What are you doin'?' Lee went on.

'Nothin'. What the hell are you doin'?' Ty replied, sounding less nervous than she felt.

'Nothing. I'm sitting here in jail,' Lee replied.

'Yeah, that's what I heard.'

'How . . . what are you doin' down here?' Lee asked, suspicion rising, but fighting it.

'I came here to see what the hell's happening.'

'Everything's copasetic,' Lee reassured her. 'I'm in here for a . . . a . . . uh . . . carrying a concealed weapon back in '86 . . . and a traffic ticket.'

Gently, Ty began to rope Lee in to her imaginary scenario. She was scared (that much was true) and damn worried. The cops had been up to her parents' home asking questions and looking for her. Lee soothed her, her voice sweet. Ty had nothing to worry about. And she missed her.

'Do you miss me?' Lee asked in a small voice, hoping desperately for some declaration of affection in return.

'Nahhh,' Ty said in the manner of a transparent lover's bluff, pretending to be above it all.

'Kinda?' Lee persisted, her voice still childlike.

'Evidently I do or I wouldn't be here. I guess I worried about'cha . . .'

Ty went on to tell Lee about her factory job in Ohio, how she was saving money, how she'd hopped a bus to come down to Florida. Unable to stay away from the fire, it was Lee who raised their problem; she told Ty she'd been reading the paper and that she wasn't 'one of those little suspects'.

'And I'm gettin' really pissed off, them accusing us . . . uh, me. You know?' Lee continued, switching then to her old, familiar tack. ' 'Cause just . . . I'll have a lawsuit out.'

'Will ya?' Ty replied.

'In a heartbeat.'

Her confidence riding high again, Lee felt she needed to re-assure Ty about the storage unit. It was gone, got rid of, she lied. (By some strange quirk of fate, her claim coincided with the day investigators finally swooped down, seizing everything in it.) The call ended with Lee going off to get some visiting information and promising to call back. She wasted no time, and by then she had cold feet.

'I gotta ask you something. Is there anybody in that room?' she asked immediately.

Somewhat reassured by Ty on that score, she said she didn't think it was such a good idea for Ty to visit the jail. She just wanted to get the warrants cleared from her name, then to see Ty again. Dinner interrupted the second call.

Lee's third collect call arrived so soon after she hadn't had time to digest her food. Her agenda by then was to claim that those pictures in the paper were all a case of mistaken identity. Someone at the Casa Del Mar must have said it looked like them. Mistaken identity, that's what it was. Ty wasn't buying it and argued with her: 'I just know I didn't fuckin' do anything and I don't want to get . . . into any shit. I don't want my life messed up because of somethin' that you did.'

She hadn't done anything, though, Lee insisted. Ty told her not to lie, reminding her that she knew 'damn well that I've seen some of the cars and heard it on the news'. She'd just be making it harder on herself if she lied, Ty said. Lee stayed in the denial mode. It wasn't going to be easy. She then accused Ty of having someone there with her, listening in, and then shifted gears. Any car she had was borrowed. You know we're not the people, she cajoled Ty.

Ty then drove home a hard fact of life. She'd tell what she knew if she had to.

'To save my ass?' Ty said. 'You're damn right I will. 'Cause I'm not gonna go to fuckin' prison for somethin' that you did. No way.'

Lee told her she loved her and missed her like hell, then, the little gremlin of suspicion prodding her again, asked how Ty could afford these phone calls! They weren't long distance, Ty assured her, maintaining her charade. Lee went back to hammering home her mistaken identity claim. She bet someone at Ty's job had told that Ty had a heart tattooed on her arm. Fear breaking through, she shed a few tears. Anyway, Ty had nothing to worry about, she'd been working the whole time and could prove it.

'I'll betcha ten bucks,' Lee warned Ty, 'they'll say, "Oh, well, we found fingerprints" just to scare the shit outta you to see if you're gonna say somethin', but it's not true.'

Ty tried drawing Lee out by asking about the car they wrecked, but Lee played dumb. She didn't know what Ty meant. She started muttering about two guys that picked them up. It was Ty's turn not to understand.

Over Ty's denials, Lee said it again: 'I'll bet you ten bucks you got somebody sittin' there and you got a little tape recorder and you're tryin' to pin me with this shit.'

The suspicions kept flooding back. It didn't make sense, Ty coming all the way down to Florida to talk to her on a phone. But she loved her. Ty was the best woman she'd ever known, and she wouldn't let her get into trouble. She'd gladly die for her, and wait to see her in heaven. Would Ty just do her a favour and try to keep her mouth shut?

'This is so sickening,' Lee said, softer. 'How did our life fall apart? I miss you and all this stupid, stupid fucking warrant . . . I just hope I get over this warrant and get out.'

She had nothing to do with anything, she said, alluding obliquely to the murders. Then why, Ty coaxed, had she said she did?

'I was bullshitting,' Lee replied.

'Oh, that ain't nothing' new.'

'I know. I'm the biggest bullshitter, right? . . . Just trying to be a bad ass, I guess.'

Lee told Ty to try to forget what she'd told her.

'I try to forget a lot,' was Ty's revealing response.

Lee didn't want to be pinned for something she hadn't done. 'You know, if one of these guys that got killed and my prints happened to be in their vehicle, it was not me that did it.'

As far as Lee was concerned, those two guys she'd referred to were the motherfuckers that wrecked the car. You know I'm not a very good liar, was Ty's response.

Tears began falling at both ends of the phone line. Then Ty signed off so she could go and buy beer.

And if Ty did not sound fearful, beleaguered or submissive, or anything resembling a subservient wife, Bruce Munster put that down to the fact that she knew by then that the relationship was over. She was afraid of Lee and wanted no part of her, but, for now, Tyria was in control.

Lee called the motel for the fourth time that day at 6.20 p.m. She had something else to tell Ty about the car: she didn't think there were any prints, so everything was cool. Just do me a favour, she asked, and keep your mouth shut.

Ty, pausing for a loud and decidedly unladylike belch, sat back on the bed in her room and listened as Lee talked around and around the familiar topics. Ty had nothing to worry about; she had proof she had been at work. Sandy or one of the others at the Casa Del Mar must have said the drawings resembled them. How could Lee help it if she was in a car that somebody got hurt in a week later?

She spoke of her fate. She imagined she'd have to stay in for ninety days before her trial, then she'd either get probation or have to serve a little more time.

She switched back to the sketches. It was because she and Ty wore hats and glasses all the time and looked like damn cops, that's why people thought it was them. Because they were together like glue. But they didn't have concrete evidence, Lee said.

'This is gonna be one hell of a lawsuit if they start on me.'

What she'd told Ty? Most of the time she was bullshitting. Always trying to be a big bad-ass. The toughies of Daytona. Getting eighty-sixed from every bar. Ty laughed. For a minute, they sounded like any old couple, reminiscing.

'Remember that three hundred and twenty-five bucks you blew on stuffed animals?' Lee asked.

'Yeah, I remember that.'

Ty made a noise down the phone. Awww, said Lee, touched,

blowing a couple of kisses back. No, it wasn't a kiss she was sending her, Ty corrected her, it was a drink of beer.

Unable to leave the mistaken identity tack for long, Lee bet Ty ten bucks it was the two chicks from Minnesota they really wanted, the two who go around ripping off cars and pretending they're cops. Ty should say nothing about the storage, Lee reminded her. It was gone. Gone with the wind. It would be best if Ty forgot about their place on Burleigh (where they moved the day of Richard Mallory's death) and didn't even mention it. They partied too much over there.

Get drunk for me, Lee instructed Ty as she excused herself to go and get something from McDonald's.

There was a fifth call that night. Lee had been wondering if Tracey, Ty's sister, had said anything to the cops. Ty brushed that off.

'I want to know if you're alone or not?' Lee asked.

'Yes, I am.'

'Tell me with all your heart you are?'

'Yes.'

The sketch, Lee reassured Ty, 'definitely does not look like you, darling.'

'Really?' Ty asked.

'Uh, uh. I mean, she's really fat looking. I mean, real blown up in the face.'

Signing off, Lee told her to have fun.

'I'll drink one for you. Don't worry,' Ty said.

'Fuck one! Drink ten.'

Ty's long, taxing day wasn't over. At 9.50 p.m., Lee came back on the line with her latest thoughts. It would be best if Ty just went back home and didn't try to visit her in case they started hassling her or arresting her.

Was there any way—Lee had been fishing throughout to find out how much money Ty had—that Ty could leave ten bucks for her? She spoke, too, of Ty's move up north, carefully laying the blame for it elsewhere.

'I understand you going up there since you lost your job. That stupid dick-stain made you lose your job. Ahmad's such a jerk . . . everybody loves you but he didn't.'

She went back to trying to deter Ty from visiting the jail saying, 'This whole accusation shit has really got me fuckin' fired up.' She'd been stunned, her eyes were popping out of her head, when she read the newspaper reports about a woman suspect being picked up in a bar. Lee blew Ty a goodnight kiss which Ty did not return.

Call no. 7 arrived early on Tuesday 15 January, with Ty yawning exaggeratedly. Lee anxiously reassured her that if she hadn't been questioned thus far, she had nothing to worry about. She should get on with her own life.

'Ty, you write me a letter first, OK?'

'OK.'

'And then . . . and then I'll write you back. Then we'll start like that, OK?'

'Mmmm . . . mmm.' Ty was still playing sleepyhead.

'Awww. Ah, I can just see what my little baby's face looks like. I remember how you used to wake up, mmm, cute little . . .'

'Yeah,' Ty said, with a hint of sarcasm. 'Look like shit, probably, right now.'

Lee suddenly did an about-face and began talking about two pretty little crystal balls she'd put in the storage unit. It made what later sounded to the detectives as if she was trying to get a message across without spelling it out.

'If you wanna go and get 'em,' she told Ty, 'just take a hacksaw and open it up and get what you want outta there. OK?'

The previous day, she'd told Ty the unit was gone, but evidently she'd since been fretting about what was in it. She made what sounded to the listening detectives like another thinly disguised reference.

'You know that, uh, water pistol I have?'

Ty chuckled in response.

'I gave that away.'

She told Ty she could take what she wanted from the storage unit, including the Eagle blanket. There was a little computer, a little duck, a dog and a butterfly. The crystal balls were in a little plastic bag with her gold chain, on the left side of the unit.

323

'All you have to do is get a little hacksaw, saw off the fuckin' lock, no biggie,' she asserted.

Lee gave Ty a taste of her life behind bars, describing the funky, whipped, pukey-looking orange jumpsuit she was forced to wear. There was an orange cell and a yellow cell, but she was confined to the blue, maximum security cell, purportedly 'the baddest cell around', where the officers never took their eyes off the inmates. Wow, Ty retorted.

'It's a joke,' Lee said. 'It really is. And they treat us like we're really criminals . . . you know?'

She veered back to the storage unit and mistaken identity, before warning Ty: 'I'm just worried about ya because I know how the Volusia County fuckin' cops are. They're . . . they're typical jerks. They . . . everybody's a criminal and they are just angels, and they're not. . . .'

Since Ty had landed a job so fast up north, Lee thought she might go up there, too, when she got out. Then she reminded Ty: 'Whoever's been fucking killing these people, you were at work all the time.'

If she was approached, she should demand proof, Lee advised. That's what she intended to do.

'. . . I'm gonna throw a lawsuit on you people. Big time. And I'm not talking about thousands. I'll go for the millions.'

Call no. 8 began with Lee's idea of good news. A friend behind bars who was going to be a paralegal had told her they'd got a couple of people up in Minnesota with the same modus operandi.

Lee believed she'd be coming before Judge Gayle Graziano. 'I heard she's a real bitch,' she added. (Played later in the courtroom in front of none other than Judge Graziano herself, that tape segment raised a few wry smiles.)

While Lee rambled on, Ty's contributions to the conversations remained largely monosyllabic, almost uncommunicative.

'. . . You know, today is the 15th and twelve o'clock tonight is the beginning of a war. And it'll be eight o'clock in the morning in Iraq. And there's gonna be the bombshelling. And they're . . . they're checking out for terrorists in the United States because . . . they're probably planted. They're infiltrated all over the United States and they're just gonna start . . . some shit.'

Ty told Lee that she'd rather nurse a beer in the bar even though it cost $1.50, than sit in her hotel room alone at night. Lee's voice turned soft and hopeful: 'Do you think we could ever get back together?'

'Oh, I doubt it.'

'I mean as roommates?'

'I doubt that.'

Presumably not surprised, and definitely undeterred, Lee said she hoped they could just be friends and live near one another and party down. She said she was drying out from all the alcohol and intended to stay sober; her kidneys couldn't take it any more. When she got out, she'd just be a good girl and work, eat, sleep and pay bills, like everybody else in the human race.

'So, Ty, you've been honest with me about everything?'

'Mmm . . . mmm.'

Saying goodbye, Lee praised Ty for being 'the beautifullest person I've ever met'.

At 8.30 p.m. Tuesday evening, Ty was interviewed in-depth for two hours on videotape by Larry Horzepa and Bruce Munster at the Volusia County Sheriff's Office operations centre.

When Ty's phone first rang on the morning of Wednesday 16 January, it was a false alarm—Ty's brother, Brett. When Lee rang through, Ty swiftly took the initiative, switching to a more confrontational stance. She was supposed to be leaving for Ohio that day, so it was becoming a case of now or never. Ty plunged in: 'I don't . . . what the hell's going on, Lee? They've called . . . they've been up to my parents again. They've got my sister now, asking her questions. I don't know what the hell's going on.'

They were coming after her, she knew it. Her family were nervous wrecks, her mom had been calling.

'You evidently don't love me any more,' she continued. 'You don't trust me or anything. I mean, you're gonna let me get in trouble for something I didn't do.'

'Tyria, I said I'm NOT. Listen. Quit crying and listen!'

'I can't help it. I'm scared shitless.'

Lee told Ty she should tell the police whatever she needed to tell them. She loved her.

'I'm not so sure any more,' Ty replied, sounding weak.

'I love you. I really do. I love you a lot.'

'I don't know whether I should keep on livin' or if I should . . .'

'No, Ty. Ty, listen. Ty, listen,' Lee said, cutting off her negative train of thought.

'Why?'

'Just go ahead and let them know what they need to know what they wanna know or anything, and I will . . . I will cover you, 'cause you are not . . . you're innocent.'

'I know I am.'

'And I know you are. I will let them know that.'

Ty went off to blow her nose while Lee held on.

'Tyria, listen, honey,' Lee continued.

'What?'

'I'm not gonna let you go to jail. Listen, if I have to confess, I will.'

There it was, the elusive promise. Unable to hear but getting the gist of what was going on, the officers in the adjoining room held their breath. Ty pushed her luck further, asking Lee why she'd done what she did? Lee didn't know. Suspicion rising again, she asked Ty if she had come to Florida to talk to detectives. Ty denied it.

'Ty, listen to me. I don't know what to say, but all I can say is self-defence.'

'OK.'

'All right? All I can say is that, all right? All right? Did you hear me?' Lee asked, nervously.

'Yes, I heard ya.'

'I'm not letting you go to jail.' Lee muttered something Ty couldn't hear. '. . . 'cause you didn't do anything. I love you. I won't let this happen to you.'

Ty was crying quietly, but Lee wouldn't let her hang up the phone. She couldn't bear the inevitable parting just yet.

'I just don't understand why you did it,' Ty went on.

'I don't either. I'm telling you, I don't. Tyria, I'm so in love with you, I never wanted to leave you. You don't know how much I love you.'

Then Lee let slip her intention to revert to her earlier line of defence—that she couldn't help it if she rode in the car of someone who got hurt later. Hearing that, Ty insisted again that Lee must tell the truth, that she wouldn't lie for her. Lee told her she didn't have to, she didn't know what happened anyway. Lee offered to say she was driving the car they wrecked, but Ty refused.

Lee's tears were tumbling, too, as she promised the woman who was surely the love of her life that she wouldn't let her take the fall for her, even though the price she'd pay would be death.

'You want me to ask one of the guards to come to the door and let me go ahead and talk to 'em and tell 'em I'm the one?' Lee asked.

'If you want to.'

'I will do that for you.'

Suddenly, Lee felt motivated to call her sister, Lori, and tell her what was going on. She wanted Ty to try to call her. Alluding to them cryptically, never using the word 'murder', Ty said, 'I mean, I know of three, so . . . I mean, that's bad enough right there.'

They took a ten-minute break then Lee called Ty back. She was ready to get on with it. But she wished none of this had happened, that they still were together.

They must have got fingerprints from that car, Lee speculated. She loved Ty, who was as innocent as apple pie, right next to God. She'd get into the Bible real hard, and die knowing she'd go to heaven and would see her mother.

'When I die,' she said, 'my spirit's gonna follow you and I'm gonna keep you out of trouble and shit, and if you get in an accident, I'll save your life and everything else. I'll be watching you.'

'OK.'

'I won't watch ya when you have sex, though. When you have sex, I won't watch ya, but I'll watch ya every other way. OK?'

Suddenly, she was facing her future, wondering what happened to people on Death Row. Did they keep them in a cell their whole life, or what? Ty came out with another suicide threat, more direct this time, but Lee shouted her down. She would confess, and Ty wouldn't even have to go to prison.

'And I'll probably die of a broken heart or a heart attack. I probably won't live long, but I don't care. Hey, by the way, I'm gonna go down in history.'

'Huh,' Ty said.

'Yep. I'll be like . . .'

'What a way to go down in history,' Ty interjected in disgust. 'That's something really to be proud of, isn't it?'

'No. I'm just saying . . . if I ever write a book, I'm gonna have . . . give you the money. I don't know. I just . . . let me tell you why I did it, all right?'

'Mmmm . . . mm.'

'Because I'm so . . . so fuckin' in love with you that I was so worried about us not having an apartment and shit, and I was scared that we were gonna lose our place, believing that we wouldn't be together. I know it sounds crazy but it's the truth.'

Ty agreed it sounded crazy. She persuaded Lee to let her off the phone so she could go and buy some beer to help calm her down. Lee said she would call back in half an hour. It would be their last call. Ty had promised to catch the 3 p.m. bus out of town.

Lee renewed her resolve to tell all. Her life was messed up anyway, and she didn't want to go on wandering and wandering. Her life was a fucking wreck. She didn't deserve to live any more . . . but she wasn't going to commit suicide or anything. She was a good girl. She just didn't understand what she'd done.

Ty grabbed her chance and went on one last fishing expedition for her own sake and for the cops: 'How much of it don't I know?' she asked.

Lee declined to answer that. The less she knew, the better for her. She loved Ty because she was sweet and innocent and kind. Too kind, perhaps, Ty asked? Lee was sorry if she'd taken advantage of her. She'd been really in love with her and still was.

'Well, you'll probably have to get over that now,' Ty retorted, not unsympathetically.

Ty could hear Lee call across to Officer Marjorie Bertolani, saying she needed to talk to her when she got off duty. She was a good woman, that officer, and Lee had decided she was going to confess to her. Her thoughts were coming fast and furiously.

'I knew that my life was fucked when I left home at fifteen. I've had my glory days. I've had my fucking fun. Now it's over.'

Lee didn't want to hang up just yet. She knew it would be their last call. If they'd stayed in the trailer for $150 a month, this would never have happened. She wished she'd never met Toni and another woman, Barb, who turned her into a lesbian. Then she fucked up, she mused, because when she loves someone, she loves them with all her heart and soul and mind and she'll do *anything*. She'll go nuts. She didn't want to hurt people. She did go nuts. Right in her soul, right then, she couldn't do what she'd done. She regretted it all. And she thought she deserved to die. She hoped they would go ahead and fry her. Then she'd go up to Heaven and get right with the Lord.

'And just do me a favour,' she told Ty. 'Be good. Don't ever get involved with somebody like me and don't get involved with anybody, because you never know what that person's gonna do. Love does strange things.'

37

Sobbing and distraught, Lee flopped down on a chair in the day room. Across the table was Marjorie Bertolani, the officer she'd called out to from the pay phone as she was giving Ty her word that she'd make a clean breast of it. Bertolani had told Lee she'd be off-duty at 4 p.m. and could talk then, but Lee couldn't wait that long. It was 10 a.m. and suddenly everything was going haywire. Bertolani, who'd got wind of what to expect from the cell block's 'mystery guest' via inmate gossip, listened intently as Lee announced that she'd done something terrible, something she had to get off her chest.

Safely assured that Bertolani was a Christian, Lee told her of her drunken confession one night to her female lover (whom Bertolani thought Lee called Tessie) regarding a murder. Bertolani quickly made one thing clear: anything Lee told her couldn't be in confidence. She was duty bound to repeat it to her superiors. Lee kept talking. She desperately wanted to go to heaven and was afraid she wouldn't; that's why she was compelled to confess. She'd talk to investigators, police, anyone.

'What would *you* do?' Lee implored Marjorie Bertolani.

'I'd ask for forgiveness. And I'd forgive myself,' the officer replied, making a mental note that Lee might be a suicide risk. Soon after, she and several other officers were escorting Lee down to the office of the superintendent of corrections.

Larry Horzepa had snapped to attention the minute he received a phone call summoning him to the operations centre. As he pulled into the parking lot, Sergeant Jake Erhardt greeted him with news that was music to his ears: 'Wuornos wants to talk to local investigators, and you and Bruce Munster are going to go on over there and speak to her.'

Jerry Thompson was originally lined up to do the all-important interview with Munster, but since Wuornos was being housed in Volusia's jail, one interviewer needed to be local. Horzepa, the Mallory expert, was the natural choice to supplement Munster, who had an overview of all the homicides from his task force work.

Munster's adrenalin should also have been pumping at what was, by anyone's standards, a career highpoint, yet he felt as sick as a dog. Struggling under the effects of flu, he fantasised about being tucked up in bed. Who'd want to conduct the ultimate, crucial interview feeling like that? Just his bad luck.

Outwardly calm, Larry Horzepa was nevertheless on full alert as he finally came face to face with the woman he believed had killed Richard Mallory. Horzepa gave great credit to Ty Moore's contribution for having brought them thus far. Had Lee not been utterly convinced that pressure was being brought to bear on her beloved Ty's family, and that police had been in Ohio 'harassing' them, he strongly suspects Lee might now still be languishing in jail without having spoken a single incriminating word.

Horzepa was reasonably confident that Ty had not played an active role in at least Mallory's homicide, but didn't see her as lily-white either, and was decidedly curious to hear what Lee would say on that score. Had Ty been covering up for her? Had she sold any of the victims' property or helped Lee out somehow?

Interviewing Ty between the crucial phone calls, he'd been struck by her matter-of-factness. As far as he could tell, she'd been truthful. Everything he tried to verify checked out. 'I felt that she was giving a hundred per cent when she was talking to us,' he recalls.

Then again, she came across like a woman who had control over her own life: 'I really didn't see her being manipulated by Lee.'

His prime agenda that afternoon was to do everything in his power to ensure that when Lee Wuornos walked into court the case would be watertight. He wanted the jury weighing the facts to have not a shadow of doubt that it was she who'd ended Mallory's life. He wanted them to realise, as he did, that she possessed the kind of detailed information that could only have come from the murderer.

Events were suddenly moving fast, but the interview strategy had been carefully planned. Two inquisitors seemed the optimum number with which to get the best out of a delicate situation. They didn't need too many voices chiming in. It would be too distracting. Besides, extra officers might make her more apprehensive. They definitely wanted her as calm and relaxed as possible.

Horzepa and Munster faced an enviable challenge but a somewhat daunting task in confronting this alleged serial killer. The pressure was on: they had to deliver the goods. While all indications pointed to her being ready to spill the beans, no one knew her true state of mind or quite what might happen once she faced two officers in an interview room. This apparent willingness and resolve to come clean to save Ty's skin might be very shaky indeed. One wrong word could make her clam up.

If she requested a public defender and heeded their inevitable advice not to say any more on the grounds that what she did say might incriminate her, the whole thing could all be over in a flash. Bang might go their only bite at talking to her directly.

Horzepa and Munster were in total accord on one thing: they needed to cover their rear ends in every which way possible. If Lee Wuornos did confess, they didn't want to leave themselves vulnerable to the slightest suggestion of impropriety later as to just how that confession was elicited. Gearing themselves up for what inevitably would be a potentially controversial piece of evidence in terms of its admissibility, they took the precaution of having the videotape and audio recorders whirring when they and Wuornos first walked into the empty interview room.

The tape began with a close-up on an empty chair and the officers introducing themselves to Lee. (Larry Horzepa, of course, had arrested her outside the Last Resort but she apparently did not recognise him.) This introduction ritual would have been ludicrous had Munster and Horzepa already spent time with Lee, and would become important later.

Sauntering in, their casual demeanours belied the full agendas they carried close to their chests. Including their own cases, they were questioning on a total of eight homicides in which Lee was a suspect.

Richard Mallory.

Troy Burress.

David Spears.

Dick Humphreys.

Charles Carskaddon.

Walter Gino Antonio.

There were also the two disappearances where cars had been found but no bodies. Peter Siems, and Curtis Reid (the Titusville man who went missing in September), might or might not have met tragic ends at the hands of Wuornos. (The case of Douglas Giddens, the Marion County victim with the .38 bullet to the head, had been solved. Someone else had killed him.)

Privately, Munster thought Reid's disappearance was probably unconnected. His Olds Ciera had been dirty and the car keys were found under the seat, yet it was found parked near an interstate system. That much fitted the picture. Other things bothered Munster, however. Reid's car was found in a shopping mall lot. Wuornos generally tried to hide cars in the woods or some other out-of-the-way spot.

More crucial, to him, was that she'd driven Walter Gino Antonio's maroon Grand Prix during the same time span. How could she drive two cars at once? But he knew enough to know that nothing could be taken for granted or assumed. She couldn't be eliminated from Reid's case.

As they began, the investigators had no clue what was in store, but as the interview got under way, Horzepa felt a small surge of confidence. It seemed clear that 'she was relieved that we knew, and that she just basically wanted to get it over with'. He could hardly fathom the stress of keeping such crimes buried inside her.

Sure enough, Lee did exercise her right to have a lawyer present. Larry Horzepa swiftly excused himself and put in an urgent call to the public defender's office. They promised to dispatch an attorney, and fast. While they waited, Lee's verbal diarrhoea continued, confirming Horzepa's belief about her need to get it off her chest.

He and Munster, meanwhile, sat back and listened, mindful of the fine line they were treading, hands metaphorically shackled behind their backs. Their goal was to interact with Lee just enough to sustain her mood of co-operation. But it was imperative that they didn't question her about the crimes. More than once, the officers interrupted her self-incriminating chatter: 'Lee, let me stop you just a second,' Munster said at one point. 'You know, you've exercised your right to have an attorney here and maybe you shouldn't be talking about these things.'

Inadvertently adding a little levity to the proceedings, Munster brought Lee some coffee in a mug bearing the slogan 'If it feels good, do it. If it feels great, do it again.' Reading it aloud, Lee laughed.

'I guess I should have read it before I brought it in,' Munster said wryly.

'That's fine sexually,' Lee added. 'But don't go around killing somebody when you don't have to.'

When Mr O'Neill appeared, sporting an Irish brogue you could cut with a blunt butter knife, he cautioned Lee that these investigators were *not* her friends, but were police officers doing their jobs. He consulted with her privately but his repeated attempts to show her the wisdom of silence (at one point, hammered home in a marathon forty-minute session) were brushed aside with complete lack of interest. Lee was hell-bent on giving the interview whatever he said. Would Lee like him to stay or leave? She didn't care.

What followed was a certainly voluntary confession that, despite off-the-record breaks when O'Neill periodically talked further to Lee, gave birth to three hours of videotape. What propelled Lee was difficult to miss. Over and over, she reiterated her desire to clear Tyria, to distance her lover from her crimes. Ty didn't know those cars were the cars of dead people, she claimed. She'd told her she borrowed them. She didn't know anything, other than what she'd heard Lee mumble or murmur in her drunken state which could all have been lies. She had told her about Richard Mallory and the body beneath the rug because she knew she'd see it on the news. 'I was trying to be a show-off is what I was doing,' she said. Apparently, to Lee, murder was an achievement to brag about.

The session rambled, veering somewhat chaotically from victim to victim, with the detectives struggling to keep it on a comprehensible track and to pin down the key elements they needed. Horzepa's focus was on Mallory, of course. It was his jurisdiction and would probably be the first and a crucial case. Lee's own testimony could provide a massive missing piece in what seemed an astonishingly complex puzzle. He wanted to hear everything that transpired that night between her and Mallory and he told her to take her time telling it.

She claimed that it was only in the past year she seemed to have hit all these problems with guys giving her a hassle.

'People just started messin' with me . . . they just started comin' like flies on shit, startin' to mess with me,' she said.

What would turn out to be crucial later was that at no time did Lee claim that Mr Mallory had beaten, raped or brutalised her.

'In my sixteen years of law enforcement experience,' Larry Horzepa later reflected, 'any time that I've dealt with a rape victim, or a victim of a violent crime, the first thing that comes out—after being able to positively identify the person that did it—they'd give me a very descriptive, exact, detailed account of what happened to them. And she never did that in any of the cases.'

If anything, this suspected serial killer seemed singularly unaffected by her plight and by the stories she told detectives. Bruce Munster and Larry Horzepa registered, without showing it on their faces, the truly chilling measure of her dissociation. Horzepa wanted to pin her down as much as possible. 'Let me ask you something, Lee. Uh, you said that you carried the gun for protection. Is that correct?'

'Yeah. Yes.'

'OK. Uh, from all the shootings that you have told us about, for the most part, you've always gotten the drop on these guys. You've been able to get your gun and point it at them.'

'Uh-huh.'

'Right?'

'Right.'

'OK. At that particular time, you were in control. Why didn't you just run? Why didn't you . . .'

'Because I was always basically totally nude with my shoes off and everything and I wasn't gonna run through the woods and briars and the . . .' her voice trailed off.

'No, but still. Like I say, you're in control. You got that gun. You could go ahead and get dressed while you had, you know, them do whatever you basically wanted. Why did you go ahead and shoot these people?'

'Because they physically fought with me and I was . . . well, I guess I was afraid, 'cause they were physically fighting with me and I . . . what am I supposed to do, you know? Hold the gun there until I get dressed and now I'm gonna walk outta here? When the guy, you know, might . . . you know, run me over with his truck or might come back when I'm walking out of the woods or something . . . uh, have a gun on him, too, or something. I didn't know if they had a gun or not.'

'So was it . . . was it your intent, during each of these times, to kill this person so that they couldn't come back at you later?'

''Cause I didn't know if they had a gun or anything. I . . . once I got my gun I was like, "Hey, man, I've gotta shoot you 'cause I think you're gonna kill me." See?'

'What about the ones who didn't have a gun, like Mr Mallory?'

'I didn't know they had . . . didn't have a gun.'

'OK,' said Horzepa, 'so you were taking no chances.'

Among the many muddled story strands Lee gave the two investigators was a lead on the missing Peter Siems. She told them that she'd dumped his body somewhere up in Georgia, but even with aid of a map, she was unable to remember where.

(Criminal Intelligence Analyst, Claudia Swain, who had already enlisted the FBI's help in searching for all unidentified bodies reported by law enforcement agencies between November 1989 and January 1991, compared their data with Wuornos's input, but drew a blank, too.)

By the conclusion of their interview, despite the repeated

warnings of public defender O'Neill, Lee had effectively incriminated herself in seven homicides.

The investigators knew, however, that there was a good chance that there might be more victims out there; victims who might never be discovered.

Mary Ann was still terribly shocked and upset when Henry got there. She just couldn't believe that her stepdaughter was mixed up in something like this. Tracey was also distraught. But they were both co-operative, and Tracey presented Henry with a pair of scissors which had come from Lee and a Sea World brochure from her visit there in Siems's car.

On 17 January, a dive team finally recovered Lee's nine-shot .22 calibre revolver from the bottom of Rose Bay where it lay in a suitcase along with a set of handcuffs and a flashlight.

Also on the 17th, Sheriff Moreland notified the press that the 13-month-long investigation was over and that Aileen Carol Wuornos had been charged with one count of first-degree murder. Other charges were pending.

On the night of 18 January, just two days after Lee's confession, correctional officer Susan Hansen was perched on a chair outside her room, watching her through the glass. Lee's every word, cough or bathroom visit was being logged while she was on 15-minute watch in the medical segregation unit which was occasionally used to isolate an inmate. (She was not ill, but had at the time been prescribed a mild tranquilliser.) Susan Hansen, like her colleagues, had been instructed not to initiate any conversations with their celebrated inmate, but merely to document whatever she said. They were to restrict their comments to 'Here's your food' or 'Do you need to take a shower?'

Medic Robert John Heaton III, a staff nurse, somehow missed that briefing, however. When he walked back to the filing cabinets to retrieve a chart, he noticed Wuornos poring over the local Daytona paper's story about her, making comments and laughing. Struck by how cheerful she was, he asked her if any of what was printed was true? Not all of it, said Lee, claiming that she and Ty had been together six years, not four. Was she really a working girl, Heaton asked? Both Heaton and Hansen looked a little aghast as Lee boasted of having had over 250,000 men in the past nine years.

When Heaton left, Lee, who was standing with one foot propped on the room's open toilet, asked Susan Hansen if she'd read the story too? Hansen hadn't, but that didn't stop Lee chatting on for hours without encouragement. Hansen struggled to keep up, taking notes as she spoke. When Lee asked if she was going to report their conversation, she merely shrugged non-committally. She was afraid to say anything because she'd been explicitly briefed not to.

Instead, she jotted the crucial words and phrases Wuornos uttered. Lee spoke, specifically, of shooting the guy with the .45 (Charles Carskaddon). If she hadn't killed him, he would have killed other people. Hansen just listened. And some of what Lee said lodged permanently in her brain. She would remember it, with or without notes. At one point, Lee said: 'I figured if these guys lived and I got fried for attempted murder, I thought, fuck it, I might as well get fried for murder instead.' She reported one victim as saying, 'I'm going to die. Oh, my God, I'm dying.'

Hansen also reported Lee saying that she was doing some good, killing these guys because otherwise they'd have hurt someone else:

'I had lots of guys, maybe ten to twelve a day. I could have killed all of them, but I didn't want to. I'm really just a nice person. I'm describing a normal day to you here, but a killing day would be just about the same. On a normal day we would just do it by the side of the road if they just wanted [oral sex] or behind a building or maybe just off the road in the woods if they wanted it all.

'On a killing day, those guys always wanted to go way, way back in the woods. Now I know why they did it: they were gonna hurt me.'

Hansen noticed that Lee was almost jovial, laughing easily. And she seemed calm, not sad.

'Never once,' Hansen reported, 'did she say, "I'm upset about this."'

Reflecting on the confession, Bruce Munster felt it had been curiously anti-climactic. Lee had held no great surprises for him, somehow. He rated her a smart criminal, well above average. Her curiosity about how she had been caught was largely intellectual; like that of a professional, interested in why a plan hadn't worked as expected. She'd forgotten the thumbprint on the pawn shop receipt. His theory was that her motive was purely monetary.

'She's a pretty rough-looking girl right now, but if you look at the pictures of her when she was younger, she was an attractive young lady. I think she was able to get money, either hustling, scamming the guys out of it, or as a prostitute.

'The latter years, she's pretty rough looking, she's drinking. She's obnoxious when she drinks. I don't know where you draw the line. Is it one beer, two beers, three beers, a six-pack, a twelve-pack, or whatever? But at some point in time, when she's drinking, she's obnoxious. She needs money. She's got bills that she has to pay, just like she said. She needs the money, and I think that she took these men out and she killed them. She definitely says she killed to eliminate the witnesses. She says, "You don't understand. I couldn't do my job. If I didn't kill these guys, I couldn't do my job." Why? "Because the cops would have my face plastered up everywhere, and I couldn't work."'

Larry Horzepa observed that 'She ran through the gamut of emotions. She went from basically almost defiant, all the way to crying. My personal opinion is that there was no doubt or no mistaking what she did. I have no doubt at all that she meant to kill these people. But as far as remorse? There was no remorse I could detect.'

The overriding impression to strike Horzepa was the way she tried to justify what she had done, claiming none of it was her fault. She'd been backed into a corner by Ty, and since she had no choice but to talk to officers in great and incriminating detail, she seemed determined to try to show herself in the best possible light. Larry Horzepa had this sense of the underlying message: 'It was like, "Hey, I've had a terrible childhood. This is rough, and none of this is my fault. I'm just a victim of my upbringing, and these people deserved it because they were trying to hurt me.'"

He did not doubt that she was the product of her environment, but he was no bleeding heart for Lee Wuornos. He felt her crimes were planned.

'She had her mind made up. I have no doubt about that . . . that there was something that occurred between these men and her that made her decide that these men were going to die. And, you know, there was absolutely no doubt in her mind that she was going to do this, everything from wiping down the cars to getting rid of the evidence in different locations. And she was going to do everything in her power not to get caught, so that she could continue to enjoy her freedom.'

He was puzzled and intrigued by what set her off after not 250,000 men but 'I'll conservatively say hundreds', and spent many long hours pondering why. But there were no concrete answers.

'For someone to talk about going out and doing their job as a prostitute and then going ahead and differentiating between having a regular business day with customers and a killing day, you know. Obviously when someone is in a mind-set of "I'm going to kill today" then as far as I'm concerned, they've got it planned out. They know exactly what they're going to do, how they're going to do it, and where they're going to do it. It's just a matter of picking the person that they've decided is going to fall prey.'

38

Even though the suspect was behind bars, FDLE agents systematically combed through the list of men whose business cards had the dubious honour of taking pride of place in Lee's wallet. None belonged to cops, despite her repeated boasts, but each card owner had a story to tell.

She had told George Trujillo, who gave her a ride in his truck in the spring of 1988, that she was hitchhiking to Fort Myers to pick up a Corvette. He couldn't remember giving her a business card and suspected she must have taken it. 'That's her!' he said, picking Lee out of the photopack special agents Walter Rice and James Brady showed him.

She flagged down Joe Palak in Pasco County in the summer of '89. It was on 52 just past a traffic accident, which is why he was moving slowly enough for her to bend down and knock on the passenger window, asking for a ride to I-75. Spotting the holster he had in his car by the console, she asked if he was a cop. The holster might explain why she didn't proposition him sexually and seemed in a hurry. Palak also picked Lee out in a photopack line-up.

Pompie Carnley picked her up in the spring of 1990 on I-75 and I-4, the same junction where Richard Mallory picked her up. It was raining. He didn't think she looked like a hooker or a hobo, so he took her back to his home for a couple of beers, then invited her to ride with him further up I-75. During that leg of the journey, he claimed she repeatedly offered sex for money. Her car had broken down in Sarasota, and she needed $200. Could he help her out? She would do anything for the money. He turned her down but the requests didn't stop until he showed her his empty wallet. He kept a pile of loose change in the car, to which she helped herself.

At the intersection of US 98 and 19, she asked him to turn south on 19, then instructed him to turn down a side road where they stopped after twenty-five yards or so to answer a call of nature. Making it sound like some kind of werewolf-like transition, Carnley, a veteran of Vietnam and Korea, then claims that Lee changed before his very eyes and as she came around the back of his jeep behind him, the hairs on the back of his neck jumped up on end. He had to get out of there, so he hopped in the Jeep and drove away, leaving Lee just standing there.

They were within half a mile of the area where David Spears' body was found on 1 June 1990.

In February '91, Jim Brady and Walter Rice also interviewed Dennis Sobczak, the man who'd reported his .38 stolen by Lori Grody back in 1985. He couldn't pick her out of a photopack; it had been too long.

After Lee's arrest, newspapers reported how she'd slept in a drunken stupor on the old tan car seat on the porch outside the Last Resort on her last night of freedom. And a handful of women, heartbroken over missing husbands, descended on the biker bar clutching photographs of their men, hoping someone had seen them. Sad, Cannonball thought. But he didn't recognise a single one of them.

When Lee Wuornos was newly behind bars, Lori Grody's 8 a.m. lunch break (she did shift work) was interrupted when her boss told her that four policemen were outside asking to speak with her. Immediately, she thought it must have something to do with Aileen. 'I knew I didn't do nothing wrong, and who else is there? I thought, "Oh, shoot!"'

Nervously, she went into the office to meet them. It seemed to Lori that the two senior officers, Detective-Sergeants Leonard Goretski and Gregory Somers, were inexplicably cheerful and smiley as they enquired whether she had a sister named Aileen Wuornos.

'Yes. Is she dead?' asked Lori. Her first thought was that they were there to tell her that her sister had ended up in the bottom of a ditch somewhere, having finally hitched the wrong ride. In the months before the police picked her up at work, because it had been so long since she'd heard from Aileen, Lori had taken to scanning the newspaper's deaths column, half expecting to read that a transient girl had been shot or killed. Usually the calls from Aileen came every year or so. It had been so long, she *must* be dead.

'No, she's not dead,' the officers replied, still very cordial.

'I take it she's in trouble?'

'Yeah.'

The officers had Lori accompany them to the police station in Traverse City some forty miles away, where they quizzed her about Aileen's visits to Michigan. They declined to enlighten her any further about what was going on. Aileen hadn't yet been arrested or formally charged, they explained. They couldn't elaborate in case Lori opened her mouth and told anyone. In her usual passive fashion, Lori didn't push. But during the four-hour interview, their line of questioning about Aileen's troubled past led her to speculate. If Aileen wasn't dead, perhaps she had killed somebody? While it was a truly preposterous and irrational line of thought for most sisters, to Lori it seemed almost logical. She did learn that Aileen had stolen her i.d. years earlier and had been using it in Florida with her own picture imprinted on a driver's licence in Lori's name.

'They said they knew who I was, but they had to prove it because she'd used my i.d. when she was arrested. I had a list in Florida against my name with so many tickets she had and arrests. They said the way to clear my name was to prove who I was with fingerprints and credit cards.'

Meanwhile, Ervin's aunt, who worked with Lori, had telephoned his parents who in turn called Erv at work to let him know his wife had been taken in for questioning. Erv telephoned Traverse City. 'My wife was abducted from work tonight by four policemen,' he said. An officer quickly came on the line to reassure him. They didn't believe Lori was in any trouble; she was just helping them with their enquiries.

'I hadn't hung up the phone more than ten minutes, when four

343

of them were right at the house,' Erv recalls. 'Two of them were left with me, and the others took off.' He had no better luck than his wife in eliciting information. When the Grodys were reunited later that night, they spent a fitful, sleepless night.

The next day, Erv was interviewed again at work. He was shown his wife's 'rap sheet' from Florida. He thought back to the day Lori had been stopped for driving with a headlight out. The officer planned to run a check on her, but was interrupted by a call for an accident down the road. Erv realised Lori could easily have been arrested.

After everything they'd been through with Aileen, nothing could have prepared them for the moment they heard that the police believed that Lori's troubled sister had been involved in multiple murders.

Stunned, Lori didn't want to believe a word, and at first she didn't. Ultimately, it was TV that made the horror of it all sink in. Even so, there was something surreal about hearing that Aileen was suspected of murdering seven men. The first two reports Lori saw didn't carry Aileen's photograph, then suddenly, the third did. Up popped Aileen's face looking so terrible, so manly, so rough and rugged, her skin all pitted, that Lori could barely believe it was her. Watching in her bedroom, Lori broke down, her body racked with sobs. She felt anger, fear and shame, humiliation and guilt. The hardest emotions in the world collided and all began their painful procession.

For shell-shocked Lori, hearing her long-lost sister's voice on the other end of the line, calling from jail, was the next emotional assault. Within moments, all her fury at Aileen for bringing disgrace on the family, for shattering her life, *all* their lives, bubbled like bile to the surface. She could hardly hold it back.

Aileen, on the other hand, sounded soft and gentle—if not exactly remorseful. Repeatedly, she denied to Lori that she was guilty of the murders.

'I know what you did, and all you have to do is just admit it!' Lori cried in exasperation. 'Admit what you did and get the trials over with. And you'll probably get the electric chair!'

'Who told you that?' Aileen demanded agitatedly.

'Nobody. To me, it just seems automatic after murdering so many men that you'll get the electric chair.'

'Don't listen to the news reports and don't listen to other people,' Aileen advised her.

Lori soon realised that Aileen simply didn't grasp the fact that she was in deep, deep trouble. Clearly, she was not prepared for the possible eventuality of being sentenced to death. If anything, it sounded to Lori as if she truly expected to be set free and let back out on the streets at any moment. The more Aileen talked, the more Lori's frustration mounted. Obviously, she didn't think she'd done anything terribly bad. If anything, she seemed to think she'd done some good. Putting her behind bars clearly had been a major mistake that would quickly be rectified.

To Lori, she sounded like a child being slapped on the wrist for doing something wrong, who takes the slap fully expecting that then all will immediately be forgiven.

'It was like she knew, but she didn't know,' Lori recalled. 'I think her mind is so messed up, she's not dealing with reality.'

Another call followed shortly after, but Aileen's mood had done an about-face. The conversation was laced with screaming abuse. To Lori, it was the last straw from this sister who had caused her so much pain.

'Don't call here again!' she shouted finally, exasperated and furious.

'I won't!' Aileen retorted.

And she didn't. She wrote instead. But the letters from those first days in jail were equally dramatic in their contrasts. Sisterly love and nostalgia one minute, ready to meet her maker the next, followed by anger and venom. For all the lashing out and hateful words they exchanged, however, Lori never seriously doubted Aileen's deep affection for her.

It was telling that when she was arrested, one of her very few personal possessions in the whole world was a letter from Lori, written way back in 1975, which had somehow survived with her the intervening years. From town to town, sleeping rough, hustling, living one day to the next, she'd clung to that letter. In it, Lori had given directions to her home in Mancelona. Symbolically, to Aileen it represented tangible evidence that somebody wanted her. Perhaps for that reason alone she'd kept it close to her heart through thick and thin.

'I don't care what she says, I think she still loves me dearly,' Lori observes. 'That letter was the only thing she had left from family to hang onto. That's a long time to keep a letter, and living the life she lived, it's amazing that anything survived all her travels, isn't it?'

In the first days after Aileen's arrest, Lori had limited capacity for such reflection, however. She was consumed with terror about how her friends and workmates would react. What if everyone looked the other way or turned their backs when she walked into a room? What if her sons were ridiculed at school, or treated like outcasts? How would she bear it if everyone ostracised them, or her and Erv? In reality, she found everyone worlds more supportive than she could ever have hoped. All her fears proved unfounded. No one judged her or blamed her. In fact, no one even broached the subject unless she did so first.

'People know it's not my fault, and I didn't do it, and I'm not her,' she muses. 'But I couldn't believe it, because I went to work just like this—bawling my eyes out—because I didn't know what they'd do, and they were so nice.'

All the same, she felt reluctant to contact any of their old childhood friends. Perhaps they wouldn't like hearing from her? Maybe they wouldn't want anything to do with it, or her. She certainly wasn't keen on talking about it any more than she had to. Whenever she did, it was like a dam bursting, and she just cried and cried. Couldn't stop herself. She was only thankful her mother wasn't still around. It would have truly broken her heart.

Shame crept over her, deeper and more painful than she could ever have imagined. Lori was so ashamed that Aileen knocked down her ex-husband, Lewis Fell, that she couldn't bring herself to admit to the police that that was what had happened. Instead, when questioned, she simply perpetuated Aileen's lie that he'd attacked her. And if she found that well nigh impossible to swallow, this went beyond anything she could describe.

If there was ever a time in Lori's life when she might have gladly relegated Aileen to the position of being her niece, this surely was it. But, no. Murderer or no, Aileen would always be her sister.

As the weeks and months slipped by, Lori found herself running the full spectrum of feelings, plagued by a traffic of conflicting emotions. It was all so confusing. Sometimes she felt she hated Aileen when her head swam with thoughts of the victims and their families and what they'd all suffered. At other times, she just cried and cried and she'd realise that the tears she was shedding were for Aileen. Still loving her. Feeling sorry for her. Wondering what she could or should have done for her to make her life turn out differently. Waiting for news that she can't help feeling is inevitable: that Aileen has killed herself in prison. Wondering why it had to be this way.

'I still cry that we rejected her when she was little. The times she wanted to play and we wouldn't let her,' she reflects, her eyes brimming with tears.

She can't help feeling that had Aileen's uncontrollable tantrums and outbursts happened in the more psychologically enlightened eighties or nineties, rather than the sixties and seventies, someone might have paid attention to the danger signs, and Aileen might have gotten some psychiatric help.

'I think it started when she was little and I think there's always been something wrong up there,' says Lori, tapping her forehead.

At times, she'd feel a strong impulse to contact Aileen, but she'd quash the urge, still bound by her inhibitions about how she's perceived by others.

'It's image,' she admits. 'If I go see her, what are people going to think?'

Swallowing hard, she gives voice to the most difficult words of all—her opinion that her sister should die in the electric chair.

'I still love her, but there is no help for her. Not any more. No pills, no people to talk to. Even if they declared her insane, it wouldn't help for her to go somewhere or be locked away. I think she needs to be gone to relieve her own mind. Even though she may not believe that. Because I think if she ever got out, she'd do it again.

'The way her mind is about men, anyway, that's never going to change. Not after all these years. I think she should [die] just

347

to end her own life and end her misery, because it's never going to get any better now. Seems like if I was in her shoes I would want to die, just knowing what I did.'

In Ormond Beach, a stunned Sandy Russell had a lot of thinking to do. 'Oh God!' she thought, appalled. 'I've been sitting in the same room with this woman who killed all these people!'

Groping to understand what Lee had done, Sandy's mind worked overtime. If Lee killed Richard Mallory, she did it a few days after that first Thanksgiving Dinner when they met. She'd known Lee was uncomfortable around her at first. Could Lee have thought she was going to take Ty away from her? None of it made sense.

Tyria's role in the whole business was what Sandy had to fathom. Instinctively, Sandy felt sure that her friend couldn't possibly have been a party to murder, or have played any kind of active role. Never. Not possible. If anyone was able to prove to her that Tyria did have some involvement, 'I would really be shocked!' she said emphatically. 'I really don't think she could pull anything like that.'

Nevertheless, she still had to face some harsh realisations. Ty's complicity bothered her greatly.

'She knew what was going on and didn't do anything about her. She maybe could have saved somebody's life. Maybe *several* lives. That bothers me. I always thought Ty was stronger than that, that she could have done something. But you don't know how a person like Lee is to live with.'

Once Lee was behind bars, Ty telephoned Sandy; a call that took some courage.

'She was real shaky,' Sandy recalls. 'I guess she didn't know how I was going to react. I still care about her as a friend. I wanted to know why she couldn't come to me, and why she let this go on without doing anything. That's why I talked to her. I asked her all that. She said she was afraid of Lee and what she might do.'

Exactly why Ty was in fear of Lee mystified Sandy. 'That's what *I* couldn't understand. As much as Lee was in love with

Tyria . . . and Ty was a pretty strong person. How could she be afraid of Lee?

'I couldn't care less about Lee, but I still think a lot of Tyria. But it's wrong that she knew all of this, and had all of this stuff that didn't belong to her, and didn't think she could come to me or somebody else. I thought we were pretty close, too.'

Sandy ran her theory past Ty: could Lee have felt threatened by her presence? Ty didn't comment. She was too preoccupied with her own fear. She only prayed that Lee hadn't killed for the money.

At first, Cammie Greene felt sorry for Ty when she learned that Ty's lover was behind bars, but the twinge of sympathy was short-lived. The more she pondered the situation, the more her conviction grew that the two women had been planning this together all along. And she was shocked and full of disbelief that Tyria had gone along with it. Because she must have gone along with it. For all their fondness of Ty, Cammie and Dinky didn't buy the idea.

'Tyria was strong,' Cammie recalled. 'Tyria could take care of herself. One time, you could hear the walls banging and stuff and I opened the door to see what was going on and they were falling around fighting. Tyria told me to get out, that she could handle it.'

No, Ty hadn't been scared of Lee. But then, if Lee was killing guys and Ty was the only one who knew about it, perhaps that changed things.

Cammie also found it hard to believe that Ty would cut Lee off if she tried to tell her she had killed someone. If Lee had told Ty anything like that, she thinks Ty would have believed her and would not have been surprised. *She* certainly would have believed her and would not have been surprised. And she would have gone to the police.

Cammie still felt an abiding affection for Ty, despite their ugly parting, yet seeing Lee up on murder charges, she couldn't help feeling that justice wasn't being done while Ty walked away scot-free.

'She had to know about it from the beginning. I'm sure that's what that conversation was about,' she fretted. The way Cammie looked at it, 'Ty was tested by God, and failed, because people lost their lives . . .'

Cammie could see a certain perverted logic to the whole scenario, though. Neither Lee nor Ty had wanted to make it in the real world. They spurned responsibilities like paying rent and utilities. Lee was getting older and losing her looks. She had nothing saved for her future; no resources to fall back on. Cammie is sure she had the whole thing planned, and that stealing her licence was part of the scheme and a way of involving her.

Around the time of Lee's arrest, Cammie had learned of her own dose of unwelcome notoriety for which she had Lee to thank. Police officers and an FBI agent had called at the Publix store where Cammie supervised the meat and cheese sections. They'd found a lot of stolen property in a pawn shop under her name, they said. It was nothing to do with her, of course. She couldn't even remember the last time she'd been in a pawn shop. She was shown photographs of Lee and Ty and asked if she knew them, or had loaned either of them her licence. Cammie identified the pictures and explained that her licence had gone missing years ago. They seemed satisfied, and left.

Cammie saw Ty's role in the scheme as largely passive. Possibly nothing more than keeping her mouth shut. And once Ty left for Ohio, Cammie could envisage Lee waiting to get caught. Getting caught wasn't that big a deal, given her belief that she would get off with self-defence. Cammie thought she knew she'd be labelled a serial killer, but didn't think she'd get the electric chair:

'Because she was saying that she was going to do something that no woman had ever done before—and that would be being a serial killer.'

Looking back, other things would fall perturbingly into place. She did bring home an awful lot of cash to have made in prostitution. She wondered, too, about that mysterious white car they'd turned up with the day they'd moved out of her home? Thinking about it, she concluded that Richard Mallory was probably not Lee's first victim.

Dick Mills neither read the newspapers nor followed the news on TV, but his daughters, Tammy and Reveshia, upon whom Lee had made such an indelible impression, did. It was they who first heard of the arrest of Dick's unsavoury companion. Dick, putting together the pieces, realised a call to the cops might be in order. He had a hunch they'd be interested in the storage unit he'd once driven her to.

Dick, a man of no small temper, wasn't a bit thrilled to hear that he'd been featured in one of the less salubrious supermarket tabloids, the *Globe*. He'd spoken to a reporter who represented himself as being from the BBC, and taped an interview for that sterling organisation—only to find the *Globe* was carrying stills lifted from the tape and a ludicrous story about how he'd wanted to make the serial killer his bride. Livid, he took a yellow highlighter pen to it, marking all the 'errors'. The article was a blaze of yellow.

The piece said that Lee had revealed her secret fantasies to Mills, saying that a favourite involved having a black hood put over her head while tied to a tree in a forest.

'Then a guy would come up to her, rape her and then shoot her in the head,' Mills was quoted as saying. 'She said the killing would make her climax.'

Mills said he had talked to a lawyer about taking the *Globe* to court but was told that unless he could prove financial loss as a result of the story, it wouldn't be worth his while.

In fact, Lee did speak of a black hood, of a fantasy that she'd be lying in a cabin up in the mountains and a man would come through the window and have sex with her all night long. A not uncommon fantasy, say psychologists. The mystery, faceless stranger relieving the woman of responsibility for her lustful feelings. In Lee's case, it was also possible such a fantasy might pertain to subconscious memories of childhood sexual abuse.

Either way, it is a far cry from the idea that being shot in the head would make her, the victim, climax. The wild story made Dick Mills furious.

Looking back on his five wild days with Wuornos, Dick would not change his lingering feeling that she was a whole lot brighter than people had her pegged for. He felt that what she had 'was a whole game she's running. That's just what it is to her. And regardless of the outcome . . . she still plays rather brilliantly.'

With Lee's arrest, the victims' families had something new to come to terms with, too, and for Letha Prater, Troy Burress's sister, one of the hard parts was seeing Buddy turn into a faceless statistic, just one of Wuornos's victims.

'Buddy was not a group, he was a man,' she explained. 'A little boy that had a beautiful smile and he had pretty blue eyes. And I saw him grow up, you know? He was a decent person. He had a family. He liked to tell jokes; he had a million jokes. He loved to go home to his horses. This was his life. And it was taken by this person. The other men, too. They had their own lives. Seven slayings. And he's just a name. If you're going to give her a personality, give him a personality, too.

'From the word go, she has been nothing but a pain in the neck to anybody that was ever around her. Her childhood is not a concern of mine. My brother is my concern. I'm not concerned about her. My concern is that she die in the electric chair. That's what I want to happen, and I want to be there when she does.

'It don't get better. Not with his mother. And it don't get better with me. I've learned how to cope with it.' She sighs. 'It's never going to get any better. You have to try to let go, but it's hard. I say out loud, "He's gone. I'm never going to see him again." I think I have to, because I don't really want to admit he's gone, you know? You think, "Maybe that wasn't him?" I know it was! I just can't quite say he's gone.

'And I can't call him and say, "Hey Bud, my car's broke down. Will you give me a hand?" "Sure, where you at? Alaska? I'll be there." That's what he would have said. I tried not to abuse that. A lot of people never had that and never will have it, and I miss him, but I am so thankful that I did have that. I had fifty years of unconditional love.'

She weeps. An escape valve for some of the pain. She loved him so much. And although she has a husband and a daughter, Buddy—Buddy had been in her life so much longer. He was her best friend, her best buddy. It is one thing to lose someone you love who becomes sick and dies. But for a man who would not have hurt a soul to meet a violent death is something else again.

39

While getting caught may not have been on their agendas—consciously, at any rate—many serial murderers ultimately bask in their notoriety and relish all the attention. For someone very inadequate, which the serial killer most commonly is, to grace the cover of a magazine can prove a heady, seductive experience. A highly appealing perk.

Aileen Wuornos's craving for fame was in place long before she got her first taste of media power, indeed, long before she started looking for a writer to work on her autobiography. Cammie Greene could never get out of her mind Lee and Ty's talk of a mysterious scheme and how Lee said they'd be like Bonnie and Clyde.

Given Lee's determination to carve a place for herself in the spotlight, there was considerable irony in the fact that when her long-awaited shining moment in the public eye finally arrived she was overshadowed by global events, namely the Gulf War. Even after the Gulf War ended, her dubiously elite status as possibly the first full-blown woman serial killer didn't receive the scrutiny or attention one would have expected. She never did command equal time with Jeffrey Dahmer and his cannibalistic killings. While Dahmer's indescribably heinous crimes scored high on the revulsion scale, Wuornos's were continually downplayed by the national news.

The distinction seemed lost on Aileen, however. Behind bars, she revelled in the attention she did get, spouting more grandiosities than ever.

But the paucity of the coverage was curious none the less. It seemed that scrutinising the actions of the clearly deranged (if not legally insane) Mr Dahmer was much more compelling than analysing what had made a woman like Lee crash through the feminine taboos against violence, aggression and bloodlust.

Certainly, the public's imagination was grabbed by Dahmer and the horrifying revelation that police had instead of rescuing a victim who ran to them for help, led him back into Dahmer's chamber of horrors to meet his death. Wuornos, thankfully, was never so gruesome. But should not the public's imagination have been equally grabbed by the first woman to go out and kill a string of strangers in cold blood?

The discrepancy was sufficiently blatant that it begged the question: is the very idea of so cold-blooded a woman killer simply intolerable to many men? Men in droves lambasted the film *Thelma and Louise*—as if its cathartic enjoyment for women, and smorgasbord of vengeful fantasies, threatened their very beings—so perhaps Aileen Wuornos and the ramifications of her existence were too ugly a prospect to contemplate.

Women have long been accustomed to their vulnerability, to co-existing with the ever-present fear of being overpowered, to living daily with the need to be careful. For a man, the idea that he might be murdered while with a woman, and perhaps while anticipating sexual pleasure to boot, is anathema.

'If a man who thinks he's going to get a blow-job is suddenly blown away instead, that's pretty scary stuff for other men to deal with,' says film-maker Jackelyn Giroux, who did a deal with Aileen for her life story rights and who experienced first-hand the reluctance of male film and TV executives to discuss the subject matter.

Perhaps Wuornos is an extreme symbol of the suspected bottomless pit of women's rage. Perhaps, in an unwritten, unspoken way, the (predominantly male) media's collective unconscious decided to ignore her, to give her less air time and column inches, in the hope that she and what she represented would go away.

Aileen from a very early age was determined to make her mark on the world. And make it she undeniably did. That desire, that need, seems to have been a motivating force in a largely aimless life. With her notoriety comes an immortality, too. Truly lasting fame.

Over time, Robert Ressler, formerly of the FBI's Behavioral Sciences Unit, had come to believe that among male serial killers a desire for notoriety can be subtly motivating.

'I say subtly because what you'll find . . . often times, the men who get involved in these types of crimes are very inadequate, unsure people who start feeling an omnipotence and a control over society, and, of course, eventually a recognition as a serial killer. Some of these people actually enjoy the title.'

It may not be what she had in mind, but, perhaps, one day Lee Wuornos will, too.

Ironically, in her wish for fame and fortune, Lee could hardly be singled out for criticism. Her methods were, of course, truly abhorrent, but that's a different story. In looking for the lime-light, however, she merely represented the most visible tip of the heap.

Back on 4 February, Jackelyn Giroux was told that three Mar-ion County law enforcement officers were involved in a script that was in the works on the case and were supposedly involved in a deal with CBS and Republic Pictures. That very day Giroux heard the same story a second time from a Lorimar TV execu-tive with whom she was discussing her own script. Could three officers be involved in a movie deal so soon after the arrest and so far before trial? Giroux learned from Brian Jarvis, the man who had supervised the major crimes unit when the investiga-tion began, that he'd been moved sideways allegedly to make room for others. There were question marks, too, about the in-tegrity of the investigation. Ty Moore was rumoured to be in-volved in the deal, too. Had she been let off the hook because playing her as the innocent made a better story? Had Lee Wuornos become the fall guy?

Suddenly, the story of the three cops and their alleged movie deal became big news, and as the scandal took on a life of its own, Sergeant Bruce Munster, Captain Steve Binegar and Major Dan Henry would each come to rue the day they'd heard the names of Aileen Wuornos and Tyria Moore.

There was Geraldo Rivera's *Now It Can Be Told* producer,

Linda Sawyer, doggedly sniffing around town pursuing her story on Hollywood perhaps interfering with the course of justice.

There was Jackelyn Giroux on the warpath because she believed she'd been discriminated against. Everywhere she went in Hollywood, she was told that they couldn't read her script or do her movie because of the 'three cops', Republic Pictures, and CBS. Yet, officially, that deal was a figment of someone's imagination. Everyone denied such a deal existed.

To Giroux, hearing those repeated denials uttered while film industry folk kept telling her a script was being developed, was maddening. Signing up Wuornos's life story rights by 30 January, just three weeks after her arrest, had been an enterprising if controversial achievement on Giroux's part. (It was through Giroux, whom I knew from her days as a photojournalist, although our paths had not crossed in a decade, that I first learned of Aileen Wuornos.)

She pulled it off with the help of attorney Russell Armstrong, to whom she was referred by Lee's then defence attorney, Ray Cass. Jackye's passion was to tell the child abuse story that she suspected must have led to the killings. Pursuing her movie, Jackye would be accused of glorifying a killer and lining that killer's prison jumpsuit pockets. And when she received a letter from the office of Florida's Attorney-General, Robert Butterworth, she was frankly amazed.

She was, of course, already aware of the Son of Sam law, prohibiting a criminal from profiting from their crime, so was not surprised to learn that the State of Florida would attempt to put a lien on any money Lee might make. (Lee did not take this news so well and had in fact called Jackye, hysterical, a few days earlier, after receiving a similar letter.) It was a bridge Giroux had decided to cross when she came to it. But meanwhile she couldn't help wondering about these three officers and their potential profits.

She felt there was a little housecleaning that needed to be done in Florida before anyone chastised her. She was a professional film-maker, this was her job. What were cops doing, pretrial, talking about a deal with a woman like Tyria? Tyria may have been the prosecution's potential star witness, but she was no paragon of virtue. She had known about the murders and could have saved lives. She hadn't been arrested even though she'd gone back to Ohio with some of the dead men's possessions.

In fact, Tyria fell into a shadowy area of US law. Prosecuting her wouldn't have been quite as easy as everyone imagined, according to Ric Ridgway, who would have been the man to do it in Marion County. Ty wasn't an aider and abettor or a principal, who knew in advance of the murders, and assisted in the planning and carrying out of the crimes. So that was out. To charge her with being an accessory after the fact would require her to have done something to cover up the criminal's crime, or to help the criminal get away, or to have knowingly taken stolen property. Therein lay the rub. Ty was adamant that while she may have *suspected,* she did not have actual knowledge of the crimes, and it would have been tough to prove otherwise. In some states it is a crime to know of a homicide and not to go to the police. But under Florida law, to know what Lee had done and not to tell, did not actually constitute a crime.

Given the consensus that she neither encouraged nor participated in the murders, she was left alone.

Ultimately, of course, she had, however belatedly, also played what was viewed as a crucial role in bringing Wuornos to justice. She was a little fish, used to reel in a bigger fish. A common tactic. Everyone denied that she'd been given any kind of a deal or immunity. Nevertheless, the fact that Ty walked away and might end up making money from a movie bothered many. It seemed downright unfair.

Then when it came out that Ty was supposedly involved in some fashion with the three police officers and their possible movie deal, her not being prosecuted was viewed with even greater suspicion.

Most damning of all for the 'three cops': there was Sergeant Brian Jarvis, one of their very own brotherhood, popping up on TV and tossing lighter fuel on the fire. He had been elbowed out, he claimed, to make room for glory-seekers who suddenly smelled fame and fortune and wanted to be in on the triumphant arrest.

Within the department, the story went differently, of course. Jarvis had been moved because he wasn't performing. Whereas he'd claimed that the computer program he devised came up with the four names ultimately responsible for locating the two suspects, there was another side to the story. The counter-attack was that he'd ignored an earlier warning about spending undue amounts of time fiddling with computer programs, his great love, rather than keeping abreast of his investigation work. Certainly, Jarvis's claim to have been the first person to have realised that the killer or killers were female, seemed debatable.

In any event, he went out on a limb and started lobbing hand grenades back into his old department. Amidst a flurry of charges of sour grapes, he kept repeating his charges that evidence that suggested Tyria Moore's presence at one or more crime scenes was not followed up on. Usual procedure, he maintained, would have been to investigate those leads to the full before letting Tyria off the hook in return for testifying against her lover. Those three cops, he felt, had other motives for not following through, and weren't interested in pursuing those leads that might implicate Tyria Moore because she was more valuable to the movie as an innocent party.

Ignoring evidence for monetary motives was a serious charge. It was ugly, all of it, and it wasn't going away.

Why, Brian Jarvis wanted to know, had Dan Henry emerged from his usual supervisory stance to leap on planes and conduct the hands-on investigation in Ohio? (Jarvis wasn't alone in that observation, even within the ranks of law enforcement.) Jarvis and Jackelyn Giroux contended that Henry was playing a more colourful part with one eye on the future screenplay.

Captain Steve Binegar, an ex-FBI man, had fallen into the role of team commander on the Wuornos investigation. While there was no formal chain of command in effect between the different agencies people looked to Steve because of his rank. And when he and Henry went off on what might very easily have turned out to be a wild goose chase, eyebrows were raised all around. It seemed amazing that they were leaving the ship without a captain. Binegar later maintained that it wasn't unusual for him to travel on a major homicide case. (Binegar was also a close personal friend of Major Henry's; indeed it was Dan Henry who recruited him back from the FBI.)

Ultimately, Brian Jarvis's charges seemed shaky. Anita Armstrong, for instance, the cashier at the Speedway store in Wildwood, whose account (which put Ty in the vicinity of Dick Humphreys) he claimed had not been properly investigated, was discredited.

There was a fatal flaw in her eyewitness account that effectively demolished her credibility. One of the two women she'd seen that she believed matched the drawings was, she thought, black. By anyone's standards, this was no small discrepancy. Tyria, with her pale, freckled skin and Irish colouring, couldn't even pass for olive-skinned.

If more thorough investigation of Armstrong's story was, as Jarvis contended, a piece of detective work that fell through the cracks, unfortunately for him it turned out not to mean very much.

Meanwhile, the thrower of darts had left his own back exposed: he himself had signed a curious deal with agent/writer/entrepreneur Michael McCarthy to tell his own story. McCarthy paid $1 to cement their agreement and Brian Jarvis gave him $500 to get him started on trying to secure them a deal.

As Ric Ridgway observed, 'When cops and lawyers and murder defendants need agents, we've put the cart before the horse here.'

When in the summer Sheriff Moreland requested an investigation into the propriety of Munster, Binegar and Henry's behaviour, it was undertaken by the State Attorney's office with considerable vigour, but no differently from anything else the office approaches.

But Ridgway felt Bruce Munster and Steve Binegar erroneously suspected it had been undertaken with extra zeal because Ridgway's and Brad King's noses had been so visibly put out of joint over the sudden arrest. Had they been a little too thorough? Were they settling the score?

In fact, the investigation exculpated the trio of the allegation that they had actually received money for a movie deal and Ric

Ridgway trusted its findings: 'I don't believe they were paid anything. Now, if you come in and prove to me they did [receive money], I won't fall over dead, but I just don't think so.'

Bottom line, he says, 'If anybody was paid any money, then somebody's guilty of perjury, and I just don't see any of those guys risking their careers over $10,000 or $5,000.'

And $50,000? That was the amount bandied around and the amount that Ty Moore supposedly said Bruce Munster had mentioned. As he learned a little more about the entertainment business than he'd ever expected to, Ridgway came to believe that would be an unlikely sum to pay up front for an assignment of rights before a project was even underway.

Ridgway and an investigator visited Tyria Moore at Twyla's home as part of the enquiry and came away convinced that if Ty had been paid, she had hidden it very well.

'We were convinced she was being dead honest with us and she made clear that she hadn't been paid anything. She wouldn't *mind* being paid, she wouldn't object if somebody came along and gave her money, but nobody had.'

During the investigation, the three officers' bank records were not subpoenaed. Had they been, the antagonism would have ballooned, and for what? Hypothetically, the reasoning went, had money changed hands, it would not have been sitting smack bang in the middle of a cheque account. It would not have left a visible paper trail. It would have been, perhaps, stashed in a safety deposit box somewhere.

A New York magazine cover story by Eric Pooley in March 1992, entitled 'Cop Stars', pointed out another salient fact with regard to true crime films in an anonymous quote from a Hollywood producer: 'There's so much competition, you *can't* wait that long. So you have a wink or a handshake with the key players while the case is still going on. It's a huge grey area.'

Frayed nerves and friendships were put under even more stress by the circulation of the movie script itself. Either screenwriter, Fred Mills, had glamorised the roles played (not to mention the superior brain power and deductive abilities) of the three named cops, or the cops had done it themselves in telling their stories. Either way, it wouldn't sit well with the other key players.

Inevitably, the screenplay form telescopes events, and that compounded the erroneous impression given that the three officers had found Aileen Wuornos almost single-handedly. Munster always said it was very much a team effort, but that wasn't the way it was going to play on TV.

John Tilley and David Taylor were just a couple of other Marion County investigators who had made valuable contributions. And Brian Jarvis, while not exactly the man who solved the case either, also played a role.

Yet Taylor, Tilley and Jarvis, as they were moving in for the climax, suddenly found themselves out investigating old robberies while other officers were out there making the arrest.

All but the names of the three cops and Tyria Moore had been changed, too, reinforcing the assumption that those parties had been reimbursed. Yet none of the other key characters involved needed to be psychic to spot themselves in this *roman à clef.* Enough of the details were spot-on for them to know that the screenwriter had been privy to inside information.

The most likely scenario seemed to be that Munster, Binegar and Henry had begun talks for some kind of deal with enthusiasm and a surprising, but not implausible, degree of naivety. At the right time—after trial and conviction—there would have been nothing wrong with them telling their stories. Indeed, there would have been nothing new about it either. What *was* different and unpalatable to colleagues and victims' families alike, was the premature timing. When the unpopularity of the steps they had taken manifested itself so rudely, it seems they slammed on the brakes and backed off. By then, it was too late for the Teflon effect to save them.

Steve Binegar said in his deposition in January of 1992 that it was his understanding that before a movie could use his name they would need his permission. And he said, under oath, that he had not given it. He admitted to the negotiations between the cops' attorney, Robbie Bradshaw, and various movie production companies but said that 'that never got past first base as far as I'm concerned'. He also said he had no knowledge of a sum of $50,000 and hadn't received it. He claimed the only figures he heard were those repeated to him by people writing books.

Before the end of his deposition he did admit to having met with Chuck McLain of Republic Pictures who had a person with him whose name he couldn't remember but who could have been Fred Mills. He also met with a woman from Carolco Pictures. But he emphatically maintained he had not sold permission to use his name to anyone in the entertainment industry, nor had he sold or given out the Wuornos videotape.

During his deposition, Tricia Jenkins, Lee's defence lawyer, questioned him on why, if there'd been no discussion of money and no deal done, a statement was issued saying that the proceeds would be given to a victims' fund that in essence did not exist? Binegar said the victims' fund was something to be established later if any of this ever came about, and if money was ever received. That was said, he claimed, in the window between those early talks and their decision to back away and tell Mr Bradshaw, 'No deals.'

He was very firm on one thing; whatever Tyria's alleged involvement in any potential deal, he had no part in that.

'. . . as far as I'm concerned, she was never a part of any package deal. I don't put myself in package deals with people who live the lifestyle that . . . that Tyria has lived. She's a witness in the case.'

Entertainment law is complex and constantly in flux, and the 'rights' situation is especially volatile, but one school of thought was that, by then, the interviews they had freely given were no longer theirs to control. That since they were freely given, they had become Fred Mills's to do with what he would, just as would an interview given to a journalist or author.

Meanwhile, relations were strained between Munster and Binegar and the State Attorney's office. Among big boys, the damage clearly ran deep. There were a lot of hurt feelings that might never heal completely.

Among the ranks of cops and investigators themselves, the Munster, Binegar and Henry triumvirate—what Brian Jarvis's collaborator, Michael McCarthy, privately came to call 'the unholy alliance'—was no more popular.

There was much mud flying and some of it was sticking to the office. No one liked that.

40

Arlene Pralle was another moth to the flame of fame. The diminutive, featherweight-fragile package is deceptive. Arlene Pralle admits to being drawn to living life on the edge. It does not require a quantum leap, then, to envisage notoriety also appealing to her. She found it in abundance when she began communicating with Lee Wuornos at the end of January after Lee's arrest and all the more so when the following fall, she and her husband Robert adopted her. Arlene was 44, Lee 35. Arlene believes they were brought together by divine intervention. But while she had some supporters, most saw her as misguided or crazy.

Arlene's place in Lee's turbulent life seemed to nourish her in various ways.

First, it allowed her to be notorious while also being good. She was the angel of mercy, the do-gooder, the soul-saver, the bearer of a knowing, beatific smile. Implicit in that was the message that everyone who didn't share her perspective was unenlightened. The ridicule and nasty, hateful comments she garnered only fed that picture of her as the loving, wrongly maligned martyr.

Then there was the living-on-the-edge factor. That was present in abundance. The daily dramas, the soap opera-like sagas, the fraught phone calls with Lee, the moods, the tension, the intensity. So long as her demanding, difficult, adoptive daughter remained behind bars, Arlene could fly close to the flame without risking everything. She might get singed, but she would not get fatally burned. She could relish the potent danger close by, knowing she was safe.

She and Lee could fantasise freely about being together on the farm—Oh, what a time they would have!—without Arlene having to confront the reality of what that would actually be like. Judging by others' past experiences, it would be far from idyllic. Eventually there came moments when Arlene recognised that.

In some ways, Arlene portrayed herself as a kind of baby-talking good girl, a perennial child, but, through Lee, she could also voyeuristically live out some bad-girl fantasies.

Curiously, both Lee and Arlene seemed to share the illusion that they were the powerful one in the relationship.

Arlene had been Lee's counsellor, her adviser, the only person who could calm Lee, the only person she loved and who loved her back. More pragmatically, she was the person who, acting as Lee's agent, decided whom she would allow into Lee's life. She would either champion someone trying to visit her, or block their path. She'd speak and Lee would listen.

The flipside of that was Lee, sitting behind bars, pulling at the strings of her puppet on the outside. ('Don't you know who I am! I'm Aileen Wuornos of television!') Lee could, when a documentary crew from England paid a $10,000 fee (via Steve Glazer, the lawyer who handled the adoption and with whom Lee later replaced Tricia Jenkins) for interview access, dictate how that money would be divided up.

Dawn Botkins, newly embraced by Lee after writing to her and offering to testify on her behalf, would get the first $4,000, Lee declared, because she was ill with multiple sclerosis. Arlene, Lee decided, would wait for her $2,500. Arlene, who had accepted Lee's costly collect calls on the special phone line she'd had installed for her, and who had been paying for extra help on the horse farm she ran whenever she made the long drives to visit Lee on Death Row, felt betrayed. Lee knew how much financial stress she was under. After being on the receiving end of some of Lee's less attractive behaviour, Arlene's patience seemed stretched to the limit. In the heat of the moment, her fury erupted.

Interestingly, the Dawn Botkins, Lee's old schoolfriend, who suddenly usurped Arlene in the summer of '92 was the same Dawn that Lee wrote about to Lori Grody in March of '91, saying: 'I hate Dawn's guts. We never were friends. You know that. I get sick thinking of her. Uk! Puke! (spit)'

No one is exempt from Lee's volatile temper. Not Lori. (Not Lori whom Arlene Pralle, when Pralle first entered Lee's life, was presumptuous enough to call and tell: 'You don't know your sister.' Lori hung up. Ms Pralle would find out for herself soon enough about her precious sister. No, Lori was not exempt.) Not Dawn. Not Tricia Jenkins. Not Jackelyn Giroux (whom Lee repeatedly maligned, while meanwhile continuing to take small sums of money from her and writing or calling, demanding more). No one was exempt. Arlene Pralle's mistake was in thinking that she would be different.

What would be diagnosed as Lee's borderline personality manifests itself with her 'splitting' behaviour, her way of seeing things and people as black and white but never grey. As good or bad, but never a truly human mixture of both. And Arlene, after the initial honeymoon period, has discovered how painful it feels to fall foul of that, to go even briefly from being the best-loved to the bad guy.

In fact, her rose-tinted, glowing picture of Lee was rocked to its foundations soon after they met. While smiling publicly, Arlene endured a mixed diet of sweetness and abuse from her new friend. Phone calls in which Lee was 'so ugly' to her left her weak and tearful. Yet she went ahead and adopted her anyway. Arlene would claim that she was giving Lee the unconditional love she'd never experienced. But Arlene had a history of taking in lame ducks only to have them turn on her—one friend she helped threatened to kill her. Somehow, she was drawn into adopting Lee despite the warning signs.

For instance, Lee suddenly decided that in 'protecting' her from the feminist writer Phyllis Chesler, Arlene had kept her from the one person who could have championed her. (Dr Chesler had written in the *New York Times* that Lee was spending 'long periods of time in solitary confinement, freezing and naked . . . denied . . . permission . . . to see a gynecologist for her almost continual heavy bleeding'. Pralle denies telling Chesler that Lee was bleeding.)

For a long time (right through the first trial and conviction),

Arlene held fast to her denial that Lee was a serial killer, clinging to what Lee had told her, to the self-defence arguments, even after weeks of evidence and testimony in court, after viewing segments of the confession tape and hearing Lee herself describe killing.

Women who love men who kill commonly exist in a state of denial of their loved ones' crimes. That is how they are able to do what they do and to keep their fantasies alive. Yet on some level most do know the truth and are titillated by it. Lee confessed to her crimes and confession makes denial harder to support. Arlene, one got the impression, accepted what Lee had done, she just didn't admit it out loud. It was the circumstances of Lee's killing that were in dispute, rather than that she'd killed.

There *was* denial, and the extent of that denial seemed to ebb and flow. Her original cries were that all of the men were brutish beasts who had hurt Lee badly. (Cries that naturally enraged the victims' families.) Those cries had softened over time, but occasionally crept back in diluted form. Who did what to whom varied, too. Speaking of the men her adopted daughter had killed, Arlene vacillated. At one time she would say, for instance, that two were beasts, but the rest were not. At another, that one man had treated Lee nicely, but the others were awful.

This shifting judgement seemed manipulative. Almost as if even truth itself could be controlled, could be rewritten at whim, could be doled out as a reward to someone currently in favour.

Visiting prisoners as a socially conscious act is hardly new, but Arlene Pralle does not belong in that category. From day one, she did not check her feelings and objectivity at the door. The fervour with which she pursued this relationship with Lee echoed the phenomenon of women who fall in romantic love with convicted male murderers: a documented syndrome. Lee happens to be female, Arlene happens to be married to someone else, otherwise the features are remarkably similar. Arlene has said that she loves Lee more than she loves her husband. He shares an apartment in Chicago, while she lives in Florida, but how must he have felt to hear that?

In the endless speculation about Arlene, the money question

inevitably reared its head. From the beginning, Arlene herself blew smoke clouds of confusion over her motives in the entire affair. She spoke of putting up her horse farm, Maranatha Meadows, to pay Lee's legal costs, and of hiring Lee a couple of ACLU lawyers, but ultimately said that Lee didn't want her paying $50,000 for them. She didn't say that she didn't have $50,000, she said that Lee didn't want her paying it. If she really had that kind of money, it rendered all her other desperate cries for money suspect.

Despite various requests for sometimes quite large sums of money from Jackelyn Giroux and the media, Arlene had always said she wasn't in it for the money. And she said that by becoming Lee's parents, she and Robert would also be forbidden from reaping the rewards under Son of Sam. That, she said, would prove they weren't in it for the cash. As cheques come in, it will be interesting to see if the State of Florida, which warned Jackelyn Giroux, will go after Lee's and the Pralles' earnings.

In one of her times of frustration in dealing with Lee and Arlene, Giroux admitted she had a fantasy. She'd like to see Lee and Arlene living on the farm alone together, cut off from the world, 'with barbed wire all around, and not allowed to receive any money or receive any publicity. Then let's see how long it would last!'

41

Awaiting trial in Volusia County in the spring of 1991, Aileen Wuornos showed two faces. Sure enough, there was the grandiose Aileen, opinionated, demanding, and strident. Warmed by the glow of media attention, and enjoying the newfound feeling of power.

But there was also evident at least one other Lee, who spoke in a softly gentle, girlish voice and in whom a palpable, creeping, cold fear became increasingly visible. Became visible, perhaps, because of the slow but inevitable dawning of the realisation that she had perhaps chosen a doomed path of glory.

She swung between personalities, but whatever fantasies of Ma Barker and gang molls may once have excited her, they were surely crumbling, confronted as she was with the harsh reality of incarceration, her impending murder trials, and the dark, looming shadow of Florida's active death penalty.

Preoccupied in her own way with her appearance and with keeping her hair looking immaculate, jail came as a jolt, if not a new experience. She was forced for most of the interminable days and nights to use the unshielded toilet facility in her cell—a loathsome experience, and at first, she ate as little as possible in the hopes she could cut down on the frequency of the ordeal. Behaviour that doubtless contributed to her weight loss in an environment where the stodgy cuisine usually guarantees the opposite effect.

When Lee's 'killing day' remarks seeped out and were reprinted by the press in cold black and white, they sent shock waves through a close-to-unshockable society that is literally battle-fatigued by the daily onslaught of violence in the news. And in jail, there was no denying the hard shell around Aileen

Wuornos, accused cold-blooded killer. But it wasn't a one-dimensional picture. Reaching behind that atrocious veneer there was also, lurking in there somewhere, a frightened, disturbed woman who wrapped her arms tightly around herself for comfort and rocked back and forth, still the rejected little girl, desperately craving love, safety, attention, warmth and affection. She drank iced water, watched TV, played Monopoly and cards (when she was in the general prison population), and cried over missing her 'baby', Ty.

To some inmates, it seemed Lee had three distinct personalities, not two. She could be the sweetest, nicest person in the world, she could be depressed, or she could just snap. She once asked another inmate's middle name and out of the blue, slammed her fist on the table and shouted: 'Bitch, I will kill you! You don't want to fuck with me!'

Guards came running and moved her to lock-down. When she got angry, Lee also spoke of sharpening her spoon and using it to stab someone.

In calmer moments, usually over communal meals, she told some of the other women that she'd killed the men because they were all cheating on their wives and deserved it.

'How do you know they were cheating on their wives?'

'Because I had sex with them before I killed them.'

Again, evidence did not bear out the claim about their marital status nor the sex, but it represented another variation on her story.

Men, Lee said, were maggots. During meals, she also infuriated other inmates who had enough difficulty handling the jail fare, which was prepared by male inmates, by glaring at it and saying: 'Man, you never know what these men did to our food before it got to us. They could be coming in our food, spitting in our food. This is a man's jail!'

'Shut up!' cried the others. 'We're hungry!'

To Puff, a fellow inmate who was in on prostitution and drug charges, Lee came off as a heavy-duty homosexual, linking up with a hefty black girl called Virginia. (Lee told Karen Collins, the Pasco County detective who went undercover in jail, that she'd had a black girlfriend in prison in the early 80s.) Lee was jealous of anyone else getting Virginia's attention and couldn't stand it when she hung around other 'girls'.

They were seen coming out of one another's 'rooms', which was an absolute no-no. Getting caught doing that meant big trouble. But, of course, homosexual relationships, many of necessity rather than natural inclination, were prevalent. Puff admitted she'd stood guard for girls many times.

Besides Doral Menthol cigarettes (she'd switched brands), when Lee got her commissary allowance, she loaded up with Pepsi and with junk food like Swiss rolls, cakes and brownies. The other 'girls', who knew nothing of Lee's history of buying friends, suspected Lee was ordering Virginia a lot of commissary with money from Pralle and Jackelyn Giroux, who sent Lee sixty dollars a month. (Despite all she said, although Lee sometimes refused Giroux's money orders at first, they were always ultimately cashed.)

Puff heard some of Lee's morning ritual phone calls to Arlene Pralle and concluded that, despite Pralle's denials, there was a lesbian undertone to their conversations. 'I've been in these places too long,' she said firmly, 'I know how they act.'

Arlene Pralle has said, 'I am not, nor will I ever be, Lee Wuornos's lover.' And of course, Puff only heard one end of the conversation. Also, Lee reputedly manipulated Arlene frequently when she wanted money and favours. She was furious if her money for commissary was late in arriving.

When her commissary privileges were taken away as a punishment for some incident, she briefed Arlene to deposit some money into another inmate's account, and Arlene rushed to do as she was asked. Speaking from behind bars, Puff had Lee in full view as she expounded her theories on the Pralle relationship; theories that seemed to have a ring of manipulative truth.

'I've been a prostitute, and I find men that will do that for me,' Puff explained. 'Like older, lonely men. It's sad, but I'll be honest with you, I prey on that loneliness. And I make them think I'm in love with them. And I keep a fat account over here and get whatever I want from them. And I think she does the same thing with that lady.'

By a quirk of timing, Lee's jail time coincided with that of another celebrated inmate, Virginia Larzelere, who with her son was accused of murdering her husband for financial gain. Lee couldn't stand having to share her spotlight with Larzelere and was infuriated when the stories about their cases ran side by side in the newspapers.

'I'm going to kick your ass for the 4th of July,' Lee was heard to yell at Larzelere that day during linen exchange. When Larzelere complained of threats by Wuornos, she also said she'd been warned by her not to say she had been threatened when she talked to the officers. One officer noted that Larzelere, herself no prize, at least gave the appearance of being scared and upset. And by the time the officers interviewed other inmate witnesses, it appeared that some of them had also received a pep talk from Wuornos. One inmate told an officer that she couldn't hear what was said between Lee and Virginia Larzelere, but that no one had been threatened. How could she know that, asked the officer, if she couldn't hear what was said?

On 19 July Lee was reported for insolence towards the staff after officer Edwards inspected her cell and Lee said, 'You're gonna be in one big lawsuit for harassment!'

'I'm scared,' the officer coolly replied.

Changing tack, Lee said, 'Guess what? I'm gonna be on *Geraldo!*'

'I'm sorry, I don't watch TV, so I'm afraid I'll miss that one.'

'Bitch!' Lee retorted.

Edwards returned with her disciplinary report for Lee to sign as required, but Lee snapped, 'Forget it! I ain't signing it. Fuck you!'

When the report was read to her, as required, Lee's response was that she'd have her attorney contact them because there would be a huge lawsuit coming for mental cruelty. She said she wasn't going to kill herself because she'd rather have a lawsuit. The ACLU (American Civil Liberties Union) would come down and get them all for what they'd done.

(On another occasion she shouted that she was going to 'sue the motherfucking jail', adding, 'just wait till Geraldo Rivera gets ahold of this!')

More serious, of course, were the accusations that Lee and Arlene Pralle repeatedly levelled against the jail for maltreatment. Puff, like most inmates, had no great love for life behind bars or her jailers, yet she denied Lee was ever badly treated while she was around her: 'The guards don't like her, but they don't really fool with her unless they have to. They do not abuse anybody in here.'

If Lee was locked down, Puff said, there was a reason and that reason was that she repeatedly threatened people. With her violent history, if she'd hurt someone, the jail might be sued. Of course they segregated her. They had to. Certainly, the jail records seem to bear that out.

Lee, however, complained that inmates filed reports against her that weren't true and indeed for a time she did seem to fare better in segregation.

The grandiosity was clearly apparent in her behaviour. In June, she had a verbal confrontation with another inmate and she refused to stop arguing. Officer Marsee wrote in her report: 'She continued to make statements in an angry/demanding tone, and stated: "Do you know who I am? I'm Aileen Wuornos of television!"'

Marsee ordered her to her cell, from which Lee called out, once again in a demanding and angry tone: 'I'm in here for murder!'

'This is not the first time inmate Wuornos has tried to control the cellblock due to her celebrated status,' Marsee wrote in conclusion. 'Actions should be monitored closely to avoid any incidents.' Marsee had also overheard Wuornos say of a fellow inmate, 'If she provokes me, I'll take care of her myself.'

Lee, of course, saw all of this very differently. She felt it was she who was being picked on, telling another officer: 'I've been in here long enough for you to know that I'm not the one who causes problems here.' She claimed to have a sweet, loving, kind nature. The reports were falsified, she said, and 'actually in all reality is a reversed situation'. The reverse theme is, of course, a familiar one—she accused Lewis Fell of beating her with his cane, and the men she murdered of holding guns to her head.

In August, she lodged a request to have a cell from which she could see the TV once her trial began.

By November, she was spending some time on suicide watch. She was also threatening lawsuits for inhumane treatment. 'This is harassment!' she said. 'You take my cross! My jumpsuit doesn't fit! I wish you'd leave me alone.'

After yet another incident, a fellow inmate reported that Wuornos had told her to go in and talk to all the other white girls and ask them to back her up by saying they'd heard someone threaten her. The inmate refused. If Lee was the Christian she claimed, she wouldn't ask her to lie for her.

Lee had been indicted on three charges in connection with Richard Mallory's death back in January. These were: First Degree Murder, a capital felony; Armed Robbery with a Firearm or Deadly Weapon; and Possession of a Firearm by a Convicted Felon. They were the first in a long line of indictments.

Not long after, holding court from her new home behind bars, Aileen had also told Jackelyn Giroux that she picked Mallory up outside a topless bar and negotiated a $35 fee with him for a varied sexual menu called 'around the world'. The terms agreed, Mallory drove them both to a spot on a wooded dirt road. Aileen asked for her money. Mallory slipped the cash in the ashtray, closed it, and said, 'You can have the money after it's over.' He took off his jacket and unbuttoned his shirt. She then unzipped his pants and performed oral sex. Afterwards, as she reached for the money, he picked up his gun. Simultaneously, she reached for her plastic bag of clothing which concealed her .22. Aiming her weapon through the bag, she said, she shot her client.

In May 1991, Aileen told Giroux the story somewhat differently, claiming that she and Mallory got out of the car for the sexual encounter and that he moved aggressively toward her with the .45, forcing her to act to defend herself. Knowing what we know now about the weapons and about Lee's confusion over her victims, it is of course possible that she was describing her version of her encounter with Chuck Carskaddon. In any event, getting out of the car would indeed be logical and more comfortable for the full sexual service she said he requested. And Carskaddon was naked. Mallory, of course, was fully clothed at the time of his death.

'She told me that each and every one of the murders was self-defence,' Jackelyn Giroux continues, 'that each and every one of them had a gun, and that some of them she killed because they didn't pay her. She decided to take what was hers, which was the money.'

If there was one thing guaranteed to make her really mad, it was not being paid what she was due.

In time, Giroux also discovered that the very old friends that Lee had specifically asked her to track down and contact turned out not to be old friends at all. Not of hers, at any rate. They were buddies of Lori's and Keith's. Mostly, they had belittled, rejected or ridiculed Aileen. Or, worse still, turned their backs and ignored her. Now, it seemed, Aileen wanted them to hear all about her. Now, she was sure they would change their minds.

42

What preceded Aileen Wuornos Pralle's dance of death—the disfigured childhood and flawed genetic heritage—is infinitely easier to pinpoint than precisely what it was that set her off on her murderous path. What, in her case, made the bough break?

Again and again she was humiliated, abandoned, rejected. Her world was filled with pain, rage, and alcoholism. And she was desperate for the world to notice her. Desperate for love.

But there are multitudes of harmless, upstanding citizens who suffered far worse. Being made to eat a baked potato retrieved from the trash is cruel and unusual punishment, but pales by comparison with some of the nightmares child welfare professionals encounter every day. Children who have been burned and battered and tortured but who somehow rise above their deadly beginnings and end up as law-abiding bank tellers.

Why one person takes the homicidal road and another doesn't, remains a tantalising mystery. So, too, is why, despite various experts' estimates suggesting there could be between two and thirteen million people in the U.S. with anti-social personality disorder (meaning their actions are not inhibited by guilt or moral boundaries), very few kill.

One driving force known to propel serial killers is an urgent need for power, for domination, and for control. Those serial killers are predominantly rather ordinary if inadequate white men in their thirties. And, however hard it may be for us to connect a woman, the giver of life, with brutality, violence, blood and gore, with the cold-hearted selection of victims, that same hunger for power by the powerless was at work with Aileen Wuornos.

The serial killer enjoys playing God.

Deciding the fate of another human being.

Determining who will be allowed to live.

And who will die.

By making a man suffer, Aileen transformed herself from victim to victimiser, grabbing that power for herself with both hands, regardless of the consequences.

She was also a robber. Long familiar with theft. And money, too, empowered Aileen.

Female serial killers, still a comparative or complete rarity depending upon your definition (criminologists and psychologists all have their own interpretations), are propelled by some different issues from men and have traditionally operated in different arenas.

Women have killed children, husbands, lovers. Black widows, killing off their men for money. Spurned wives murdering those who've betrayed them. Mistresses out for revenge. Crimes of passion. Crimes of lust. Crimes of jealousy. Crimes of greed.

Women, who are meant to be selfless nurturers, have also positioned themselves in the caring professions and in nursing, only to do the unthinkable and take the lives they're entrusted with: babies, children, the elderly. The small, the weak, the infirm. Those who can't fight back. There, too, Aileen Wuornos is different. Her victims were anything but infirm.

Mary Beth Tinning, of New York State, allegedly killed a total of nine of her own babies by suffocation. Because they were labelled accidental or SIDS ('cot') deaths and because she kept moving home, she survived undetected for a long time.

Dolores Puente, a Sacramento landlady, preyed on the elderly, allegedly drugging then killing nine of her senior citizen tenants so she could collect their Social Security cheques.

What women have done very little of, relatively speaking, is killing strangers in cold blood. Which is why Aileen Wuornos was leapt upon as being the pioneer of a new breed: the preying hitchhiker, stalking the highways. What women have also done very little of is killing for sexual kicks.

Looking into the minds of murderers, the perpetrators of some of the most gruesome and heinous killings imaginable, might seem a strange way to earn a living, but criminologists who study serial killers are a vital cog wheel. Such killers, a minor but menacing plague lurking in the shadows of society, must be caught so we can sleep at night.

Realistically, there is as much chance of winning the Lotto or of being struck by lightning (or, for that matter, of being murdered by one's own spouse) as there is of falling prey to a serial killer. Yet their modus operandi threatens us. Unlike mass murderers who kill a number of people in one impulsive, isolated spree, serial killers threaten us with the implicit message that they will kill again, and again, and again . . . until stopped.

The seemingly unfathomable way they operate, striking in an apparently random fashion without visible motive, chills our blood. But, to some extent, they are fathomable—and they certainly have motives. Figuring out that motive lights up a pathway to catching them.

Chicagoan, Robert Ressler, co-founder of the FBI's psychological profiling programme and one of the country's preeminent authorities on serial murderers, has over thirty years in criminology and was credited with coining the term 'serial killer'. Ressler began teaching at the FBI training academy in 1974 and was a supervisory Special Agent at Quantico, Virginia, until, in 1990, he left to set up shop as a private consultant. That his business is flourishing is a sad testament to the violent state of the world in which we live. During his FBI years, Ressler pioneered criminal profiling and was behind establishing the FBI's National Center for the Analysis of Violent Crime (NCAVC) and the FBI's Criminal Personality Research Project. The latter led to the book *Sexual Homicide: Patterns and Motives,* by Robert K. Ressler, Ann W. Burgess, and John E. Douglas: a handbook on catching and understanding sexual serial killers.

The Special Agents in the FBI's Behavioral Science Unit at Quantico, Virginia, first began profiling such criminals back in the early seventies, culling information from crime scenes to learn more about the offenders and looking for common factors. The engaging question of what lies in the mind of a serial murderer stimulates more than idle or voyeuristic curiosity: their psychological fingerprints help lead to their capture.

Local police forces, detectives, investigators and federal agents alike, turn regularly for help to the data available to all law enforcement via the FBI's computerised clearing-house.

During his time at the BSU, Robert Ressler put the magnifying glass to more serial killers than any other human being walking the streets. He came the hard way to his conclusion that serial killers (once labelled 'lust killers') always operate from sexual motives, be they blatant or hidden. Just because a murderer does not rape a victim does not mean the sexual motive isn't there. Overtly, there may be physical evidence that a male killer had sex with the victims; the victims may be disrobed or positioned in a sexual manner, their bodies may bear semen. More covertly, the killer's sexual arousal can come, for example, from torture, from overkill (using more bullets or stab wounds, say, than is necessary to kill), or from dismembering a corpse.

For male serial murderers, the issues of power and sex become highly and inextricably intertwined. The feeling of power being sexually arousing. As with rape, so with serial murder: the manner in which that arousal is come by has more to do with violence than with sex.

Where Robert Ressler's expertise falls short, as he'd readily admit, is in the area of women serial killers. A largely uncharted territory.

Ressler, who says he didn't feel qualified to draw any conclusions about serial killers until he'd interviewed, in depth, over fifty of them, insists that there are 'no hard and fast rules in the serial murder game' and accuses journalists and writers of repeatedly over-simplifying. Yes, Ted Bundy's victims did look alike, with their curtains of long, brown hair, but for every such example, Ressler can find its antithesis. Whether it's concluding that all serial killers emerged from impoverished homes or all were sexually victimised as children, Ressler strongly discourages generalisations.

His is a world full of 'mights' and 'maybes' and 'mosts'. 'So, when people start talking about rules and serial killing, they just don't really know their business,' he says flatly.

The definitions laid out in Ressler's book were formulated from a study of 36 male serial and sexual killers. Traditionally, women have not met those same criteria, and simply to transfer the serial killer label, based as it is on a male sample, and apply it to a female multiple or serial killer is like mixing apples and oranges.

Would Ressler's underlying sexual motive theory hold water for Aileen Wuornos? Quite possibly. At any rate, the label 'female serial killer' is not a misnomer in her case. She is unarguably female. She is also a serial killer who meets the FBI criteria of having killed three or more times, in more than three different locations, on more than three separate occasions, with a cooling-off period in between.

'Aileen Wuornos is the first one that would be defined as a serial killer based on the model of, say, Ted Bundy or someone like that,' Ressler observes, 'where they're separate events, separate times and locations, and in fact seeking out an individual and killing them for whatever reasons. There's just no comparison for Aileen Wuornos.'

Women do not customarily plumb the depths of depravity and sexual sadism either, mutilating their victims in horrific fashion. Carol Bundy, lover of Doug Clark, the man nicknamed the Sunset Slayer, decapitated her neighbour (and sometime lover) and helped Clark murder a prostitute.

Two factors are unusual with Bundy. First, she voiced the unthinkable, actually telling police that killing was 'fun'. When she talked on the telephone to a police officer prior to her arrest, she told him, 'The honest truth is, it's fun to kill people, and if I was allowed to run loose, I'd probably do it again.'

Secondly, she shot her neighbour twice in the head, stabbed him more than twenty times, sliced his buttocks, then decapitated him. Trophy-style, she took his head with her. She claimed she wanted to make the crime look gory.

Like Aileen Wuornos, Carol Bundy began shoplifting at a tender age, and has made various attempts at suicide. Unlike Carol Bundy, Aileen Wuornos apparently did not mutilate her victims. But when she fired nine bullets into Charles Carskaddon and seven into Dick Humphreys, she certainly journeyed into the province of overkill.

If Aileen Wuornos is only the first of a new breed of murderous woman, the potential ramifications for society are horrifying, but Robert Ressler isn't predicting an epidemic. Far from it. It's his belief that women are not capable, either psychologically, sociologically, or physiologically, of moving into what for centuries has been the largely unchallenged domain of men. He cannot see areas such as rape, or even property crimes, being infiltrated by women on a large scale.

'At the same time, because of the evolution of violence in society across the board, I think that it's very appropriate that she has done this right here in the emergence of the nineties, and on into the year 2000. Because I think that throughout the decade of the nineties, and beyond the year 2000, we're going to see more Aileen Wuornoses.

'We've had women now who have shot up shopping centres. Sylvia Seegrist in Pennsylvania. We had a 16-year-old girl shooting up the school yard in San Diego. We're seeing women doing these violent, male-type things, but we're still only seeing one here and one there. We're not seeing it on the media on a daily basis. We're seeing women who are sexually assaulting and abusing children, but again, it becomes a speck of sand, compared to a beach of sand with men.'

As a known prostitute, some of whose victims were nude, Aileen's crimes immediately took on a sexual connotation. Condoms were found at one crime scene. Yet contrary to this superficially sexual picture, it is not definitely known whether Aileen Wuornos was a sexual serial killer. We may assume that at least one of her male victims completed a sexual act, and with the naked victims, we may assume some sexual activity took place, but those assumptions are only assumptions and ultimately tell us nothing definite about the female aggressor's state of sexual arousal . . . or lack thereof.

Males leave a calling card of tangible evidence of their arousal on or near their victims in the form of semen. Women offer up no such clues.

But the absence of physical evidence does not negate the possibility. It is one to which Mr Ressler has given thought. He consulted with author David Lindsey on his novel, *Mercy,* which features a female sexual serial killer. (Another writer, Lawrence

Sanders, took a prophetic fictional journey with a female serial killer still earlier, in his 1981 book, *The Third Deadly Sin.*)

The vast preponderance of the research done on arousal responses to violent sexual imagery has been, of course, on males. One University of California Los Angeles study found that 30 per cent of men (not criminals or offenders, just men) responded to portrayals of violence against women by becoming sexually aroused, the researchers' deduction being that they fantasise about those kinds of violence. But it is important to note that being aroused by a particular fantasy is not in and of itself a sign of perversion. The dividing line between normal sexuality and perversion is foggy, but one rule of thumb is that it's a perversion when an aberrant fantasy must be brought to mind in order to facilitate sexual arousal and orgasm.

In 1991, a study was published by a group of Australian psychologists on women and fantasy: the first objective study, in that it measured genital blood flow in some of its subjects during sexual fantasies. (Once again, the research was not of female criminals or offenders.) We don't know whether Aileen Wuornos's body responded with sexual arousal and release on her killing days. It would be enlightening to know, but we don't.

It is plausible and indeed likely that her 'killing days' were precipitated by personal crises or extra stresses in her home life. As her feelings of powerlessness heightened, those feelings could in turn have triggered an escalation in her need to exert control over another human being. Male serial killers commonly admit that an argument with a woman or parent preceded a murder. Of those in the FBI study 59 per cent specifically mentioned conflict with a woman. Lee had direct conflicts and problems with Ty at the time of the murders of Mallory, Spears, Carskaddon, Siems, Humphreys and Antonio. Either Ty was threatening to leave, or the presence of a competing force for Ty's affections had made Lee fear she might.

Sandy Russell appeared in Ty's life just a few days before Lee killed Richard Mallory. When Tracey visited, Lee killed David Spears, Charles Carskaddon and Peter Siems. Ty was fired by the Casa Del Mar and talking about leaving Lee and Florida in the week preceding the murder of Dick Humphreys. Ty had left for

Ohio for Thanksgiving with talk about making a break from Lee when Lee killed Walter Gino Antonio. It is not a great stretch to imagine that something was afoot between them at the end of July when Lee murdered Troy Burress.

Candice Skrapec, a Canadian psychologist who teaches criminology at the John Jay College of Criminal Justice in New York City, has interviewed serial killers and has been studying them since 1984. She points out that there is no single explanation, motive, or factor, but many.

'Human behaviour is so complex,' she says. 'It's a product of our biology, our psychological make-up, and our environment, and how those things interact with one another.'

If Aileen's abandonment fears were triggered, they could indeed be very powerful and become a predominant motivating theme. If she was finding herself less effective as a prostitute as she got older and put on more weight, she might well be more vulnerable. And when those feelings surfaced, even subconsciously, they might well fit into the equation. Then opportunity occurs: meeting a man with over $300. Suddenly, it's a homicide, rather than a prostitute and a potential client.

Skrapec points out that there were probably many occasions when such stress factors were in place and Lee did not kill. 'So what is the difference? Is it opportunity?'

Did Lee find herself confronting a potential victim but, not having left the house that day feeling threatened, let the opportunity pass her by? Faced with opportunity, perhaps something one man said or did triggered her in a way another did not.

Clearly, given her longtime lifestyle, Lee spent a lot of time in the woods with a lot of men she did not kill. She had opportunities she did not take. When she did take a life, almost all the victims we know of had in common the fact that they were carrying rather large sums of cash. There were two possible exceptions. Charles Carskaddon, Lee claimed, had only around $20. Yet there is no reason to doubt Florence Carskaddon's belief that her son should have had approximately $300. It would be more logical given the long journey he was making.

Dick Humphreys, Shirley believed, had only around $45 on him the day he was murdered, but ask most women to tell you how much cash their husbands have in their pockets at any given moment and they will be wrong. Unlike some of the other victims, Dick was moving around locally and did not need a large sum, yet people often carry around some extra undeclared cash for no other reason than the feeling of security it gives, of being prepared. He might have had more.

When spinning her tales to the men who picked her up, when chatting to them in their cars, perhaps she somehow elicited from them the fact that they had a considerable amount of cash on them. Perhaps that knowledge played a part in determining her killing days.

Perhaps, in times of pressure, she went back to what she'd always done, even as a child, and tried to empower herself with money. To avert her loneliness and isolation by having cash. Maybe it was to try to soothe Ty and ensure her continued presence that she wanted to take home a wad of bills.

Robert Ressler's studies have led him to conclude that serial killers themselves do not have the introspective capability to understand or reflect on what triggered their crimes. If Richard Mallory were indeed her first victim, her reasons for killing him ranged from the rape and brutalisation story to the accusation that he didn't pay her, to the accusation that he *had* paid but she was afraid he'd take his money back, to the fact that he wouldn't take his pants off.

The sexual serial killers studied, however, were driven by their fantasies, and, although the research thus far pertains to men, Ressler suspects females may turn out to be similar to males in this area.

He has learned that with serial murder, 'You just don't start thinking about it and then start doing it.' The bizarre thinking might gestate for eight, ten, or even more years before it's acted upon. And 'unaddressed traumatic and early damaging experiences to the murderers as children set in motion certain thinking patterns'.

While Ressler cannot speak for the Lee Wuornos case specifically, the BSU has learned the following, he says: 'Life circumstances all shape the direction that these people go, and, generally speaking, there are precipitating stress factors that will move a person towards acting out their bizarre thoughts. A divorce, job loss, some financial setback, loss of loved ones, something like that. In other words, a normal person has all these circumstances happening to them, but they don't have the early bizarre fantasy development, and hatred, and hostility, and anxiety and a need for dominating and controlling people.

'When all these criteria are in line, and then you start having these events, say, after this has been around for ten or twelve years, you'll find that these people gravitate towards moving to acting out. And once they act out, and if they find their act satisfying, they desire to repeat it . . . and they start considering the repetition of their crime.'

Skrapec points out that after Wuornos began killing, she remained a person continuing to experience the world, and that each experience could shape her future behaviour.

'As she becomes more empowered, for example, by these killings—"Look what I can do!"—then that could even change future killings in terms of what precipitated them. Whether she chooses to kill one person and not another.'

Aileen Wuornos exhibits something that Skrapec has observed as predominant in male serial killers, but not in females, and that's a sense of entitlement. It may have begun quite differently. As a child she was treated unfairly and reprehensibly by the males around her and was indeed entitled to better, and perhaps may have been bright enough to realise it. That, coupled with anger, may have been transformed into a sense of righteous entitlement. The media coverage would feed that. And as her killings progressed, by, say, the fourth rather than the second, that sense of entitlement, that sense that she had every right to do this for herself, might have grown too.

43

It's tempting to jump on the bandwagon and conclude that as Lee took the lives of her victims, somewhere in the dark recesses of her mind, she was killing her abusive grandfather over and over again. Lauri was 45 when she was born, 56 when she began her sexual acting out and 65 when he died—in the age range of her victims. And male serial killers do sometimes, but not always, seek victims that are in some sense symbolic of a person who has harmed them.

Ted Bundy, who was electrocuted in Florida in 1989, confessed to further murders before he died. He killed, it is believed, over thirty times, and his young, female victims certainly shared the parted curtain of long, brown hair, worn by his rejecting first love. But Aileen's whole client base was focused on middle-aged men, and most lived to tell the tale. She herself was furious when she learned that her trail of carnage was being blamed on her rage at men stemming from being abandoned by her father and emotionally abandoned and abused by her grandfather. One suspects, however, that her outrage related to control. She couldn't accept that theory because it wasn't her own. She liked to control everything, especially her own life story. But in this instance, she may be right.

What was at work in the selection of her victims may just as easily have been the trouble at home overlaid by the client's available cash, for argument's sake. Or a casual remark about her being 'crazy'. Or her indignation at a wrong remark made about her worth. In her chat with undercover officer Karen Collins in jail, she'd said: 'I'm worth more than twenty dollars.'

If the killing-the-grandfather underlying motive does exist, realistically it will take years of careful study to slice through

Aileen's self-serving rhetoric to reveal and confirm it. Until then, says Robert Ressler, we're shooting in the dark.

Some serial killers have the strong sense that they're ridding the earth of people who don't deserve to live—prostitutes (commonly murdered by men whose mothers were prostitutes), homosexuals or domineering, manipulative women. But when Aileen said her victims were old, their parents were probably dead anyway, and that they were cheating on their wives, it seemed more like a rationalisation of what she'd done than a motivation. Implicit in her remarks, however, is the sense that while their families or parents might have warranted consideration, the victims themselves were less than human.

By virtue of the terribly young age at which she began prostituting herself, Aileen was certainly a victim. We don't know exactly where she learned her behaviour, but psychology, research into the backgrounds of prostitutes, and even plain old common sense, all suggest that at least one adult had abused her sexually when she was very young. Lauri was publicly dead-set against sex before marriage. Nevertheless, Aileen was selling sex at the age of eleven at a time when her peers were, possibly without exception, virgins. Statistics show that the overwhelming majority of prostitutes were sexually abused children.

Aileen has claimed at different stages to have been sexually abused by her grandfather, but has spent far more time denying it. Lauri is dead, as are Alfonse Podlack, Keith and Britta. And Aileen is once again quite likely the only living witness to her own early betrayal of innocence.

Like other victims of abuse, she may also have a vested interest in keeping family secrets, or even in denial. Shame at what took place, too, might be playing a part. A family trance of denial, a kind of self-preserving amnesia, is also common in incest families, along with a need to hide potentially embarrassing material. On the other hand, Aileen has pulled no punches in denigrating her grandfather in other ways, and hasn't seemed concerned to protect him.

Lori Grody gives short shrift to a completely unsubstantiated rumour long-circulated in Troy that Lauri was in fact Aileen's real father via an incestuous relationship with Diane. Were it true, given the patterns of incest, such a relationship may well have repeated itself one generation down. If, in some way, Aileen and Keith were ever-present reminders of Diane and his feelings for Diane went beyond fatherly, or he'd been rebuffed by her, it might go some way towards explaining Lauri's especially antagonistic relationships with them.

But this is pure conjecture, undertaken in the spirit of 'we know there was a terrible car collision, let's try to figure out how the cars were positioned'. And Diane, while having called herself the victim of 'almost sexual abuse', has categorically denied that penetration took place.

After revealing to investigating officer Bruce Munster the incident when Lauri came into her bedroom in the dead of night and sexually propositioned her girlfriend who was sleeping over, Diane said something that seemed classic for someone brought up amidst denial: 'I wish my girlfriend had never told me about this . . . because then I wouldn't have to think about it.' She also went on to admit: 'But yet, there may be some unconscious stuff that's bothering me.'

Harking back to that bedroom incident also set Diane wondering and questioning. 'That makes these other incidences about how he touched me or how he held me . . . and stuff like that . . . ah . . . more dramatic.'

Britta's harsh treatment of Diane may well have been the behaviour of a woman fearing desperately that abuse might occur and that if it did, she would have to leave her man and would never be able to manage. Instead, Diane said (making a slip that revealed her unwarranted feelings of guilt), the woman turns on the kid 'that is doing it . . . I mean, that is the target.'

In January 1991, Bruce Munster asked Diane about Aileen's pregnancy and if she'd had any questions about it. Diane said she'd blocked the pregnancy right out. When Munster asked if there was any chance that Keith had ever been bothered in the family, sexually, Diane's nervous answer again revealed repression: 'I can't say that Keith ever said anything and I would never even right now . . . talk with you . . . ah . . . if it happened . . . Keith is . . . you know, Keith died of cancer. And ah . . . if it happened . . . ah . . . I don't . . . we should not be discussing this.'

The second time she was interviewed by police, she added a telling coda to her account of Lauri sexually propositioning her friend that showed how well-trained she was in silence. In a household such as the one in which she grew up, you were not supposed to tell what went on, she explained. Nobody exactly tells you not to, it's just an unwritten rule. Diane said that after giving them her statement about Lauri sexually propositioning her friend, she'd woken up a couple of days later: 'And this horrible fear came in me—"You told!"'

Given the repressive atmosphere in the home—swearing was not allowed, sex was not discussed—just what might she have forgotten? (Interesting, too, that Diane never heard her father utter a swear word, yet neighbours often referred to his colourful language.)

In the months after the arrest of the daughter she had abandoned, Diane Tuley spent many long hours pondering over what had happened. Diane had recently taken a year's sabbatical from the food store supervisory job she'd had for 24 years, and much of her energy during that year had gone on reading about abuse and trying to unravel the mysteries of her own childhood. A perhaps fortuitous preparation for dealing with what was to come.

The great majority of multiple criminal offenders, men and women alike, commonly had ineffectual parenting and emerged from dysfunctional family backgrounds. And the vast majority of serial killers came from families with alcohol abuse, emotional abuse (including indifference), verbal abuse and humiliation. Frequently, they were unwanted children who had in effect been punished for existing.

While a severe mental disorder may conceivably override a troubled childhood as a cause, it is unusual. Robert Ressler's never seen it. And he simply doesn't believe that somebody who behaves like Aileen Wuornos or John Wayne Gacy (who killed over thirty young boys) came from a model family.

With the wave of self-help and twelve-step groups, and what is seen by some as a self-indulgent tendency to blame all ills on the parents, there has also been a backlash against holding the parents responsible for any sins of the child. To Robert Ressler, that can be an easy way out for the parents of people who commit awful crimes.

'They say, "By God, it's not me! Don't look at me! It's not me! I didn't do this!" My position on that is: "If it's not you, let's prove it." Kids don't grow up without a strong influence from the parents. And it can be overt and aggressive activities—sexual, psychological, physical abuse—or it can be absence of nurturing, and ignoring behaviour.'

The John Hinckley case was a classic example. The Hinckleys were a wealthy family with everything going for them on paper, yet their son shot the president. Experts and laymen alike scratch their heads and wonder what went on in that home. (Ressler's several attempts to interview Hinckley were rebuffed.) Mrs Bundy clung desperately to the veneer of normality she painted on her family right through Ted's execution in 1989.

'Who wants to admit to raising or giving birth to a monster like Ted Bundy?' Ressler concedes. 'The man is probably one of the worst examples of humanity ever to come down the course of history. And my heart goes out to these people that have been parents. I'm a parent. And most parents get upset if their kid has an auto accident or throws an eraser at school. It's not an easy cross to bear, but the fact is these people know what they raised. They know how they raised them. And getting at that information is difficult because nobody's going to tell publicly what has gone on here.'

Interviewed by police on 29 January 1991, Diane Tuley described herself as 'the natural—not the legal mother' of Aileen Wuornos. After her marriage to Leo Pittman ended, Diane immediately reverted to the name Wuornos when applying for her driver's licence and upon Aileen's arrest, the reluctant interviewee reflected on the irony of that choice. Had she not put the name Wuornos on the form, she doubted (rather naively) that police would have been able to find her.

'Things will come back to haunt you . . . no matter how you try to get away from them,' she told Bruce Munster in their telephone interview.

Twenty-six years after Leo's death, Diane told Munster she didn't know of the end Leo came to in prison. On hearing the story, she said: 'What a life, huh? No wonder the reporters would like to get a hold of it.'

But when Munster offered to show her some papers about Leo, she declined. At 51, she didn't care about it. She'd tried hard to put that part of her life behind her. She'd also tried hard to put her first- and second-born children behind her. Obviously she'd been singularly unsuccessful in the case of Aileen.

With hindsight, she viewed her decision to leave her babies with her parents as 'probably the biggest mistake I have ever made in my life'.

Now recognising herself as something she didn't back then—a victim of a form of child abuse—she felt she'd have done better to let strangers adopt them.

'My father was verbally abusive . . . my mother verbally abusive and we were always told we were no good . . . we didn't do good enough,' Diane told Bruce Munster. 'My daddy was the meanest man in the neighbourhood . . . everybody would say that.'

Both parents struck her. 'We got whippings all the time with belts, and that was the normal way to treat children,' she told Marvin Padgett in March 1991.

Until a few years ago, however, she kept her mother's maltreatment and seeming hatred of her to herself. It finally came up with Alma and Ben one day when they discussed her dad's suicide and Britta's curious death. 'Diane, it must have been awful for you,' Aunt Alma sympathised. 'We had no idea.'

Those who subscribe to the 'bad seed' theory would find amply rich pickings in Aileen's deeply flawed father whose violence, criminal career, and eventual suicide in prison, inevitably made the issue of genetic predisposition loom large.

If research showed it was common for people with anti-social personalities to have come from at least one anti-social parent, Leo Arthur Pittman did not disappoint.

For Barry Wuornos and Lori Grody, of course, nothing could be tidier than the explanation that it was Aileen's bloodline and heritage—somewhat different from their own—that delivered the recipe for violence. That the bad part of her was the part that came from Pittman. There is strong evidence to suggest that perhaps it was, at least to some noteworthy extent. Heaven knows, it was understandable that Lori and other members of the Wuornos clan would clutch at this theory as a straw of relief, a life-raft of vindication. Its implicit message was that Aileen didn't learn her wicked ways in her family; her family was a good family. Since thankfully few of us can imagine the horror of learning that one's flesh and blood stands accused of brutal, cold-blooded murder, it is hard to blame them for that.

It is certainly true that with the benefit of hindsight, some curious parallels and eerie foreshadowings of Aileen's path were evident in Leo Pittman's short anti-social life.

Like Aileen and Keith, Leo Pittman (who was abandoned at five months old) ultimately had a new birth certificate registered in his name listing his grandparents as his parents. (He was seven at the time.) Like Aileen, Leo freely confessed to his crimes, only to claim later that he'd been coerced. Father and daughter both unsuccessfully attempted to get their confessions kept from their trials.

Like twins separated at birth, father and daughter both exploded in heinous fashion and, most uncanny of all, faced charges that could bring the death penalty.

Behaviourally, they shared a lifelong pattern of explosive tempers, of outbursts of violence and of a dire reaction to alcohol. They both lied at the drop of a hat and changed their fanciful stories repeatedly.

Both treated their partners more as hostages than lovers and were exceedingly jealous and possessive. Both had marriages in which they successfully managed to conceal the worst of their behaviour until the union was sealed, although Aileen's marriage to Lewis Fell was, of course, dramatically shorter than even Leo's to Diane. Leo's treatment of both his grandmother and Diane was violent, that much we know. And his crime against the little girl was brutal. That, too, sent him down a path that Aileen would also walk.

When Leo was arrested, he had a fake sheriff's badge he claimed he bought in California. Aileen claimed to be an undercover agent in Colorado and to have once wanted to become a cop, and two of her victims carried law enforcement badges.

Both were highly manipulative personalities. In an especially unappealing parallel, neither showed true remorse for their crimes. Like Leo before her, the only pity Aileen seemed able to dredge up appeared to be for herself. When Leo's guilty verdicts were read, he remained emotionless. But although Aileen appeared likewise flabbergasted into momentary silence in court, she soon exhibited less impulse control than her dad, spewing abuse at the jury.

Prison records show that while doing his time, Leo destroyed a state-owned dustpan. He wanted a new one. Like a petulant child, he was furious when that demand was turned down by the officer in charge, who'd decided there was nothing wrong with his existing one. In retaliation, Leo then bent it so badly out of shape that it couldn't possibly be used. Just as Lee once painted her Daytona apartment without permission, so Leo painted his cell a different colour without authority to do so.

Aileen's time in jail awaiting her first trial might easily have been far more disruptive, although full prison records for Leo Pittman's day-to-day behaviour were not available. Also, Aileen lived under the cloud of the possibility of multiple death sentences.

During Leo's trial, the *Wichita Eagle* reported Prosecutor Keith Sanborn's closing statement to the jury in which he acknowledged the tough task of defence counsel Fettis. It was a message that 26 years later might have applied perfectly to Aileen's team. Sanborn said: 'It isn't a pleasant job to defend a person like this, gentlemen, and don't you forget it. They don't call you a hero, but it's your system of justice and you have provided that [Pittman] is entitled to the best counsel obtainable, and you know he has had good counsel.'

Yet another curious quirk in this story: when Leo was arrested in Wichita, he was wearing his red hair in a long curl that hung down the back of his neck. Up until the time of trial, Tyria Moore, whose colouring and even physique so resembled his, wore her red hair with a long red strand hanging down at the back. (She'd said she intended to let the strand grow until Aileen was convicted, then to cut it off and mail it to her, but it was gone by January 1992.)

It is truly frightening to contemplate, but Leo Pittman did have at least one more child (and indications are that there were probably more) after his failed marriage to Diane, so Aileen has a sibling or siblings she does not know. And somewhere out there in the mists of adoption secrecy, Aileen, too, has a male heir, carrying on her bloodline. Leo Pittman's genetic heritage, it seems, has become the lot in life of several persons unknown. It would be fascinating to know what became of them.

Criminologist Robert Ressler happens not to subscribe to the 'bad seed' theory, largely because he hasn't studied the proper correlations, but given mental illness's known potential for genetic carry-over, neither does he reject it. The crime man points his finger to history. There were many lawless families even in the Wild West who, over the decades, went on to produce multi-generations of bandits and killers.

This, of course, is where the nature versus nurture argument rears its head again.

Aileen and Leo never came face to face, yet studies have shown that there does appear to be a biological or genetic component to some criminal behaviours. Even if a child is separated from a parent very soon after birth and raised in a different environment, if the biological parents were criminally inclined there is a greater likelihood than usual that the child will also engage in criminal or delinquent acts and ultimately be arrested.

'We have a child coming out of the chute who has a certain kind of genes,' Candice Skrapec admits. 'If neither the biological parents nor adoptive parents are criminally inclined, especially in terms of property type crimes . . . the research has shown that the child, sort of by chance, may grow up and offend. But if the adoptive parents have a criminal record, then the probability the child will also have a record goes up.' But it does not go up as much, however, as if the *biological* parents are criminally inclined.

'So there does appear to be some overriding genetic kind of factor here that contributes to the criminality of the individual,' Skrapec acknowledges.

Perhaps in Aileen's case that 'nature' legacy, coupled with the cold, unloving, violent and alcoholic personality of Lauri Wuornos to which she was exposed during her 'nurture' stages, combined in a lethal way. Perhaps Lauri was the extra fatal ingredient in the mix.

44

In March 1991, Tricia Jenkins, Chief Assistant Public Defender for the Fifth Judicial Circuit, was appointed to replace Ray Cass as Lee's counsel on the Richard Mallory case in Volusia's Seventh Judicial Circuit. Jenkins was by then already representing Wuornos in Marion County (Jenkins's home turf), and she would also be handling Citrus County's David Spears case. The move marked yet another step in the difficult passage of bringing Wuornos in front of a jury.

In January, when Ray Cass put movie producer, Jackelyn Giroux, in touch with Russell Armstrong, the Daytona lawyer who'd represented Lee back in 1981 for her armed robbery charges, Armstrong executed the agreement between them.

Cass, who as a public defender, was not allowed to be involved in any civil matters, believed he had acted properly by merely introducing the parties then withdrawing forthwith. Judge Gayle Graziano (who later withdrew from the case) said that Cass should never have made the referral. She believed that there had been at least the *appearance* of impropriety.

By the time Lee sought to replace Cass as her defence counsel, Cass had also filed a motion to withdraw because he felt he was in an untenable position. It was granted on 1 March. But, he said, 'I assure you there was no impropriety. I was not brokering for anyone.'

Cass had also taken some flak from Lee as she went through her on-off periods of disenchantment with the contract she'd signed and with Jackelyn Giroux. As Giroux battled to get her film made, she continued to send Lee the allowable monthly sum of $60 as promised, but the problem wasn't difficult to pinpoint. Lee had expected to get rich quick. Not just rich, but ultra, mega-

397

wealthy. In reality, the film industry with which Giroux was grappling was fickle and difficult. Lee's expectations, in this as in so many things, were outrageous multi-million-dollar pipe-dreams. Of course she wasn't satisfied.

Lee was not happy with Cass anyway, movie contracts aside. Cass and his colleague Don Jacobsen had failed to accept all her collect calls and had not visited her as often as she wanted. With input from Arlene Pralle, Lee had decided she wanted a woman lawyer, and when Judge Graziano approved the switch to Jenkins, Cass, for one, certainly didn't lose any sleep over it.

One of the most crucial battles facing Lee Wuornos's defence lawyers was to keep their client's highly incriminating video-taped confession out of the courtroom in the Richard Mallory trial. A hearing was held in December of 1991 in front of Judge Graziano to determine whether it would be suppressed. The question was whether it would be more prejudicial than proba-tive. In other words, whether showing it would compromise Lee's right to a fair trial more than it would illuminate the events that had taken place.

The tape's mere existence had already sown a powerful seed of presumption of guilt in the minds of the public. If it were re-leased to the press and public, it might contaminate the minds of the entire jury pool. It would be hard, if not downright impossi-ble, the defence argued, to find impartial jurors.

Of course, the videotape was not Lee's only confession. (Hearing of the motion to suppress it, Bruce Munster quipped: 'Which one? There've been so many!') Indeed, some of those in-criminating statements Lee made in jail had already leaked out to the press. Then there were the taped phone calls. Transcripts of them had been making the rounds on the black market with a high price tag attached. Various writers had been offered a copy.

But in December, Judge Graziano took the steam out of the black market in one fell swoop by agreeing to the tape's public release. She also judged it admissible in Lee's first murder trial. Immediately, extracts from the videotape were given wide play on television and in the newspapers, irretrievably cementing in the minds of many Lee's status as a cold-blooded killer. It was a rare piece of footage in every sense and destined to gain notoriety fast.

To the families of Lee Wuornos's victims, it was a double-edged sword, at best. Its content was hardly objective, since it presented at length the accused's highly dubious, yet uncontested, account of the murders. It came from the subjective, self-serving perspective of a self-confessed murderer. An alleged murderer whose victims were all too painfully absent and unable to defend themselves.

While some of the men were found nude, others were fully clothed and found with no evidence to suggest sexual activity had taken place. True, Wuornos was a career prostitute, but police heard from and contacted a number of men who'd met and encountered her with no sex involved. Even allowing for their reluctance to admit to sex, at least some seemed to be telling the truth. Those men had given her rides and had heard her 'cons.' The sob stories of kids she couldn't feed and of broken-down cars. The requests for money.

In spite of these factors, many of the press had taken to lumping together all Lee Wuornos's male victims as men soliciting the services of a prostitute, ignoring any evidence to the contrary.

Yet Shirley Humphreys cried with relief when Judge Graziano ruled in favour of releasing the confession tapes to the media. Although Wuornos, before trial, had already succeeded in conveying to many (through the printed word) how callous she was, Shirley felt that the tapes, in their ugly, unemotional and visual way, would show the world just what this woman had done.

Shirley had borne the pain of hearing Wuornos say: 'I felt sorry for him 'cause he was gurgling. Well, I shot him in the head and tried to put him out of his misery.' And she, for one, had little patience with hearing about the highway harlot's terrible childhood. Nor was she swayed by the news that Wuornos had been born-again in March of 1991. And she found some solace in knowing that with the videotape everyone would witness first-hand Lee's lack of remorse.

But it was painful, nevertheless.

'Every time you pick up a newspaper article, you hurt,'

Shirley said. 'Every time you see a picture splashed in the paper, you hurt. Turn on the boob tube, you hurt. The tapes that Geraldo Rivera did—you hurt. There's just no getting around it. Hell, that woman will outlive me! She has to be judged by her maker.'

Saying this, Shirley trembled, her palpable anger barely reined-in. She wiped away a tear before conceding, 'Some days are worse than others. Some days you feel like somebody kicked you in the stomach, just riding down the highway. And I am out on the highway a lot.'

Personally, Shirley Humphreys had no misgivings or doubts whatsoever about the propriety of her late husband's conduct. She cited, to support her total conviction, the autopsy report, the absence of semen or condoms, and the fact that he was fully clothed. She spoke of this difficult subject with the quiet, matter-of-fact dignity of the wife of an ex-cop. The wife of a man who had spent the bulk of his career in law enforcement or investigation.

How painful for her to have to deal with seeing him referred to, shorthand-style, as one of the male clients killed by this woman prostitute. How painful for all of the loved ones and friends of these men to see footage of Lee Wuornos recounting how they'd met their deaths. To listen to her unconscionable lies about their violence.

Letha Prater hadn't seen the videotape in December of '91 and didn't know exactly what was on it, but she hoped it would at least seal Wuornos's date with the electric chair. But Dee Spears fretted that David's name would never be cleared, would never be free of Lee's vile accusations that he was going to attack her with a lead pipe in the back of his truck.

For the dark side to all Lee's cries of self-defence was their implicit message that branded her victims attackers. They were being portrayed as violent, aggressive rapists. Salt in the wounds of the bereaved.

Letha Prater didn't pretend Buddy was a paragon of virtue. He might, if provoked, have gotten into a fight. Neither she nor Wanda doubted that he'd get physical if anyone threatened his family, or if his own life was in jeopardy. But they were all certain that if Wuornos offered sex and he wasn't interested, Buddy wouldn't turn rough or mean. He certainly wouldn't have beaten her up. He might have pushed her if she wouldn't get out of his truck. Letha couldn't actually imagine her brother being interested in sex with Lee Wuornos, but, unlike Lee Wuornos, she wouldn't presume to speak for him.

And rape? Never. Had he wanted another woman, he could have found one without picking up someone as scruffy as Lee, and without paying for prostitution.

Lee Wuornos raised a rare issue. Just as no family wants to accept that a daughter is selling her body, no family or wife wants to believe that a man they love is out on the highway negotiating for prostitution, or having sex in the woods with a less than salubrious woman. The unpalatable news that this might sometimes be the case, with the arrest of a prostitute, is mortifying. And the assumption of the victims' complicity in sex with Wuornos added a salacious taint to an already unbearable situation. It was an added burden in a horrendous ordeal for the already shattered and devastated families behind the headlines.

In the fall of 1991, Lee's lawyers tried to make a deal with the various counties in which she'd been indicted, so as to offer her life sentences in exchange for five guilty pleas. Four counties were ready to settle, but James Russell, Pasco County's State Attorney, demanded a death sentence. Lee had murdered Charles Carskaddon with nine bullets.

Once the deal crumbled, the defence changed tack. With no choice but to go to trial, they would argue that Lee killed in self-defence. It would be a tough nut to crack, of course. Self-defence once, maybe. But seven times? The defence also planned to attack the way the investigation had been tainted by the split loyalties of three key law enforcement officers—Sergeant Bruce Munster, Captain Steve Binegar, and Major Dan Henry—whose negotiations for a movie deal, the defence contended, had got in the way of their police work.

In July 1991, there'd been an official investigation into the officers' actions, initiated by Marion County Sheriff, Don Moreland, and headed by Chief Assistant State Attorney, Ric Ridgway. The resulting report on 13 August showed no wrongdoing. Nor did it find evidence to support the claim that their work had been affected because of improper motives. But it did suggest that some investigative leads needed further following up. The defence planned to capitalise on that as much as possible in January.

45

Aileen Wuornos Pralle's trial for the murder of Richard Mallory began in DeLand on Monday 13 January 1992. Theatre-like, the courtroom rapidly took on its distinct flavour, echoing the foibles, quirks and personalities of the key players, most especially Judge Uriel 'Bunky' Blount. Presiding in no uncertain terms, he was officially retired from the bench but retrieved his robe for this one last important stand. A gruff, mildly curmudgeonly fellow with a ready reprimand but an equally ready smile, he commanded immediate respect.

From the start it was apparent he would tolerate no foolishness and brook no delays. He conducted his courtroom decisively with the sure and fearless hand of a virtuoso. With his silver, spiky, flat-top brush cut, his squat face sinking into his robes in repose, he resembled an approachable bulldog. Out of sight of the jury, at the end of a long day, while inquiring into the welfare of the inhabitants of his packed-to-capacity press gallery, he'd slip off the robe to reveal a pastel polo-shirt beneath, topped with a formal, black bow-tie.

Before him that first morning stood the defence team, led by Tricia Jenkins, Chief Assistant Public Defender of the Fifth Judicial Circuit, a husky-voiced, confident ex-journalist with angelically waved blonde hair and a penchant for print, Puritan-style dresses. Forty-two-year-old Jenkins had represented Danny Rolling, a suspect in the Gainesville student slayings, on robbery and burglary charges, and, over nine years, had represented around fifty alleged murderers. She'd been in charge of all death penalty cases in her area for five years.

At Jenkins's elbow stood Assistant Public Defender Billy Nolas: short, dark, bookish, bespectacled and with a razor-sharp legal mind. Deceptively youthful-looking, 33-year-old Nolas was a graduate of Georgetown Law School, the son of immigrant parents 'who kicked me through school, so I finished a couple of years ahead of schedule'. He came to the Wuornos case a veteran of over a hundred capital cases, having spent six years as the Chief Assistant at Capital Collateral Representatives, working on appeals. A one-time law teacher, he soon revealed himself as the most vocal defence counsel, armed with a wealth of case law and a ceaseless supply of objections.

A third, quietly spoken attorney William Miller, played a low-key role throughout most of the trial. He and the team's often-present, pony-tailed investigator, Don Sanchez, were kept busy listening to the defendant's comments and complaints.

For also present at the defendant's table, of course, was the star of the show herself, Aileen Carol Wuornos Pralle, newly trimmed down by around 25 pounds, her skin prison pale. She looked oddly vulnerable in an inappropriately transparent white blouse that, according to her frustrated adoptive mother, Arlene Pralle, was intended only to be worn beneath a jacket.

Across the courtroom sat Volusia County's wiry State Attorney, John Tanner. The head man himself, trying this most public of cases in an election year. David Damore, the chief of the felony/homicide division and the Assistant State Attorney who had led the case thus far, sat beside him as co-counsel. A tall, dark, moustached and rather dashing figure, Damore's volatile energy balanced well with Mr Tanner's unruffled calm.

The search for jurors quickly clarified the prosecution's and defence's diametrically polarised aims. On voir dire, the prosecution repeatedly probed what was for them a crucial issue: willingness to dish out the death penalty. Were they to win a conviction on one or both counts of first-degree murder, when the penalty phase followed, they didn't want anything short of the electric chair. That meant weeding out bleeding-heart liberals, the faint-hearted, and all points in between. They didn't want anyone unduly squeamish because of sexual bias. If someone felt incapable of voting to put a woman to death, they wanted to know now. With the death penalty currently the law in Florida, they could discount anyone unprepared to live up to its letter.

Times were more liberal than when Leo Pittman faced a capital charge 26 years earlier; then only seven of 151 prospective jurors were excused because they felt unable, under the circumstances, to impose the death penalty.

The defence fished hard among the prospective jurors for signs of a capacity for mercy and a willingness to consider mitigating circumstances. The defence also pursued what it had deemed impossible to find: a jury untainted by the flagrant media coverage. The team was especially intent on sniffing out those who'd been exposed to the so-called tabloid TV shows, such as Geraldo Rivera's *Now It Can Be Told, Hard Copy* and *A Current Affair,* all singled out for such scrutiny because they had aired segments of Lee's controversial confession tapes. Anyone exposed to that little lot, they felt, would be irreversibly prejudiced against Lee.

Their interrogation of prospective jurors would have warmed the hearts of the circulation directors of *National Geographic* and *Reader's Digest*—but revealed an astonishing dearth of viewers of the highly successful TV tabloids. Some folk admitted to having seen the lot. Others said they'd seen limited coverage and felt they could put it aside in the interests of fairness, and could judge the defendant's guilt or innocence on the evidence offered in court alone.

Arlene Pralle immediately made her presence felt in court revealing both her devotion to Lee and her sense of drama. She arrived with tales of the death threats and weird mail that had come to the house. At each break, she signalled Lee, carried on mouthed conversations, slipped notes to her team and updated the media on Lee's latest woes and complaints. That very first day Arlene learned to her chagrin that even as the defendant's adoptive mother she didn't get a vote in jury selection.

Pressing on with their task, the defence team looked for people who hadn't been the victims of major crime, who weren't closely tied to law enforcement, and who harboured no deep-seated prejudices against prostitutes. More vital by far, they sought jurors who appreciated the defence's lack of responsibility to prove anything, and who understood the prosecution bore the burden of proof. If Lee declined to take the stand on her own behalf, they didn't want that interpreted as a reflection upon her innocence.

On Tuesday, Pralle sat with tears flowing after a prospective juror disqualified herself, saying she'd been awake all night and had decided she couldn't support a death penalty vote under any circumstances. Praise the Lord, Arlene cried. She was also upset because her requests to visit Lee after court so that they could pray together, had been denied. Lee was in lock-up for some infraction which precluded phone contact, too. Deanie Stewart, sister of the missing Curtis Reid, was in court and generously offered Arlene a comforting hug. Mrs Stewart's ire was not so much for Arlene but for Tyria Moore; she felt it horribly unjust that she had not been charged with any crime. Because the seat in Corky's car had been pulled all the way forward, she'd become convinced that if Lee and Ty had killed Corky, then Ty, the shorter of the two, had been driving his car.

By the middle of Tuesday afternoon, 58 prospective jurors later, the panel was seated and included a lady jeweller with a taste for historical novels, an equestrienne, a chemist and a high school English teacher.

By Wednesday morning, when the prosecution and defence teams were due to lay out their cases, elder statesman Judge Blount had ably demonstrated why he was so respected a local character. A charter member of a local breakfast group, The Loudmouth Club, this George Burns of judges was undaunted by retirement and continued to meet his cronies daily at Hunter's restaurant.

Stories about 'Sometimes in error, but never in doubt' Blount abounded. Besides being fast with the gavel, the native Floridian was a hanging judge, they said. But not heartless. On Christmas Eves, legend had it, he used to dress up as Santa and set free jail inmates who were facing misdemeanour charges—as long as they first sang 'Jingle Bells' for him. He'd often determine the need for a recess by looking at the jury and seeing 'a lot of hairy eyeballs over there'. He had not been hard to persuade out of retirement for the case: 'You know what they say about old fire horses! You aim for the bell!'

A judge since 1955, 'before TV was allowed in the courtroom', he was adamant that there would be no William Kennedy Smith-style circus with him on the bench. To this end, the 65-year-old jurist had insisted on using his old, familiar (but exceedingly small and stuffy) courtroom in DeLand. Consequently, the three designated press rows on the left were overflowing, and the floor between the benches was a minefield of electronic equipment and wires feeding off the pool TV camera. Curious spectators sat across the aisle. Outside, a metal detector had been hurriedly installed: a last-minute nod to Wuornos's high-profile case.

As the attorneys took up their places, Lee turned to smile at Arlene who was seated behind Shirley Humphreys and her daughter, Terry Slay. Arlene was most afraid of the wrath of Shirley Humphreys and of Letha Prater.

John Tanner, a zealous porn-fighter, ardent Christian and member of the Assembly of God, had spent seventeen years as a defence attorney. The 52-year-old prosecutor had 22 years' experience in court and was a private criminal defence lawyer before joining the State Attorney's office. He felt some sympathy for Arlene Pralle's role in Wuornos's life because he himself had developed a relationship with serial killer Ted Bundy and had worked hard on saving Bundy's soul before he was executed. Tanner felt the death penalty was sometimes warranted, however, and would spare no effort in ensuring that Aileen Wuornos got to meet 'Old Sparky', as Shirley Humphreys so wanted her to.

Adjusting his spectacles, Mr Tanner began his opening statement by explaining to the jury that Aileen Carol Wuornos stood charged with murder in the first degree, by premeditation, and with armed robbery. The evidence they would see and hear would show that Richard Mallory did not know that 30 November 1989, a little over two years ago, would be the last day of his life.

'He didn't know that in less than ten hours he would be robbed, murdered, his body left to rot in the woods. Of course, he didn't know that he was about to pick up a predatory prostitute who had sex with over 250,000 men by her own admission. He didn't know he was about to admit into his car Aileen Carol

Wuornos. Her appetite for lust and control had taken a lethal turn. She was no longer satisfied with just taking men's bodies and money, now she wanted the ultimate control. She wanted all that Mr Mallory had—the car, property, his life.'

Tanner then detailed the discovery of Mallory's abandoned car, followed two weeks later by the discovery of his decaying body, bearing four bullet holes. He told the jury that after killing Mr Mallory, Wuornos returned to 'her lesbian lover, best friend, Tyria Moore', and used Mr Mallory's car to move them to another residence. He told of her confession to Deputy Sheriff Larry Horzepa, of Lee's several accounts of events, and of how she'd admitted to soliciting Richard Mallory for prostitution by saying she needed money for rent and they'd finally ended up, hugging and kissing, in the woods.

Tanner then spelled out Lee's conflicting accounts of what followed. There was the version that he'd paid her in advance but she became concerned he might try to take it back, so she jumped out of the car and told him to do the same. In another version, he'd stayed in the car, she didn't tell him to get out, and she shot him behind the wheel. Tanner told how she'd said they'd been having fun together in the woods for five hours, that she'd decided he was a nice guy and abandoned her usual practice of demanding her money first because she really didn't feel she needed to. But all that changed when he wouldn't take off his clothes and wanted just to unzip his pants, and she didn't like it that way. Then she'd said, Tanner reported, 'Oh no, you're not going to just fuck me!', and shot him where he sat behind the wheel.

In both stories, John Tanner pointed out, she had admitted that he was sitting in the car, fully clothed, when she shot him. (Something that would become crucial later on in a way that even John Tanner could never have dreamed.) That Mallory then crawled out of the driver's door and shut it. Tanner had a point to make: 'Because on the other side of that doorway was a woman who was pumping bullets into him. She says he crawled out the door and then she ran around to the front of the car. Difficult to imagine,' he said, his voice rising, then pausing for effect, 'but she shot him again. He fell to the ground and she shot him again.'

Mr Tanner then moved on to list the several different reasons Lee had cited for shooting Richard Mallory. She didn't really understand why. He didn't pay. He was going to try to take his money back. He wouldn't take his pants off. Then Tanner reached a crescendo.

'From her statements, we know that it was partly because he was middle-aged, and according to her, it didn't make much difference if she killed him because he didn't have any parents. The real reasons, as you sort out the evidence in its totality, are not all that complex. She said she doesn't really know why she killed him, but the evidence tells you why she killed him. She killed him out of greed. She was no longer satisfied with $10, $20, $40. She wanted it all. And she had to take it. And she did. And she used a gun to take it. And she shot him to keep it.'

Next, Tanner wanted them to know that Lee had told Larry Horzepa that she needed to kill Richard Mallory dead because if she didn't, she couldn't go back out on the highway as a prostitute. Intent, Mr Tanner reiterated, hammering home the key point to the watchful jurors—she said she *intended* to let him die.

'Ultimately, the bottom line is the evidence in its totality will show that Aileen Carol Wuornos liked control. She had been excercising control for years over men. Tremendous power that she had through prostitution. She had devised a plan now and carried it out to have the ultimate control. All that Richard Mallory had, she took, including his life. Under the law, *under the law,* she must pay with her life.'

Then it was Tricia Jenkins's turn to state her case and of course it all sounded quite different. Her evidence would show that when Aileen Wuornos got into Richard Mallory's car that rainy night, 'She had no idea that she was going to be travelling with him into a nightmare . . . and that ride would ultimately bring her into this courtroom today.'

Jenkins painted a picture of a vulnerable woman taking shelter from the rain in the shadows beneath a highway underpass. A woman who was scared. A woman who'd lived on the road. who'd been a prostitute, who'd stayed in motels when things were good and she could afford it, who'd been finding that life on the road was getting more dangerous. Time after time after time, the defence counsel said, she'd been raped, beaten up, not paid, and she had finally armed herself.

Jenkins then offered a different account of the tentative way her frightened client got into the car, anxious to get home to Ty, and therefore taking Richard Mallory up on his offer of a ride all the way to Daytona. 'She knew that her very best friend, her roommate, the person that she was helping to support, would be waiting for her and wondering why she was out so late.'

Lee drank out on the road for Dutch courage, Jenkins contended, and accepted the mixed drink Mallory offered her, but refused his offer of marijuana. She told of Lee worrying that Mallory was drinking too much, of him buying beer for her on the road, of his looking for a good time and of Lee needing to earn money for groceries and rent. Jenkins told of them talking, drinking and having fun in the woods until 5 a.m., of Lee feeling comfortable and deciding she could trust him. Then Mallory asked her if she was ready to earn her money and requested she remove her clothes, which she did while he went to the boot. Lee had heard the boot shut and the car door open. That door opened a nightmare for Lee, Jenkins said imploringly to the jury, 'of bondage, rape, sodomy and degradation. And Lee was a victim of that.'

Contained in her dramatic remarks was the first glaring clue that Lee Wuornos's tale had changed in tone and thrust from the one she had related to Larry Horzepa and Bruce Munster. Bondage, rape and sodomy?

All eyes were fixed on Jenkins as she elaborated, saying that as he abused her, Mallory told Lee he had done the same to other women and that he wanted to see her pain. Lee had been able to get the weapon she had in her purse on the floor of the passenger side and she shot him. She got out of the car and warned him not to come closer or she'd shoot again. He was cursing, wounded and angry, Jenkins said, and he kept coming and she shot him again. Terrified, frantic, trying to get away, Jenkins continued, Lee had driven off in his car. Lee knew she couldn't go to the police or tell anybody: who would believe her? She was a prostitute. Mr Mallory was a businessman. She *did* go to Ty, and told her. And Ty said that she *should* defend herself, that she *shouldn't* be treated like that. Now Ty was under fire with Jenkins's allegations.

'You're going to hear that Ty has kind of changed her mind about that. You're going to hear that she changed her mind when there was a composite on TV. And you're going to hear that Ty agreed to assist law enforcement and come down to Florida and help them catch her friend, her love. And you'll hear that she did that.'

Jenkins said that Ty had been put up in a motel and had worked with law enforcement to get Lee to confess and to say that Ty hadn't had anything to do with it, and didn't know about it.

'Finally, after Ty threatened to kill herself, after Ty had told her that her family was being threatened, she finally convinced Lee to tell law enforcement about it.'

Jenkins had to address the videotape, to take a pre-emptive strike against it, to prepare the jury for seeing an interview with law enforcement that was not only incriminating but was also shocking. She had to take the sting out of it as best she could.

'Contrary to what the prosecutor has told you, you are not going to hear several stories about what happened. You're going to hear her say, "I will protect Ty, I will do anything, I will even die for her", and you'll hear her give one version of what occurred. And you will also hear her saying, "I was so drunk—I was just so drunk." She will say, "I was drunk royal."'

They would also hear, Jenkins promised, how Richard Mallory got violent with her client. She did not want to labour the points. Wrapping it up, she said solemnly: 'Ladies and gentlemen, Lee Wuornos is not guilty of first-degree premeditated murder, or armed robbery. She defended herself. She had had enough. Not one more time could she take it. Not one more time.'

Never far from the surface bubbled perhaps the most crucial issue in the case, and the one weighing especially heavily on the defence: the extent to which counsel could mention the other murders for which Lee had already been indicted. Judge Blount

411

had yet to rule on the Similar Fact Evidence, or Williams Rule, as it is otherwise known. For now, they would have to wait and wonder.

The prosecution began its procession of witnesses with Sergeant John Bonnevier, previously a deputy, who had discovered Mallory's abandoned car. As they were introduced into evidence piece by piece, Bonnevier described Mr Mallory's belongings that were found near the car. On direct, Tanner established that they had been not just tossed out, but furtively hidden in the sand by Lee.

On cross-examination, Billy Nolas established that they were only partially hidden.

A sequence of evidence technicians, sheriff's deputies, and crime lab analysts stepped up, escorting the jury along the investigative journey. Finding the body. The condition of Mr Mallory's clothing (pants fully zipped, belt buckle off to the left side by four to six inches). The blood on Mr Mallory's car seat.

Jeff Davis, the son of Richard Mallory's ex-girlfriend, Jackie Davis, took the stand. He'd worked for Mallory but had since become a parole officer. Davis identified the picture of his birthday party that depicted Richard's maroon Polaroid camera, then identified the camera itself. The OK Pawn Shop's owner's daughter was put on to tie in the thumbprint left on the receipt with the person who'd pawned the camera using Cammie Marsh Greene's driver's licence.

FDLE fingerprint expert, Jenny Aherne, brought together Lee's various aliases. She testified that the Cammie Greene thumbprint, the Lori Grody prints, and those she took of Aileen Wuornos in jail in January '91 were one and the same.

Lieutenant Carl Clifford, a member of the diving team that recovered Lee's .22 from Rose Bay, identified the rusted gun and the Styrofoam cooler he'd used to keep it in stable condition while he transported it to the laboratory. At 4.30 p.m., the judge called it a day.

Former medical examiner and forensic pathologist, Dr Arthur J. Botting, was the first witness in the box on Thursday 16 January. John Tanner had him take the jury methodically through the findings of his autopsy on Richard Mallory and of the bullets that had killed him. The jury saw Mr Mallory's shirt, complete with dark brown bullet holes. Dr Botting concluded that of the four bullet wounds, it was the two that struck the left lung that caused the fatal haemorrhaging.

Over the objections of the defence, Mr Tanner was able to convey to the jury the clear impression that death was not instantaneous. He gave them a palpable sense that Richard Mallory would have struggled desperately for air until so much blood was lost that his life simply ceased.

William Miller, on cross-examination, hit a few salient points. The bullet in the back of Mallory's shoulder-blade had entered from the front, not the back. Botting could not know what had happened between the shots. Couldn't know what the victim was doing to the assailant. Couldn't know the position of either party. Couldn't know whether Mallory was reaching out. His subtext was obvious: Mallory could all the while have been trying to hurt her. Miller also hoped the expert would say that the .05 per cent blood alcohol level meant that Mallory was under the influence, and might have been more so because the decomposition could have broken down the true amount of alcohol in his system. Dr Botting, however, had seen no sign of the bacteria growing in the blood sample that would have led him to believe that it had altered Mr Mallory's blood alcohol level.

FDLE agent, William 'Ward' Schwoob Jr, a crime scene analyst, was the prosecution's next witness. He'd searched Lee's storage unit and, with Larry Horzepa, had videotaped the locker both before and during its opening and as it was being searched. Schwoob was the man who'd documented and inventoried the eclectic contents and tried, in the lab, to lift latent prints from them. Assistant State Attorney, David Damore, after opening some big, brown, sealed evidence bags, presented Schwoob with a procession of victims' items for identification. Among them, a brown wallet whose contents included a driver's licence receipt for Ty Moore.

One primary defence goal was to tie in Tyria as much as possible, to let her enigmatic presence around Lee cast shadows of doubt on what Lee had actually done herself and on the presumption she acted alone. To the prosecution, Ty was a red herring. They pointed out that the receipt found in the wallet in Ty's name was just one of a collection of papers in the storage bin that even included an i.d. of Susan Blahovec's.

Lee, throughout this long process, busied herself repeatedly whispering in the ear of whichever counsel was currently seated beside her. What was keeping her spirits up through her ordeal, Arlene Pralle confided, was her fierce desire to get on with writing her autobiography.

Next up was Donald Champagne. Like Judge Blount, retired but brought back for the trial. The silver-haired, silver-bearded veteran was previously a FDLE firearms examiner, with 23 years' service. He was an ex-Royal Canadian Mountie to boot.

'Even a screwdriver makes individual marks,' he said, explaining to the jury his field and its intricacies. He testified that the .22 calibre revolver was indeed one of the calibre of weapons used most often. 'In my experience, yes, they do kill a lot of people.'

After identifying the CCI brand, .22 calibre, copper-coated, hollow-point Stinger cartridges, he admitted, under Tricia Jenkins's questioning, that he couldn't say they came from that weapon.

John Tanner couldn't let that impression linger: 'The class characteristics of the weapon you examined and the one that fired those projectiles [are the same]?' he asked.

'They are the same,' Champagne agreed.

'But there are other brands the same?' Tricia Jenkins came back.

'Yes,' the witness admitted, before finally being allowed to step down.

After lunch, Susan Komar, an FDLE firearms crime lab analyst who had studied Richard Mallory's shirt, testified that the bullets had been fired from within six feet. There were a total of seven holes, she said, but possibly fewer than seven shots. And the hole in the back of the sleeve would be consistent with the muzzle of a gun being aimed from the back side of the arm. The chest shots could have been fired from the front; the arm shot could not.

The holes in the collar, she said, meant that the gun would have had to have been aimed at the collar.

She did not know, William Miller got her to agree, whether the individual was sitting, standing, or doing anything else.

Word had filtered through to the press corps that Tyria Moore was to be the state's next witness. For the current contingent of spectators, the presence of Wuornos's 29-year-old, lesbian ex-lover was a welcome bonus. The long, punkish ponytail-strand of red hair that hung down her back in December had been cut off. Rumour had it that law enforcement had persuaded her to clean up her image for court.

David Damore led nervous Tyria through a potted autobiographical sketch, then had her describe the morning Lee showed up with Mallory's car and told her they were going to use it to move home immediately. She confirmed that she was not expecting to move that day. Later, Lee had come home and said she had shot and killed a man that day, that she'd taken his car and put his body in the woods. Ty told of the jacket and scarf Lee gave her, and the other items she'd brought into the apartment.

Crucially, Ty testified that she had seen no sign of injury on Lee whatsoever.

'How long did you remain living with the defendant after she told you she shot this man?' asked Damore.

'Approximately a year.'

'At any time, in the period of that relationship, as lovers, as roommates, as friends, did she ever advise you that the man she had shot had done anything to her?'

'No, she didn't.'

'She never suggested she'd been raped by this man? Did she ever say anything?'

'No.'

'Did she ever give you an explanation as to why she had shot this man?'

'No.'

'Was this a close relationship between you?'

'I believe it was.'

'She never, ever suggested that the man she told you she shot on December 1, and whose car you used to move to Burleigh Avenue, had done anything to her, on the morning of December 1, 1989?'

'No.'

Ty had known of Lee's prostitution, had never known her make a living any other way, and knew she owned a firearm for her protection.

'During that period of time, from the time she told you that she shot the man on December 1, 1989, back to when you first met her, did she ever indicate to you that she had been beaten and raped and robbed by people that she was going out and prostituting herself to, while you two lived together?'

'No.'

William Miller cross-examined Lee's ex-lover, establishing that Lee supported her when she was unemployed. That Lee rarely told her about her work because she knew Ty didn't like her doing it. That Lee had told her life on the road was dangerous. Ty also conceded that Lee had told her of being raped and beaten prior to their meeting. Miller established their heavy drinking habits. His next goal was to have Ty confirm some of Lee's good points. She had never been physically abusive to Ty. Never struck her. She was protective of her. Loved her. Said she'd do anything for her. Even said she'd die for her. Said it over and over again, Miller asked?

Ty hedged. She didn't know if it had been said more than once. Miller reminded Ty that in her deposition, given the previous November, she'd said that Lee said exactly that throughout their relationship.

'If it's there, I said it,' Ty shrugged.

Miller wanted the jury to know that Lee had been drunk that morning she returned with Richard Mallory's Cadillac. He also wanted the jury to know that Ty had left Lee when the composite sketches were released and she became afraid.

'You were scared you might be arrested?'

'Because I knew I was driving the car when it happened . . . and I wrecked . . .'

'And so, you went to Pennsylvania?'

416

'No.'

'I'm sorry, you went to Ohio?'

'Yes.'

Miller had suddenly had Tyria teetering on the brink of Williams Rule territory. As those privy to the case knew, but the jurors did not, the car she referred to was that of Peter Siems, the missing missionary. Quickly, Miller changed the subject.

He led Ty through being contacted by investigators Bruce Munster and Jerry Thompson in Pennsylvania, being brought to Volusia, and making the recorded phone calls that led Lee to confess. Yes, she wanted Lee to say certain things in those calls, to clear herself. Yes, she had lied to Lee about her reason for coming to Florida, about who she was with, and about the calls not being recorded. Miller also wanted the jurors to see the treachery. While Lee had continued to reaffirm her love for Ty, to say she'd do anything for her, Ty had used a suicide threat to bait Lee into confessing.

'I really don't know why I said that,' Tyria said flatly and unapologetically. She was worried and very scared. Miller wanted to drive home that it wasn't enough for Ty to have Lee clear her, she also wanted Lee to confess.

'You wanted her to say that she *did* do it, that she did all the homicides?' Miller asked.

'Basically, yeah.'

'So, her saying that you were totally innocent didn't have anything to do with any of this, is that right?'

'No.'

'There were at least ten phone calls, and it was only at the end of those calls, on the last one, that you got what you wanted? Is that true?'

'I believe so, yes.'

The jury and the witness, Tyria Moore, had been ushered from the courtroom while Judge Blount instructed the defence on what was and was not beyond the scope of direct examination with regard to the much talked-about movie deal and Bruce Munster's dealings with Tyria Moore. The judge had no intention of allowing the events of January 1991 to impede justice being served on the events of 1 December 1989.

After everyone trooped back in, Miller questioned Ty on Bruce Munster's suggesting that he get her a lawyer.

'And that lawyer's name was Mr Bradshaw?'

'Yes.'

'In case someone came to you about a book and movie deals?'

'Right.'

'And Mr Bradshaw was assisting Mr Munster in his book and movie deals, correct?'

'I know he was an attorney that Mr Munster had spoken with.'

'And Mr Munster was asking if you wanted to get in with him, right?'

'Asking me if I would like to use the same attorney, yes.' Miller brought up her relationship with FDLE agent, Rose Giansanti, who had often been assigned to accompany her. (Away from the court, Pralle wondered if the two women's relationship went beyond the professional.) Ty valued Rose's opinion.

'You liked to talk to her about things like that, correct? I mean, she's someone you trusted?'

'Correct.'

'And you called her and asked her opinion on the book and movie deals?'

'Correct.'

'And when you did that, you spoke with her about some monetary figures?'

'Something that, yeah, was mentioned.'

'In fact, the figure mentioned was $50,000, correct?'

'That could have been, yes.'

Ty betrayed her lover, Ty was in with the cops, and Ty was out to get rich, so the message went.

David Damore stood up to question Ty again. He showed her a photograph of Peter Siems's car and had her confirm it was the one she referred to when she said that she and Ms Wuornos had been in a wreck in July. A different car from the one in which they'd moved. Damore had her reiterate that Lee had never complained of being physically abused while they lived together. That she'd never seen her looking as if she'd been beaten.

Damore then sought to redress the balance on the phone calls. Lee wasn't the poor victim the defence made her out to be. During those calls, Lee had repeatedly asked Ty to lie for her, to lie and say it was mistaken identity.

'When you told her that you wouldn't lie for her, did she tell you that it was mistaken identity, that the police had the wrong woman?'

'Yes, she did.'

'Did she ever suggest to you during any of those three days of telephone calls to your hotel that she had been raped or harmed in any way by Richard Mallory?'

'No, she didn't.'

Neither had Lee ever suggested that Richard Mallory had done anything to provoke her attack on him, Ty agreed.

Damore also wanted the jury to know that Aileen had written to Ty and told her that she wanted her to be the beneficiary of any proceeds from a movie deal. And he wanted them to know that Sergeant Munster had said that no one in law enforcement would profit from any deals.

'Isn't that true that he told you that they couldn't get one red cent?'

'Yes, I believe he said that.'

'Isn't it true that you told him you wanted nothing to do with the movie deal? That you didn't think it was right for *anybody* to get a penny?'

'At a point in time, yes, I did.'

Damore's voice was strident and emphatic, underlining each word, as he went on to say: 'Have you ever taken one cent from anyone involving a movie deal, or the knowledge you have in this case, or the story, or your life with Aileen Wuornos, since the first day that you met with police officers and told them that she had told you about shooting Richard Mallory?'

'No, I haven't.'

Damore kept going. 'Isn't it true that you wanted to be left alone? To be able to live your life . . .'

Billy Nolas, who had been making repeated objections, was

419

thoroughly frustrated. 'Objection, Your Honour. There's a witness on the stand, we're not at the podium.'

Undeterred, Damore moved on: 'The defendant wrote to you and offered to pay you money, did she?'

'Yes.'

'And *she* wanted to be involved in a movie deal, to sell her story, didn't she?'

Billy Nolas was back on his feet, complaining again to the judge about Damore's leading questions. Damore changed tack. 'When you told Aileen Wuornos that you wouldn't lie for her, she then tried to come up with "It was a mistake"?'

'Correct.'

Damore hadn't finished. 'Did she tell you what she would do to the authorities if they couldn't come up with some evidence to tie her into it?'

'I believe she put it that she would have a big lawsuit on them.'

'Yes. Lawsuit-happy.'

'Yes.'

'Objection!' cried Bill Miller. The judge sustained his objection but the jury had heard Mr Damore's commentary.

William Miller stood up. He was going back to Ty's conversation with Bruce Munster about a book and movie deal. Hadn't Munster said that only a portion of the money would go elsewhere? Ty reiterated that Munster had said they'd get no money from it. But Miller brought out that Ty had been told she *could* get a portion of it, though.

'Do you recall having conversations with Rose Giansanti wherein you said to her, "Do you know what I could do with $50,000?" Do you recall saying that?'

'No, I don't.'

'And in fact, if Miss Giansanti says that you did say that she's—'

'Objection, Your Honour!' Miller was interrupted.

He changed direction. 'Regarding the statements on the phone, in fact, Lee Wuornos did tell you several times that she acted in self-defence, did she not?'

'I don't recall that.'

'You don't recall?'

'No.'

Bill Miller had had the final, anticlimactic words with Tyria Moore.

46

The prosecution next called investigator Horzepa. And the officer who had heard the defendant confess to seven murders would bring the Williams Rule issue to a head.

Under Tanner's questioning he moved from the discovery of Richard Mallory's body to the focus, almost a year later, on the suspects, Tyria Moore and Cammie Greene. He painted the picture for the jury. The pawn shop search. Cammie Greene's thumbprint on the ticket that led to Lori Grody, who then turned out to be Aileen Wuornos. The arrest. The taped calls between Ty and Lee.

John Tanner set about clearing up any impression that there was any evidence whatsoever that Ty was involved in the Mallory homicide or the theft of his car. In referring to 'the Mallory case', however, Tanner kept veering into the province of the admissibility of mention of the other homicides to which she had confessed. Billy Nolas made repeated objections and moves for a mistrial. The judge noted both but moved on.

Tanner led Horzepa through the evidence, the Polaroid camera, the storage unit key. He established that Lee had been read her Miranda Rights by Bruce Munster before he and Horzepa taped her interview on 16 January. Horzepa conjured up for the jury a word picture of the three-hour exchange that followed and what it had revealed. But the Similar Fact Evidence issue kept rearing its head. At one point, Tricia Jenkins herself wandered into the danger zone, asking Horzepa, 'When you talked to Aileen Wuornos, January 16, she told you over and over and over, she'd acted in self-defence, didn't she?'

'Not in reference to Mr Mallory,' Horzepa answered.

And there it was again. Once the jury had left the courtroom,

Judge Blount pointed out to Jenkins: 'You elicited the answer, ma'am!' But he announced that he would hear the lawyers and make his ruling first thing the next morning. The jurors returned to their seats and Jenkins resumed her questioning of Horzepa.

She didn't name Chastity Marcus but she did want the jury to know that another woman, a nude dancer, had once been arrested for Mallory's murder and extradited from Louisiana. She definitely wanted them to know that Mallory frequented seedy establishments. She would have liked them also to know that Jackie Davis had told Horzepa that her ex became paranoid when he'd been drinking. The judge sustained the prosecution's objection. But the jury had heard it. In similar fashion, they got the message that Mallory liked porn.

(Out of the presence of the jury, the prosecution had already accused the defence of trying to assassinate the dead man's character with hearsay testimony.)

Jenkins also noted that in her videotaped interview, Lee had said both that she wasn't about to let someone rape her, and that the killing wasn't intentional.

Redressing the balance on redirect, John Tanner read to Horzepa, from the transcript of the videotape, some of Lee's more damning statements. During Larry Horzepa's eventful afternoon on the stand, four motions for a mistrial were denied.

The prosecution made a persuasive argument for having their Similar Fact Evidence included. They'd prepared a huge chart tabulating the similarities, and very compelling they were, too. Besides being able to tell the jury about Lee's bloody handprint being found on Peter Siems's wrecked car, the prosecution wanted them to hear about all the other common factors. That personal property had been stolen from all the victims. That the car keys had been taken. That a number of the men's pockets had been turned inside out.

Tanner wanted to be able to hammer home with full force all the evidence that pointed to a robbery plan and premeditation. All the victims were white males who'd picked her up hitchhiking. John Tanner argued that if the similar fact was allowed, he could establish her pattern of killing along the Florida highways and that would speak specifically to Lee's self-defence plea. Not only was Ty not present, but during some homicides she wasn't even in the state, he argued.

David Damore pointed out to Judge Blount that they would establish that some victims were shot in the back when helpless. Shot in the back while in locations and positions where they couldn't have inflicted any injury to Wuornos.

John Tanner enumerated the findings of the various cars and bodies. The videotape, he argued, was virtually impossible to edit so it would pertain only to Mr Mallory. Looking thoughtful, he read quotes from the transcript of that videotaped confession to the judge. Of Dick Humphreys, Tanner said, Wuornos had told the investigators that she thought she shot him three times.

"I think. Oh, yeah, he stumbled and fell. Oh, yeah, I remember . . . 'cause he pissed me off and everything. I felt sorry for him 'cause he was gurgling. Well, I shot him in the head and tried to put him out of his misery.'

Bunky was getting the picture.

Billy Nolas argued for the defence. He claimed that the state had put forward a propensity argument and that that was what the jurors would hear, that it didn't meet the Williams Rule, and that the collateral crimes evidence would become the thrust of the trial: 'It'll be, either Miss Wuornos is guilty in all these cases . . . or in none of these cases.'

Richard Mallory, and the specific charges Lee was facing, would get lost in the shuffle, Nolas argued.

He also pointed to discrepancies between the homicides: in where the men were shot, their ages, how they were clothed, geography. The area was northern Florida which covers a lot of ground, he pointed out. 'We could say it happened in the western hemisphere!'

Judge Blount rubbed his chin thoughtfully, but his mind was made up. The Similar Fact Evidence would be allowed by the court.

The prosecution downplayed their pleasure, at least in public. The judge's ruling was a major victory for them—and a serious blow to the defence who would, of course, have Judge Blount's ruling at the forefront of any future appeals. But the jurist was not weighed down by any doubts.

After the jury was seated, he explained that they would be hearing of other crimes allegedly committed by the defendant, Miss Wuornos, but that they'd be hearing about them for very specific reasons: 'For the limited purpose of providing motive, opportunity, intent, preparation, plan, knowledge, identity, the absence of mistake or accident on the part of the defendant. And you shall consider it only as it relates to these issues.'

The defendant, he said finally, was not on trial for any crime not included in her indictment in that courtroom.

Lee, meanwhile, was grimacing, visibly furious. Turning around to look at Arlene Pralle, she hissed, 'I can't believe this! I'm up on one case!'

Once back on the stand, Larry Horzepa explained the prosecution's body-and-car map to the jury and used it to point out where Richard Mallory and his car had been found. The prosecution was ready to roll. Horzepa was succeeded by a long procession of detectives, investigators, crime scene analysts, pathologists, evidence technicians. All the bearers of sombre news, confirming the prosection's contention that these men had each died at the end of a .22, and had each been robbed of their personal property and vehicles.

Every witness, adding their particular piece of the puzzle, helped build for the jury a horrifying picture of multiple murder. Hearing about the other victims, even in this limited fashion, drove home the chilling nature of the case. Their faces didn't say it, but how could they help but think it? One time, it might have been self-defence. Maybe twice. One time, it might have been accidental or unintentional. Maybe twice. Maybe three times. But the jury was getting a loud and clear message about the abundance of evidence against the defendant.

Lee drummed her fingers on the table and hissed more furious comments, this time in the ear of William Miller, seated beside her. Meanwhile, the jury heard exactly what the defence had hoped they would not. Like how Dick Humphreys died as the result of seven bullets, one to the back of the head. It would be hard for the jury to suspend their doubts about Lee's guilt in the face of this authoritative onslaught. Although many of the gory photographs were kept out by Nolas's arguments and the judge's rulings, the point was nevertheless seeping across. The men had met horrible deaths, their bodies had ruthlessly been left to rot.

Observers could not help but note the difference in the demeanours of two key figures in the courtroom. Lee and Letha Prater. As John Tanner read aloud some of her killing quotes, Lee, her mood improved, grinned cheerfully at Arlene Pralle, oblivious to any incongruity. At other equally inappropriate moments, she mouthed, 'I love you!'

Letha Prater was having a hard time sitting listening to the evidence, 'and looking across and seeing her there and knowing what she did'. Investigator John Tilley had tried to persuade her to leave when testimony began on Buddy and she'd planned to, but she changed her mind. She sat, still, staring into space. Her ashen face, a study in quiet, dignified pain, was turned away at a right angle to the court.

Six bullets in David Spears's body. Lee's bloody palmprint on Peter Siems's car. Donald Champagne, the soft-spoken firearms expert, returned to compare the bullets from one homicide to another. Those in Richard Mallory's body were the same CCI Stingers brand as those in Dick Humphreys'. Same six right-twist, all hollow-points. The bullets in David Spears had been examined microscopically and also fitted those criteria.

The attorneys fought to drive home their points. For the defence: that Champagne couldn't be sure in all cases that those bullets had been fired in the weapon found in Rose Bay. For the prosecution: some had definitely been fired in that weapon. And those that might not have been still shared the same class and characteristics.

As Billy Nolas and Tricia Jenkins cross-examined and re-cross-examined witnesses, Nolas repeatedly leapt to his feet with mistrial motions and objections. He was laying the foundation for appeal, of course, but Judge Blount's patience wore thin. It wore thin, too, with the verbal sparring between David Damore and Billy Nolas throughout the trial. He chastised them like a couple of unruly sons.

426

On Tuesday 21 January—Monday having been Martin Luther King's birthday—the process continued. The spoils of Lee's robberies that had been found amidst the clutter in Jack's Mini-Warehouses were trotted out, items tied to victims; other victims whose stories were slowly told.

Nine bullets had killed Charles Carskaddon, the jury heard. Throughout it all, the prosecution's highly visual body-and-car map was building.

And the crowd in the courtroom was shrinking, driven away by the tedium of technical evidence.

The task of adding the human touch and re-engaging any flagging attention fell to Stefan Siems, son of the missionary whose body had never been found but whom Lee had confessed to killing. Stefan identified his dad's luggage, his radio tape player, his windbreaker and toiletry bag, all of which had been seized from Lee's storage unit.

Peter Siems's niece, Kathleen, was called to testify about her 'Uncle Pete', but kept getting the date of his disappearance wrong by a year. Broad hints by the prosecution failed to get her back on track so she ended up a wasted witness. No matter. The prosecution could afford to lose her.

That day, during recesses, Arlene Pralle chatted about her and Lee's plans to sue Volusia County Jail for alleged mistreatment of Lee. They would use, Pralle said, the same attorney who had handled the adoption, Steve Glazer.

Everyone noticed it. At times, Lee looked so bubbly and downright cheerful that it was hard to believe she was on trial for her life.

On Wednesday 22 January, Walter Gino Antonio's fiancée, Aleen Bury, testified. Struggling to control her emotions, she identified his property. Dr Margarita Arruza, the forensic pathologist who carried out the autopsy on Antonio, hurried State Attorney Tanner towards his goal of blowing Wuornos's pleas of self-defence out of the water.

As the jury viewed a gruesome photograph of the back of Antonio's torso, Dr Arruza pointed out the wounds, testifying that all four bullets, including the one to his head, had hit him in the back. The courtroom was silent, but the point was definitely taken.

The doctor had noted that Antonio wore a ring (he had a tan-line) but that it was missing from the body. He had no dentures, she said.

'It was like he'd been stripped of everything that would give him identity.'

Billy Nolas got her to agree that she couldn't tell which bullet had been fired first, or if Mr Antonio had been standing or sitting. She also agreed that the bullets were fired in rapid succession. Billy Nolas wanted the jury to think that it happened too fast for premeditation or cold calculation. But Nolas's by-then-familiar point that the victim could have been in any position or doing anything when he was shot, carried little weight in light of the damning testimony that all four shots had hit him in the back.

Even so, John Tanner didn't let it go at that, getting the doctor to agree on redirect that death would not have been instantaneous and that Antonio would have had to bleed to death.

'You didn't list excessive bleeding as a cause of death?' asked Billy Nolas, hoping to recover somewhat. It was a bad call.

'No. That's what usually happens if you're shot,' the doctor replied coolly.

All told, it was very damning stuff. The Fairview Motel's Rose McNeill followed, then Bobby Copas and James Dalla Rosa, two men who'd picked up Lee hitchhiking and lived to tell the tale.

Copas's testimony was particularly colourful. Overweight, nervous, and embarrassed about repeating Lee's graphic language, the likeable witness nevertheless told how she'd offered him 'the best damn blow job you ever had in your life'. The jury listened attentively as he described her violent reaction when he tricked her out of his car. She'd whirled around, mad as hell, and said, 'I'll kill you like I did them other old fat sonofabitches! Copas, I'll get you, you sonofabitch!'

Mesmerised, the jurors no doubt believed his closing claims that he was 'scared to death', and it was an experience he'd remember as long as he lived.

* * *

Larry Horzepa, by then a familiar face, went back on the stand, as John Tanner took him through the circumstances under which he and Bruce Munster had elicited the confession. (Despite leading the task force, Munster had been pointedly absent throughout. It seemed the prosecution didn't want to put him on the stand and give the defence a chance to keep bringing up the TV movie saga.) Tanner established the propriety of the setting when the videotape was made.

He then went on to Lee's various versions of the time when things went awry during her encounter with Mr Mallory.

'Did she say it was a surprise that this man wanted to lay on top of her, after she took off her clothes and lay on the front seat?' Tanner asked incredulously.

'No,' Horzepa replied.

'Point of contention was, he didn't want to take his pants off? That was the point of contention, wasn't it?'

'Yes, sir.'

Tanner also established that Larry Horzepa had let Lee talk without prodding her and had given her plenty of opportunity to describe the sequence of events with Mr Mallory.

The following day, Thursday 23 January, the famous videotape took centre stage, although the prosecution ultimately decided to show just an edited, twenty-minute version, keeping their focus firmly on Mr Mallory. They'd won on the Williams Rule issue, but the other cases could not, by law, overshadow the one in hand.

The defence trio didn't know whether to consider the showing of this truncated tape a blessing or a curse. There were points for and against. The full tape would show the jury Lee's remarks about self-defence and her repeated professions of love and concern for Tyria. But if they asked for the whole thing to be shown, they'd jeopardise their chance for later appealing the Williams Rule decision. Their hands were tied.

The jury watched the edited version, the picture of stillness. As usual, their faces betrayed very little, but this day, flickers of dismay and discomfort were detectable. The schoolteacher fore-woman looked the most visibly pained.

Commenting on the tape later, Arlene Pralle again reinforced the impression she gave of being in deep denial about Lee's crimes. She had not seen the tape before but her reaction was unlike any other courtwatcher polled. The observers were, without exception, struck by Lee's underwhelming remorse.

She did not cry—and she sounded casual, as if reminiscing about a vacation.

But her adoptive mother had a very different take on all this. Arlene Pralle hissed, to the amazement of all within earshot, 'Those men were animals!'

With a few last words from Larry Horzepa, his soft voice barely audible in the further reaches of the courtroom, the state announced that it was ready to rest its case.

Belatedly, Aileen Wuornos Pralle cried, her head cupped in her hands. She was grieving, the timing unfortunately seemed to say, for her own plight rather than that of her victims. As she was led away, she waved Pralle a tearful goodbye.

Outside the courtroom, Tricia Jenkins was still hedging on the defence strategy. It could run anywhere from an hour to two days. And no, she was not prepared to say if Lee would take the stand.

47

It was the moment the courtwatchers had hoped for. The moment the prosecution dreamed of. And the moment the defence could only have dreaded. A charge of anticipation coursed through the spectators, and adrenalin kicked in, reviving the most jaded reporters.

The defence had called their first and ultimately their only witness, Aileen Wuornos Pralle. Otherwise known as Lee.

She'd been the source of a year of news coverage, interspersed with titillatingly horrific snippets from her various confessions. Now the defendant had her day in court. Lee wanted to have her say, but she would purge herself of her latest version of events at considerable cost to herself and against the strong advice of her counsel. The defence team could see what Aileen could not. Lee was a loose cannon who had problems controlling herself. They were afraid she would hand the prosecution everything they wanted on a plate.

Wuornos, looking particularly pale, oddly pretty and strangely peaceful, made her way to the stand. The box of pink tissues that was always placed so pointedly in front of her also made its way to this new location. A signal that some emotional revelation could be expected.

('They've put them within reach of the judge,' one veteran reporter drily observed, singularly unmoved.)

Somehow, that simple box of tissues stood as a curious symbol of what might and should have been. It remained untouched by Lee throughout what should have been, for her, in any context a devastating experience.

What unravelled under the gentle guidance of Tricia Jenkins was an account of events that bore no resemblance to anything previously heard. It began simply enough with Tricia eliciting basic data. Lee, looking positively demure—mirroring her counsel in a white blouse with puritan collar, long floral print skirt and blue velvet jacket—was startlingly composed. First she gave an account of her background. Aged 35, from Troy, Michigan. Left home just prior to turning fourteen. Hitchhiked alone to Florida because she'd been sleeping rough in the snow and it was too cold. Supported herself with a couple of jobs but earned only 75 cents an hour, so was basically a career prostitute from the age of sixteen on.

When she hitchhiked, when men approached her asking if she wanted to make some money—the kind of offers she's sure were extended to any young girl travelling the highways—she accepted. She had a child at fourteen, but was made to give it up by her grandmother. (A perhaps revealing slip, in light of her unaddressed anger at Britta.) She then corrected herself. She was made to give up the baby by her grandparents. Her grandparents had raised her, she informed the jury.

She pursued her prostitution work three to seven days a week, riding with anywhere from eight to fifteen men a day, servicing anywhere between three to eight of those sexually. She worked from highway exit to highway exit. If a sexual deal wasn't struck, she asked to be dropped at the next off-ramp to try all over again. She spoke softly, her account surprisingly devoid of street language.

Tricia Jenkins then steered her questioning into the relationship with Tyria Moore. It was in this emotionally charged terrain that Lee's dramatic change of heart about her lover revealed itself, in public at least, for the first time. The room was hushed as she spoke, calmly and softly.

'From the very first day I met her, we fell head over heels in love. The first year we were pretty sexual. The second year, and as it went on, we became like sisters. I loved her very deeply. She loved me very deeply, but we didn't care about the sex part any more. We just cared about each other.'

'Did your hustling stop once you got into the relationship with Ty?' quizzed Jenkins.

'No. She . . . as a matter of fact, she quit her job that week.

The first month that I was with her, she quit her job. I told her I was making $150 a day and you only make $150 a week, so if you want to quit, I'll support you. She continued to support me like a cheerleader. She *wanted* me out there,' she alleged.

After that allegation, Lee then testified, and this is where her tone took on the first hint of an edge, that during their last year together, Ty didn't like trailer living.

'She was just constantly telling me I wasn't providing enough for her. She wanted me to go out there and make more money.'

At Jenkins's prompting Lee went on to claim she was pressured by her lover.

'She'd tell me to go on out there and if I didn't, she was going to break up with me and find another girl that would take care of her.'

'Did you talk about your experiences on the road with her?'

'Not really. She didn't want to hear it. She never . . . she had me totally not talk about it. She didn't want to hear what happened to me.'

'Did you try to talk to her about Richard Mallory?'

'Yeah, I did, but she didn't want to listen.'

Lee's tone sounded as if she hoped to elicit considerable sympathy on that score.

'And during the times that you were with Ty, she never worked?' Jenkins enquired.

Lee could no longer disguise her feelings or keep the edge of sarcasm from her voice. Ty had worked for a month at the El Caribe Motel, then she had taken care of her. Ty then worked at Zephyrhills Motel but she didn't get any money there, so Lee still took care of her. She'd worked in a laundry, but that didn't last.

'The only solid job she ever had was at the Casa Del Mar last year.'

'Was she working when you two split up?' Jenkins enquired, ready to cast her own shadow over Tyria.

'She got fired.'

'Do you know why?'

'She beat up her boss,' Lee replied sweetly.

While Lee had wanted to save up for a house and a pressure-cleaning business, Ty was a spendthrift, Lee alleged.

'Every time I came home with money, she always wanted to go to the mall.'

Meanwhile, Lee didn't buy clothes for herself, didn't seem to care about herself, and even wore 'a bra with Band-Aids on it'. The self-serving note that had worked its way into her still-ladylike voice was unmistakable.

When she was prostituting out on the road, she would consume anywhere from two to six beers.

'Why?' asked Jenkins.

'It was like my tranquilliser. I was shy. I was sometimes too . . . just shy. I was embarrassed about my body. I was scared, nervous.'

That admission of vulnerability regained her a little ground in the sympathy arena, although her claim of shyness (one repeatedly reinforced by Arlene Pralle) strained credibility. Speaking clearly on the stand and with the appearance of ease, this woman had shown no glimmer of this supposed shyness throughout her year of media exposure.

Did Lee purposely solicit an older clientele? Jenkins asked her, harking back to a point made earlier on by John Tanner.

'Yes, I did. The young guys, I decided not to deal with, because I'd learned throughout time that they were always high, always stoned, or something. They just seemed a little more aggressive and like a violent attitude. I didn't trust them. It was obvious they were stoned or something, and I don't do drugs.'

Next Jenkins wanted the history of abuse brought out. Lee was still operating within the realms of plausibility as she described a profession and a world that is generally recognised as hazardous. Few prostitutes escape abuse at the hands of at least some of their clients, and it would have been odd if Lee were any different. Her claim to have twice had mace guns taken from her was feasible. While she lived on Oleander Avenue between 1986 and 1988, she said, 'A couple of guys raped me without any weapon. I got hurt on that.'

She then described an attack by a man in Jacksonville. 'He beat me up so bad I couldn't describe my face. I got away from him, and finally got help. The police arrived and they told me that he'd raped a police officer's daughter . . . and that he'd killed two teenagers and they were in the backyard of his house, buried. That was one. I got away.'

Why did she stay on the roads after she'd been so badly hurt? 'Because it was my only way.'

She'd tried to get churches to help her, but was turned away because she wasn't a member of the congregation. She'd also tried to become a correctional officer, she said, seeming unaware of the irony of this revelation. The Salvation Army offered her refuge for one night only. She'd even tried to get into the military. Ultimately, prostitution was her only option.

Tricia Jenkins was ready to lead Lee into the testimonial mine-field that centred on Richard Mallory. Lee amplified the account Ms Jenkins had outlined in her opening statements. She had been coming from Fort Myers where she had spent a couple of nights. She saw one head in Mr Mallory's car, an indication she would be safe in accepting a ride. Her responses became lengthy and descriptive, forming an almost uninterrupted narrative that gripped the attention of all present. She was fleshing out the story with the colour and detail only she could provide. It was the very kind of intricacy that could lead her into treacherous waters. And indeed, she wove a tangled web that stretched the sympathies of even the most open-minded onlookers. One could only hazard a guess at the impact on the jury of the contradiction-laden, implausible and convoluted versions of events that emerged. Their faces were like masks.

She said she'd had a gun for protection for at least six months before Mr Mallory's death. He'd offered her a drink. She recalled seeing tonic bottles, what she thought was a Smirnoff vodka bottle, and perhaps orange juice. He'd offered her marijuana but she declined.

They chatted about their respective lines of work: Mr Mallory's video business and Lee's pressure-cleaning business. He said he was heading for a topless bar in Daytona and asked, Lee said, if she knew any girls out there, claiming he paid $2,000–3,000 or more for these sessions. Lee told him she didn't.

She was getting drunk, having emerged from the Office Pub

in Fort Myers with a few beers already inside her before hitching her ride.

She did not proposition Mallory for sex, she told the jury, because she was exhausted, had made enough money on her trip, and was anxious to get back to Ty. By her own account, Mallory was pleasant company and complimented her on being such a good listener that she was almost like a psychologist.

When he first suggested they stop somewhere, she'd been reluctant. She didn't have a key and was afraid the dog would bark if she tried to slip in late, which might wake up the motel manager. Plus, Ty had to get up early for work. But when he pressed her, she relented. It was his car; he was at the steering wheel.

Lee suggested a spot near Bunnell and once there, they talked for perhaps a couple of hours with Mallory returning repeatedly to the subject of porno movies. He'd smoked a lot of pot, but was handling it. By then comfortable with him, Lee admitted that her real occupation was hustling. Mallory seemed surprised.

'You mean for sex? I thought eventually we would get it on. But you don't do it for free?'

'No, I don't. This is my job. This is what I do for a living.'

'How much?' Mallory pressed.

'A hundred dollars an hour.'

Lee told the jury that she'd explained rubbers were mandatory. Mallory had some in his trunk, but wanted to move to a still more remote spot before they began. Lee suggested another place so dark and wooded that they couldn't even see down the deserted trail. He'd retrieved a flashlight from his glove compartment and put it on the dashboard, then suggested they both disrobe. Lee did so first, while Mallory went back to get his condoms and a blanket, 'so we wouldn't get anything on the car seat'.

Lee was half-undressed by then and said, 'This ain't fair', still in good humour. She mentioned her stretch marks and beer belly but he'd thought her not bad and said, 'You'll do.'

She'd suggested he take off his clothes so they could get started because it was cold in those first few hours of December 1989.

'He ignored me, and he was starting to act like he was unbuttoning his pants, unzipping his pants, and he said, "What if I told you I don't have enough money?"'

She asked how much he *did* have and when he said he only had a little for breakfast and gas, she told him no way. She wasn't there for her health, they'd have to call it off. She'd turned to grab her clothes which she'd put in the back seat and as she did so, she saw him coming towards her.

'I was going to turn to look at him, and before I even got a chance to turn and look at him, he wrapped a cord around by neck and pulled me towards him.'

Here it was then, the bondage to which Tricia Jenkins had alluded. After establishing that Lee had said 'no' to sex with him by then, Jenkins said, 'Tell us what happened after you felt the cord around your neck.'

'. . . I'm really nervous, and really shy, and embarrassed—and this is hard for me . . .'

Her words were falling on an unusually rapt courtroom. 'He said, "You're gonna do everything I tell you to do, and if you don't, I'll kill you right now . . . just like the other sluts . . ." He said, "It doesn't matter to me. Your body will still be warm for my . . . huge cock." And so, he was choking me and holding me like this, and he said, "Do you want to die, slut?"'

She said he'd then told her to lie down on the car seat and to give him her hands.'

'He lifted up my hands like this . . . and tied my hands to the steering wheel.'

He was sitting in the driver's seat. She was lying down.

'He told me to slide up and get comfortable, he was going to see how much meat he could pound in my ass.

'And he walked around from the driver's seat—opened the door—the door was closed. He was very aggressive so he got in and he lifted my legs all the way up . . . then he began to start having anal sex.'

Under Jenkins's probing, she went on. 'I was crying my brains out . . . he was saying that he loved hearing my pain and he loved hearing my crying, and it turned him on.'

Leaning forward, her forefingers pressed against her temples as if in extreme concentration, she told her hushed audience that

Mallory had bruised her cervix and ribs. Then, she claimed, he'd got out of the car, taken his clothes and walked back around to the driver's side. He'd fetched a red cooler from the boot, containing what she thought to be two large bottles of water, plus a tote bag and towel.

Still tied to the steering wheel, she said she turned her head, straining to watch.

'What are you doing?' Lee said she asked.

'I'm full of surprises,' her alleged attacker retorted, producing a bar of soap, toothbrush, rubbing alcohol and a small Visine bottle, then holding them in front of her face. No one in the courtroom could imagine what was coming next.

She continued: 'This guy begins to take a bath, because he had blood all over his face. And some other jazz which I don't think I should say.'

Lee told the jury that Richard Mallory poured the water all over himself while saying that he had to clean himself because the last sluts he'd been with had given him terrible diseases.

'I thought to myself: "I think this guy is going to kill me . . . dissect me or something. I don't know what he's got in his bag."'

Lee's horrific tale ran on.

'He puts his clothes back on. He gets the cooler, brings it back to the trunk, he puts everything in the tote bag, he leaves it there, he goes around the passenger side—grabs the bottle of Visine and goes around the passenger side—and he says, "This is one of my surprises."'

The defendant looked worn. She mumbled and sighed. She then described what Mallory had done with the Visine bottle.

'He lifts up my legs and puts what turns out to be rubbing alcohol in a Visine bottle, and he sticks some up my rectal area. It hurt really bad because he tore me up well.'

She'd been crying, and he also squirted rubbing alcohol up her nose. And for a moment, tears seemed to well up in Lee on the stand, but they subsided. She then described the way Mallory put the items back in the tote bag and the tote bag back in the boot. She was breathing hard as she said that his door was open and that she, still tied up, was freezing to death.

'I'm thinking he's going to kill me. I'm trying desperately to

438

get untied. I tried a million times. Finally he even said, "I can see you moving in there, don't worry, you're going to get untied." I kept trying. I kept moving my body.'

After what felt like an hour, he finally grew cold outside in the winter weather that he said he loved, and got back in the car. Lee went on with what he'd said: "'I'm going to untie you from the steering wheel. You'd better be a good girl." He untied me . . . put the rope around my neck and held it like a noose so he could hold me. I moved over, he moved in. He closed the door. He was still saying all kinds of jazz about what he wants to do. So then he told me to turn toward him, lay down, spread my legs. He had all his clothes on. I guess he was just going to unzip.'

At Jenkins's prodding, Lee said she may have asked why he had all his clothes on but she wasn't sure. It was hard with the alcohol-induced blackouts she'd had, to recall every incident, every word.

'He had me turn and wanted to start having sex with me . . . I later learned it was jacks to a stereo or TV or something. So, he was holding me like this, like reins.'

She held her arms up to her neck to demonstrate a restraining hold. She then grabbed for the cords, she said, thinking that she'd got to fight or she was going to die.

'He's already said he killed other girls. I gotta fight.'

She'd been working her way closer to her bag which she'd put near the hump between the seats. Then Mallory grabbed her and slapped her really hard in the face and started choking her. She jumped to her feet and, as he got onto his knees, pushed him back. They struggled.

'I jumped up real fast, and I spit in his face. And he said, "You're dead, bitch. You're dead."'

She lay down quickly and grabbed her bag as he started to come towards her.

'I grabbed my bag and whipped my pistol out towards him, and he was coming towards me with his right arm, and I shot immediately. I shot at him.

'He started coming at me again. I shot. He stopped. I kind of pushed him away from me. He kind of sat up on the driver's seat. I hurriedly opened the passenger door, ran around the driver's

439

side, opened the door real fast, looked at him and he started to come out. And I said, "Don't come near me, I'll shoot you again", or something like that. "Don't make me have to shoot you again", something like that. He just started coming at me and I shot him . . . he fell on the ground.'

She then described what happened after she shot him for the last time. 'I stood there and looked at him. Thought what I'm going to do with the car, and just said, "I gotta drag him away from the car", 'cause he's near the car. I dragged him away, got back in the car, totally nude.'

She'd reached to turn the ignition key, but it wasn't there. She said she hurried back to Mallory's body and frantically searched his pockets. She then spotted a piece of carpet.

'I didn't want birds to be picking at his body, so I grabbed the carpet and threw it over him.'

She drove back to Quail Run, crying and shaking. She had to get dressed, had to think. She went to the car boot and cleaned herself with the things Mr Mallory had used.

'Sat there, didn't know what to do. Drinking a beer and thinking what am I gonna do?'

Deciding she'd have to lie low, she cleaned off the fingerprints and put what was left of his marijuana in her own tote bag. She was scared while she was throwing stuff out. Looking at his watch, she noted it was 6.30 a.m. She recounted her thoughts to the jury: '"I've gotta hurry up and get back to Ty. I'm tired and beat up. I'm hurting all over. My crotch hurts, my vagina hurts, my nose hurts. I'm freaking out. I've gotta go take a shower." These are the things that are going through my mind.'

Her most pressing need was to dump the car. She'd planned to drive it through a car wash but instead went straight home to the Ocean Shores Motel. She said that Ty opened the door for her and that she immediately saw that their dog, Maggie, had wreaked havoc, ripping the furniture and the curtains. She told the jury that, coincidentally, they were supposed to move that day. Everything was ready, packed in boxes. Anticipating a visit from the cops once the motel manager saw the damage the dog had done, Lee said she called over to the new apartment and said they were coming right over. (Her report, of course, contradicted Ty's.)

Yes, Ty had quizzed her angrily about what she thought were hickey marks on her neck, but she'd brushed off the accusation, saying she must have scratched a mosquito bite. Once they'd moved their belongings to the new apartment, Lee drove Tyria back to the motel where they picked up Ty's moped, which she drove to work, and Lee's bicycle, which she put in the boot. She then went to the car wash and cleaned off the car.

'I forgot the glove box, and that's where his . . . I found his wallet underneath the seat.'

She scanned its contents, verifying that the man she'd left in the woods was indeed named Richard. And she found she'd also forgotten to get rid of all the stuff that was under the seat.

'Everything. I was finding like pens, tumblers, business cards, vodka bottle.'

So she threw it all out near where she left the car.

Did she take anything out of Mr Mallory's wallet? Tricia Jenkins enquired. She believed she had retrieved somewhere between $38 and $42. Had she taken his credit cards? She had not.

Jenkins went on to let the jury know that Lee had a prior felony conviction, defusing the impact of that news on the jury. She also established that Lee had never had anal sex before this occasion with Mr Mallory. What had she said to her attacker, Jenkins wanted to know, when he turned violent?

'I couldn't. He was choking me so hard, that blood was running to my head, spots were before my eyes.'

It was 11 a.m. when Jenkins announced that she had no further questions.

John Tanner would cross-examine the defendant in what seemed a wise and calculated strategy. If the mild-mannered Mr Tanner could unnerve Ms Wuornos, it would be enormously more effective than if it were done by the combative (and consequently less sympathetic) Mr Damore. Yet John Tanner wasted no time with pleasantries, heading straight for the blatantly apparent weaknesses in Lee's tale of terror.

She had seen the video the day before, along with the jurors, had she not? And she had not made one single mention of anal rape, or of being tied up, or of having alcohol squirted in her rectum, had she?

Lee sounded mildly indignant when she replied, 'I told you that he was getting violent. Also, I told you before, in the first confession, that he was talking about anal sex.'

'Did you, in fact, anywhere in that videotape, or did you tell Detective Horzepa at any time, that you were strangled with a cord by Mr Mallory?'

'Every time I tried to start telling him about what was happening, he'd interrupt me and ask me, "How many times was this person shot? What kind of items did you take? Did he say anything after . . . when you shot him? Where did you leave his car?" I never got a chance to ever express myself. I was always interrupted.'

Here she was really straining credibility: the jurors had seen the videotape. They'd also seen the real-life presence of Larry Horzepa on the witness stand and had seen him to be an apparently gentle, soft-spoken fellow. They'd also seen him give her a chance to express herself.

When John Tanner reminded her that Horzepa had in fact said he *wanted* her to tell him all the facts, she switched tactics. She explained that her main, in fact *only,* purpose in being there to confess, was to proclaim Tyria's innocence. She could remember nothing, she said. 'I was hysterical. I was shocked. And they had forced me to talk, saying they were going to arrest Ty Moore if I don't answer their questions on the case, which I didn't want. I was only there to confess about Ty's innocence, 'cause I had just got done talking to her on the phone and told her I was going to confess to clear her. I didn't even know I was going to have to talk about anything because of that. If I did, believe me, I couldn't remember nothing. I was totally out of it.'

John Tanner challenged her further. 'You could remember being anally raped if you'd been anally raped, couldn't you?'

'I wasn't even interested in telling them certain things, because I was interested in Tyria Moore, and I was mad that they had threatened me that if I don't talk to them, they were going to

442

arrest Ty Moore, so I was pretty well belligerent and stubborn,' she said.

Foolhardily, she expanded the accusation, saying that these threats had come before the camera was turned on. Of course, the jury had seen for themselves the previous day what were clearly the interview's first, introductory moments in glorious videotaped colour.

Tanner went on to have Lee again make her claim that she didn't talk about the anal rape and the alcohol and being tied up because the detective had cut her off. Was it, he suggested, that she'd forgotten about it? And now she'd given another reason for not mentioning it, he reminded her. She'd said she was just there to talk about Ty Moore and was stubborn.

Lee said there were a lot of reasons why she hadn't brought up the anal rape. 'I was there to confess that Tyria Moore was innocent.' She took a breath, then added: 'That was pretty much a flat-out lie because I loved her so much I was protecting her.'

'Well, are you lying to protect her today?'

'Oh, I'll be more than happy to explain that Tyria Moore knows more than she's saying, that she knows it's self-defence,' Lee said, sarcasm creeping in.

'Are you lying to protect her today?'

'No, I'm not. I will tell you all about Tyria Moore.'

John Tanner took Lee back to her accusation that she'd been forced to talk. Yes, she'd been advised of her rights, but she'd spent fifteen minutes with the deputies before either the tape or video was turned on.

'That was when they threatened me.'

'They threatened you?'

'Yes, they did.'

She rambled on, but her claims had a hollow ring.

Lee's statements took another startling turn when the lover to save whom, she claimed, she had confessed, became the target of her accusations. She had never publicly said a bad word about Ty (whom privately she called 'butt-face') before this day, yet now her negative feelings came spilling out, laced with sarcasm.

She'd been pretty amazed to find that her ex-lover had been taken into protective custody, she said sarcastically.

Clearly, the long, lonely hours in various Florida jails had provided Lee with ample time to think. And she'd come to the hard realisation that Tyria had betrayed her to save her own skin. She'd also realised that Ty had repeatedly lied to her during those incendiary taped phone calls between them. The calls that had led her to confess and landed her in this mess. There was no mistaking it. The woman she loved so very desperately had abandoned her and turned on her.

Now, with her own neck on the line, Lee siezed what might be her last chance to strike back and blurt some accusations of her own. It seemed she was about to verify rumours that she wasn't willing to go down without implicating her oh-so-innocent ex-lover.

Ty knew a lot more than she was letting on, Lee enigmatically informed Mr Tanner and the jury.

Rising to this irresistible bait, Mr Tanner asked just what exactly it was that Ty had knowledge of, but wasn't telling. A hush fell over the spectators: were they now going to hear that Ty had played an active role in the homicides? Would they hear that the original second suspect who'd been out walking the streets, was indeed guilty of murder?

Lee's response was decidedly anti-climactic: 'She knows that it's self-defence, but she is not telling anybody anything. That's basically about it.'

There was a pause, but she seemed to know she had to say more.

'She knows it's self-defence, and she's not saying anything because she's involved with these books and movies. And she's involved in her family, not losing her family. I know her very well. She doesn't want to lose her family, and she's willing to lie for that. She's also worried about being arrested for accessory to the fact, after the fact.'

John Tanner zeroed in on a gap in logic. 'If it was self-defence, if you *really* feel Mr Mallory was self-defence, how would that jeopardise Tyria Moore?'

'Because Tyria Moore was interested in making the five hundred million dollars that . . . has already been offered her.'

She had just cited a truly ludicrous figure, but she went on to claim that the people involved in books and movies needed her blood in order to get their money. Her voice rose in anger. 'She doesn't want to say it's self-defence, because I believe she is involved with millions of dollars for books and movies. And she doesn't want my acquittal, because if I get convicted, she gets multi-millions.

'So does Mr Horzepa, whatever his name is, Munster, and a lot of you other detectives and police officers that are involved in this. And also, that her family is really . . . she loves her family to the max. Her family's rejecting her. That's tearing her up because I know her to the max.'

Mr Tanner was getting to Lee, who was intelligent enough to realise that she was not gaining any points at this stage. Suddenly, she went for sympathy. And she accused Ty of having amnesia. Ty was acting like she didn't even know how long they were in the Zodiac Bar the first night they met, acting like she didn't know where Lee lived. Ty knew she was living in a car because she'd just broken up with her former female lover, Toni. Tyria, she sniped, was lying to keep herself from being an 'accessory to the fact' about everything.

Lee had a capper: 'I've got two hundred and eighty-nine lies in her deposition that she gave. Just flat-out lies.'

Was there anything else Ty knew about Mr Mallory that would incriminate her in his death? the prosecutor asked. Lee backpedalled: Ty merely knew a little bit about the murder. 'She's always telling me, "Don't tell me the rest or I won't pass the polygraph!"'

Ty *had* witnessed the bruises and signs of her attack, Lee contended. She'd only been covering for Ty when she told Larry Horzepa that Ty didn't know anything, she said, breaking into a wan smile.

So she'd *lied* to Larry Horzepa?

'Yeah.'

Tanner next tied Lee in knots in another area full of contradictions. Had she told Ty she'd found a guy in the woods or that she'd killed a guy in the woods? And exactly *when* had she told her what she told her? Lee complained that Ty didn't believe her when she described what had happened and said it had been fourteen days after Mr Mallory's murder when she told her. When she knew she would probably see Mr Mallory's car on television and recognise it, she'd said, 'Remember the day you saw bruises on my neck?'

(This delay in telling Ty represented yet another deviation from Lee's 'I killed a man today' version, which was also what Ty had testified had happened.)

The picture Lee painted of her and Ty veered back and forth between one of loving trust and closeness, and one reflecting deep anger at Ty's betrayal.

'So you didn't even tell her this rape story until two weeks after it happened?' John Tanner prodded.

'I was scared to, because I didn't want her to worry or get scared. She loved me very badly, and I loved her very badly. I didn't just want to sit here and tell her what happened.'

'And then you say that you told her all these details about the alcohol and the anal rape and the tying up and all of that?'

No, she hadn't, Lee insisted. But she and Ty did have a tight bond: 'Very close. Like two peas in a pod. Right arm, left arm, moved together. We loved each other very much.'

What broke up this trusting union? Mr Tanner enquired. Lee responded that after seeing the police sketch on TV of two females, she told Ty she'd have to leave.

She'd talked to the investigators for Ty's sake, to prove her love, but had come to realise Ty was working with them to trap her, and now she knew Ty wouldn't help her out. 'I never knew she had a black heart.'

Inevitably, Tanner pointed out that not once during the eleven phone calls had Lee said a single word about being raped. That was because she was totally focused on clearing Ty. Tanner wanted to clarify that although Ty knew some of what happened she didn't participate in any way.

'She *knows* that I was raped, not in detail, but she knows I was defending myself.'

More than sixty-five times in those calls, Tanner said, Lee had said it was either mistaken identity or that Ty was innocent. It was a tactic, Lee responded, just in case Tyria was lying to her about the calls not being taped. She didn't want to say anything to put Ty in jeopardy.

'Or yourself?' Mr Tanner sniffed.

And hadn't she more than twenty-five times suggested Ty lie for her? Hadn't she briefed Ty to tell the truth but not to mention her?

'I don't recall that. If I did, then I said next that it's a very confusing situation. It's a very intense, scary, shocking moment . . .'

Those casual calls to her best friend weren't shocking, Mr Tanner scoffed. And since she'd suspected the police were listening in, 'Wouldn't those calls have been the ideal time to have said, "You know I had to do it because I was raped so brutally and had to defend myself"? Wouldn't that have been something to say for the police to hear?'

Lee's response was that she didn't want to say Ty knew anything and to make her an accessory. Tanner quickly torpedoed that argument. Saying that Ty knew about the murders had been almost the first thing out of Lee's mouth. He was on a roll by then.

Lee had been quick to suggest Ty's greed regarding a movie and book deal, but hadn't she herself signed a contract with filmmaker Jackelyn Giroux?

'We have a lawsuit going on,' Lee retorted. 'We are filing a lawsuit.'

'You talked about if any money was to be made out of this, you'd like Ty to have it?' Tanner persisted.

'No,' Lee shot back. 'If I said anything to her, in a letter . . . which I can't understand how I could have wrote her while I was in jail—because as soon as I got done talking to the detectives, they stuck me in solitary confinement, lock-down, shoving pills down me, and got me messed up on drugs, forcing me. And I didn't have any pen or pencil or paper to write. And you people are saying these letters came in January in jail. I don't remember writing any letters whatsoever.'

'Who was this that was forcing drugs down you?'

Tanner's question was calm. He didn't have to do anything. Lee was doing quite well on her own.

'They had me on Vistaril. They had me where I didn't have any commissary. Not even a Bible or books, nothing to read . . . they'd come up and say, "Do you want your pills so they'll help you go to sleep?" Of course I took them to sleep. Vistaril, I was taking 2,800 mg a week, sixteen pills a day. Almost killed me. They almost killed me.'

As if all that were not dramatic enough, she added that it was the detective's idea.

'You're saying that Detective Horzepa was forcing you to take pills?' John Tanner asked, incredulously.

'It was the plan, I believe,' she said coolly.

John Tanner could no longer tolerate such blatant misrepresentation by the almost-cheerful star of the prosecution's explosive videotape. Had she *seen* the video? Did she *see* herself shaking? Hadn't she been smoking?

She'd been shaking like a leaf, very nervous and cold, Ms Wuornos replied. That's why she'd been wearing a detective's jacket.

Tanner moved on to point out that she'd never once said on the telephone that Mr Mallory had tried to rob her. Lee had an answer for that, too. Why should she? All she was thinking about was clearing Ty.

Hadn't she also said she was planning to sue law enforcement? The defendant's response was casual. 'Who knows? I was withdrawing so bad from alcohol . . . I was so confused and so scared about Tyria that I couldn't function properly. I don't know what I was saying. I was totally in another . . . I was in Pluto. Scared out of my wits. Caring about Tyria, loved her to the max. Must have told her twenty-five times a day, "I love you."'

Taking a few more swipes at Tyria, Lee said she'd supported her for three and a half years. Tanner spotted another contradiction and pounced on it. Then why had Lee told detectives that Tyria did nothing *but* work from morning to night? Lee's confusion was now glaringly apparent. She stumbled to keep her stories straight, as Tanner put it.

The prosecutor switched back to the subject of prostitution, suggesting that she was in it for the money; good money. Lee agreed. He elicited her price list: $30 for head, $35 for straight sex, $40 for half and half, $100 an hour. She could make anywhere from $600 to $1,000 a week then? Tanner asked. And it all went on Tyria, buying her fancy clothes, Lee came back. (This raised a chuckle in the gallery. Ty in fancy clothes?)

Lee said she was a prostitute because she didn't have the qualifications for a normal job. She'd never been able to hold one down; had always been fired. And she liked prostitution? Tanner asked. Lee admitted to liking the sex and some of the clients. Some became like brothers. But it was a job. Tanner's next question was asked in a voice laden with sarcasm. 'It was kind of a rolling road party, wasn't it?'

For a moment, Lee almost laughed at the idea. But she went on to answer seriously. 'No, because you have to watch yourself and be careful and keep a level head on your shoulders. It's a job. It's not, like, super-exciting.'

Lee told Tanner that she armed herself purely for protection. She'd been raped many times: three times while with Tyria. (Tears of sympathy rolled down Arlene Pralle's cheeks.) She'd needed to defend herself five times. She'd needed to defend herself before Richard Mallory, but couldn't because she didn't have a weapon.

So, she was saying that if she'd had a gun she would have used it earlier? Tanner enquired. She didn't know. Every situation was different. How could she answer that? she complained. But she tried.

'If it's very violent and physical, I'm going to defend myself, yes. Everybody has a right to defend themselves. That's what I did. These were violent, violent rapes, and the other ones I had to beg for my life. I had a double-barrel shotgun against my head. I had a .357 magnum against my head.'

Despite prostitution being illegal, she defended her career, saying three million other women do it. She was kind and nice in her work, and even talked to the men about religion and Jesus coming soon.

Did she think it was OK to violate the law if a lot of other people did? Tanner wanted to know.

'Everybody prostitutes, even housewives. And so do the men. They're out there, they're the ones with the money, putting it on the hood, saying to us prostitutes, you know, "Here we are." If they'd keep their money in their back pockets and their penis in their pants, they wouldn't be feeding prostitution. They're the ones who feed it. We're just out there making our money.'

She wasn't hurting anyone by selling her body. It was a job, and if anyone was the victim, she was. Mr Mallory had no reason to rape her. She didn't provoke him or any of these men. They hurt *her*. She came close to death so many times.

Just as she was on the brink of launching into a speech about the years taking their toll, Tanner cut her off with another question. Lee's team objected before she could answer his loaded probe on whether she was the victim in every case where she'd hurt someone. He rephrased it: 'I'm only trying to ask you why you killed six other men.'

Lee retorted that she was only there on trial for one man. Richard Mallory. One trial. Tanner went on to ask about her prostitution clients, and who propositioned whom, but when he mentioned the previous day's witness, Bobby Lee Copas, Lee claimed she had never set eyes on him before in her life. She believed Copas had been put up to it by Jackye Giroux to get some media attention.

He wasn't the kind of guy she mixed with. She didn't go to truck stops; truckers were too dirty. Nor would her gun have fitted in her purse the way he'd said it did. She carried it in her tote bag. And she would never have dealt with someone that fat. He was lying.

Mr Tanner asked whether she'd practised how quickly she could pull her weapon, quick-draw style? Lee laughed sarcastically. 'Oh, yes! I doubt that!'

She'd never done that in her life. When she got home from work she was far too tired for anything like that, she said disgustedly.

She smiled when asked if she was aware that it was against the law to carry a firearm. Then, full of righteous indignation, she explained that as a convicted felon she was denied the right to buy a firearm legally. Otherwise she would have bought one. It was obviously a pet subject. A lot of nice, decent people are convicted felons coming out of prison, she continued. A lot of them turn to the Lord. They have to have some way to protect themselves.

Somehow, she'd cast felons in the curious role of deprived citizens.

'You're even a victim of the law?' Tanner asked.

'We can't use our *hands*. That's what I'm saying. You have to have a weapon. Or are you trying to tell us convicted felons to not defend ourselves? We have to have a way to defend ourselves.'

'You think that all convicted felons . . . should be allowed to carry guns?'

'A lot of them do turn to the Lord. And a lot of them are very decent people. Very straightforward people. So, they broke the law. Everybody breaks the law. I bet you do too.'

'And some of them shoot men to death in cold blood, don't they?' ventured Tanner, his voice rising.

'No, they don't! I didn't shoot anybody in cold blood.'

There was a pause.

'I don't have the heart to shoot someone in cold blood!'

'Did you ever shoot a man in the back of the head because he was gurgling?' Mr Tanner said forcefully.

'Objection!' cried Tricia Jenkins.

'Sustained,' ruled the judge.

As Lee's counsel fought to quieten her, David Damore chimed in, then Billy Nolas, prompting Judge Blount to actually dispatch a deputy to bring him a roll of masking tape which he threatened to use on the two lawyers.

(Was the judge in the habit of taping the mouths of unruly counsel? the journalists later asked. 'It wouldn't be the first time,' Blount said with a wry chuckle.)

Moving on, John Tanner began zeroing in on Lee's inconsistencies. She'd earlier accused Mallory of being unwilling to unzip his pants. That didn't gel with this latest Visine/rubbing alcohol/rape account. Lee was indignant.

451

'I told you guys about anal screwing with Mallory in the beginning!'

She complained about having been questioned improperly in the confession. She'd been on a five-week 'royal binge of drinking since Ty left me and I was all bummed out about her leaving me'. The drink had given her blackouts. She was incoherent, in shock, interested only in clearing Tyria Moore, and now she was getting just as confused again! (As indeed were those listening.) She tried asserting that the complaint about Mallory being unwilling to unzip his pants referred not to immediately before the shooting but to earlier on in the ordeal.

Time and again, Tanner drove home the inconsistencies between Lee's convoluted stories, the failings in logic. And time and again she blamed them on her total incoherence, her hysteria, her distress. Emotions that were glaringly absent during her confession. The jury could not fail to notice the great discrepancy between Lee's visible demeanour in the videotape and what she was asking them to believe.

Far from incoherent, tearful and 'freaking out', she'd seemed for the most part rather cheerful, almost to be enjoying herself. And far more concerned with how detectives had found her than awash with remorse for her victims. Tanner asked about her nine-shot .22 gun. She'd thrown it away, she claimed, as advised by Tyria Jolene Moore at the end of their relationship. She also claimed Ty had told her to make sure she cleaned the vehicle real good if she ever ran into anything like that again.

Tanner wanted to establish that her gun was not an automatic, but that she'd had to pull the trigger and cock it.

'It shoots real easy. It's got like a hairpin trigger,' Lee blithely replied, seemingly unaware of the point he was scoring for 'intent'.

Tanner also confronted her with her sudden recollection of details like the rubbing alcohol, details that had never, ever been heard of or mentioned before.

She snapped back: 'And I can talk about every one of them today, but I'm not going to.'

Moving on to the bullets, Tanner pointed out that on the video she'd stood up and shown Horzepa where the first bullet had struck Mr Mallory on his right side. Her account of what happened in the car didn't gel with that either.

'I guess that's what I said,' Lee allowed. 'I can't take the typing and erase it . . . but this is an incoherent mish-mash.'

'You certainly are willing to admit he was behind the steering wheel when you shot him, aren't you?'

'I was lying down in the passenger seat. Lying down across the whole car.'

'He was behind the wheel?'

'He was up on his knees, one leg down, one knee up on the seat.'

'And you were lying down?'

'I was . . . my legs were up. He was having me spread my legs.'

'Can you explain why the bullet, which you shot in his side, didn't enter low and go upward and high if you were lying on the seat shooting up?'

'I thought he was so decomposed you couldn't tell. How come you say that?' she retorted. Her detachment was shocking.

Moving on, Tanner had other points to drive home: 'You shot him immediately, didn't give him a chance to say anything, did you?'

'What am I supposed to do, stop the clock and rationalise with this guy who wanted to kill me?'

'You didn't give him a chance to say anything when you shot him the first time, did you?'

'No, I didn't.'

'What about the second time?'

'No!'

'What about the third time?'

'No.'

'What about the last time when you shot him on the ground?'

'I didn't shoot him on the ground. I shot him as he was coming out of the car.'

She decided to explain further. 'I didn't know what the dickens he was doing, I didn't know if he had another gun under the seat, and I didn't know if he was going to reach for another weapon. I didn't know what he had.'

453

'He didn't have a weapon in that car, did he?'

'How do I know?' Lee replied, all sarcasm.

Tanner got back to the robbery aspects. She had dipped into Mr Mallory's pockets. She'd contended she turned them inside-out, not to steal his money but to retrieve his car keys and that he was wearing tight jeans.

'They were still zipped up, weren't they?'

'Yes, they were.'

'He had his pants on and that's what made you mad? He wouldn't take them off?'

'That's not what happened!'

Lee had pawned Mallory's radar detector for $30 because she needed rent money. And she'd had the car washed to get the fingerprints off. She'd shot him because she had no choice. But she denied Tanner's contention she had intended to kill him.

'I'm not the greatest aimer,' she said.

Revealing further the fracture in her loyalty for Ty, Lee admitted to keeping the razor belonging to one victim because Ty wanted her to. She addressed the issue of the stolen property: 'I felt like what he did to me was unnecessary, and so therefore, when I took his property . . . I figured, well, like . . .'

Jenkins hurried to halt her, but Lee finished her sentence anyway:

'. . . he owed me for what he did to me.'

Tanner wanted to address the issue of motive further.

'Isn't one of the reasons you killed Mr Mallory because you didn't want him to tell on you?'

The question prompted a halting, rambling reply. 'I had to do what I had to do. If he would have been alive, he would have probably told the cops I tried to rob him and kill him, which is not true. I am a prostitute. Nobody is going to believe that I'm a prostitute and that he raped me and that he tried to strangle me and kill me. And he was going to probably do all kinds of other things to me throughout the whole day and the next morning, or whatever . . . how long he was going to keep me. I don't believe anybody would have believed me.

'We've got prostitutes out there that are being killed every day, and nobody cares about it. And we've got women being raped every day, and it doesn't seem that they are prostitutes, that nobody cares about. I have witnessed with my own eyes, reading the newspapers, numerous, numerous, numerous times. I believe that nobody would believe me. So, when I made that statement, I meant, referring to the fact that nobody would have believed that I was raped, and that I had to defend myself.'

'So you decided that you had to kill him?'

'He was dying. I'm talking about other . . . different situations. I'm telling you, I'm not talking about Richard Mallory now.'

'Well, what had you decided after you shot him the last time, square in the chest?'

'When he was coming out of the vehicle? That's where it was very obvious to shoot at . . .' her voice trailed off.

'And you say that, here you were, a woman who was ravaged and naked, right?'

'Yes, I was naked.'

'Cord marks around your neck which had been strangled, right?'

'Yes.'

'Bleeding from the anus where you'd been raped, right?'

'Yes.' Her voice was barely audible. She seemed reluctant to answer.

'Alcohol in a Visine bottle, where this torture took place, right?'

'Alcohol to drink?'

'The alcohol that was squirted up your anus.'

'Oh. Yes.'

'A cord with which you had been tied to the wheel and held by the neck, and no one would believe that you'd been assaulted?'

Tanner asked the question rhetorically, his voice rising in a crescendo of barely disguised disgust. The marks on her neck were very small, she said.

'Well, how about your anus? You said that was bleeding and ripped?'

'The way I was, it was too much for me to walk out of there

nude with a gun in my hand and walk down the road and say, "Someone help me!" No way.'

She, like everyone else, had the right to defend herself.

'And you never even bothered to tell your best friend, until the news of the murder came up on television?'

Tanner managed to get that in before the judge sustained an objection by Billy Nolas, cutting him off.

Lee Wuornos's imagined moment of glorious vindication had disintegrated into disaster. She had realised her counsels' worst fears.

And as the court adjourned for lunch, the pink tissues in front of the defendant sat pointedly unused.

48

After lunch, Jackie Davis, Mallory's ex-girlfriend, took the stand outside the jury's presence so that the defence, who had not had the chance to depose her, could decide whether or not to call her. After Lee, Davis was anti-climactic, to say the least. She seemed to all assembled spectators to be fudging the answers to Billy Nolas's questions. She had suffered a head injury a few years earlier which she now claimed meant she was unable to remember portions of her interview with Larry Horzepa two years before. Yet her responses, and the instances of 'amnesia', seemed spotty, hopping around in a manner consistent with someone who simply didn't want to testify.

Richard Mallory, she agreed, had told her he'd been charged with a burglary in his teens and had been put on a rehabilitation programme. She wasn't clear what kind of rehabilitation. He'd had an involvement with an ambassador's wife and had thought at times that he was being followed. Yes, she remembered telling Horzepa he was paranoid.

Nolas asked if she recalled telling detectives that Mallory had said he'd been in jail for ten years? She did not. Perhaps this sea change had less to do with her injury, more to do with the fact that upon reflection she felt less comfortable with repeating gossip she'd heard. And Mallory's obsession with washing himself? She'd forgotten that completely.

The jury did not see or hear Jackie Davis, for the defence decided not to call her, after all.

Instead, they saw Lee returned to the stand (looking drained and subdued) as the defence went on to formally rest its case.

John Tanner recalled Larry Horzepa to clarify once and for all that his and Munster's interview with Wuornos began and ended with the tape rolling, that he did not try to cut her off, and that he never once threatened her, or threatened to arrest Tyria Moore if she didn't confess to the murders.

The jurors had the weekend to relax. On Monday, they would hear closing arguments.

Speaking that weekend from her home behind bars, Lee Wuornos admitted that she'd been 'scared shitless' before testifying. There was a new piece of evidence, she said, sounding optimistic. It would prove she was raped and the jury would have to be crazy not to believe her. (Supposedly a photograph of scratch marks on Mallory's steering wheel, it was never presented in court.)

By Monday morning, back in DeLand, the judge (wearing a dusty pink jacket and white polo shirt that he topped with his robes for the jury) asked the defendant if she had any questions. Lee spoke softly, her voice childlike. 'No, sir, I don't think so; I trust my lawyers.'

Before William Miller and John Tanner went on to present their closing arguments, the judge tossed out a word of warning, a classic example of what those assembled had come to recognise as a true Bunky-ism: 'I only remind you, counsel, that the mind can assimilate only what the posterior can endure.'

A low communal chuckle rippled through the gallery.

William Miller, who had been on the sidelines throughout much of the trial, had been selected for this crucial task. Speaking softly, he went straight to what was for the defence the veritable heart of the matter. So much of what the jury had heard had nothing to do with Mr Mallory, Miller said imploringly. It was their task to consider Mr Mallory that night—and other juries would consider the other men they'd heard about. He reminded them that Ty was a suspect, and requested that they ask themselves, maybe Aileen Wuornos *did* act in self-defence?

He hit home again with the way Ty had coerced Lee, who loved her. How she had lied to her and threatened suicide and made those taped phone calls. Ty had said that never once in their time together had Lee laid a hand on her.

Larry Horzepa, Miller said, going back to something that had come up in the trial, had written a note to himself in the margin of the typed transcript of Wuornos's confession, a note saying, 'Don't use'. Miller's voice rose in indignation, planting again the suggestion that the investigator had been intending to edit what transpired in that interview to the benefit of the prosecution: 'You're to hear that Lee shot Richard Mallory—but you're not to hear why!'

Just like Ty Moore, Miller went on, Horzepa didn't want to hear about the rape. He also addressed the way John Tanner had so tied Lee in knots. 'Lee Wuornos may have been confused, may have been rattled by the skilful cross-examination of Mr Tanner. Don't forget Mr Tanner is here before you, asking you to send her to her death.'

Richard Mallory, Miller contended, had ultimately tortured Lee. She'd been a prostitute for some seventeen years prior to Mr Mallory. As a prostitute, Lee had been beaten before. Richard Mallory raped and tortured her and she finally took a life. Maybe something had finally snapped in her, Miller suggested. And she finally took a life. But 'Far from being the predator that John Tanner describes, Lee Wuornos is a victim; victim of a brutal attack.'

After lunch, it was John Tanner's turn to talk about premeditation. Premeditation, he wanted the jury to be assured, did not mean, as they may have in their minds, long-range planning.

'It may only be the time between picking up a firearm and firing. Or it may only be between the first and second shot. But surely by the third shot, and certainly by the fourth shot.'

He told them they would be called upon for two verdicts. One, on the robbery. Wuornos could be guilty of armed robbery; robbery with a deadly weapon but without a firearm; robbery without a firearm or a deadly weapon; robbery without a weapon. She could also be guilty of petty theft. Or she could be not guilty.

On the murder charge, she could be guilty in the first degree of premeditated and felony murder as charged. She could also be guilty only of first-degree, premeditated murder. She could be guilty of first-degree felony murder; or of second-degree murder; or of second-degree murder with a firearm. She could be guilty of third-degree murder; or of third-degree murder with a firearm. She could be guilty of manslaughter, or manslaughter with a firearm. Or she could be not guilty.

The judge would instruct them on all their alternative findings. Mr Tanner went on to say that Aileen Wuornos, despite the way she had been portrayed by the defence, was not a victim in any sense of the word. She was not a victim because she was a prostitute. She was not a child but a grown, healthy woman. She was a prostitute because of money. She indicated she liked sex, and there was nothing wrong with that, said Mr Tanner, Daytona's famous porn-buster. He harked back to Tricia Jenkins's story of Lee being afraid as she hitchhiked that night. Of what? Mr Tanner asked. This was what she did. Hitchhikers are usually delighted when a car stops for them!

Tricia Jenkins, Tanner went on, had said that her client was beaten and raped repeatedly. Yet not once had she told anyone! Not even Ty, her best friend, during four and a half years of living together! He also disputed Lee's contention that she was royally drunk. Mallory had bought her a six-pack of beer and she'd had at least one left after the murder. That was not a person who was royally drunk out of her mind.

Similar fact evidence, he told the jury, was not that unusual, and it *was* relevant and material and admissible in court. The other victims *were* key issues in this case, and they were all relevant. It was relevant to prove identity, opportunity, preparation, planning, pattern, intent, motive. And in this case the absence of self-defence was relevant.

All the men were travelling major thoroughfares alone.

'Each of them made one fatal mistake—they found Aileen Wuornos.'

She left no witnesses. Stripped their vehicles. He stacked up the points against her. Her pattern had begun to change, Tanner contended. Her appetite to control men—shared by most prostitutes—was tremendous. There was only one thing left; and that was to kill. He pointed out that the bullet holes were not consistent with the picture Lee painted of a man on his knees on top of her.

Tanner also asked them to think about why Ty Moore would come in and lie. Had Lee in fact acted in self-defence, that might have given some moral justification for Ty not reporting her crimes. If that were true, it would have been better for Ty to have said so. Lee had said that Ty would make a lot of money lying about the self-defence issue. Untrue, Tanner said.

'Wouldn't it be a much more interesting story, a much more sellable story, if this poor, pitiful prostitute who was simply doing her job and some guy does horrible things to her—she killed him in self-defence? Now, that's a good story.'

Tanner had the courtroom's full attention.

'And then her girlfriend who knew all about it got on the stand and told the jury how it was self-defence. How when Aileen came in, she had bruises on her neck—she could hardly talk, he almost choked her—and had been beaten brutally, and that she administered to her private parts of her body because they were torn . . . and there was blood on her clothes and underwear, and that this was a terrible thing.'

All of that, plus how she'd been a victim of the state of Florida, he contended, was a good story. 'That would sell a lot of books.'

Tanner criticised, too, the defendant's attacks on Deputy Horzepa. She had told the jury that everyone had lied, from Richard Mallory to Mr Copas, whom she'd accused of wanting publicity.

Tanner then went right to the heart of the matter: 'Well, did Richard Mallory give her money in advance which she then was afraid he'd take back, as she said in her first statement? Or was he just a nice guy, and she decided she could trust him and wasn't worried about the money until they had an argument about unzipping his pants, as she said in her second story? Had she had the gun two months or two days?'

She knew what she was doing, she wasn't missing a lick, he said, repeating her damning comment about thinking the body was too decomposed for law enforcement to be able to tell the angle of the bullets. She had, Tanner said, carried her pattern of manipulation into the courtroom to try to manipulate their verdict. He pointed out that there was no physical evidence found to tie with her claims of brutality: no cords, no rope. He then went on to her suggestion that she'd been threatened with the persecution of Ty Moore if she didn't confess.

'I think you have a clear choice here. Either Deputy Horzepa planned to sit there and not tell you the truth, or she's not telling you the truth. There's no grey area there. Someone of the two is not telling the truth.

'In fact she told us in her testimony; she said, "I'm the *only* one telling the truth. Everybody else is lying." She said that in court. That everyone else is lying—to convict an innocent person?'

Tanner then moved on to Tyria Moore. She'd told Ty just enough that she wouldn't flip out when she saw the car, but didn't tell her everything. And Ty should have come to the police.

'Maybe, just maybe, it would have stopped right here. Ty Moore is not on trial. Aileen Wuornos is.'

Ty hadn't wanted to get involved. People don't want to get involved. The system cannot work that way, Tanner opined. Ty's refusal to accept and believe, her not telling anyone, had perhaps cost six men's lives.

'That doesn't hold her up with anything respectful or honourable at all. But by the same token, if she'd been told this was a brutal, anal rape, etc., it would at least give her some moral justification for not saying anything. She knows that. And she would have said that if it was true. Because it's not true, she didn't say it. It was bad enough that she didn't come forward. But at least she didn't sit on that witness stand and lie to you to perpetuate and protect this woman who killed Mr Mallory.'

That point forcefully made, he closed by hammering home the portrait of a murder born of greed: 'This was a woman who could make, according to her own testimony, $30–50,000 a year, and squander it just as quick. This is a woman moving out of power and control into a new and unfathomable—for you and I—area of domination, to the extent of snuffing out a life.'

His voice rose with horror. 'It became obscenely simple to have it all!'

She chose her life, Tanner said, and she had left the jury with no reasonable choice but to find her guilty of murder in the first degree, and of armed robbery.

The defence had more to say on behalf of their visibly furious client. William Miller was rapidly back on his feet, suggesting that Mr Tanner was dealing with speculation not proof. Tanner had argued that Ty would have been on high moral ground if she had come in here and admitted that Lee told her about being anally raped by Mr Mallory. Miller argued, unclearly, that if Ty knew everything, there was no better reason for her not going to the police.

'Mr Tanner spoke some about the robbery charge in this case. If you listened carefully to the robbery charge, and you've listened to whether or not there was any evidence that Lee Wuornos threatened anybody, or killed anybody, or did anything to get property—is Lee Wuornos guilty of theft? Sure. Find her guilty of that. She should not have taken that property.'

He suggested to the jury that Lee's actions and her state of mind meant they should not find her guilty of murder. 'I'm not asking you to feel sorry for Lee Wuornos. She doesn't need your sympathy. She needs fairness, she needs justice, she needs you to understand what really happened.'

He went back to the self-defence claim. 'She had every right to shoot Mr Mallory. She had every right to shoot him not once, not twice, not three, but four times. She was terrified. She was drunk. She was naked. She was tortured. And she defended herself. That's not a crime.'

He referred to Tanner's point about Lee's chosen way of life as a prostitute. 'But did Aileen Wuornos ask to be slapped? Did she ask to be tied to the steering wheel? Did she ask to be anally assaulted? Each and every one of you, in jury selection, indicated that you could be fair. Each and every one of you indicated that a prostitute, yes a prostitute, can be raped. Mr Tanner suggested that somehow she brought this all on herself because of her profession. She was raped and she was brutalised, and despite her profession, she had a right to defend herself.'

John Tanner stood. He'd plucked a few last words of testimony to highlight. The defendant had told Horzepa that when someone gave her a hassle, she had to kill them because she didn't want to leave a witness. There was her intent.

And Deputy Susan Hansen had heard her say in January of '91 that sometimes she felt guilty, but at others she felt like a hero or something.

Aileen Wuornos did not even have remorse for the life she had taken. And for that murder, if the jury found her guilty in the first degree, she would get death, or a life sentence with a minimum 25-year mandatory sentence.

Judge Blount briefed the jury. Aileen Wuornos sobbed at the defence table as the people who would decide her fate were told there was no time limit on their deliberations and were led out. They only needed 91 minutes. At 6 p.m., they were back.

Guilty on the first count. Guilty on the second count. Aileen crumbled as did her sobbing adoptive mother, Arlene Pralle. A scan of the faces in the courtroom could not pick up any other expressions of surprise. Emotion, grief, relief and pain, yes. Shock, no.

Shirley Humphreys, weeping silently, was led out by her daughter Terry. The verdict wouldn't bring Dick back, but it was justice. Justice at last.

Then suddenly, Lee's shock turned to fury, manifesting itself in a snarling parting shot to the jury members sombrely filing out across the courtroom: 'Sonsofbitches! I was raped! I hope you get raped! Scumbags of America!'

There it was again. Her inability to control herself, to resist even the most foolish or self-destructive impulses. In what could hardly be called a politic move, she had just cursed out the very people who would, the next day, begin to decide whether she would live or die.

49

On 28 January 1992, judge, jury, and the by then familiar cast of players reconvened for Lee's sentencing: for many the most suspenseful part of the hearings, in which the jury would recommend to the judge whether Aileen Carol Wuornos Pralle go to meet her maker via the electric chair, or serve a life sentence with the possibility of parole after 25 years.

Judge Blount instructed the jury to weigh aggravating versus mitigating factors, then John Tanner launched into his opening statement, pointing out that a verdict to recommend the death penalty need not be unanimous, but required a majority vote of seven jurors. He said that they should consider that while the burden of proof still rested on the state, most of the aggravating factors had already been proven in trial.

Aileen turned and grinned at Arlene Pralle, apparently oblivious to what was being said. She had tuned in by the time he listed the factors that could lead them to recommend death: such as murder in the first degree committed while in the act of robbery, or murder committed for the purpose of financial gain. Tanner said the state believed that the evidence supported their contention that Aileen Wuornos deserved to be put to death. Suddenly, her grin was a glower.

Billy Nolas stood to address the jury. They'd heard, he said, two weeks of the state's evidence regarding Aileen's guilt and they'd had an opportunity to observe her demeanour.

'I daresay that many of you are sitting there, thinking to yourselves, "Why? Why is Lee the way she is?"'

Now they would get those answers, he promised, explaining that Lee did not simply fall from the sky. He spoke of her sad background; of the father who hanged himself in the penitentiary, of the mother who abandoned her, of the biological, genetic and environmental factors. He spoke of the child whose school records noted a need for help she didn't get. The alcoholic, abusive grandfather and the meek, humble grandmother who couldn't deal with what was going on. The fire in which Lee was burned, her problems with her self-image, her rape at fourteen and pregnancy, her being put out of the home at fifteen with no skills.

He cited her way of life selling her body, being abused, and being alcoholic. And he cited the young man who left her whom she loved so much that she shot herself in the stomach. And he refreshed in the minds of jurors that, to Lee Wuornos, the world was a hostile, frightening and bitter place that she simply didn't understand.

John Tanner recalled Larry Horzepa and after once again laying to rest any ghost of a doubt cast by Aileen on the fairness of the videotaped confession, he asked what the detective had heard about Lee's reasons for killing Richard Mallory. Horzepa, quiet and believable, delivered the damning message. Aileen had claimed that in her heart she didn't really want to kill, but she couldn't leave witnesses. She didn't want to get caught.

David Damore then used Deputy Susan Hansen, the jail officer, to describe Aileen as animated, laughing and joking behind bars. During their couple of hours' chat, Aileen at no time mentioned that Richard Mallory had attacked or raped her.

Billy Nolas got Susan Hansen to concede that there was another side to the story and that Aileen had also said 'Sure I shot them, but it was self-defence. I've been raped eight times in the last nine years, and I just got sick of it.'

He also elicited from Hansen the fact that Lee became angry at times, and could be laughing and angry within the same conversation.

With those preliminaries out of the way, out trotted the first of the defence's procession of expert witnesses, designed to provide real insight into what had made Lee kill, and into why she couldn't control her impulses.

At 2.55 p.m., Billy Nolas called Elizabeth McMahon, Ph.D.,

an expert in neuropsychology, clinical psychology and the study of deviant human behaviour. McMahon, a diminutive, elfin figure with short silver hair, dressed in a pale blue sweater and navy suit, was in for a long session. She described how she had evaluated Aileen five times for a total of twenty-two hours and did over six hours of neuropsychology testing on her.

David Damore pointed out that she was like a doctor in English, who cannot prescribe drugs. He also pushed across the impression that she was in the habit of testifying for the defence by asking if she'd ever been retained by the state. Dr McMahon believed so, but couldn't remember.

In assessing Aileen, she'd also reviewed depositions, school records, police reports, prior psychiatric evaluations, and had talked to people who knew her. She'd also run a battery of tests. Her suggestion that Lee might have some cortical brain damage was doubtless clinically sound, but came across as too nebulous to be effective in swaying a jury. Her primary diagnosis, however, was that Lee was a borderline personality.

Dr McMahon described borderline personality for the jury as someone who has intense and unstable personal relationships; who is very labile in their emotions, like a roller-coaster—one minute happy, one minute sad, one minute angry, one minute laughing, and subject to very rapid mood changes. A borderline is impulsive and has a regular problem with intense anger and cannot moderate it well. They may behave self-destructively, either very overtly in the form of suicide attempts, or more subtly. Borderlines commonly have identity disturbances: 'And by that, one may mean a gender identity disturbance, or disturbance in terms of long-range goals, values, what they want from life. Someone who experiences high feelings of emptiness, alienation, and who has a great fear of aloneness and abandonment. These are people who have what's called impaired cognition in terms of the way they view the world and the way their thought-processing operates. They have very intense, overwhelming feelings that they have a great deal of trouble modulating, and their life tends to revolve around two primary feelings: victimisation and alienation. I could go into more detail, but that's a thumbnail description.'

Dr McMahon then explained that borderlines incite strong feelings in others and because of their intense emotions are difficult, unpredictable people to deal with, tending even to wear out their therapists. They're unhappy people who project that unhappiness on the world.

Nolas asked what precipitates a borderline? The doctor explained that there was often some cortical dysfunction and as a result they, among other things, are never able to assess what's going on around them accurately. The second theory concerned very early abandonment. The third, that their family dynamics make the borderline susceptible to what's called splitting.

She then described Aileen's history as she understood it, recapping on much of what had already been heard. Of Lauri, she said, 'Miss Wuornos's biological mother had described him as the meanest man in town, that he was verbally abusive to her growing up.' She pointed up Lee's descriptions of Britta, her grandmother, as being like an angel who could do no wrong, and who loved flowers and trees. Bad Lauri, good Britta. To Dr McMahon, Lee's perception typified splitting. And she cited Diane's description of Britta as not being that way at all. Britta had been verbally abusive to Diane. She obviously wasn't a saint.

McMahon reiterated Aileen's difficulties in school, her vision problems and hearing loss in one ear, and her grandmother's refusal to get her help. At fourteen, said Dr McMahon, Aileen was raped by 'a gentleman who said he was a friend of her father's, and offered her a ride home'.

(The problem with all of this and with much more that Dr McMahon repeated, was very evident. It was based purely on Aileen's version of truth. For instance, Aileen told Dr McMahon that she began prostitution at the age of fifteen when in fact she had been no more than twelve.)

McMahon revealed more about the cortical dysfunction explaining the split between Aileen's verbal IQ and performance IQ.

'A split of that magnitude immediately tells us the brain is not working in concert. One of the things that is necessary for us to function in the world is for our brain to work in unison. It *must* work in concert. It must work as a whole. Either all the parts are in unison or they're not. And if you're going to be able to have a smooth, melodic effect, then it all has to be working together, and if it isn't, you get sort of . . . lost.'

In and of itself, that split alone would tell you there was something seriously wrong.

'By the same token, the kind of cortical dysfunction that she has is not . . . I'm not saying that there's anything wrong with the structure of the brain. In other words, if she were to have an EEG or a Cat-scan or an MRI, she would show up fine. Everything is structurally intact, but it's not functioning right.'

Suddenly, she delivered an analogy that rendered the whole thing more comprehensible. She likened it to a car that is OK and has its motor: 'But it's as if you had sand in the gas line, let's say. Then you go to drive your car, it's going to splutter, it's going to maybe cut out on you. It may not start. You drive it a little way, then it may stop, start, sputter. It is that way with Ms Wuornos's brain.'

Billy Nolas wanted the jury to know that all this was a physical problem and not a choice. It is not something anyone would choose, said McMahon, because borderlines are very, very unhappy, discontented individuals who cannot function in the world and cannot figure out how to get their needs met. 'It's like they go through life and they sort of have some sense that other people out there are getting it OK, and they're not. They can't figure out how to do it.'

'A person like Miss Wuornos, is she mature?' asked Nolas. 'No. Ms Wuornos is probably one of the most primitive people I've seen outside an institution. By that I mean that she functions at a level of very basic—by basic, I mean, small child—needs. I'm talking about food, shelter, clothing, and an attempt at some sense of security. An attempt at some sense of OK-ness and contentment.'

Most people have gone way beyond that and are concerned from adolescence on with, for instance, making relationships. 'You're no longer at the level of basic trust and security needs. These are things that you provide for infants and small children. That's the level at which Ms Wuornos operates.'

Billy Nolas led Dr McMahon to Aileen's self-destructiveness. There were the blatant acts, the suicide attempts, McMahon said, but in addition to that, her whole life was self-destructive. The drinking, the drugs (although she claimed to have stopped them at seventeen), the living on the edge, the living in a state of danger. McMahon said that Aileen today, although 35–40 pounds lighter, looked 'immeasurably healthier in terms of her skin, her eyes, her hair, everything' than when she first saw her a year before.

Dr McMahon addressed the abandonment by both parents and the emotional abandonment by the grandfather, and the flaw in Aileen's angelic portrait of her grandmother. The very fact that she was afraid to tell anyone she was pregnant for six months indicates she didn't have anyone that was there for her. Aileen, she said, had poor judgement, poor insight, and if you asked her to reflect on her situation, to say how she thought she got there, she had no idea.

There was a lot of what McMahon called 'externalisation'. Everybody out there was responsible. Borderlines don't see themselves as the actor, only the reactor. Everyone else is in control and making the decisions. They don't understand how they get from A to B.

Nolas asked how Lee viewed the world.

'She's a victim, her paranoia is frequently sky high. It's an angry, unpleasant, out-to-get-her place.'

Billy Nolas wanted to hear what the doctor thought regarding the Mallory incident. She prefaced her answer by saying that she was dealing with Ms Wuornos's account, then said, 'In my clinical opinion, Ms Wuornos saw herself as threatened, saw herself as in severe, imminent danger. Whether that was accurate or not, whether that was a distortion of what was going on, I don't know.'

Dr McMahon did not believe Lee was capable of conforming her conduct to the requirements of the law.

'Could she distinguish right and wrong?' asked Billy Nolas, tapping the core issue in this, the courtroom.

Dr McMahon found that a complex question. She believed that if you removed Aileen from that place, that night, and asked

470

her in a calm situation, sitting on the beach, if it was wrong to take somebody's life, she'd say 'yes'.

'At that moment, feeling threatened, the question of whether it was right or wrong becomes irrelevant.'

Dr McMahon believed that Lee felt she was in a life-threatening situation, that legality didn't enter into it. She'd simply reacted and done so with less thought than the average individual, given her impairment.

As Lee listened straight-faced, Dr McMahon pointed out that she didn't see that she'd done anything other than defend herself. To her, shooting Mr Mallory was the only way she perceived of getting out of the situation. She didn't see her responsibility for what happened. Her actions, like her lifestyle, showed poor judgement, impulsiveness, very poor skills. Given her history, dynamics, view of the world and cortical dysfunction, McMahon believed that Lee could see no alternative.

Would it matter, Billy Nolas enquired, if Richard Mallory did none of the things she said he did?

'It matters to the extent that if he did *none* of them and she is so firmly entrenched in her belief that he did, then I think my diagnosis would change and I'd say we're dealing with a psychotic. But what generally occurs with folks like this is that there is some truth; it may not be all, but what truth there is gets distorted.'

She explained a psychotic as being someone who is out of touch with reality.

'What if Mr Mallory did nothing, and she's just lying about it?' asked Nolas, obviously aware of the answer he'd get.

That would be inconsistent with the material McMahon had seen and read. She, unlike those in the courtroom, said that her various encounters with Wuornos and the stories she'd heard had been fairly consistent. And the thread of self-defence had run through their conversations. Lee saw people as angels, wizards, ghosts and evil spirits—her emotions overwhelmed her cognition.

Enter David Damore, who had been itching for his turn at the witness. He rapidly established that Dr McMahon did not consider Lee legally insane, that most of the time she knew right from wrong, and that she understood the consequences of her actions.

'She knew when she shot Mr Mallory over and over again, that what she was doing was wrong, legally?' Damore asked.

'At that moment, I do not think that that was a relevant . . . or even a consideration.'

'So, then you say that Lee Wuornos is not responsible for her actions?'

'I don't say she's not responsible. I think she's responsible.'

Damore pointed out that all of McMahon's assessments were based on Lee Wuornos's perception, that truth had nothing to do with it.

'Now, the fact that someone has a borderline personality disorder doesn't make someone a killer?' Damore asked.

'Does it make them a killer? Not in and of itself.'

Damore got Dr McMahon to concede that Aileen had been similarly disordered since the age of fifteen but that those disorders had not driven her to kill then—according to her account. Damore seemed impatient. Under his probing, McMahon admitted that the prognosis was not good for helping Lee, that she would need intense therapy.

'With somebody as primitive as Lee it would be very difficult. Is it possible? It's possible.'

Damore shot back: 'It's possible! It's possible for me to be the next man on the moon but it's not probable.'

'Objection!' said Billy Nolas, his voice audibly weary of Mr Damore's sarcasm. The judge overruled Nolas, however, and Damore moved on to the defendant's childhood, pointing out that the doctor had based her conclusions on information that either came from Lee or from other people who might not have been telling the truth. For instance, the account of Lee's teenage rape came from Lori's interview with the police.

(Lori who didn't believe Aileen's account. The doctor was not to know that and nor was David Damore. Yet he addressed that very issue.)

He said Dr McMahon didn't know if Lee had lied to her sister, or if it was perhaps easier for Lee, six months' pregnant, to have lied about a rape than to have admitted to having had consensual sex. Damore also brought out that Lauri had allowed Aileen back into the family home after the pregnancy, and that she at least had a family unit. Yes, the doctor agreed, also sounding weary, Lee had been fortunate enough to have had a family unit.

They got into the alleged abuse. 'The worst thing he ever did, according to her, was to strike her in the face with a buckle.' David Damore was firing questions so quickly that the doctor couldn't get a word in edgeways.

'Your honour, the witness should be allowed to answer *something!*' Billy Nolas piped up.

The judge agreed. 'Let the witness answer the question.'

Dr McMahon read from her notes that Lee had told her that her grandfather hit her with a belt but only on the butt and the legs. There'd been just the one incident where he'd struck her in the face with it.

Damore ventured into Lori and Barry's police accounts of the childhood. Dr McMahon had talked to a distant cousin and to a gentleman who had spent six days with Lee in 1990. Damore pointedly asked if she'd spoken to, or tried to speak to, Lori Grody, Barry Wuornos or Tyria Moore. Dr McMahon answered 'No' to each question. She'd read the sworn statements and had gone no further.

Damore brought out that it took Lee from the first interview in February 1991 until December of that year to recount to her that she'd been raped by Mr Mallory.

'I didn't see her between then and December, so yes.'

Damore also elicited from McMahon that Lee had described her criminal history as being lacking in violence and theft. The doctor admitted that Aileen's criminal history was irrelevant to her diagnosis. The violence, the robbery, the use of aliases, all of it. Irrelevant. Whether she'd stolen or lied. Irrelevant.

'Isn't it a fact that the defendant provided you with a history of manipulation and lies to people before Richard Mallory?'

'Manipulation yes, lies no.'

Damore then returned to the damning absence of mention of

the rape by Richard Mallory. She did not tell her she had not been—she didn't tell her she had been, McMahon fudged.

'Do you think that a woman who'd been anally raped and sodomised and vaginally attacked and brutalised to the extent that she claims to have been . . . would be able to forget it?'

'Would she be able to forget it? In terms of both her condition at the time she was arrested and the time [I saw her] after that, I can see where she may not have related it. Yes.'

Dr McMahon was doing a sterling job of remaining calm and unruffled on the receiving end of David Damore's often abrasive questioning. It was clearly designed to shake her, but did not. Ultimately, the impression jurors carried away from all this would probably be largely determined by their feelings about psychology.

Damore wanted to go back to the self-defence issue, asking the doctor if she was familiar with the autopsy on Walter Gino Antonio. (Alluding, obviously, to the bullets in the back.) That time, Nolas's objection was sustained. Damore reworded his question, asking if Dr McMahon had considered any autopsy reports, including that of Mr Mallory, in an attempt to establish whether Aileen Wuornos was telling the truth. Again, McMahon said it was not relevant. It was not relevant to her diagnosis, what had happened out there.

Dr McMahon also said that while she entertained the possibility that Aileen might have an anti-social personality disorder, she found that not to be the case. The diagnosis calls for three or four characteristics by age fifteen and she found Aileen did not meet that criteria.

'In my clinical opinion, she is not an anti-social personality, she is a borderline personality.'

Dr McMahon felt that sometimes Aileen lied, sometimes she told the truth, and that she wasn't delusional. She was aware of Aileen's arrest history, but didn't consider her recent offences to be an escalation from that, calling them qualitatively different. She was aware of her history of manipulating and using aliases. About lying, she wasn't so sure.

'I can tell when she thinks she's telling the truth,' Dr McMahon said, but reiterated that for her purposes, Aileen's percep-

474

tions were more important. And she readily admitted that she did not know what had truly transpired with Richard Mallory. She also admitted what Lee had denied. Yes, Ms Wuornos had told her that she had practised drawing her gun quickly.

Billy Nolas then questioned Dr McMahon on redirect.

'Are what you understand to be her interactions with men while prostituting consistent with the way prostitutes are?'

'No.'

'What's inconsistent about it?'

'The very fact she enjoyed it, stated that she enjoyed it, stated that it was both emotionally and physically gratifying to her, stated that she would spend more time with them than the contract she had with them . . . holding hands, kissing, affectionate type of engagement. This is not typical.'

McMahon found it telling that Aileen would want that physical contact and enjoy it even from a stranger, without closeness. And her premature sexual behaviour wasn't appropriate either.

Billy Nolas had done his very best to elicit from the witness a digestible explanation for his client's behaviour. And court was in recess until 9.30 a.m. Wednesday.

The defence began the second day of the penalty phase hearing, Wednesday 29 January, by calling Dr Harry Krop, a clinical psychologist, an expert forensic psychiatrist and an expert in sexual abuse.

Billy Nolas began by eliciting from Dr Krop that he had treated over 4,000 sex offenders and had evaluated 435 first-degree murder cases, only 40 or so for the defence. After assessing Lee Wuornos and all her files, his primary diagnosis, in line with Dr McMahon's, was that she was suffering from borderline personality disorder. Of the eight criteria listed in the DSM-111, of which five are supposed to be met in diagnosis, Lee had all eight. She was a classic case.

Dr Krop had interviewed Lee's cousin and heard about the dominant, very critical and (when drinking) violent grandfather, and about the passive grandmother who drank intermittently and was ineffective in praising Lee or intervening on her behalf. Dr

Krop naturally covered much of the same ground as Dr McMahon. He testified that when sex is prevalent from a very early age there can be one of two outcomes: hyposexuality (a withdrawal from sex) or hypersexuality. Lee belonged in the latter category. Sex was her way of gaining acceptance and she became sexually aggressive.

She had told Dr Krop that she'd been gang-raped at sixteen and tied up and raped at seventeen. He, too, had been told the story of rape by her father's friend leading to the pregnancy. From thirteen on, Dr Krop said, she'd had a tremendous amount of sexual experience.

Dr Krop mentioned Lee's school report and the observation that her IQ had been rated, he said, as low dull normal, which was borderline retardation.

This comment precipitated a stifled guffaw from Lee, and Billy Nolas seized the opportunity. His client had just encapsulated the very heart of her problem right before the jury's eyes. And he badly wanted them to understand her. Nolas walked behind Lee and laid his hands on her shoulders. Lee had just heard that she possessed very limited mental capacity and yet she found it cause for laughter, Nolas pointed out: 'Is that typical of a borderline personality?'

'Yes,' the doctor replied. 'She doesn't view herself as being disturbed.'

In his opinion, Lee still ached for family ties. 'Lee still has the fantasy of being part of a family.'

Billy Nolas had one more point to make. He listed all the borderline qualities from anxiety to poor impulse control. 'You see all of that here, don't you?'

'Yes.'

After a fifteen-minute recess, John Tanner questioned Dr Krop.

'Good morning,' Tanner said.

'Good morning,' Dr Krop replied.

'Did I just attempt to manipulate you?'

With that device, Tanner then launched into a demonstration of the dissension within the psychiatric field and an attack on the professional bible, the DSM-III. Krop admitted that, like Dr

476

McMahon, he too had based most of his assumptions on reports and documentation. The first time he had heard the anal rape/Visine story had been ten days earlier. Krop also said that Lee didn't meet even three of the twelve criteria that would cause him to diagnose her as an anti-social personality.

Dr Jethro Toomer was the third expert to testify for the defence and he confirmed the conclusions of his colleagues.

Lee, sitting at the defence table, being discussed like a specimen in a scientific study, for a moment looked unusually vulnerable. But an outburst of furious gestures just before the lunch recess quickly diluted the impression. She had just heard that Lori Grody and Barry Wuornos were in town to testify for the state. Lee had been promised that if that were to happen, Dawn Nieman would fly in to testify on her behalf. Now it was too late to get Dawn, and Lee felt betrayed.

On the stand, Dr Toomer continued building the picture of a borderline personality that so described Lee. Borderlines lack core self-esteem and their underlying message is, 'Please like me! Please accept me!' Unfortunately, the sheer weight of the psychological testimony was taking its toll: one juror had actually dozed off.

Under John Tanner's questioning, Dr Toomer said that he hadn't diagnosed Lee as an anti-social personality for a number of very significant reasons. One being that an anti-social personality is someone without a conscience which didn't, to him, describe her. In his view, she manifested remorse. Anti-socials constantly violated social norms. Again, he didn't find that the case with Lee.

What John Tanner described as her lying and changing stories, the doctor described as 'her recall and reporting facilities break down under stress'.

Billy Nolas brought out on redirect that Lee was unpredictable in her relationships and that Lori Grody said she never knew what to expect. Dr Toomer elaborated: 'Ms Wuornos does that. She'll find one person, put all her focus on that person, like everything about that person, then she'll switch around and she'll hate their guts that fast.'

The idealising was typical, the doctor said.

'The defence rests, your honour,' Tricia Jenkins said, stirring the drowsy courtroom.

Dr George Barnard from the University of Florida, a forensic psychiatrist who'd examined Lee earlier that month, took the stand for the prosecution. Under questioning, Dr Barnard stated that the day of their interview, Lee had arrived in an agitated state, claiming that the jail officers who'd escorted her had made sexual remarks she considered inappropriate. Her accusations fluctuated, but she was offered a rape test which she declined. Dr Barnard was the gentleman who evaluated Lee for the court back in 1981 at the time of her armed robbery conviction. Barnard agreed with the borderline personality diagnosis but also diagnosed her as an anti-social personality disorder. He said, however, that Lee appreciated the criminality of her conduct, and that neither diagnosis would take away that judgement. He didn't think people chose to have such disorders, but they might choose some of the behaviours.

John Tanner asked him, 'She had intent to shoot Richard Mallory to death and she shot him, didn't she?'

'Yes.'

The prosecution's next witness was Barry Wuornos, a squat man with thinning hair, spectacles, a double chin and a maroon-striped shirt. The state had decided not to call Lori Grody. David Damore took Barry through the by now familiar childhood terrain. His father was a strong character, a disciplinarian, gentle, strong rules, a man you could look up to. Did he beat his children? Absolutely not. Aileen had not been denied medical care, he said. Mom he described as quiet, studious, laid-back, very much in the background and much easier-going than dad. Dad was strong on school. Aileen was no differently treated from the others.

Lee did not hide her anger. As Barry spoke, she shook her head in disbelief. First, that Barry was up there testifying against her, then that he was denying she'd been treated abusively. She scribbled copious notes on the pad in front of her.

'Did you ever ask them to let you talk to Lee?' Billy Nolas wanted to know.

'No. There was no reason to ask to talk to her. She'd been in various trouble, and I just thought, here we go again.'

'Did you ask how Lee was doing?'

'No.'

'Did you ask to talk to Lee's lawyer?'

'I didn't even know she had a lawyer.'

Billy Nolas's tone quietly conveyed it all. It was OK for the prosecution to give Lee a hard time. It was expected that most of the rest of the world would turn away from her, but hadn't this brother of hers any compassion for his own flesh and blood? Didn't he at least want to hear her side of the story and find out what had happened to her?

Diane, Barry described as a normal older sister. Leo, with whom she had an on-off marriage, was a rousty individual who'd once thrown Barry down and threatened to choke him.

Barry, Nolas learned, had never heard of Lee needing a hearing aid. He'd heard of the shoplifting and, from Lori, the fire-setting. But he hadn't heard of much else. Despite his departure from the home when Lee was around ten, it seemed he'd grown up in a different household. All of this had nothing to do with me, his stance seemed to convey.

Lee's mouth was set in a rigid line of anger and her eyes were downcast as Barry stepped down from the stand. Without looking across at her, he walked from the courtroom. It was a truly distressing scene to watch.

Thursday 30 January was the final day of this, Lee's first trial. She arrived in a flowery blouse. Larry Horzepa sat in the back row. Arlene Pralle was tearful and agitated. I asked her if Lee had been prepared for the worst. Arlene didn't know. The strain was certainly showing on Lee's face. It seemed she'd aged ten years overnight. She had a quiet, angry outburst with the beleaguered Billy Nolas at the defence table.

When the jury filed in, Lee was red-faced and crying.

As John Tanner made his closing argument, she sobbed openly. Nolas put his arm around her to comfort her. Tanner went on to list Lee's aliases, and to inform the jury that their advisory sentence would carry great weight with the judge who would have the final say.

'Your responsibilities are here and now. It began in Volusia County and should end in Volusia County. The finality of Richard Mallory's death, and what is to be done about it, rests with the jury here.'

Of the eleven possible aggravating factors, Mr Tanner felt they had proved six. Listening, Lee shook her head. He reminded the jury that she had previously committed a violent crime and that she killed Mr Mallory during the course of a robbery, acted to avoid arrest, acted for financial gain, and acted with premeditation.

He addressed the mitigating factors the defence would bring out. Dr McMahon had said she could tell when Aileen Wuornos was lying. 'But McMahon based her whole opinion on the alcohol, rape and bondage story. She accepted that as fact. You rejected it.'

Aileen was sobbing noisily.

He called the suggestion of sexual abuse by Aileen's father a dirty little innuendo. Summing up, he said that what the doctors had really told them was: 'She just doesn't think like others. You knew that!'

He wanted to bring Richard Mallory, the victim, fresh back into the jurors' minds before he wrapped it up.

'It became obscenely simple for Aileen Wuornos to kill. In one moment Richard Mallory was eliminated and by that act of her will, he was no more. Simply was no more.'

He brought up Lee's own words. She said she deserved to die. And John Tanner agreed.

'Aileen Wuornos deserves the ultimate penalty provided by the state of Florida.'

A few of the jurors looked almost as shaken as the defence team. Tricia Jenkins, as she stepped forward to speak, was on the verge of tears. She faced an unenviable task.

'I must ask you to save Aileen Wuornos. How do people who live unimpaired know what it is like to live impaired? Everything goes through that filter of impairment. She is not like us. I don't know what to do or say to convince you Lee should live. I only know that she should.'

Two female jurors were working as hard as Jenkins to fight back the tears. As she took them once more through a synopsis of the events of that night, Lee sobbed loudly. So did Arlene Pralle, seated behind her.

'Travelling through the world, always on the outside,' said Jenkins. 'Living in a world which to her perception is violent and frightening.'

She was, Jenkins said, 'intensely needy, intensely afraid of being abandoned.'

Lee's body was heaving with sobs, perhaps crying for this vulnerable self that Jenkins described. A damaged, primitive child.

'Not being able to make people like her. Always turning on the very people trying to help her.'

Eloquently, Jenkins told the jury that Lee was incapable of doing anything to help herself. They had learned, she said, 'that Lee can't control impulses, and I think all of you have seen that. Think how frustrating that must be.'

Jenkins decried Barry Wuornos's testimony of this normal family. Even Dr Barnard, the prosecution's own witness, agreed that Lee came from a dysfunctional family.

'Barry came into this courtroom against Lee in a proceeding in which the state is trying to kill her. What does that tell you about dysfunction?

'Ladies and gentlemen, Richard Mallory is dead and that's a terrible, terrible thing. We're not asking that you forgive that . . . all of mankind is diminished when someone dies at the hands of another.'

What she was asking was that they show mercy. Life in prison without possibility of parole for 25 years. Wasn't that enough?

'When she longs for the comfort of human touch, she can't have it. She has been free, out in the open, most of her life. She'll go to sleep in a metal cage. If she's lucky, it will have a window.'

Tricia was making a moving speech.

'She's always maintained a degree of hope. When she leaves

481

this courtroom for the last time, she'll have lost her hope. Please go back there and decide that this is punishment enough.'

Word came back after 108 minutes. The jury had reached its verdict. Lee was shepherded back into the courtroom, looking deathly pale but composed. She even managed a small smile. Jenkins put her arm around her client's shoulders.

Ms Mills, the forewoman, was crying. The equestrienne, Ms Staten, looked terribly shaken, too. Yet their verdict was unanimous: 12 votes for death.

For a moment, Lee looked as if she might collapse, swaying visibly under the supporting arms of her counsel. William Miller took off his glasses and wiped his eyes, and Tricia Jenkins appeared just as upset. Nolas looked ashen.

Outside the courtroom he spoke of Lee's mental state. She was very emotional, naturally.

'She knows that there will be court tomorrow and when you're dealing with somebody like Lee, that's as good as you're going to get.'

No one doubted for a moment that he would, and the next day, Friday 31 January, Judge Blount made it official. Before he did so, Lee stood and spoke.

'First of all, I would like to say that I have been labelled a serial killer, and I'm no serial killer,' she began.

She repeated all her familiar arguments, throwing in a few new accusations for good measure. John Tanner, she said, was part of a conspiracy, too. She'd been coerced into confessing. She alleged that Tyria knew it was self-defence but was lying through her teeth . . . Judge Blount listened patiently, but eventually it had to come: 'It is the sentence of this court that you, Aileen Carol Wuornos, be delivered by the Sheriff of Volusia County to the proper officer of the Department of Corrections of the State of Florida and by him safely kept until by warrant of the Governor of the State of Florida, you, Aileen Carol Wuornos, be electrocuted until you are dead.'

Lee was fingerprinted and led away.

A crowd had gathered outside to see her depart. As she was ushered into a car behind the court building she had one last outburst for the gaggle of press microphones extended in her direction: 'Bust these crooked cops and their conspiracy, please! I'm innocent!'

Arlene ran as close to the car as the deputies guarding the area would allow.

'Bye, Lee. I love you!' she called through the closed window.

While Lee was on her way to Broward County to take her place on Death Row, Billy Nolas's mind was already looking ahead to the inevitable appeals.

But he reflected on the curious sight of jurors crying as they sentenced Lee to death. That had been a new experience for him. So, too, was seeing a defendant's brother take the stand as Barry Wuornos did, trying to help seal his sister's fate. 'I have never in my life seen a family member testify for the state,' he said later. 'It was atrocious.'

His sadness was evident, and his feelings obviously went beyond the call of duty.

'One of the tragedies of Lee's life is that folks like her brother who should be supporting her just aren't there. She had been basically abandoned by *everyone*.'

Barry's act of unkindness did not go unrewarded. When, in March, Lee gave an interview to talk-show host Montel Williams, she had by then shifted the blame for her introduction to sex at age twelve, and laid it firmly at Barry's door. 'Sex was a new . . . well, we were finding a lot of dirty books from our brother Barry in the closets, and sex kinda started opening to us when we found those dirty books in the closets,' she said.

Barry might well have belatedly wished he'd conceded the point on how well he knew Aileen. But while Aileen's anger at Barry, the author of yet another betrayal, was understandable, what also came across was her readiness to re-fashion her tales at whim and to tailor them to serve her interests of the moment.

50

Arlene Pralle called him a 'giver of great bear hugs', but 38-year old Steve Glazer was also a man with a legal mission only marginally less challenging than Mount Everest. On May 4, 1992, he faced an unenviable, if voluntarily undertaken, task in Marion County.

Lee had pled 'no contest' to the murders of David Spears, Troy Burress and Dick Humphreys back on March 31, negating the need for a trial. So at the May penalty phase hearing a jury would decide if she would get life in prison or be sentenced to death for the three homicides. Utilising a format resembling a mini-trial, it gave both prosecution and defence a forum in which to lay out their cases to a jury unfamiliar with the details.

Chief Assistant State Attorney Ric Ridgway had been shocked back in March when Lee not only appointed Steve Glazer her defence attorney after dumping her three court-appointed public defenders from Volusia County, but also immediately entered three 'no contest' pleas.

He was also concerned. Glazer, a former public defender, had handled Arlene Pralle's adoption of Wuornos, but Ridgway didn't know if he had prior experience in capital cases or if he'd even attended the educational life or death seminars given to public defenders and was anxious to get the issue of Glazer's competence addressed on the record. His main goal was to protect the case against later allegations of ineffective assistance of counsel.

"I was concerned with: could his competency be demonstrated, put on the record," he explained, "and the defendant accepting his representation of her, in spite of the deficits or deficiencies that might exist in his experience."

Ridgway was not alone in his concerns. He noticed that Judge Tom Sawaya also did, "vitually everything he could to talk Aileen Wuornos out of entering that plea." But enter it she did.

So in May, Ridgway's aim, along with his co-counsel, David Eddy, was to hammer home to the jurors the sheer heinousness and cold-blooded calculation of Lee's crimes, urging them to recommend to the judge that the fitting punishment was death in the electric chair. The guilt-versus-innocence phase required a unanimous jury verdict to convict but the penalty phase required only a majority verdict to determine Lee's fate.

Although Lee spoke of an urge to meet her maker, Glazer would do his best to convince the jury that spending the rest of her natural life on Death Row without possibility of parole for at least 25 years per sentence, would be punishment enough. Glazer, with his confessed multiple-murderer client, would attempt to prove that there were mitigating circumstances that went some way towards offsetting the brutality of her crimes, and would urge the jurors to show mercy.

Glazer was working pro bono for Lee. In return, his career would receive a desired infusion of publicity and notoriety. A burly figure in a navy-blue suit topped with a mass of fuzzy black hair, Glazer had suffered a major heart attack in December 1991 and had since lost 125 pounds. A high school dropout, New Yorker, and sometime musician, affable Glazer seemed to relish his renegade outsider role.

Indeed, his controversial tactics (underscored by his own Judeo-Buddhist—he called it Judhist—philosophies and approach to life on this planet) had earned him biting criticism from his peers. After the bombshell of Lee's 'no contest' pleas, his crassly-commercial telephone number DRLEGAL, practically begged the nickname that sprang up: 'Dr. Lethal'.

In court for the first day of the penalty phase, the defendant looked like some product of a less advanced nation, her uneven teeth veering off unchecked in conflicting directions, her skin rough and blotchy, her dishwater-blond hair in lacklustre condition.

Lee did two things. Fought for the right to sit out the remainder of the hearing in her Death Row cell. And made a rambling, self-serving speech that reeked of a persecution complex, reading from handwritten notes and unwittingly reading one page twice. The diatribe unwound painfully slowly and laboriously, until finally Judge Tom Sawaya could stand it no more and enquired how much longer it would take. Solicitous, Lee promised to speed it up.

She was supposedly admitting to her crimes and voicing her sorrow, yet the old blame and self-defence notes kept creeping in.

Ultimately, she got what she wanted. Gentlemanly Judge Sawaya, with his low-key voice and manner, would allow Lee to sit this one out, but only on condition that Glazer confer with her daily and that she reiterate during each telephone call her continuing desire not to be present. She could change her mind at any time. She had only to say the word. The judge insisted on it, mindful of heading off any future procedural appeals. (Her absence infuriated victims' family members, however, who felt the very least this creature could do was to face them—and the music—in court, not languish back in her cell eating popcorn.)

In fact, Lee's desire not to be present played right into Steve Glazer's hands. She could rant and rave out of the presence of the jury. Meanwhile he hoped with the help of Arlene Pralle to give an impression of a new, saved—or at least salvageable—woman.

Yet leaving court that first day, triumphant in some small way, Lee did not radiate the happiness that Pralle claimed she felt so much as outrage. That evening, she snarled and sneered out from TV sets on the nightly news.

Why so furious? Word was out that in Hollywood, actress Jean Smart, latterly of the TV show, *Designing Women,* had been cast to play Lee in the long-denied TV movie, *Overkill.* It was moving forward just as Jackelyn Giroux and Geraldo Rivera's *Now It Can Be Told* had claimed all along, with CBS, Republic Pictures and CM2 (Chuck McLain's production company) the players in the deal.

The cast of characters, detailed by Breakdown Services Ltd. to bring in submissions from actors hoping to audition, was also just as predicted by Giroux in February 1991, over a year earlier.

The key characters whose real names remained in place were the three police officers, Munster, Binegar and Henry, and of course, Tyria Moore. Certainly, Lee's belief that all those people (not least Ty) would be making money off her life story was enough to fuel her ire.

But seeping through again came the unmistakable impression that some plan had gone horribly awry and that the reality of her situation had begun to truly sink in.

In her contorted thinking, had Lee perhaps envisaged the scenario thus? That she would pay a price for her crimes (serve a sentence mitigated by a successful plea of self-defence), then reap handsome rewards from books and movies? Utterly convinced that her self-defence stories would be believed, had she thought she'd spend a limited time behind bars (nothing she hadn't done before), then be liberated to capitalise on her unique place in history?

Serial killer is a factually accurate description of Lee, but the chord it strikes is worlds less sympathetic than that of a victimised woman, brutally and repeatedly raped, driven to exact the ultimate revenge. The portrait she tried to paint of herself.

It's a fair bet that Aileen Wuornos did not anticipate being labelled the world's first female serial killer (a term she disgustedly decried as just one more con on the part of authorities). Rather, she saw herself being viewed as some kind of trailblazing, suffering heroine. Someone who would command respect. And along the way (and no less importantly), she, like so many others before her in the time-honoured American tradition, would get rich selling her story.

Back in court, without Aileen, prospective jurors were quizzed as they'd been in Volusia County, on their ability to render the death penalty, their awareness of pre-trial publicity, their open-mindedness.

'Are you going to ask me to prove to you that she deserves to live?' Glazer enquired of one potential juror, who was quickly dismissed after answering affirmatively. Another, who believed in an eye for an eye unless it was proved otherwise, quickly followed suit. A German-born woman was excused because, having grown up under the totalitarian Hitlerian regime, she could not help sentence a fellow human being to death. Reality setting in, many were simply afraid of making the weighty decision required of them.

One man admitted to having read the Sunday paper and, mindful of his upcoming jury service, to thinking, 'Lord, let that not be my trial.' 'Well, your prayer was not answered,' Judge Sawaya replied. 'Is that going to bother you?'

With the Los Angeles riots of the previous week still tumbling indigestibly in everyone's minds, Steve Glazer, in a clumsy attempt at levity, asked one citizen if 'we shouldn't change the venue to Simi Valley or anything like that?' With no co-counsel at his side, Glazer received the occasional fold-up note from Arlene Pralle, giving her input as a kind of informal jury consultant.

Across the cramped, modern-looking, yet poorly designed courtroom (with its unavoidably creaky chairs and doors and resulting poor acoustics) sat a varying but solid contingent of victims' family members.

When the jury was sworn in at 3:35 p.m. and the courtroom cleared of the remaining jury pool, a small press corps and a few interested court employees remained. Then there were two factions, glaringly disparate. Arlene Pralle, adoptive mother and curiousity, on the one side. And those who had lost their loved ones at the bloodied hands of her adoptive daughter, on the other.

After the judge instructed the jury, Ric Ridgway launched straight into his opening statement, outlining his evidence. Ridgway, a tall, bespectacled and (in this arena at least) rather serious 40-year-old in a pale beige suit, had graduated from the University of Miami Law School and had been with the 5th Judicial Circuit for ten years. As Chief Assistant State Attorney, he had tried around ten capital cases in Florida. With the help of David Eddy, Ridgway would show the jury that Dick Humphreys had died a cruel death:

'Dick Humphreys had been beaten, and shot seven times. He had several bullet wounds in his chest, one in his right wrist, and several in his back.'

The jury listened intently as Ridgway explained that the decomposed condition of the bodies of David Spears and Troy Burress made it impossible to prove whether or not they too had been beaten or abused.

'These murders were committed in a cold, calculated and premeditated fashion. These were not spur of the moment . . . they were carefully thought out, planned-in-advance murders.

'Dick Humphreys was brutalised and abused before he was killed. And his murder was committed in a manner that is heinous, atrocious and cruel.'

Steve Glazer then stood up and argued that the facts would prove beyond any reasonable doubt that the jury could return with a verdict of life and would have done its job. He said they'd see the three-hour confession videotape and that they would hear Lee often mention self-defence, or answer, 'I don't remember.' They would also hear Arlene Pralle testify that Ms. Wuornos's life had changed.

Yes, he conceded, the state would prove aggravation, but the mitigation would outweigh that. But Steve Glazer did acknowledge his uphill battle, saying, 'I don't even want to use the word good . . . but there's some spark of hope here that this person, Miss Wuornos, does not deserve death.'

The jury would have to make a life-or-death decision without the benefit of hearing all the evidence presented in a full-scale trial, and from the outset it was clear that Ric Ridgway would be the soul of level-headed, sound reasoning. When he called his first three witnesses, law enforcement investigators, he immediately began cleverly and economically to thread his miniature tapestry of evidence into a cohesive, digestible whole.

Amidst the expert witnesses and law enforcement officers, he came up with the perfect tool with which to show the fragility of the veneer of the much-advertised reform in Lee. Although part of her reason for pleading 'no contest' to these charges had supposedly been to avoid putting the victims' families through the ordeal and to save the state money, when she thought she wasn't going to get her own way about being in the jail she chose, she threatened to change that plea at the last moment and to have a trial after all.

And during the four and a half hour drive from Broward Correctional Institute to Marion County for the March 30 hearing, she'd threatened jail transporter, Paul Laxton. Ric Ridgway had him testify to their exchanges that took place just hours before she claimed to be a changed person.

'She made a statement that she'd kill me if it took her ten years to do so,' said Laxton.

'Anything else?' enquired Ridgway.

'She also made a statement, something about shooting me in the back of the head, and her words were, cutting off my dick and sticking it in my mouth.'

'Did she make any statements referring to a change in society that she would like to see made?' Ridgway probed.

'She talked about creating . . . a society where . . . they would shoot police officers between the eyes, and the police would have to walk around with bullet-proof helmets.'

'Did you respond?'

'No.'

The jury also heard forensic pathologist Dr. Janet Pillow tell of the doughnut-shaped abrasion on the side of Dick Humphreys's body, consistent with the shape of a gun barrel, and pushed there with enough force to scrape off the top layer of skin.

This jury, unlike the one in Volusia County, saw the videotape in its entirety on May 6. Journalists, a cynical bunch by definition, are not necessarily the ideal barometer by which to gauge the emotional temperature of juries, but it seemed to all present that the jury members shuffled in their seats with noticeable discomfort. They appeared mildly shell-shocked. And two men exchanged a fleeting glance of what looked like disbelief.

The videotape patently did not vindicate her, as Lee had imagined it would, by pointing out her painstakingly tallied number of self-defence pleas. It merely prolonged the horrific impact of her degree of denial of what she had done, her lies, and the sheer improbability of her story.

The victims were muddled in her mind, perhaps due to her inebriation at the time of the murders. Yet, curiously enough, some facts seemed to come easily. She'd asked the investigators if any prints had been found on the car she'd wrecked? She'd been worried that she hadn't covered her tracks in her usual careful fashion in that instance, and she was right: both her and Ty's prints were found.

Taking the stand immediately following the videotape could not have been worse timing for Arlene Pralle, who was primed to launch into her 'Lee is a wonderful, compassionate human being' speech. The jurors' ears were still ringing and their minds reeling from the emotionless recounting of seven slayings. And they were in no mood for Pralle's saccharine tale of first setting eyes on Wuornos and knowing in her heart that 'this woman was no serial killer.'

Amidst the visible pain of the victims' families, Pralle recounted her own tale of woe, from her mother's death to her father's massive heart attack, then, wisely urged by Glazer to move forward into her relationship with Lee, she quoted unquestioningly from Lee's litany of stories: from being abandoned at six months old and discovered in an attic covered with flies, to a story the jury was in even less of a mood to hear. Lee's least favourite food was baked potatoes and when Lauri once found she had dumped one in the trash, he made her retrieve it and eat it. The baked potato incident was Pralle's anecdotal crescendo.

Pralle said that since her adoption, Lee felt complete and total and now had a family and people who loved her.

'Since she's found Jesus Christ, I suppose she's a perfect angel?' asked Steve Glazer.

'She's not an angel,' Pralle responded with a smile, but she had nevertheless seen lots of changes. Lee listened to her now, and followed the Bible. She had nightmares about what she had done and felt really bad. She had been treated terribly by her jailers, she said. Lee's state of mind now was such that at times she was very depressed. She would never be able to drive a car again. And Arlene Pralle read the jury a letter from Dawn Botkins that said that Lee had had a rough deal in life and been treated terribly as a kid.

Pralle's earlier sob story about incurring over $5,000 worth of telephone bills while talking to Lee in prison was presumably meant to tug at the heartstrings of the jury. A jury she approached as if they would automatically sympathise with her higher calling and not question her sincerity.

The sum total of Pralle's plea for her daughter, her excuse for her behaviour, seemed to be that Lori was the favourite in the house.

Pralle was right about one thing. Barry Wuornos was indeed absent during Aileen's crucial adolescent years. But this nugget of truth was most probably lost on a jury floundering in a swamp of accusations.

And of course Lee's claim of her prayer that God send a Christian woman to befriend her sounded totally incongruous with telling the jailer who transported her that she'd kill him if it took her ten years. When Ric Ridgway questioned Lee's adoptive mother he scored more points when he established that she could not really explain her converted Christian daughter's outbursts against her jailers.

Ridgway pounced on Pralle, cutting her pious certainty from under her, and some witnesses to his cross-examination, while mindful of the sobriety of the proceedings, had to stifle an impulse to cheer.

Eventually, he cut straight to the exposed jugular. He had a revelation to make that would shake Lee's oft-repeated bleating about cops' movie and book dealings tainting her right to a fair trial. Pralle's reputation as the probably well-meaning, Christian crazy lady also took a turn for the overtly mercenary as Ric Ridgway established that she had recently received $7,500 for a television interview. Ric Ridgway had puréed Pralle's already shredded credibility.

After the jury was escorted from the courtroom on the afternoon of 6 May 1992, normally placid Judge Sawaya's frustration with Arlene Pralle was apparent. She had already angered him by telling the press that the proceedings were a waste of time. Now, in the courtroom, she pleaded for mercy for Lee. Yet in the press, she espoused the desire to help Lee get what she wanted and therefore dispatch her as quickly as possible to meet her maker.

Not the judge's words, but his message was clear: she speaketh with forked tongue.

Pralle offered him an extraordinary explanation for her apparent diversity of opinions. What she said to the jury came from her heart (i.e. her faith in Lee's finer qualities and redemption); when she spoke to the press, she was speaking for Lee (i.e. her disgust at the system, lack of hope in justice being served, the proceedings wasting taxpayers' money).

Ric Ridgway stepped up to present his closing argument. He pointed the jury towards the physical evidence surrounding the death of David Spears, who may or may not have accepted Aileen Wuornos's offer of prostitution.

'Now why he came from his intended route of Ocoee near Orlando and drove all the way to a remote section of Citrus County to pick up a thirty-dollar hooker isn't clear. There's a lot about his death we will never know. But what is clear is that whatever David Spears had done or agreed to do . . . shot six times including at least twice in the back, is not self-defence. David Spears, whatever he agreed to do, whatever he was misled into doing, died as a result of a robbery.'

From Bobby Copas (the witness who'd had a frightening encounter with Lee after picking her up and had also testified in DeLand), the jury could see, he said, 'That you didn't have to accept Aileen Wuornos's offer of prostitution for her to turn violent. All you had to do was disappoint her. All you had to do was have something she wanted.'

Her crimes were not spur-of-the-moment killings, he argued, but the killings of a woman who went out hunting men to kill and rob. Men she'd tricked into secluded areas. Hers were not the actions of someone who'd just been almost killed.

'Common sense says that a person is not going to have to use deadly force to kill another human being in self-defence seven times in one year . . . a police officer on the street every day, dealing with criminals, doesn't have to kill seven people in a year. Most of them don't kill one in a *lifetime*. Yet they want you to believe that she ran into seven men within one year and had to kill them all.'

Killing to avoid arrest, Ridgway pointed out, was an aggravated circumstance. After the men had been shot once or twice and it was no longer necessary to shoot them just to rob them, once they were obviously no longer in any condition to resist, she'd shot them again, and she'd kept on shooting.

He pointed out to them the bruise on Dick Humphreys's abdomen and the small bruises up near his armpit. 'When you consider what you see on Mr. Humphreys's body and what Mr. Copas told you happened, if you said 'No' to Aileen Wuornos, you were going anyway. But Copas had the presence of mind and pretended to go along until he could trick her out of his car. The physical evidence says that Humphreys couldn't trick her out of his car. Saying 'No' to her only angered her. He wound up where he wound up, at the end of a gun, knowing that he was going to die.'

Steve Glazer stood up and told the jury that he had to prove to them that Aileen Wuornos's life was worth saving. He made a valiant try. The tack he took, arguing for a life sentence over death, was that 'Aileen can never and will never repeat that past. She'll never walk the streets again.'

He believed she had now taken responsibility for her own actions and that she was sincere in her professed wish to get things right with God. She had found, her lawyer said, 'a glorious new belief.'

Steve Glazer took a reel of tape and while the courtroom waited, he eased his bulky body down to the floor and marked off a rectangle 6 feet by 8 feet. That, he said, was where she was living. Her plea of no contest had probably saved the state of Florida $20-$30 million, and she'd considered that as well in deciding to plead 'no contest'.

In the weeks preceding this hearing, investigator John Tilley, anxious to find Peter Siems's body and hoping to give Siems's family some peace of mind, had approached Lee for help regarding its possible location. Together, they had taken a trip to South Carolina, where she'd come to think she might have left him, but the trip drew a blank. Now Steve Glazer was citing that trip as evidence of the change in Lee.

'Is this not an act of unselfishness?' he asked the jury. 'It may even somehow qualify as an act of kindness. An act of kindness from a killer.'

He had not burdened the jury with psychiatric and psychological testimony or stories of her being dropped on her head as a baby. He did not even think his client killed in self-defence. He did believe, however, that *she* thought she acted in self-defence. Glazer continued: 'I keep walking on the border of this taped-off area. This could be all the space left for her on this planet.'

As he described the harsh reality of her life on Death Row and his intention to tell the judge that Lee should be put away for a minimum of 75 years, Shirley Humphreys left the courtroom. She need not have worried. When the jury returned after less than four hours of deliberation, they had voted to recommend death, by ten votes to two. When Judge Sawaya confirmed the sentence, Lee was facing four death penalties. Dixie County and Pasco County, with their victims, Walter Gino Antonio and Charles Carskaddon were still waiting in the wings.

The day after the Marion County jury's verdict, Ric Ridgway admitted that when he'd learned at the eleventh hour of John Tilley's proposed trip with Lee to South Carolina, 'I went ballistic.' To Ridgway, the timing was awful and reeked of manipulation. And what a position to be in. If word leaked out that Lee was willing to help and they'd turned her down, that would have looked dreadful and deservedly so.

'On the other hand, I see this freight train is going to run me over in the courtroom.'

Ridgway had hoped the trip could be stalled until after the hearing, but in the end he told John Tilley that if it became now or never, he should go ahead. By then Ridgway had thought it through, and felt reasonably confident that he could impress upon the jury that it was a ploy on Lee's part to make herself look better.

Tilley had ended up in this slightly rocky position because he was the only officer from Marion County that Lee would deal with. And he was torn. He knew he was due to testify for the prosecution, but he was also supposed to be trying to find Siems's body. By letting Lee help, he was certainly opening himself up to some potential problems. On the other hand, he and his fellow officers had travelled the interstate in Georgia and had got off at each and every exit as they headed north, to search in vain. He'd also been back through two whole years of records of unidentified bodies from the medical examiners' offices for Florida, Georgia, South and North Carolina, Virginia and Tennessee. None matched up to Peter Siems's dental records. He was clean out of ideas.

Ultimately, Lee and Tilley did take their little trip before the hearing, and, besides being unsuccessful, it was a security nightmare. Tilley had to consider that since Lee might well be about to receive her second, third and fourth death penalties, she didn't have much to lose any more. Perhaps she saw this as her big chance to escape. It would not look good if he lost her somewhere. Tilley didn't *think* escape was in her mind, but who knew?

He'd returned from South Carolina without finding Mr. Siems but with added insight into the defendant. He viewed her as a totally callous woman who'd used self-defence as an excuse. In his opinion, she was meticulous, knowledgeable, and thorough in her killings. And he'd learned that a clever and manipulative serial killer can be very adaptable, and can sometimes adjust his or her crimes specifically to throw off investigators. She'd broken her pattern with the length of time she kept Peter Siems's car.

The thought had been, she might also have broken it in other ways with Corky Reid, who was still missing in May of '92. Then, suddenly, in August, he turned up alive and living in Las Vegas. Lee had always maintained he wasn't a victim and she was proved right when he was picked up during a routine traffic offence. Apparently he was one of the surprisingly large number of people who disappear each year, mysteriously walking away from their lives.

Unhappy about being found, Reid declined to discuss with his relieved but pained family what had driven him away.

51

In June of 1992, Aileen pled guilty to the murder of Charles Carskaddon. At the penalty phase hearing, her lawyer presented a letter from Dr Harry Krop saying she was delusional and incompetent to stand trial. Based on that, she was sent for further evaluation by Drs Donald DeBeato and Joel Epstein. Those experts, however, found that while she suffered from a personality disorder, she was competent to proceed.

There was one bright spot for Steve Glazer—in August, his wife gave birth to their son Kody. But the year was fraught with sleepless nights. When he says, as he is fond of doing, that, 'I literally gave my heart to these cases,' there is harsh truth behind the laughter and glib one-liner.

In November, Steve suffered another heart attack and underwent double bypass surgery. While in the hospital, his mother died and he missed her funeral. And more work with Wuornos lay ahead. Weathering the criticism from fellow lawyers, many of whom treated him as a pariah for 'helping' a confessed killer die, working gruelling hours—the personal sacrifices involved were enormous.

'If you asked me would I do it again,' he reflected in 2001, 'the answer would be "no," just because I couldn't put my family and my health through it again.'

By February of 1993, however, he was back at Aileen's side when she went before Judge Wayne Cobb in Pasco County for sentencing for Charles Carskaddon's murder. Glazer's legal representation of Aileen ended thirty days later and by then she had already received her fifth death sentence in Cross City for the murder of Walter Gino Antonio, with the jury voting 7 to 5 for death.

At her sixth sentencing hearing, Lee waived her right to present mitigating evidence and Glazer went along with her wishes. She griped that she'd already received five death sentences, whereas male serial killers like Ted Bundy, usually only received a couple! On receiving her sixth death sentence, Lee launched into a by-then typical litany of complaints and profanity, causing Judge Cobb to threaten to bind and gag her unless she stayed quiet. Ultimately, he let her address the court. Again, she complained about her inability to receive a fair trial due to all the sensational publicity. Again, she said she'd acted in self-defence.

With six death sentences on the books and still no sign of Peter Siems's body, Lee settled into her cell at Broward Correctional Institute for the long haul. There was no air-conditioning in the Fort Lauderdale prison, which can be swelteringly hot in South Florida's humid climate, and Death Row inmates, distinguished from other inmates by the orange t-shirts they wore with their prison-issue blue pants, could only shower every other day.

They were allowed a radio and black and white television in their cells and could watch church services on closed circuit TV. They could receive letters during the week and have non-contact visits, but no phone calls whatsoever. Lee got three square meals a day, the first at 5 a.m., the last around four o'clock in the afternoon.

At Broward C.I., which was originally intended for male prisoners but has only ever housed females, Death Row inmates were counted at least hourly and were moved around in handcuffs, which they had to wear at all times except in the shower, the exercise yard or their cells. And they were generally in their cells 23 hours a day.

Among Aileen's neighbours were Judias 'Judy' Buenoano—who became the first woman to die in Florida's 'Old Sparky' on March 30, 1998—and murderess, Virginia Larzelere. But they were not allowed to socialize together in a common area.

For better or worse, this was Aileen's home. If she ever harboured hopes of a new trial or even release, nothing was happening soon. The gears of the judicial process grind very slowly and what lay ahead was a very long road, littered with appellate proceedings.

Aileen had more cause to hope for a new trial than most Death Row inmates. While she was awaiting sentencing, NBC's Dateline TV news show uncovered new evidence that she felt sure would help her. When they voted for the death penalty in the Richard Mallory case, had the DeLand jury unknowingly sentenced her to death for murdering a convicted sex offender and rapist? The flashiest issue her lawyers could raise on appeal to try to save her life would be a bonafide miscarriage of justice, if they could find one.

On November 10, 1992, Dateline aired a segment in which reporter Michele Gillen revealed what Aileen's defence team had not—the specifics of Mallory's criminal history. On the face of it, it sounded like huge news. At her trial Aileen had accused Mallory of brutally raping and sodomizing her. If the jury had heard that this man spent years locked up for a sexual offence, wouldn't they have given her the benefit of the doubt? Certainly her self-defence claims would have seemed more credible.

So, when Aileen appealed the Mallory death sentence, her team contended that she was not told that law enforcement had interviewed Jackie Davis, Mallory's girlfriend. They claimed that Davis's testimony would have established Mallory's prior violent disposition toward women. However, the Justices disagreed, responding that Aileen's defence team had been given details in a timely manner and had chosen not to present them, or Davis herself, to the jury. Davis's problem as a witness was that other than hearsay, secondhand reports or gossip, her own experience was that Mallory had been gentle towards women.

There were other problems with using Mallory's record as a mitigating factor to somehow lessen the apparent cold-bloodedness of Aileen's crime, most notably its distance in time. His crime took place in 1958. Mallory was a married, acne-plagued, nineteen year old just a few days shy of induction into the army and very stressed out at the time. His crime was breaking into a woman's home and trying to assault her. When she resisted, he fled immediately. He pled insanity and was convicted of housebreaking with intent to commit rape and assault, and sentenced to four years in a Maryland psychiatric facility.

A doctor who examined him found Mallory immature, with feelings of inadequacy with women which he covered up with fantasies that he was irresistible. The doctor also found that he had poor control of his sexual impulses. Once, he even gave up a job as a beverage delivery boy because of his strong urges to have sexual relations with the different women to whom he delivered packages. Indeed, the woman whose house he broke into was on his route and he'd seen her once before, lying across the bed, sleeping. He'd wanted to have sex with her then, he admitted. But then, as at all previous times, he had been able to suppress his inappropriate sexual desires.

Mallory was diagnosed with 'personality pattern disturbance, schizoid personality,' and he was deemed a 'defective delinquent' and confined to the Patuxent Institution.

There, he told a psychiatrist that he had, 'no hope for the future, nothing to live for,' and was, 'of no use to anybody.' He thought that his wife would be better off if he were dead.

Ultimately, Mallory held a job in the institution as a hospital clerk; a pat on the back for his progress. But he backslid and had to be removed from the job in August 1960 after making, 'a molesting gesture towards the charge nurse, with sexual intent.'

Early in 1961, he escaped from the institution but was caught and returned there. That year, a report on Mallory read: 'It is the feeling of the staff that this individual is quite unstable emotionally and lacks sufficient inner controls to warrant any change in status at this time. It is strongly urged and recommended therefore that he still be considered a defective delinquent and remain at Patuxent in an attempt to mitigate same.'

Richard Mallory was finally released in 1962, and in April 1968, was found by the Circuit Court for Montgomery County, Maryland to be 'completely relieved of the status of defective delinquent.'

As an adult, Mallory was a fan of porn and girlie bars but that is hardly synonymous with violence towards women. And his criminal record had been clean since his youthful offence, thirty years before his fateful encounter with Aileen Wuornos.

In short, his long-distant past was hardly a magic bullet and raised in Aileen's appeals, it was dismissed as irrelevant. When a defendant claimed self-defence, only two kinds of evidence could be admitted to establish the victim's character. One, evidence that showed their general reputation for violence in the community. Non-existent with Mallory. The second allowed testimony about specific acts of violence committed by the victim, but only on condition that it was first shown that the defendant knew about these same specific acts. Aileen did not know of any such acts.

Her lawyer tried to use Mallory's history to appeal the Charles Carskaddon conviction, but Attorney General Robert Butterworth and Assistant Attorney General Scott Browne, wrote in response:

'The defendant has failed to show that the extremely remote in time 'conviction' or incarceration of the victim in her prior murder case was relevant and admissible in this case.' They continued: '. . . even if Mr. Mallory's stay in a Maryland Institute for Sex Offenders from between 1958 and 1962 for a 1957 offence of housebreaking with intent to rape was somehow admissible in the Volusia County case, there is no reasonable possibility that this evidence would have resulted in a different result.'

They also argued that, 'It strains credulity to suggest that the outcome in the instant case would have been any different if only Mr. Glazer (Steven Glazer was Aileen's counsel in the Carskaddon case) had investigated the background of Mr. Mallory and learned that he had a "conviction" for an offence that occurred more than thirty years prior to his murder.'

The court agreed. And Steven Glazer, for one, was not surprised. He'd never viewed Mallory's history as particularly helpful to the case and is sure that even if all the specifics had been available at Aileen's trial for Mallory's murder, they'd have made no difference there either.

'They wouldn't have at all,' he reflected in 2001. 'To test the waters in case it came up in the Dixie County case, if you look at the record, you'll see that I tried to enter it into evidence. And it was objected to based on the fact that, number one, it's too old. Number two, Mallory's not on trial. It was not relevant.'

In appealing the Mallory trial verdict, the numerous issues raised included the fact that the jury was allowed to hear testimony about the other murders to which Aileen had confessed, prejudicing her case. The Justices noted that *all* evidence of a crime prejudices the case, in effect. Question was: Did it do so to an unfair, and therefore unlawful, degree? They thought not. The evidence was used to establish a pattern of similarities and to rebut Aileen's claim that she was defending herself while under attack: a proper use of the information under the Williams Rule. As the only witness to Mallory's murder, Aileen claimed he'd viciously abused her and threatened he might kill her. Had the jury heard that alone, they might have concluded that the murder was not premeditated and didn't reach the standard of first degree homicide. The prosecution was within its rights to use the 'similar fact evidence'.

The Justices *did* agree with the defence's contention that the trial court should have weighed Aileen's alcoholism, difficult childhood, and some kind of mental disturbance and impaired capacity at the time of the murder—especially since even the State's psychological experts agreed on this. But they found that since there were no other mitigating factors that should have been considered, given the record as a whole, the omission was harmless in that it would not have changed the outcome.

And so, on September 22, 1994, the Florida Supreme Court denied Aileen's appeal in the Mallory case, upholding her death sentence. Justice Kogan rendered a special opinion in concurrence, noting the discrepancy between the two pictures of Aileen—one as a victim of violence, lashing out at one of her victimizers, the other of a cold-blooded robber and killer. He agreed that the jury and court had been within their 'lawful discretion' in recommending and imposing the death penalty but went on to write about society not yet having confronted the problems arising from women forced into prostitution early, often to escape an abusive home environment:

'The tragic result is that early victimization leads to even greater victimization. And once the girl becomes an adult prostitute, she is labeled a criminal and often is forced into even more crime, as the only means of supporting herself. Few escape the vicious cycle.'

On October 6, 1994, the same appellate panel considered Aileen's appeal against her murder convictions for Dick Humphreys, Troy Burress and David Spears. The court did not agree with Aileen's argument that her 'no contest' plea was not voluntarily or intelligently made. Aileen had been extensively questioned by Judge Sawaya before her plea was accepted. As to another argument made by her counsel that her plea was improper because she pled no contest while continuing to insist that she'd killed in self-defence—that didn't help her either. The court held that the two were not inconsistent, noting that it's common practice for a guilty plea in a murder trial to be followed by an appeal for mercy.

Amongst the issues Aileen's team argued was that she did not murder for monetary gain but took the victim's property only as an afterthought and as revenge for having been abused by them. The court was not persuaded. Another round lost. Ultimately in 1994, the Florida Supreme Court upheld each and every one of Aileen's death sentences.

And so it went. Hearing after hearing. As Lee's various appeals crept forward, several key issues—like the question of Mallory's history—came to the fore and were repeated in each venue. Some trial and penalty phase errors were found but each error was ultimately judged harmless. In short—none would have affected the guilty verdicts and death sentences.

In 1999, CCRC (Capital Collateral Regional Counsel), whose state-paid lawyers work strictly on death sentence appeals, appointed Joseph Hobson as Aileen's lawyer. Hobson had his work cut out for him from day one.

When Aileen hired Steven Glazer, her goal was speedy execution and although over the years, she vacillated somewhat, her wish to die, to get right with God, remained a constant underlying theme. How does a lawyer fight for a client who one minute wants to live, the next, to throw in the towel and die?

'Representing Aileen Wuornos was clearly the most difficult and almost confounding challenge I'd ever had as an attorney,'

Hobson recalled in 2001– by then working in private practice with McFarland, Gould, Lyons, Sullivan & Hogan of Clearwater, Florida. Looking back, he believes he saw his duty not so much as to carry out her wishes but as to represent her interests.

'I wrestled with this,' he said, explaining that he talked it over with many other lawyers, too. 'And to my mind, I was really always kind of saddened that Aileen wasn't a more willing client because I thought she had some good issues.'

In February 2001, the issues Joseph Hobson referred to coalesced at an evidentiary hearing in Ocala, Marion County, where he set out to show that all the procedural errors added together had led Aileen to face execution rather than perhaps life, or life without possibility of parole.

Steve Glazer testified at the hearing, as did Tyria Moore, who arrived with her current life partner. The two women dressed in matching outfits which victim Troy Burress's sister, Letha Prater, took to be Ty's way of thumbing her nose at Aileen, and saying, 'Look, we're together.' (Lee grinned and tried to catch Ty's eye in court but Ty kept her eyes downcast and walked straight by without meeting her gaze.)

Incompetence of counsel is a death penalty appeal classic and Tricia Jenkins came under fire as well as Steve Glazer. Like Glazer, she took some hits for failing to present any mitigating witnesses. Childhood friend, Dawn Botkins, who saw adolescent Lee living rough and sleeping in cars, was all geared up to tell the story as were other childhood acquaintances who could have told of Lee's drug use in her teens and pre-teens, beatings, incest and sexual abuse. (Lee said the witnesses would not give accurate testimony: she'd had a good upbringing.) Filmmaker Jackelyn Giroux had also unearthed information about abuse in Lee's childhood that Pralle was convinced would have helped keep her off Death Row.

'It has always troubled me, too, that there were several witnesses who wanted to testify for Wuornos, but Jenkins never brought them in,' said Giroux, who would have been willing to testify.

Nor, Hobson and his CCRC colleague, Ruck DeMinico argued, did Jenkins pursue Lee's level of intoxication the night she murdered Richard Mallory. Voluntary intoxication can be a mitigating factor when weighing the intent behind a crime. If someone is falling down drunk, arguably, they cannot form the intent necessary for a murder to reach the level of heinousness found in Aileen's murder of Mallory and that warrants the death penalty.

An 18-year veteran of the Public Defender's Office, Tricia Jenkins had spent over 15 years as Chief Assistant, but at the time of the 2001 hearing had recently resigned to go into private practice. When defending Aileen, she had sixteen capital cases and over one hundred first degree murder cases under her belt.

Tricia knew Steven Glazer from his approximately two years with the Ocala Public Defender's Office. She was his supervisor . . . and his friend. And when Arlene and Aileen were desperate to have contact visits prior to the Mallory trial, it was Jenkins who referred Arlene to Steven Glazer. Not that Jenkins ever envisaged her *adopting* Wuornos. But she knew Glazer to be a member of the American Civil Liberties Union—he always wore a little ACLU pin—and he seemed ideal to handle the women's visitation issue.

Jenkins, like Ric Ridgway, was shocked when, during preparations for Aileen's Marion County trial for the murders of Burress, Humphreys and Spears, she learned that Glazer had become far more deeply involved than that and was planning to take over Wuornos's case. Personally, she would never have assigned Glazer a capital case, wouldn't even have appointed him second chair on one. He just didn't have the experience, she said, testifying in front of Judge Musleh, who presided over the Evidentiary Hearing.

'I would have wanted him to have co-counsel at least through a few felony cases,' she said. She also testified that later, in private conversation, Glazer had referred to himself 'as the Dr. Kervorkian of the legal community.'

Their friendship was quickly history. The vehemently anti-death penalty Jenkins was appalled by Glazer's handling of Wuornos's case and his 'no contest' pleas and she felt he had sold Aileen out.

Assistant State Attorney Jim McCune, the prosecution's main player at the Evidentiary Hearing, quickly brought out that Jenkins and Aileen weren't getting along when Aileen changed her plea on March 31, 1992:

'Well, isn't it fair to say that Miss Wuornos didn't want anything to do with you after the Volusia trial?' asked McCune.

'I think that that's probably a fair comment,' Jenkins replied, 'but that changed off and on, just like it did during my entire representation of her almost on a daily basis.'

52

Things got uglier and more personal for Steve Glazer than for any other player in Wuornos's legal drama. He was genuinely taken aback by the barbs flying in his direction.

'A lot of people have crucified me,' he reflected late in 2001. 'I do have a bitter taste in my mouth.' He was just following his client's wishes. And Aileen was very clear: she wanted it over with fast and didn't want anything happening that would give rise to a slew of appeals.

Other lawyers might have weighed her state of mind—she was depressed, surely, after recently being sentenced to death, and might soon start to feel quite differently about wanting to die—but Glazer was led by the lawyers' rules of ethics he felt appropriate.

'The defence client controls the litigation,' he explained. 'The next thing I have to find out: Is she sane? Can she make these decisions? I knew of her evaluations in Volusia where she was considered sane. I had her evaluated. While I represented her, I believe five separate doctors told me she was competent. So I had no doubt.'

He wouldn't have proceeded if he'd had any misgivings and always felt that he did the right thing. Seeing Aileen still chasing death nine years later only reaffirmed his belief. But his personal convictions didn't convince his critics and he flinched when he saw a criminal defence lawyer pontificating on television, saying, 'What Steve Glazer did was an abomination.'

The other thing was: his client's wish to die made sense to him.

'All I can tell you is that if it was me, I'd like to die as soon as possible,' he'd later explain. 'I wouldn't want to sit there for ten, fifteen, twenty years, waiting for the electric chair. I think that's part of why I helped. I could put my feet in her shoes . . . it's what she wanted.' He also knew Florida law and speculated, 'We're looking at twenty years, sitting on Death Row in that little cubicle!'

Glazer, who still practised criminal law in 2001 but had determined never to handle another death case, admitted he was stunned by the empathetic feelings he'd developed for Lee. With just two years in age between them there was rite-of-passage common ground, plus Steve's a musician and they enjoyed some of the same music. 'She understood The Beatles' "A Hard Day's Night",' he said wryly.

He continued to send her birthday and Christmas cards once he was no longer her counsel—with his representation of Lee an appeal issue, there could be no more contact than that. When they saw one another in court in February 2001, 'She smiled and we blew kisses at each other. I believe that if you asked her, she would say, "Steve Glazer's my friend." I would hope so. I think she would.

'I thought that she had three strikes against her by the time she was fourteen. What amazed me was how I could grow to really, really like someone who killed six people. I'm shocked. But I consider her my friend. Again, as a defence lawyer, you do not judge people. You help them. That's it.'

One thing was certain, he looked on Lee far more kindly than he did Nick Broomfield, the British documentary-maker who made the 1994 film, *Aileen Wuornos: The Selling of a Serial Killer,* portraying the money-hungry characters around Aileen. Broomfield, Steve believed, was bent on destroying him.

Steve Glazer's actions as a deal-broker for Aileen with media folk like Broomfield also came up in Aileen's appeals. Did he jeopardize her case by putting his time and energies into them? Did he have a conflict of interests? (He was charged with representing her best interests in her death penalty cases, yet meanwhile, he made money from being the liaison on some media projects like Broomfield's.)

At minimum, when Glazer brokered a deal with Broomfield and agreed to be interviewed along with Arlene Pralle and

Aileen for the documentary, it was a p.r. disaster. The already-embattled Glazer was seen taking money on camera and smoking marijuana during a drive down to visit Aileen. It was all captured on film for posterity . . . and ready to come back and bite him.

What most hurt Steve personally was learning that in a short-lived, San Francisco–based opera about Wuornos, his character was called Buffoon. 'That's where I sting,' he said later. 'Buffoon! They're talking about me!'

Yet Broomfield's portrayal of him as a mercenary, pot-smoking incompetent who seemed to find things rather amusing harmed him far more. Jovial by nature; that side to Glazer wasn't easily suppressed. Yet he truly believed he always acted in Aileen's best interests, and at her behest.

'I did not sell a serial killer,' he insisted. 'And just because they say it's a documentary, it doesn't mean it's true.'

The only money he received came from Aileen, and, 'What's so strange about a lawyer taking money from a client?' he puzzled. What's more, he was representing her free of charge in her criminal case because she was indigent and because, 'In my heart, I felt that if that's what she wanted, that's what she should get.' He had a clear conscience, thank you very much.

As he sipped a cup of coffee at the February 2001 evidentiary hearing in Ocala, Steve watched with interest as Tyria Moore arrived to testify, but he was then shocked to see his nemesis Broomfield being allowed to take a camerawoman inside the courtroom to record the proceedings. He kept his cool, though.

'I shook his hand, smiled, and said, "Fuck you." Steve recalled, chuckling despite himself.

Broomfield testified that his first take on Glazer was that he was acting more like a sales agent than a lawyer focused on the merits of Aileen's case. Quickly intrigued by the story's business angle, Broomfield had decided to start filming his negotiations with Glazer and Arlene Pralle.

Aileen's lawyer, Joseph Hobson, had Broomfield point out pages in his film's transcript that illustrated the fact that the money discussions with Steve and Arlene began at their first meeting.

'Arlene is talking, saying: "It's a neat story, but I can't tell you until you pay,"' Broomfield recalled. 'And Steve is asking for the $25,000 dollars. And they are basically trying to sell the story. That's what the scene is about.'

Apparently, Glazer sought different fees if Broomfield wanted to film Aileen's drawings or also use her poems.

'Mr. Glazer is a very amusing and jokey guy,' Broomfield told Hobson, recalling that he often sang songs.

'Did he appear to approach his duties as Ms. Wuornos's attorney in a serious manner?' asked Hobson.

'I think that Steve was . . . in essence, very concerned about the case. I think he felt, and I felt he seemed, very overwhelmed by the case, and it was quite apparent.'

Hobson then asked about Arlene Pralle's conduct regarding requesting a fee for the interview.

'Well, she—I felt she had a very strong mercenary interest, which I actually stated to her,' said Broomfield. 'I was surprised that with all the sort of love and devotion that she was talking about, that her main—I mean, all she was really talking about was the money involved.'

Did Glazer share that mercenary interest, Hobson asked?

'I felt he was part and parcel of that,' Broomfield replied.

Hobson successfully argued to be allowed to bring Mr. Glazer's marijuana use into the record, 'Because it goes to a possible habitual use that might have gone to the degree . . . of impairment that attended his representation of Ms. Wuornos.'

Broomfield had filmed Glazer smoking marijuana while driving with him to visit Lee down at Broward C.I., where Steve was scheduled to discuss the Carskaddon case with her.

'I think he said it was a seven-joint ride,' said Broomfield, who felt it was an inappropriate time for Glazer to be indulging in drugs.

On cross-examination, Jim McCune presented a photocopy of a bounced check that Broomfield had written out to Glazer. The judge cut the discussion short, but not before an impression was given: could Broomfield have purposely bounced a check so that he could hand cash to Steve and capture that damaging image on film?

Jim McCune pointed out that in two parts of the dope-smoking scene, Glazer was wearing different coloured shirts: one blue, one white. Might the footage have been cut and pasted to make it look like something that hadn't happened? Broomfield countered by saying that Glazer might simply have wanted to change his shirt before the prison visit after a long drive in the Florida summer heat.

Although Glazer represented Aileen criminally pro bono, Broomfield's film portrayed Aileen as the lamb sacrificed on the altar of his and Pralle's greed. In truth, behind bars, it was Aileen calling the shots and designating who would get how much of each fee that came in.

'I never took a penny from anyone but Aileen,' Glazer testified. 'Never. I think it came down to, I got $7,500 from her—three separate occasions of $2,500, and that was my total compensation for two or three years working with her.'

One $2,500 came from Broomfield's ultimate payment of $10,000 to gain access to Aileen to interview her.

'I think it's ludicrous to think that I could have talked her into anything,' Glazer said later. 'Do you think anyone could talk her into anything? I did what she wanted me to do.'

All her life, Aileen had craved attention and even on Death Row, enjoyed being in demand and the feeling of power it gave her. Tellingly, early in 1992, she asked for permission to receive a book at Broward—*Writing For Publication*. Apparently, she was still bent on having a book about her life.

Ultimately, Steve Glazer would be delighted with Judge Musleh's order after the hearing. 'It finally vindicated me,' he recalled late in 2001. 'Because the nature of the hearing was an attack on me and he just exonerated me; sang my praises.'

Put in a more formal way: 'The court finds counsel did not render ineffective assistance of counsel.' And the 'Order Denying Defendant's Motion for Post-Conviction Relief' issued by the Circuit Court, 5th Judicial Circuit, Marion County by Circuit Judge Victor Musleh on June 7th, 2001 found: 'Counsel was competent to represent Wuornos and assist her in her decision as to whether to plead guilty, and to assist the Defendant in a determination of what matters should be presented in mitigation.'

Musleh noted that although Glazer was strongly opposed to the death penalty, he also believed that a competent client had the right to make the ultimate defence decisions. Even so, he noted, 'Counsel was successful in presenting significant mitigation on behalf of a very difficult defendant who wanted no mitigation presented on her behalf at all.' And, he went on: 'Because of counsel's strategic decisions, the trial court found evidence of remorse, found evidence of a religious conversion, and found the Defendant suffered a deprived childhood.' Musleh also wrote: 'The relationship between Glazer and Wuornos appears to have been one of benevolence and mutual respect.'

He again vindicated Glazer regarding his role as intermediary in Wuornos's financial dealings with the media:

'The fact of the matter is the Defendant fired a highly trained and dedicated team of public defenders in favor of private counsel who would handle matters according to her directions. There was no testimony trial counsel's actions were unauthorized. The court finds Glazer acted on Wuornos's requests and that there was no conflict of interest. The payment of $2,500 to Glazer is neither shocking, nor unreasonable, in light of the pro bono work he performed on Defendant's behalf.'

Steve Glazer felt much, much better.

Arlene Pralle also rued the day she met Nick Broomfield. In his film, she came across as money-minded, with questionable motives for involving herself in Aileen's life. Of course, her adoption of a confessed killer was always, to most people, mystifying.

A onetime secretary who took up horse breeding in 1986, Arlene married Robert Pralle in 1974 and they had no children . . . until Aileen. Although they'd thought about adopting a child back in the 1970s, Robert had backed out of the idea.

Arlene, who became a born-again Christian at age twenty, had only recently moved to Florida when she read about Aileen's arrest and felt moved to write to her. Being deposed in January and June of 2000, Arlene was questioned by Joseph Hobson about the beginning of their relationship.

Her first letter to Aileen was about helping her save her soul, she recalled. 'I told her about Jesus. I told her I could help her.' Arlene admitted to Aileen that she felt scared to write to her, but was doing so because she'd been instructed to contact her by God: 'I have to obey God and I am writing to you because, and solely because, I want you to have peace in your heart and accept Jesus.'

Apparently not realizing how curious it sounded, Arlene then testified that although her husband was 'a Martian;' Robert felt similarly moved to reach out to Aileen. To avoid confusion, Mr. McCune had her clarify that she was referring to the *Men Are From Mars, Women Are From Venus* variety of 'Martian', made famous by John Gray's bestselling book.

The Pralles just saw something in Aileen's eyes that was calling out for help, said Arlene, and her letters soon led to weekly visits. But at Volusia County Branch Jail, those visits could only be through glass. Aileen, said Arlene, 'kept saying, "I wish I could be part of a family and see what it really feels like to be part of a family."' But the adoption was less about that than facilitating contact visits that only family members were allowed. Arlene said it was Steve Glazer's idea that the adoption could be a solution.

Theoretically, Arlene had much to offer Joseph Hobson as he worked his way methodically through Aileen's appeal topics. She had been close to Aileen during the Mallory trial, she'd had contact with Tricia Jenkins and the other lawyers, and she'd been enraged when they failed to present witnesses to Aileen's abusive childhood.

In 2000, under Hobson's questioning, a behind-the-scenes picture emerged of the Wuornos team during the Mallory trial when Hobson asked Pralle how involved she was and if she helped Aileen's defence attorneys.

'I tried to, but they told me to mind my own business, that they knew what they were doing and that I was being more of a hindrance,' said Arlene, describing Aileen's pre-trial behaviour as erratic.

'Some of the time she was right on target, and sometimes she would blow off just hysterical . . . either crying or using horrible, foul language. One end of the extreme to the other. There was one time where she threw a chair at Tricia.'

'In the course of a visit?' Hobson asked.

'Yes,' said Pralle, explaining her use to the defence team as a calming go-between. 'Tricia said it was like I had Valium on my hands, because whenever I would go in and just hold on to her (Lee's) hand and say, "Look, just talk to Tricia, she is trying to help you," she would calm down. And if she was screaming, she would stop screaming. If she was crying, she'd stop crying.'

'In your visits with Lee did it ever seem to you that she was losing contact with reality?' Hobson asked.

'No, not when we were alone. When Tricia would push her and the trial would come up and things like that, she would just go off. In her more recent letters from Death Row, yes, I would say she is losing perspective.'

Hobson tried to bring out whose idea it was that Aileen should switch from Tricia Jenkins to Steve Glazer.

'I think it was Aileen's, because she was very destroyed, as I was, with the entire team of Tricia, Nolas and Miller. And she asked me to find her another lawyer because she just thought they screwed up. I thought they screwed up, too.'

Pralle admitted that Glazer had expressed 'great reservations' about taking on the case but that she and Wuornos had pleaded with him. Back then, Arlene said she believed Lee's claims of self-defence regarding Richard Mallory. Some victims, Pralle believed, had hurt Lee; others she questioned in her heart.

Hobson asked whether subsequent to the Mallory trial, as her mother, Pralle had felt it in Aileen's best interests to plead 'no contest' in the Marion County cases rather than go through a trial. Yes, Pralle had encouraged that:

'And all I was interested in was her salvation; going to heaven if she died. That she would make it to heaven. If she was lying on any of those cases just to, quote, escape, get out of jail, she would be in hell. To me, as a Christian, I thought she needed to tell the truth even if the truth meant she wound up in prison the rest of her life, or the death penalty. The truth was what needed to come out.'

And Arlene believed Aileen did tell the truth. She also confirmed that Aileen wanted to get the death penalty and to be done with it.

Questioning then switched to all the media interviews. Initially, it was, said Arlene, 'Lee pushing, pushing, pushing, "Do it, do it, do it." Tricia saying, "Don't do it, don't do it, don't do it." And Lee wanting me to do it.'

No money changed hands before the Mallory trial—which, Arlene revealed, caused Aileen to have a fit. But once she was on Death Row, money was taken for interviews for shows like Montel Williams, which paid $10,000, and was split between her, Steve and Lee.

'Steve got money. Lee got money. I got money. And this was where the mistakes started. I never, ever, ever should have taken ten cents for doing any of these interviews, but Lee was the one who pushed them. Steve Glazer said, "What is wrong with it? Your daughter wants you to do this, do it."'

'And that is where I feel the line was drawn. I crossed over. And if I could go back I would not have accepted ten cents from any of these, it was Montel Williams and that other creepy guy . . .'

'Nicholas Broomfield?'

'Broomfield. Those were the two.'

Broomfield's $10,000 was split between Lee, herself, Steve and Dawn Botkins, she said.

'There is a portion of the Nicholas Broomfield documentary, *The Selling Of A Serial Killer,* said Hobson, 'in which it is depicted that you and Mr. Glazer and Aileen were requesting $10,000 to do any interviews. Is that inaccurate?'

'Totally, one hundred per cent inaccurate. Aileen wanted $10,000 or, she said, "You will not talk to anybody. This is stupid." And this was when she started losing reality. She was the one that was pushing.'

In the years since Aileen was first sentenced to death, the relationship between adoptive mother and daughter had gone through some rough patches. Late in 1993, Arlene's six-month absence to go to Tennessee and aid a sick friend, for instance, upset Aileen. So, later, would the news of Arlene's move to the Bahamas in 2000, prompted because her husband wanted to retire by the ocean.

'It is not a thing like, "You are abandoning me,"' said Arlene. 'It's . . . "they pirate the high seas, you're going to get yourself killed." My father says she has more sense than I do. I don't know.'

Although Arlene couldn't phone Death Row, she could visit, but no visits were imminent in 2000.

'Right now, she is just angry,' she said. 'And until she gets over being angry, if I went down there, I am sure the only thing that she would do would be yell at me for the entire visit. So there is no sense spending several hundred dollars on airfare just to have her sit there and yell at me for a Saturday and Sunday. So I am letting her get over the anger phase of me moving, and then I will go see her. So our relationship is the same as it has been except she is just feeling angry that I am moving.'

Pralle admitted that there were times when she'd felt very isolated with no one to talk to about her relationship with Lee.

'Tricia won't even talk to me,' she testified. 'Because of convincing Lee to plead guilty, Tricia thinks I am the scum of the earth—and sending her to the electric chair—so that entire team absolutely will have nothing to do with me.'

On June 16, Arlene Pralle testified for a second time. Why? Upon reflection, she wasn't happy with her January deposition and contacted Assistant State Attorney Jim McCune, to ask to speak again. 'Because I felt in my heart that there were things that, although they weren't blatant lies, they were withholding some truths I did not specifically bring out,' she said. 'My husband and I talked about it and I just felt that, as Christians, we had left the door open to Satan by not being completely, one hundred per cent honest.'

She was particularly keen to correct the record on her portrayal of Steve Glazer. Earlier, she'd testified that he had spent as much time brokering movie and book deals as working on the criminal case. This was unfair.

'He did a wonderful job defending Aileen Wuornos,' she said.

516

'I feel he did a far better job than Tricia. That was proved by the fact that he got some of the jury members to vote for life in prison, not unanimous death sentence, which Tricia got.'

She didn't believe that Steve had any conflict of interests as Joseph Hobson, in an effort to save Lee's life, had been trying to show. Why this change of heart about her testimony? Besides the second thoughts about Glazer, she'd also received a letter from Lee:

'She said, "I read the deposition. You led people to believe total untruths. I don't know if you said it that way, or it was written that way."'

Lee did not like Arlene suggesting that her husband Robert had promoted the adoption idea. In fact, Robert and Lee had only spoken by phone a couple of times in 1991.

'But other than that, he's not like, quote, a father, and he wanted all of this,' Arlene admitted. 'He just merely went along with it. It was one hundred per cent my idea, my prompting.'

Arlene said that Lee also was really bothered by her claim that they still had contact. Contact was very limited, she admitted, in response to Jim McCune's questioning:

'. . . before we were seeing each other a lot. We were writing back and forth every week. After Nick Broomfield, it really shattered the relationship.'

(Arlene alleged that Broomfield played a kind of divide and conquer game with them, telling Lee things Arlene had supposedly said and vice versa.)

Finally, sometime the previous year, Lee wrote to Arlene seeking forgiveness. 'She realized that Nick was quote, unquote, a jerk. She asked if we could start over. I very willingly agreed. I wrote to her. She wrote to me faithfully.'

However, Arlene testified that she'd told Lee, 'I don't want you to use me as a puppet. I am not doing any media things for you. I will be your friend, period . . . but I am not going to be manipulated. I am not going to jump, "Well, I want you to do this, I want you to do that, go talk to these people." If you want only a friendship, this is fine. And I am glad you forgive me and you realize the Broomfield thing was not my fault.'

Arlene felt some guilt that the year she was busy selling her horse farm, she'd only visited Lee once:

'And she wrote to me a lot. I was the one who failed to communicate back with her and she felt very abandoned. It had nothing to do with abandoning her, but that's how she perceived it . . . she said, "You dropped me like a hot potato. And in the deposition you said we have contact all the time. That's an out-and-out lie." Lee is correct, our contact has been very limited; not her fault, my fault.'

When Arlene sent her birthday cards and Valentines, 'She just was furious and said, "Why are you coming back now when I needed you before?" So that is the absolute truth.'

Summing up, she said, 'I feel I did abandon her.' And yes, she could and should have organized her time better, 'because I promised I would be there for her and I was not.'

53

Lee was furious about the television movie, *Overkill: The Aileen Wuornos Story,* which fed right into her deep belief that others were getting rich off her story. The progress of *Overkill* also infuriated Jackelyn Giroux, who had signed up Lee's life story rights in January 1991, just three weeks after her arrest.

The Hollywood grapevine being what it is, Giroux was tipped off very quickly that 'the three cops,' as Munster, Binegar and Henry came to be known, had been brokering a movie deal. To her mind, that was a real conflict of interest at a time when the officers should have been focused on protecting the case against Wuornos. Officers whose salaries were being paid by taxpayers, no less. She was also livid because another fast-moving Wuornos movie project, one with sources inside law enforcement, could thwart her own. In 2001, she testified that she had an unwritten deal with Lorimar Productions to make her movie which fell through when Lorimar couldn't get the rights to the officers' part of the story. Suddenly, everywhere she went in Hollywood, she was hearing about 'the three cops' project.

Much later, Giroux would see memos sent by Kevin Mills of Republic Pictures to attorney Robert Bradshaw, an ex-reserve cop and close personal friend of Major Dan Henry's, indicating that by January 28, Bradshaw had been enlisted to represent the officers and was at least *talking* to movie folk about Tyria Moore as well. The day before Giroux signed her deal with Lee, Kevin Mills received a memo from Adoley Odunton, also of Republic Pictures, asking him to structure a deal with 'Major Dan Henry, Bruce Munster and Captain Vinegar (sic).' Tyria Moore's name had been handwritten in on the memo, along with the notation, 'Les. Lover.'

Kevin Mills' January 29 handwritten notes from a conversation with Bradshaw bore the words, 'confession on videotape.' They also noted: 'Son of Sam Laws? No but Robbie is checking.' (The so-called Son of Sam law was intended to prevent criminals from profiting from their crimes.) The memo set out a tentative deal which was formalized on January 31 in a letter Kevin Mills wrote to Robbie Bradshaw, entitled: 'Re: Motion Picture Rights Option/Purchase.'

On February 5, Republic issued a second letter addressed to Bradshaw naming 'the three cops' and Tyria Moore and monetary terms. The letter had space for signatures, yet remained unsigned. Signed or not, in February, writer Fred Mills was hired to write a teleplay. Work was moving ahead, with or without the cops.

For Aileen's various appeals, including the Ocala Evidentiary Hearing in February 2001, precisely when the officers began talking movies with Bradshaw would be a key issue. The sooner the talks took place after Lee's arrest, the more mileage her CCRC defence lawyers could get out of arguing that the movie issue might have tainted the purity of the criminal investigation. *Overkill* was an obvious topic to raise because it hinted that Lee might have received less than a fair shake from law enforcement.

Had the allure of a movie, and the tempting prospect of seeing their investigative handiwork depicted on screen, led the officers to compromise their investigation or to corrupt her trial? Had Tyria Moore's possible involvement in the homicides been fully explored? At the very least, the officers had exercised poor judgment—as key players in the case against Lee, they might be called as witnesses at trial.

From the moment the tantalizing word went out that police were seeking two women for the Florida murders, media interest was at fever pitch. Captain Steve Binegar fielded all related enquiries—a job commonly tackled by a public information officer. Enterprising Hollywood producers always chomped at the bit to sign up the main characters in any juicy crime saga but would usually hit a brick wall or two when seeking cooperation from law enforcement during an active case. (The three cops weren't the only ones crossing the line. All media has access to information once it's made part of the public record but transcripts of Aileen's three-hour videotape confession were somehow circulating before that happened . . . and long before her trial. Some journalists keen to get an early jump on the story were quietly offered black market copies for thousands of dollars.)

Testifying in court hearings in both 2000 and 2001, Munster, Binegar and Henry admitted movie deal discussions took place but said they were quickly aborted. Red flags went up as soon as they ran the idea by Sheriff Moreland who said that no one in the department would make any money from such a deal. He suggested they might establish a victims' fund with any proceeds, but things never got to that stage.

'We started getting a lot of flak over it,' Bruce Munster testified. 'I guess that we were all pretty naïve in being involved in something like this and we quit it.'

When Dan Henry went under oath, he denied knowing that Munster had told attorney Robbie Bradshaw that Tyria might be party to a deal. He also denied entering into a contract with Republic Pictures. He assisted them, 'No more than I did anybody else that came and asked questions.'

As far as receiving money? He might have gone to lunch with somebody, but he wasn't sure about that, and normally paid his own way at lunches. He had trouble remembering the names of media folk or writers he might have met with.

All three officers stood firm: *Overkill* came to fruition, but their own deal did not. That didn't negate Bruce Munster having discussed the subject with Tyria Moore, a suspect and possible co-defendant. Munster contended that he simply gave Ty Bradshaw's phone number in case she was interested; there was no persuading her to join forces with them.

The three officers said that all discussions happened *after* the investigation was over, *after* Aileen confessed, and *after* Tyria was eliminated as a suspect. Nevertheless, this was almost a year before Aileen's trial. Just talking to Ty about movie deals smacked of a conflict of interest, with Aileen the loser. An aroma of impropriety wafted around the whole business.

Detective Munster had thirty-one years in law enforcement, a job liaising between the sheriff's office and the Department of Child and Family Services reviewing child abuse cases, and retirement looming, when he was quizzed at the 2001 Marion County Evidentiary Hearing.

Munster saw no conflict in talking to Tyria, he said, because he was satisfied that she had no involvement in the murders. He'd been active in creating a timeline of Aileen and Tyria's movements, checking with Tyria's former places of employment and interviewing ex-neighbours.

'When we met her up in Scranton, Pennsylvania, she was interested in exonerating herself,' he said. 'She was very helpful. She was agreeable to come back to Florida to prove that she wasn't involved.'

'Did you tell her: "Tyria, you're off the hook. Don't worry about it,?"' asked Lee's lawyer, Joseph Hobson.

'Never did,' said Munster. He certainly didn't have the power to grant her unilateral immunity, and with five counties involved, she remained subject to prosecution by any of them if ever any new evidence came to light.

'This investigation was being conducted by several different State Attorneys' offices and several different police departments and sheriff's departments, and everybody had access to her,' Munster explained. 'If they wanted her, go get her.'

Except for the wrecking of Peter Siems's car, he said, 'There was absolutely no evidence that I could find that these two girls had ever hitchhiked together or been involved in anything together.'

Yet, Tyria had not officially been ruled out as a suspect and however innocent they believed her to be, they were in effect throwing their hats in the ring with her. Not clever. Looking back, the officers would not disagree.

The feelings of elation soon faded, but Bruce Munster remembered initially being quite dazzled by the idea that there might be a movie about the case:

'I thought that was pretty neat. I'd never been involved with anything like that before.' Clueless about Hollywood's ways, Munster claimed he had no idea what he was getting himself into. 'I didn't know that you sold your rights and people paid you money and stuff . . . I was naïve.' That, he says, is precisely why they involved Robbie Bradshaw.

With hindsight, suggested Assistant Attorney General Scott Browne, 'Would it have been wiser, perhaps, to wait until after a conviction to even talk about a movie deal?'

'Absolutely,' said Munster. 'Hindsight being 20/20, I've learned a lot, my agency has learned a lot, and I don't think you would ever find us being involved in anything like that again.'

Captain Steve Binegar, an ex-Marine and ex-FBI agent (now a Chief of Staff at the Marion County Sheriff's Office) was commander of C.I.D. and Munster's superior during the Wuornos investigation. Originally he got caught up in the excitement too:

'It was almost an ego trip for me, personally. In hindsight, I would have ran from these people. With the benefit of ten years of more maturity now and—you know, we were just blown up with the idea that we had participated in a case of this magnitude . . .'

'Was it fair to say you all got caught up in it?' Joseph Hobson asked.

'I think that's fair to say,' admitted Binegar.

Yet he maintained his actions weren't affected by a possible movie deal, nor did it in any way affect the Wuornos investigation. And he'd never signed a contract with anyone.

'Did you receive any compensation, a free meal, a free trip to Hollywood?' asked Scott Browne.

'No sir,' said Binegar. 'Nothing but heartache, really.'

Looking back on the episode, he saw their blunders in glorious technicolour:

'Even by considering it in our naïve state, we gave . . . you know, we handed the defence in my opinion, a . . . something to hang their hat on. Because the case itself, the real case, the case that's made for who actually killed these people, that was rock solid, in my opinion.' He continued, 'But . . . we had nothing to say: "Big red flag. Yo." We certainly do now.'

Jackelyn Giroux, for one, found the officers' claims of naivete hard to swallow—especially in the case of Binegar with his FBI background. Under questioning by Joseph Hobson, she had to concede that she'd never seen a contract or cheques or cash change hands. (Nevertheless, it remained her personal belief—and still does—that the three officers had an unwritten deal with Republic Pictures.)

Besides criticism from Giroux and Tricia Jenkins, the three officers also had to contend with their own colleague, Sgt. Brian Jarvis, who also testified at the evidentiary hearing. Jarvis, the supervisor of the Major Crimes Unit, was Bruce Munster's immediate superior and friend, and created the computer programme that collated all the phone leads generated by the sketches of the two suspects seen leaving Peter Siems's crashed car. But as Wuornos's arrest grew closer, Jarvis was increasingly left out of the loop. 'I was in charge of the investigation and I was the only guy at home,' he complained to a journalist in 1991. He was subsequently moved from Major Crimes to Property Crimes, and Bruce Munster was promoted to fill his slot.

Feeling slighted and pushed aside from the excitement of this big celebrity case, Jarvis hired his own representative, Michael McCarthy, who tried (unsuccessfully) to sell Jarvis's own version of the Wuornos story.

By 2001, Jarvis was ensconced as chief of police for the Chester Police Department in New York State, a small department with eight officers. He testified that he left Marion County, where he worked from 1985 to 1991, of his own volition, after becoming a sergeant in major crimes in November 1988 and receiving several medals of commendation.

To Jarvis, there was something wrong when his colleagues not only didn't charge Tyria but actually referred her to their lawyer. However, he could not point to any specific harm that had resulted and could only speculate that there may have been a basis to bring charges against her: 'There could have been. I think the leads needed to be investigated further.'

Under questioning by Hobson, Jarvis claimed that some of Dick Humphreys' property was located on both sides of a dirt road which seemed to him to suggest at least two people in a car, throwing things out on either side. The clear inference: Tyria Moore could have been involved. (Munster's account disagreed with Jarvis's. He said, 'The stuff was strewn everywheres.')

Weakening the impact of Jarvis's arguments: once the case extended beyond Marion County, his involvement really ended at the computer and he'd never interviewed Wuornos or Tyria Moore.

Jarvis found it odd that later in the investigation, Binegar and Henry got so deeply involved, stressing that Captain Binegar hadn't gone out to the sites when Mr. Burress's and Mr. Humphreys' bodies were found.

Was it really so surprising to find senior officers jumping in with both feet once they realized they had a search for a prolific serial killer on their hands? Maybe not. But to Jarvis, it was. And it was odd to see Binegar and Henry go out in the field conducting background investigations where Wuornos and Moore grew up.

'What if anything struck you as unusual about that development?' asked Joseph Hobson.

'The unusual part initially was that Captain Binegar and Major Henry were not investigators,' Jarvis replied. 'They were administrators. They had not done investigations before, they had not become involved in investigations before. So I thought it was a little odd, but I really didn't know of any motive or anything; just that it was happening.'

Jarvis's comments skirted this: Binegar was in a desk job but with his FBI background, was far more than just an administrator. Jarvis traced his troubled relationship with Binegar back to mid-September 1991 when Jarvis re-released the composite sketches of the two 'wanted' women to the media and suggested the crimes might be linked:

'He criticized me for releasing that information. He said, furthermore, he didn't feel females were involved; it wasn't any more than a fifty per cent chance that they were involved.'

Jarvis told of his desire to write a book about the case, and of receiving one dollar from Mike McCarthy on signing their agreement and in turn paying McCarthy $500 to help him research and write it.

'The next day, (McCarthy) called me back and asked me who Binegar, Munster, Henry and Moore were,' he said.

Then Binegar called him in to his office. 'And I was chastized for wanting to write a book. After that point, I could tell my job seriously changed. And this actually happened right after her (Aileen's) arrest. I was removed from major crimes and Bruce Munster was promoted to sergeant and put in charge of major crimes. And then Captain Binegar was basically criticizing every bit of work that I was doing, no matter how minute it was.'

Jarvis testified that the focus on two female perpetrators also died away once Wuornos was located. After that, 'There was never the mention or the implication of two females; only one. My concern was a large portion of evidence which linked two females to these cases. It was not followed up on.'

'What evidence are you referring to?' asked Hobson.

Jarvis cited Mr. Humphreys' belongings being found in Pennsylvania with Tyria. He suggested other avenues of investigation, like finding out if Tyria was in the area of any of the murders:

'I checked her time cards to make sure she wasn't working during that time, and I got copies of the time cards from her employment that showed she had been released a week prior to Mr Humphreys' disappearance and murder. But that was never followed up on.'

(Bruce Munster asserted that he was satisfied with Tyria's timeline.) Jarvis also found it odd that in *Overkill,* only the names of Binegar, Munster, Henry and Tyria Moore were not fictionalized.

Scott Browne asked Jarvis if his departure from MCSO was 'fairly acrimonious?'

'I left because I didn't feel safe here,' Jarvis replied.

'In fact, were you disciplined for removing items and information from a computer?' asked Browne.

'Yes, I was,' he replied.

Browne noted that a State Attorney's investigation found no serious or criminal misconduct by Munster, Binegar or Henry: 'You are aware of that conclusion, are you not?'

'Yes I am,' said Jarvis.

On redirect, Hobson brought out the fact that the disciplinary action against Jarvis came within weeks of learning, 'that there was a movie deal involving my superiors.'

Why *did* he remove the computer programme he'd devised?

'To prevent myself from being subject to copyright infringements,' he said.

When Tyria Moore testified, she said she heard nothing about any 'movie deal' until after she'd told the police everything she knew relating to the crimes—and after she had helped the police secure Aileen's confessions via those taped jailhouse telephone calls.

Ultimately, two official movie-related investigations took place. To testify about the one instigated by Marion County State Attorney Brad King in July 1991, the state called Ric Ridgway, who had prosecuted Lee in the Spears, Burress and Humphreys murders. Ridgway's office had conveyed to the sheriff concerns about the movie issue, 'as to the obvious impeachment issues it would create for the witnesses,' and subsequently headed the investigation.

'What conclusion did you reach,' asked Scott Browne, 'as a result of your investigation, with regard to what impact, if any, the movie deal had on the prosecution and investigation of the Wuornos murders?'

Ridgway explained that there were two key issues—was there anything in, 'What was commonly referred to as "the book and movie deal" that would have interfered with our prosecution of Aileen Wuornos?' Secondly: 'Was there any evidence of the involvement of Tyria Moore in the homicides that had not been properly developed or found, either because of the book and movie deal, or any other reason?'

Tyria's involvement was, Ridgway admitted, 'Always kind of an open question. There was always a question she was involved; and if so, to what extent?'

Ridgway confirmed that the five different Florida sheriff's offices and his own investigation came up empty-handed regarding evidence of Tyria's criminal involvement:

'There was never any credible evidence, or there wasn't any admissable evidence, that Tyria Moore had any involvement, either as a principal or as an accessory after the fact on any of the homicides.'

Tyria was neither offered nor granted immunity by Ridgway's

office. 'She never asked for it,' he confirmed, 'nor was she ever offered it. There was never any deal cut for her testimony.'

In August '91, the investigation's report concluded that a document outlining a payment scheme in a potential movie deal existed, but that contracts were never signed and the officers never received any money. It found that the deal idea was aborted because it might conflict with the investigation.

In 1993, the FDLE carried out a rather different investigation. Triggered by Bruce Munster's deposition for a civil lawsuit between Aileen Wuornos and Jackelyn Giroux, it involved some odd telephone communications between Munster and Henry.

The background to the Wuornos/Giroux legal battle lay in a 'declaratory judgment action' that Steven Glazer filed on behalf of Wuornos in September 1992 against Jackelyn Giroux, Jackelyn Giroux Productions, and Russell Armstrong (the lawyer who had originally liaised between the two women.) Wuornos wanted to repudiate the January 1991 contract giving Giroux rights to her life story. Later, Giroux learned that Lee was angry when she filed her suit because she was under the erroneous impression that Giroux was cooperating with the Republic Pictures-CBS production of *Overkill*. Nothing could have been further from the truth, of course.

The Giroux defendants lodged a cross complaint against Wuornos for the right to continue to exclusively own her story as she had told it to Giroux. Then the Giroux team deposed various players including the three police officers because, Giroux said, 'I believed they had intervened with my communication with Aileen Wuornos and additionally, I believed that the depositions would give me discovery—insight into what transpired between them and Republic/CBS.'

Ultimately, Wuornos and Giroux dropped their complaints against one another. Meanwhile, those were tense times for 'the three cops'. Just before Bruce Munster was deposed, he received a curious voice mail message on his pager (possibly two, he couldn't recall) that sent him straight into self-preservation mode. Major Henry's voice was asking him to call back 'Mr. Nobody' at a different extension from his own in the sheriff's office. So, Munster testified:

'I recorded those (one or two voice mail) pages that made me suspicious and made me believe that I was going to be asked to do something, or say something, that wasn't true. And it was just a feeling that I had.

'And I called the office and I recorded that conversation in which Major Henry told me that this conversation that he and I were having never occurred; that he wanted to discuss the depositions.'

Munster said that Henry told him that if he was asked if they'd discussed his deposition, he should say no.

'Now Mr. Hobson, I don't lie, period, and I'm not going to do it,' Munster testified. 'Even if it jeopardizes my job, I don't lie.'

Munster turned over the tapes to a lawyer and ultimately they were given to Sheriff Don Moreland, leading to the FDLE's investigation.

'After the investigation, isn't it true that Dan Henry resigned?' asked Hobson.

'That's correct,' said Munster.

(When Dan Henry testified about his 1993 resignation, he said, 'I wasn't being terminated but I felt like it was the best thing to do at the time.' Five months after the FDLE investigation cleared him, however, then-sheriff Ken Ergle rehired him. And by 2001, like Binegar, Henry was a Chief of Staff in the Marion County Sheriff's Office.)

'Did Captain Binegar resign?' Hobson asked Munster.

'No, he did not,' said Munster. 'Captain Binegar hadn't done anything.'

Munster also denied a common rumour that he himself had been demoted:

'In June of 1992, I had given up my stripes and my position as a sergeant in the major crimes unit and had taken a position as a school resource officer,' he explained. 'So that happened in '92. This happened in '93.'

Speculating on what might have prompted Dan Henry to conjure up this fantasy character, 'Mr. Nobody', Munster could only guess that Henry was being overly cautious in a contentious climate. And the way he did it came back to bite him.

'. . . it was just a knee-jerk reaction that there would be—he would be criticized in some way for the answers that he gave, or something,' said Munster. 'I don't know. But there wasn't anything to lie about. We didn't do anything wrong.'

'The only really questionable conduct he engaged in was trying to do something that might have been perjurious or less than truthful testimony?' Hobson asked.

'Well, this was the second most powerful man in this agency,' said Munster. 'He was right under the sheriff. And this man was telling me that this conversation never took place . . . and for me to go into a depo the next day and to say he and I never talked, I wasn't going to do it. Not for anybody.'

Hobson then asked about the suggestion that Tyria was never charged with a crime because she was tantamount to the officers' commercial colleage.

'That's ridiculous!' said Munster, citing the fact that the investigators didn't find a single witness who put Tyria and Aileen together on the highways. All evidence pointed to Aileen travelling alone while Ty had a job or stayed at home.

'I don't want to call her a wife, but that's basically what she was,' he explained.

Munster wouldn't have been surprised to learn that a proposed contract for a movie existed, but he personally never signed anything and he strongly doubted that Binegar or Henry would have done so either:

'I would find it very hard to believe that they did because that would be their careers.'

When it was Dan Henry's turn to testify, Joseph Hobson asked: 'Do you remember why you were so eager to talk to Deputy Munster about your testimony?'

'I've been waiting ten years to say this,' Henry replied. 'If all my phone calls were recorded all my life, I probably wouldn't be a policeman today. You know, people say pretty dumb things when they don't realize they're being recorded, and I said some pretty dumb things.'

'But that conversation, you took efforts to conceal?' said Hobson.

'Excuse me?' said Henry.

'You identified yourself as "Mr. Nobody"?' Hobson clarified.

'I don't recall that, but it wasn't concealed. It was on the telephone.'

Before releasing the witness, Scott Browne elicited Dan Henry's testimony that he'd never received a single dollar in relation to a movie deal.

For Munster, what had begun as the most exciting case of his career, had turned so sour that later, he seriously considered leaving the department. 'I was tired of all the stones that were being thrown and backstabbing,' he said. Being deposed in 2000, and again in 2001, wasn't pleasant either.

'You know, the movie thing, it was so innocent,' he said. 'I mean, of course, today it doesn't seem like that. But it was so innocent. There was nothing unscrupulous or anything going on.'

He wanted the story told right, he said, and making money was never his objective although, 'No one is averse to making extra money.'

Well, apparently Tyria Moore was. For a while, anyway. Tyria, who worked as a forklift driver and by then had lived in Pennsylvania for eight years, said she knew only of the Richard Mallory murder and had no suspicions of any others. (This sounded at minimum disingenuous, and if Tyria thought that the dead men's belongings she took to Pennsylvania were gifts from Aileen's clients, what did she tell herself about the procession of strange cars that Aileen brought home? That question wasn't asked.)

Tyria admitted to being 'very scared' when police first questioned her.

'Did they give you the impression that you could be prosecuted?' Joseph Hobson asked.

'Yeah. They never told me that I couldn't be,' she said. 'There was no guarantee that I would ever not be charged.'

'So in your mind, it was a real fear that you could be charged?'

'Correct.'

The only thing she'd ever heard about any movie monies perhaps benefitting the victims' families came from what she read in a newspaper. She recalled being contacted by Robbie Bradshaw and the suggestion that she, Munster and Henry, 'Should stick together and have one attorney.'

Hobson questioned her more closely: 'So you went from being a possible co-defendant, to a partner in a business enterprise?'

Scott Browne objected so Hobson scratched the word partner.

'So you went from being a defendant to someone who was going to go in on book deals with them?'

'That was what they wanted. Yes.'

Tyria told Hobson she'd had no previous thoughts of book deals herself.

'What did you think of the idea as they proposed it to you?' he asked.

'I didn't want anything to do with it,' she said firmly.

She responded to a letter from Mr. Bradshaw saying she wasn't interested and at that time, didn't entertain the idea at all.

'At any time, did you?'

'Later, yes.'

Hobson wanted to know why Munster would approach her and how he knew she was interested.

'I don't know,' said Ty. 'He didn't know I was interested, because I wasn't. I made it very clear that . . . I could not make money off of this. I just can't see the fact of profiting when someone else lost their life. That's just not me.'

A transient philosophy apparently. Later, Tyria was open to telling her story to Jackelyn Giroux . . . for a price. In May 1992, the two also joined forces in Giroux's effort to have an injunction issued to stop *Overkill* from being aired. That month, Giroux hired lawyer Jonathan Lubell of Morrison, Cohen, Singer & Weinstein in New York City, impressed by his track record in cases against CBS. However, Giroux contends that to her horror, she discovered that Lubell did not immediately notify CBS or Republic Pictures of her grievance, as she'd requested—and didn't do so until November. The month *Overkill* was due to air.

Lubell then told her the court venue was changed to Los Angeles and suddenly put another lawyer on the case. To Giroux's dismay, the L.A. judge ruled that the complaint was filed too late and *Overkill* could air as planned. However, he did note that Tyria Moore and Giroux could try to claim damages afterwards, based upon their claim that the CBS/Republic movie invaded Tyria's privacy rights—rights which Giroux obtained from Tyria in a September 1992 contract.

That summer, even State Attorney Brad King felt moved to write to Jeff Sagansky, then head of CBS, to lobby for CBS to drop *Overkill*. He urged him to reconsider: he'd read Fred Mills' script and found it a 'substantially inaccurate portrayal of the role of law enforcement in bringing Aileen Wuornos to justice for her crimes.' He complained about Aileen being portrayed as a, 'sociological victim instead of the cold-blooded killer of reality.' He asked that CBS not give Aileen Wuornos any more attention. But his pleas fell on deaf ears. *Overkill* aired on television in late November.

'We had planned to continue fighting,' Jackelyn Giroux recalled in 2001, but she received a massive lawyer's bill and simply didn't have the funds to continue. 'Plus, I was advised that Tyria's damages could never recover that enormous legal fee.'

Giroux felt that she got a raw deal whereas, in her opinion, Binegar, Munster and Henry got off very lightly for their little foray into the wilds of Hollywood during an ongoing case.

'I think they were very, very lucky,' she said. 'And if it happened in a large city, they would have been dismissed in a heartbeat. We can all say we were naïve and we are sorry, after the fact. But they have never come clean. When you read their depositions and they cannot remember who sat next to Tyria Moore on a plane and Henry can't remember who he gave information to while mowing his front lawn—well, why would you want them in law enforcement if their memories are that bad?'

54

Lee's wish to die led to a competency hearing in Marion County preceding the February 2001 Evidentiary Hearing. It fell to Circuit Judge Victor Musleh to decide if she was competent to make the monumental decision to end all appeals of her six death sentences and proceed to execution.

Psychologist Bill Mosman thought she was not, testifying that Lee suffered from paranoid delusions and believed prison officials were trying to change her thought patterns via radio waves, and to poison her food.

Dr. Michael Herkov, a psychologist, associate professor at the University of Florida College of Medicine and consultant to the FBI, had a different take. He interviewed Lee in her room for a couple of hours, initially focusing on retroactively reviewing her competency back in 1992 when she decided to plead 'no contest' in the murders of Burress, Humphreys and Spears, then her current competence. Unlike Mosman, Herkov found her competent.

After hearing conflicting testimony on February 18, Judge Musleh ordered Herkov to re-evaluate Aileen. At 7 a.m. the next morning, the two talked for an hour in the jury room adjacent to the courtroom while Herkov took notes on his laptop computer.

There was no doubt in the doctor's mind that Lee understood all that she needed to. At the time of her trial and convictions, she'd understood the nature of her crimes and the range of possible penalties. And now she knew what she was doing in wanting to hasten her journey to execution. She *was* a little confused regarding that step's absolute finality. So Herkov explained to her that waiving her appeals would close the door on *all further appeals*. Understanding that, she chose to still leave that door open just a chink. She asked to be allowed to drop her appeals without prejudice . . . just in case she later wanted to re-file.

'It is my professional opinion within a reasonable degree of psychological probability that Ms. Wuornos is competent to proceed today,' Herkov told Judge Musleh. She had changed her mind on important issues but was not psychotic and her inconsistency was not evidence of incompetence.

One of Aileen's defence lawyers, Mr. Reiter, pressed Herkov about Aileen's mood swings: happy one minute, sad the next, friendly one minute, screaming outrageously the next.

'That would tend to confirm a borderline or an antisocial (personality disorders),' Herkov testified. 'They tend to do that. But just because you become irate, just because you have poor control over your anger and then you have mood fluctuations, doesn't make you psychotic.'

Yes, Aileen had in the past complained that someone had been 'messing' with her prison food, but given the prison environment with its pervasive culture of suspicion, that was not a delusion either. Food was a constant topic of discussion among inmates, and Aileen didn't think she was being poisoned.

With her behavioural changes and mood instability, Herkov said, 'I think that Ms. Wuornos is classic, and very much antisocial and borderline.'

Dr. Herkov agreed with Mr. Reiter: it was distinctly possible that Lee might blow up in court. 'But,' he added, 'if you're talking about a capacity to be able to control it, I think she has the capacity to do that.'

Someone with mood instability might be *able* to control their behaviour, he explained, 'And may simply be so angry that they choose not to do it.' That was the case with Aileen whom he believed could confer with her lawyers in a reasonable manner. He noted that personality disorders like Aileen's are difficult to treat.

On February 20, Herkov took the witness stand again. Assistant Attorney General Scott Browne asked about Ms. Wuornos's flip-flop decision first to waive, then not to waive, her appeals. Herkov explained that she wasn't contesting her fate but wanted to keep the appeal process going a little longer to give her, 'some time to get right with God before her execution.'

535

She did not like her lawyer, Joseph Hobson, apparently, because she felt he'd pushed her to keep trying for a new trial or even to perhaps get her sentence overturned.

'But she did not believe that he was trying to cause her any harm,' said Herkov. 'She thought that he might be trying to enhance his own career, but she felt that he was working in her best interest from his point of view. She just did not agree with that and just did not want that.'

True, Aileen had waived her right to be present during the current important hearing but, 'She gave a very cogent and plausible answer, that she doesn't like it here because of the clothes, because of the shackles. They're uncomfortable. Because of the belt (around her) that if she gets unruly . . . they can hit her with a jolt or something that she doesn't relish very much. Also, the conditions here, I guess in this jail, at least in her opinion, are dirty and much less clean than her cell down at Broward C.I.'

Lee told Herkov that Jesus was influencing her mind, telling her to tell the truth. That did not amount to a delusion. And she'd denied hearing any voices.

True, Lee had thought she was being monitored via an old, disused P.A. system from which she'd occasionally hear crackles or whining noises. Again, Dr. Herkov didn't feel this was delusional. The apparatus existed. Sound might have travelled along it in some fashion.

Herkov wasn't remotely surprised that she didn't trust the correctional officers because, 'There is a culture of distrust of correctional officers in the prison, be it founded or unfounded.' He explained the importance of context and the environment. For instance, if he thought his colleagues at the University of Florida were trying to poison him, that would be more likely to be delusional than the same assertion made by someone in the prison population where food might indeed be 'messed with'.

Dr. Herkov defined a delusion as a fixed false belief that is contrary to observable reality. 'The person is unable to accept that their opinion, belief, may in fact be wrong,' he said. He said folks who believed the earth was flat were not delusional. They had false information and false information does not make something a delusion.

Dr. Herkov was aware that Dr. Mosman disagreed but in his professional opinion, as long as Lee could give plausible explanations for her beliefs—which she did—that, 'does not border on psychotic and, therefore, does not meet the criteria for delusion.'

Going back to the food, he noted, 'If you look at the BCI (Broward C.I.) records, she refuses relatively few meals. You can count how many times she's refused a meal, which may have some bearing on how strong her belief was that she was actually being poisoned.' ('If I thought *I* was being poisoned, I might eat less and certainly might refuse more meals!' he said later.)

Joseph Hobson asked an intriguing question: is not wanting to fight being executed, or actually wanting to be executed, suicidal? Again, Dr. Herkov felt Aileen's reasoning was sound.

'. . . she felt that the evidence was so overwhelming in the Volusia case with the confession, that it really wasn't surmountable. And as she has said many times: "How many times can you kill me?"' There was also her faith—she was unafraid of dying, had made peace with God and was looking towards an afterlife. Herkov admitted that his ears perked up at first since religious delusions are common. But it wasn't as if she was saying God had been telling her to lie in return for eternal bliss. What Aileen said was rational.

Persuaded, Judge Musleh ruled Aileen competent to make decisions about her case. She could have ended the appeals process right there, but she wasn't *quite* ready to.

To the shock of many, Aileen Wuornos suddenly abandoned her decade-long claim to have killed in self-defence. On February 10, 2001, a Miami television station aired an interview in which she confessed she'd lied when she said that she shot her seven victims to save herself.

By April, she was ready to take another step towards death. She wrote to the Florida Supreme Court and to Assistant State Attorney Jim McCune, saying:

'I'd kill again. So let's cut with the chase and head for a hearing to get evaluated for, and proceed as sentenced.'

In June, Aileen again wrote to the Florida Supreme Court and to each county's prosecutor asking that they end her appeals and carry out her execution. On June 13, the Florida Supreme Court referred the competency issue back for a hearing in the Daytona Beach Circuit Court.

'There's no question she did it, she's confessed to it and she's ready to pay the penalty—what's the hold-up?' asked Volusia State Attorney John Tanner.

One of Aileen's CCRC lawyers, Richard Kiley, indicated that they'd make further attempts to have her declared incompetent. Lee, though, had no doubt that she was quite sane, very sensible and completely competent. She apologized to the victims' families for her crimes and said that there was no point in more taxpayers' money being spent on defending her:

'There's no sense in keeping me alive. This world doesn't mean anything to me.'

Nothing if not consistent in her inconsistency, talking to *Ocala Star-Banner* reporter Rick Cundiff, late in June, she said, 'I can't really say I regret what I've done. It was an experience.' So much for apologizing to victims' families. She again said that none of the murders involved self-defence, just robbery and hatred. 'I can't say I have regrets for anything. I'm too cold, man, I'm too cold. I don't care.'

It struck him, Cundiff wrote, that she seemed to think that telling the truth alone would be enough to secure divine forgiveness.

'There's no sense in dying in lies, man,' she said. 'I can only see going to hell for that.'

When Steve Glazer heard that Aileen had finally confessed to killing her victims in cold blood without provocation and was heading towards the fast-track to execution, he was not surprised. 'She's asking for the lethal injection as soon as possible,' he said. 'That's the same thing she asked me to do for her nine years ago. Nothing's changed.'

the country's prosecutor asking that they and her appeals and out her execution. On June 13, the Florida Supreme Court.

55

And so the wheels of justice ground slowly on. In Daytona Beach on July 20, Circuit Judge R. Michael Hutcheson questioned Lee closely and at length. He wanted to be very, very sure that she understood the rights she'd be giving up by abandoning further appeals. A ruling from him that she was competent meant that the case would be returned to the Florida Supreme Court where Lee could ask for permission to fire her lawyers and ask for her execution to go forward. A death warrant could then come quite quickly.

Did she realize she could then be on what's known as 'a fast-track to execution?' the judge asked her.

'Yes, sir,' she said. 'I'm not scared by it. I know what the heck I'm doing.'

Aileen had arrived in court that day, all smiles. She laughed, and at times she cried hysterically. She spent around ninety minutes on the witness stand and when she described the murders, tears flowed. 'This is harder than I thought it would be,' she sniffed. But she also said something chilling:

'I want to tell the world that I killed these men. I robbed them and I killed them as cold as ice, and I'd do it again too. I'd kill another person because I've hated humans for a long time.'

Again, the conflict, the contradictions. After all, she had also recently voiced regrets, saying, 'After you're done killing a person and you realize what you've done, it will haunt you the rest of your life.'

Calling for further psychiatric evaluation, and hoping to have her declared incompetent to fire them, her attorney Richard Kiley said, 'Wuornos is using this court as merely a vehicle for state-assisted suicide.'

Under questioning by her own lawyers, Lee's tone turned hostile.

'I am a serial killer,' she said. 'I killed them in cold blood, real nasty. Right after they picked me up and we parked in the woods, I whipped out my gun and killed them.'

She said that her lawyers had lied when they said that she was raped by her father and that her mother was an alcoholic; lied to try to have her life spared. Clearly, she was still as horribly uncomfortable as ever about admitting anything negative happened in her childhood.

'I am ready to die,' she said.

The judge's mind was made up but before ruling her competent, he wanted to know one more thing: would she like other lawyers to represent her?

'No! Not even if they were [Robert] Shapiro and [Johnnie] Cochran!'

That day, Troy Burress's sister, Letha Prater, wanted to thank Lee for finally admitting that there had been no rapes or abuse or brutality by her victims and for clearing her beloved brother's reputation, but she was not allowed to speak to her directly for security reasons.

'I don't hate her. I hate what she did. Hatred is lost on her,' said Prater. 'She said she wanted to pay for the crime and that she wanted to die . . . and we want the same thing, so let's get on with it.'

Wanda Pouncey, Troy's daughter, agreed: 'It's time for all this to be done instead of dragging this on.'

Had Letha been granted her wish to speak to Troy's killer, what would she have said?

'I would say thank you for doing the right thing and stopping the appeals, because it will help,' she explained. 'I know it is not right to wish somebody dead. I know that in my heart. But I just don't want to see her face anymore.'

To anyone who'd watched Letha Prater in court during Richard Mallory's trial or spent time with her then, her strength and composure in 2001 was a relief. Nine years earlier, one could not help wondering if she would survive the loss of her brother, 'Buddy'. A private nurse, Letha had also served as a deputy sheriff and had no problem getting tough when the job called for it. But that woman was gone in 1992, replaced by one so utterly devastated, that she seemed as if she might somehow simply dissolve.

'It wasn't an accident, it wasn't a death by illness, his life was taken from him,' she explained. 'I can't get past that. It was senseless. I hated her with a passion for a long time. I was very resentful. I had to mend.'

Now, it bothers her that Tyria Moore was able to walk away from her life with a serial killer without any repercussions. Whether or not she was present at any of the murders, Ty had Wuornos's victims belongings and had been told point blank by Lee that she had murdered Richard Mallory. 'And,' said Letha, 'I resent that she got off scot-free.'

She is not a bloodthirsty woman, but she still wants to see Aileen executed. She favours the death penalty because she doesn't trust that a life sentence without possibility of parole will turn out to be that. After all, the death penalty was banned in 1972 after the case of Furman vs. Georgia was decided by the U.S. Supreme Court, which held that capital punishment was unconstitutional and struck down death penalty laws across the nation. Ninety-five men and the one woman on Florida's Death Row had their death sentences commuted to life in prison. That decision was eventually overturned when the Supreme Court upheld the constitutionality of the death penalty in Gregg vs. Georgia. Executions resumed in Florida in 1979.

If Aileen was allowed to live, Letha would never be free of the fear that one day she might be back on the streets.

'I feel she would do the same thing—and she said she would. You take a rabid dog and you put it asleep, then you don't have to worry about it getting out. If they get out, they can do a lot of damage. And I feel that she could and would do the same thing.'

Troy Burress's family was warned that the appeals process would take at least ten years, but still, it hadn't been easy:

'You have this woman's face on T.V. and she is laughing and carrying on and it just kind of hits you It's hard.'

Meanwhile, Letha's life had changed a lot. Her fifteen-year

marriage to Bob Prater ended in 1995, something she considered a casualty of the tragedy. 'I tried to work through all of it, but I didn't have the strength or energy to keep trying,' she said. (She's since remarried.)

'Bob said when Buddy died, I died,' she explained. 'I didn't but it changed me so drastically. I think he felt like I loved him much more than anyone else in the family. And I did. I was just devastated. I kind of got the wind knocked out of me when my Buddy died. I lost heart and I never could seem to get back to what I was before. I got a lot of it back, but I never will be the same.

'Someone asked if I was surprised when Wuornos said that the men didn't try to harm her? I don't know the other men but I know my brother, and I knew that all along. I am surprised she admitted it, but I am glad.'

Revenge fantasies are common, and seeing Wuornos in court sometimes sparked enormous anger.

'There has been a time or two I wanted to do something physical,' she admitted. 'When I think: that is the last face he saw. I used to hate her with a passion. I used to think of things I would like to do to make life horrible for her. But that doesn't help you. It just makes you bitter. And I got past that. I'm ready for her to get this sentence. But actually saying I hate her as a person? I hate what she did because she caused such a change in so many people's lives.'

Letha will attend the execution.

'Oh, definitely. I just want to be there. I want to see it. I know to some people it sounds cruel, but if it is, it is just cruel. That's how I feel. I think a lot of it is loyalty. To his memory and maybe to myself, too. Then I know I won't have to hear a lot more about her. Because each time there is a hearing and they bring all this stuff up, my heart breaks all over again.'

56

'This is where you get answers . . .' Billy Nolas had promised at Lee's trial for the murder of Richard Mallory. If only that were so simple.

We are still in a bind. There is an ever-present conflict between our wish to understand and feel compassion for the influences and events and psychological hiccups that turned someone like Lee into a cold-blooded killer, and our reluctance to forgive the end product.

The prime flaw in any psychological defence, or defence based on childhood abuse and trauma, is the overwhelming amount of cases that can be cited in which heroic souls have triumphed over adversity and become the stronger for it. They have not turned around and slaughtered their fellow men. And often the abuse they have suffered is more horrific than that sustained by the thankfully few who mock the rules of society.

Billy Nolas was right. Aileen Wuornos did not drop from the sky. But while psychology and psychiatry set out to comprehend, understanding does not equal defence.

So it is that while we can feel compassion for the pain of a mistreated child we can also, without contradiction, expect, require—demand—that the adult that the child has become should set aside his or her handicaps and live up to the same standards and rules we set for ourselves and society.

And the courtroom is the ultimate province of those rules and standards.

By default, any psychological diagnosis—any listing of biological, genetic and environmental factors that may have contributed to make the murderer—may be affecting, but remains, for the most part, an ineffective teardrop in the bucket of blood.

Compounding the problem in the case of Aileen Wuornos was the diagnosis of her as a borderline personality. It is a diagnosis that even within the therapeutic professions has become tainted, however unfairly, as a kind of catch-all. Because it lacks the drama inherent in, say, a layperson's perception of a multiple personality disorder or a psychotic, its effect on the jury in this case was probably tantamount to that of hearing that Aileen Wuornos was overstressed.

At the time of Aileen Wuornos's trial, Robert Ressler described 'borderline personality' as a useful phrase for psychiatrists to employ when they were not sure what they were dealing with. One murderer Ressler interviewed in-depth was 6 foot 9, 295-pound Edmund Kemper who killed his grandparents when he was fourteen. After being released from a mental hospital at 21, he killed a further six young people, having sex with them after their deaths, then dismembering them. Finally, he murdered his mother and her best friend. He propped his mother's severed head on the kitchen table, reporting that it was the first time she had actually shut up.

Kemper, Ressler found, was something of a psychology buff; an articulate, literate man with an IQ of 136. And when Ressler asked Kemper where he thought he fitted in the DSM-III, the psychiatric diagnostic manual then in its second edition, Kemper replied, 'Somewhere in the seventh or eighth edition.' Ressler likened it to medical science's understanding of AIDS: We know a little bit about it, but can we cure it or stop it?

'And I think it's the same thing with Kemper. Psychiatry can't deal with Kemper. They can't deal with Dahmer. I sat in and listened to the psychiatrists testify on Dahmer, and he had six or seven psychiatrists, and they all had a different opinion.

'If they understand it, they should all have the same diagnosis. Prosecution and defence, as well. And they don't. One guy said that he was psychotic . . . most said that he wasn't psychotic. One guy said he was not psychotic, but he was worse than a psychotic. It makes sense to me, but to the layperson? That's saying it's worse than the worst. More severe than the most severe mental illness. I mean, what does that mean?'

Ressler felt that just as Dahmer defied pigeon-holing or categorising, so, too, did Lee. While the four experts in her first trial agreed she was a borderline personality, only the prosecution witness, Dr. Barnard, diagnosed her as an anti-social personality. The others said she didn't meet more than three of the twelve criteria then required by the DSM-III by the age of fifteen. (Hearing that, Robert Ressler said, 'My God! What do you consider her to be?')

Those criteria for anti-social personality disorder were: frequent truancy; running away from home overnight at least twice (or once without returning) while living in parental home; initiating physical fights; using weapons more than once; forcing someone into sexual activity with him or her; physical cruelty to animals; physical cruelty to people; destroying others' property (other than by fire-setting); deliberately engaging in fire-setting; frequent lying (other than to avoid physical or sexual abuse); stealing without confrontation of a victim on more than one occasion (including forgery); stealing with confrontation of a victim (i.e. mugging, purse-snatching, extortion, armed robbery).

A layperson with greater access to Lee's childhood might have suggested that she met at least five of the criteria and that her anti-social behaviour was evident very early on.

Certainly, she did not exhibit the mask of charm so often present in sociopathic personalities. As psychologist Candice Skrapec noted in 1992 (although she didn't personally examine Wuornos), where that charm is lacking, it's often replaced with a superficial but convincing way of making you feel sorry for them.

In court, Lee did not exhibit judgement or discretion about how she was perceived. Ted Bundy would never have been caught cackling or grinning wildly when the jury was viewing photographs of a bloody victim. Lee was manipulative. But her manipulation had its limits. Skrapec suggested that those limits may have been imposed by her IQ.

Borderlines have unstable relationships, are impulsive, anxious, prone to intense anger, and take desperate measures to avoid being abandoned. That shoe certainly fit, but away from the courtroom we cannot be too quick to label her. There is an enormous amount of overlap in the various types of behaviours with borderline, narcissism and anti-social personality disorder. And none of these disorders could specifically explain her compulsion to kill.

While psychological testimony has become a necessary part of the adversarial system, and is needed as we examine the issues of responsibility and culpability, it is also open to abuse. Outside a courtroom, why try to pigeonhole her? Candice Skrapec feared that if we did so, we would only close the door prematurely, and may lose a lot of what we might otherwise learn about her.

Labels aside, what is abundantly clear is that Lee lives her life governed and handicapped by an emotional language that blessedly few humans speak. And as in trying to comprehend any other foreign and unfamiliar language, we must seek to unlock the mysteries, taking the clues she has handed us and making stumbling attempts at translation.

What is Lee trying to say? What does her behaviour mean? Why does she think the way she does? What motivates her? And why did she do what she did?

Underlying any effort in this direction, however, is the difficulty in dealing with her over a period of time, the grating unpalatability of the borderline personality. We are talking now not of murder, but of the problems of basic social interaction.

Lee's borderline world is stark black and white. Her inability to tolerate ambiguity does not allow for human shades of grey. People, to Lee, are either angels or demons. Britta was an angel. Lauri was a demon. Tyria was first an angel, then a demon. Dawn Botkins has been both. Jackelyn Giroux has been both, as has Lori Grody and Lee's various lawyers. In time, Arlene Pralle met that same fate.

In writing this book, I came to believe that never, not even in the grip of her most negative moments, did Lee envisage herself landing on Death Row. I believe that in her mind she saw it differently. She would have respect. Power. Money. And then they would all look up to her. Death Row didn't feature in her plans.

Her ultimately fatal inability to foresee consequences, to grasp cause and effect, had effectively distanced her from the existence of any such ramifications. Speaking on the telephone the day before the verdict in the Richard Mallory trial, she left me in no doubt whatsoever that she was completely, frighteningly, unprepared for being found guilty. This despite the best and repeated efforts of her considerably more realistic counsel to prepare her for the worst.

She was unequivocally convinced that the jury had believed all her cries of rape and self-defence. In her mind, it was simple. She'd said it, so it must be true. Those jurors would have to be crazy not to know that. Just as she could accuse Larry Horzepa of bullying her and expect the jury to believe her.

As ever, she had no useful grasp on the effect she had on others. She'd been oblivious to the discreet squirming in the jury box, to the subtle flickers of horror and distaste that, despite their best efforts, crept periodically across the jurors' generally expressionless faces.

'It might be just that she was naïve enough to think that, indeed, the righteousness of her actions would somehow shine through and save her, spare her, and indeed glorify her,' suggested Candice Skrapec.

Had she deluded herself into thinking that she was on some kind of mission to save women, she might well have not even entertained the consequences of her actions. The psychiatrists did not find her delusional. Nevertheless, one cannot help feeling that, as in most things, it is a matter of degree, and in the months after her arrest, her grasp on the reality of her plight was decidedly shaky.

'What I want to do when I get out is I want to help women,' she said. 'I'm going to go into the women's liberation field, get a foundation going for the women, that will be hopefully under my name. Because they'll understand who—knowing who I am and everything, they'll understand. "Oh, go to Aileen Wuornos, she can help." I want to help. And I'm going to try and glorify the Lord and try to get people saved and everything if I can. This world is evil and needs help. It really does.

'I'm going to be like a trumpet for the women. I feel like I'm a martyr for the women.

'And if they convict me, and send me away to prison for life, or the electric chair, or send me to prison for years and years, you know, I hope to God—and I'm sure that it will happen—that there is going to be one hundred jillion women out there, millions of women, that are really going to be pissed. Really. For sure.'

Yet Aileen 'Lee' Wuornos had never been on a mission to save women. Her dream and ambition was to do something no woman had ever done before, and as a result, become famous and rich and respected. Looked up to. And thereby become a hero for women.

A short in the wiring could allow the co-existence of two seemingly incompatible agendas. She craved fame, power, glory and recognition and she would earn them for herself with her outlaw life—or her outlaw life would earn them for her. She would have books written and films made about her, and the world would listen to her.

Enter the short in the wiring. It would seem that there was a fatal flaw in this plan from the word go. If her recipe for this attention was to have murdered six men in self-defence, rousing the women of the world to seize upon her as a heroine and join her in her corner, there was also at least the possibility that she would at some point end up behind bars. She might be forced to pay a price (however minimal) for her crimes (however justifiable). Battered wives who have killed their husbands, for instance, regularly serve some time in prison, self-defence or no.

Was that a price she'd recognised and was willing to pay? A necessary sacrifice for a greater goal? Or had she just not thought it through?

Candice Skrapec floated this possibility: 'Here's this woman who's really quite naïve and maybe is operating a few bricks short of a load, and maybe her IQ just doesn't allow for a lot of creative thinking in terms of alternatives. Like, "What really could happen to me here?"'

Just as the delusional thinker who kills is mystified when society snaps on the handcuffs—they'd been doing society a big favour, hadn't anyone noticed?—Lee's own perception was out of whack. What we would regard as highly irrational thinking was to her perfectly rational.

A personal theory, which will likely never be anything more: I suspect that Lee may have killed before but that she confessed to a specific number of murders—six—that she felt befitting her role as heroine. Six put her in a league of her own but was perhaps also a number that seemed to her to work with self-defence.

We can't let the confessions lull us into thinking that she has revealed the full extent of her killing sprees. She lied and lies as easily as pouring a cup of coffee. The stories about her babies and dead husbands dropped from her lips on a daily basis. They were cons, pure and simple. People would repeat her rape/pregnancy claim without question, yet she herself contradicted it on many occasions. With her history of invention, who would relish trying to judge her murder accounts? The facts would have to speak, as they did in court, since the victims could not.

She had a .22 back in 1986 when she was arrested. Carrying a gun was nothing new. Then there was the .38 she stole in 1985. Many experts in serial murder would agree that 33 (her age when she killed Richard Mallory) is a somewhat late start for a serial killer.

When confessing to Larry Horzepa and Bruce Munster, she said she had killed six men, yet she spelled out the details of seven murders. Questioned by the investigators on this discrepancy, she still maintained there were six.

We are not speaking here of cups of coffee, but the snuffing out of human lives.

Her confusion on this crucial point could not be easily explained away. Even if never before, hadn't she run through in her mind the list of men she'd murdered during those first days in jail when she feared she was a suspect?

For a variety of reasons, some of those involved came strongly to suspect that Lee was killing before Richard Mallory.

When Larry Horzepa questioned Lee about the things she'd pawned in December '89 and asked if they belonged to Mallory, her answer was oddly revealing.

'I would have to say so . . . 'cause if that's what time it was, it was his stuff then. But I don't remember. See, 'cause . . . all these vehicles these guys usually had, you know, some clothes and stuff and I just threw the stuff away, you know, and kept what would be worth money, you know, so I could get some money off it.'

She pawned those items just a few days after what she claimed was her first killing. You'd think the whole incident would be hard, if not impossible, to forget. Serial killers often relive every detail of their crimes in their minds. What did it say if that killing, supposedly separated from the next by five and a half months, didn't stand out in her mind as memorable? If that nightmare attack had blurred in with all the rest?

If Lee had killed more and decided not to admit it even to Ty, she undoubtedly could have kept quiet. Some serial killers become competitive, statistically ambitious, about the number of people they've killed. Lee never wanted to be a serial killer. Ultimately, she confessed to seven murders, but we honestly don't know that that wasn't part of a manipulation, too. The BSU studies found that lying to investigators was another way for killers to have some form of control.

Lee was good at keeping her own counsel. Always had been. Dawn reiterated this as the reason why she found it entirely believable that Ty didn't know about the murders. Lori didn't know about her young sister Aileen's hooking. And nor did Dawn, her best buddy, ever hear it straight from the horse's mouth.

It is possible that another paradox was at work in Lee Wuornos. There was her silence on the murders, brought about because on some level she recognised that what she had done was not acceptable. And, tugging against that, was a desire for recognition for her actions. Such a paradox can precipitate what might seem to the rest of us blatantly self-defeating behaviour.

Keeping Peter Siems's car for almost a month. Keeping the dead men's possessions. Storing things for which she really had no use in a warehouse unit. Risk-taking. Stupid or careless? And if careless, was it deliberately so? Consciously, she did not want to get caught. But there may well have been, and frequently is in such cases, some subconscious need to take risks to ensure being caught and punished for bad deeds.

Also at work with serial killers, Candice Skrapec had learned, could be a need to command our respect. In Lee's case, was this the underlying message: 'Come on! Look what I've done, and no one's paying any attention to me!'?

Indeed, Lee did speak of 'showing off' when revealing to Ty the death of Richard Mallory. She said, 'She doesn't know, basically, anything except for the fact that I could have murmured or mumbled or said something while I was drunk, which she would either believe or not believe or whatever . . . like be in awe.'

It was also possible, Skrapec pointed out, that although she trusted that Ty would not go to the police, on another level she thought that she might. And that, too, would lead to her needs being met because it would mean she would be caught.

Skrapec wasn't fond of labels but had a name for the risk-taking behaviour she'd observed in serial killers: false bravado.

'They have so much to lose, but they really feel invincible, like they're almost invisible and can walk amongst us and we don't see them. From that, they glean this bravado. They experience it in terms of "Well! You can't catch me!" And really, of course, it's false bravado in that it's not grounded in anything.

'In this case, she was driving the car around. It was perhaps only a matter of time before someone might have linked her to the car, but they crashed it anyway. But to take such a risk in light of what she stood to lose, is really kind of consistent, to my mind, with a false bravado type of behaviour.'

The underlying desire to get caught is not inconsistent either with the desire for recognition from the world and for respect from the men who had otherwise used her.

Another calculation on her part, misguided as ever, might have given rise to her having a clear picture of how she would be viewed by us. She wanted to control that, too. And she grew furious when the world began going its own merry way, making assumptions about her and labelling her a man-hating serial killer in a way that didn't fit in with her vision.

From Death Row, she told talk show host Montel Williams that when the press first labelled her a serial killer, she 'almost passed out'. Unequivocally, I believe that.

While she had no qualms about her adoptive mother hearing her shocking accounts of her murders on the videotape, she for a long time did not share with Arlene her sexual history. Jackelyn Giroux was the first to uncover just how young she'd been when the sex started, but Lee called Jackelyn a liar. What would Lee have to lose by admitting to that? Why would she expect to be rejected over childhood incidents over which she had far less control? If anything, it might engender sympathy. But that's not the way her disjointed thought patterns operate.

'Jackye Giroux was telling the truth about the abuse and the sex with the guys,' she later admitted to Arlene Pralle. 'I couldn't tell you before because I was ashamed. I was afraid you wouldn't like me anymore and you'd be disgusted if you heard that stuff.'

Candice Skrapec suggested that it might be possible that other more calculating and practical motives were at work. If Lee had admitted to early sexual abuse, might the court system see her as a man-hater who'd gone out and hunted men? Not just the court system, perhaps, but the world. (It is interesting that Wuornos made a point of saying on the stand and to the psychiatrists that she liked guys and she liked the sex. Yet she also referred to men as maggots.)

'She might have felt that at all costs she could not be perceived as a man-hater,' said Skrapec. 'In fact, she would have to project that she enjoyed sex with men. To portray to the world a non-man-hating female who did not have a vendetta, who did not have a mission to kill men, who really loved men, enjoyed sex with them. But these guys just were going to kill her and she had to protect herself.'

It might all have been the product of the distorted thinking of a mind that while not legally insane, was hardly a model of health.

The same kind of thinking that could have determined that six was the number of men to whose murders she would safely and gloriously confess.

EPILOGUE

Los Angeles, December 2001

Aileen Wuornos has occupied a Death Row cell—that confining space that Steven Glazer paced out in the Ocala courtroom—since 1992. In fact, Broward Correctional Institute's Death Row cells are six by nine feet; a foot longer than Glazer indicated, but let's not split hairs. This is no spa. It's claustrophobia with bars and in summer, an open-plan sweatbox.

Nowadays, you can take a virtual tour of a Death Row cell on Broward's Web site, panning around from the narrow bed's skinny, comfortless mattress to the unshielded stainless steel facilities.

Since Judy Buenoano's 1998 execution in the electric chair, Broward's female population on Death Row has numbered three. Floridians now have the option of seeking death by lethal injection and Lee, who considers the chair 'barbaric,' has chosen to end her life via chemicals and the less-fearsome needle.

If she is on the fast track to death, she might soon be contemplating her last meal. The menu can be of her own choosing but must cost no more than $20. After the Governor of Florida signs a death warrant for Aileen—and one death warrant on one of the murders is all it would take—she will be moved to a Death Watch cell to sit out her last hours on this earth.

First, the Florida Supreme Court has to review Judge Hutcheson's decision that she is competent. If it finds no technical errors, her attorneys and remaining appeals will be dismissed. If it approves Hutcheson's decision, Governor Jeb Bush will sign a death warrant for Wuornos and set a date for her to die. It could all happen quite quickly, according to death penalty experts.

No one can predict Lee's state of mind when her wish to die by lethal injection finally becomes an imminent reality, rather than a wearying, decade-long, abstract topic of debate and court hearings.

On that day when the state takes her life, others who have been touched by Aileen—many in an unspeakably negative fashion, some less so—will doubtless also experience powerful and somewhat unpredictable emotions.

Some of the main players in the drama of Aileen Wuornos's life have moved on: some have passed on. Shirley Humphreys, sadness etched on her face like an inescapable reminder of the abominable nature of Wuornos's crimes, succumbed to the cancer she bravely fought for so long. Troy Burress's mother, Clara, who thought the pain would get better but found it never did, also died. Judge Uriel Blount, who came out of retirement to preside over the Richard Mallory trial with a firm, experienced hand, has passed away. So, too, has Detective Tom Muck of Pasco County, an active player in the unofficial task force that brought Wuornos to justice; the advocate, if you will, of the victim who took his last breath in Pasco County—Charles Carskaddon.

Circuit Court Judge Thomas Sawaya is now a state appellate judge. Marion County prosecutor David Eddy is now a Circuit Judge. Munster, Binegar and Henry are still in Marion County, with Binegar and Henry both now chiefs in the sheriff's office. And Detective Larry Horzepa, who, with Munster, interviewed Aileen Wuornos during her startling three-hour confession—and who put his jacket around Aileen's shoulders because she was chilly and because he wanted her to keep right on talking—now works in Volusia County's Sex Crimes Unit. Tyria Moore has her job as a forklift driver. Diane Tuley, Lee's birth mother, continues to elude the spotlight. Aileen's son—who was adopted at birth and is now thirty—doesn't know her. Nor she him.

And then there's Arlene Pralle, still something of an enigma with her story of being drawn to something she saw in Lee's eyes—the same eyes in which others, like lawyer Joseph Hobson, would see nothing. A blank. No connection.

Arlene's new life in the Bahamas inevitably curtails regular contact with Lee, but one can't help but sense a sea-change in

Arlene anyway; a distance. It must have been gruelling, their incredibly intense, emotional rollercoaster ride of a relationship. Certainly, during the early '90s it was, when she was Lee's emotional support and on-call day in, day out, for hours upon hours of telephone calls.

Only Arlene knows for sure why she was moved to reach out to a violent stranger in prison and, within a couple of months of 'knowing' her, agree to adopt her. Then again, perhaps even Arlene doesn't fully understand it herself.

However, after enduring a heart attack, Arlene was willing to look inward and examine her feelings. She found herself thinking about the victims' families.

'Tragedy and grief are universal,' she wrote in a recent letter, 'though the circumstances for each of us are different, the feelings are the same. And those feelings have to be dealt with correctly or we will become the next victims, eaten alive by bitterness and hate. Enduring a heart attack, resulting in us selling our farm and having to move, brought this fact home to me in a very real way. I had many issues to deal with in my own life, just as the victims' family members had been doing. My prayer for them is they can find closure and peace.

'We reached out to Aileen Wuornos as a result of what we still feel was a prompting of God. I am not sorry we did that, though at the moment I'm not at all sure what good came of it. We tried to be friends with Aileen and bring her to a knowledge of Jesus Christ as her personal saviour. That was the only motivation for writing that first letter.

'Initially, I saw her only through "Pollyanna eyes" and really thought she was telling the truth when she said she was innocent. When she, on Death Row, later confided in me that she was guilty and wanted "to get right with God", I honored her request by getting Steve Glazer to end further trials. Aileen herself said she didn't want the family members to have to endure anymore. She just wanted it over and to pay for her crimes. We support her decision.'

Reflecting further on their interactions, she wrote:

'Our relationship over the years has been rocky. The first couple of years I visited her faithfully on Death Row. Starting in October of 1993, I spent nearly a year in Tennessee. Needless to say, during that period, I was not able to visit Aileen. Our communication was only through letters. That put a wedge between Aileen and I. Nick Broomfield also added great stress to our relationship. We both became angry with one another and communication broke down for a long while.

'My one and only regret is that I ever accepted money. I never wanted to—not once. Aileen pushed the issue relentlessly until I finally gave in. Ironically the same Aileen Wuornos who pushed me to do interviews and accept money for them, is the one now falsely accusing me. She says the only reason we reached out to her was for financial gain. I only wish I had never taken a dime. But God knows our hearts and the truth. In that knowledge we find peace.'

Over the years, Jackelyn Giroux found herself unable to let go of Lee's story and in September 2000, she finally raised enough money to begin shooting her film, *Damsel of Death*. An ex-actress who appeared in *The Cross and the Switchblade* and *To Live and Die in L.A.*, Giroux's tie to Lee grew even tighter thanks to a curious turn of events in a saga full of them. She had problems with her lead actress and to stay within her thinnest of shoestring budgets, had to not only direct the film but to take over the lead role too. She had to *become* Lee for a while; the woman who'd been inside her head for so long.

Some time after Lee and Jackelyn Giroux dropped their lawsuits against one another, Giroux received a letter from Lee.

'She apologized for mistrusting me,' Jackelyn recalls. 'But it didn't mean anything to me then, as it means nothing to me now. In my opinion, Aileen Wuornos is a little girl who will do anything for attention, even murder. And I believe she would do everything all over again for the same attention and fame she has received.'

Even so, Giroux will take no pleasure in it when Lee is tethered to a gurney with wrist and ankle restraints. Two saline I.V. lines will be started, one in each arm, and then used to deliver lethal chemicals like sodium thiopental, which will render her unconscious, then pancuronium bromide, a muscle relaxant to stop her breathing by paralyzing her lungs and diaphragm.

'When I think of Aileen Wuornos, I think of a wounded animal,' says Giroux. 'With each bullet, the animal gets weaker yet fights more ferociously. With each year of abandonment, Aileen became just as ferocious and desperate. I realize that I am in the minority here, but I don't think justice is served through murder. Whether that be taking a life unexpectedly, or by lethal injection, it is still murder in my opinion.'

MORE MUST-READ TRUE CRIME
FROM PINNACLE

HORRIFYING TRUE CRIME
FROM PINNACLE BOOKS